OF THE SHADOW SOUL

The Unanswered Questions Series

The Unanswered Questions
Of the Curatrix Code
Of the Shadow Soul

THE UNANSWERED QUESTIONS

BOOK THREE

OF THE SHADOW SOUL

LAUREN D. FULTER

Paperback: 978-1736114643
Ebook: 978-1736114636

First Paperback Edition December 2022

Edited by Micheala Bush & Ariana Tosado
Cover Art by Klymenearts
Cover Layout by Beck Michaels
Formatting by Benita J. Thompson | Kairos Book Design

laurendfulter.com

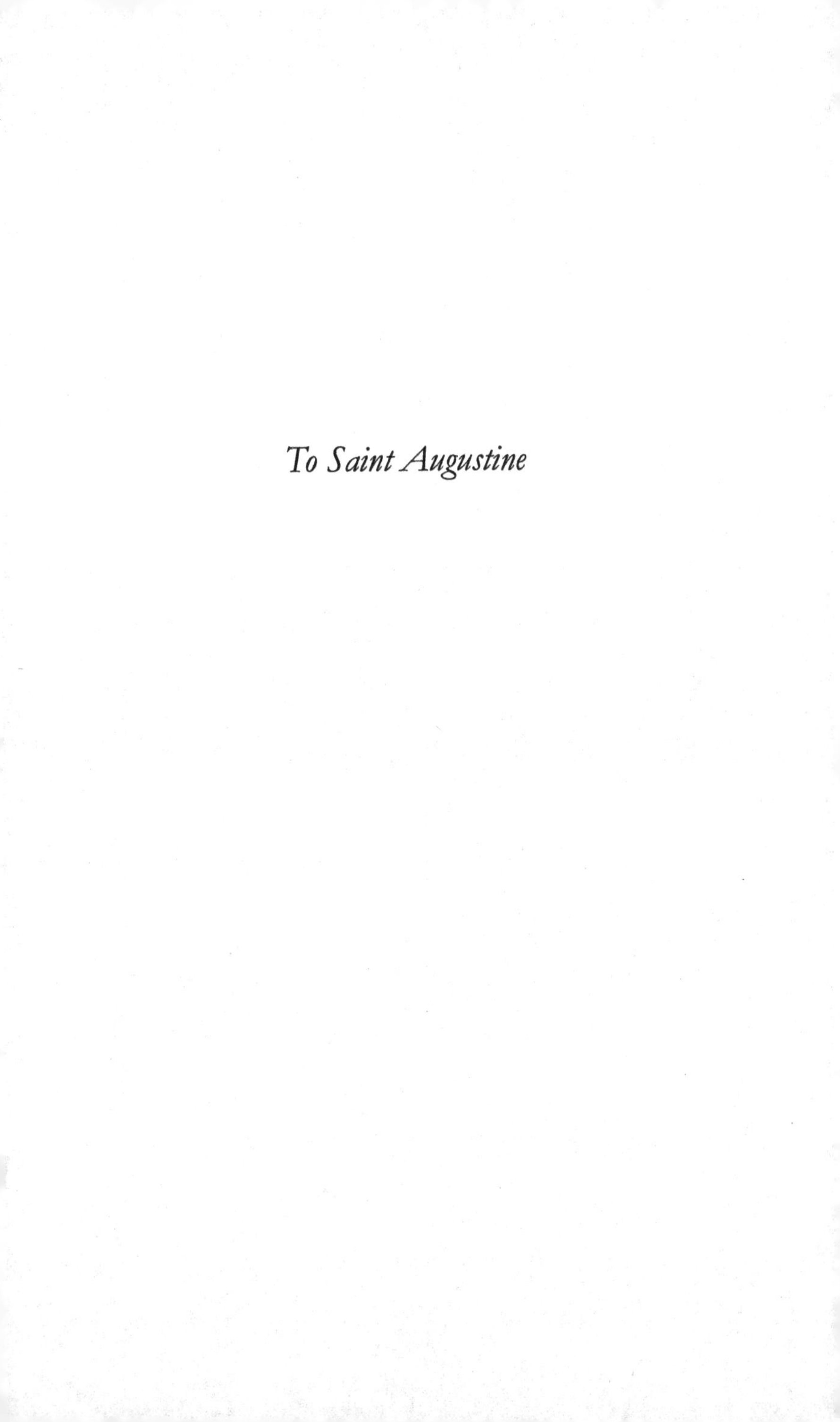

To Saint Augustine

PROLOGUE

I'VE HEARD MUCH about you, little Aguirre. It took so long to break you. It took death.

Who are you?

The Lady of the Universe.

What is your name? How do you know my name?

Have you not learned, little Aguirre, that names hold power? You will lead me to Algery.

I won't do anything for you. Where am I?

Oh, foolish child. How little you know....

The Ewyon Coastal Alliance Palace—Before Recorded Time

There was no person less deserving of the ability to breathe than one who sympathized with the very kind of people who'd murdered her mother.

Adrienne peered into the room, the golden light spilling from the slowly spinning chandeliers that cast shadows of the brightly colored women, and the glittering weapon at every lord's side. No, they had not killed her mother nor even sided with the Oquelite that did, but the fact that some dared question her aunt's decree against the Shadow Soul made them just as evil.

"I do not belong in there, Sergia." Adrienne let out a sigh, avoiding the sliver of light that fell across the floor.

"Adrienne, you don't have a choice." Sergia looked more stressed than Adrienne. She played with her long, dark braid, too busy all evening to care to fix the hair that fell loose across her face, though with her sparkling eyes and dark complexion, the maid always managed to look stunning, even if Adrienne was sometimes bothered by her mothering.

"Do you understand what this integration into the court means to your aunt? What it should mean to you? I thought you were anticipating this."

A display of power to the entire court. A great honor.

Adrienne looked down at her hands before clenching them into fists. "What if they ask questions?"

Sergia paused. "No one will. It would be rude of them to second guess the Queen…your aunt's judgment."

"I know. I know." Adrienne took a deep breath, looking at her handmaid. Sergia was only seven years her senior, but maturity set in well with her proud smile. "I will. Only because you say so."

Sergia pat Adrienne's shoulder. "Don't be so hard on yourself."

Adrienne snorted. "How do you think I've made it this far?"

Sergia only laughed softly.

Everything she'd worked for came to this. She pushed through the doors.

No one seemed to give her much notice, most young and giddy in tightly fit dress and glasses full of golden liquid bubbling in hand.

Most entered the court at fifteen, not the eighteen years that Adrienne held. Even Cal, now thirteen, had been permitted for his "extraordinary essence form," even though Adrienne knew that it was mostly Carastene's bias toward her spoiled son.

Her cousin knew how to irk her, and the little devil knew a perfect high-pitched cry to get a report written straight to Carastene for "hot-headed nature."

Better to be hot headed than sympathetic.

She adjusted the circlet on her head. She'd take what compliments she could get no matter their intention.

She glanced desperately back at Sergia, who ushered her off with her hands and a confident grin.

The white-uniformed guards unlinked the red rope. Adrienne smoothed the front of her gown, rolling her shoulders back.

She walked into the crowd. The music was melodic, the shimmering, glass chandelier dancing with the purple flames, mimicking the dancers across the center of the polished, marble floor, with the smell of perfume thick.

Adrienne kept her fists to her side as she walked through. She'd never seen the ballroom so full. No doubt that every Ewyon noble family was in attendance.

"Lady Adrienne." An attendant swept to her side. "Our Highest Queen Carastene requested your attendance nearly an hour—"

"We ran into a delay. Everything is sorted now, sir."

The attendant nodded, quickly leading Adrienne through the crowd. Eyes cast upon her, parting the way. Eyes grew wider as she approached the elevated platform where Carastene sat, her head held high in an air of superiority.

Adrienne quickly dropped a bow. "Our Highest."

"Adrienne, you are late."

Adrienne bit back a remark. "My utmost apologies."

Carastene sighed, rubbing the crease between her perfect brows. "Now that you have arrived, Ireward, please prepare the other entrants."

The attendant bowed and rushed off.

"This is a high honor, Adrienne. You must take it seriously," Carastene said, her cold features turning back to her niece.

Adrienne sighed. "Oh, I'm very serious, Your Highness."

"Stop the sarcasm, Adrienne. People are watching."

Adrienne pursed her lips, glaring at a man sipping a glass nearby who quickly looked down to the floor.

Carastene rose, and the crowd grew quiet.

A row of young teenagers lined in front of the queen, of which Adrienne stuck out like a sore thumb above them. An attendant was quick to move Adrienne to the end of the line, next to a short, freckled girl, who sent her a wide grin.

"Today we are present for the Court entrance of the birthright nobles." There was a pause. "And those noble born."

That was her only claim. Her mother had been a noble, and everything else was a disgrace.

"Children of Ewyon, take your knee and bestow your essence."

In an instant, they fell, the lights falling with them.

This was the moment she'd begged for. She'd spent countless nights *pacing and sweating over essence scrolls.*

One by one, the adolescents' appearances became enlightened, growing richer and older, the slight glow protruding from under their skin. It was a simple yet magnificent trick that every Ewyon child could embrace.

One by one, the line came closer to her. The girl beside her glowed, her lips filling and curls rising.

Now all eyes were on Adrienne. A sensation should arrive in her chest, a burning in her veins as the essence would overcome the demand of her mind.

All she felt was cold. Completely and utterly empty.

Every glowing face was staring at her.

No.

Carastene looked away. Whispers flooded the hall.

No.

"I, therefore, accept this guild into the court."

The lights burst on, the glowing faces fading, and the entire world seemed pinned on the Ewyon woman who couldn't do a task as simple as shift.

Slowly, the room began to move back to life. The music picked up, and the conversation began to hum. It all blurred together in Adrienne's mind.

She turned away from her aunt, not willing to face her disapproval. She pushed through the crowds. It was easy to do when they all moved away from her anyway.

Whispers flooded the air around her.

Weak.

Weak.

Weak.

She clenched her jaw, flinging the door open to the balcony. She was anything but weak.

She ran to the edge, throwing herself against the railing. She had failed. In the face of mere children. A simple task. What was wrong with her? Why didn't she have power like the rest of them?

"Don't be too hard on yourself," a cool, young voice chuckled.

Adrienne whirled around, bracing herself. A young man stood behind her in the dark frame, holding a champagne glass, silhouetted by the lights dancing beyond him in the open doors.

"Nerves really mess with essence."

Nerves? He thought she was anxious? She snorted. "Thank you," she spat bitterly.

He took a swig of his foul substance, walking up beside her. She ignored him, staring down at the glow of the village far below.

"Hadeon, by the way," he said, leaning against the rail. "Son of Abaddon."

"Don't know him."

Hadeon paused in surprise. "You are still new to this court life."

His eyes studied her every inch.

She sighed, turning to him. "And to whom would that matter?"

"Oh, no one," he insisted quickly. "You are very...different."

"And not taken by flattery."

He snorted. "A tongue to suit her beauty."

"I regret that I cannot return the same remark."

"It's always banter that fuels a passion, my lady."

"Why did you follow me?" she said. No one ever seemed to stick around long enough to converse with her.

"Forgive me." He cleared his throat. "I saw a woman unable to use abilities and with a remarkable face. I take a special study to oddities. I, myself, am one helping execute the Shadow Soul."

Adrienne's heart flipped. "You are?"

He smiled. "Does that intrigue you?"

"I am pleased to hear that someone is doing something about it."

He chuckled and took a sip before looking at her for a long moment. His finger dared to trace the curve of her ear. "Your point is shorter than most. Are you aware?"

She raised a brow. "Does it matter?

"I suppose not," he said, his voice thick and deeper. He took another sip.

Shorter ears...Even Sergia's were longer. Maybe this obnoxious boy had a point...

"You really ought to practice your abilities more, my lady." Hadeon mixed his drink with his fingertip. "I heard that it helps."

She bit back a scoff. "And if it does nothing?"

He winked at her. "Perhaps you'd like to call for a little help, Lady..."

"Adrienne," she said. "House of Emberson."

"I knew you looked familiar." He took her hand and kissed it, sending a distasteful shiver crawling through her skin.

He swept his cape in an overdramatic flourish and strode back inside to the gala. Adrienne turned away. She clenched her fist, staring down at it. Perhaps she would call on him. He could be useful.

She, instead, turned to the thin steps crawling up the palace wall, toward the soft glow of the higher balcony. She climbed higher, hearing the murmur of voices and bursts of laughter.

What were people doing up here?

The flickers of light revealed the figures of young men and women sitting and standing among the lounge chairs in their own private escape from the event.

She turned and looked down over the balcony, grand and connected to one of the dining halls. It lacked any stone railing...not like any average Ewyon needed one.

She removed the golden circlet from her head, focusing on the weight of it in her hands. Everything she studied said that she should have abilities.

A minor setback, she assured herself. Hadeon was right. She needed more training. She needed to focus harder.

But what if that wasn't it? What if she wasn't—?

The circlet slipped from her fingers.

It all happened in a blur. The golden weight of the past fell before her eyes as her mind acted before she could.

Screams. Rushing to the ground.

Snap.

Pain. Pain. Pain.

Warmth threatened to take the pain of living, but it held back.

Pain. Pain.

"She's dead!" Another shrill scream.

Was that her shoulder? She couldn't feel her neck.

Pain. Pain.

Strength burned into her arms. The smallest movement forced a cry from her arms. Why couldn't she turn her head? Why was her body burning?

Shaking, she sank to her knees, the world black and blurred. She slowly raised her trembling arms, holding onto her face, and turned to face her shoulder. With a quick jerk, her head snapped forward with a crack that pulled a scream from her lips.

Another echoed from the stairs above. Footsteps rushed. Voices shouted out.

Adrienne's vision wavered. Her gaze fell to her hands. Red. Blood.

"Her neck! It snapped!" a terrified sob cried out.

Adrienne's vision blurred.

"She put it back!"

"Someone get help!"

"Why isn't she dead?!"

Dead. Dead.

She should be dead.

"You! Are you all right?"

Dead.

She closed her eyes, letting herself crumple over. She was anything but dead.

PART ONE

THE SEPARATION

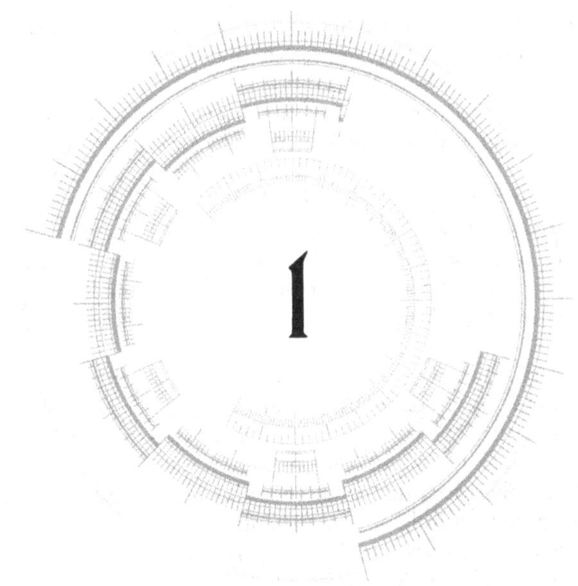

1

North Cordell, 29 Days Until

THE LADY OF the Universe is Coming.

Cold. The world was so bitter cold. And…wet.

His eyes burst open, and with a gasp for air, he sat up. Wind howled around him. Snow was now as slosh as the light rain. The hills were empty, and the sky was clouded with the dark, rumbling storm clouds.

Lincoln's head throbbed. He'd been knocked out. His heart skipped a beat. How long had he been out? He scrambled to his feet, one thought pounding in his head that sent a shiver through him.

She was *alive*.

"She's alive," he breathed.

He looked around, finding the Cube lodged in the mud. He quickly tore it off, cleaning it away with his jacket. His breath caught in his throat as he saw the red light still blinking strong.

She was alive. But for how much longer?

He broke out into a run, following the Cube's guidance. Nikki hadn't lied. She knew that this couldn't be the end. And he almost hadn't trusted her.

He jumped over a fallen tree, bursting past the blasted bus, slowing and sinking into the hillside in the mud. But how? He'd been right here when he saw the image that would forever haunt his mind.

Blood. So much blood.

He met the small river at the base of the mountain, running and crashing as it rose from the rainfall. Lincoln dashed over the little, rickety bridge. She was alive. She had to be.

What if he was too late? What if he was supposed to find her weeks ago? What if by the time he got there—?

He thrust the thought from his mind as he ran farther into the thick of the woods that were riddled with nostalgia. The past five years had made them his refuge, but he wasn't an insignificant, little boy on the run now.

Now he, apparently, had a purpose. Being part of a Council that had killed his friend.

But she wasn't dead. She was alive.

The snow was deeper as he climbed, the rain not falling as heavy. The trees cast shadows along the ground from the hidden evening light. It would be dark soon.

The red light was glowing brighter now. He was close.

He shouted her name with all his might. *It's me, Lincoln. Can you hear me?*

Nothing.

He pumped his legs faster. He cried her name over and over till his voice grew hoarse. He didn't care if she couldn't hear him. He didn't care if anyone else did. He just wanted to say her name and know that maybe, just maybe, she'd hear it again.

The Cube gave a low beeping noise, slowing Lincoln. He was close now. He stopped, his breath burning in his lungs. His heart froze as he scanned the woods. There was nothing here.

He'd failed her. Only snow carpeted the ground—snow.

His eyes grew wide. Of course, it was snow. He zoomed in on the cube and stepped forward ten steps, and dropped through the ground and, with his bare, raw hands, began digging. He couldn't feel the bitter cold biting at his fingers, only the slow, angry burn in his chest driving him harder and harder. Faster, and faster.

What if it's hopeless?

Tell me your name, and I will assure you that it is not.

Get out of my head.

You want to find the girl, don't you? Let me prove myself, boy.

His fingers hit stone ground. Lincoln's heart lurched. *No.* She wasn't here. The Cube had been—

Wait, boy.

Then he frowned. The stone ground wasn't stone. In fact, he wasn't sure what it was. It shimmered green, like a hologram.

His heart thundered in his chest, scrambling to brush the snow from the rest, even if it took till he froze. Till every inch of himself went utterly frostbitten and his bare fingers were raw and bleeding.

He wouldn't care. Not until he saw her face again as it had been two weeks ago. Healthy and alive.

He brushed a final scoop of snow away, and the supernatural cocoon dissolved.

Lincoln's heart stopped in his chest. The voice had known.

"Nikki," he breathed.

The voice had been right.

There lay an untouched girl, her skin a light shade of brown and her dark waves of hair damp from the snow, her stature short and especially small, as she was curled up. A crackle of green energy escaped from her small, enclosed fist at her chest.

The Ewyon Stone.

Lincoln couldn't move. This couldn't really be happening.

She was breathing. The subtle rise and fall of her chest proved that much. The wound on her face looked as if it had just been cut, and the fatal strike in her side, with its blood still fresh.

Wait…fatal.

Lincoln's heart leapt. The wound was quickly dampening her shirt with crimson red. She wouldn't be able to survive much longer.

With shaking hands, he fearfully pressed his hand against

her non-bloodied cheek. He almost drew away. She was burning up. She hadn't come back to life.

No. They'd only delayed her death. And this time, he was going to save her.

Oh, boy, can you? Have I not proved myself yet?

Lincoln gently scooped up her unconscious body into his arms, careful with her hanging head that lolled against his chest. A small, pained groan escaped from her lips, mumbling something under her breath.

"Hang in there, Nik," he choked. He refused to let his eyes burn.

He broke out into a run, letting the strange burn overcome him. Faster. Steady. *Faster.*

How much time did he have? She was alive. But for how much longer?

He'd have to watch his friend die twice. He shook it off and ran. He couldn't fall. He had her in his arms, and he wasn't going to let go.

He saw the camp nearing in the distance. "Help! Please someone help!" he screamed. Screw it if he was too far for them to hear. "Help!"

He nearly stumbled forward into the mud, quickly catching his balance. He grit his jaw. *Never again.*

Yes, boy. Your energy is strong. You are angry.

He held her tighter, checking to see if she was still in his grasp, as if he'd dreamed the whole thing. He could feel the fever rolling off of her, the emotionless face absent of those blue eyes.

"Hang in there, Nik," he begged, trying to run as quickly as his heart banged in his chest like a click reminding him of how little time he had left.

He had to save her. He refused to let himself fail her again. No one would stop him this time.

2

Kennedy, 30 Days Until

RAPHEAL MATHEWS WAS not one for asking for directions. Instead, he was relying on his strange, pulsing headache.

How many things could go wrong in the span of twenty-four hours?

He sat cross-legged on an icy bench, shivering, clenching his jaw to keep it from chattering. He should've packed more than just his jean jacket and one of Lincoln's hoodies…That one was an accident. Their cabin was such a disaster that it was hard to tell what he'd grabbed on his rush to the SpeedRail, which he'd caught going the wrong way, having to use his food money to pay for a new ticket to the region of Kennedy.

And no one had warned him that it would be this darn cold.

He shook his Comm in frustration, the eternal, blue circle seeming to mock him with the flashing

13

"CONNECTING" as it continued to not connect. How was he supposed to start his search now?

He sighed, leaning back into the cold, metal bench, watching an occasional auto glide over the worn, jagged road. A few scrawny trees scattered the sparse landscape of the small region town. Government-issued cube buildings were scattered about the main roads, most closed by now, a few bots tending to the windows and residents scurrying off down the sidewalks, not one batting an eye at the sixteen-year-old boy with deep lines under his golden eyes and an ancient sword at his belt.

Taryn would kill him if she found out that he'd stolen it back. His conscience told him that it was wrong. He didn't deserve to hold the Shadow Blade. They still hadn't figured out what was wrong with his brain yet, and all thought that he was a lunatic when he tried to blame the stupid voice. But Taryn had already made him go on a mission alone so that he wouldn't go psycho on the other Members, so it was only fair that he got his sword.

The energy still pulsed against his head. Whatever it was…it was powerful, but Ray would at least like to have a working GPS before investigating the supernatural.

He was going to find the Council Member Officer that Miriam Outown had heard about in Kennedy and prove to everyone once and for all that he *wasn't* a lunatic, and could use his Oquelite blood for good. First things first, he actually needed directions so that he could actually begin to enact his grand plan.

So far, that wasn't going so well.

He let out a frustrated sigh, shoving his Comm into his pocket, rubbing his temples. He was here to find a Council Member, so if he could get that out of the way, he could go back to North Cordell and act like he didn't just blow all of Taryn's money.

All he had to do was follow the surge of essence pounding at his skull. Easy enough.

He didn't stick out from the other dirty civilians littered on the streets, sitting on a curbside with a cigar and a good coat or two warmer than him.

The energy drummed like a pulse against him. No one else on the streets seemed to feel it.

A man plopped down beside Ray on the bench. Ray jumped, nearly clambering off the bench, swiveling to meet the newcomer.

"Hey, kid," the man, maybe in his mid-twenties, said with glints of amusement in his brown eyes that didn't show through on his bored face. He wore a thick, worn coat and had long, blond hair tied up behind him. He had a sharp nose and a bold jawline and sat taller than Ray.

Something about him and his brown eyes seemed very familiar, but Ray wasn't in the mood to try to place it.

Ray cleared his throat. "Hey."

The man only smiled and turned to the tele in his hands, leaning back into the seat.

He had a tele. With connection. Maybe he could—no. Was he stupid? Asking strangers? They'd think that he was some stupid kid in need of a guardian or somthing.

"Sir, have you seen anyone suspicious lately?" he blurted out. *Great going, Ray.*

The man didn't look up, continuing to scroll. "Why?" he asked in the most monotone, bored voice possible.

"I'm on a search." He tried to sit up straighter as the man raised a brow.

"Need to call your mom or something?"

"No! I'm traveling on my own."

"How old are you? Twelve?"

"Sixteen!"

The man turned, scanning Ray up and down, before frowning. "So you're short."

Ray jumped to his feet. *Now* he towered over the man. "I'm not that short."

The man shrugged, turning back to his tele. "Whatever you say, kid."

Ray huffed, crossing his arms. Maybe he should ditch the effort and go find a nice alley to sleep in.

"Where you from?" the man asked.

"Glorgory."

"Isn't that the region with the rebellion over a decade back?" the man said, narrowing his eyes at Ray.

"Yes, now, about any suspicious sightings? Strange people?" *Anything?*

"Sure," the man said, chuckling. "I saw a guy eat a

cigarette off the sidewalk this morning."

Ray blinked. What? "That's not exactly what I meant." He paced. "Think mysterious. Ominous. Strange. Defying nature."

The man continued to stare at his tele and scroll. "Like the things that wrecked Imperial?"

Ray stopped short. "Sure."

"Yeah, dunno any of those."

Ray was one of those.

Ray tore his fingers through his hair and groaned. "Nothing? Absolutely nothing? Is this town so boring, people only eat weird stuff off the sidewalk?"

"One time I saw a guy on a bench eat—"

"I get it!" Ray rubbed his temples, his head still throbbing. He tried to focus on it. Where was the power surge coming from? *Come on, Ray. Focus.* "Anywhere...on the northside?"

The man suddenly pocketed his tele and jumped to his feet with a yawn. He adjusted his beanie, brushing a strand of blond from his face, shoving his hands into the pockets of his baggy pants. "I think I got a place, kid. North, you say?"

Ray frowned. "You do?"

"Yeah, yeah." The man made his way down the road. "You wanna eat, kid?"

Go with a strange adult to eat? That didn't sound like something well advised...but this was his only lead. He was an Oquelite. He could handle himself.

"Sure," he said, racing to catch up. "As long as it's not off a sidewalk."

REMEMBRANCE MOTEL. WALK-INS WELCOME, OR BOOK ON RM045.NET.

The hologram flickered at the end of the small, auto-parking lot in front of a homey, weather-beaten, blue building. It stood two stories high, the multitude of windows trimmed with white and the paint chipping, a few bars from railings missing. The twin-door entrance was propped open by a stand and a broken stereo, the air humming inside with the sound of voices and a faint drone of music.

The man strode right past the sign, his hands in his

jogger pockets, as if he owned the place. Ray scrambled to catch up. "This place seems pretty...normal."

In fact, even his throbbing headache had subsided. Had he gone in the wrong direction?

"Well, I'm hungry." The man shrugged, spitting out the toothpick from his teeth and ascending the stairs.

Ray had no other choice but to follow him.

Inside was a spacious room full of round, wooden tables and chairs and booths in the corners. Yellow lights hovered above the tables, most crowded with people of all ages and regions, their winter wear shedded to their chairs. The aroma was pleasant, and it made Ray realize just how hungry he was.

How long had it been since he last ate? Over thirty-six hours? Right. Since he'd had to pay for an extra SpeedRail ticket. He had a total of maybe three pounds left. With a quick glance at the holographic menus hovering over an occasional empty table, he had enough for a medium drink.

Great.

Live off of a soda for the rest of your trip, Ray. It'll be great.

He hoped that the man had been onto *something* about leading him here.

The man took a booth by the wall, a hologram popping up as Ray sat opposite him. The man adjusted his ponytail, yawned, and took out his tele and began to scroll.

Ray scanned the room. Anyone suspicious was a lead. Hair that was *too* colorful, someone *too* nervous? Maybe a blue tint to their fingers—oh, wait. That was nail polish.

"Kid, you gonna get anything?"

Ray turned back to the man, looking up at him. He shrugged. "I don't have any money."

"I can pay."

Ray was about to reject when he caught himself. Turn down free food? What was he? Cole? "Thanks, guy."

"'Course." The man continued to scroll. "Lucas, by the way."

Ray tapped his fingers against the table, narrowing his eyes at a serving bot that swerved between tables, one of its screens glitching. Its wavering path did make it look a bit suspicious, didn't it?

His gaze followed the struggling bot as it threaded

through the tables with an occasional bump to a chair before pulling up to a shaded corner booth, the hover light gone out above it. A bulky man with broad, hunched shoulders sat in the corner seat, his shaved head shadowed with new hair, a tablet in hands, tattoos decorating his arms built with muscle.

The small serving bot ejected its thin, metal arms to extend the plate of steaming meat to the table. The man looked at it hesitantly before glancing in Ray's direction.

Ray looked away, pretending to suddenly be very interested in the zipper of Lucas's jacket.

"I think I see them," Ray whispered. "The person you were talking about."

The man raised a blond brow. "Really?"

"Yeah." Ray glanced back at the bulky man, now soberly eating his meal. "I'm going to go confront them."

The man chuckled. "Good luck with that."

Ray frowned. "What do you mean?"

"They're feisty. Don't get on their bad side or you're pounded." The man shrugged.

Pounded? Ray didn't like the look of the meaty fists already, and the thought of them in his face sounded like bad news. "I can deal with them. Thanks for the tip."

Ray rose from his seat, trying to act casual, shoving his hands into his pockets. He wove his way through the tables, trying to keep his eyes anywhere but the corner.

Act confident. Act like the almighty Shadow Blade Holder you're supposed *to be.*

And the almighty Shadow Blade Holder tripped over a serving bot, slamming right into a man walking through the front door.

He stumbled back, his headache suddenly rearing back. He stumbled back, clearing his throat as the man gave him an eye from under the brim of his hat, flaring his nostrils.

"Sorry." Ray coughed, swiftly turning around, trying to ease the headache. The essence was near. Was it that guy? He didn't have time to investigate Hat Guy.

He moved over to Tattoo Guy, clearing his throat.

The man looked slowly upward.

Ray scrambled to adjust himself, straightening his shoulders, clearing his throat, and crossing his arms.

The man's shadowed eyes bore into him. "What der you want?" he mumbled.

"I—I—" What did he want? "You know what I want."

The man huffed, turning back to his foot.

Assert your dominance, Ray. Come on. He slammed a hand down on the table. "Hey. Don't you dare ignore me."

"Or what?" the man said softly, a bored look lingering in his eyes.

"What do you know about the Members?"

"I don't know no members."

"That's exactly what someone who knew about Members would say!"

The man grumbled something under his breath and continued to eat.

This wasn't going anywhere. Ray grabbed the man's plate and slid it from under him. That's *all* he did. The next thing he knew, the guy had a hand on Ray's wrist and he was flung to the floor. An uproar went through the room.

Ray tried to recover from his shock, scrambling back, trying to regain his footing. "Ha! You thought I'd be—be an easy target! You're a big guy and I'm small?"

Apparently that didn't help, because now the bulky guy full on barreled at him, tossing the plate at him. Ray barely dodged it, food splattering his front. He rolled to his feet, unsheathing his sword.

It had been a long time since he'd done that, and it felt good.

The room was upended, people cheering and jeering.

The swell of power knocked on his skull. He was close. It was close.

Ray drowned them out. The burly man took a chair, throwing it; and without warning, Ray blipped from his feet, crashing down onto a table. People scrambled away but seemed hardly fazed by the teleportation.

He'd subconsciously teleported?

Someone pushed the table out from under him. Ray jumped, taking hold of the light and jumping to another. Someone took up a chair, swinging it, crashing up against the blade. Within moments, the chair was cut clean in half.

The man pushed through the crowd, smashing his hands down onto the table. Ray teleported, dropping down onto the man's shoulders, which proved to be a bad idea, as it took them both down and earned him a face to the floor. He tried to scramble away before the man got to his senses.

He didn't need to. A sharp tug on his ear was enough to pull him out.

"What is the meaning of this?" The shout echoed. Ray was tugged back by his ear, holding him steady by threat of pain. "Who started this?"

No one paid attention to his captor besides a few frantic diners.

"He did!" A groan came from the floor where the burly man lay, cowering away from Ray's captor.

"I did no—ah!" A sharp tug to the ear upward. "Stop that!"

With a swift jerk of his ear, Ray was whirled around to face his captor, and he almost stumbled back had she not gripped his shoulders.

A girl?

A really tall girl. She had dark-brown skin; round features contorted with a stone glare; large, brown eyes; and well-tamed, curly hair tied back...

He didn't have a moment to focus on her further. His ears began ringing as the entire world slowed.

And then he spotted the knife.

He quickly threw himself onto the girl, knocking her to the ground. The world spun back to life as the knife clattered to the ground. The girl looked far more distubred at the fact that Ray was on top of her as she shoved him off. "What the—?"

Ray rolled to his feet, catching the eye of Hat Guy, who turned and ran out the back door. Ray didn't hesitate to run after him, weaving through the crowd and bursting out the door.

The man started shooting.

Ray whipped out his Blade. "Who are you? Who sent you?"

"Does that matter? Just here for the reward." The man gave a smirk, removing a familiar, red blade from his belt. He'd seen it before—

The man slammed into Ray. Ray spun out of the way, but the man anticipated it, sending the blade scraping across his cheek.

Ray turned, the Voice raging to life in his mind. The man reached for his throat. Before Ray could stop himself, a blast of energy exploded from his hands.

The man flew back.

The voice let go of Ray's mind. The Blade fell from his hand, and he ran for the man, now crumpled to the ground, clutching his wound.

"Get away from me!" the man shouted.

"I—I can help!" Ray's throat began to close. "I'm a Me—"

"They said the Soul was dangerous," the man choked. He reached for his weapon, cocking it. He dragged himself away from Ray with a quivering hand holding the weapon up.

"Please, listen to me!" Ray couldn't breathe. They didn't have time for this.

He missed Ray by a long shot and crumbled to the ground, lifeless. Ray's blood went cold, his lips trembling wordlessly.

No.

Ray fell back, scrambling away from the body, gasping for air. The body was swallowed whole by a burning, red energy. Tears burned in his eyes. What Soul? He wasn't anything. He didn't mean for any of this to happen.

He'd overestimated his own abilities. He hadn't meant for the blast—

His stomach revolted. He could feel whatever essence the man had inside rolling through his veins.

He turned away and vomited, crumpling to the ground. It hadn't even been two days, and he was already being reminded that he was the monster.

He squeezed his fists, trying to hold back a scream. He was tired of the monster.

The girl wasn't only tall, but impressively strong. But he wasn't taking a lot of time to admire her muscle tone as she insisted on using it to drag him into the back kitchen and shove him onto a stool.

"Who are you?" she snapped, grabbing a wooden spoon from the counter, keeping a safe distance from him across the counter. "Do you have any idea how much a *table* costs these days? And you're going around smashing them like it's no one's business! And you…you—"

Killed someone. He'd killed someone.

Ray tried to snap a snarky comeback, but her glare choked it down in his throat. "They—they tried to kill you."

The girl flinched. She pushed a loose curl out of her face. She was wearing a baggy jacket, but he still caught sight of a light, curling mark on her dark skin up her neck.

He frowned.

"What are you staring at?" she snapped, swinging the spoon, quick to adjust her jacket.

"Look. I'm not going to hurt you." Ray felt too nauseous to try anything like that. "I *saved* you."

"She warned me about this." The girl began to pace, a hand twirling through her hair.

"Who warned you about some magical boy—?"

"'Magical?'" The girl stopped, giving Ray a disgusted look. "What are you doing? Making jokes?"

Ray blinked. She hadn't seen him teleport?

"How do you think I'm supposed to pay for the damage, idiot?" she said, swinging the spoon back in his face.

"Well, how do you think *I'm* supposed to pay for it?" Ray shouted back. It was just a table or two…and a man. He was a broke teenager. What was her deal?

She cursed under her breath. "Who the heck are you? And why did you save me?"

"Rapheal Mathews. My friends call me 'Ray,' but I can guess from context we're *not* friends. And I'm just a really nice, good-looking person."

The girl scowled, her jacket slipping again. The lighter spirals along her dark complexion flexed with her muscle, her loose curls thrown out of place from the scuffle, almost framing the perfect image of rage—

"Stop staring, Mathews!" she said, swinging her spoon to get his attention. "You started a fight in *my* place, and now—"

"Aren't you a bit young to own a restaurant?"

"Aren't you a bit young to own a weapon?" she said in a mocking impersonation of his voice.

She made him way too high pitched, but he guessed that she wasn't in the mood for criticism.

She rambled on in his face. "Grandmere will be furious about this."

"Look!" Ray shouted before she could say another word and drive him insane. "I. AM. SORRY!"

The swinging door banged open. "Remembrance, some ki—"

Lucas froze in the open doorway, both Ray and the girl frozen, staring back. The serving bot spun around Lucas's feet, racing for the girl.

Lucas blinked a few times before frowning. "Well, I see you've met."

The girl quickly stepped behind the bot as if the rusting, three-feet tall trashcan could protect her. "Mechanic, you brought this disaster here?" She quickly turned to the bot. "He didn't hurt you, did he?"

"Hey! Watch it. I saved your life…and you're talking to a bot."

The girl just scowled.

Lucas shrugged. "He said he was looking for weird people."

The girl frowned. "And you brought him to *me*?"

Even the bot made a whirring, offended sound.

"Dude, why be so offended? I'm looking for a *cool* weird person." He knew that it was petty, but he didn't exactly care. "And besides, it seems like some weird people found you first."

Lucas quickly snatched the spoon from the girl, stopping her from probably committing murder as Ray winked at her.

"Remembrance, calm down."

"I am calm," she snapped.

Ray snorted. "Your name is 'Remembrance?'"

The girl opened her mouth, but Lucas quickly talked over her. "Introductions?"

The girl hesitated, but Lucas gave her a reassuring look.

She stared at the counter. "Mercy Remembrance. Sixteen. Kennedy. And no one calls me 'Mercy.'"

Too late. His mind has already registered her as Mercy. "Remembrance" had way too many letter for him to remember. "Wait, your name is two words?"

"And yours is just two regular names, *Mathews*."

He scrambled to find a response, but all he sputtered out

was, "Yeah, so?"

Mercy's body tensed. "So, you owe me, Mathews."

"And you owe me."

"For property damages." She opened her eyes to glare at him, though she didn't look convinced.

Ray looked to Lucas, who just shrugged.

Ray let out a long sigh, enjoying the panic that he saw in Mercy's eyes. She needed him. "Look. I'm broke. Like, really broke. I used all my money on the SpeedRail ride over. And I need everything I have to get back."

"I can call the Defenders on you."

Ray fell quiet. Well, that backfired.

If Taryn heard of this, he was done. That Oquelite boy had screwed up once and for all.

Lucas stood off to the side, watching with as much enthusiasm as a media broadcast break with a long, loud slip from his drink.

"You have to work for me," Mercy said, straightening with a new, authoritative air that made Ray want to scream.

Ray's jaw dropped. *Work for* her? He was on a mission. A mission that could prove that he wasn't just the pathetic, crazy Member. He couldn't be stuck—right. He had no other option.

"How long?"

Mercy clicked her tongue and shrugged. "Two weeks, at least."

"Two weeks keeping you alive?" he jabbed.

He couldn't argue. He didn't even have any money to stay anywhere else, and sleeping on the streets or a Defender cell would not be helpful toward finding a Member.

Besides, this girl intrigued him. He saw the way her shoulders relaxed when he didn't argue.

She wanted him to stay. Why? He was a murderer. And she was obviously annoyed by him, but that feeling was mutual.

"Fine," he grumbled. "We all know you need a bodyguard, anyway. Your trashcan bot doesn't seem too ferocious."

She glared right back at him, not denying the fact. "So you accept?"

Ray crossed his arms. "I do."

"And his name is 'B0bbl3.' B-0-b-b-l-3." Mercy turned on her heel to a cabinet in the wall, withdrawing a blank card, scanning it over a machine clipped to the side. She tossed the card at him, the card smacking him in the face before he could tease her on the fact that she named a bot.

"Ow!" He picked it up from the floor.

She had regained her composure, her face not showing a crack of emotion now. She waltzed over to him. "Room 14. Go drop off your bag."

He nodded, wanting to hurry away as soon as possible to get out of her towering gaze. Something about her was unnerving.

"Oh, one more thing, Mathews!"

He stopped at the door, gritting his teeth. "What?"

"After that, meet back here. I think there's a nice pile of dishes waiting for you."

And, of course, it was after that snark that Ray came to the absolutely worst and horrible realization: *this* was the potential Council Member that Lucas had been talking about.

3

Court Illegia, 29 Days Until

TABITHA DELOROUS TECHNICALLY hadn't been discharged from the Medic Center. But with the chaos of the attack and all the new incoming patients, it wasn't hard to slip out. Really. They should probably look into security.

She didn't think that it was possible for the air to smell of both rain and smoke. Or maybe it didn't. Maybe she was just imagining things.

She rammed into a couple rushing past her, who shoved her back and against the fall. She tried to turn and catch herself with her hands. She cried out, falling back. She looked down at her hands and cursed.

They were bandaged. Right. She'd burned them in the fire.

The fire. The fire that *Cole* started. Her head hurt.

How much farther was the Lopez house? She was drenched and felt as though at any moment, she'd fall to the ground and never get up.

Coleson Johnson, the timid, quiet boy in the back of the class, had set a building on fire. He'd burned her hands.

He also saved your behind.

Or, at least, she thought he did… Her memories were hazy.

She couldn't help but feel nauseous. Guilt gnawed at her insides, among other things. She'd been the one to give the idea to go to the museum to the potentially dangerous *Mors Vis* when information was uncovered that the *Cors Vis* would potentially *help* the Wingor Member. Her eyes burned.

She had been right, but at what cost?

Now the *Cors Vis* was destroyed, so it didn't even matter.

She knew that she wouldn't be in great enough condition to go back to North Cordell just yet. She needed to stay behind in Court Illegia and help fix this mess.

The Lopez's side gate caught her eye in the flash of lighting. She gave a shuddery sigh of relief, rushing across the street, throwing herself against the gate. It creaked open, and she slipped into the courtyard.

The lights were dark in the windows, which didn't surprise her. It had been a long night...or day. How long ago had it been? She ran to the door, out of the rain under the porch roof. She scrubbed her cheek dry and pressed it against the sensor. The door swung open.

Tabitha was quick to shut it and turn up the light switch with her nose to a dim setting. She breathed in the dry air and collapsed onto the couch, trying to catch her breath. The aching of her body and the pain of the burns came down upon her all at once, forcing out a small groan.

Oh, mortals, that hurt. Everything hurt. Everything was soaked. Everything was miserable. And her best friend hated her...and she had to admit, she kind of didn't really like him right now.

And that hurt the most.

She missed Felicity, and she missed the warmth. The assurance that she hadn't ruined everything.

The kitchen of the west wing was in the same room as the living room, and the white counter was littered with documents and sleeping holograms and plenty of empty, plastic cups of coffee. Muddy boots ranging from large Defender uniform wear to little, pink ones of a child piled at the door. Coats were sprinkled around on chairs. Tabitha frowned, noticing a broken plate on the floor by the oven.

She was too tired to really be concerned. She tried peeling her wet jacket off, but her stupid, bandaged bands were proving difficult. She was too tired to get up and try and wriggle it off.

Could she use her teeth?

"Tabitha?"

Tabitha froze. Her heart crashed. *Cole. Don't look at him. Don't you* dare *look at him.*

"Yeah, that's my name," she grumbled, her voice cracking, burning at the words. "Help me take this off."

She heard the crash of something, and Cole rushed quickly to her side. She tried to pretend that she hardly cared as he gently helped her remove the stupid jacket and hung it on the arm of the couch.

There was a long moment of silence. Tabitha didn't look at Cole, and she didn't doubt that he was doing the same.

"Tabitha, why are you out of the Medic Center?" finally came Cole's quiet voice. "Please don't tell me you...walked."

She wished that her first instinct was to turn around and tell him that he couldn't control her and it was her business. But she didn't feel the burn of anger. Nope. Only the feeling of wanting to vomit.

She broke her rule and swiveled around on him. "I *did* walk, bozo. Get me that blanket."

He blinked with surprise and did as she said without a word. Her heart settled a bit, seeing that he was mostly unharmed, besides a healing scratch on his lip. She reached for the blanket with her stubby hands, but he draped the blanket over her shoulders for her before stepping back and letting her adjust it herself.

"Are you okay?"

"Me? Oh, yeah, I'm fine," she said, wiggling her stub-hands.

He didn't laugh, and neither did she. She just watched those stupid, green eyes stare into hers. She'd seen them so passionate and furious, energetic and alive, but now, they were utterly crushed. Dim and glassy.

And she hated it.

"T—Tabitha—"

"I know you're sorry," she blurted out.

Cole jumped, frowning. "How'd—?"

She pulled the blanket tighter, wanting to curl up into a ball. "I didn't," she said, quietly. "I just...That's what I wanted you to say."

He leaned forward. "Then let me," he said. "I am sorry. I am so, so sorry. I was so stupid. I should have considered what you were saying. I shouldn't have said those terrible things. That was stupid. You didn't deserve that. Stupid. So stupid."

Tears burned in her eyes. She snorted. "You going to apologize for being born too?" she said, her voice threatening to break.

Cole opened his mouth.

She kicked him. "I'm *joking*."

He frowned, bewildered. His dumb, little face pinched, his green eyes brightening with a sliver of life. "Why—why aren't you angry?"

She shrugged. "I am angry," she admitted, her gaze falling. Her stomach churned. Whom was she angry at? Herself or Cole? Her voice cracked. Not now. "I don't want to lose you."

Silence.

"Lose me?"

Tears collected in her eyes as she forced them to meet his, those stupid, green eyes again, pained and wide. "Tabitha, please don't cry. I'm sorry. I don't want to make you—"

"Just stop. It just makes it hurt more," she choked, wiping her face. "I can't lose you, Cole. Because if I lose you, I don't even know what. I don't even know what I'm supposed to do with myself! You and your stupid eyes mean so much to me and I don't even know how it happened."

She hid her face into her arms, unable to breathe, feeling sick. "I hated you for making me believe for a moment the last person in this world that really loved me had tossed me out. I feel so stupid for even thinking for a moment you—"

"Tabitha—"

She squeezed her eyes shut. Why did he matter so much? She knew that she had more people in her life than Cole. She had Felicity, but it always felt like *Felicity* had Tabitha. Tabitha loved Felicity. She really did. But then why did this hurt so much more?

"I want you to prove it."

"I'll do anything." There was no hesitation.

She looked up, wiping her nose. "I want twenty pounds and salted potatoes."

The confusion that flooded his face lifted so much of the pain nagging at her. "Okay."

She smiled, leaning back in the sofa. "Okay, number *two*. Are you keeping track?"

"Yeah."

She glared at him.

"I am!"

"Good," she said, clearing her throat, trying to blink away the tears. "Number two, do something impulsive."

Cole frowned for a moment before letting out a sigh. "That's fair."

She smiled. "Number three, give me a souvenir."

"From where?"

"I know you're running away, idiot," Tabitha said, gesturing to his fallen bag by the stairs. "I want a souvenir."

Cole's eyes widened. "I—I'm not running away."

"You're a terrible liar."

"Look, I'm leaving," Cole said with a heavy sigh. "But Nigel will approve once I tell him...after I leave. If I stay any longer, I'll screw up things more. I have to learn how to handle this."

Tabitha faltered. He was really leaving? She didn't want him to leave. She didn't want to be alone without him. Why? Wasn't she busy being angry at him?

"Oh," was all she managed to say.

Cole nodded solemnly. "So, is there a number four?"

Oh, right. "Number four," she said, biting her lip. "Write a song."

"A song?" He wrinkled his nose.

"I need something to start my new binder." She shrugged.

"I can't write—okay. Fine. I'll do it."

She sat up straighter, scooting closer toward him. "Good, and the final point?"

Cole perked up.

"Be proud of yourself."

"How is that supposed to prove anything to you?"

"Because you're a good person, Cole." Tabitha rolled her eyes. "And you don't ever seem to realize that. You're a good leader too when you don't have the stakes of the world on you. You screwed up, sure. We both did."

I don't want you to leave.

His eyes fell. "Tabitha, I lit a building on fire. I yelled at you. I *yelled* at you like a total idiot. You're right about that."

She kicked him again. "Hey! No self-degrading!"

He looked up, the smallest smile on his lips that apparently wanted to break her heart when accompanied with those sad, lost eyes. "I don't ever want you to think I'd toss you out ever again," he whispered. "I care about you too. More than I probably should. I'm not going to let you down."

I care about you too. More than I probably should.

Tabitha leaned her forehead against his. "Thank you," she whispered, staring into his eyes, which were full of tears as they tried to keep up with her own. *I care about you more than I should too.*

"I'm going to come back as someone you deserve."

She didn't feel like she deserved anything.

She didn't know what to do. She wasn't sure whether to hug or punch him.

She gave in and threw her stubby hands and arms around his neck and hugged him. He hugged her back, holding her tightly against him. She buried her face into his neck, wishing that she didn't have to let go. Wishing that everything was really okay. Wishing that he didn't have to leave.

But she had to push away, forcing a shaky smile. "Go be a stupid knight in shining armor for me now."

He tightened his grip on her shoulders. "I'll try."

"No. Repeat after me: 'I will.'"

"Seriously—?"

She deadpanned at him.

"Fine, fine. I will."

"Very good, goldfish," she said, patting him on the head with her stubby hand.

She swore that she caught a hint of a smile. He set her back onto the couch, getting to his feet. "Goodbye, Tabitha Delorous."

Tabitha swallowed hard, her chest twisting with emotions that she couldn't read. It burned…Anger? "Good luck, Coleson Johnson."

Come back for me.

He picked up his bag and moved to the door. He opened it, looking back over his shoulder. They shared a long look before he stepped out, closing the door after him.

If she wasn't so tired and hurting, she would've ran back out into the rain. Maybe beg him to take her with him, but the other side was bitter. Let him go.

Maybe that was the punishment. Separation.

For a Council meant to be stronger together, they were all on their own now.

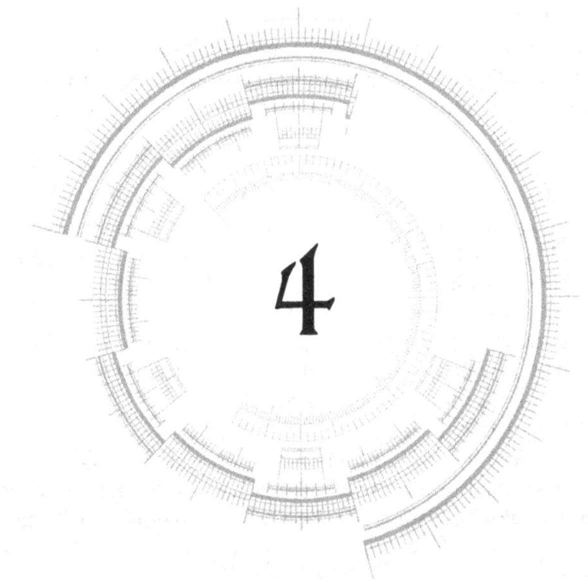

4

North Cordell, 29 Days Until

THE SPEEDRAIL FLOOR became more interesting the longer you were forced to look at it.

The car was mostly empty, understandable for this late at night. Worn, brown, leather seats were empty; the dim lights flickered over a harsh turn; and uncared-for food wrappers rolled across the floor. The sound of the rackety seats became a hum in the back of his mind.

Lawrence Williams's mind was fighting him.

That fact was nothing new, but right now it was more uncontrollable than it had ever been in years. Anxiety pounded his skull, threatening to break his stone disposition glued to his face.

The boy beside him had almost let himself die. Why did that fact hurt him so much? It wasn't like Lawrence hadn't had the same...if worse...thoughts. Maybe that's why it hurt. The boy reminded him of a dark side of himself that he never wanted to see again. He never wanted anyone to go through that.

Lawrence glanced hesitantly upward. The boy was asleep, his legs pulled up to chest, his face pressed up against the window, the quilt still held tightly around his body. He looked so *peaceful.*

He was safe now from the Oquelite, but not from himself.

Lawrence itched to punch something. But he had to settle for clenching his fists so tight, it hurt. He tapped his foot rhythmically against the floor, looking back to Matteo, as if he'd just disappear.

It wouldn't bother him so much if Lawrence didn't know how Matteo felt. No one deserved that in their mind.

He took a forceful, deep breath.

"Approaching North Cordell #512."

The only North Cordell town with a SpeedRail station, and it proved to be the only thing in the region even remotely worth visiting. Maybe it would be good for Matteo to start here before being thrust into the vastly different world of camp.

The SpeedRail began to slow.

He swallowed his anxiety and turned to Matteo, still curled at the window. Lawrence reached his hand out, hesitating, before he gently shook Matteo's shoulder. "Come on. We're here."

Matteo's eyes opened slowly, blinking a few times, before he frowned, his body freezing. He searched the car, confused, till his eyes settled on Lawrence, and his brown eyes widened.

He muttered something that Lawrence didn't understand under his breath.

Matteo's hair stuck up from lying against the window, an indent on his cheek from his headphone, and his eyes were still swollen and hung with sleep. He draped the quilt like a cloak and held it around himself, only making him look more like a little kid.

His glances darted around, studying the Rail car, before turning once again to Lawrence.

"We're in Town #512," Lawrence said, clearing his throat, wanting to do anything but continue to stare at Matteo in deafening silence. "It's about a day's walk away from where we're going."

Matteo nodded. His silence only made Lawrence's concern grow. Back in Court Illegia, he hadn't been the world's most outgoing person, but now, it seemed as if every word was suppressed and locked up, and Matteo looked like he needed a week's worth of sleep.

"Are you feeling fine?" Lawrence dared to ask. Matteo was his responsibility, after all.

Matteo nodded again.

Did the boy know how obvious it was that he was lying?

The SpeedRail came to a sudden stop. Lawrence threw his arm out in front of Matteo to keep him from crashing into the seat in front of them.

"Arrived at #512."

The scratchy announcement closed off with a bang, and the mostly empty SpeedRail shuffled to life. Lawrence glanced at Matteo, his eyes still wide in a daze. Lawrence cleared his throat and got to his feet, taking his lone bag from the seat. Matteo gathered the quilt around him and followed closely after Lawrence.

The doors opened to an anxious crowd.

Great.

The projections were already full of the attack on Court Illegia, the sparkling city now besieged with fires and Defenders by the truck load. Lawrence moved quickly, hoping to get out as soon as possible. Matteo couldn't have a moment to dare look at the projections. That would be too much.

Lawrence stepped off the platform with urgency, but Matteo hesitated, staring at the floor a long moment before taking the step.

Lawrence took a deep breath, resisting a groan. Time to face the crowd.

He walked through the storm, instantly regretting it. All those sweaty bodies, moving around so close. A shiver went down his spine. He dodged a group of racing children and stepped over a fallen suitcase, turning and colliding into a distracted man on his Comm.

"Watch it!" Lawrence shouted.

The man shot him a dirty look and shoved past him.

Lawrence scowled, looking over his shoulder. "Okay, we

just have to—Matteo?"

He was gone.

Lawrence's sweat went cold. It had hardly been a minute and he'd already lost him?

"Matteo!" He shoved through the crowd, his heart hammering against his chest. He caught a few frowns. "Matteo Lopez! Where are you?"

No boy with a blanket cape anywhere.

"Matteo!"

A warm hand suddenly grabbed his arm. Lawrence jerked back, swiveling around. Relief flooded over him. *Matteo.*

Lawrence cursed under his breath. "You're here. Oh, gosh." He took a breath again. "Stay close to me, got it?"

Matteo nodded, gently grabbing Lawrence's arm. Lawrence held back a cringe at the touch. He had promised Nigel that he'd make sure that Matteo was safe. And he intended to see that through.

He pushed through the crowd to the glowing door of freedom, pushing through the line to the hovering checkpoint. A woman adjusted her cap, blinking herself awake as they approached.

"Car number," she grumbled, drawing up a hologram.

"91."

"Name, age, registered home region."

"Lawrence Williams, seventeen, North Cordell." He glanced at Matteo, who still stood quietly beside him, gripping his arm. Lawrence held back a sigh and turned back to the checkpoint. "Matteo Lopez. Sixteen. Court Illegia."

Instantly, the woman was wide awake. "So you're Skyline refugees, then? The attack there is all anyone's talking about. He definitely looks like a native pre-earthshaker southern regioner. Can he speak in Anglis—?"

"Yes," Matteo snapped suddenly. "He can."

Matteo's glare shut up the excited woman. She cleared her throat. "Any luggage?"

Lawrence blinked with surprise. "O—only this," he said, showing his satchel.

She shook her head and tapped a few times on her screen, and then the metal gate opened. Lawrence practically ran out the gate, away from the stuffy station and into the cool, open North Cordell air. The sky was grey, as usual, with a brewing storm. The wind picked up, and the strong, familiar smell of rain was strong. The uniform, steel, cubed buildings lined the streets, each with their diversified window sills and advertisement bots zooming about and waving little signs. People, mostly dressed in work clothes, bustled with bags and sacks in arms, farm trucks parked along the sides of buildings.

Lawrence spotted one with a red cross painted on the side, the Health Care Society's adopted sign, of one of the trucks, a few men loading crates into the back. No doubt for those suffering from the fever, a flu caused by the poor conditions of many of the farming settlements across the region.

Lawrence considered himself lucky to have never contracted the disease that nearly killed his sister and her unborn child. They were staying with the Defenders now, and the new Inn would be a much healthier stay. So, hopefully, no more almost dying instances.

He turned to Matteo, frozen beside him and his eyes wide in wonder, taking in the stark, new surroundings.

"So," Lawrence said, breaking the silence. "You hungry?"

Matteo jumped out of his trance. "Sure," he said, quietly.

At least he was talking.

Lawrence straighted. "All right. Let's find something then."

He needed to make sure that Matteo didn't get lost this time, which proved too simple since Matteo seemed too terrified to go anywhere else. They finally made a stop at a department store with a small, indoor coffee shop that was definitely overpriced, but Lawrence was too tired to care.

They took advantage of the empty restrooms to clean up. Lawrence was now sitting in the hall, coffee in hand, ignoring any curious looks from passersby and blowing a wet curl from his face.

His foot tapped impatiently. Matteo had been gone awhile. Matteo wouldn't run away…would he? He wouldn't try and—

Lawrence shook off the thought, though it still pounded his skull. Matteo was fine.

A minute passed, and Lawrence couldn't take it anymore.

He jumped to his feet, rushing to the back hall, ready to run up the stairs when he nearly collided with Matteo.

Matteo stumbled back, staring in shock before he gave a sigh and a wave. Lawrence sighed and stepped aside to let Matteo pass him out of the hallway. Lawrence wanted to facepalm himself.

He wore his bright-green shirt, still a little marred with scorch marks and tears. His usual grey undershirt was reduced to the strips. Matteo had wrapped and tied it along his lower arm.

So that's what had taken him so long.

Lawrence didn't ask. Instead, he cleared his throat.

"We should be heading out soon. We're not too far," he said, trying to muster some authority. "Once we're at camp, we should be safe."

"'Should be?'" Matteo's brow lifted.

"We *will*," Lawrence insisted. "Don't worry. The Sergeant has it all under control."

Sergeant Taryn Hunter, the only living member of the famed Curatrix team, had anything but control, but Matteo didn't need to know that.

Lawrence glanced over his shoulder at Matteo, who was rubbing his bare arms under his quilt, his eyes stuck on the ground.

Darn it, Williams. How could he have ignored the fact Matteo didn't even have a *jacket*? If he pointed it out, would it embarrass Matteo further?

"We need supplies first, of course. You'll need a coat. Maybe a new shirt too, considering the weather."

Matteo looked down at his quilt.

"A real one."

"Like your trenchcoat."

Lawrence frowned, looking down at his coat that reached down to his knees. "It's not a trenchcoat."

"It is a trenchcoat."

"It's warm and that's what matters."

The smallest hint of humor glinted in Matteo's eyes.

Lawrence made sure *not* to buy a trench coat, though he was tempted. He selected an undershirt, though Matteo hadn't requested it. The quilt and strips of his past T-shirt weren't doing the best job at covering his arms.

Matteo sat staring at a display of bright-green shirts, which, considering that that was all that Lawrence had ever seen him wear, seemed to be a favorite of his.

Lawrence stepped beside him. "Are you ready?"

Matteo's eyes narrowed. "Flip it?"

"Flip what—?" He turned to see a crumpled shirt with the odd words "flip it" printed on the front. He wasn't really with the trends, but he was sure that that was no popular saying. He picked it up and shoved it into the bag. "Consider it a welcome present."

"The Council gives out free shirts?"

"Yes."

And then they were back on the road with a less terrified-out-of-his-mind Matteo at Lawrence's side, despite his coat still wrapped in his quilt. They hit the dirt road, out of the town, and toward the camp.

Matteo looked up to Lawrence for a long moment, chewing on his scabbed, bottom lip. "I'm sorry."

The words caught Lawrence by surprise, and he nearly choked on his coffee. "For what?"

"Making you take me here."

"You didn't make me," Lawrence said quickly.

"Right," Matteo said. "I'm just your job."

"It's not like that."

Matteo shrugged, his eyes darting up for a moment. "It's okay," he said. "I'm used to it."

"It's not babysitting," Lawrence insisted, not sure why it got him so worked up. "You're not a child. You're an extremely important Council Member."

Matteo turned to him with a frown. "You saw how I acted. Aren't—aren't you going to mention that?"

"The way you act is *fine*," Lawrence insisted, trying not to see his own younger self staring back at him. "You are allowed to be scared, kid."

Matteo looked at him, surprise flashing through his eyes. He didn't respond.

Lawrence tightened his fists and continued ahead. They were alone now. No weapons. No Defenders. Only two boys in a race against whatever the world threw at them.

"Stay close!"

Lawrence knew that he didn't really have to remind Matteo of it. The boy was practically glued to his side, never daring to stay far away. Lawrence still had eyes on the road that they'd left an hour ago. Going through the fields would shave a few hours off of the journey. At this rate, it wouldn't be much longer. At least, he hoped so.

The sun was going down, and the air was threatening to grow colder, and the clouds echoed of a storm. The fields were definitely less safe than the road, but he didn't have much of a choice. Besides, Matteo didn't even need to know that.

The long grasses rustled in the distance. Not by wind. Something was moving. Lawrence took a breath…

…and Matteo cried out.

And then there was a bark.

Lawrence's eyes widened with a laugh. "Fire Wolf!"

A firey head poked out of the grasses bounding for him, leaping straight on top of him with a thump. Matteo scrambled away.

Fire Wolf tried to lick Lawrence's bare face as Lawrence tried to shove him away. "No, bad. Stop it! It's good to see you too. NO!"

The wolf rolled off and sat back. Lawrence sat up, turning to Matteo adjusting his quilt. "Are—are you okay?"

"Uh-huh." Matteo didn't move.

"Don't worry. He may be supernatural, but he has nothing to do with Oquelite," he said, getting to his feet. His heart was still racing, reminding him that the threat was still looming. "This is Fire Wolf. He's—uh—a wolf that can light on fire. Fire Wolf, Matteo. Matteo, Fire Wolf."

Awkward silence followed, only disrupted by the whistling of the wind.

Fire Wolf watched Matteo curiously before nudging Matteo's leg with his nose.

Matteo scrambled away, stumbling to his feet, clutching his quilt around him. Fire Wolf titled his head.

"He won't hurt you," Lawrence said. "He might not look like it, but he's hardly more than a puppy with half the brain."

Fire Wolf snarled at Lawrence.

Matteo still moved quickly to Lawrence's side, not saying anything.

So they were back to this?

Lawrence got to his knee, and Fire Wolf trotted to him excitedly, accepting a scratch behind the ears happily. "He only ignites when there's danger. There's nothing to worry about."

Matteo didn't move.

Lawrence sighed silently. He looked at the wolf. "Camp? Can you get us there fast?" And before any real danger came out.

The wolf just stared at him.

"Sergeant," Lawrence pressed, imitating Taryn's eternally disappointed expression. "'The Council this. The Council that. Williams, stovetops are for food, not fists.' The Sergeant?"

Fire Wolf didn't give a satisfactory moment of a bark and chase of his tail in excitement, but simply trotted forward in the direction that Lawrence was already planning on going in.

He pretended that he'd made a revelation with the wolf anyhow, adjusting his coat and ushering Matteo after him. "We'll be safe this way."

Matteo didn't look sure, but he followed Lawrence regardless.

They trekked through the long grass field in silence. Lawrence counted two hours passing, the farmed land increasingly becoming more and more familiar as the rolling hills became sharper and the mountains nearer.

Matteo began to struggle to keep up, and Lawrence had no doubt that it had to do with all the walking by the pain he tried to hide in his face.

The foreign, nervous energy still hummed in Lawrence's chest, and he couldn't push it away. These intrusive feelings had been showing up ever since he got the unexplainable pain when Cole destroyed the *Cors Vis,* and he didn't particularly enjoy it.

He shoved it aside and tried to ignore it. Instead, he turned his attention back to Matteo. "You nervous?"

Matteo didn't respond, his eyes still on Fire Wolf leading them on. He gave the tiniest shrug.

"Really, camp's all right. No Oquelite there." *How much can you promise to him that you can actually ensure?* "I was born here, and never left."

Technically, his mother was from Algery, but his father was from North Cordell and Lawrence had inherited his paler skin and not a single word of his mother's native tongue.

"The people?" Matteo's question was so quiet, Lawrence almost missed it.

"The Council or…?"

Matteo nodded.

"Uh, the other Members are great." "Great" was a word for it. "You haven't met Lincoln, or Ray. There's another named 'Felicity.' She's cool, I guess. There's also the Sergeant. She's all right. Oh, and then my siblings."

Matteo perked up. He spoke in the language that Lawrence didn't understand, but he caught something like "family" out of it.

A lump formed in Lawrence's throat. "Yeah. I have a sister, Isabel. And a little brother, Charles."

Matteo watched him expectantly, as if there was more to say.

"My parents are dead," Lawrence said, knowing what he was wanting. Matteo's eyes flicked with surprise.

Neither said a word in any language for a long moment.

Fire Wolf bounded excitedly toward the road that sprouted from the road. Lawrence's heart leapt. He definitely knew this road. It had been redone not long ago after the Oquelite destroyed it. Not far at all now.

"I'm sorry," Matteo said, his voice louder now. "About your parents."

Lawrence shrugged, though he felt as if he'd been punched in the chest. He was already an orphan by the time his mother died. His father's sanity died with her.

He hurried forward, clearing his throat. "We should start moving quicker. Camp's coming up. If we run, we could be there in maybe fifteen."

Fire Wolf liked this idea and Matteo not so much, but he didn't complain. The cold was quickly setting in, and the hills rolled like waves as gusts of winds blew against them. The ever-growing woods stood, mostly likely growing closer by the week. Lawrence shivered. His experience there hadn't been pleasant.

Fire Wolf gave a bark of delight. Lawrence saw the cabins rising into view now and the Inn standing triumphantly on the close hill. It looked like an actual building now: impressive on its two stories as it faced the road, its back facing the glowing sunset.

Fire Wolf and Lawrence turned down the torn path to the camp. Lawrence frowned, noticing that Matteo wasn't beside him. He stopped and turned. Matteo stood at the beginning, watching the camp with distracted eyes.

Lawrence pressed his lips together firmly and walked to Matteo's side. "Come on. It'll be fine. You'll hardly be noticed. They're used to new kids and explosions."

Matteo's eyes widened in horror.

"Well, not anymore—it was a joke." Lawrence offered his arm. "You're going to be fine, kid."

Matteo narrowed his eyes but still took Lawrence's arm as if there was nothing else keeping him up, and they went down the road.

The guards saw them approaching first. But they weren't alone. The whole camp was already alive: lines of black, uniformed Defenders swarming about, construction workers hurrying off paths. What was going on?

They approached the cabins. Matteo squeezed Lawrence's arm.

"Lawrence Williams!"

The last remaining member of the famed Curatrix team, Defending Sergeant of North Cordell, came bounding through the camp with a youthful, determined energy. She came to a halt in front of them, hardly having to catch her breath. Her dark hair was swept up in a messy ponytail, new stripes of her natural blond showing through. Her eyes had a slight shimmer to them as she turned to meet Lawrence.

Lawrence nodded. "Sergeant."

Taryn acknowledged him, turning quickly to Matteo. "I take it this is the Wingor."

Matteo hid his face deeper in his makeshift hood of the blanket.

"His name is 'Matteo Lopez.'"

Taryn's brow raised. "As in Nigel Lopez?"

"His nephew."

"Huh." Taryn studied Matteo, bending her head forward. "I forgot he had a nephew. He talks much of nieces, though."

That was proving to be a trend.

"Matteo, do you speak?" Taryn asked gently.

Matteo didn't move.

"Could I at least see your face?"

There was a moment of hesitation before Matteo let the blanket hood fall to his shoulders, revealing his messy, brown hair; youthful, round face; and the two large, frowning, brown eyes.

"You do look like him," Taryn noted, crossing her arms. "Now, I—"

"Taryn!"

A scream tore through the camp, a young Defender shoving her way through the rushing crow. An eyepatch may have concealed her right eye, but not the sheer terror on her face as she bounded torward the Sergeant, her short hair whipping in the wind. She nearly doubled over as she came to a stop.

"Miriam!" Taryn grabbed Officer Miriam Outown by the shoulders, steadying her. "What is going—?"

"You have to see." Miriam gasped for air. Her face had gone pale, her pupil small and trembling. "Taryn. Oh, my mortals. Oh, gosh, Sergeant."

Miriam crumpled to her knees. Lawrence and the Sergeant dropped down beside her.

"Outown, *breathe*," Taryn commanded, grabbing her shoulder firmly. "What is going on?"

Miriam looked up to the Sergeant, gathering her breath. "N—Nikki."

At the name, a hundred horrifying possibilities flooded through Lawrence's mind, and not one of them could possibly have prepared him for the words that Miriam spoke as she turned her eye to him.

"She's alive."

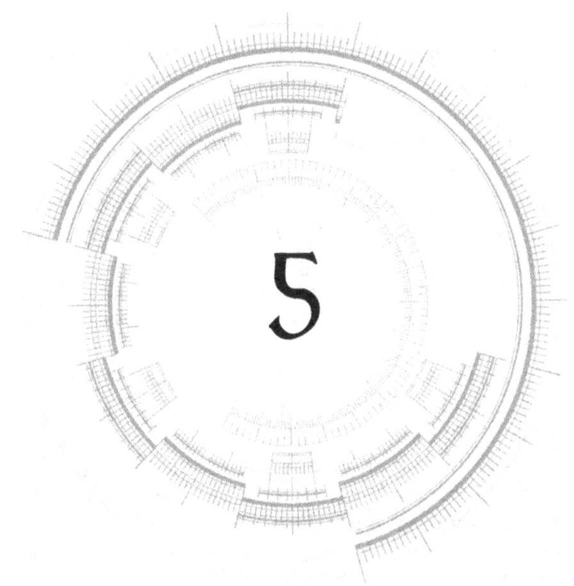

Kennedy, 29 Days Until

RAY HATED DOING dishes, almost as much as he hated trying to remember the bajillion confusing Impure and Council things. Tabitha, apparently, was very bored and had provided a very helpful breakdown on the Council, which Ray downloaded right after he desperately messaged her, hoping for some sort of interaction.

The facts were simple. There were twelve Council Members, all representing some aspect of existence, and all fit together to be the most powerful force of all time.

So far they had eight, leaving four yet to be found…five if you included the fact that they still had no idea which Member Felicity was.

Aguarious: represents the race of Water and Sea. (Fun fact: Zita Klirkpatrick was one!)

Sublinight: represents the race of Emotions and Feelings (fun stuff).

Oquelite: represents the race of Oquelite…needs no further explanation.

Guardian: represents the Mythic, A.K.A. those magic creatures in the woods and stuff.

Keyper: doesn't represent anything. Meant to be the "key" to the Council. A binding force. Not much is known.

The Member in Kennedy could be any of them, though the signs pointed more towards Keyper or Guardian. Ray just hoped that Mercy wasn't either of them and he would never have to deal with her again.

He couldn't help his eyes falling to his own Member: *Shadow Holder (RAY!): represents the dark, the shadow, etc. Has the Shadow Blade.*

He clicked off his Comm. Even Tabitha couldn't make the Shadow Holder Member status seem less daunting. Was he just the embodiment of evil?

That was his only thought as he soothed his raw fingers under his pillow and stared into the dark, watching his Comm. Any moment now. He was sure of it.

His friends were bound to check in. If not them, definitely Cole.

It was hours past midnight, and the Comm screen had been dark since he'd arrived. It was pointless. They weren't going to. Why did he keep hoping?

He rolled over to face the wall. *I could—*

He shook the voice away. He hated the stupid voice. That stupid voice was the reasons they ignored him, the reason even his own brother was wary of him. What about his mother? He hadn't spoken much to her in the last few months. How could he? What did he even say to her when all he could think about was the fact that she had known this whole time what a monster she had as a child?

He squeezed his eyes shut. Even his own voice was bothering him. *You are a monster. I can help you.*

This was his chance to start over and prove himself, and he was stuck with some overbearing, *tall* girl till he paid off a debt.

But she doesn't know you're a monster yet.

Shut up, Ray. Just pretend you're normal and sleep.

"Mathews!" The door banged open.

Ray's eyes flew open.

"Time to get up!" came the unbearable human's voice.

Ray frowned. What? "It's too early," he groaned.

"It's 6.30."

It was what? Had he not slept at all?

"I can—"

Ray shot up, shooting her a glare. His body felt heavy with sleep. "Fine! I'm awake!"

"Good." Mercy held a stone face, crossing her arms. "Now, get a shirt on and meet me downstairs. We're going shopping."

She turned before Ray could spit out a response and recover from his blush. He scrambled out of the bed, slamming the door shut.

Stupid Mercy.

He tried to think positively as he pulled his bag out from under the bed. Shopping meant walking around the town, right? Maybe he could even manage to slip away and do some exploring of his own.

He found a shirt that he wasn't sure was clean and gathered his two jackets from yesterday, which he already knew were *not* warm. He dug, trying to find a sweater of some sort, till he pulled out a green and brown sweater vest.

Cole's, no doubt.

Ray groaned outwardly, but the smallest bit of warmth clung to him. He stepped out of the room, feeling ridiculous. He leaned over the railing, looking down at the large dining room. The broken tables had been piled in a corner by the door, and Mercy was busy adjusting her scarf and gloves, careful to cover her neck.

She glanced up. "You coming?"

Ray deadpanned at her. "What? You want me that bad?"

She looked at him horrified, without a response turning to adjust her thumb rings. He tried not to stare when he realized that she had two anklets too, but with a small, glowing, red light. He decided that it was best not to ask what they were for.

He took his time down the stairs, checking his Comm. Still nothing.

Mercy apparently didn't really care how long he took, opening the door and walking right out, leaving Ray to scramble after her, closing the door behind him.

The cold slammed into him as soon as he set foot

outside. He felt slightly warmer, but for how long? He jogged after Mercy, who walked quickly down the dirt parking lot to the street, scrolling through her tablet.

"So where are we going?" he asked once he caught up beside her.

"You mean *I'm* going and you're following?"

"Makes things easier for me," he said, shoving his hands into the stolen jacket of Lincoln's.

"Ahnah's Deli. We're almost out of meat for the night rush."

"We're going *grocery* shopping?" He had been hoping for something a little more interesting.

Her glare shut down his hopes for clarification. "All right. Fine. Sure. Grocery shopping it is, lady."

He trailed beside her begrudgingly as they started down the sidewalk of the run-down downtown of the Kennedy city. Like yesterday, no one seemed to be lingering about, besides a few ragged people sitting on benches. Everyone else was rushing about in regular business, not paying attention to the two teenagers making their way through.

Mercy made a pretty good scene of not being associated with him. She scrolled through her handwritten list on her tablet. Her gloves were fingerless, revealing the metal thumb rings that he'd noted yesterday. There must have been something mechanical about them as light on it glowed green. She had similar ones on her ankles, which her jeans cut off to reveal. The rest of her body was entirely covered, a stark contrast to her outfit yesterday, and hardly any hint of the curious marks on her body.

"What are those things for? The aesthetic?"

Mercy glared at him. "None of your concern, Mathews."

"My name is 'Ray.'"

"I don't do first names."

"I would call you 'Remembrance,' but that's way too much work."

Mercy halted in her step, her eyes widening for a split second. "Then, just don't call me anything. You hear me, Mathews? Don't you dare call me—"

She stopped herself before she could say her own name, shaking her head and moving forward quickly.

Well, that was weird.

Progress with Mercy, therefore, was limited. He'd learned that she didn't like first names at least. Was she embarrassed of her own, so she had to punish anyone in her sight? Kinda rude if you asked him.

She seemed unbreakable. There wasn't a moment longer than a second that she wasn't tense.

He guessed that they'd arrived at whoever-Ahnah-was's deli when they pulled up outside a shop with a simple hologram framed above the display window: AHNAH'S DELI.

Mercy pushed the door open, a bell going off. Ray followed tentatively after her, creeping into the warm shop that smelled overwhelmingly of cleaning products and lunch meat.

The floors were orange and yellow tile, and there was a long counter with a protective, half-dome, glass covering. A woman appeared behind it, adjusting her cap that wasn't holding most of her dark hair. "Remembrance." She nodded monotonously.

She had sharp features and a large nose that complemented her face well. Her eyes were dark and seemed to be in the constant mood of judgment. Other customers filed along the counter. Mercy forced herself into line, and Ray sighed and followed.

He strained his eyes amongst the crowd. There had to be *someone* here who could prove to be a lead to a Member. He couldn't take *Mercy* back with him.

That would be terrible. For the Council. Definitely not just for him.

It didn't help that everyone here seemed just as boring as the next. Tired and drinking coffee. Scratching mud off the bottom of a tennis shoe. A guy with a holographic lip ring. However cool and awe inspiring, Ray was left disappointed. Nothing.

"I don't believe I've ever seen you with a companion before," a youthful voice said, pushing between Mercy and Ray.

Ray jumped back in shock. A girl only a year or two older than him at least stood with her arms full of a basket and packages, a door swinging behind her. She looked strikingly like Ahnah. Her hair had an undercut, and the rest was left in a braid.

"He's not a companion, Nakasuk."

"A companion doesn't break your grandmother's rules, does it?" the girl said with a quipping smile.

Grandmother?

Mercy forced a laugh, though she shifted uncomfortably, before reaching into her bag, pulling out a wrinkled, plastic bag. "I finished these for you. One's for your sister."

Nakasuk's eyes widened as she took the bag. "Oh, my gosh, really? You know I was only joking when I said I wanted an earring set to match—"

Nakasuk didn't even finish as she ripped through the brown paper, and she pulled out a piece of cardboard with two earrings stuck through it. Two crescent moons looked like they were shaven from white glass attached to obviously hand-bent wire, but Nakasuk looked thrilled nonetheless. "Remembrance, these are adorable!"

Mercy seemed to be fighting a smile as she nodded. "Waning crescent. They're the hardest to make out of a broken plate."

"Hopefully B0bbl3 helped out." Nakasuk laughed, quick to switch out her earring pair.

Mercy rolled her eyes. "Mechanic can't make him that advanced."

Ray noted that she called Lucas "Mechanic." Did he not have a last name?

"Had no idea you were a jeweler, Remembrance," Ray said with a smug smile. "Why don't you have your own?"

Before Mercy could respond, Nakasuk said, "Oh, she's not allowed."

"Not allowed?"

Mercy glowered at him. "It was just paying her back for the meat delivery last week."

Couldn't she see how obvious it was that she was avoiding the real question? Ray was tempted to stick his tongue out in immature defiance.

"I haven't seen you around here," the girl said, turning to Ray with a frown. "Uki Nakasuk, eighteen, Kennedy."

"Rapheal Mathews, sixteen, Glorgory."

Uki raised a brow. "Glorgory? What is someone from there doing here?"

Ray straightened his jacket. "Important business—"

Mercy watched him from behind Uki.

"—and repaying a debt."

Suddenly, a force slammed through his senses. Ray stepped back, catching his lost breath. His senses vibrated, his vision going out of focus for a moment. The energy was suddenly overwhelming.

"Sounds fun," Uki said. "I'm Ahnah's sister. Never been to Glorgory. I've actually never been anywhere but Kennedy."

Ray nodded through gritted teeth, shoving his trembling hands behind his back.

Essence. He was feeling power.

Uki turned to Mercy. "Are you going to the market fair this weekend? There are going to be lots of craft sellers…"

"Remembrance."

"I—I'm not sure I can," Mercy said with a sigh.

"Remembrance!" Ray jumped between her and Uki.

Mercy scowled at him, glancing at Uki. "What is it?"

"I—I think, um, I see something low-key suspicious."

Mercy grabbed him by the shoulders, spinning him around the wall. "What do you mean?" she said in a hushed voice.

Ray searched the shop.

A glint of red. A straw hat.

His heart leapt. "There!"

"Where?"

Ray shoved her out of the way, grabbing a baguette from the shelf and swinging it at the man as he burst through the crowd. "Hands up, Glowing Eyes! I know who—"

The man staggered back, his *brown* eyes looking horrified back at Ray.

Shoot.

Mercy took back the baguette, faking a laugh as she glanced over her shoulder for a split second to glare at Ray. "Sorry, he's a bit…stupid. Just *really* likes bread."

She pulled Ray back into the line, his eyes unable to move from the guy straightening his coat. "What do you think you're doing?"

"Uh, being your super-awesome bodyguard."

Mercy frowned, bewildered. "You just threatened the

mailman with bread!"

"I swore I saw something!"

Mercy scowled. "Just…stop. Make a bubble in your mouth, and stay low."

"Fine."

"Where's your bubble?"

"Seriously?"

Mercy glared. Ray formed a bubble in his mouth and glared at her.

His Comm went off in his pocket. He resisted from picking it up.

He'd felt something. He was sure of it, and he knew that Mercy did too. The way her eyes darted around the shop was hard to hide as she folded the brown paper bag, her focus gone from Uki's rambling. He watched her grow tense. That big-tough-girl mask had a crack. And he itched to shatter it.

Who was hiding under there?

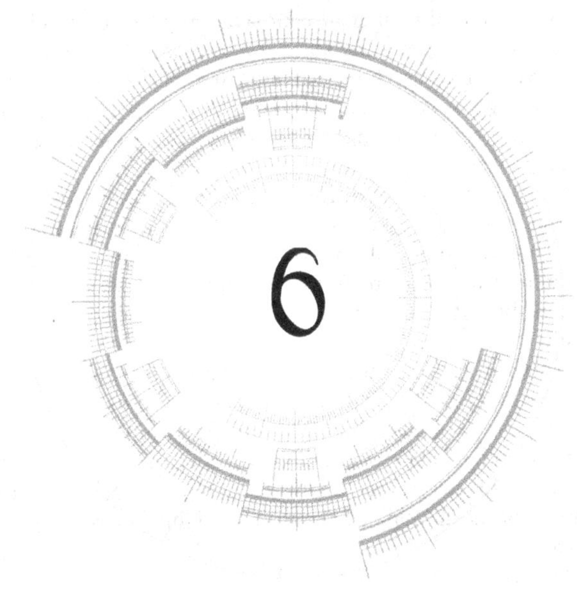

6

Isledowle, 29 Days Until

COLE HAD LOST count of the hours since his last recharge. Maybe four in Midventern? Who knew? He'd been driving aimlessly, and every spot of adrenaline had evaporated, and he was left to the echoes of the taunts in his mind. He knew that he was acting on his emotions again.

You know how well that went last time.

You don't have a plan.

You'll screw it up.

You're going to hurt her again.

He tightened his grip on the wheel, his fingers digging into the leather. Focus on the *road*. Focus.

Should he go to Imperial to the Outowns? They were his patrons, after all. But would they change their minds seeing him disgraced?

What region was he even in? The town reminded him of a more worn-down North Cordell, but with low-ceiling, brick buildings; fluorescent-colored window lights; and a run-down road that hadn't been paved in what seemed like a decade. The roofs of the shops were made from sheets of metal with pipes as chimneys, emitting smoke out into the near freezing weather. The windows displayed an occasional shadowed person in a bar or two, but most were closed up for the night.

Maybe he should restock. His food supply was two granola bars and a bottle of water. He had been in a bit of a rush, and meeting Tabitha had thrown off his focus. He meant to run away from *her* to learn to get better at his abilities, but of course, when she was sitting right there, he couldn't walk away.

Would it look strange for an underage teenager to walk into a bar and ask for food? He was eighteen, sure, but what if someone recognized him from the holograms?

He decided against it, turning the corner.

The next street was oddly dark. No lit signs or street lights. Not an illuminated window in sight. Maybe this was the exit—

Thump.

The hit came from above. Cole went rigid.

It was nothing. Maybe just a rock?

He tried to keep his eyes forward, ignoring his thoughts waging a storm now.

Two pairs of glowing eyes dropped right in front of him through the window shield, staring right at him.

He swiveled back. The truck skidded. His vision blurred. Everything slowed. He slammed his foot on the brakes. The tires screeched, glass shattered, and Cole slammed back, his ears ringing, his vision blacking out.

He smelled smoke. Alarms.

Something sharp grabbed onto him and dragged him out, his body dropping.

His eyes burst open, his head searing with pain.

He squeezed his eyes shut, trying to breathe. The darkness only made it worse.

He was dead. In the most pathetic way ever.

"Don't fall asleep!"

His eyes burst open, the world becoming painfully clear. A stranger stood above him. And out of nowhere maybe four...five leather-clad persons appeared, a few standing on the opposite rooftop.

Where was Glowing Eyes?

"Get to auto! Contact Cecileo! I'll deal with them!"

Cecileo—? His head punished him, spiking with splitting pain, leaving him helpless to watch as a woman expertly descended from the roof, landing flawlessly on her feet, whipping out two hilts from her belts, bolts of an electric blade.

Looking at them was a mistake. His head was not having it.

He looked away, his eyes watering. He heard a shriveled cry and a zap. A few crashes.

He felt so heavy. Maybe if he just—

Slap!

The woman squatted next to him. "Do. Not. Fall. Asleep," she repeated, tucking her hilts back into her belt. "We need to get you out. Can you walk?"

The woman's form was split into two now.

"Y—yeah."

"Good. Let's go."

With help from her impressive grip, Cole was hoisted to his feet. His head rocked, threatening to take his body with him. Nausea shook him. His head spiked.

He was fine. He deserved this. Just endure.

One step forward, and the whole world slipped.

You, nameless boy, are incredible. I came to torment you and you've already done more damage in your mind than I could ever dream.

Cole jumped up with a splitting headache and the dim room rocking. He narrowed his eyes, his vision beginning to calm down. He still felt heavy, wanting to sink back down and sleep, but he fought it.

Where was he?

The wood walls surrounded the small room that he was confined in. There were no windows, and the only light source was the light spilling out from the doorway, blocked by a thin curtain. He sat on a thin mattress, and his bag sat beside it. A jug of water was set on a stool beside him, the Medallion lying next to it.

Cole's heart skipped a beat. They'd taken off the Medallion?

He quickly grabbed it, clipping it back around his neck. The memories slowly trickled back.

He'd *crashed.* No wonder his head felt like it was on fire.

"You're awake."

Cole jumped, scrambling back from the figure in the doorway. The voice was familiar. He frowned, his vision adjusting. His eyes widened.

It was the woman. The woman who'd saved his life.

She had dark skin and dark eyes to complement. Her hair was made out of tight braids, randomly assorted with purple weaved around a silver circlet on her head. Her left hand was made entirely of metal, and on the right hand, she had a red, glowing DNA ring. She wore mostly leather and a belt around her waist holding the two hilts that he remembered vaguely from before.

But he couldn't stop looking at her hand. A metal hand? How was that even manufactured?

Where had she come from?

"I imagine you're confused." She laughed, taking a seat opposite him on the floor. "Concussions can do that."

"C—concussion?" No wonder.

Great job, Cole. Stuttering away like an idiot.

"You'll be all right. You were only out for a few hours. The burn was an easy treat, but the head injury took a bit more of a dosage. Those creatures didn't seem to be very interested in you, anyway. Headed north for Liberty."

So he hadn't been hallucinating. He'd really seen the glowing-eyed people again. How much did Cole owe this woman now?

"Thank you," he managed to say.

"It's my duty," she said with a playful smile. It faltered, her eyes studying him. "Looks like you have a long history of being burned. Where's the scar from?"

Cole frowned. What scar? He looked down and realized that she meant the faint scar across his chest. "I—I was burned as a baby," he said simply. That's the most his father ever explained of it at least.

"Ouch." The woman cringed. "Well, survivor, I'm Echo."

No formal regional introduction?

"I'm—"

"Coleson Johnson, known better simply as 'Cole.' Eighteen years. Sulfur." Her eyes glinted with humor. "I know."

Cole's jaw dropped. "You—how…? What?"

"I think it might help if I mentioned I was a Marketeer."

Well—that explained almost everything. It had been seven months since he first encountered the rebel group of counter-culture misfits who lived within "markets" hidden in city walls, with a strong hatred of Defenders.

They were the ones who'd given him the Illuminate.

Cole's eyes widened. "I need to go back to the Market with you," he gasped, starting to get to his feet, before his headache split. He stumbled back, gritting his teeth.

Echo jumped up after.

"Please?" he pleaded painfully. "I—I have to."

"Whoa, whoa. Kid, chill." She grabbed him by the shoulders, easing him back down. "You're still recovering."

"I *have* to go to the Market." He clenched his fists in frustration as his head throbbed.

She frowned. "Why the sudden urgency?"

"I need a teacher."

"A teacher?"

Cole nodded. His head begged him to forget it and lie back down.

Echo pinched her lips, studying him intently. "The Market isn't the best place for a young Council Member under a Defending Sergeant's rule—"

"I burned down a building," Cole broke in, laughing hoarsely. "I doubt they want me."

"And your brother crashed the Glass Tower. It could be worse."

She had a point…

Echo looked at him curiously and then sighed. "Look, I'll check with some others, and I'll get an answer back to you. Sound good?"

Better than good. "Amazing," he breathed. "Thank you. Thank you so much."

She clapped his shoulder, giving him an assuring smile. "Now, get some rest. Got it?"

Cole nodded back.

"Good." Echo got back to her feet. "I'll check on you

later."

She slipped out the curtain, leaving Cole alone now, sitting in the dark. His heart was racing, and despite the pain in his head, he felt…hopeful. He would overcome Tabitha's list, and he'd learn what he needed to be better.

A Marketeer teacher. A solid plan.

But his plans had grown a habit of going wrong.

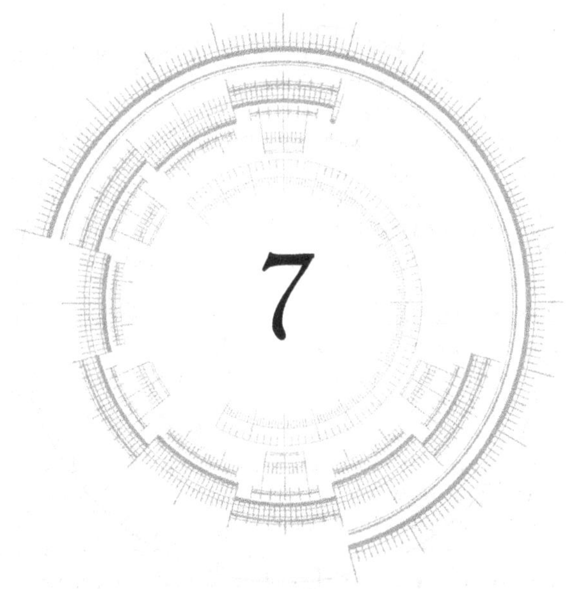

7

North Cordell, 29 Days Until

MIRIAM WAS GETTING Taryn. That was the only thought keeping Lincoln's sanity at bay.

He wasn't crazy.

No. He could feel the warmth of her in his arms and the distant heartbeat in her chest. He clung her to him tighter, keeping his face hard in a scowl to anyone who dared come close. That was the only thing keeping him from sobbing. He couldn't be weak. He needed to protect her.

"Lincoln," Sergeant Rayder Dow said, stepping forward. "I need you to let me examine her."

"No," Lincoln gasped, shaking his head. "Don't take her—"

"I won't," Dow said, his voice steady and cautious.

Lincoln watched, his throat closing up as Dow gently pulled Lincoln's grip around her looser. Dow hesitated and then pressed his hand against her face.

His eyes widened, drawing away. Lincoln's heart dropped.

"She's burning up."

Lincoln held her closer, and she groaned slightly. Unintelligible words slipped through her lips.

You can't save her without me.

The border patrol was sent into panic when they'd seen him running toward camp. A few had rushed to stop him, fully convinced that he'd gone mad until they saw that the body in his arms was, in fact, *alive.*

Miriam promised to get the Sergeant. They were running out of time.

"Oh, my mortals." Taryn stopped dead in her tracks as she turned the corner. "Oh, my gosh."

Her eyes went wide. She clasped a hand over her mouth, smothering a cry. Dow went to her side.

She's a mortal. Your Sergeant cannot help you.

"Don't get too close, Hunter," Dow said. "The boy's being awful protective."

Taryn didn't hear him. "She's—"

"Dying," Lincoln spat out. They didn't have enough time to gape over her being alive. She would leave again. He wouldn't be able to stop it—

Dow began rattling off a list. "She has a high fever. I couldn't examine the wounds, but most likely blood loss. The wound is likely infected by the Oquelite blade—"

"Lincoln, get to my truck right now! Dow!" Taryn snapped out her daze. "Dow, keep talking!"

Lincoln rose to his feet, but he didn't let her go. He had to save her.

Taryn began barking orders, breaking out into a run. "Notify the MedTent! Alert the patrol!"

With the click of her tele, the doors of her truck flew open. Taryn tore into the driver's seat. Lincoln stumbled into the back with a shove from Dow, who climbed in after him. As soon as the door shut, Taryn slammed on the gas.

Dow flew forward, clinging to the seat in front of him. "The infection might have potentially been stalled by her stasis—"

"Stasis?"

"Lincoln found her protected by the Stone."

"That means her essence rates must also be failing," Taryn snapped. "The longer she's away from the Stone producing essence, the weaker she becomes to whatever darn Oquelite is fighting to control her essence."

Right. Someone had *killed* her. Had Silas planned the whole thing? Who was responsible for this?

Whoever they were, he'd kill them over and over until they felt this pain.

I could help you tear their throat out.

Lincoln looked down at Nikki's face. She looked so peaceful amongst the commotion.

"I don't think she'll make it," Dow said.

Lincoln's heart lurched. His mind was frantic. Control your emotions. Don't be weak. Don't be weak. She couldn't die. No.

Please don't die. Please, Nik—

"She won't!" Taryn shouted, taking a jerking turn in the mud. "I'm not letting her."

The white tents of the field hospital shimmered in Taryn's headlights, the sun beginning to submerge below the mountains. Taryn sped up. The front flaps opened. Medics scrambled out of the way as Taryn came to a sliding break right in front.

She slammed the door open. "Out! Now!" She ran out of the truck, shouting. "We don't have any time!"

Lincoln stumbled out the auto, Nikki tensing in his arms, the cold night air nipping at his numb face.

Taryn practically dragged a Medic to them.

One glance, and the Medic gasped. "Oh, mortals."

Lincoln flinched.

The Medic drew out their wrist band, scanning it over Nikki's forehead. The wristband beeped, glowing red, displaying, "105°F."

Lincoln almost forgot how to breathe. He could hear the voice echoing in his mind its temptations.

It will be your fault.

"Sergeant, I—" The Medic gulped before looking into Taryn's glower. "We don't have any open availability."

"You what?"

"Jessica, calm down." Dow grabbed her arm.

No room. There was no room to treat her. No doctor.

The world was spinning. He pressed his forehead against hers, squeezing his eyes shut. *I'm sorry, Nik.*

She didn't respond. Of course not.

You could've saved her. Don't make the mistake again.

"You can't do *anything?*" Taryn shouted, her voice cracking into almost a scream.

"Sergeant?" A new voice broke in.

Lincoln looked up. It sounded familiar.

The shadow of a man paused. "You're that boy," the man breathed. "The one who fixed the generators before the flood."

The hospital director from a few weeks ago.

He stepped beside Lincoln. Taryn went quiet.

"Can I see her?" he asked.

Lincoln didn't move.

"Lincoln." Taryn's voice was on edge.

"Don't hurt her," he warned, his breathing quickening.

The directors placed a firm hand on Lincoln's shoulder, loosening his grip to let her face roll back. Lincoln refused to process the symbols that appeared on his hologram. "We don't have room. Medic's right, but we do have an empty storage room."

"A what?" Taryn snapped.

"I'll try and clear a room," the director said. "Most of the patients are near the end of their fever term. I can send in oxygen and any stabilizing equipment I can find."

"Hurry," Lincoln said. *Thank you.*

"This way. I'll send a nurse for a full-scale inspection as soon as I can find one."

They were rushed into the tent. Lincoln tried to stay level. *Don't show weakness.*

Taryn shouted for people to clear out. The lights were bright, and everything was a blur. It was at least warm.

The director stopped and pulled away the flap to reveal the small, empty room, a cot already set. It was pushing it to cram four people in it. The director left in a hurry, and within moments, a woman ran into the room. A field Medic who wasn't fazed at all by the bloody, dying girl in Lincoln's arms.

"He's not letting go of her," Dow warned.

"We don't have time," the Medic said, rushing to Lincoln. "Just from examination and the director alone, if we don't do anything, she'll be gone within the next hours."

"Lincoln." Taryn gave him a warning look.

Lincoln wished that he couldn't feel her weak heartbeat as he let the Medic and Dow carefully cradle Nikki out of his arms and set her onto the cot.

Everything felt so cold.

He itched to reach her hand hanging limply off the cot. The smallest groan escaped her lips. Lincoln's heart skipped a beat.

The Medic began tapping away at their projected screen, another nurse pushing in the stabilizing tech that the director was talking about earlier.

"Blood loss is the second greatest factor. Her wrist is also broken."

"We know," Taryn said. She wavered a moment, paling. Dow wrapped an arm around her shoulders.

"What's the first factor?" Dow asked.

"How—how did she receive these wounds?" The Medic looked up hesitantly.

Lincoln's heart seized in his chest.

"Oquelite attack," Taryn said, squeezing the bridge of her nose. "Please don't say—"

"I'm afraid so, Sergeant," the Medic whispered. "Something must have momentarily stopped the infection, but it's spreading rapidly now. Just like it would right at the moment the victim was impaled." The Medic took a deep, shaky breath. "We don't know any doctors who can treat anything like this. Even if we did manage to heal the wounds, the venom would still kill her first."

Kill. Kill. Kill.

Lincoln squeezed his eyes shut, trying to banish the word from his mind. The Stone had only been able to stabilize her for so long.

"There has to be something!" Taryn shouted. "Anything!"

Breathe. Breathe. Breathe.

"We don't have a specialist here," the Medic said, cowering.

Lincoln stopped. An Oquelite specialist.

His eyes rose, his fists shaking. "I know someone."

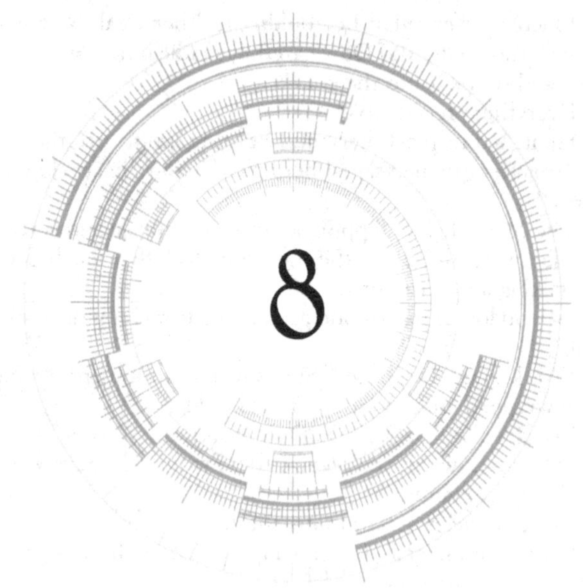

8

Kennedy, 29 Days Until

"SHE'S ALIVE."

Ray's heart dropped as his phone nearly slipped out of his hands as he closed the door to his room.

"I need your mom's ID."

His blood went cold.

She's alive? He couldn't mean Nikki. He couldn't. She'd been pronounced dead for two weeks…but here was Lincoln saying the opposite.

"Nikki," he whispered.

He didn't even stop to process, pounding his mom's ID into the message.

His heartbeat echoed in his ears. This was impossible.

He moved to the group chat, instantly demanding some explanation.

She was alive. And suddenly, everything became possible. All memories of the morning were washed away and he didn't feel like vomiting out the nothingness in his stomach.

His friend was defying death.

His other friend had messaged him. *Twice.*

Ray was prepared to meet the jerk eye to eye as he threw the washroom door open…and Mercy dashed into the room.

Ugh. What was she doing in here? So soon too?

She slammed the door behind her, her eyes wide and frantic, holding her hair back with her hands. B0bbl3 zoomed in with her, spinning in a glitchy panic. "Do you have a hair tie?"

"You can't just barge in here like—"

"DO YOU HAVE A HAIR TIE?"

"Do I look like someone who'd have a hair tie?"

Mercy stared at him. Even the dumb, little bot stopped spinning to stare at him.

Ray sighed. "Dresser. Second drawer."

Mery tore his drawer open, scavenging through it for a tie like her life depended on it. Ray pretended to ignore her, inspecting his busted lip in the mirror. Why was it so important that she had her hair up at all times?

She hurriedly put her thick, curly hair up in a bun. She whirled around to him. "Where's your jacket?"

"Why the heck do you—?"

"Mercy!" A shrill, sing-song call echoed outside the door.

Both Mercy and Ray froze. Someone was here calling her by her first name?

She quickly turned to check her thumb rings and anklets. "Stay put," she shouted with a whisper.

She ran out the door, closing it gently behind her now.

"Ah, there you are!" came the voice.

Ray ignored Mercy's command, which was easier to do when her dumb face wasn't here glaring at him, and crawled to the door.

The cheerful, homey voice took a sudden, cold turn. "What are you *wearing?*"

"It has been a rushed day," Mercy replied quickly.

"I don't remember that jacket."

"I—Papa—it's Papa's."

A moment of silence. Ray stiffened. Anyone could see through that stiff lie.

"All right." A small chuckle. "Let us go downstairs, *mon héritage.*"

It only occurred to Ray as the footsteps echoed down the hall that the woman hadn't been speaking in Anglish. Did Kennedy have many people who spoke with pre-earthshaker languages? He racked his brain. The *francé*, perhaps?

Why had the woman been so picky about Mercy's clothing? Seemed a little obsessive to know when an article of clothing was out of place.

Mercy had told him to stay put. But she was a jerk, so why did he have to listen?

He got to his feet and did a twirl for the fun of it, landing promptly behind the coat hanger with a thud.

He froze.

"Did you hear something?" the older woman said, her voice darkening.

Ray's sweat went cold, willing himself invisible.

He spotted the two persons coming down the stairs, an older woman, her curly hair cut short with brown skin a shade lighter than Mercy's, towering above her.

If that woman was taller than Mercy, Ray didn't want to be caught beside her.

The woman narrowed her eyes, scanning the room as she stepped off the staircase. Her eyes stopped on Ray. He froze, his breath seizing in his chest.

She moved on, adjusting the hair tie in Mercy's hair.

Mercy followed after her, her eyes quick to dart in his direction and then right back to the ground as she twisted her long sleeve. "I didn't think you were coming for another week," Mercy said, her tone softer than usual.

"I saw a withdrawal in the motel finance account. And I heard rumors of an…attack." The woman straightened, drawing out her tele in hand. "You know I take every matter very seriously."

"It was just some broken tables," Mercy said quickly. Ray saw her tense, her eyes becoming panicked as she stepped back. "I—I'm paying off the debt right now."

The woman raised a brow. "And you hadn't told me of your plans before."

Mercy opened her mouth and then paused. "I'm sorry. I should have."

"I expected responsibility. You know I don't like you being here alone. And what of this attack? What did they do to you?"

"It was nothing. I—I'm okay. They…they were nothing," Mercy said quickly.

This time the lie didn't pass. The woman shot her a glare, and Mercy fell back.

"Perhaps you don't need to know of your papa's whereabouts if you can't handle how serious the idea of people using you is." The woman tucked her bag under her arm and began to walk toward the door.

Using her? What was Mercy's deal?

Mercy jumped, racing after her. "You know more?"

The woman stopped, turning on her sharp heel. "I've received some word. But irresponsible little girls cannot possibly handle it, as I've learned. Too emotional. Too willing to put the legacy at risk."

"He's my fath—" Mercy stopped herself, rigid with horror at the woman's furious glare. "I—I'm sorry. I—I shouldn't have talked—"

"You've been doing an odd amount of talking back today." The woman stepped closer.

Ray caught Mercy cringe.

"Maybe I should restrict your visits with the Nakasuk sisters as well."

Mercy's lips twitched, but not a word left them. Fear was welling in her wide eyes that Ray could no longer find the smallest twinge of snark in. The eyes of a child.

Ray ran out, dropping his invisibility, making a loud thud. Mercy and the woman whirled around. Ray froze as if he hadn't noticed them prior. He gave a wave. "Oh, hey!"

Mercy's expression quickly hardened to the I'm-going-to-murder-you look from behind the woman.

The woman frowned, slamming her tele onto the table. "Who are you?"

"Ray," he said stupidly. "Who are *you*?"

The woman straightened her posture, upturning her nose. "Virtue Faithful."

"That's a name?"

Mercy appeared to want to throttle him as she tore her fingers through her hair.

"Who is this boy?" The woman quickly turned to Mercy, who dropped her hands behind her back.

"A—uh, customer," she said, obviously uncomfortable as she shifted on her feet, her eyes darting anywhere but Virtue's face.

Was she that bad of a liar? He'd imagined that she was good at all arts of the cruel tongue.

"I'm looking for my colleague," Ray said, turning Virtue's attention back to him. "Last I heard, they were here in Kennedy."

Virtue raised a brow.

"He was interested in the art of sandwich making. *Remembrance* gave me some great rates for a room."

"Do not elaborate on your details," Virtue said with a growl. She pinched the bridge of her nose, shook her head, and turned back to Mercy. "I see at least you're abiding by at least one of the rules."

She turned for the door, not bothering to look at Mercy as she pushed through the door. "I'll be back for another inspection soon. I expect better results."

Mercy stood still for a moment before watching the door as if it would open again and the woman would come back to eat her alive. She suddenly snapped out of it, shaking her head. She didn't even look at Ray, just stormed past him, purposefully ramming her shoulder into him as she passed into the kitchen.

"How about a thank-you?" he grumbled. The whole thing had been odd. Virtue storming in just for a simple withdrawal? Then yelling at Mercy for wanting to know information about her father?

A small part of Ray felt sorry for her. His memories of his father were all vague, happy, sure, but tainted after a decade without him. Yes, he'd gone to take care of Cole, but it didn't soothe any of the pain clawing at him. The pain of leaving his mother all alone with *four* children.

He clenched his fist, trying to shake the thoughts away.

How long had Mercy's father been gone? What happened to him? Had he left her, just as Ray's had?

He turned and looked to the table, a glint catching his eye from the sunlight. His heart skipped a beat. There was Virtue's forgotten tele, alone on the table top.

He couldn't help but smile. Perhaps there was a way to get answers.

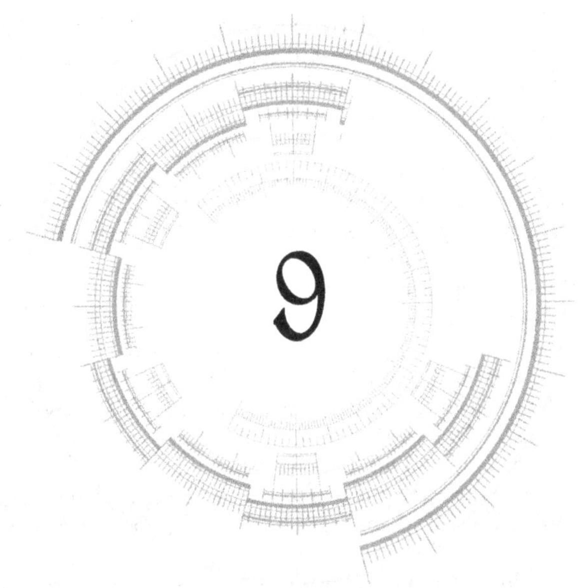

9

"DOCTOR MATHEWS!"

"Lincoln?"

The joy in Ray's mother's voice gave Lincoln room to breathe. His hands were shaking, and he thought that they'd never stop. He needed to get back to the room, but he called the only person that he knew was capable of healing Oquelite-infected wounds.

The only person who could save her.

Since I can't save her.

Oh, foolish boy. You can save her. You only need my *help. Only for a name.*

How can I trust you?

Dow sat across the hall, watching Lincoln intently.

"Doctor Mathews, we need your help." His throat threatened to choke him. Tears burned again in his eyes. "Please."

"Lincoln, what's—?"

"The Ewyon girl," Dow cut in. "Nikki. She's suffering from a deadly, Oquelite-inflicted wound to the side, spreading rapidly as of an hour, on top of other things. Lincoln says you know how to deal with these types of inflictions."

Lincoln clenched his jaw, trying to keep the feeling away. What if she was too far? What if she said *no*? They were too late, weren't they? *Why were his thoughts torturing him*? His own mind physically hurt him.

But didn't it have every right?

I can heal you.

I only want to heal what's done to her. And destroy who's done it.

"I'm coming." Dr. Mathews's voice rose. "Give me an hour. Keep the girl's oxygen stable, and in a stable state!"

"I'm afraid we might not have that time."

"Then *make* it." Dr. Mathews hung up.

"I see where Raphael gets his gallantry," Dow said, though neither of them smiled. "I'm going to inform the director. Get to Taryn."

Lincoln's heart raced with a new urgency as he rushed back into the room. Nikki was hooked up to more machines and collectively less bloody. She looked as if she was only asleep, if you ignored the bandaged half of her face.

Taryn turned away from the monitor, her body tense and eyes wide. "Lincoln," Taryn said, her voice soft.

He tried to calm his breathing. "Doctor Mathews. She— she'll be here in an hour."

Taryn paled. "An hour?" she shouted. She stopped, shaking her head and turning back to Nikki. She pressed a cautious hand to her forehead. They had cut uneven bangs away from the bandaged part of her face. The marred right side of her face was the least of their worries, but it still pained him.

He slumped to the floor beside the cot. All he could do was wait and ignore the voices.

An hour.

Message Ray.

LINCOLN: Thank you for being a Mathews.

Forty minutes.

Lincoln's hope was falling, just as Nikki's vitals seemed to be fighting to do. A dip, an alarm went off. The glowing, green Stone flickered.

Lincoln shot to his feet. "No!" He ran, but Taryn grabbed him, forcing him to face her.

"It's okay, Linc," she said, turning him away, her breaths ragged. "She's okay."

He refused to look her in the eyes. The burning inside of him wanted to fight her. But he felt weak, and he couldn't show weakness. Not to the Sergeant.

"No," he said, coldy. "She's not. She's not okay."

"Don't think like that. She's escaped death before." Taryn pushed the damp hair from his eyes, but he was too numb inside to feel its comfort. "Before she was born. Full-blooded Ewyon and Aguarious are illegal. Executive Dean convicted the Aguirres, they lost the trial. I thought Dean had been successful in killing the unborn child."

Taryn's voice choked up.

Lincoln had almost forgotten that Taryn had been friends with the Aguirres…Nikki's parents. She'd watched her friends on trial, *Nikki* on trial, for simply the child they'd conceived and watched them lose.

Nikki had been condemned to death before she was even born.

His sweat grew cold.

"But I was wrong, Lincoln. I'm not going to let her die." She grabbed his shoulder and held him to meet her eyes, glassy with tears and an anger that Lincoln had never seen before. "Not another Aguirre will die on my watch, you hear me?"

She held his shoulders, staring into the depths of his eyes. The Sergeant's face softened like he'd never seen it before. Those clouded eyes of hers seemed to break, and for a moment he thought that he could almost see through them. "Don't let this get in the way of your judgment."

Lincoln opened his mouth to argue, but he couldn't force a word out. He only looked away with a scoff.

"I know how it feels to be angry," she said, a delicate edge to her voice. Her voice quieted. "I don't want you going down the same paths I did."

"And what paths were those? You're still an infamous Defending Sergeant. You're in charge of the Council operation. What would you know?" The words came so quick, he didn't even know where they were from.

You spoke the truth, boy.

Then why did the surprise in Taryn's face only seem to shatter his heart further?

"They called me insane for ten years," she said firmly. "I know what it's like to watch someone you love die."

"The Curatrix Team didn't die in front of you," he muttered, the heat only building inside him even though he knew she was right.

"But ninety of my officers did."

Lincoln froze, the flame quenching.

"There's a reason it's codenamed 'The Ninety-Five Massacre.'" She turned from him, her gaze fixed on Nikki and the monitor. Her finger trailed slowly as she scrolled down the darting pulse record. "Ulysses died then."

"Who?" he asked gently, his face heating, instantly wanting to take back everything he'd said.

Taryn only gave a harsh laugh that sounded so distant, so lost, but no further explanation.

"His eyes…his scream," Her words were so quiet, he doubted that he was supposed to hear them. She shook her head. "Don't do that yourself, Lincoln. Please."

Lincoln couldn't face her, too embarrassed and too panicked to think that he'd even be able to say the right thing. How much about the Sergeant did he not know?

Neither of them seemed able to speak. He sat down, trying to remember how to breathe.

I won't let another Aguirre die too, Sergeant.

Twenty minutes.

You're running out of time. Let me prove myself.

Nikki gasped.

"Nikki?" He jumped to his feet, controlling himself from running to her before Taryn. A Medic ran through the door.

Nikki shifted uncomfortably, as if she were struggling to fight.

"She shouldn't be conscious," the Medic said, shouting into their wristband words that Lincoln drowned out. He couldn't move.

Let me help you, boy.

Taryn ran from the room.

Nikki? He stepped closer to her, looking at her pained

face, his ears ringing. He tried to drain out the voice. *Please, Nik. Please hang in there.*

He gently unclenched her hardened fist, closing his eyes, drowning out the shouting and the blaring machines.

She froze. For a moment, he thought that she'd respond. Did she hear him?

Taryn burst back into the room, shouting. Lincoln opened his eyes. A nurse followed her, too shaken to even bother casting Lincoln a second glance.

"It's the natural progression of the infection, Sergeant," the nurse said nervously, checking the vitals. "Since we can't tend to the wounds till it's removed…there is nothing we can do."

"Nothing?" Taryn shouted, causing the poor nurse to flinch. "There isn't anything?"

"Pray. Beg." The nurse watched the vitals, turning to Nikki, whose hand grasped Lincoln, her breathing harsh and rapid. She was struggling.

Tell me your name.

Lincoln froze. Not now. Not again.

Tell me your name. And I can save her.

Taryn sank down in the corner and closed her eyes, her forehead leaning against her clasped hands. Bags were forming under her eyes from the long night. Defeat had caved into her brow.

Nikki's grip loosened, her face suddenly softened—

The alarm went off.

Taryn jumped to her feet. "Dow!" she cried out. "Director!"

Lincoln's heart seised in his chest. *Resist, Nik. Resist it!*

The Voice echoed against his skull, begging for his name. He couldn't hear his own thoughts.

Nothing happened. No one came. Just the deafening sound that forced bile into his throat. The taunts in his mind grew louder and louder and—

"Soul," Nikki gasped. "Soul…Linc…"

The voice silenced his mind with a blow. So weak. So soft. He thought that he was going mad. He whirled around, unable to breathe, but gasping for air all at the same time. "Nik!"

"Lincoln!"

A new voice stopped him dead in his tracks as a woman tore through the flap. The woman didn't stop to stare. She dropped her satchel, pushing Lincoln aside. She tossed a device into the air, a hologram bursting from it. It ran over Nikki. She snatached it back and clicked it into her watch band.

Soul. His head was spinning. What had Nikki meant by "Soul?"

Dr. Mathews didn't pause to think, turning to the nurse and shouting, "Open a surgical dock!"

The nurse froze. "You're not—"

"Now!"

The nurse ran off. Dr. Mathews turned on Taryn. "Any medical experience, Sergeant?"

"Only field operations."

"That's enough. Come with me," Dr. Mathews said, signaling Taryn to follow. "I don't trust University students."

Taryn's eyes widened only for a moment before they narrowed and she nodded. One thing was clear. Dr. Mathews was the superior. And Lincoln trusted Ray's mother with his life…and Nikki's.

"A room has been opened!" The nurse burst back in, followed by a train of Medics rolling in a wheeled stretcher, Comms going off and abuzz.

Dr. Mathews moved to Nikki. Lincoln froze, allowing himself to be pushed out of the way and into the crowd.

They were taking her away.

He could only catch a glimpse of her as Dr. Mathews lifted the small girl gently into her arms and to the stretcher. If she died, he wouldn't be there to stop it.

What if she left again? There wasn't another second chance.

He felt numb, feeling Dow's strong hand on his shoulder to keep him from chasing after them as the crowd rushed out. His knees felt weak.

He couldn't see her anymore, only hear Dr. Mathews's shouts. "Room 356 now!"—"Patient 9074 vitals falling!"

He stumbled, feeling cold and empty. He stared blankly forward. He felt so numb.

So helpless.

And that sparked the smallest burn in his chest.

A hand clamped down onto his shoulder. "Lincoln, you need to get back to the camp."

"What?" Lincoln turned on Dow, wrenching his shoulder out of Dow's grip. "I need to stay here. I need to be here once she gets back."

"You're too emotionally unstable in this situation. It's best if you're out of the way." Dow's face pinched as he spoke.

Lincoln backed away.

Tell me your name. It burned brighter, painfully. The voices grew louder. *Tell me your name.*

"I need to stay. I can't leave."

"Lincoln…"

Tell me your name.

His heart felt as though it were on fire. He clamped his hands onto his chest, gasping in pain. He couldn't hear Dow's shouts now. What was happening to him?

"No!" he cried out.

Tell me your name.

He buckled over, closing his eyes, praying something, someone that would put him out of his misery. He wanted a bitter sleep. A sweet relief. But the burn only grew stronger.

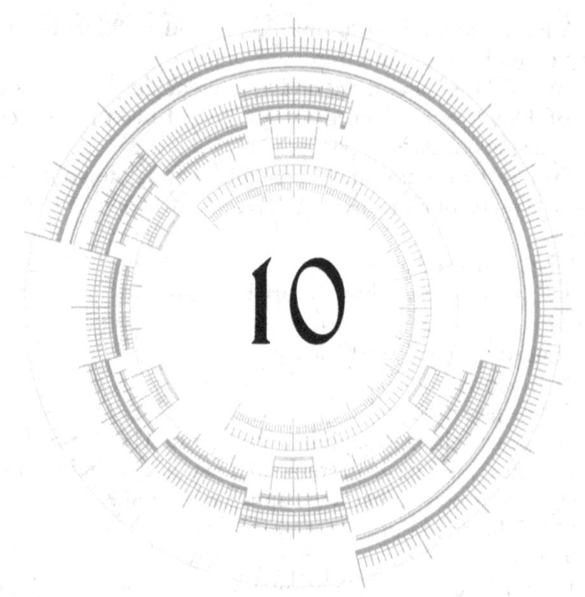

North Cordell, 28 Days Until

YOU CAN NO longer trust them. My offer is still open.

A cold, hard surface pressed against his cheek. Everything was sore and heavy.

His eyelids fluttered, everything a blur. Lincoln groaned as he pushed himself off the floor, blinking a few times at the Sergeant's makeshift office in her cabin. Boxes were stacked up in the corner, a folding table being used as a desk full of monitors and the all too familiar Curatrix machine.

Lincoln frowned, his head rocking. He was still dressed in his damp clothes and only had a thin sheet as a blanket. He sat up, rubbing his temples. How had he gotten here?

The last he remembered was Dow towering over him and a cold sensation flowing from his forearm. And then it dawned on him.

They'd *sedated* him. And banned him from seeing Nikki.

He leapt to his feet, nearly toppling into the wall behind him.

They've betrayed your trust, boy. I will not let you down.

"Shut up," Lincoln grit under his teeth.

He wasn't sure whom he was angry at. The burning in his chest still lingered, sore as he rubbed it to soothe it.

The cabin was quiet, besides the walls creaking under the wind and rain. No doubt that the snow would be nothing but slush and mud. Not that he minded. His first experience with snow was anything but pleasant.

He picked himself up from the ground, his head rocking, flinching as pain searched his skull. Stupid sedative.

Suddenly, the pain washed away, only leaving a small hum through his head. He froze, hesitant to dare take a deep breath.

There. See? I told you I could help.

He paused. The…voice had done that? He shook it off, not willing to respond to give it any more fuel to its ego.

He stepped out onto the cold, wood floor of Taryn's office, frowning as he realized that his boots were gone. He scanned the room. His boots were nowhere to be seen.

He rushed to the door. The handle was locked.

Lincoln stepped back, unable to breathe, noticing a paper pinned to the door. He tore it off, his mind too panicked with the fact that he'd been locked in to even be frustrated that he didn't recognize half the letters on the page. Not being able to read was becoming an ever-growing problem.

He dug his hand into his pocket, fishing out his ear buds, cursing as one glitched in his hand, crushed.

He stuck the functioning one into his ear, scanning over the paper as it was read aloud:

It was collectively agreed the best decision was to not have you near the MedTent till we know for sure the status of the young Aguirre. You're needed at camp and might interfere with her at the MedTent.

This restriction is in place for all Council Members.

I will be back soon to check on you.

I'm sorry, Lincoln.

– Sergeant Rayder Dow

He was sorry? He'd locked him in a room, for crying out loud. They'd banned him from seeing Nikki. They were trapping him back at camp right after he'd tried to run away from it.

The only reason he'd come back was because he knew

that they were Nikki's only chance at survival.

He ripped the paper in two, crumpling it in his hand. He let it fall to the ground. Heat clouded his eyes, but he quickly blinked them away. His feelings were the reason they were keeping him away. His stupid feelings.

Suppress them. Once nothing affects you, anything is possible.

Suppress them.

Lincoln scanned the room before his gaze rested on the Curatrix machine. Nikki's voice echoed in mind. *Soul.*

Dow didn't want Lincoln near her, but that didn't mean that Lincoln couldn't stop helping her. And where was a better place to look than the information device created by the Aguirres themselves?

Lincoln jumped into Taryn's hover chair, swiveling to the desk, tapping the machine on.

Lock On.

Lincoln cursed, trying to scramble his brain. The key to the machine was Nikki's DNA. His heart skipped.

Lincoln removed his jacket, praying that the blood stained in the fabric wasn't too saturated as he pressed it against the sensor.

He held his breath in what felt like the longest seconds of his life.

Access Granted.

The holographic screens blew up on the screen. Little dots marked the tracking device. The red, an unclarified source; and the purple, the Oquelite.

Currently, the Oquelite clustered in North Cordell, but the red were sprinkled all about, and considerably less of them. The largest cluster of red resided with the Oquelite. No doubt some sort of co-conspirator.

He swiped the tracker aside, pulling up a search code. Quickly, he spoke the word. "Soul."

About a dozen files came up. Great.

He clicked on the first. A particularly boring research paper on how the Oquelite body's soul adapted to immortality or something.

The next was a bunch of backup source code that, somewhere in the hundreds of words, had "soul."

The next was a cluster of files simply labeled, "A-Lot-Of-Woods." A bit of a silly title that Lincoln almost scrolled past. Woods. Did it have anything to do with the woods that were rapidly growing across the regions, bringing mythical creatures with them?

It couldn't hurt to look. He clicked.

To his surprise each of the files were hologram recording files, each with equally quirky titles such as, "don't-eat-the-purple-ones," "magical-defender-warriors-maybe," "play-fire-is-more-than-jess," and more.

Lincoln's eyes stopped on one file, not labeled like the rest. *SSoul.hol*

Maybe it was just a typo.

He clicked on it, almost flying out of his seat as a blue hologram jumped up in front of him out of the machine. His heart hammered in his chest as the blue, un-colorized hologram glitched into place, portraying a young woman most likely in her late twenties flipping through a series of discs, her messy hair kept back in a loose braid, one piercing on her left ear.

Lincoln was speechless as she looked up toward the camera. He'd seen her face so many times. Yet, somehow, when the dead woman looked at him now…he didn't know how to feel.

The recording of Agent Reyna Wents Aguirre cleared her throat. "Good day to whoever has come across this. Hopefully, it's you, Jess, or perhaps Nik, but that's beside the point. The conference in Calidor is in a few days." Reyna's tone shifted. Her voice was rich and authoritative with an air of confidence. It struck Lincoln as familiar. Nikki was soft spoken, but the moments she raised her voice, it was undeniably her mother's.

"Twelve hours ago, I met with Executive Cadissa Dean. Ten hours ago, Aaron was attacked in Liberty."

Lincoln's heart seized. Had this been made during the attacks on the Curatrix team?

"He's all right. Hardly scratched," Reyna continued with a fake laugh. "But it only confirms what Lyell and I only thought to be theories. We don't have much information, Jess. All we could gather from our venture into the woods in northern Court Illegia was a few documents…dated before our time. You're probably rolling your eyes at me now; but, Jess, I know it's a rare occasion, but I'm being dead serious."

Reyna adjusted the discs in her hand, and Lincoln inched closer in his seat as though Reyna were looking right at him.

"There is one thing clear in all of them. A warning. And I think it's related to Dean's hatred for us. A Council. It's a petty reason, but I think it's because the first Council *created* something, Jess. And the fact its name literally translates to 'Shadow Soul.'"

Lincoln frowned. Never in his history of Impure knowledge had he heard of such a thing.

"The Oquelite know of it," Reyna said with a heavy sigh. "And I have no doubt it's somehow connected to them. I wish I had more insightful information to provide, but Jess...I have this feeling I don't have much time left to collect it all." Reyna shook her head, laughing softly to herself. She looked back to the camera, her face hardened with determination. "But if anything, I fear the Shadow Soul will be coming. I think that's why the forests are reawakening. It has to be connected to the Oquelite somehow...and, most importantly, the Council."

Reyna was cut off by a young voice. "Ma?"

"One moment, Nik!" Reyna jumped to her feet. "And if our theories of this Soul are true...the next resort is the NMA files, right here in this very computer. We'll figure it out...Coming!"

The recording shut off.

Lincoln slumped back in his chair, speechless. How long had it been since someone heard the words of Reyna Aguirre?

And little Nikki. So much was here in that one short file. And he knew exactly what he needed to do about it.

He leapt from his seat.

Ah, yes. I sense a bit of rebellion from you.

"The Oquelite and those red dots are all located in the woods. The same supernatural woods Reyna Aguirre was dealing with ten years ago," Lincoln said, trying the handle on the office door again. "In Avalon's tower, Nikki found documents. The Stone is connected to the Council, and if anywhere has any lead, it has to be that stupid rock's castle."

A fair conclusion, the voice said, sounding pleased at finally being acknowledged.

Now his only problem was how he was going to get

there…

The voice chuckled. *Boy, let me show you your power. The Aviduous are supposed to be durable, aren't they?*

"My essence hasn't broken yet." Lincoln scoffed, not fond of the sultry voice. Was this what Nikki felt like with Avalon?

"I'm back!" The front door of the cabin swung open, Dow's voice echoing through.

Lincoln's heart stopped. No. Not now.

Dow knocked on the door.

Lincoln took one look back and jumped out the window, rolling into the muddy ground below to a stand. To his surprise, he couldn't feel anything at his feet.

Your essence may not have broken yet, little Aviduous, but I can give your power to you early…all for the price of your name.

"Prove yourself first," Lincoln said, breaking out into a run. The sky was too dark and the storm too heavy for any camp guard to notice him.

He was going to the woods. He was getting answers. And, like the voice said, he would suppress any feelings that got in the way.

UNKNOWN ID #.

Lawrence jumped up, his heart racing as he looked around the boy's cabin, dazed. He didn't remember falling asleep. Charles was asleep on the floor beside him, and Fire Wolf only perked up at the sound of Lawrence's movement.

Matteo peeked his head out from his quilt in the corner. He'd been avoiding sleep, but Lawrence almost couldn't blame him.

They'd been confined to the cabin, not allowed to follow Taryn to the MedTent. Lawrence tried arguing, but it only ended in "Someone needs to look after Charles and Matteo," and he knew that he was stuck.

What was he? Council babysitter?

He pulled the Comm out from his pocket, silencing it. A message read clearly. *Look outside.*

His heart skipped a beat, slowly turning his head to Sergeant Rayder Dow standing in the window with a white grin and a thumbs up. Way to scare the crud out of someone.

Dow motioned for Lawrence to meet him. What did the

forgein Defenders Sergeant want with him?

He tucked his little brother into a sleeping bag on the floor. He rose to his feet and carefully moved across the wood floor to the door.

He heard a sudden shuffle and turned to see Matteo pressed against his corner, watching him with wide, fearful eyes.

Lawrence gave him a reassuring nod and opened the door to a cool burst of air. He shivered, creeping out the door, Fire Wolf squeezing his way after him.

The sky rolled with thunder, and the thick smell of rain and biting cold hit him like a wall. If only the apparent fire that burned inside him helped with that.

He closed the door tightly behind him, turning to face the Defender dressed up in his Sergeant uniform, raincoat, and Comm in hand.

"How is everything?" Dow asked, tucking his hands into his pockets.

"Fine," Lawrence grumbled. Fire Wolf brushed up against Lawrence's leg, the warmth comforting.

Dow let out a sigh. "Good. Good. Lincoln's been secured in the Sergeant office. And the Wingor?" Dow asked, ignoring the rain. "I heard he's a Lopez."

"'Matteo,'" Lawrence corrected.

"Yes, him. Odd how yet another Council Member has some sort of Curatrix relation. Nigel Lopez competed in the same Trial as the team and I," Dow said. "How is he?"

Did Lawrence lie? Tell him that Matteo was fantastic and how he could handle it? That he wasn't totally terrified of being a Member?

He couldn't trust these Defenders. They hadn't done a thing for him or his family their entire life.

"He's...okay."

Dow's eyes shifted in the window, no doubt baring down on Matteo now. "I can see that. He's glaring at me through that cocoon of his."

"He doesn't want to be here," Lawrence said. Matteo already worried Lawrence, and the fact that he was showing signs of being hypersensitive to sound specifically. This felt like too much to push on him. Not without understanding Matteo and his secrets first.

"He has to learn to adapt somehow and soon." Dow sighed. "Sergeant Hunter knows your Council better than anyone, but she's occupied as of the moment."

Lawrence nodded, hoping that this marked the end of the conversation and they could leave the matter of Matteo to Taryn.

"The Outown kid is a Wingor," Dow said, his face brightening. "She'd be able to train him. Passed flawlessly in combat during her post-trial exam."

Being a darn *Wingor* had nothing to do with it. Lawrence nodded anyway. "Do you think the…*Cors Vis* situation will interfere?"

"That whole thing is confusing." Dow sighed. "And to be honest, I don't exactly understand Delorous's theory. *Cors Vis* or *Mors Vis*, it still destroyed buildings. How is it supposed to help the Wingor in anything?"

Lawrence bit his tongue. He couldn't argue with the Sergeant. Dow was right. It didn't really make a lot of sense, but Lawrence had been the one to go and help Tabitha prove her point. He'd seen how the *Cors Vis* had rejected Iracema. And he'd felt the unexplainable pain when they'd been destroyed. It was nothing like he'd ever felt before…and that was coming from someone who could hold fire.

And it made sense. The Wingor was the only Member that got its power all at once. Lawrence most definitely hadn't learned all his Ywondie abilities, but once Matteo got his wings…he got everything. Miriam wasn't even half as powerful as a Member would be. How would she be able to help? It just made sense that some supernatural force would be there to help…like *Mors Vis*…*Cors Vis*. Whatever it was called.

Well, it was gone now.

"I'll send her by tomorrow," Dow said, crossing his arms in pride.

Dow started down the cabin steps. He looked over his shoulder. "Thank you, by the way, kid. If no one told you that already. You deserve a lot more credit for what went down in Court Illegia than you get."

"T—thanks," Lawrence said, his heart leaping, his face growing warm.

Dow nodded again, walking off into the growing storm.

A Defending Sergeant just *complimented* him?

Don't let it get to your head, he snapped at himself. He couldn't help but feel the small swell of pride in his chest.

The elated thoughts were quickly cut off by Fire Wolf's bark, followed by a howl.

Lawrence frowned, quick to crouch beside the Wolf, the fur on his back beginning to smoke.

"What is it, boy?" Lawrence whispered.

He could only hear the distant shouts of the camp guards, which were faint over the wind of the rainstorm. Fire Wolf growled, looking back to Lawrence, antsy on his paws, and he jumped farther out into the darkness.

"Something's out there?" Lawrence slowly got to his feet. He'd promised to stay back and look after Matteo and Charles.

But who was he, following the Defender's every order? And it wasn't every day that something irked the usually playful Fire Wolf.

"Fine." Lawrence sighed. "But we're only checking it out. That's *it*."

Fire Wolf took that to be enough, leaping into a run, his entire coat igniting even in the pouring rain. Lawrence took a deep breath and ran after the wolf into the dark.

Fire Wolf was considerably faster, but seeing as the glowing ball of fire was hard to miss, he wasn't hard to follow. Why was he even doing this? He could be back in the cabin, warm and comfortable, not following a *dog* into the place that the Defenders explicitly said not to go due to danger.

That's what it was. Doing things he was explicitly told not to do. Something about it made him feel a little less lost. Like he was still in control. No one could control him. Not ever again.

A cry broke out in the darkness.

Lawrence braced himself as Fire Wolf stopped, his flames running in circles. It could be anything. An Oquelite. A red-eyed guy. A warl—

"Fire Wolf! Get off!"

"Lincoln?" Lawrence frowned, rushing to catch up with Fire Wolf. He couldn't believe his eyes when he reached the wolf, pinning down an unpleased Lincoln, drenched and his clothes stained still stained of blood.

"Lincoln, what are you doing here?" Lawrence snapped, shooing Fire Wolf off of him, grabbing Lincoln's arm and hoisting him to his feet, firmly taking the boy by his shoulders.

Lincoln tried to shrug him off. "Williams, I don't have time to stand around."

"You've been banned from seeing Nikki, if this is what you're trying to do."

"You think I'm stupid? The MedTent is in the other direction." Lincoln scoffed, rolling his impossibly dark eyes. "And we're *all* banned from seeing her."

Lawrence grimaced at the reminder. "So you're intentionally heading for the woods? What, are you insane?"

"If that's what you call trying to get things done." Lincoln tore free from Lawrence's grip, stepping back. "I'm not going to be locked up in a cabin when Nikki gave us the biggest lead we've had since Imperial."

Lawrence's brows furrowed, looking to Fire Wolf to see if he sensed that anything was off. "What do you mean?"

"She mentioned a Soul. It was the only word she managed to get out. I...I kinda broke into the Curatrix machine—"

"You what?"

"Look, that's beside the point!" Lincoln said, slowly inching backward. "I found a file of your aunt, Reyna Aguirre, talking about a Shadow Soul. Something related to the Oquelite...but created by the Council. It's connected to Nikki now too, and I need to find out what it is, and what it's done."

Lawrence paused, hating to silently admit that it sounded a smidge reasonable. "And you're going to find this Shadow Soul in the woods?"

"That's where Reyna found her information on it. And the palace we ran into last time once belonged to the woman inside Nikki's stone, the sole reason Nikki isn't...dead." Lincoln stared him hard in the eyes. "If she kept Nikki alive, there was something she wanted us to know."

Lawrence was speechless. Could this explain the weird happenings that couldn't just be blamed on the Oquelite? Was there really something more?

"Look, if you're not coming with me, I'm going no matter what."

"I'm coming," Lawrence snapped, feeling Dow's praise leave before his eyes. "Just to make sure you don't get yourself killed."

Lincoln laughed. "Admit it, Williams, you want a little revenge too."

Lawrence ignored the comment, marching with Fire Wolf after Lincoln. "Revenge" was a broad term.

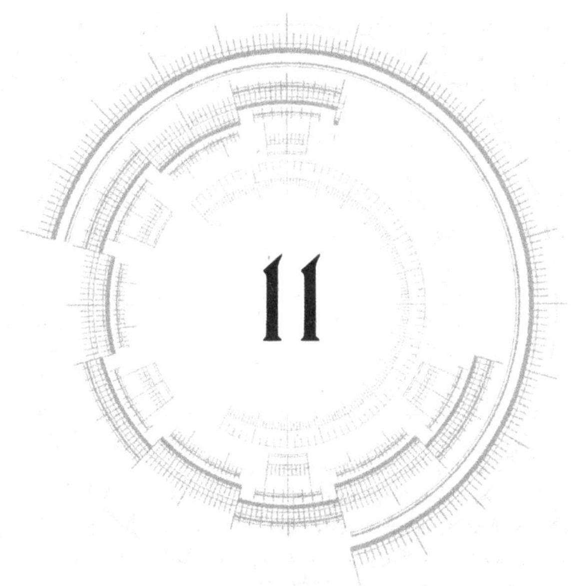

11

Unknown Region, 28 Days Until

COLE HADN'T EXPECTED to fall asleep in the midst of the splitting headache and the new, adrenaline-driven hope racing through him. But a Marketeer shook him awake, and his eyes burst open back to the dark closet.

It took him a moment to process. He was in a closet…Right. He'd asked a person named "Echo" to take him to the Market. How long was he out? Had he slept at all?

"The Mater requests your presence," the gruff Marketeer grumbled, tossing a satchel at Cole and marching from the room.

Cole sat up, rubbing the lull of sleep from his eyes. His head still ached, but he ignored it. He had much more important things to worry about.

He untied the satchel, finding an odd change of clothes. Pants with loops and more pockets than he'd ever need, a loose shirt, and a leather jerkin. He changed quickly, deciding not to question it.

He turned, catching a glimpse of the Illuminate leaning in the corner. He wanted to look away and leave it. The sword felt so much heavier to bear now. He could still see her terrified eyes as he held the hilt of the flaming blade so near to her. He squeezed his eyes shut, trying to shake it off.

He grabbed it, buckling it around his waist. He hated how natural it felt to have it swinging it at his side. How familiar the deadly weapon he hardly knew how to control was to him.

He looked down to the Medallion hanging loosely on his chest. He took a deep breath, tucking it away in his shirt.

Clear your head, Cole. You're going to go insane. It sure felt like it.

Cole only paused for a moment before stepping out from the curtains. He cringed at the bright light, his headache spiking for a moment as his vision adjusted.

"Ah! You're looking better today, Coleson."

He was behind a bar, Echo sitting nearly opposite of him, turning away from a Marketeer mid-sentence. The room was empty besides the few scattered Marketeers at the bar tables and a tender checking his Comm in the corner.

"I feel a bit ridiculous," he admitted, gesturing to himself. "But much better. Thank you."

"You look stunning. I'm glad the painkiller is effective." She laughed. Echo waved the Marketeer away, patting the stool beside her.

Cole easily obeyed her. Something about Echo felt safe. He caught himself. He couldn't trust a stranger. He had to be cautious. He couldn't screw up again.

"Eat, and I'll be able to tell you the situation," Echo said.

The bartender slid a meal over with perfect timing, and Echo slid back a coin.

"So, I spoke to Cecileo, the Pater…Market leader, while you were out." She sat cross-legged on her stool yet still managed an air of dominance and authority as she adjusted her circlet. "In discussion with him, the conclusion was made to grant your request to come back to the Market to find a way of training in your Illuminate duties."

Cole almost choked. *They'd what—?*

Echo gave an amused smile, handing him a water glass. "One condition."

He gulped it down. "Anything!"

"You help me with my position on the side when needed," Echo said. "It's all simple things, such a running test on neural tech and disinfecting."

Cole blinked. "D—did you say *neural* tech?"

"What? Is that surprising?" Echo said, flexing her hand. "How do you think I can control this hand if it's not connected to my brain?"

"So no new limbs come with the job?"

"I hope not," Echo said with a mischievous smile. "Perhaps you'd look good with a metal hand."

Cole nearly laughed back but smothered it. He should be learning and working. Not enjoying himself.

He got up from his seat. "Tell me when we leave," he said simply, turning from Echo.

Echo got up after him. "I will," she said. "We board a Rail to Liberty in thirty. Our trucks are parked outside. Don't get left behind."

She patted him on the shoulder and went to join the other Marketeers.

Cole stood alone, staring at his feet, the weight on his waist suddenly becoming apparent. He wasn't sure what hurt him more: his aching head or the gnawing in his chest that already missed his little brother and the chaotic girl he cared too much about.

But neither mattered.

He decided to get a head start, heading out the door.

It didn't take Cole long to notice the Marketeers' distrust of him. They sent him occasional glares to the best of their efforts, studying his every move as he sat petrified in his SpeedRail seat. He wished that he might be able to relax and take in what was the only time he would ever see a First Class car.

It was spacious with deep-red carpet and wallpapered walls, and a holographic keyboard with which you could request a server from. A glass light fixture was crafted into the ceiling, and little lace curtains framed the windows, and instead of seats, reclining couches were bolted to the floor. He sat on the edge the entire time, distancing himself as far as possible from the nearest glowering Marketeer.

Echo offered him lunch, but he shook his head, not willing to draw more attention than he already was just sitting there.

"I hear you've previously *been* to a Market," Echo said, pouring herself a glass of an emerald liquid. "I heard all about how the Illuminate was found stumbling into the Market after a girl over a stolen bag."

The Marketeers chuckled.

All thanks to Tabitha. As usual.

Cole nodded. "It was a…productive moment."

"I'm sure," Echo took a long sip, setting the glass down. "Now, Coleson, what do you hope to do this time?"

"Learn," he said, simply. Isn't that what he'd told her before?

"What exactly?"

"How to be the Illuminate."

"Seems oddly broad," Echo said, examining the faces of her companions, who gave no comments, only a few smirks or eye rolls. "No specific role?"

"Not one I'm deserving of."

"Oh, screw that," Echo huffed. "What is it?"

Cole's gaze fell. "I thought I was a leader," he said quietly. He remembered the moment Ray stood up against the obnoxious Officer Giles and claimed that Cole was just that. Cole always denied it, but in that moment, he felt pride in it. Being trusted with such a high position. To *lead*.

"You thought?" Echo said.

"I realized that it wasn't for me," Cole said quickly, sitting up and keeping eyes away from the floor.

Echo narrowed her eyes at Cole for a long moment. "All right," she said finally. She took back her cup and her tele. "Whatever you see fit, Illuminate."

Whatever *needed* to fit. He would be much better at following orders.

The SpeedRail stopped less than half an hour later, drawing into a nearly empty station. Cole followed after the Marketeers into the station. The place was enormous compared to North Cordell's single station, with soaring walls and mopped tile walls and floors. A giant holographic clock hovered above the exit.

12.31.

The night didn't seem to be much of an issue for the Marketeers, who walked right past the suspicious eye of the ticketmaster and out the door into the cool night. The cold pierced right through the thin material of his shirt. The streets were mostly empty, and the buildings were nothing like Cole had ever seen before. There wasn't a single steel, cubed building in sight. Only brick and wood and paint and paved roads with glittering hologram signs…and a giant, glowing, blue dome in the distance.

Cole stopped. Not just any dome…The Dome.

Echo laughed. "I see you've never been to Liberty," she said, clapping her hand onto his shoulder and pulling him forward.

"There are cities *outside* the Dome? I thought the land was mostly inhabitable, except for the Dome because of its artificial resources."

"Someone reads tablets," a Marketeer grumbled.

Echo ignored them. "That was true three centuries ago. And thank goodness for it, a Liberty market wouldn't survive in that stuffy Dome anyhow."

"Why was Cecileo in Elery six months ago and now here?" Cole asked. Liberty seemed like a more ideal location.

"Elery is our closest Market to Imperial," Echo said. "And if you recall, that's when the attacks were happening. Pater Cecileo wanted to be as close to the action as possible to watch the Defenders crumble."

"Why does that matter—?" Cole shut his mouth as quickly as every Marketeer turned to watch him. Personal thing. Got it.

Even Echo seemed a little swayed, clearing her throat and turning her vision straight ahead. "It isn't wise to explain our position on government here," she said with a forced smile. "Now, we should hurry before the gates close."

Echo hurried back to the front of the group, leading them quickly down the streets. The gates, Cole quickly learned, were what they called the walls that opened at Echo's touch, pushing apart only momentarily for the entire group to rush through.

Cole's body didn't hesitate to run after them, but his mind was still spiraling entirely unprepared as he burst out onto the dirt street of the Market, the walls shutting behind him.

The rush didn't wait for him to catch up.

At night, the Market was elaborate, catching his breath from him. He stumbled after Echo, trying to take it all in. Lanterns hovered and glowed above the streets, and colorful tents were set up as booths on either side, some packed up for the night and others just getting started. They were dressed in their leather and painted skin, many barefoot and flaunting their various missing limbs and malformations and screaming for customers over each other.

Slowly, the street began to change.

One by one, the Marketeers following Echo veered off till it was only Cole turning the corner to a quieter street. Larger tents occupied it now, their heavy carpet material intricate and making up several rooms. A dog was tied at the stake in front of one, barking at their arrival. Some had their door flap propped open. Children peered outside in curiosity, ducking their heads away when Cole waved.

They took another turn, and finally, Cole saw an ending. The entire street was occupied with thin, white tents, silhouettes of working figures inside illuminated through the glow. At the very end was an enormous tent that nearly seemed to command the silence on the street Cole hadn't heard anywhere else in the Market. Hundreds of golden pins were attached to the tassels of the tent. Poles and supports held the crimson tent almost as high as the building concealing it.

Cole felt wrong just approaching it.

"Take your shoes off," Echo commanded.

Cole did as he was told, and Echo did the same. She handed him a wet cloth after quickly wiping off her own feet and waited for him to do the same before drawing back the flap of the tent.

Cole sucked in his breath and followed her inside.

The tent smelled of an old closet but in a homey sort of way. The setting was dim by the candles set on either side of a low desk, scattered with papers and tablets.

"Echo?" The flap opened from behind the desk. A man in his mid-twenties, with hair part white and part black, an eye that appeared to be real besides its mechanic glow stood in the light, his hair disheveled, and his shirt untucked and barefoot. If Cole had to guess, he'd just woken up.

An ideal state to reunite in.

Echo stepped back to reveal Cole. "I have the Illuminate."

Cecileo Reuder's face quickly faltered to a frown, stepping out into the room. "Well, this is a pleasant surprise," he said, tearing his fingers through his messy hair. He shot her a look. "You know how to make things awkward."

Echo shrugged. "I thought you two'd met before."

"Kid, pretend you've only ever seen me with a sword to your throat," Cecileo said, waving him off. Turning to the desk, he picked up a tea kettle and rummaged through the desk, pulling out a small cup.

"Coleson, I'm sure my husband needs no introduction."

Cole blinked. "Wait…husband?" He swiveled to Cecileo, looking back and forth between him and Echo. "You two are married?"

"No, she was clearly joking," Cecileo said, his sarcasm thick.

Echo elbowed him, causing him to nearly choke on his cold tea.

"We are." Echo sighed. "What happened to being the almighty Pater?"

"Almighty Pater hours are *not* after midnight."

Echo hid her amusement. "You're impossible."

Cecileo smirked. "Truly." He looked to Cole, who shifted uncomfortably by the door. "So, kid, why did you request to come here? I heard it was something about a teacher."

Cole nodded. "I—I need someone to teach me how to handle the Illuminate," he said. "And since the Market is connected to it…I assumed it was the best place to start."

The long silence made him want to take it all back.

"I have the perfect choice," Echo said.

"Who?" Cecileo and Cole said together. She already had someone in mind? Cole's heart leapt. That meant that he could start learning as soon as possible and start making it up to Tabitha. And—

"You, Cecileo."

Cole fumbled. *Cecileo?*

"Me?" Cecileo blinked away his shock before chuckling. "Echo, really? No! That would be insane."

"You're good with swords, among other traits."

Cecileo shook his head. "Echo, you can't trust a *Council Member* with my hands. I have too much that people already hate me for. I don't want to throw an insecure kid in with it."

Cole's face burned. "I'm not insecure."

"There's no one else." Echo looked at him longingly, her brows pinched to a frown.

"Echo, there's plenty—"

"Aren't you the protector of the Illuminate?"

"The *Blade*, not whatever kid comes on the side."

Cole felt like any spark of energy in him had just died. He wanted to step away and apologize. What could he do now?

"If you protected the Blade for so long, maybe you know *something* about it that can help," he interrupted.

"It was given to the Market when we stole it off some guy over a century back." Cecileo shrugged. "I know as much about it as you do."

"Then maybe teach him to learn," Echo said.

"I'm not qualified. And it doesn't concern me."

"It concerns *everyone*."

"There is no such thing as a creature and some soul that's going to kill us all."

A soul that was going to kill everyone? A creature? What creature? What the *heck* was Cecileo talking about?

Echo spoke too quickly for Cole to try and ask, and he decided that it was best not to. "I never said it was true, but we *do* have Oquelite on our hands."

"That's a Defender problem." Cecileo set down his cup, taking a deep breath.

"And once they crush the Defenders, where do you think they'll head next?"

Cecileo gently grabbed Echo's shoulders, steadying her, as she looked like she might slap him at any moment. Instead, she glared at him for a long moment before taking a deep breath. "Just let him try with Doran," Cecileo said.

"Doran is *not* you."

"Doran is a teacher. He taught me. He's served the Market longer than me. Trust me, it's the best choice."

She raised a brow. "I trust you, but I disagree."

He patted her shoulder, turning to the desk. "I'll take that as a yes."

"Take it as a future I-told-you-so."

Cecileo only laughed under his breath as he picked a paper from his desk. Echo rolled her eyes. Cecileo tore away an edge, scribbling something down. He turned to Cole, holding out the paper. "There. Got you a trainer."

"You're an idiot, Cecil." Echo sighed.

Cole took the paper. *Second left after bathhouses, two rights through general market area, gate behind red tent. — Authorized by Pater Cecileo Reuder.*

Cole wasn't sure what to say. Doran, the guy who'd shown him how to hold the sword in the first place? Is that what he needed? "Thanks?"

"Good. Great." Cecileo dusted his hands off. "See, Echo? It's all settled."

Echo rolled her eyes, turning and disappearing behind the flap into the back rooms of the tent.

Cecileo gave a heavy sigh, watching her go. He took a moment before turning back to Cole. "Should I get a guide to show you to your tent?"

His *tent?* He would have one of those?

"I can find it," he said, not wanting to drag anyone else into his mess this late at night.

"Take a turn back onto that residential street you passed. Easy," Cecileo said, taking back his tea cup and turning to follow after Echo. "I trust you're smart."

Cole nodded. "I sure hope."

Cecileo just chuckled and disappeared behind the tent flap. Cole left in a hurry, struggling to pull on his boots while rushing down the street.

This was a ton to process. Doran was his teacher… teaching him sword fighting. Why did that make him uneasy? Isn't that what he wanted?

Cecileo had been right. Finding the tent was easy. It was a cute, little, blue tent that stood out against the larger, deeper-toned tents, which had mostly gone dark inside. A few persons were walking along, hauling their carts behind, but didn't seem to give Cole much notice as they passed.

No doubt that they were used to newcomers.

Cole tentatively pushed through the flaps into the dark tent. No automatic lights. Of course not. It's a *tent*, Johnson.

He searched the tent, hitting a lantern on the table, and

the tent burst to life. It only consisted of one room. A bed was made up of a mattress and a plethora of organized pillows and blankets and two side tables decked with little vases of greens. Carpets covered the floor, all of various designs and colors. An armoir was against the only mostly empty wall, which Cole found held a large assortment of clothing, varying in size and dress. Did the Market have visitors often?

The table in the center of the room was empty.

Cole searched for a chair but saw nothing but hard, stuffed cushions. He checked the corners, and behind the mass of pillows in the bed. Were chairs evil?

He ducked under the armoir. There. A single plastic folding chair. It kind of ruined the aesthetic, but it would do.

Something stuck out under the armoir with a chair. Bigger, bulkier, and more solid.

Maybe it was another table.

His curiosity won over and he pulled it out from underneath the armoir. He froze. It wasn't a table at all. No, its black and white keys and buttons running along the black bar were an all too familiar sight.

He didn't even think about how a keyboard ended up here. He just turned it to face him and flicked on the power button. The keys were smooth and cold under his fingers.

Memories flooded through him. Sitting alone in the kitchen with his keyboard plugged in by the microwave, a small Scroll set up on the counter as he followed key by key.

He pressed down. He cringed as the smooth sound rang loud.

Cole hadn't touched a keyboard since he lost his place in the University. Not like it mattered anymore, anyway. He doubted that he'd ever need to play one ever again.

Well, what was he waiting for? Push it back under the armoir and tell Echo about it tomorrow and go to bed.

He ran his fingers along it anyway, feeling the overwhelming, forgotten adrenaline of home. One by one, he wanted to drown out his thoughts. The faults that he'd caused his entire Council. The pain of the emotions every time he thought about her tears caused by *him*. The stupid voices taunting him over and over in his head.

He wanted to drown them out, and the rhythm felt so

familiar. So calming. So in symphony with the chaotic chorus in his mind.

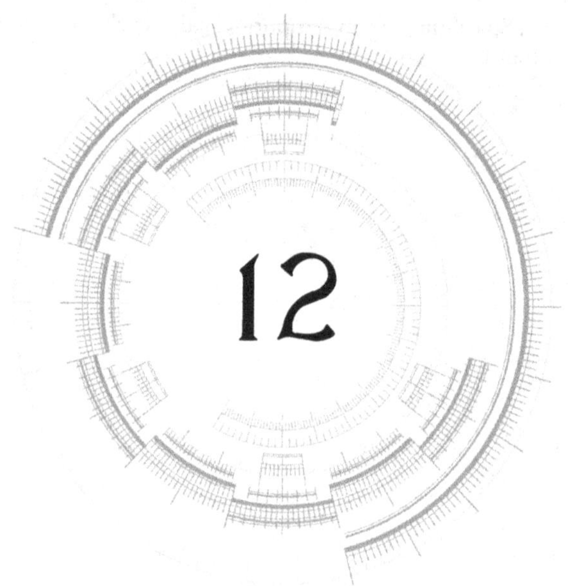

12

North Cordell, 28 Days Until

MATTEO JUMPED UP, gasping for air, grabbing his ribs with a cry. Pain seared through his side.

Almost as quickly as it came, it left, leaving Matteo gasping for air and his chest flooding with a tight anxiety. He tried to shake it off, to pick up his quilt around him, wrap himself up and lie there, ignoring everyone in this strange region, but it nagged at him.

That wasn't normal…That wasn't natural.

Something rang in his mind. Something was wrong.

"*¡No es cierto!*" he whispered harshly, drawing the quilt back over his head, pulling his legs to his chest, trying to bury his face. It wasn't like the intrusive feelings were new, but this time they felt…different. Like they were coming from something outside him. Like something his father might've said when he offered a piece of sweet bread so that it could dispel the fears, or stopping Calynda from sweeping over her feet because, if so, she'd never get married.

That one had her for years.

Matteo never believed them. Because if there was really some mysterious power and rules for life, why didn't they ever seem to turn out to be true?

The feeling continued to eat at him. Maybe he was just hungry. He hadn't eaten since he left Court Illegia, and the thought of sweet bread really awoke that sense. But that meant *leaving* and that meant *Defenders* and that probably meant *having to* talk *to people*, and that sounded like a lot.

"Mister Teo, are you awake?"

Matteo flinched at the sudden sound of the little boy's groggy voice. A youthful voice nonetheless with a slight pitch to it, and a light sleeper from how alive he managed to sound.

He tried to stay quiet, hoping that the little Lawrence would go back to sleep.

A finger poked him through the blanket. *"Hello, mister."*

The next poke landed in his face, and Matteo shrugged the boy off.

"You *are* awake! I heard your stomach. Do you want to get donuts?"

Matteo didn't answer him, turning his back to the little boy.

The little boy, who apparently knew nothing about personal space, draped himself over Matteo's back, playing his head like a drum. "Come on, mister. Everyone likes donuts. Do you not like donuts?"

The boy gave a horrified gasp at the thoughts. He rolled off of Matteo and onto the floor with a thud.

"Or have you never had a donut before?" The boy popped his head under the blanket, forcing his best puppy eyes.

Matteo jumped, scrambling backward, hitting his head on the cot behind him.

The boy giggled behind his hands. "I'm not scary. I'm Charles."

Charles. That's what Lawrence mentioned his little brother's name to be. Matteo stared at him, not sure what he was supposed to say now that he'd been exposed. He glanced away nervously.

"You're Teo."

"Yes." He fumbled out a reply without bothering to correct him. Why was this so hard? He didn't have a problem with little Cielo at home. Charles wasn't going to drag him away to some Defender…was he?

"How old are you, Teo?" Charles crawled closer. "I'm five."

Matteo noticed that his eyes were green like his brother's, but something in them held so much joy and innocence that went well with his little smile. Like Cielo when Matteo would greet her after a shift, her brown eyes lighting up like his father's did.

Matteo slowly sat up. "*Di*—no. Uh…I—I'm sixteen."

"You're almost as big as Lawrence. He's going to be eight and teen in the summer," Charles said proudly.

Matteo decided not to ruin the moment with the fact that he'd only turned sixteen a few weeks ago. A very boring and unexciting event, but he considered it a successful one, seeing as his family usually awkwardly talked about how he would even function on his own once he was older.

He tried to shove the thoughts away. *No pienses como eso.* Don't think like that.

"Do you want to get donuts?" Charles asked again, stretching out his little hand.

"I—I guess so." He slowly reached for Charles's hand, who enthusiastically grabbed it, pulling him forward with an impressive grip.

The two stumbled to their feet, Charles practically jumping. "I love donuts," he squealed, looking up to Matteo with a huge grin. "And frogs."

Matteo gave a nervous one in return. "Frogs are cool."

Charles grabbed his little coat from Lincoln's messy desk and led Matteo to the door. Matteo stepped out into the cold, shivering as he heard the rain pour down, hitting hard against the cheap roofs of the makeshift cabins. The feeling crept back into his side.

"Are you okay?" Charles asked, pausing for a moment.

Matteo grimaced. Where was the feeling coming from? "I'm fine."

A howl broke through the falling rain. Matteo jumped.

Charles let go of his hand, stumbling down the steps and running out into the storm. "Fire Wolf!"

"Charles, wait!" Matteo ran after him. What would the Defenders have to say when they found out that their pathetic Wingor Council Member *also* lost a child?

The Defenders guarding the central fire jumped up at the shout, and panic ran through Matteo. He stopped in his tracks.

To his relief, he heard Charles's laugh not far off.

Once he managed to free himself from his freeze, he turned to see Charles riding atop the panting Fire Wolf. "Aw, Teo. He's bleeding," Charles said.

The little boy looked up, his big eyes now glassy as he held up his hand smeared with blood.

Matteo's heart leapt, quick to pick Matteo off the Wolf, wiping his hand off. He looked back to the wolf, his heart hammering. Where was Lawrence?

"Who hurt him, Teo?" Charles said, with a small whimper. "I want Cents."

"Cents?"

"My brother," Charles said, hiding his face against Matteo.

Matteo placed a hand on Charles's damp hair, looking at the wolf's glowing eyes that seemed to be begging. The feeling burning inside grew stronger.

Lawrence was in trouble. And what was he supposed to do about it? There was no way he could help—

"Teo, I don't want a donut anymore." Charles's voice was so small.

An image flashed before his eyes, but it wasn't as hallowed as the sounds that echoed with it. The sounds that took every ounce of innocence…

"I'm going to find Cents," Matteo said, dropping to his knees, trying to hide the fact that he was shaking as he took Charles's little shoulders. "Go to those Defenders over there while I bring him back, okay? They'll get you a donut. Donuts make everything better." They weren't the sweet bread that his father insisted vanquished fear, but they were something.

Charles looked up, nodding slowly. "Yeah, donuts do make everything better."

"I'll be back really soon," Matteo said, forcing a queasy smile. Good thing it was too dark for Charles to tell.

The little boy hugged him. "Thank you, Teo! You're my number four favorite!"

Matteo froze, not expecting the sudden affection, but resigned himself to patting Charles gently on the head before shooing him off to run to the Defenders guarding the central fire.

Matteo took a deep, quaking breath before he looked Fire Wolf in his glowing, red eyes. "Let's go."

Fire Wolf didn't hesitate, igniting his coat into flames and bounding off into the darkness, leaving Matteo struggling to keep up. His legs were already sore from all the walking, but he forced himself to keep on. He hadn't moved so much in so little time his entire life.

The sky was finally beginning to lighten…or as much as it could with a storm veiling it. It was nearly 4.00 in the morning, and Matteo was running on only a few hours of sleep.

But Lawrence had saved him from the Oquelite…and maybe from himself.

He tried to shake the voices away.

The woods came closer, and Matteo's throat tightened. They were enormous when he saw them from afar, but now running toward them, they were a hundred times more daunting with their shadowy presence and impossibly ancient-looking trees that entwined together as they stretched toward the sky.

Fire Wolf slowed as they approached the entrance of the woods. He looked behind timidly, almost fearful to enter as Matteo caught up, his lungs burning. He nearly toppled over trying to catch his breath.

All this working out better be worth it.

"Are—are they inside?" he said, looking to Fire Wolf, before he realized how absurd Iracema would say it was to be talking to a dog.

Fire Wolf paced in a circle before finally creeping forward. Matteo glanced behind him, at the dim lights of the camp and, with an exhale, began to follow.

"Hey! Where do you think you're going?"

Matteo froze midstep, and for a split moment he thought that he was done. He'd screwed up and a Defender was about to come and report him to the Sergeant and he hadn't even been there for a day and already messed up his Member-ness.

And then he realized that the voice sounded way too young.

He slowly turned on his heel, surprised to see two young teenagers staring right back at him.

A boy and a girl, obviously siblings, with black hair and striking, golden eyes that made an appearance even in the dim light. The girl's hair was frizzy…though he could guess that it was curlier when it wasn't pouring.

"Into the woods," Matteo said, wanting to groan at how dumb that sounded.

"Without us?" The girl gave an overdramatic gasp. "Dude, do you know how off limits those are? Some Defender probably spent a whole half hour repeating it."

"Then why are you here?" Matteo dared to ask.

The siblings exchanged glances.

"I was following *you*," the girl said.

"And I was following her." The boy shrugged.

"You're a Council Member, right?" The girl stepped forward, her eyes lighting up and her voice hopeful and pleasant to the ear. "I heard someone say you were. My brother is one too."

"I—I guess so." Their brother? Did Lawrence have more siblings? No. They didn't look anything like Lawrence.

"So you know where Lincoln went?" the girl said with a smile. "I went to the office to let him out even though that Defender guy said not to…and he was gone."

Is that where Lawrence went?

"I don't know." How many kids were intent on following him?

"I'll help you find—" Her brother cleared his throat from behind her, and she sighed. "*We* can help you find them. I'm training to enter the medical program at Imperial's university."

She looked awfully young, but from the looks of the blood on Fire Wolf, they might need it.

"All right," he said, though he felt like they'd come whether he let them or not.

"Jenna Mathews," the girl said with a nod and two-fingered salute of respect. "Fourteen. Glorgory."

"Noah Mathews," the boy said, crossing his arms. "Fifteen. Glorgory."

So who was their brother?

"M—Matteo Lopez. Sixteen. Court Illegia."

"And what member are you?" Noah asked, raising a brow.

"W—Wingor."

"Holy cow, what?" Jenna squealed. "The ones with the wings? Dude, you can *fly?*"

Matteo swallowed hard, the pain spiking in his skull saving him. He grimaced. "We have to hurry."

"Why? Are they in trouble?" Jenna's face paled.

Fire Wolf howled for them in the woods.

"I think so," Matteo said, hoping that the answer was sufficient enough as he chased after Fire Wolf into the woods.

"Wait up!"

Jenna and Noah followed close behind.

The woods were oddly still and quiet. But not the quiet that Matteo was fond of. The kind of quiet that was made up of all the other little noises that crowded together in a symphony of catastrophe. The crunching of wet leaves, the whistling of the wind through the branches, and the moaning of the bending trees…and the little, unnatural *scratch-scratch-scratch* noise that seemed persistent. Too persistent.

"Something is above," Matteo whispered.

"What did you say?" Jenna called out after him.

Scratch-scratch-scratch. Much closer this time.

"Right above us!" Matteo cried, throwing himself back and shoving the siblings as a horrifying lizard creature dropped from the trees with a blood-chilling cry.

Jenna screamed.

Fire Wolf leapt onto the creature. The burning in Matteo's chest grew stronger, pulling him to go forward. His heart was hammering, echoing in his ears as he tripped over his feet into a run, grabbing Jenna's arm frozen at the sight of the creature.

Scratch-scratch-scratch.

They were everywhere. Dozens of them.

Jenna tightened her grip on Matteo's arm. A thud came

from behind them, followed by a whack and a grunt from Noah, but Matteo couldn't look back. If he looked back, it was over.

He broke out into a clearing, smoke rising into the air, his eyes widening as he caught sight of an enormous, burning tree that crossed over an enormous split in the earth.

Keep running. Don't stop running.

Matteo ran, despite everything that the senses in him told him to, stopping only when he nearly toppled off the edge. He stumbled back, Jenna clenching his arm so hard that he could hardly feel it, coughing on the smoke.

The split in the earth wasn't as deep as he'd anticipated, but a good thirty feet down for sure.

Then his eyes stopped, landing on a boy that Matteo had never seen with dark, black eyes…and he was kneeling beside a motionless Lawrence.

"Lincoln!" Jenna cried out.

"Jenna?"

The boy's eyes widened.

He must have been the "Lincoln" that Matteo kept hearing about. "Jenna, what are you doing here?"

"Looking for you!"

"What are you doing standing there?!" Noah's voice shouted from behind.

Matteo and Jenna turned around, Matteo's heart dropping into his stomach. The creatures were bounding toward them now.

"What do we do?" Jenna cried out, looking around, panicked.

There was no option.

The noises were getting louder: the creatures' nails scraping against the dirt and stone, Jenna's panicked breathing, Matteo's own heartbeat.

There was nowhere else to go. Nowhere else to go but down.

Jenna seemed to have made the same conclusion as she met Matteo's eyes. "You can fly us down, right?"

"I—"

"Go!" Noah shoved them both before Matteo could even answer.

He couldn't tell who screamed, only that he was tumbling

down the muddy side of the gorge, his thoughts as tumbling as his body till he hit the bottom with a thud. He lay motionless for a moment before he realized that he was alive. In fact, he wasn't even injured, just sore all over from running.

He sat up, his heart racing, trying pointlessly to scrape away the mud and scramble to his feet. Matteo ran to Lincoln's side and froze, seeing Lawrence still unconscious.

"He fell from there," Lincoln said, his eyes casting up to the burning tree bridge. "Straight down. Much nastier fall than sliding down the edges."

Jenna rushed over, shoving Lincoln out of the way. "Who's this? What happened to him?"

"He—he fell. He was conscious for a bit. It was his side…and then he just blacked out."

"His side? " Noah said, dropping onto the other side. He and his sister exchanged glances. "And he's *lucky* if that's all it is."

"Can you do anything?" Lincoln asked.

Matteo couldn't speak, watching them all glance at each other.

"If it's not severe, yeah. I have field medic training," Noah said, patting his bag. "And supplies. I always keep things just in case…especially with my condition."

"Condition?"

"Diabetes. No time to explain." Jenna sighed, removing Lawrence's glasses and handing them to Matteo. "The best we can do is painkillers and tending the wound…and then hope for the best."

And hope that those creatures didn't get the nerve to crawl down here.

Matteo glanced upward, seeing the little, beady eyes staring down at him. No Fire Wolf. No Defenders. No one. Just a bunch of kids stuck in a ditch.

Lawrence had felt pain before. In fact, he'd bruised a rib before…but breaking a few was way worse. Breathing was his worst enemy, and the moment he woke up, he wasn't sure if his vision was blurry because he wasn't wearing his glasses or because it hurt too much to process vision.

The first moment was getting whoever was touching him

away, no matter how badly it hurt. He clenched his jaw, struggling to breathe for an extra solid minute when a voice spoke to him.

"Woah, chill, dude." A young female voice.

"He's usually like this." Lincoln's voice was too far off.

"The pain shouldn't be too bad in a second once the meds start kicking in. They're weak, but they should do something." Another voice he didn't recognize.

Where were all these people coming from? He clutched his painful side.

A hand reached out for him. He quickly squatted it. "Don't you dare," he growled.

"How can you see my hand without your glasses?" the girl said with a defeated sigh.

"I'm not blind. I can see your blurry hand." Lawrence half-rolled his eyes before grimacing. "I'm fine."

"Jenna, don't bother him." A figure knelt closer to him. "I'm Noah Mathews, and this is my sister, Jenna. We're Ray's siblings."

"And that makes you trustworthy?" Lawrence snorted, which was a mistake, forcing a groan from his lips. What were Ray's siblings doing here?

"The fact you survived with only a few busted ribs is a miracle," Noah continued. "Your coats and the mud no doubt were helpful factors."

"I've been through things before," Lawrence grumbled, tired of the lectures. "Now, can I have my glasses? If only we still had snow. The ice would help the swelling."

"Is that safe?" Jenna teased.

"You really are related to Ray," Lawrence said, trying to give a glare in what he hoped was the right direction.

"The suspiciously quiet guy has your glasses," Lincoln's voice said.

Lawrence frowned. "Matteo?"

There was no way he was here. Not until he saw the blur of the familiar bright green and the frame of his glasses nudged in his hand.

He took them gratefully, but he was too stunned to waste a painful breath on a thank-you. He slipped the glasses in place, fighting a groan as he saw that one of the lenses was cracked.

This made the second pair in the past two weeks.

It still functioned, and he could see Matteo's mud-streaked face looking concerned toward him.

"So who are you?" Lincoln asked bluntly.

In the light, Lawrence could see him more clearly. The dark lines under Lincoln's black eyes were darker than ever, his hair a mess and muddy, and his feet were bare.

"He's a Council Member," Jenna said. "Just like you, Lincoln. And, apparently, stick-in-the-mud here. You—you don't know each other?" She looked at them, confused.

"He's the Wingor, remember? We just got back from Court Illegia," Lawrence said, slowly easing himself back, his face contorting in pain. "And now we're stuck in a ditch on the hunt for some Soul."

Lincoln winced at the mention of his goal.

Matteo frowned. "Soul?"

"It's important," Lincoln said defensively. He got to his feet, turning away from the rest of them. "All I know so far is that it's connected to the Council and the Oquelite. And it could potentially be super important."

"So running to the woods was your smartest idea?" Jenna said. He could hear the judgment in her voice.

"There is a palace here. We've been once before. I saw on the Curatrix machine a bunch of Oquelite were gathered there, and I remember a document in a tower written by some ancient woman named 'Avalon.'"

"Do the Defenders know about this?" Noah asked.

"Nope." Lawrence sighed. Of course they didn't.

"Look. I didn't have time to ask Taryn, and Dow would've said no flat out." Lincoln spun back around on them. "The longer we stand here, the more the woods grow and the farther the palace goes. And your mom will actually *kill me* when she learns you two came along. Is Adam here too?"

"Not the reunion I was expecting," Jenna joked half-heartedly. Why was Lincoln being so harsh?

Lawrence didn't want to blame him, especially considering the Nikki situation, but something seemed… unusually tense.

"No, Adam is back at the cabin we were supposed to be staying in," Noah said, shooting a glare at his younger sister.

"At least something went right." Lincoln sighed, looking up toward the rim of their prison, where an occasional pair of beady eyes would stare down at them. "We need to get out."

"Even if we could, we'd be eaten alive by those things," Lawrence said, letting himself lie down on his back to ease the pain as he stared up into the gray sky as rain fell gently.

"Where's Fire Wolf?" Matteo said.

"Not here. So not helpful." Lincoln groaned.

"Chill out."

"How can I 'chill out,' Lawrence?"

"Maybe breathe?"

"I am breathing."

"Fine, then. Be that way." Lawrence didn't want to waste any precious, painful word on the pointless argument. If he weren't feeling like his side was being crushed under an ax, he'd happily slap Lincoln across the face and demand for his senses.

All four of them were quiet for a long moment.

"Does anyone have a rope?" Matteo asked.

"You think a rope will get us out?" Noah said.

"No, wait." Lincoln perked up. "He might be onto something."

Lawrence pushed himself up, his brows knitting as he watched Lincoln dig through his bag, pulling out his Cube. "I made an ejected rope line...for climbing trees."

"How high does it go?" Jenna said, her eyes lighting up.

"Not this high. Maybe seven feet." Lincoln scowled. "It's never been tested and can only carry about one at a time."

Lawrence looked around before his eyes settled on a crumbled, little ledge a few feet away and above. "If we can get up there, we can probably reach. But with those repitox up there, you would hardly have a moment to gain balance and run."

"Well, it's either die down here or die up there," Lincoln said.

All four of them shot him either a glare or a horrified look.

"Good to know the legendary Council is a bunch of loser pessimists," Jenna scowled, rolling her eyes and beginning to storm off.

Lawrence and Lincoln exchanged a glance. For a moment, the stubborn exterior melted and Lincoln quickly jumped to grab Jenna's shoulder. "Look, we're just being realistic."

"Realistic? You're a group of magical teenagers who fight bad guys trying to take over regions. How is that realistic?" Jenna's brows furrowed as she pulled out of Lincoln's grip. "I came to North Cordell *excited* to see you. It's good to know on top of Ray going berserk and my apparent half-brother we didn't know we had until months ago is setting buildings on fire. And now this."

"Jenna." Lincoln's eyes widened.

She ignored him, turning her back with a huff, her brother running to comfort her.

"We're going up that ledge," Matteo said softly. Far from a declaration. He turned to Lawrence and hesitantly offered a hand.

Lawrence took a deep painful breath before taking it. He struggled to his feet, the sharp pain shooting up his side. He grit his teeth.

Lincoln looked at him, surprised.

"She has a point," Lawrence said. "You had a mission to help the Council, and we're not giving up on it."

Lincoln's eyes faltered before he gave a shaky, singular nod.

Noah looked to them, hopeful now that a decision had been made, but Jenna's face still looked red enough to punch something. Lawrence didn't want to add anything more to the poor girl's flame.

They trekked over the ledge, every step making every breath harder. It was a burden to simply breathe.

The repitox above grew excited that their prey had begun to move, scampering around. The climb up the incline was a tortuous one, and Lawrence bit the inside of his mouth so hard that he could taste blood. It didn't compare to the fire in his side. He was grateful for Lincoln's help, pulling him up finally onto the safety of the ledge.

The rain had begun to pour down harder, the ground below their feet shifting, growing more unstable by the minute.

Jenna's eyes were glassy, and she hugged herself in the

cold with a sniffle. Matteo offered her his jacket.

Lincoln fumbled with the Cube, taking a deep breath. He looked over his shoulder for a moment to Jenna, who refused to look at him and only at the zipper of Matteo's jacket.

Lincoln steadied the device in his hand, and with the click of its side, a wire shot out. Lawrence held his breath as it flew, digging into the edge of the ditch.

"It worked," he said.

"Don't get too excited." Lincoln looked around. "Who's going up first?"

The newly excited screeches of the repitox above were not comforting.

Lawrence looked around to the young faces around him. Jenna was on the verge of tears, Matteo was looking like it took every bit of his sanity to keep from panicking with one earbud in, and Noah was hard and unreadable as he stood at his little sister's side.

"I'll go."

"What?" Lincoln gaped. "But your ribs. Shouldn't you wait—?"

"I'll. Go." Lawrence stepped forward, trying to hide a pained grimace. "I can try and keep them off as you guys climb out."

He wouldn't last long, but it was their only chance.

Lincoln held his eyes for a long moment before he sighed. "Fine." He scowled.

Lawrence caught Matteo's wide eyes and the tiniest shake of his head before turning for Lincoln. "All right. Let's get this over with."

Lincoln instructed him to put his foot up against the Cube as a support, cringing as his precious creation was touched by Lawrence's boot. To Lawrence's surprise, it was fairly firm, but the racing of his heart wasn't exactly helping the pain that made every breath a burden.

"Ready?" Lincoln said, for once the look on his face uneasy. He looked up to Lawrence.

Lawrence shrugged, careful not to laugh. "As I'll ever be."

"Hit your foot on the left side."

Lincoln stepped back, and Lawrence did as instructed,

and almost instantly, he was lifted up. He hardly had a moment to process when he was scrambling to pull himself over the edge. He gave out a pained cry as his side pressed against the ground. He pushed himself up, rolling onto the ground.

A high-pitched shriek of delight made his blood run cold.

There was no time for rest. Even if it felt like he'd be breathing boiling blood if he moved anymore. Lawrence scrambled to his feet, clutching his side with instant regret. The repitox crouched cautiously.

"Yeah? Remember last time?" Lawrence said, having no idea why he kept talking to animals. "The guy with the fire?"

It didn't seem like it had fazed them too much as they crept toward him.

"Noah's up next!"

Lawrence scowled. "Great!"

They had a matter of seconds. Clutching his side, he snatched a stick from the ground, holding it out in front of him, preparing himself. One reared up to pounce.

And then the creatures froze. Were they really afraid of sticks?

A howl broke through the air, the power bellowing to an echo. Not just one howl…multiple.

Lawrence's heart dropped.

Before he could process the rocks bouncing at his feet, the creatures began to scatter, their slithering bodies scrambling into each other in confusion.

An enormous wolf tore from the woods, its body aflame and its eyes aglow. It had to be at least seven feet and sent the repitox running. More trickled out, easily chasing after the repitox creatures.

The largest stared hard at Lawrence, a snarl following on his lip as he stepped forward.

Lawrence shoved a petrified Noah behind him and held out his stick, his heart beating against his ears.

A small yip came tumbling out the woods, a Fire Wolf running toward Lawrence, ramming into him with a full force of excitement. Lawrence cried out in pain. He dropped the stick, crumpling over onto the ground, throwing his arms around Fire Wolf's neck.

"Don't do that." He gasped, burying his face in the wolf's coat, struggling to breathe. "Good boy. You're such a good boy." Lawrence sat back, holding Fire Wolf's big face in his hands as he panted with delight.

Lincoln cursed from behind him. "When did they get so big?"

The giant wolf stepped forward tentatively.

Jenna dropped beside Lawrence. "You okay?"

"I am now."

The girl glared at him. "Don't lie."

Lawrence was glad that Fire Wolf bit the end of his coat and nudged him forward. He ignored Jenna's call and let Fire Wolf lead him to the big wolf. He ignited himself, nudging his head forward to Lawrence's hand.

"You want me to…hold it?"

Fire Wolf nudged again. Lawrence looked up at the bigger wolf with a gulp, taking a handful of flame from Fire Wolf's coat. Fire Wolf yipped with joy.

The larger wolf was still for a moment before bowing its front leg.

Lawrence stumbled back, the fire going out in his hand. "What the—?"

Lincoln gasped. "You're a Ywondie, Lawrence. That's the reason Fire Wolf follows you around, since the Ywondie are their creators…These must be ancient creatures." For a moment, the childish delight returned to Lincoln's face as he stepped forward, his eyes aglow.

"You must be the first Ywondie they've seen in literal centuries," Noah breathed.

Fire Wolf was growing impatient, yanking at Lawrence's coat and dragging him to the wolf's side.

"It looks like he wants you to climb on." Jenna laughed.

Matteo looked at her in horror at the suggestion.

Lawrence had to agree. He glanced at Fire Wolf before climbing onto the enormous wolf's back. A few other wolves began to do the same.

"We get to ride wolves too?" Jenna squealed, shaking her brother. "Wait until we tell Adam!"

"We're not telling anyone." Noah grabbed his sister's hand, carefully helping her up.

Lincoln climbed up fairly easily, the numbness settling

over his expression. That left Matteo alone, glancing around at the others. Lawrence urged the wolf forward.

"Hop on."

"Maybe I should—"

"No way we're leaving you behind." The wolf lowered. "Come on."

A small wave of relief fell over Matteo's face as he joined Lawrence. The wolf rose.

The wolves all met at the edge of the woods, Lawrence stepping in line beside Lincoln and sending him a smirk. "You gonna thank me for getting you a free ride to your castle?"

Lincoln rolled his eyes and set off.

Lawrence wasn't prepared for the harsh jerk and the wolf punching into a run. His ribs were going to kill him…if whatever danger they were throwing themselves into wouldn't take him first.

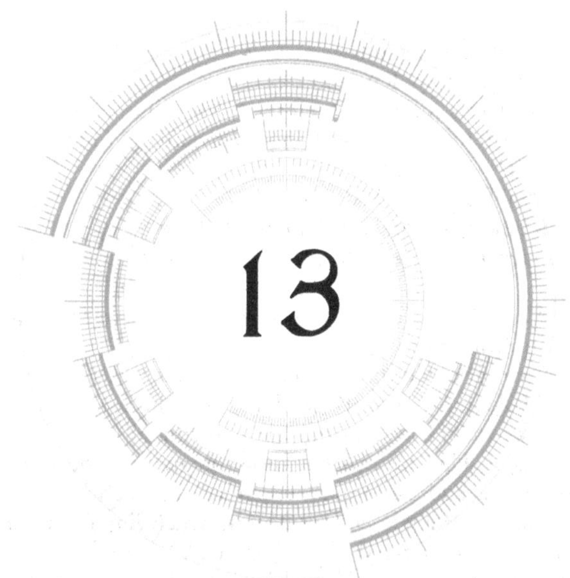

13

Kennedy, 27 Days Until

"REMEMBRANCE, I THINK I know where your dad is."

Those were the words that caused Mercy to drop an armful of pots and spin on Ray, her mouth gaping without any hesitation. Her stupid bot even raced to protect her. "You what? How? Wait…how do you know about my dad? Are you stalking me?"

She grabbed a pan swiftly from the ground, swinging it out in front of her like a weapon.

Ray stepped back. Stupid decision. He should've prefaced that better. "Your grandmother mentioned him. That you were looking for information about him, right? I assumed he was lost." He wasn't lying about that part.

Surprise flickered in Mercy's eyes, which confirmed it. The speck of emotion vanished as her face quickly hardened. "Then how the heck do you know where he is?"

"So he is lost?"

"*Tell me*," she growled, raising the pan. "Or I knock you

out."

"I'd like to see you try—"

She began to pull back.

"No! I was joking! I'll tell you!" He whipped the sticky note out of his pocket, shoving it forward. "I found this in my room."

Mercy frowned. "You what?"

"Behind the dresser. I think it fell there."

In your grandmother's phone. I think you aren't supposed to know this.

He kept his hand steady as Mercy crept forward, swiping the note from him.

Mercy set down the pan on the counter, unwrinkling the note. "Lakehouse. Local's Soul Night." She looked at him and frowned. "How does this mean anything?"

Dang it. Had he made it too ambiguous? The original message was addressed to an unnamed contact and the only other one on the tele besides Mercy, which Ray found odd. They briefly mentioned "Remembrance," and then she told the number to meet her at the lakehouse, on the locals' "soul night." He was hoping that it would trigger something.

"Uh, I thought it was something like directions," Ray said, rubbing his neck. *Think quick.* "I mean, it doesn't look like a grocery list, does it?"

"How do you think it relates to my father, though?" Mercy said. "Or written by my grandmother at all? What if whoever those attackers were wrote this?" Her eyes narrowed at him. "Or maybe *you*?"

Ray snorted. "What motivation would I even have to try and trick you into finding your dad?"

To learn answers about your weird family and region, maybe…

Mercy raised a brow. "I guess you wouldn't know about the lakehouse." She sighed.

"Wait, you know about the lakehouse?"

Mercy tensed, as if she hadn't expected him to hear it. "Y—yeah," she said, stepping back. "My dad used to take me when I was little."

"Look, you seem to really want to find your dad, so what if this is a lead? Maybe your only lead?"

Mercy looked down again at the note for a long moment. She set it on the counter and shook her head. "No," she said, her voice falling. "My grandmother is looking for him. And I should stay here and tend the motel."

She knelt down and began to gather the fallen pots. How was she so stubborn?

He dropped down to help her. "So you're just going to sit around like a passive, helpless kid while your grandma does all the work? She literally threatened not to tell you stuff about your own *dad* and you just take it."

"Look." Mercy tore a pot from Ray's hand. "She's kept me safe for my entire life. I owe her that."

"Safe from what?"

She didn't answer, kicking the bottom drawer open to the cabinet open, dropping in the pots with a clamor.

Ray got up after her. "You'd just abandon your dad like that?"

Mercy swiveled on him, and he instantly regretted every word. "I'm not!" she shouted. "And how *dare* you accuse me otherwise?! You have *no* say in what it's like to lose a father."

"Oh, you have no idea," he snorted, clenching his fists.

"You're only here to repay a debt, not lecture me on my dad," Mercy reminded, grabbing a washcloth from the sink. She wrung it with all her fury. "You don't know what I'd do to get him back."

"Are you saying I've had it easy?"

B0bbl3 threw a washcloth at him with its tiny bot arm. He caught it with ease, trying to contain the burning inside him.

"From the way you've pranced around like some egotistical prat for the past few days, yeah, actually." Mercy didn't even look up from the dishes.

"You're impossible," he spat, spinning around, scrubbing the counter, hoping that he was as obnoxious as possible.

Mercy seemed to have the same plan, banging every utensil that came within her bowl.

He was sure that it would've worked. How could she just blow off an opportunity like this? Was he just stupid thinking it would work?

Crash.

Mercy cursed, and the sudden smell of burning exploded in Ray's senses. He whirled around, ready to knock the jug of water over onto the stove from there before catching himself. Mercy just coughed and watched the batter that had spilled over a flaming kitchen stove. Ray ran from the jug, dumping it on top, quickly turning off the stove.

They both stumbled back, choking on the smoke.

"Not again," Mercy gasped.

"Again?"

"You distracted me!"

"*I* did?"

Mercy looked away, her fists squeezing, her shoulders heaving. It hit Ray: she was trying not to cry.

Ray's face softened. "You really do want to go and look for him, don't you?"

She was quiet for a moment.

"Look, Remembrance." Ray opened his mouth, shutting it. Was he really about to dump his life story on this unbearable girl? "If I had had the chance to find my dad before it was too late, I would've taken it," he said quietly.

It felt…wrong. He knew that he was lying to her. He just wanted her to look for her father so that he could get information out of her. But something inside of him *did* envy her. She at least had an opportunity to find her father, whereas he was only a five-year-old waiting at the end of a driveway with his hands over his ears so that he couldn't hear his mother say that Dad wasn't coming back.

"I'm sorry." Her voice was so small, he almost missed it.

He swallowed hard. "Did—did he run?"

Mercy slowly turned back to him. "I—I don't know."

She took out a new towel and began to clean up the mess in silence. Ray went back to the refrigerator, putting back Mercy's odd ingredients. The two worked in silence, and he preferred it. That way it was easier not to feel guilty about using her situation for his own gain. A situation that felt oddly personal.

Mercy took the order pad and slipped quietly outside of the kitchen, leaving Ray to prepare the breakfast orders by himself. He didn't mind the time to think.

Hours must have passed when Mercy slammed the order pad back onto the counter. "Take a break," she said suddenly. "You can do dishes later."

Ray frowned.

She headed for the exit of the kitchen. She stopped when

she realized that Ray wasn't following and ushered him to follow her. "Come on."

This was new.

He ran after her through the door. He burst into a dark hall he hadn't bothered to notice before. It smelled mustier…and older than the rest of the house, and the floorboards were creaky under his and Mercy's steps.

"Where are we going?"

"Somewhere you shouldn't be." Mercy stopped, fishing a rusted, golden, burnished key out of her pocket. She dug it into the doorknob of the door, and it opened with a click, and the door swung open.

Ray's breath caught. The walls were lined in *bookshelves*, with the various paperbacks in all sorts of faded colors on the dark, wood shelves. Windows lined the back wall, letting in light pouring into the room and over the large desk with a green grass lantern on top and a small stack of papers weighed down by a glass case.

The parts of the walls not covered by books were covered in framed photos and paintings of the moon and charted stars. Even the rug on the floor mapped out the moon cycle.

"This place is incredible." Ray gasped, turning as he followed her, trying to take it all in.

"The 'Soul Night' did remind me of something that *does* sound like my grandmother," Mercy said.

Ray turned his attention to her and followed Mercy's gaze to the charts along the wall.

"She loves the night. The moon, specifically."

"Why?"

"I have an idea…but you can't know, nor do I think it's really related." She glared at him, so he didn't dare ask. "But it's not beyond her to use her knowledge to set up a date."

Ray's heart leapt. Mercy was *actually* considering his note. She was cooperating…as long as he pretended that she was the one in control.

"So do you know what 'Soul Night' means?" he asked.

She shook her head, turning to sift through the shelves.

Soul. The word liked nagging at him. Was it connected to the Shadow Soul that echoed in his mind?

"The note mentioned it being a local thing," Ray said,

wandering around the room, a large book striking his interest on the desk. It looked useful. "Is there any way we can ask people around?"

"By 'local,' she must mean the EarthShaker settlers." Mercy's eyes brightened. "After the EarthShaker, a large group came to reclaim their homeland from before the EarthShaker, accepting anyone who came with them as their own."

"Are these people hard to find?"

Mercy laughed. "Hard? They're 90 percent of this region's population. Some of my family is part of it."

He made a mental note of the book, stepping closer to the desk. A photo sat beside it. A woman with curly hair, big earrings, and a big smile. She had marks like Mercy that curled up onto her cheek. She was beautiful.

Ray's fingers brushed against the frame.

"Don't!"

Ray pulled back, turning to see a frozen Mercy, her arm outstretched. She quickly composed herself and cleared her throat.

"Sorry. Is that your grandmother?"

Mercy tensed at the question, shaking her head quickly as she wrung her hand through her curls.

"Oh. Well, I just thought...since she looks like you, but with your hair down."

Mercy froze up. "I—I can't. No hair down. Let's move on."

"I didn't—"

"We're moving *on*, Mathews."

He swallowed hard. Yikes. Another rule?

"So where do we *look*, then?"

"A bit harder." Mercy bit her lip, her eyes drifting to the bookcases. "The farmer's market. That's where we'll go."

Ray groaned. "More grocery shopping?"

"Important grocery shopping," Mercy said with a smile. She took the Comm out of her pocket, walking to the wall. "Ahnah will be there, and her family. I'm sure they'll have answers."

Mercy clicked her screen, and the shutter of the camera went off and she slipped it back into her pocket. "Maybe you are helpful to keep around, Mathews."

"I'm very helpful."

Mercy smirked with a roll of her eyes. "Now, wash those dishes."

"Really?" Ray whined playfully.

"Come on!" she called, rushing out the door. "I have to lock the door. Don't you *dare* touch anything."

Ray's hand wavered to the nearest shelf. "What happens when I—?" She glared at him, and he just laughed. "Harsh much?"

He followed after Mercy and she closed the door, locking it firmly. He watched her as she tucked away the key into her pocket.

"Can you keep a secret, Mathews?"

"I keep quite a few."

"Good. No one, I mean absolutely *no one*, can know about this." She once again towered over him, her glare boring into him. "Do you understand?"

"You can trust me, Remembrance."

"Can I?"

"I'd never lie to such an esteemed person as yourself." Ray gave a small bow, feeling his face burn.

"Good." Mercy began walking back toward the kitchen. "Because you're the first person I've ever given a secret to keep."

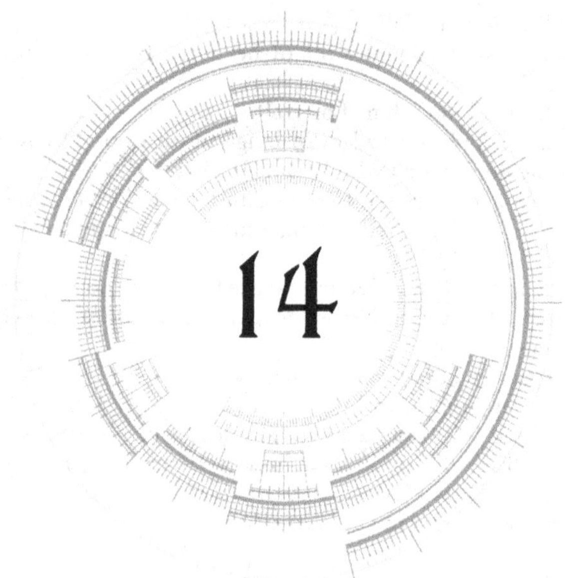

14

North Cordell, 27 Days Until

LINCOLN TRIED TO keep his focus ahead and trust the animal that made his scientific and supernatural knowledge clash. All thanks to one person…and Lincoln couldn't bear looking at him.

He had watched Lawrence fall, and for a moment his own thoughts were louder than the woman in his head. He'd slipped down the muddy side, scrambling to Lawrence. He was struggling to breathe, clutching his side, trying to push Lincoln away.

For a moment, Lincoln thought that he was dying. He had killed another one of his friends. All because of a stupid goal and—

Why do you doubt yourself so? He was the fool who fought off that Repitox when he knew he would most likely fall.

But he was doing it to protect—

Exactly! A foolish decision. First things first, to survive, you must prioritize your own well-being.

I guess that makes sense…

You cannot guess. You must be more assertive. It does make sense. If you want to survive, you must be a priority.

It sounded selfish. But Lincoln didn't want to dwell on morals. So far, the voice in his head hadn't done any wrong. She'd helped him. She'd even offered to help him get his abilities early and was trying to help him heal Nikki. How bad could she be?

A shiver overcame him. He knew that that wasn't right. But he also knew that he didn't have much of an option now. Once he got back to camp, no doubt that Taryn wouldn't be so forgiving, seeing as he ran away against direct orders.

"Is that it?"

Lincoln looked up, peering through the woods when his wolf came to a halt, nearly throwing him off. He swung himself off with the sudden momentum, rolling to his feet.

Despite his feet not feeling much thanks to the Voice, he still wasn't comfortable with the fact that the ground was wet. In fact, it was too soft. Fog was hanging over the soggy ground. The palace stood in the woods, trees seeming to take nearly no notice of it, their trunks up against the stone walls and branches flowing into the windows of the numerous towers that rose up and disappeared with the thick branches that surrounded it.

"The closest access point is that second floor window," Lincoln said, remembering their escape from the palace through the tower. "It's as simple as climbing a tree. We get to the tower. Find the documents. Then get out and back to camp. Simple as that."

"Very simple." Lawrence sighed. "And no way I can join you."

Everyone went quiet, their eyes trailing to Lincoln.

Lawrence groaned. "Which means you have to lead them in. And I swear, this better not be a mistake."

"Let's get this over with, shall we?" Jenna said, her curly hair now a mess and a scratch across her cheek, with her dark brows still furrowed in a frown.

Lincoln's heart swelled, opening his mouth.

Don't bother with the child. Her opinions of you shouldn't affect you, fool.

He closed his mouth quickly and cleared his throat. "Let's

go."

He led them up the enormous tree trunk, which was easier than he remembered it being. His mind sorted through it easier, and his skin felt more gripped to the bark as he crawled his way up. The smell of the dirt was enticing and the earth around him exhilarating, like it just gave him energy to be among…

"Lincoln, wait up!"

Lincoln stopped, turning to see the others farther behind him. He resigned himself to waiting, finding it oddly easy to find a safe position. He watched Jenna, who seemed determined not to look in his direction.

Matteo, the new Member apparently, trailed behind her, his eyes darting nervously from Jenna to the ground, steadying her when her hand's grip slipped.

He tapped his foot impatiently. "I'll meet you all up there," he decided, quickly turning to run for the window.

He heard Noah call after him, but he didn't wait. Lawrence had named him leader, so why should he? He was giving them a head start.

Lincoln easily leapt through the window, hitting the wood floor with a thud, sending dust flying from the boards. He got to his feet, coughing, and stopped to scan the room.

For the most part, he found it to be empty. A few ancient, broken bed frames and littered lace curtains and torn mattresses, and a closet with the doors ripped off and a few plain garments hanging loose on a rack. Nothing really to his use.

Exactly. No use to you. So why stand around aimlessly?

Why would he abandon his friends?

They're not your friends. Two of them are the siblings of the boy who tried to kill you.

That wasn't Ray's fault.

Then whose was it?

Lincoln paused. "I—I don't know," he admitted out loud. "Something told him to…in his head."

How pathetic. The fact still remains. And the other boy? You hardly know him. And don't try to "But he's a Council Member" me. We all know you tried to run from the Council.

Lincoln's face heated. "Fine. You're right. I should start looking."

He had to force himself not to look over his shoulder as he pushed open the heavy, wood door. He peered out into the hallway. This one was far grander than the previous that he'd been in. A small draft ran through the hall. A moldy, red carpet ran through the entire hall, the ceiling stretching upward with gold-crafted chandeliers…that were lit.

Lincoln's heart leapt in surprise. Fire?

The hall broke into another hall passing horizontally in front and more naturally lit. He crept down toward it, his feet suddenly cold against the stone. He moved slowly forward, feeling more uneasy now that the stone surrounded him.

He tried to shake it off. What was going on in his head?

Suddenly, something jerked him back, thrusting him against the wall, and before he could cry out in defiance, Noah shoved his hand over his mouth. In Lincoln's horror, over Noah's shoulder, he saw an Oquelite, dressed in a ragged uniform, charged right across the opposite hall.

They were done—

Bang!

The Oquelite collapsed to the floor, and Jenna looked proudly at the heavy Medic bag swinging in her hands. Noah let go of Lincoln to help Jenna drag the Oquelite into the dimly lit hall.

Lincoln blinked in shock, turning to find Matteo beside him.

The Wingor didn't look at him. In fact, Lincoln doubted that he could hear with earbuds in. Matteo rushed to help Jenna, and she panted with adrenaline as she collapsed in the hall.

"It's Oquelite occupied," Lincoln breathed. Of course it was. All the dots indicated that the Oquelite were in the woods, but *in the palace?* This made things levels more complicated.

"They don't seem too hard to beat." Jenna laughed softly, though terror was evident in her wide eyes.

"There's no way we can beat them like this." Lincoln began to pace. Even with the Super Cube, it wasn't enough.

"Do we need to beat them?" Matteo's voice was soft.

Lincoln turned around to find one bud removed. He wasn't making eye contact with anyone, just staring at his shaking hands.

"Don't we just need to get past them?"

Lincoln frowned. He had a point.

"We have a disguise right here," Matteo pointed out, shifting uncomfortably from the unconscious body.

"Who's going to disguise as an Oquelite?" Jenna said, wrinkling her nose.

"How about the Oquelite here?" Lincoln said, looking at the half-Oquelite siblings, who looked back at him with surprise.

"Oh, right," Noah grumbled.

"They're out of it enough to assume you as Ray," Lincoln said. "Same dark hair, gold eyes. It would work."

Noah's head fell with a small nod. "It's a good idea."

Lincoln guessed that they hadn't processed their Oquelite lineage much. And after what happened with Ray, he could feel why they wouldn't want to.

The Voice tried twisting the pity away from him.

Lincoln looked around his group, trying to ignore the fact that none of them looked willing to go forward. "It's settled, then."

Lincoln blamed himself for not being able to stop Ray. And seeing the familiar, golden eyes behind the hood of an Oquelite uniform reminded him more than anything had in the past seven months.

It took him a moment to adjust himself when Noah first stepped out shyly. "I hate this. It smells like sweat and dirt."

Lincoln wanted to tell him to be more serious when his subconscious reminded him of Noah's age. And now they were following a fifteen-year-old dressed as his older, powerful brother down the echoey halls of a quite possibly enchanted palace.

Lincoln kept close behind Noah. So far they'd spotted no Oquelite. They must have all been down on the lower layers.

They ran down the large hall, lit by an enormous, fractured, stained-glass window of a woman with dark-brown hair cascading around her in royal colors of purple that brought out her bright-violet eyes and the impressive crown sitting upon her head full of the green stones. Artifacts of the same stone as the Ewyon Stone. Vines hung across it, as well as moss that grew along the border, and no one else seemed to pay it a moment's more attention than needed.

"The tower is on the south side of the palace," Lincoln whispered, remembering the spire from the outside.

Noah nodded, taking a quick turn through the left hall. The steps ascended a short flight of stairs till they entered a new hall with a patterned carpet runner and one wall completely gone. The glass shards scattered across the hall, leading Lincoln to assume that the wall had been made of it. It looked out into a courtyard, now overgrown with shrubbery.

"The carpet," Jenna choked.

Lincoln looked down, realizing that the carpet had no pattern at all. It was stained with blood.

Jenna's face was pale, looking sick enough to vomit. Matteo was frozen at the edge of the hall.

"You two should stay behind," Lincoln decided. "This place seems tucked away enough to where no one will find you. Noah and I will be back in a second."

"You want to leave them alone?" Noah said with a frown, looking from his sister to Lincoln. "That doesn't seem safe."

"They'll be fine as long as we hurry. Come on!"

Lincoln wasted no time dashing across the blood-stained, glass-ridden carpet. He could see the shadows of the spiral stairs in the doorway from here. He heard Noah sigh and run after him. They reached the doorway; and, correct to Lincoln's suspicion, a stone, spiral staircase ran up the long shaft and went even farther down, no doubt the basement area that they'd first been trapped in.

He flew up the steps, his heart racing.

He pushed through the heavy, wood door at the top, nearly stumbling into the tower room. It was almost exactly as they'd left it, except the branch sticking through the window had grown larger, beginning to infest the room.

The room was quiet, and Lincoln paused for a moment. He could hear his heart racing in his chest. Was this a good idea?

His eyes slowly drifted to the papers on the desk. What he'd been searching for this whole time. They were right there.

He moved slowly toward it, picking up the crisp paper in

his hand, yellowed with age, and, to his surprise, finding another beneath. The scribbles were nothing similar to Anglish.

"Whoa," Noah breathed. His hood has fallen to his shoulders, the uniform a bit big for the boy, his eyes wide and mouth hanging in amazement at the sight. His golden eyes stopped on Lincoln. "Is that what you came for?"

"I hope so," Lincoln said. If it wasn't…then he'd come all this way and put everyone in danger for nothing. "I can't even read it. It's not even Anglish."

Not that it mattered. He couldn't read, either.

Noah looked over his shoulder, and his breath caught.

Lincoln looked to him with a frown. "What is it?"

Noah took the paper from him, beginning to pace. "'Dearest sister Carastene, I know the past few months have not been ones of peace between us. I know you blame me, and you and the entire court have full right to do so. But refusing to speak to me is a grave mistake. There is so little you truly know.'"

Lincoln's jaw dropped. "You can *read* it? Dude, that is an ancient script!"

Noah cringed. "Our mother brought us up learning about our Impure heritage."

"But how could she know—?" Lincoln stopped himself. He knew the answer. Richard Mathews, their father, must have taught her. "It doesn't matter. What does matter is that you can read it. Does it mention anything about a Shadow Soul?"

Noah's eyes drifted quickly down the page. Lincoln's heart pounded.

It felt like an infinity before Noah's eyebrows shot up. "She did," he gasped, his hands beginning to shake. "'The Shadow Soul is a force you do not understand. You only know it from the Council's decrees, but what you don't know is that the Council created the Shadow Soul.'"

"But what is it?" Lincoln urged, wishing that his eyes could process the scribbles on the page more than anything.

Footsteps caught him off guard. Lincoln and Noah froze.

"Up here! I heard voices!" Gruff voices. They didn't belong to Matteo or Jenna at all. Oquelite.

They were found.

Lincoln tore the letter from Noah's hands, shoving it into his bag. He glanced around the room for a weapon. Nothing.

"There! The Aviduous!"

Lincoln had no time for hesitation. He spun on Noah, grabbing his shoulders; facing his wide, terrified eyes; and whispering one word. "Run." And then he shoved him to the ground.

"He's attacking!" Two Oquelite guards jumped through the door.

Noah scrambled to his feet and, with one desperate look at Lincoln, raced down the steps.

Oh, foolish boy. When will you admit you need my help?

An Oquelite lit his hand with purple flames and, with a cry, dove at Lincoln. Lincoln dodged.

And then something strange happened. It felt as if the world slowed with him as he skidded down to the floor. The burning energy in his chest returned, and, as if it were an extension of his own body, a branch from the trees spilling in from the window reached up and whipped his Oquelite opponent into the wall away from him.

The world flew back to normal speed, leaving Lincoln breathless.

Embrace it, Aviduous.

These were his abilities. He hardly thought. His vision blurred, coming clear into focus as everything registered in an odd, focused blur, the Oquelite appearing red against the black and white canvas.

The voice in his head was giving him his abilities before his essence had broken yet.

It wasn't ethical.

He didn't have time to dwell on it. He rushed for his other opponent, now panicked, feeling every wisp of the earth around him, and leapt, finding a branch catching his foot, blocking the exit.

The Oquelite ignited his hand, but Lincoln swatted it away, willing the branches to come forward, swallowing the Oquelite with a scream.

His vision flew back to normal. His heart was racing, the burn still in his chest.

Don't you see what I can make possible for you? All I need is your name and you can have them forever.

Lincoln looked down at his hands, dirt ridden and blistered. He could finally be the Aviduous he heard about in legend. He could be powerful.

He shook it away, gasping for air as he stumbled back. What was he thinking? What was getting into him?

"Not now," he breathed, turning to race down the steps. First, he had to get out of here.

Matteo heard the Oquelite first.

He hated a lot of noises, but he decided that the sound of heavy boots and imminent death had to be the worst. He hadn't been able to sit still, pacing in place, not daring to get near the bloodied carpet. Jenna was curled up by the wall, her face buried in her matted curls.

"Are—are you all right?" he asked.

She nodded and cast him a small smile before curling up again.

Something like Jadie would do when she scraped her knee and came to him to help repair her jeans that she'd ruined. The thought of his younger sisters he'd left behind pierced him.

Not that he'd been able to take care of them. He could hardly take care of himself.

He knew that they were doomed the moment he heard the Oquelite racing through the hall. Jenna perked up at the noise. Matteo raced to her and, without a second thought, grabbed her wrist, running for the shattered, glass wall and out into the courtyard, slipping behind the wall and into the corner.

He flattened them against the wall, holding his breath. Jenna was shaking, grabbing his arm and squeezing it tightly. A lump formed in his throat.

"Up here! I heard voices!"

"No," Jenna whispered. Her eyes became glassy. She tried to jump up, but Matteo grabbed her. She spun on him. "They're going to find Noah and Lincoln." Her breathing was harsh, her eyes looking every which way.

"I—it's okay." It wasn't okay. "We need to get out of here."

Once they got to Lawrence, they'd be safe. Lawrence

could protect them.

Jenna froze, a single tear slipping down her cheek. Matteo tried to stop his shaking. How was he supposed to comfort her? He was just another mess.

But he was a Council Member. One Lawrence believed in. And Matteo trusted Lawrence. Lawrence had been able to help him calm down.

He gently took Jenna's hand. "We're going to do this."

She gave him a shaky nod, holding onto his hand tighter. "O—okay," she breathed.

Matteo took a deep breath. *No te asustes. Don't freak out.*

He led Jenna out. Peering into the hall and seeing it clear, they broke out into a run. If they just ran the same way they'd come, they could get out and meet Lawrence in the place they left him. Easy.

Until the pounding of the stupid boots echoed in his ears again. He drew Jenna back into a corner. Only shadows protected them now. A wrong glance would reveal them to the Oquelite marching down, his cape flowing behind him. Jenna pressed herself against him.

"Are you sure they weren't seeing things?" The Oquelite scoffed. "Her Ladyship will not approve if this turns out to be a silly mission driven by madness."

"She *is* the one causing the madness," his shorter companion said with a cough. "Whoever thought this was a good—?"

Fire caught onto the taller Oquelite's fingers. "Choose your next words and loyalties very carefully."

The two stared at each other intently.

Footsteps echoed from the hall Matteo had just left, and the two spun around to face the newcomer.

"Soldier!" the Oquelite shouted.

The small Oquelite halted in his steps before the other two. Matteo's heart dropped seeing Noah's familiar, frazzled face.

"H—hi," Noah blurted out.

Jenna tensed at her brother's voice.

"I don't remember sending you to clear the tower," the taller Oquelite said, glaring down at Noah, whose foot began to tap. "What is your name, soldier?"

The other gasped. "He's the hybrid boy, sir."

"That is me," Noah said quickly.

"No. That mortalizer's son left with the Council months ago."

Matteo's heart sped in his chest. Not now. Not when they were so close. They couldn't be discovered.

Noah's fists clenched, biting his lip with a hoarse laugh.

Jenna slowly sat up, quietly undoing the buckle on her bag.

No. No. No. She was about to do something stupid.

"I came back," Noah choked out.

The Oquelite weren't buying it. One stepped closer to Noah.

Matteo couldn't take it. He was pressed against the wall, trembling with fear, but if he didn't do anything—

"Hey! Over here!"

Jenna jumped out of the shadows. Matteo's jaw dropped as she grabbed the cape of the taller Oquelite, spraying the disinfectant toward his face. In rage, the Oquelite shoved her off of him, knocking her to the ground.

Matteo jumped to his feet, his heart hammering, his mind screaming at him to move.

"It's a female version," the shorter Oquelite gasped.

"Get over here, you little—"

Jenna sent another pathetic spurt of disinfectant spray, scrambling to her feet, and ran right through the arch leading into the main hall. The taller Oquelite took no hesitation to disappear into thin air.

"Jenna!" Noah screamed after her.

Matteo shook himself to his senses. He couldn't let them get hurt. He grabbed a fallen vase beside him, smashing it against the back of the Oquelite's head.

"That was awesome!" Noah said, giving a panicked smile.

Matteo still felt like every inch of him was shaking. The air was getting too loud. The footsteps were storming. The two ran out into the main hall. Jenna was running for the stained-glass window. Shouts came from behind.

Matteo regretted the decision to look behind and saw about half a dozen Oquelite racing up the steps and toward them.

They were trapped.

The voices were getting louder. He needed to get away.

He couldn't take this. He couldn't—

Jenna screamed.

The tall Oquelite dropped to the floor out of the air. Jenna ran, throwing her back against the stained-glass wall, holding out her disinfectant spray.

The Oquelite stalked toward her.

Matteo broke free from his mind and ran for her. Time was against him. His own mind was against him. Panic was rising in his chest to his throat.

He threw himself in front of the Oquelite, nearly tripping over the step leading up the stained-glass window, trembling. The Oquelite spoke, but Matteo couldn't hear him. His vision was spotting.

Keep it together, Lopez. Keep it together.

And then he saw the Oquelite's hand glow with a violet blast. An exploding pain in his side, Matteo heard his name screamed as he was sent sliding against the floor, hitting the wall with a definite thud.

He groaned in pain, his eyes burning.

He rolled himself over. The Oquelite was at Jenna now. He tried to reach out. He tried to scream for her.

The ground shook. The smell of burning rubble exploded through the air. The Oquelite spun around. Matteo craned his head to look. Through his blurry sight, he saw flames.

The palace was on fire.

And then an enormous figure stepped out, followed by something bounding toward him. He tried to scramble up and away. He almost cried out before something wet hit his face. His vision cleared. "F—Fire Wolf?"

The wolf tugged at his collar.

Matteo looked up, seeing Lawrence atop one of the enormous wolves, clutching his side painfully as he held himself high, sending a streak of flames down on the descending Oquelite. Lawrence wouldn't be enough to hold them off. Especially not in his state.

"We can't go," Matteo choked as Fire Wolf tugged him to his feet. He coughed, his throat feeling raw. "Not without Jenna!"

He turned for Jenna, the Oquelite now putting his hand on her, tearing her disinfectant spray from her hands.

Matteo stepped to run for her, but pain shot up his leg, the echoes crashing on the sides of his skull. He couldn't breathe.

"Matteo!"

He was frozen in place as Lawrence tore by. Fire Wolf shoved Matteo forward as he collapsed into Lawrence's grip, heaving up onto the back of the leaning creature before it jumped back up and bounded for the exit.

"No!" Matteo shouted, trying to fight against Lawrence's hold. "We need to go back! We need—"

He looked back, and with horror, the Oquelite and Jenna were gone.

He stopped fighting, hearing Lawrence's pained breathing. His eyes burned. "No."

He'd failed.

No, no, no, no, no, no.

He was whipped back around by the wolf's sudden turn, nearly colliding with Noah squeezed in front of him. Matteo couldn't bear to see Noah's face. The entire world burned as he saw the exit, the now busted-through wall coming into sight.

The green of the trees surrounded them as the wolf burst into new speed. They'd escaped. They'd made it out alive.

He could only muster enough energy to slip in his buds.

But Matteo didn't feel relieved. He'd let his weaknesses overcome him.

He felt his chest tighten. He wasn't giving up. He was going to free Jenna. Next time, he would be ready.

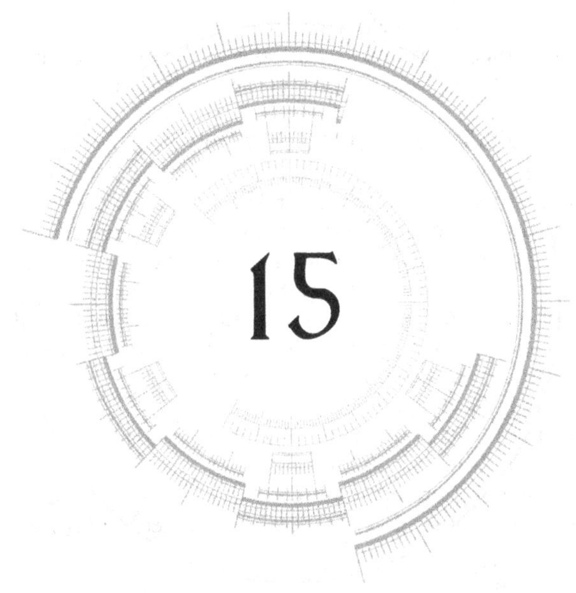

15

Liberty, 26 Days Until

COLE WOKE UP feeling heavier and more tired than when he fell asleep. That's what he got for staying up impossibly late all to try and remember something of his University days when he wasn't some magical Council Member with a fire sword.

He winced at the light stinging his eyes as the new world came into focus around him. He narrowed his eyes at the tent flap, slightly ajar. He was sure that he had closed it all the way last night.

Oh, well. It must have been too late to tell.

He sat up among the pillows and blankets, rubbing life back into his face. It was oddly quiet. There was the soft talking of conversation outside and creaks of carts, but it sounded so calm compared to waking up to the sound of Lincoln and Ray arguing at inhumane hours of the morning or Tabitha banging on the window if he was a minute too late.

Nothing. He was all alone here.

He took a deep breath. Maybe it was better that way.

His Comm vibrated on the carpet. He rolled off the bed, snatching it from the floor.

*MESSAGE FROM 4 OTHERS. 45 MINS AGO**

Cole tapped the message, reading it over. He sat back down onto the floor. Lincoln had a point, and Cole didn't know why it made his heart beat stronger to read something from one of them. Someone knew that they needed to get things done. Too many things. Red-eyed murder guys had to be a priority right up there with the Oquelite…but he had to meet Doran today to start his training. He groaned internally.

Talk in a few hours?…I have something huge.

"Ouch! Don't hit me!"

Cole frowned, looking up. Was that a…child?

"You're being too loud!"

"You woke him up, dummy!"

Cole quietly set down his Comm and crept to his feet.

"Amie, you're on my foot!"

"I am not!"

Cole carefully gathered the tent flap in his hand.

"*I* saw him first!"

"Nuh-uh!"

He pulled the tent flaps back with a jerk, sending three kids screaming back onto the dirt.

"He *is* awake!" A young boy with dark, black hair and thin, dark eyes darted behind a little girl, her box braids decorated with charms that jingled as she moved.

"You said he had a tail!" the little girl shouted, turning on the third child.

"He did last night!" the other boy said. His skin was pale, much like his tightly curled hair.

They couldn't all have been more than eight years old. Cole fought back an amused smile.

They all froze, realizing that he was still standing there, listening.

The little girl cleared her throat and stepped forward. "Hello, man. Where's your tail?"

Cole swallowed a snort. "I—I'm afraid I don't have one."

"I *knew* Amie was lying. I bet you were lying about last time too," she said, sending a glare at the pale boy. She turned back to Cole. "I'm Dana, a wolf-man catcher, and I think you need a bath."

Cole blinked, subconsciously looking down at himself. He hadn't bothered to change last night, his clothes still dirty and sweat ridden, and dirt and dried, bloody scrapes adorned his showing skin. He wrinkled his nose. "You know, kid, you might be right."

"We can show you to the bath house!" the boy behind Dana said, poking his head out. "I'm Tiez."

Cole nodded in acknowledgement. The bath house was part of Cecileo's directions to reaching Doran.

Perfect.

"That would be very helpful," he said.

"We *are* very helpful," Amie agreed.

Dana shoved him. "I'm the one who said it first!"

Cole let the children fight it out as he slipped back into the tent, grabbing his satchel and quickly attached the Illuminate to his belt. He decided that it was best to leave the boots behind, noting the children and the general public's bare feet. He folded Cecileo's note carefully and put it into the bag.

The moment he stepped out, Dana grabbed his arm, her youthful force nearly dragging him off his feet as she pulled him into the street.

The morning was alive. More were out than the day before, hanging clothing on the lines above the streets or driving their carts or rushing through the crowds to make it to the Market quicker.

"What's your name?" Tiez asked.

"'Cole.'"

"Why's your name 'Coal?'" Amie said, taking the lead, his chest puffed out with pride. "Did your Ma and Da have a lot of coal?"

"Uh...no." Cole laughed. "My father named me 'Coleson' after my mother."

"That's a weird name," Amie said.

Dana agreed. "That's like having some stuff and then putting 'son' after it. Like 'Noodleson.' I wanna be 'Noodleson' now."

Tiez ignored them. "Your ma's name was 'Coleson?'" he said with a small frown.

"'Colette,'" Cole corrected. That was the only fact he knew of her, and that she supposedly died when he was only a baby, but Cole wasn't sure whether he trusted that, either. His father had kept an entire life secret from him, and it was hard to trust anything now. "So, to answer your question, not really about stuff."

Dana huffed in disappointment.

Amie burst in with another question. "Have you met the Potter yet?"

"It's '*Pater*!'"

"I have," Cole said.

"Whoa," Dana breathed, holding Cole's hand tighter. "He really *is* special."

Cole snorted. "Not really."

"You are!" Dana declared. "And I want to marry you!"

Cole blinked. "Wha—?"

Tiez and Amie both groaned. "Not this again, Dana! You said you were marrying Ezra! He didn't even say yes."

Dana looked up to Cole. "Do you say yes?"

How was he supposed to respond to *that*? He faked a thoughtful expression. "Hm. I've never been asked that before. I don't think *I'm* old enough for that yet. I'm sorry, but I'll need more time."

Dana sighed. "Bummer."

"We're here!" Tiez declared.

Cole turned his attention to the direction of the little boy's voice. The bath house wasn't hard to miss. It was a relatively large building, seeming to be the only one that wasn't a tent, with only a few small windows and heavy curtains to each entrance.

"Should we wait for you?" Dana said, all three Marketeer children turning to look at him with their big eyes.

Cole shrugged, patting her on the head. "It's up to you three."

Honestly, having the three talkative children around kept his attention away from the anxiety of being swallowed into the chaotic culture of the Market, but he didn't want to hold the kids he hardly knew to any promises. For all he knew, they had much more important things to do…like chasing people with tails.

He entered the humid building cautiously, finding it

crammed with dozens of stalls and mostly empty. He showered quickly but spent a total of fifteen useless minutes trying to re-buckle his jerkin correctly. He was slightly disappointed to find that the children had gone when he left the building. He took out Cecileo's note, now having to navigate the chaos on his own.

He moved quickly. The faster he moved, the more it would look like where he was going, right?

Second left after the bath houses.

He glanced around, thankful to see that no one really minded him any attention, more engrossed in their carts and companions. The carts were curious contraptions: ones that had no electric power, which seemed most of the Market lacked. Why *was* that—?

Something slammed into Cole's side, knocking him off balance. He slammed against the dirt road without a moment to react to the cart coming for him. He rolled quickly to his feet, dodging quickly out of the way, falling back into the stunned crowd. His body was trembling, his mind reeling.

A blur of someone ran to him, a grip on his bad shoulder. "Sorry about that, kid. I didn't see you—"

Cole pulled away, trying to push back into the crowd and disappear. "I—it's fine, sir. I'm fine."

"You okay?" the man asked again.

"I'm fine. Really."

He turned and tore through the crowd. He had to get out of there. He just needed to find Doran and get all this over with.

He turned the corner, reaching for his bag's pocket. All he needed was—

His blood went cold. The note.

He'd taken it out, and his hands were now empty. He slowed to a stop, searching his pockets. His satchel. Nothing.

He had to have dropped it on the road. He needed to go back. But where was back? Left, right, forward?

The streets were unfamiliar. Shops lined the walls with growing, rush-hour crowds. No towering carpet tents. No familiar Celiceo or Echo.

For a moment, Cole felt like he was seven years old again: alone in the Sulfur streets, his father disappearing for months, his caretaker dead upstairs, and no one looking for him.

He was alone. And completely and utterly lost.

First things first, do not *freak out.*

It was easier thought than done as the suffocating crowd seemed to drag him along, the shoppers rowdy and aggressive, everything Cole was not. He was well aware that he stuck out like a sore thumb among the Marketeers and their missing limbs, who occasionally sent the lanky, pale, blond boy a curious scowl.

The farther he went, the more strange and unfamiliar it became—the tents dirtier and the walls older and crumbling.

His anxious fingers itched to cling to the Medallion, but he denied it. He needed to be stronger than this.

The Market was clearly at its prime time: shop owners shouting, shoppers conversing, others packing up and driving through from the night sales and pawning at various stalls. The Marketeer society felt so forgein and disconnected from the ordered, manufactured, outside world he knew.

They comfortably had children, family, and…lives. It was incredible.

The crowd was becoming stiffer, people beginning to stop moving. Cheers roared through the crowd. What was going on?

Cole pushed through the crowd, reaching to see a bare circle in the middle of the crowd, a middle-aged man with a well-trimmed, black beard walking around a leather bag unbound as shouting and cursing Marketeers tossed coins inside, some directly aiming for his face in anger.

He spat at the offender and closed the bag. Something about him stood out from the Marketeers…less cultured, and more practical.

"That's *nine* wins, people!"

"And one loss!" someone screamed from the crowd, but no one seemed to be swayed by the remark.

"Anyone willing to give our boy another chance?" The word used for whatever "boy" this man was giving another chance was far more explicit.

Cole's heart skipped a beat as said person was shoved to the middle of the circle, tripping over the leather straps tied loosely around his ankles. He caught himself on his knees.

He didn't look much older than Ray or Lincoln. His skin was tanned. He was slim and underfed, the only meat on him seeming to be some muscle. He had dark-red marks wrapping on his collarbone and his arms and along his cheek bones.

And a muzzle around his face.

This was no doubt a street fight. And that was no doubt a *human* captive. Was this allowed? Wasn't the Market a *safe* place for refuge?

"I bet ninety pounds. Biggest amount of the day for sure," the man shouted.

The crowd was undecided, murmuring through consideration and insulting the man all at the same time. Cole prayed that they'd all decide to turn and walk away, but he knew that deep down that was hopeless.

"No one?" the man scowled. "Come on, the scared lot of you!"

Cole saw the relief in the boy's eyes. That was until the man shouted, "I'll throw the runt in for a win too!"

The boy's body went rigid, his eyes wide in horror.

That got the bloody crowd's attention, roaring on bets and shouting for a fighter. It seemed like Cole was the only one who noticed the boy struggling against the bonds that bound his hands behind his back in a desperate attempt, searching the crowd.

And then his odd, yellow eyes met his. And now Cole couldn't turn away.

He tore through the crowd without thinking. He broke out into the circle. "Stop!"

The man froze, turning slowly to meet Cole, examining him. He snorted. "You placing bets, kid?"

"I'm ending your stupid show."

The man laughed, stalking toward him. "You new here?"

Cole held his ground. "Does that matter?"

Apparently, it did. Cole got a fist, punching him square in the face. He stumbled back, pain exploding through his sinuses and his concussed brain spiraling. The crowd shoved him forward, and he spun to catch his balance on his feet.

The man spat with a smile. "You can end my show when you're part of it."

Cole ignored the stinging in his face, tightening his fists.

"I'm not joining your pathetic fight."

The boy's eyes widened.

The man shrugged. "Oh, kid, you already have."

He what?

Suddenly, Cole was jerked back, the chain of the Medallion choking him. He grabbed at his throat, not reacting fast enough and thrown to the floor. He scrambled back to face a massive contestant, his eyes set on the golden Medallion now hanging loose from his shirt.

Cole cursed.

The crowd cheered. Cole went for his sword but found his side empty. *Shoot.*

He jumped to his feet, missing a near punch. He turned, pushing the man off balance and tumbling forward. He spun quickly, coming back at Cole. Cole dodged a blow to his side, landing a fist on the guy's face. He stumbled back with a groan. Cole turned to run. He wanted no part of this.

His foot was caught, something dragging him to the ground. The opponent pinned him to the ground, Cole struggling furiously. The opponent raised a hand to claim his prize, and Cole took it as his opportunity to throw his weight and turn, knocking the man off him. Before he could get to his feet, the giant hands clamped over the Medallion, and with a *snap!* Cole was sent stumbling backwards onto the dirt.

"What is going on here?"

The crowd went still and began to part, an older man sifting his way through. His sun-tanned face was hard with fury, his neatly trimmed, graying, brown hair neatly set; and with every angry step came a clank of metal when the rapier at his side hit the metal of his leg.

Cole's heart stopped. *Doran.*

He might as well have died right then and there when a younger man dressed in formal, leather apparel and a silver circlet adorning his black-and-white hair followed him.

"Victor." Doran glared at the man, whose confident smile had melted.

Cole picked himself up.

"The kid started it," "Victor" pleaded, pointing to Cole.

Cole's eyes went wide. It was *his* fault? Didn't they see the tied-up and muzzled—

He looked around the ring. The boy was gone. Cole's

stomach dropped, reaching his empty chest.

The opponent was gone…and so was the Medallion.

Doran turned to glare at Cole when his brow raised. "The Illuminate?" he said, confused, turning to Cecileo. The Pater stood with his expression unreadable, his lips pressed to a firm line.

Almost on cue, a member of the crowd dropped Cole's bag back out into the ring before rushing out to hide in the ground. Cole scanned the pile. His sword was still there, but no Medallion. He felt too ashamed to bend down and take them back.

"I expected more from a Council Member," Doran said, his face firming.

Cecileo turned to the crowd. "Go! Before I have your entrance passage revoked!"

This got their attention, rushing away quickly and melting into the usual Market traffic. Cole searched for Victor, hoping that at least he would stick around for a beating, but he was gone before Cole could catch a trace of him.

He'd failed to save the boy and lost the Medallion.

The Medallion.

"What is he doing here?" Doran swiveled on Cecileo.

"Echo brought him here," Cecileo said. "That's the pupil I was talking about."

Doran sighed heavily. "Just because your *wife* does something doesn't automatically make it a good decision," he said bitterly, surprising Cole. Doran had been understanding and authoritative when they first met, but when he spoke of Echo…he almost seemed angry.

Cecileo just glared back.

Doran turned back to Cole. "Pick up your things," he commanded, and Cole scrambled to obey. "I'm surprised I'd meet you participating in unauthorized street fights. You seemed nobler upon our last meeting."

"Doran, I don't think that is his—"

Doran held up a finger. "Cecileo Reuder, you made a name for yourself as an illegal street fighter as a youth yourself. I see why you'd sympathize."

Cecileo huffed. "If he was a real street fighter, he wouldn't have gotten beaten so easily."

Doran ignored him.

Cole clenched the strap of his bag. "Sir, I—I am—"

Doran pinched the bridge of his nose, waving Cole's words off. "I accept your apology, but I'm *disappointed*. You're a ways off from my ring, Johnson."

"I got lost, sir."

"But you found the fight quite easily."

Cole swallowed hard.

"I'll *consider* your training," Doran said with a harsh glare to both Cole and Cecileo. "Believe me when I say, Illuminate, this is not the kind of behavior that gets anything done. If anything, it only gets people killed due to selfish, reckless behavior."

With that, he trekked off into the crowd.

Cole's face burned. *Selfish. Reckless. Killed.*

Tabitha's voice echoed in the mix. *The boy who can't even stop his own brother from going crazy!*

Cecileo gave an angry sigh, watching his master disappear into the crowd. His attire demanded far more respect than last night: a blue-armored jerkin and a long jacket, his tight pants splitting at his calves and meeting the thin, leather boots bound around his ankle. His fake eye glowed dully as he watched Cole, a frown twisting his features. "He's not usually that harsh to most people."

I guess I'm just lucky. "I should be above getting in street fights," Cole said.

Cecileo snorted. "Illuminate or not, you're still a kid."

Eighteen technically, but sure. A child worked too.

"He probably doesn't need too much time to consider. He'll probably admire your determination if you go to his ring right away," Ceclieo said, shooing him off. "Go!"

Cole suppressed his surprise. Disobeying Doran indirectly? He nodded and began his way after Doran when Cecileo called after him.

"Oh, yeah. Echo wants you to stop by at dusk at the end of your week to discuss your situation."

"Okay!" At least he had something to look forward to.

"Don't be late," Cecileo said. "Doran might not respect my wife, but you will."

"Don't worry, I will!"

He pushed through the crowd. Why *didn't* Doran respect

Echo? From the looks of it, she had nearly as much power as Cecileo, and even if people disliked her, she should have some sort of formal respect.

There was too much unknown. But he knew for certain that the Medallion was no longer hanging from his neck.

A part of him said that it was planned. Something was off. Something about the bound boy with markings. The Victor man. The Medallion.

Lincoln was onto something about discussing a mission. They needed a goal. And, for once, they needed to succeed.

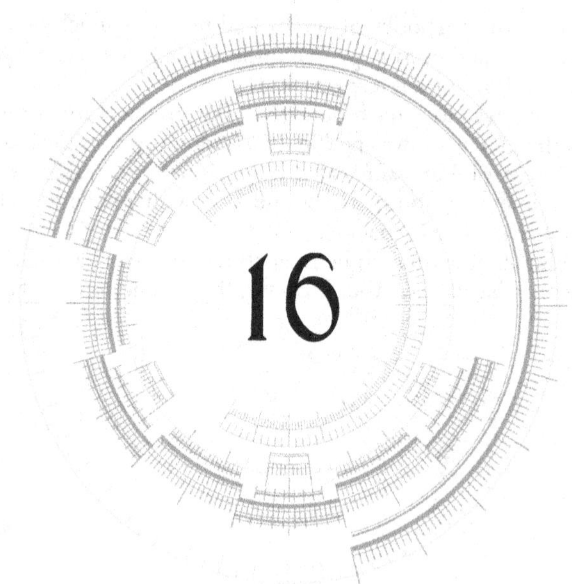

16

Kennedy, 25 Days Until

LINCOLN COULDN'T EVEN look into Dr. Mathews's eyes. He knew that she stood by the door of the cabin he was being held in, but he couldn't look at her. He couldn't face her.

"The Williams boy's ribs are doing much better, still painful for him to breathe," she finally said.

Lincoln knew that he deserved to know the pain he'd put Lawrence through.

Do not repent. You did what you had to do.

Dr. Mathews just stood there. He knew that she was waiting. She was waiting for anything. But the Voice sealed his mouth shut.

She finally let out a sigh. "I can't make you talk. I'm disappointed. I really thought better of you."

Her voice was quiet and fragile. It struck Lincoln in the chest.

She went to the door, pausing for a moment.

Lincoln raised his eyes and met the glassy eyes of a mother who now had two children out in a cruel world before she shut the door.

He knew that he deserved the cabin arrest. Every bone in his body wanted to help with the search for Jenna and apologize to Dr. Mathews for failing her children twice. He couldn't even see Lawrence to ask for updates.

But his mind…or, rather, the Voice inside it was pleased with the solitude.

His arrest ended in a few days. And he'd snuck Avalon's letter with him. So it wasn't entirely unproductive.

How much of a mess had he landed them? Why was he doing this? It was right. He knew that it wasn't. The way he was acting would horrify her, and it terrified him too. He didn't want to hurt his friends.

Why do you insist on calling them your friends? Pathetic.

"Because they *are*," Lincoln muttered, alone in the dark under the windowsill, clutching the letters in his hand. He wasn't willing to give them up.

No need to give up these "friends" of yours if you just tell me your name, boy.

A cold shiver swept down his spine.

I have given you power. I've made you strong.

The Voice had given him power. They'd helped him this far and even promised to help Nikki. The least he could do was—

His Comm went off, vibrating on the cabin floor.

He snatched it from beside him, relief freeing his lungs as he saw the screen illuminating: *Coleslaw calling Chat with Black Ey…*

Lincoln quickly joined. "H—hello?"

"He's alive!" came Lawrence's triumphant mock.

Lincoln couldn't help but smile slightly to hear that at least Lawrence was all right. He only saw him occasionally from outside his window.

"We heard you went into the woods and into an Oquelite-occupied palace," Tabitha said with a laugh. "You that lonely, Linc?"

They weren't…mad? Didn't they know that he'd gotten Jenna captured?

He forced a laugh.

"Well, now that Nikki's back…apparently, maybe you won't be." Felicity's voice was gentle, and Lincoln forgot how much he missed her.

They were all quiet for a moment. The fact seemed to have shaken them too.

Lincoln cleared his throat. He didn't want to dwell on her. "I'm going to make sure nothing like this happens again."

"You can't stop death, Lincoln," Cole said solemnly. "There's always the risk."

I can try.

"Nikki said something about a soul while she was unconscious." He took up the ancient papers.

"A Shadow Soul?" Ray said, surprised.

Lincoln frowned. "How did you know?"

"Nothing."

"Well, yeah. Something called the 'Shadow Soul.' It's mentioned in letters that were in the tower…written by the Ewyon Stone."

"A rock wrote letters?"

"No, the lady *in* the rock, Tabitha. Duh." Ray scoffed.

Lincoln sighed, pretending to be annoyed with his friends' banter that he'd grown to miss. "It's connected to the Council, and from what I've gathered from Reyna Aguirre…it's caused by the Council too."

"Hold up, 'Reyna' as in the Curatrix Member and Nikki's mom?" Felicity said.

"We don't have much time to—"

"He broke into the Curatrix machine," Lawrence said.

"Wow. Lincoln's been really naughty lately." Ray laughed.

Lincoln only managed a weak laugh. He was basically grounded and had endangered literal children. At what cost was it worth it?

Do not second guess yourself, boy.

"So, what do these letters say?" Cole said, drawing them back on track.

Lincoln set the Comm down, sifting through the papers in his hands. He took a deep breath. "I've had a lot of time to read them"—or have his buds read them to him—"but I'm not particularly sure what it all means."

Thanks to the Voice, he couldn't feel the shock of

hearing the words. Apparently, dumbing down his emotions would "help" him.

"Don't leave us hanging, what *does* it say?" Tabitha urged.

Lincoln took a deep breath, tentatively slipping the bud into his head and picking up the paper.

"The beginning was mostly Avalon, the Stone, pleading with her sister. I'm guessing they were in some sort of fight."

"Siblings." Ray scoffed.

Lincoln cringed, deciding against mentioning that he'd *lost* one of Ray's siblings. He might as well be signing a death sentence. "Yeah, well, the disagreement seemed to boil down to this Shadow Soul thing."

"Which is?"

Lincoln cleared his throat, turning to the second page as the earbud recited it to him. "*The Shadow Soul, as you know, was created by the First Council as a punishment for breaking the natural order of mortality and a way of reconstructing the balance.*"

"Oquelite!" Tabitha shouted as if it were some sort of trivia. "They're the only immortal, impure *race* we know of."

"I—It gets worse," Lincoln flinched. "*By the Council's proclamation, an Oquelite hybrid will be the one to possess the Shadow Soul and, with unspeakable power, be the one to bring on the destruction of the world.* Not just *the Oquelite.*

"*I understand the concern and urgency, sister, but what you don't understand is the fact the Oquelite people are not responsible for this. The Council is. The Council created the destruction we all know is coming.*"

No one responded. Lincoln held his breath in the silence.

"I knew I wasn't insane!" Tabitha gasped finally. "The tapestry from Court Illegia. It mentioned a Shadow Soul."

"But—but I'm an Oquelite hybrid," Ray whispered. "If that's true—"

"Don't think like that," Cole said quickly. "There have been more Oquelite hybrids. And I'm half-Oquelite."

"Cole is right," Lincoln said. "I think the reason Avalon wrote these letters is because her daughter, Kathryn, was an Oquelite hybrid…and obviously nothing happened there."

"Is that why the Oquelite were so against us?" Ray said gently.

Multiple voices spoke at once, but Lincoln drained them out, the swelling in his chest going numb. Was that the reason the Mathews family had been torn apart? Five half-Oquelite children under one roof. The Oquelite couldn't have been happy about that.

That was the curse that Dr. Mathews mentioned so long ago.

"It's so vague." Lawrence finally broke through. "How is it relevant to our situation with the Oquelite now?"

"Nikki mentioned the Soul," Lincoln reminded. "It was the first thing she said, so it has to be connected to her almost dying."

"So the Shadow Soul is here. Now," Felicity breathed, her fear evident.

"But the motives are so unclear," Cole said. "Why would the Shadow Soul destroy the world? And where are they?"

"And if we…or the past Council created it…why are we concerned?" Lawrence scoffed.

"No offense, Lawrence, but I actually do like living," Tabitha said.

Lincoln sighed, running his fingers through his hair, holding his head.

"If one thing is clear, this Shadow Soul is targeting the Council, also known as *us*," Cole said. "They've attacked Nikki."

"The Shadow Soul or whatever is apparently supposed to be some sort of punishment…destroying-the-world thing? Doesn't sound so good."

"And they're connected to Red Eye Guys," Ray butted in.

"But it doesn't make sense," Lincoln said, shaking his head. "No one is just that shallow to sit there and wake up one day and decide they want to destroy the world. Humans are just too complicated for that."

"Our biggest weakness is really our lack of information," Felicity said.

"Is it a bad time to mention there is something legit called the 'Soul Night' here?" Ray said.

"The *what*?"

"It has to be coming up soon. If it's related, this could be a great breakthrough," Ray said, growing excited. "If I can find out the date—"

"That would be amazing," Cole said, his voice firm. "If this Shadow Soul and Soul Night are connected, then we actually have a date to go off of."

Lincoln straightened. "But our priority should be finding information on what this Shadow Soul wants and who they are. If we can shut them down...we might be able to shut down the whole Oquelite mess once and for all."

PART TWO

THE MISSION

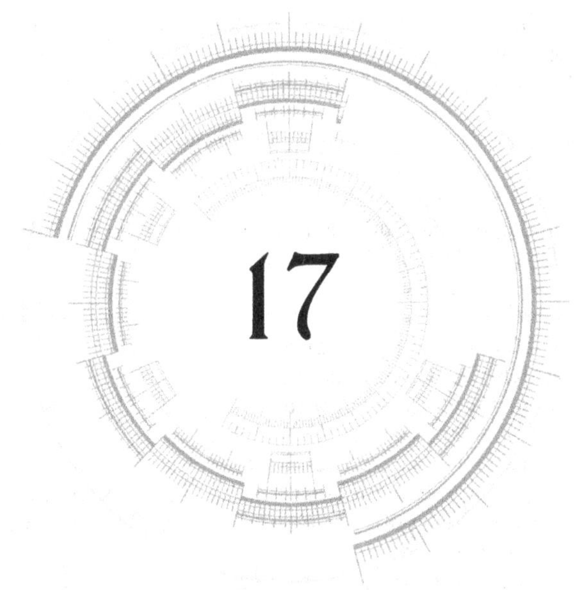

17

North Cordell, 19 Days Until

MATTEO MADE A fool of himself. He always managed to do that, and today of all days felt like the worst time to keep up that trend.

And it was even worse knowing that Lawrence watched every pathetic fumble.

Matteo *thought* it'd be better if Lawrence was there. He was the only person in the camp he felt safe with, yet now he was being humiliated out of his mind as he toppled back onto the dirt yet again.

Miriam cringed, looking away as she dusted off her hands.

Matteo's face burned. She wouldn't say it, but he knew that the Defender didn't exactly have high hopes for him.

He tried to push down the panic. He couldn't risk the noise getting louder. He had to keep control. He pushed himself back up, only glancing for a moment at Lawrence standing toward the edge of the marked-off training ground.

He looked away before he could catch a glimpse of disappointment.

"It's simple, caterpillar," Miriam said. The nickname was odd, but she insisted that it was fitting due to his first appearance of being wrapped in a quilt. He didn't argue. "Don't be too far forward on your stance, or I'll kick you in your face. Simple."

Simple, but not super helpful. Besides, his forehead still hurt from the last backhanded slap. Lawrence had reacted to it too, which was weird.

There was some sort of connection. Lawrence was feeling Matteo's pain, and Matteo was more than certain that he had felt Lawrence's. The intense pain in his ribs back in the cabin? It couldn't have been a coincidence that Lawrence had just broken his ribs in the woods.

He tried to shove the spinning thoughts away. He tried to slide his feet the right length apart. Trying to keep his breathing under control. And trying to break the intense gaze of Miriam's one eye.

He could hear Jenna's distant screams in the back of his head. Her bright amber eyes seared with fear as they were pressed against the palace wall. But even in their terror, she had determination.

He didn't know how she had managed it. How she had managed to push through. He could only hope that she was still holding onto that determination wherever she was.

¡Enfoque, idiota!

Miriam missed his face by a centimeter. Matteo didn't even see it coming, sprawling back with a spin.

Miriam dropped her fists with a sigh. "I say we end it here," she said. "I'll need to speak to the Sergeant about the...slow progress."

Matteo held back from cringing at the sting of the words, pushing himself back up to his feet and moving back to the bench quickly for his headphones before Lawrence could reach him. He didn't want to hear shame from him, either. He just needed to get rid of Jenna's cries in his head.

He grabbed his headphone, wiping the sweat from his forehead with his sleeve.

"Maybe he just needs more time."

"We don't have a lot of time," Miriam said with a sigh.

"His essence isn't breaking any time soon, and he's not even efficient in combat."

Matteo wanted to disappear as he sank down onto the bench, beginning to slip his headphones over his head when he heard a sharp radio static. He flinched.

"How do you know his essence isn't breaking? I sure didn't know when I'd be able to hold freaking fire." Lawrence's breath was pained from the snap.

He looked around for the sound, seeing Miriam's jacket, belt and radio clipped to it. The screen blinked. Someone was trying to get through.

"Miriam?" He tried to raise his voice.

"Not now, Lopez."

Matteo swallowed hard, looking to the radio. His heart skipped a beat: *SEARCH TEAM #003.*

Jenna's search team.

"Essence is broken under extreme circumstances, and unlike the other Impure, Wingor has a very physical quality: wings. It takes so much more strength to control those alone…and who knows what extra power a Wingor *Member* will be holding?" Miriam's glare was almost as intimidating as Lawrence's. Definitely wasn't a good time to butt in, even as much as he wanted to.

He picked up the radio, his hands shaking. Someone's glitchy voice was trying to get through. He had to *try* to get through Miriam. *For Jenna.*

"Officer—"

"Perhaps Tabitha was onto something about the *Cors Vis*, then," Lawrence said, stepping back. "Maybe a Wingor does need a supernatural element to fully break through their essence."

Miriam snorted. "Yeah, but he'll need a lot more than supernatural help. He's virtually useless."

Matteo's heart stopped, his face heating. He'd burdened Miriam enough. He quickly grabbed the radio. He could do it himself. He could prove to her that he wasn't useless. He would get someone to listen.

He slipped out without the two of them noticing. He doubted that they would. He was just a liability to them.

The radio continued to glitch out as Matteo ran down the dirt path. "REPEAT—LOCATION FOU—!"

Jenna's scream echoed through Matteo's mind, his entire body going to a halt. His heart thundered in his ears. He had to have heard that wrong.

The radio began to glitch. "BACK—FOUND—REPEAT—"

Had they found Jenna?

Matteo had vowed the moment he left Jenna behind in that palace that he'd get her back. He wouldn't turn back. He wouldn't run away. He wouldn't mess up again.

Don't let them think you're crazy.

You can't mess anything…anyone else up.

He tried to push down the thoughts before they could rise up. He didn't have time for a full on panic. He needed to get to Jenna. He wouldn't let her get hurt again.

He slipped his headphones over his ears to block out the noise and the snickers from the fire guards. They wouldn't believe him. No one would. He was just the scrawny, useless Member from Court Illegia. He doubted that they even knew that he understood what they said about him. Little did they know that Matteo heard everything, whether or not he wanted to.

He broke out into a run across the field.

"BACKUP!"

Was he really good enough to be backup? He could only pray that the Sergeant…someone else heard it. Was he really running into this?

Turn back.

No es su culpa que será discapacitado.

Think of Jenna.

He tried to breathe. The wind began to whip around harder as he tried to grasp onto the image of the young girl's bright, amber eyes and her frizzy, black curls that reminded him of his little sister Jadie coming in from a ball game in the courtyard, her hair in a disarray and asking Matteo to take out the sewing kit to patch up the hole in her pants.

Matteo estuvo allí por horas.

The woods were growing closer. He tried to keep his eyes trained away from the swirling storm clouds. He could feel the radio vibrating in his hand.

Matteo estuvo allí por horas.

He was already tired from the failed training session. His

lungs were burning, but it was better to focus on that pain than the echoes of the past.

Matteo estuvo allí por horas.

Get to the woods.

Él no puede oírte.

Matteo slipped on the damp earth, slamming hard into the grass, his headphones slipping off an ear. The radio crackled more clearly now: "IMMEDIATE BACKUP REQUIRED."

Era demasiado tarde.

He quickly adjusted the headphone before the noises could drown him. He pushed himself back up to his feet and he ran, forcing himself not to think of the hundreds of things that could go wrong.

He slowed as the grasses began to thin to the tilled, damp earth and the twisting roots began to curl into the trees guarding the supernatural, growing woods.

Matteo swallowed hard. Was he really going to do this? He should run back. Miriam was right. He *was* useless. Why did he think that he could do this?

He'd failed in the past. There was a reason he stayed away from situations like this.

Think about Jenna. Jenna is alive. *You can still save* her.

With that, Matteo took a deep breath and ran into the woods, this time all alone. He knew that if he stopped, he would probably faint, so he kept running. If he was going to find the search team, he needed to remove his headphones.

The thought terrified him. If he took them off, he would start panicking…and then the noises would grow louder.

No tienes otra opción.

He slipped off the headphones, and the noise exploded. Matteo's body halted. He tried to stumble onward. He couldn't stop. The rustling of the branches, the crunch of his feet. It was overwhelming. He needed to calm down. He needed to calm down—

A screech broke out through the woods. For a solid second, the woods were quiet.

Matteo's blood went cold. Human screams followed.

He was in the right place. He picked up his headphones and ran toward the commotion. Right into the face of everything he was against. He couldn't just leave them.

He was met with a wall of the overgrown trees, inter-twined with each other. Matteo began to panic. *Think. Think. Think.*

His eyes landed on the winding roots of the trees. He was small enough. He'd pushed himself through smaller cracks. He dove through the roots, pushing himself through, trying not to breathe in the dirt crumbling from above. He could see the light at the end.

The root tunnel was safe and enclosed. If he just stayed here—

The ground above him shook.

Never mind. He raced out the end, tumbling out into the open air before the dirt could lay claim to him. He lay on the dirt floor, gasping for air, not given a moment to recover before he was picked up and shoved out of the way, his earphones sliding to his shoulders. A Defender sheltered Matteo's body as the horribly eerie cry of the lizard creatures rang out.

"First it's wolves, and then it's these…and then a kid?" The Officer looked beat up, his face bruised and cut and streaked with dirt, his uniform heavy with gear as he looked down at Matteo, bewildered.

Matteo struggled to breathe and organize the words properly in his brain: "I—I'm backup."

"There is no—"

"Hicks, watch it!"

The Officer managed to drag Matteo out of the way before a creature lunged, his eyes focused on Matteo. Mateo couldn't move, frozen, staring into the beady eyes of inhuman monsters, its eyes slightly glowing in the dimly lit woods.

A gunshot only slightly deferred the creature.

"It's the Wingor Council Member!" another of the Officers shouted. They had all begun to huddle together, still holding firm a circle.

Matteo's vision began to adjust. He could hear the creatures skimpering above. Officer Hicks held tightly to his arm, holding his pistol in the other.

"You're a Council Member?"

Miriam's words echoed back in his mind. But Matteo mustered a nod. Anything was worth seeing the glimmer of hope in the Officer's eye.

"Is Jenna—?"

He couldn't finish his sentence as the hope quickly fell from the Officer's face. "We have—"

A shriek echoed louder, ringing through Matteo's ears as he stumbled back. A new pack launched themselves down the trees, breaking into the circle.

Matteo couldn't move. His vision blurred, only seeing the commotion scrambling around him. Fight. Do something. Slip into a stance. Run. Anything.

Instead, he heard someone screaming at him, and he was shoved to the ground. The world flew back into view, and Matteo almost vomited at the sight of Officer Hicks only a few feet away from him on the ground, his hand pressed against a fresh, deep scratch on his chest. Blood didn't stop coming.

Blood.

Matteo scrambled for him.

"Hicks!" one of the other Officers shouted.

Matteo scrambled to him, trying not to think about the fact that the claw mark should've been deep in himself. "Do—do you need—?"

"L—listen to me, Member," the Officer said, grabbing Matteo's coat collar harshly. The smell of blood was on his breath. "We—we have a chance—a chance to get her back." He gasped for air, tightening on his wound.

"Don't breathe," Matteo said, trying to keep his eyes from burning with tears. "I—it's okay. The Sergeant will be here."

Would she? Would anyone be here? No one was ever there. He was always left alone to watch.

"They—they've been using the abandoned depot building—they've been using it to—to pick up supplies." His eyes began to droop.

Not again.

Matteo didn't want to look.

Hicks took in a deep, painful breath. "They're planning on bringing the girl. Two days' time."

He tried to breathe, but nothing was coming. He was choking and Matteo couldn't help him. Matteo couldn't watch. He looked away.

He expected himself to freeze like he always did. Feel his body go numb and cold as the world passed around him. But instead…it burned.

He would not let this happen again. He wouldn't be useless. He grabbed Hicks's dropped bag, pulling out a tele. A tele? What could he do with a tele? And a tent light?

He got to his feet, feeling the tears stream down his face as he stared at the creatures mercilessly attacking the Defenders only a few feet away.

The wind began to howl as Matteo clenched his fists.

Never again.

The creatures began to stiffen at the cold air, leaping in aggression. Their huge, beady eyes looked around frantically.

Their eyes. Their biggest, most horrific feature.

Mateteo's heart leapt. He flipped on the tent lamp, shining the bright light meant to light a room toward the creatures. One let out a horrific shriek as he focused on its eyes.

Never again.

The wind began to howl faster as Matteo pressed forward. The Defenders began to fall back.

"Light!"

"Get light!"

"They're sensitive to light!"

One after another, they began pulling out light sources. More bright tent lanterns and flashlight beams. The wind grew faster and faster. The trees began to howl. Everything spun around him.

The creatures began to fall back, stumbling in the strength of the wind.

Matteo didn't feel a thing. He could only feel the burning anger in him. The regret that he knew too well. He'd been too late to save someone from death.

His hands were shaking, his vision blurring. It was a curse. *Never again.*

And the world slipped away as he fell toward the ground.

"Matteo! Are you okay?"

Lawrence tried not to panic as Matteo drowsily sat up in his seat as he pushed through the MedTent. He'd seen the search team come in, but it wasn't until the Sergeant of all people told him that she'd found Matteo with the group. Apparently he'd passed out and woken up in a panic to tell the Sergeant of something he'd learned about Jenna.

Miriam and the assigned nurse looked back at him.

"He's fine," Miriam said, her voice quieter than usual. "A little banged up, that's all."

"A little banged up?"

"We have bigger issues at hand," Miriam said. "You saw the wind."

"That was almost a full on *storm* out there."

"There's always storms…That's a separate weird issue. The wind. That was insane." Miriam's eyes lifted slowly. "You can't deny the coincidence."

Lawrence's heart skipped a beat, realizing what Miriam was implying as he looked back to Matteo. "There's no way—"

The small crowd dispersed, echoing conversation and murmurs as they went.

Miriam stormed over to Lawrence and Matteo with a scowl. "I hate to admit it…but they are right."

Lawrence tried to choke out something. Something to hurt Miriam with. Something to prove her wrong. But he knew deep down that she was right. And it was horrifying. It had been connected. It had been *power*.

"You aren't as weak as I thought, Caterpillar," Miriam said with a dry laugh.

"He shouldn't have had to run off to the woods in the first place! If you Defenders just listened to your darn radio!"

It could've been so much worse. It could've been Jenna all over again.

"The search team's radio was damaged. My radio was the only one close enough to pick up the signal. Don't blame the others. It was my fault, and I know that." Miriam was out of breath as she looked away.

Lawrence stopped. "If you think this is power, then how do we help him with it? We don't have a *Cors Vis*."

Miriam ran her fingers through her hair, her face hardening in thought. "The '*Cors Vis*' is a myth. It's not real. And besides, Goldfish burned it up in Court Illegia."

"Maybe the *Cors Vis* isn't gone."

Lawrence's heart jumped at Matteo's strained, quiet voice. He turned around. Matteo had one headphone slipped slightly from his ear. His eyes were swollen red, and the blood still flowed from his nose.

"What do you mean?" Miriam said, gentler now.

Matteo shook his head, using his green shirt to rub away the blood. "I—if the Wingor needs the *Cors Vis* to use abilities, then the *Cors Vis* has to be here." Matteo's eyes fell to his bloody hands, almost as if he didn't believe the words he was saying.

"Yes. That would seem the simple answer, caterpillar, if it wasn't gone."

"But if a Wingor can use abilities, then it's not gone."

Lawrence and Miriam exchanged glances.

Lawrence almost smirked. "He has a point."

Miriam opened her mouth, choking on her words, her face contorting. She shut her mouth and took a deep breath. She glanced to Matteo and then back to Lawrence. "I'll talk to the Sergeant about this," Miriam said, shoving her tablet at him. "You take him out of this commotion."

"Easy enough," Lawrence grumbled, stuffing her tablet into his coat pocket.

Miriam darted a look in Matteo's way and hurried away.

Lawrence kicked the dirt, taking everything in him not to groan. Why hadn't he said something? Because Miriam would probably ignore his suggestions? Because he wasn't even part of this Council by his own will, but by some stupid thing called "fate" and "the safety of his siblings?"

Who was he to think that his opinion really mattered to them?

Lawrence glanced up to the storm brewing above them and let out a breath.

"Let's get inside," he said, turning to Matteo. He offered him a hand, but Matteo stared as if human touch would kill him. He got to his feet, holding himself as Lawrence led them back to the mess hall before the storm let loose.

"You guys are back!"

Noah jumped up from a table, nearly spilling his mug as his blanket fell from his shoulders. Adam Mathews took his older brother's distraction as a time to take a sip of his beverage. "I was looking for you all morning."

Lawrence cringed at the joy and bounce in Noah's hopeful eyes. "There—there are no updates of Jenna."

Noah's face fell. "Oh," he said, stumbling back into his seat.

"I'm sorry," Lawrence said, not sure what else to say. He'd begged to be let on the rescue team, but he was rejected for joining Lincoln on the tirade that got Jenna captured in the first place.

Noah forced a smile and turned back to Adam, pushing his mug toward him and slumping forward on the table, burying his face.

Lawrence quietly made his way to the kitchen. At least he'd be alone there.

He slipped through the flap and sank down onto a stool by the makeshift oven with a sigh, flicking on the kettle, trying to remember how to breathe with the burning in his ribs. The ban of coffee hadn't been in his favor recently, either. Tea wasn't his favorite, but it was something.

He couldn't imagine today going any worse. They were nowhere closer to the Shadow Soul and seemed to have only set Matteo back. *Great job.*

He reached for Miriam's tablet lodged in his pocket when his hand brushed something warm. He frowned, pulling out the forgotten sweet bread carefully folded in the napkin.

Matteo had given them to Charles this morning, as the two spent the morning in the kitchen. Something about the sweet bread dispelling fear. Lawrence unraveled it from the napkin, deciding that there was no harm in trying it as he tapped the screen of Miriam's tablet to life.

His brow furrowed as the screen lit up. *Training checkpoints*, the header stated, bold and clear.

This is what Miriam was using to train Matteo? Was he supposed to be looking at this?

Wingor are masters of silence and aerial grace. As a result, attacks should appear to come from nowhere if built upon these natural components.

Seeing as Wingor were the race of the sky, it made sense why this would apply. Matteo, on the other hand, was quiet for other reasons. Could that be harbored with good intention?

—Wingor have controlled composure and ordered thought. This

helps by on-will activation of wing essence.

"Controlled composure?" Lawrence almost cringed. Part of it wasn't exactly Matteo's fault.

—Wingor emotions are strong, yet distinct. Being able to sort through them and identify them is vital for composure against a usually more physically advanced opponent."

Lawrence wanted to accuse Miriam of being a hypocrite. But it took a moment to realize that it never specified whether the emotions had to be positive or negative. A bit frightening.

Weren't the Sublinight experts on the mushy emotion stuff?

A small rustle caught his attention. He looked up, surprised to see Matteo standing in the doorway of the kitchen, his bloody nose now dried and his quilt right around his shoulders, his eyes on the sweet bread in Lawrence's hand.

"Oh, uh, Charles gave me some this morning." He cleared his throat. "It's good."

The tea kettle went off with a whistle.

Lawrence pulled a plastic cup from the stash. "Tea?" he asked.

Matteo hesitated a moment before shifting over to the seat opposite the table, his eyes down. Lawrence poured him a cup and slid it over to him. Matteo stared at it, slowly closing his hands around the warm cup.

"I think I have a lead on your training," he said.

Matteo didn't say anything, though his gaze was attentive as he tentatively took a sip.

"I'm not qualified in anything Wingor…but I don't think that's the main root of it. No one else here needs training to break our essence. It's because of that *Cors Vis.*" Lawrence picked up the page, glancing over to see if Matteo would provide a thought, but all he did was watch.

Lawrence took that as to continue. "I said I was going to help you, so I am. But I think you're going to be the one to control yourself into a powerful state. I just…might have an idea how to get there…to help you get Jenna back."

A terrible idea, including begging Lincoln for some adjustments to gloves…and figuring out how to make some accommodations for Matteo's hypersensitive hearing. But if they truly were to try and get Jenna back in two days, he wanted Matteo to be with them.

"You in?"

Matteo was still for a long moment, looking from his tea to Lawrence. "Why are you so nice to me?"

Lawrence frowned in surprise. "That's the right thing to do," he said generically. Not at all because he saw his younger, broken self staring right back at him. Not because he felt so relieved when he saw the soft surprise on Matteo's face.

Matteo's face quickly fell. "I'm sorry."

"For what?"

"I ran off. I was impulsive. I listened to the voices in my head…I'm sorry." His voice slowly became quieter.

Lawrence wanted to be angry with him. The whole situation was annoying and had made him worry out of his mind, but he couldn't help but feel pity.

"You got us information on Jenna. You were trying to do the right thing too."

"I wish more people did the right thing," Matteo said quietly. "In general."

"Only in an idealistic world," Lawrence said, scrambling to correct the cold statement. "But hey, that's what we're here for."

"The Council?" The group of children chosen by fate for the most dangerous roles of all time?

"Yeah. That's why we're here. To do the right thing." He wanted so badly to believe the words he spoke.

Matteo considered it, nodding slowly. "That's why you're a good Member."

Lawrence laughed softly. "You'd think so."

Doing the right thing? The lines had been so blurred, he was never so sure. Charles and Isabel were alive, and that's what mattered.

"I accept," Matteo said finally with a confident sip of the cup. The hood of the quilt fell to his shoulders, revealing his messy, disheveled hair that went with the shadows under his eyes.

"We start as soon as I can use some gear."

Perhaps he needed to start believing in this Council… Otherwise, he'd be sending Matteo off into something far worse.

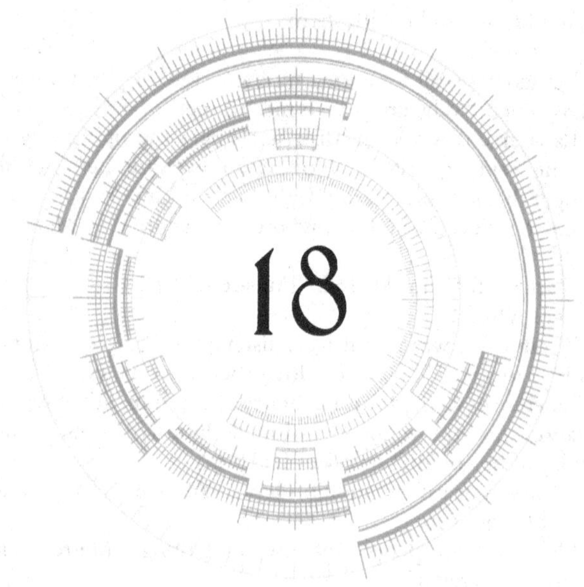

18

Liberty, 18 Days Until

"DRAW!"

Cole stumbled back, breathless, still staring at the blade that had only a moment ago been pressed against his neck. The sun was beating down on him, but he refused to let himself feel the sweat and bruises.

"Win for Ren." Doran sighed from the sidelines, darting a glare at Cole. "One again, too slow, too sloppy, and wrong starting form, Illuminate."

Ren, the girl standing opposite him, sheathed her blade, sending Cole a sympathetic smile before rushing off to join the other students by the hose. Cole knew what was coming. He switched the Illuminate, wiping his sweaty palms as Doran stalked toward him.

"What was with the hesitation? Even with your starting errors, you could've overcome her when she took that sloppy turn," Doran said, crossing his arms, his brows furrowing. Even though the swordmaster was Cole's height,

Cole always felt small compared to him.

His eyes fell. "I'm sorry. I'll work on it."

He'd noticed Ren's slipup, but he wasn't going to mention it because then Doran would drill him on why he hadn't acted on it. And why hadn't he?

"That isn't good enough," Doran said with a snap.

You're not ranting to Ren about her screwup, are you? Cole held his tongue. He knew that it was different. He was supposed to be the almighty Illuminate Holder of the Council. And here was, messing up on standing right.

"I want you to practice on swings late tonight to teach your stubborn mind to learn."

Cole nodded. "Yes, sir."

That made three days this week.

He saw the group of students watching, their eyes wide. Doran turned on them, his harsh expression immediately melting. "The day's dismissed. I'll see you tomorrow, I hope."

Doran went to collect his bag, and the students rushed past Cole to the gate leading out. They kept their distance as usual, their eyes having no sort of envy or awe. More pity than anything.

Cole clenched his jaw. Great. He was pitied by the people he was training to protect.

"Remember your stance, Johnson!" Doran shouted as he swept out of the ring.

Cole nodded, though no one would even see. No, now he was utterly alone. No one to watch him epically fail and humiliate himself as per usual. He unbuttoned the jerkin, tossing it to the dirt floor below, tugging at the sweaty collar of his shirt. He unsheathed his Blade, feeling the balance in his hands.

He closed his eyes, taking a deep breath.

Cole swung the sword through the air, moving step after step, the blade spinning in a perfect hit against the pole.

He opened his eyes, pulling the Blade free. This was pointless. It wasn't repetition he needed. He stepped back and restarted regardless.

The whole week went nowhere. Early mornings to late nights, Cole hardly got a moment to remind Doran that he needed to eat. He'd practically given up on the notion of a full night's sleep. It was the only time he had to himself and the only time he could sneak the keyboard out from under the dresser and play its keys without anyone listening.

Sleep didn't exactly come easy, anyway, when his entire body felt so sore that he might as well give up.

He'd attempted to write the song Tabitha had requested, but he only wrote a line about sheep and nothing else.

His momentum increased the faster he moved. *Thwack. Thwack. Thwack.*

Most people would say that he'd learned a lot that week, but Cole knew better. He didn't need to learn a lot, he needed to perfect it. If he didn't in time, it could be disastrous.

He turned, slashing the blade through the air. It hit the post, shaking it. He pulled it and was tugged back. Cole frowned, turning his head to see that the Blade had sunk unusually deep into the wood.

He sighed, putting a foot against the pole and tugging it free. It didn't matter how *hard* he hit, it mattered *that* he hit. That was the most difficult part.

He started again, moving foot to foot, balancing the Blade with his weight. One step at a time…

He'd nearly hit Tabitha with it. He'd hit the *Mors Vis* with it. He'd *burned an entire building.*

"Get over it!" he cried out, slamming the sword to the pole. He didn't care if it was graceful. He just wanted to cut into the wood over and over and over. He didn't have a choice. He had to do this.

The hilt slipped from his hands as he swung it through the air, flattening against the dirt floor of the ring. Cole tried to catch his breath, clenching his trembling fists.

What does this girl even see in you?

He needed to try harder. He needed to *hit* harder. He needed to listen. He needed to stop questioning. Stop feeling so much. There was so much to do.

He evened his breath, walking to the sword. He picked it up from the ground, the blade glinting as he leveled it upward. He didn't dare look in the reflection. What *did* Tabitha see in him anymore?

Don't start to think like that.

Oh, boy, please do.

Cole's Comm went off from the sidelines. He frowned. Who could be calling him now? Had the others gotten any further with the mission?

He sheathed the Blade and ran for his Comm.

*Cecileo Reuder**

Where are you?

Cole's heart dropped. He cursed, shoving the Comm into his bag. He tore out the training ring gates and ran headfirst into the bustling evening crowds. He didn't have time to carefully keep distance. No. Not when he'd forgotten a request for dinner from the literal *rulers* of this place.

How could he have been so forgetful?

He pushed through the crowd, apology on loop as he stumbled out into the residential street. Did he have time to change? What was worse, showing up like a sweaty dog to royalty or being even more late?

He decided to not rub more salt in the wound and took the fastest shower he'd taken in his entire life, still struggling with the jerkin ties on his way out the door, running his fingers through his hair as he stumbled upon the outdoor mat.

He calmed himself before hesitantly stepping inside.

Cecileo's head appeared from the opposite flap. "Look who finally showed up."

Cole set his bag down, stumbling to rush to Cecileo. "I'm so sorry. I completely forgot. I—"

Cecileo waved him off and turned to shout over his shoulder. "Echo, your charity project is here!"

Cole blinked. Was Cecileo wrong? Not entirely.

Cecileo turned back to Cole, ushering him in. Cole followed through the second flap into an entirely new room. His eyes went wide, a silent "wow" leaving his lips. He couldn't believe that *this* was a tent. A chandelier hung from the tent ceiling, the fabric walls decorated in a fine, golden design, portraying dozens of foreign scenes along them. A low table was set with unfamiliar foods, and richly decorated pillows were set around it in place of chairs.

Cecileo plopped down casually, a hair falling loose from his circlet as he massaged his temples.

Echo burst through another pair of tent flaps. Her hair was down, her braids elegantly cascading down her shoulders, her tunic a dark-fitted red, complementing the golden hoop earrings. Her eyes lit up as she rushed to greet him with hands on his shoulder. "You survived." She laughed. "Mortals, you look beat."

Cole couldn't help a small smile back, though unsure of what to say.

Echo led him to a seat, and she took the one opposite, beside Cecileo. "How did training go?" she asked, handing Cecileo a small stack of plates, and he handed them out.

"All right," Cole said. What could he say? He wasn't doing well, and that was his fault.

"Miserable," Cecileo corrected, loading his plate. "Never seen such dark circles in my life. You're also looking at the food like it'll kill you. Seriously, Johnson, you might need some before you become a full-on phantom."

"It could kill me," Cole said.

Cecilo and Echo stopped, staring at him.

"Uh, wait. No! I don't mean it that seriously, I—uh—I'm allergic to nuts."

Maybe Cecileo was onto something about eating…and probably more sleep. *Great job making things awkward.*

"Oh," Echo said, her face relaxing. "I would recommend staying away from the baked goods, then. I'm not sure what the flour contains, but I can double-check that for you next time if you'd like."

There was going to be a next time? Why did she even want him around?

"Thank you, but there's no need to go through all that trouble just for me." He shyly placed a few fruits onto the plate, his stomach too anxious already for much more.

Echo shrugged. "It wouldn't be trouble at all," she said. "Besides, I want you to feel comfortable here."

"Co, I don't think he knows what the word 'comfortable' means," Cecileo said.

"Cecileo."

"What?" He turned to Cole. "Remember your delightful street fight?"

"Very delightful," Cole grumbled.

"You tried in all noble. If you wanted to end that fight, you should've been comfortable with going all in, sword and all." Cecileo's eyes were alive with enthusiasm. "That would've been an epic entrance into the Market."

"I've tried that before…and it didn't end well," Cole said quietly.

"Were you confident? Comfortable?"

Cole opened his mouth but stopped himself. He didn't remember feeling confident or comfortable. He'd felt terrible and tired. Looking into Tabitha's eyes and the flames around him—

He shook the memory away. "No," he admitted.

"Exactly, kid," Cecileo said, taking a sip of his tea. "That's what you should be working for."

"Assert dominance," Cole said. "I understand."

"And once you've started a fight, *don't* run. Running gets your back to the enemy, making you more vulnerable. Fight them until you have a guaranteed getaway, or you're in it for the win."

Cecileo was asking Cole to be fully committed. He couldn't back out. But that's what he was worst at. He never wanted to in the first place. He didn't enjoy fighting. All it brought were thoughts of guilt…ever since that stupid incident. How was he ever supposed to do that?

"And you said you didn't want to teach him." Echo snorted.

Cecileo smirked, shaking his head. "You're awfully quiet, Johnson, unlike your tiny, yelling friend."

"I—I thought it would be rude to speak out of turn in the presence of…royalty."

Echo and Cecileo exchanged looks.

Cecileo sighed. "Yes. Very royal. Best king. That would be me."

Echo elbowed him. "Not technically," she said, turning her attention to Cole. "The Market is run in a somewhat monarcharcy with a Pater and an occasional Mater, but the idea is more based around having leaders to foster a culture and maintain order. The Market is meant to be a safe haven, not another government."

"So, if it functions as monarchy would have, is Cecileo or you the child of the previous ruler?" Apparently, unwanted library tablets could come in handy.

"Actually, no." Echo sighed. "The previous rulers had no children, and they were the first Mater and Pater. The Mater died decades ago, but the old Pater set out on a mission to find eligible 'sons' to eventually choose to become his heir in a competition."

"I wonder who won," Cecileo said.

"So yes, royalty in technicality, but in reality,"—she gave Cecileo a teasing glance—"still the twelve-year-old thief we found on the streets all those years ago."

"I don't know if you've noticed, Echo, but I've grown a little."

"So, the Pater is just to keep maintenance?" Cole asked with a frown. "Why do you go through so much trouble to find an heir, then?"

"It's politics too," Echo said. "With how large the Market's grown, someone needs to protect them. And the original rulers never intended for the son system, it was always meant for the heir to be the descendant."

Silence fell over the room.

"The son system caused way too much separation and violence. It won't happen again," Cecileo said, his voice suddenly serious now. He placed a gentle hand on Echo's knee. "Besides, Echo's masterminding of the Markets has created the best economy here the Market has ever seen."

A small smile pulled at Echo's lips. "Showing me off now, are you?"

"*You* mastermind the Market?" Cole said, his interest peaked. He couldn't see Cecileo being too technical, but Echo? Everything about her always seemed just in place in such a natural way.

"She's the brain, I'm the bronze. And a part-time peddler."

"Oh, and he's a top-wanted felon by the Defending Department." Echo laughed with a shrug.

"Top?" Cole's eyes widened.

"It's called *living*, Johnson." Cecileo refilled his tea cup. "And by the way, you sit as straight as a board, I can tell you don't know much about it."

Cole tried to quickly slouch, but Cecileo just snorted.

Echo rolled her eyes. "So, any plans for tomorrow?"

"Show up at training," he said. As he did every day, and stay up late trying to figure out Tabitha's song. He'd scrapped the "I'm sorry I blew up a building" line because it sounded desperate…and "building" didn't rhyme with "sheep."

"Determined," Cecileo noted.

Echo nodded. "Don't let Doran beat you to a pulp." She began to refill her plate when she paused. "Your Medallion is gone."

Cole reached for the empty space on his chest. "It was taken. During the fight."

"Stolen?" Cecileo said, frowning. "Why didn't you steal it back?"

"I—"

Cecileo sighed, looking at Echo. "Honestly. He knows *nothing*."

"I did tell you he needed a teacher." Echo shrugged.

"More like a life coach."

Cole held back a glare.

Echo turned back to Cole. "Do you know what the thief looked like?"

Cole described what he could remember of the man, and Echo watched with an ever-deepening frown. "Doesn't sound like a resident," she said, glancing to Cecileo. "Call a search."

Cecileo twirled his fork into a bowl of noodles. "I already did. But all I've gotten is he's a bandit slug."

Cole raised a brow. They had a lead?

"Probably a Victor leech, then." Echo scowled. "I don't see why he hasn't left yet."

"You can't kick him out?" Cole asked, scowling at the mention of the ring master.

"He doesn't sell so-called fighters in the Market, though I don't doubt he's doing it secretly. So technically, he's not breaking the creed."

"But owning human beings is illegal anywhere," Cole said. Wasn't it that simple? Just call him out for that!

Echo's eyes hollowed. "You'd be surprised."

"You have to know about bandits. You can't be that sheltered." Cecileo took it more lightly than Echo, who stared hard at the table, her expression blank.

He'd heard about them all the time as a kid. Often to scare kids to keep them off the streets late at night in fear of being kidnapped. "I—I do, I just thought they weren't successful."

"Defenders really want to keep that fact they can't get the issue under control and under wraps." Cecileo's face hardened. "Everywhere they and their buyers end up is never good news."

For the first time this week, Cole felt determined, the soreness feeling empowering. He had a target.

"We've had just enough bad news for one night," Echo interjected. She met Cecileo's eyes, and it was as if unspoken words passed between the two. Her pained expression softened his hard face, and Cecileo nodded.

"Maybe I do have some good news," he said with a sly smile. "I have a plan to get back your necklace."

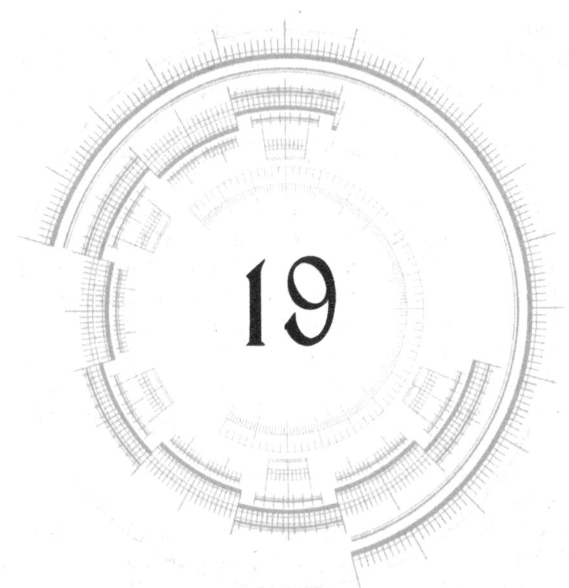

19

Kennedy, 17 Days Until

RAY SWITCHED OFF the blinking hologram, turning to face the dark, empty restaurant hall. Saturday was Mercy's off day and his second day working for her. He'd *planned* to use it to sleep in, but she'd come in with a broom to wake him up and insisted that they had things to do.

His hands were still sore from helping her scrub the floor, and he could already feel the biting morning cold from the open door behind him.

"Hurry your behind up if you don't want to get caught up in a crowd!" Mercy called from outside. "Let me tell you, it's the worst kind. Pickpockets galore."

Ray sighed, wishing that he could somehow manifest magical earplugs, and turned to follow Mercy out the door. She closed it behind him, swiping the keycard to lock it and jogged gracefully down the steps, leaving him to chase after her.

"Weird backpack you got there, Mathews." Mercy

scoffed, eyeing the bag on Ray's shoulders. The Shadow Blade's hilt stuck awkwardly out of the zipper, the bag pulled out of shape from trying to cram the weapon inside. No one was going to sneak up on him again. He wouldn't let himself make a mistake and add another pair of dying eyes to his nightmares.

He didn't try to explain himself and simply shrugged.

As predicted, she rolled her eyes at him and sighed.

The Kennedy streets seemed busier than usual: more locals out walking the sidewalks and autos parked at shops. If Mercy anticipated crowds, Ray could see why.

"So where are we heading now?" he said. "Let me guess, a bot shop, because seriously, let me tell you. A mop bot would save you, and me, so much time on scrubbing floors. A worthy investment."

"You paying for it?"

"Uh—"

"Now hurry your short legs up! It's about a kilometer out!" Mercy burst into a sprint now, running off the sidewalk, weaving between parked autos with Ray scrambling after her.

"You never answered my question!" he shouted after her.

"You never asked me a sincere one!"

He groaned. "Where are we going?"

"'Please?'" she said with a smile.

Ray frowned. "What?"

"You didn't say 'please.'"

"Are you ser—?"

She smacked him on the shoulder.

"Hey! Fine, *please*. Where the heck are we going?"

Mercy skidded out of the way of an advertisement bot, turning around to give Ray a frown before whirling around to continue running forward. "You already forgot?"

"Forgot what?"

"The harvester's market," Mercy said, her voice more sincere and her eyes wide with the smallest twinge of disappointment. "So we can find more information about this moon thing?"

"Oh, right!" Ray's heart leapt. How had he forgotten so easily? The past week was spent elbows-deep in dish water and the rest spent creeping downstairs in the middle of the night inspecting the lock.

He never tried to pick it, even though he was certain that he could. Something held him back. Something about the trust that Mercy had given him. He didn't want to betray it, but if he did, it would make things so much simpler. It was always tomorrow, but it was always the same, staring and questioning.

This provided both progress on their mission and the Shadow Soul, and it didn't endanger Mercy's trust.

"It's only a once-a-month event, and all of the locals attend," Mercy said, slowing around the corner. "And it attracts a few tourists here and there too. Uki and Ahnah have a stall. I'm sure they'll have some references."

"References? I thought *you* were a local."

Mercy shrugged, her pace slowing. "I—I don't go out much."

Right. How closed off had Mercy been? No wonder she seemed antsy about this.

"Well, you know more than me," he said, unsure of what else to say. Everything felt fake on his tongue.

"You really know nothing," she grumbled.

Can she not take anything he said lightly?

He followed Mercy down the streets. The cold chill pricked at his skin, though the sun stood out brighter than most days. The wind blew through the peacefuls streets, voices and laughter beginning to rustle. The building began to thin, and the melodic, pounding music filled the air.

Ray furrowed his brows. The melody was unlike anything he'd heard before…And what instrument was that? In a way, it was pleasant, alluring almost.

The stands and shades set up in the lot were packed with people and colorful produce, and Mercy slowed to a stop at the sidewalk across. Her lips pinched together as she stared at the people ahead.

"What? You scared?" Ray said.

Mercy didn't jab back. She let out a breath. "Don't talk to anyone who we don't need to talk to and I think it's okay," was her only instruction.

What's okay?

Ray didn't have time to ask as Mercy scurried across the street into the crowd. The crowd was peaceful, the music setting a joyous mood among the slow shoppers standing over tables of produce and crafts. So much color and style, each seeming distinct and rich. Ray's eye caught on a young girl sitting at a table, a woven blanket as her tablecloth, beaded jewelry set out in front of her. She sat looking wistfully at the passing shoppers with her face in her hands.

He stopped in front of her table and the girl perked up, her large, round, brown eyes staring up at him in intrigue. "Hello," she said, shyly tucking a braided strand of hair behind her ear.

He waved with a small smile. "You selling these?"

She nodded. "I'm old enough. I turned thirteen two months ago," she said defensively. "I made them myself."

Ray laughed, crouching down to the level of the table. "No, no. I didn't doubt it. These are incredible."

He gently picked up a wooden bracelet, made of individual squares strung through and small carvings imprinted on the front. It reminded him of the moon necklace that Mercy had made for Uki out of the broken plate.

"It's not *exactly* how I wanted to make it." The girl sighed. "My aana makes them with bone, but I only got wood. Three pounds?"

Ray hadn't said that he was going to *buy* anything, but now that the girl was staring at him so intently, he couldn't help but reach into his bags for the heavy coins. "I'll take two," he said, pushing them forward.

The girl's eyes lit up, quickly snatching the coins. "Really? Two?" She scrambled to undo another similar bracelet from her stand and handed it to him. "Thank you for your business, sir."

He gave her a small nod. She reminded him of his own sister, always ambitious in her attempts to be a better Medic than him. He didn't doubt that Jenna would be a doctor like his mother. "Happy to give it."

Ray pulled one over his wrist, finding it oddly comfortable. He put the other away into the pocket of his backpack, waving goodbye to the little seller. He moved through the rows with intrigue. The produce was interesting and all, but the art…He stared at a tiny carving statue on a table.

Mercy nearly full-on collided with him, pulling him out of his gaze. "Mathews! You can't wander off like that." She glared at him, her hand gripping his arm hard.

"Sorry," he said with a long sigh, which didn't seem to humor her. She pulled him through the rows, which he thought was rude, not even letting him get a moment to take everything in. She finally stopped right in front of a produce table. The familiar face of Ahnah stood, wrapping meat into a package for a customer. She looked up with her monotone expression to Mercy.

"Remembrance," she said with a nod. "Can I help you?"

"Nakasuk," Mercy said, moving forward in line. "I—we have some questions."

"What is it this time?" Ahnah sighed, hardly paying Mercy much attention. "Your grandmere requesting a meat tray to serve fifty now? Tell her the limit is twenty-five with a two-day notice."

"Do you know what the Soul Night is?" Ray blurted out.

Ahnah's eyes flickered with surprise, turning to Ray. "The what?"

Ray stepped forward. "The Soul Night."

Ahnah frowned, her eyes narrowing with intent. "I'm probably not the most suited to answer what I'm taking as a myth question."

"Myth or fact, I'll take anything."

"Why do you want to know?" An elderly woman pushed her way behind Ahnah, laying a hand on the young woman's shoulder. She was a plump woman, her dark hair woven into two brains, wrinkles pressing into her face. A group of children and young teens watched intently from a small circle in the grass behind her. "I didn't think the Remembrance child would be asking questions of stories."

Mercy's eyes widened before her face fell with a blush.

"She's not asking," Ray said, facing the woman. "I'm new to Kennedy and this entire culture. I'd like to know more, if possible. Especially about this Soul Night."

"That story is no party trick for tourists," the woman said, her face stern.

Ray opened his mouth, trying to fumble out an excuse. What could he say? He could pull out the Shadow Blade and—

"It's about me," Mercy said quietly. She raised her head, her eyes cautious to look up. "I need help."

Immediately, Ahnah and the woman's face softened. "You?" Ahnah said, her voice cracking with surprise, looking back and forth between Mercy and Ray.

"Well, if it's the young Remembrance asking." The older woman smiled, her eyes glinting. "Come, sit."

She led them behind the Nakasuks' table into the long grass, where children were running about throwing a ball. Ray recognized Uki among a group of other girls. She waved at them from the distance, running over to greet them.

The old woman bent over against her cane and rested herself into a seat, and Mercy and Ray sank down onto the grass as the rest of the young group scrambled out of the way to give them space. Uki ran to them. "Aana, what's going on?" Uki said, her cheery expression falling to a frown.

"Didn't know good ol' story time still interested you, Uki." Ahnah laughed.

"It's help for the little Remembrance," the woman snapped at Ahnah.

Ray couldn't help but steal a quick glance at her, sitting tall and straight, her eyes unwavering. Everything about Mercy struck him as unique, but the way the woman spoke, there seemed to be something more. Was it to do with her grandmother?

"'The Soul Night' isn't a phrase I'm too familiar with," the woman admitted. "But I can draw a conclusion as to what it stems from. In tradition, there was only one EarthShaker battle fought in Kennedy."

Uki plopped down next to Ray excitedly.

"That was the night the Sun finally left to regain energy after its perilous chase after the Moon," she said.

"Spoiling it so soon, Uki?" Ahnah snorted.

The woman sighed. "Uki is correct, according to legend. In the darkness, strength was found, but it wasn't a pleasant strength. Civilians were defenseless as a dark force, the Purizies, came without bounds and destroyed everything in their path."

Purizies. Ray's blood chilled at the term for the Oquelite. This all sounded too coincidental. Too likely but unlikely all at the same time. It felt so cheesy, yet horrifying.

The woman continued. "The strong survived and came together regardless of whether they belonged by blood. They escaped the massacre to a bunker, where they were safe during the great darkness above for those two decades."

"How did they survive?" Mercy pressed. "It couldn't have simply just been because they were strong, especially if this force was…supernatural. When *is* the night?"

"The night itself is just a dare. The important part is the power of words, child. That's always how it's been taught. Words to contradict the very darkness itself." The woman sighed. "Though, I'm sure there will be others with more to offer than I about your historic question."

Words having power? Just like names. But which word could contradict darkness? Was it as simple as a word? Or what the word could do?

Maybe stop taking it so literally, he told himself. *It's just a legend.*

But the Shadow Soul…What if it has to do with that night? What if I have to do with that night?

Panic seized him. No, he refused to think like that.

"Really?" Mercy perked up. "Where can we find them?"

"Outskirts of the main city," the woman said, settling both hands over her cane. "They hold an extensive record of EarthShaker events, getting it directly from MEDIA offices in Sycamore."

Ray's eyes brightened, glancing at Mercy. "That sounds perfect."

Mercy's face faltered, swallowing. She nodded. "Perfect," she repeated.

"But is it really true?" one of the other kids in the group asked, his face wrinkled to a frown and his nose upturned. "Purizies aren't real."

"Then what attacked Imperial, Pilip?" Uki retorted.

Ray tried to resist squirming as the two glared at each other.

The boy shot her a look. "Terrorists with supernatural alerations." He waved his hand around, making a dramatic howling noise.

Ahnah kicked him from behind.

"Perhaps you don't understand the meaning behind it," the elderly woman said. "Do the words spoken to you not affect the way you feel?"

Everyone slowly came to agreement.

The woman leaned forward against her cane, stealing a look at Ray, his heart leaping. "Then don't other words as well? The power of a name is great. The names of those living around us is the same, but perhaps we all are too human to perceive it."

"You're implying we can draw upon light?" Ray asked, slowly.

"That is what the stories say."

Then what about the darkness? What about the shadows? What about the wickedness that he felt had ensnared every part of him?

He just pursed his lips and nodded.

"Any questions, young Remembrance?"

Mercy jumped, quickly shaking her head. "No, that's all I needed," she said, getting to her feet and dusting herself off. "Thank you."

The woman nodded, and Ray got up to follow her. Mercy left in a hurry, not giving Ray any time for a farewell as he chased after her to the stands. Her head was intently forward, and cold as stone. She didn't even seem to notice as he caught up at her side.

"So, we know where we're heading next?"

Mercy didn't respond, just glancing at him.

He let out a breath. "Not this again. What did I do this time?"

"Nothing," she snapped. Her face immediately pinched. "I mean...we can't go."

Ray's heart faltered. "We—we can't?"

What did she mean they couldn't go? It was just a research facility at the edge of the city. What could possibly be stopping them now? He was *this* close to finding out when this night was and then to figure out how to connect it to the Shadow Soul, and Mercy just said...no?

"This is ridiculous," he spat. "We're going. We can't just *stop*! What the heck are you scared of now?"

Mercy turned and grabbed him by the shirt collar, tearing him from the moving crowd with a jerk. "I'm not scared," she shouted in a whisper.

He should've been more scared with her fist so close to

his face, but everything burned too much to care. "You are! I can see it in your eyes!"

Her big, brown eyes widened before darkening. "Shut up!" She shoved him back, causing him to nearly stumble off his feet. He quickly caught himself. "We can't, and that's final."

"I don't have to listen to you."

Mercy groaned, holding her head in her hands. She swiveled on him. "You do. I'll call the Defenders on you."

"You've used that threat already."

"Maybe I'll do it this time."

"I'm beginning to think you *need* me, Remembrance."

Mercy went stiff.

It shouldn't have felt as good as it did to have the upper hand. He knew that it was wrong. What was he thinking, using her father against her like this?

You were born a monster. It's not any worse.

"We're leaving," she snapped.

"Fine with me."

She snorted, turning and marching from him. He gave a dramatic sigh and followed after her. They pushed past the other shoppers, Mercy hard set on her path, not bothering to watch him. Ray wanted to be angry with her, but instead, his chest just felt twisted.

He followed along, apologizing to every shopper she barged into.

Ray froze, a burning feeling creeping up the back of his neck. He whirled around. Two glowing eyes stared from the crowd.

He heart leapt, he blinked, the world crashing back into clarity.

The hood was removed. A deathly pale man...woman, he couldn't tell, with hair almost as white braided back stared at him. A tiny smile was on their lips. Their gaze slowly turned, and Ray's went with it, landing on the storming figure of Mercy.

Ray's blood went cold. *No.*

Before he had a chance, a scream tore out in the stands. A table was overturned, produce crashing to the floor. People were running and scrambling away. Others picked up to fight.

Ray caught sight of the panicked jewelry seller's table, wiped clean of its contents, people trampling through her area. He rushed to her and pulled her out from under the table. "Are you all right?"

She nodded, tears pooling in her eyes.

"What's going on?" he asked.

"I don't know," she said, her voice cracking.

Ray peered over his shoulder. He swore that it was those stupid, red-eyed jerks. What were they doing ruining this perfectly calm gathering?

A table came flying. The girl screamed. Ray clutched her close, and in a blink, they hit the sidewalk. Her eyes flew open, her chest rising and falling, looking like she was about to scream as her eyes locked on him.

Stupid. Stupid.

He scrambled to his feet, backing away from her. "Go! Get away from here!"

He burst into a run toward the tent, the crowds running. He ducked behind a truck and reappeared atop a table inside, tearing his sword from his backpack.

A gruff-looking man wearing a black, bulletproof vest with thinning, orange hair and tattoos across his cheeks stumbled back. He had a gun in his holster and splinters of wood all on his woolen clothing.

Ray swung, leaving the man stumbling back. Ray pulled at a chair, tripping the man under his feet. Ray leapt on top of him, slamming a knee to his chest, grabbing the man's collar and shaking him. "Who are you?"

"I—I—"

"Who sent you?"

The man just stared at him. Ray let the burning infest his eyes, feeling their glow. "Tell me!"

"They're bandits, Oquelite!"

Ray's burn froze, whipping around a new face. Tanned skin, dark hair that complemented his dark eyes, and golden stripes running through his hair, an unconscious man in similar dress at his feet. He clapped his hands together, dust flying from them. He clenched his hands together and the man cried out, specks of sand crawling from the ground, whirling around him.

Ray jumped back.

The man was lifted from the ground and slammed down with a thud.

Ray scrambled to his feet, whirling the Blade around. "How do you—?"

"You teleported, genius." The man snorted.

"You have—"

"Abilities, yes." The man seemed preoccupied, rushing past Ray and into the commotion.

Ray tried to run after him. "What about the red-eyed guy?"

"I'll deal with the Exerticus!"

Exerticus? The red-eyed guys had a name.

And bandits? He'd heard of them all too frequently. Not an organization, just frequent troublemakers and thieves. And they were picking on this little town?

Out of nowhere, a fist was thrown. Ray ducked back, rolling to his feet. No time to fight.

He scrambled into the cover of the crowd. Where was the red-eyed guy? And the sandman? He knew Ray's secret. What else did he know? Ray needed to catch him.

He quickly blasted a box from one of their arms, sending it sliding to the floor, and they stared at Ray in horror.

Someone was bound to call the Defenders any minute, right?

He heard another cry and a spray of sand. *There.*

He ran through the twisty overturned rows. And then he froze.

A shiver overcame him, and as he turned to the crowd, everything slowed. He strained his eyes. All he saw were the fleeting faces of the shoppers and merchants. What was he supposed to be seeing? He needed to get the sand guy and get answers about all of this. He didn't have—

Red eyes. Moving quickly toward the exit, weaving expertly through the crowd.

Mercy.

He glanced back to the sandman, running farther. Ray cursed himself. He ran and teleported into the crowd. No one seemed to notice. He glared at the "Exerticus," giving Ray a sly smile.

Ray pushed through the crowd faster. Where was she? Had she already left? He wanted to cry out her name, but that felt dangerous.

Words have power. Could he use it?

He bit his tongue and shoved through the crowd, searching for the girl with curious marks and the look of death. They burst out into the open, Ray stumbling onto the grass.

Where was Mercy?

Ray stopped in his tracks, his heart hammering against his chest. Every inch of him cried to shout her name.

He bit down harder, feeling blood on his tongue. He ran to the sidewalk, now packed with people hurrying. He heard the distant cries of a law enforcement car.

No matter how many passed him, he couldn't see her. He scanned the crowd, spotting Uki. She held his eyes for a split moment, wide and surprised, before running.

Dread settled into the pit of his stomach.

He broke out into a run, back toward the stands. He couldn't think. He hoped that it wasn't true. He rolled into the long grass, letting the void envelope him. He popped up right behind Ahnah's stand.

"Mathews?"

For a moment, relief swept over him, but only for a moment as his senses shook him.

Mercy held fast to an iron pan, a group of the cowering pupils and the elderly woman standing huddled together behind Ahanh's overturned table.

"You came back?" Mercy asked in a hushed voice, but her face indicated a rage that he knew would've been a lot louder...but a twinge of a surprise. But her anger, for once, didn't seem targeted at him.

He crawled closer. "I've been in the grass," he lied.

She raised a brow and sighed. "Of course you were."

"What are *you* doing?" he asked, settling himself behind their shielding table.

"Their aana can't move quickly, and they refused to leave without her," Mercy said, her eyes peering over the table, not once mentioning why *she* was there.

But she didn't need to.

He crept by her side, holding out his sword.

She glanced at him, then stopped, her brows raising. She didn't ask any questions.

"I thought you said nothing happened here," Ray whispered.

"There must be a reason they're suddenly targeting here," the woman said quietly.

"What? We aren't a wealthy town. Nothing a value's here for them to want," Pilip said.

It took everything in Ray not to look at Mercy.

Could the bandits and the "Exerticus" be linked somehow?

A table across from them burst into flames. The elderly woman smothered a pupil's cry. Ray caught sight of the tall, lanky figure walking from the strokes of flame. Their red eyes met his.

Ray's heart leapt, and he pulled Mercy undercover, his heart hammering. She stared at him, confused. He put a finger over his lips. Her face softened, clenching the pan tighter in her hand.

One of the pupils sat up straight, pointing out into the field. What now? More bandits? Sand Man?

Ray's lips fell apart. A truck was racing toward them. For a moment, he panicked, prepared to jump to his feet and get everyone out of the way, until he recognized Ahnah at the wheel, staring hard at them.

He glanced at Mercy. "Go," he whispered.

"What? I can't—"

The table was torn away, sending the group running in screams. "Get to Ahnah!" Ray yelled, swinging at the red-eyed guy.

They lept gracefully back, and with the swing of their arm, red energy crept up their arm, firming around their fist, swiveling upward until it fell away and they sent a sword blade flying for Ray's head.

Ray ducked, slicing for them. They sidestepped, their blade meeting Ray's and shoving him back, moving toward Mercy. She was scrambling back onto the dirt, trying to reach for the pan.

"No! Stop!" Ray jumped and swung. He hit the arm. Red Eyes stumbled back.

Ray pulled Mercy to her feet, not letting go of her arm until they reached Ahnah's truck. They were pulled up into the bed. Uki and Pilip slammed the door shut.

"Go!" Uki screamed at her sister.

Ahnah slammed on the gas, sending everyone sliding. Ray collided with Mercy, grabbing onto the ends of the truck bed as Ahnah peeled out into a turn and took off.

He tried to catch his breath, staring at the market, low-status Defenders pulling out of cars and bandits trying to scramble away.

Red Eyes just stood and watched, their hands on the top of the sword, and shimmered out of sight.

Ray's stomach flipped. They were gone…for now.

He turned to Mercy beside him, who was holding herself in her arms, staring down at her feet. "Are you all right?"

She glanced at him, then closed her eyes. "Thank you," she said quietly.

Ray blinked. No questions? No screaming and shouting? Just "thank you?"

"You're welcome," he said gently.

She rested her head in her arms as they hit the road, Ahnah slowing. Ray didn't try to bother her. He tried calming his hammering heart. Trying to set the thoughts in his mind in order.

Red-Eyed Guys had a name.

Everything had just gotten a lot more deadly.

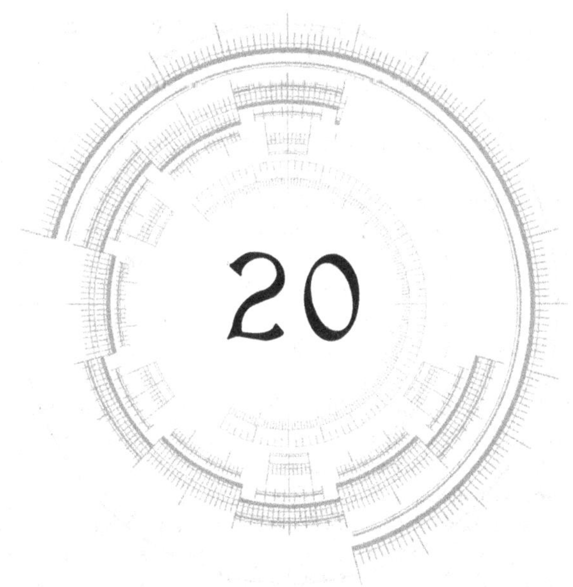

20

North Cordell, 17 Days Until

"'EXERTICUS.' THE GLOWING-eyes guys have a name."

Ray's announcement sent the entire group call quiet.

"Well, someone's been productive." Tabitha coughed. "All I've done is make a few public apologies and clean a few tables."

"It's a better lead on the Shadow Soul than anything we've had," Lincoln said, itching to move as he sat facing the screen beside Lawrence in the upstairs of the Inn. They were set to leave on the Jenna mission in a matter of minutes. "The only other connection we have is that tapestry in Court Illegia."

Cole beat Lincoln to pulling up the image of the tapestry. The borders were lined with vaguely familiar symbols. Two that stuck out were a green, crystal shard and a feather. The rest must be the other Artifacts, like the *Cors Vis* and the Ewyon Stone, Pulcheremii.

There in the middle was a cloud of darkness, woven with

silver in and out as if it were tucking all around itself in a never-ending turmoil around brash, blood-red mountains.

The words came before he even had thought them up. "The Shadow Soul."

"Yeah, we came to that conclusion already." Lawrence snorted from beside him. "There's nothing there that's useful besides a blob and a few symbols."

"Do you think their blood-like abilities have any connection to the mountains?" Tabitha said suddenly.

"How so?" Felicity asked tentatively.

"In my nightmares...I was shown blood-soaked mountains. The North Cordell mountains," Tabitha said quietly.

"Blood is in a lot of things," Ray said. "I've got blood in me right now. Punch me in the face a few times and am I suddenly one of those guys too?"

Tabitha rolled her eyes. "I'm *trying*."

"They attacked the mountains depicted." Matteo's small voice surprised Lincoln. He looked up from across the table, not facing the screen. "And—and the tapestry is—was in Court Illegia."

"Where they also attacked," Lawrence finished.

"That's just two correlations," Cole said. "It doesn't mean anything."

"Just go on with me here," Lincoln said. It was their only lead anywhere, and Tabitha was making sense. "Blood does act as a life source. Essence is commonly referred to as the 'second bloodstream.' That's what keeps the supernatural thriving, our blood keeps our natural bodies thriving."

Lincoln creased his brows. People that used blood as an ability, what kept the material part of them thriving, as ability. And seemingly from themselves too...Didn't they need it to stay alive? Unless...

"They aren't alive," Lincoln breathed.

A moment of utter silence.

"What?" Lawrence blurted out.

"That's what I thought!" Tabitha said excitedly. "Why would it matter if they used...blood as an ability and used its life force to create things if they didn't need it themselves?"

Lincoln's mind was running. "They must be almost entirely essence based then. In a body somehow. I don't know how they could do it."

"Maybe they aren't," Matteo's voice said.

Cole frowned. "Like…someone else created them?"

"But that means there has to be someone *so* powerful, they could have literal essence to bring dead to a sort of life," Lawrence said, his eyes wide, getting to his feet. "And that isn't possible! That's insane."

"You're right. It shouldn't be possible," Cole said quietly. "But I'm beginning to think it might be."

Lincoln went quiet.

Someone powerful enough to bring life into the dead. Could they also be powerful enough to keep someone supposed to die alive?

"The Shadow Soul." Lincoln shuddered, trying to shake off the thought. No, it couldn't be. He closed his eyes. *Get out of my head, for the last time!*

A deep chuckle. *Oh, boy, isn't that the power you want above all? Power to contradict death?*

He didn't want that. He told himself that over and over. He wanted Nikki to be okay.

He got to his feet quickly. "We should go if we want to get Jenna back," he said.

The room went quiet.

He frowned. What? Why were Matteo and Lawrence staring at him like that?

"Where's Jenna?"

Ray's voice made Lincoln's heart drop.

He couldn't face the screen. "Uh—Jenna. She—she's fine."

"You're lying to me, Black Eyes."

Lincoln's heart beat into his ears. He could hear the edge on Ray's voice.

"What happened to my sister?" Ray shouted, the speakers cracking. "What did you do?"

Lincoln tensed before turning to hit the end call button. Lawrence slammed his hand down against the table. Lawrence dared to look into the camera as Lincoln's face burned, staring at the floor, his hand trapped under Lawrence's. "Your sister was taken by the Oquelite. It was no one's fault, and we're on our way to try and get her back tonight."

"You mean my little sister got captured by *Oquelite* and no one thought to tell me?"

"Ray—"

"Look. I get you all not telling me things most of the time. I *get* I am an unreliable monster, but this is my sister!"

Lincoln could hear the tears that Ray was holding back.

Why feel guilty? He tried to kill you.

"Ray, you aren't a monster," Cole said. "Don't do this to yourself again."

"Maybe I'm just not the only one."

He ended the call abruptly.

Lawrence let go of Lincoln's arm with a frustrated sigh as he turned away and pinched the bridge of his nose. "You're impossible."

"Look, I didn't mean to mention it!"

"And you didn't seem to be all too willing to fix it!"

"It's not my fault Jenna got kidnapped. And it's not my job to make Ray feel okay." Lincoln snorted, pushing past Lawrence.

"Lincoln, you're the one who ran impulsively into the woods for that letter," Lawrence said, his voice surprisingly stern.

Lincoln stopped only a moment before racing down the stairs.

You did the right thing, the Voice said.

He pushed out the door, which led into the kitchen.

"Hey, Lincoln!"

Lincoln stepped back, startled by Officer Jack Sallow's voice, who stood at the counter…or what would soon be the counter. He was as lively as he remembered, his dark-brown curls a bit longer, hanging down in his face against his light-brown skin. Lincoln almost forgot that Jack was the one leading the expedition. "I've missed seeing you guys." He laughed.

"Hi, Jack. So a Defender on injury leave and three teenaged boys took the job to get Jenna back?" Lincoln tried to joke.

Jack cringed at the statement. Jack had been kidnapped by their new, red-eyed friends only weeks ago and had been exchanged to the Oquelite. It was heavily alluded to that he was tortured for information…about them, the Council.

Jack never talked about it, and his friend and only witness, Miriam Outown, never went into detail, ever. All Lincoln knew was that it left Jack unfit for duty, besides helping out at the MedTent.

He suddenly felt guilty. Curse his stupid mind. He felt so numb inside that he forgot that other people could still feel.

"Good. You two have arrived."

Lincoln stepped out of the way as Matteo and Lawrence left the door, avoiding Lawrence's glower.

"And you must be the Wingor Member from Court Illegia," Jack said, holding out a hand to Matteo. "Jackson Sallow to most. Twenty-two."

He spoke in another language, and Matteo's eyes lit up, responding excitedly.

Jack smiled. "Then we should get going."

Matteo looked to Lawrence and then quickly followed Jack out the back door. Lincoln sighed.

And back into the darkness they went.

Fire Wolf waited excitedly outside the door, eager to get his pats as he trotted in the lead.

They were taking the backway behind town, hoping that the Oquelite would be less suspicious of any sort of infiltration.

Lincoln couldn't shake the echoes of Ray's anger from his mind. He couldn't shake the feeling that maybe the Voice was wrong. Maybe Lincoln *was* at least partially responsible for Jenna's capture.

It made the pit in his stomach deeper.

That boy with the spectacles is proving to be a problem. Why do you care what he and the Oquelite hybrid say to you?

I don't know, Lincoln insisted, trying to push away his other thoughts.

Lawrence and Ray were his friends. Lawrence was older than him, and Lincoln felt an ounce of respect for him.

Why respect him? He's done nothing for you. I, on the other hand, have given you abilities, which you can keep *if you give me your name.*

Lincoln shook it off and ran after the others.

He could see the depot in the distance. He'd been inside a few times when he was younger before he discovered his cave. It was a sturdy building and kept you safe from storms, but it was hardly the size of a cabin back at camp.

Lincoln removed his bow, pulling out an arrow and bracing himself as they approached the door. While he was conflicted about Ray, these Oquelite deserved no mercy.

Fire Wolf set his coat aflame as they approached the door. Jack held up his hand for a moment before signaling to go.

They charged the door, Fire Wolf leading and barging through the door, his howl echoing off the empty walls of the depot.

Wait…empty?

Lincoln lowered his bow. This wasn't supposed to happen.

"Where's Jenna?" Matteo said quietly, stepping into the building.

His voice echoed. Where was Jenna? Lincoln had told Ray that his sister was fine, and now he felt that lie getting deeper and deeper.

He turned on the light on the Cube. The walls of the depot had been vandalized…They hadn't been like this last time.

DEATH TO THE SHADOW SOUL

THE LADY OF UNIVERSE, THE LADY OF NIGHTMARES

It was hard to find any without crude language or a language he couldn't understand entirely.

"Well, this Lady of the Universe really ticked off someone."

"Oquelite," Lincoln said. "They're the only ones who would know this language…the only others who would know about a Shadow Soul."

Everyone exchanged glances.

"I think we've discovered a lot tonight…even if it's not Jenna. We can report it to the Sergeant and do further investigation on the Soul and Exerticus," Jack said. "For now, it's probably best we all get rest."

That Sergeant controls your life, doesn't she?

"Why Taryn?" Lincoln grumbled. "Why can't we handle this lead?"

Lawrence raised a brow. "Look, the Sergeant's not my favorite, either, but she's the one who runs this operation."

But Lincoln did like Taryn. It was the Voice nagging him.

Don't question me.

"I know she's keeping secrets," he said weakly. "She mentioned some Ulysses and then quickly moved on. There could be more—"

"Lincoln." Jack's face hardened. "Ulysses Akash died ten years ago."

The room went silent.

"If she mentioned him, it must have been important to her," Jack said sternly as he met Lincoln's eyes, though they faltered with pain. "They were engaged."

Lincoln's heart lurched.

"They were what?" Lawrence's voice was quiet.

"She was a much different person before," Jack said. "Ulysses was Taryn's second in command, and according to how the story goes, he told her not to rebel against the assassins. He probably saved her life."

"But how did he...?" Lincoln's voice trailed off as he remembered. Taryn had been beaten, forced to watch her entire squadron lined up and killed in front of her before being buried alive.

She had watched him die. Just like Lincoln had watched that sword slide right through Nikki. He didn't even know how she was. If she was okay. If she was dying.

"And then only hours later, when she arrived in Imperial, she learned the rest of the Curatrix team had died...and she broke," Jack said, his voice rising. "Her own ring was lost during the attack, so when she found the Aguirre DNA ring, it was very special to her. I never thought she'd even reveal it to Nikki. Are you satisfied?"

Lincoln couldn't respond, his throat closed up.

"Now, let's get back," Jack instructed.

Lincoln didn't argue. The burning whispered in his chest, calling to him. To embrace it. To crush it.

It hurt. Everything hurt. His heart ached, and everything felt heavy.

Where had his empathy gone? Why was this emptiness torturing him?

Empathy is weak. I can bring you relief. I could bring you the Shadow Soul. You would never have to face death. All for a name.

No, Lincoln pushed out with all his might.

Fine. I have an eternity to torture your mortal soul for answers, boy.

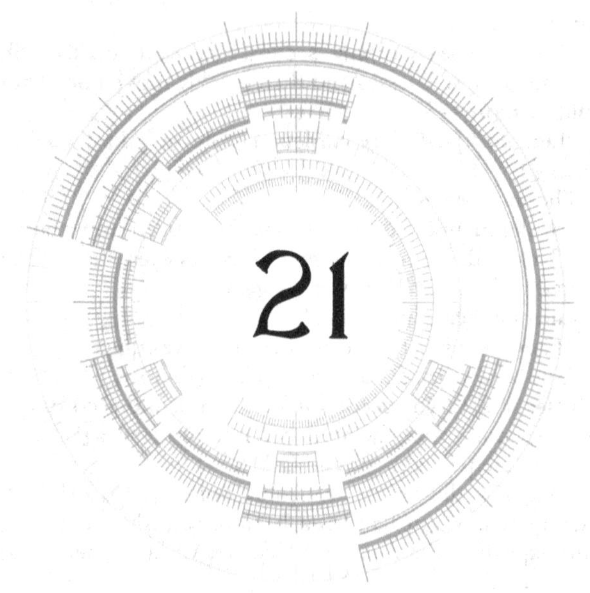

21

"YOU'RE GOING TO the festival, right?"

Cole tried to block out the other students' conversation as he settled into a stance, directly opposite of Doran.

"Of course, I am."

"Eyes here, Illuminate!" Doran snapped, his form perfect, artistically swiping his sword into place.

As usual, the entire arena went quiet at the reminder of who was in their midst. Cole tried to ignore them and his sore shoulder from Doran's last strike. Sweat glued his hair to his face, but he didn't care. He held his stance.

Cole took a deep breath and settled into the form he knew all too well, balancing his Blade firmly in his hand. He knew that his form was perfect, and he knew that Doran could see it, by the scrunch of his nose.

But anywhere past that? Cole hadn't excelled Doran's expectations. But he'd managed to knock a fellow student off his feet, and that was progress. Just focus.

"Three," Doran started, "two, one—"

"Swordmaster!"

With a thud, the Pater leapt down from the circling roof. The pupils scrambled to his feet in a hurry. Doran sheathed his sword, and Cole turned and nearly tripped over his own feet as the adrenaline died. Cecileo's eyes were glued on him.

"I need to borrow your star pupil."

Doran snorted at the comment, though the humor quickly faded. "You're not supposed to interrupt sessions. On what business?"

"The Mater's business," Cecileo said simply.

Cole saw the rest of the pupils exchange glances and a handful of frowns.

"Echo's errands do not take priority over Council affairs," Doran retorted, though his voice held much more bite than a simple inconvenience.

What was it about Echo that caused people to act so differently?

"The very fact she needs him *is* a Council affair," Cecileo said with a mocking bow. "Come on, Johnson."

Cole looked from Cecileo to Doran.

Doran just scowled. "Go."

Cole smothered a smile of relief and nodded. He quickly grabbed his jerkin and bag from the steps, though not having any time to put it back on. With almost too much enthusiasm, he ran after Cecileo. He caught up at the Pater's side, a bit difficult considering the crowd, but it was worth pushing his way through to finish a Doran session early, no matter how well it was going.

"What are we doing?" Cole shouted.

He recognized where they were going through the Market that would soon branch off into another residential street where a small emerald tent stood between a blue and red. Echo had only requested his help twice, but he cherished those moments of silence and productivity. Being in Echo's presence always helped. She always knew just what to say and how to say it.

"I don't know," Cecileo said, turning the corner.

Cole frowned, skirting around a barrelling shopper. "What?" he said. "What do you mean you don't know?"

"I'm just the messenger, kid." Cecileo shrugged. "She

knows more than I do."

"And you didn't bother to ask?"

"I didn't question it."

Cecileo trusted Echo completely, as he should have, and Cole trusted in that reasoning.

They finally pushed through into the street through the narrow gap between two brick buildings evening out into the rows of tents. The street was mostly empty at this hour, besides a few stray children. Cecileo ushered Cole after him.

They reached Echo's emerald work tent, the tent flap slightly ajar, held open with a rock. Cecileo pushed past, and Cole followed after. "Echo, what—?"

Cole froze, his entire body going and his heart racing. He forgot all about Echo. There, sitting straight across from him, was Felicity Bentsworth.

"Felicity?" Cole shouted. He couldn't believe it. She was sitting right there on a table, her orange hair tied up in a loose bun, strange, metal braces on her bare legs connected to an array of machines on Echo's desks surrounded by the hanging blueprints and colorful ornaments of the tent. What was—?

"Cole!" Felicity cried back. Her face lit up before stooping to a frown. "What are you doing here?"

"I mentioned I was in a Market, didn't I?" he said, trying not to laugh. It felt so good to see a familiar face. He had no idea how much he'd missed it. "The real question is, what are *you* doing here?"

"Why didn't you say you were a Marketeer?" Giles pushed Cole from behind with a groan. "Honestly, Johnson!"

Oh, great, *he* was here.

"Got a problem with them, Officer?" Cecileo said with a smirk before disappearing into the next room.

Giles rolled his eyes.

"I'm not a Marketeer," Cole said with a sigh.

"I—I can't believe it." Felicity laughed, leaning forward on the table she was sitting on. "I would hug you if I could stand."

Cole froze. If she could stand? "What do you mean?" he said. "You—you can't—"

It only took a quick glance back at her legs again, nearly

all the pale, bruised, purple color hanging loosely off the table, unmoving. He didn't finish his sentence. He rushed to her and hugged her. She hugged him back tightly, her grip impressive.

"You smell sweaty."

"Yeah, I know."

"So, you do know each other."

The two jumped at Echo's voice. Cole quickly stepped back, swiveling to face Echo wiping her metal hand with a towel.

"The Bentsworth had a Council kid." Echo laughed softly, shaking her head. "Who would've thought?"

"It fits their theme," Giles grumbled, crossing his arms.

"Is there a reason you—she's here?" Cole asked. He couldn't imagine that Felicity was here for training too, especially with her condition.

"A friend of mine asked for help," Echo said. "All the Bentsworths know is she's receiving treatment, and she has her Defender security." She nodded to Giles, who gave her his sullen look.

"I didn't know Renee had a connection to the market," Felicity said excitedly.

Cole just nodded along, having no idea who Renee was.

Echo tapped the screens, a hologram appearing with jumping lines and flowing data down the sides. "You're paralyzed waist down, right darling?"

Felicity's face fell. She nodded.

"And your"—Echo frowned, looking over her shoulder to Cole—"sixteen-year-old, *amnesiac* friend made her a device which allowed her to walk without pain for extended periods of time."

"Sounds like Lincoln," Cole said.

Echo stared at him blankly. "Wait, so the mullet boy wasn't lying? You're serious."

Cole nodded.

Giles huffed, patting his hair.

"You Council kids are even crazier than I thought," Echo said, laughing hoarsely.

"Very crazy," Giles grumbled.

"The creation is incredible, but not durable now that she's in a state of full paralysis. His device lacks a knowledge of neural tech." She tapped on her metal hand. "That happens to be a specialty of mine. I'm sure I can enhance these braces to function as they did before, if not better. The only issue is, no one knows how it came about."

"So you'll be enhancing Lincoln's invention to help Felicity walk?" Cole said.

Echo nodded.

That sounded amazing, if not revolutionary, but there were too many questions. Why the Market? Why Echo?

"Can I help with anything?" he said.

Felicity looked up.

"You're a Member, and Bentsworth's friend," Echo said. "I hear she struggles with anxiety, and since we can't have that…Officer lurking around too much, I thought it might be comforting to have you around. The process relies much on her mental stability."

Felicity blushed, tucking on a loose strand of her hair.

"I can do that," Cole said, trying to contain his excitement jumbling inside him, holding his hands behind his back. "Will she be staying here?"

"No, not for now," Cecileo said, entering the room from the flap behind Echo. "A few days on end at most, but to keep the suspicion low, she'll be back in the Dome frequently."

Cole's heart sank a bit, but he tried not to show it. He nodded. Still plenty of time to finally talk to someone who knew about the whole Shadow Soul mess. "That sounds good."

"Great!" Echo said, turning off her hologram, going to unplug the braces. "The next Rail to the Dome leaves in an hour. I bet you have quite a few things to talk about." She removed a disk from her machine, slipping it into her vest pocket. "Cecil, will you let Doran know?"

Cecileo pinched the bridge of his nose. "Why don't you do it? I'm not in the mood for a lecture."

"You're the man here," she quipped. With a teasing smile, Echo left the tent, Cecileo reluctantly following her.

As soon as they left, Giles turned back to Felicity and Cole. "They're an odd couple."

"They're fine," Cole said, surprising himself with how quick he bit back. "I mean, Echo is. People seem to hate her for no reason."

"Oh, you're just naïve." Giles chuckled. "People always have their reasons in places like this, Johnson. Marketeers are about as trustworthy as Defender politicians."

Cole swallowed an argument. He didn't want to waste his time on Giles's opinions. He obviously had never spent longer than ten minutes in the Market.

Wait…Defender politicians? What did Giles have against those?

Felicity pushed herself forward, Giles jumping to assist.

"I'm fine," she said, waving him off. "Your Comm number was different when you contacted us."

Cole cringed. "I—I got into a crash. New Comm."

Felicity's jaw dropped. He had a feeling that it would hit close to home. Felicity was in a horrible accident years ago. She hardly spoke of it, but she still resisted an auto ride every chance she could, and he knew that her home tormented her with the memories.

"A crash? Coleson Johnson, get over here right now. Are you okay?"

Cole sat beside Felicity, letting her fuss over him. "How bad was it? Did you hit someone? Are you feeling all right? Where is your Medallion?"

Cole put a hand over her shaking one. "I'm fine, I promise. It was minor, just got a concussion. The Medallion… was stolen."

"I told you this place was bad news!" Giles said.

"It was partially my fault," Cole admitted, though quick to assure Felicity that he was fine, guilt striking him as her freckled face welled with concern.

She nodded, as if trying to convince herself. "Good. That's good," she said, sitting quiet for a moment. "I still can't believe you actually left without Tabitha."

Cole flinched. "Don't we have bigger things to discuss?"

"Oh, no," Giles said dryly. "Did you two have a big break up?"

Cole's face flamed. "What? No!"

"You two were courting?" Felicity frowned, looking from Giles to Cole.

"We weren't!"

"Then why isn't she here?" Felicity looked at him with

her brows knit and her eyes bright with drive.

"She's back helping clean up in Court Illegia." Cole swallowed hard. "I made a bad mistake. I—I burned down a building, for one thing."

"Oh, yeah. Way to go." Giles laughed. "One way to turn off someone."

"I wasn't trying to turn anyone on!"

Felicity shook her head. "Now I'm *really* confused."

"Me and Tabitha are *not* anything, and probably never will be," Cole clarified, hoping once and for all, but it only seemed to spark more interest in Felicity.

"'Probably?'" she said, cocking her head.

Way to be brutally honest with your word choice there, Johnson. Great job.

Cole wasn't willing to pour his tangled mess out, especially with Giles's smug mouth standing a few feet away.

"We'll revisit this once we get past the whole 'you're paralyzed' and 'we're in mortal danger on a ticking clock' situation," he said, mentally adding "without Giles." "I'm taking it you found the chip."

Felicity nodded. "I did."

"Heck yeah, she did," Giles said. "It was incredible. You really should see the security feed. Never thought the Bentsworth was one for a fight."

"Wait, you fought someone?" Cole gaped, unable to imagine the image.

Felicity blushed and shrugged. "It was just…part of the mission. What about you?"

"Well, Lawrence found the Wingor."

Felicity's eyes widened. "Matteo, right?" she said.

Cole nodded. "Yes. He's back in North Cordell, as you probably know, safe from whatever chaos goes down in Court Illegia." *He would've been safer if the* Cors Vis *wasn't destroyed.*

"That's amazing news," Felicity said, a smile brightening her face. "When do you plan on going back? We're going to need you once we find out this whole Shadow Soul thing."

"Once I've learned how to properly handle the Illuminate," Cole said. His gaze fell to his callused hands.

Giles frowned. "From the Marketeers?"

"But, Cole, that sounds a bit impossible," Felicity said

bluntly. "*You* are so much more important than a Blade and it's lore."

"I know, I know. I—I just need to learn something. I tried to lead, and I messed up and I hurt people. If I'm just going to be even a self-sustainable Member, I can't be flailing around like a paranoid maniac." He tightened his fists.

Felicity placed a hand on his shoulder, and he turned to meet her eyes. "The fact you recognize you're not ready is honorable, but you can't drive yourself into an endless spiral at every mistake."

Cole didn't respond, unsure of what even to say.

"Believe me, I should know better than anyone." She chuckled.

He cracked a smile for her, looking at her high-held face. For someone with anxiety and paralysis, he hadn't expected to see her so positive.

It seemed for a moment that her smile made the doubts a little weaker. That maybe things were going to be okay.

"We got to start heading out soon, Bentsworth," Giles said, heading out the door. "Begin your goodbyes to lover boy."

Cole glared.

Giles shrugged. "You never denied it."

He slipped out the tent before Cole could argue. He sighed, turning back to Felicity. "Will you be all right alone?"

"Giles will be back in a moment. He's getting the chair," she said, her face flushing pink.

He paused, getting to his feet. "Chair?"

Felicity cleared her throat. "With wheels."

"A wheelchair." Cole's face softened. "Oh, come on, Liz. That's nothing to be embarrassed about, especially being the formidable Bentsworth thief thwarter."

She wrinkled her nose, seeming to relax a bit. "Doesn't have a nice ring to do it, does it?"

He shook his head and laughed. "Name making isn't my expertise."

"Yes, we're missing the expert."

The cheery mood vanished at the mention of Tabitha.

Felicity slung her bag over her shoulder, holding his gaze for a long moment. "And Cole?"

It took everything in him not to look away. "Yes?"

"Please. Talk to her."

Liberty, 15 Days Until

Cole was going to be rebellious.

That morning he decided to intentionally take a detour down the Market street ingrained in his mind ever since he got his face slammed into it. He didn't know how Tabitha managed living like this, with the racing adrenaline of knowing Doran's certain disapproval when Cole showed up at the gate late. Cole tried to not care.

Doran was right about one thing: Cole was the Illuminate. And the Illuminate needed their Medallion.

Cecileo mentioned something about an idea for getting it back, but Cole hadn't dared to ask more about it. He was beginning to regret that as he trekked through the morning crowd. It was a cooler morning, and the streets were not entirely crowded just yet, and all besides a few glares, no one minded him much attention.

It was a simple task today. Just check to see if Victor had started another ring fight. If not, then Cole could call it a day and, maybe if he ran fast enough, get to Doran without a problem.

"Cole-son!" A familiar, young voice called out to him, swimming from the crowd to collide into his side with a hug. Dana smiled up at him. "I knew you'd come again!" She clung to his jerkin as they made their way through the flow of the crowd.

"Hello, Dana," Cole said with a small smile. "How's wolf-man hunting going?"

Dana gave out an exasperated sigh. "No. Not much stuff has been happening," she said, only dwelling on it a moment before looking up to Cole with a new excitement in her big, brown eyes. "Did you see the stars last night, Son-Cole? Do you know what they do?"

Cole laughed. "Yeah, what do the stars do?"

"The stars are only pretty when the sky is dark," Dana noted, distracted by her bracelets dangling on her wrist. "Mama said it's silly. You ever had candied corn?"

Dana's words struck him. The beauty of stars…light that could only be seen with darkness. Just like the Illuminate and the Shadow. Two halves of a whole. He'd never seen it like that, and it took a talkative child going off about candy to bring it to his attention.

That's when Dana screamed.

Her grip on him jerked him to the side. He only had a split second to react and reached out for her as she was torn away from him and into the crowd behind a fluttering blue scarf.

"Cole—"

The cry was cut off.

"Dana!"

No one else seemed to realize that a child had been taken among them. Cole ran through the crowd, shoving through, desperate to catch a glimpse of the blue scarf. "Dana!"

And then he saw it, slim between the two closely placed border buildings. Cole didn't hesitate, tearing after them. He burst into the thin alleyway, seeing the captor to clearly be a bulkier man, his face scarred and unshaken.

The man removed his hand from Dana's mouth and went for his pistol. Dana screamed. The man shot. Cole flung himself to the ground, whipping out the Illuminate.

Another gunshot. Cole deflected, his heart now hammering, glaring hard at the man. Without warning, the Blade went up in flames. Cole didn't flinch.

The bandit didn't take any more chances, dragging Dana behind him, turning around the corner. Cole charged after him, skidding around the corner to find the bandit climbing up a thin ladder bolted to the side of one of the brick buildings.

Cole scrambled to follow, but the bandit reached the windowsill first, and with a shove, Dana landed inside with a thump. The bandit, breathless, hurried to unhinge the ladder. It bent back, peeling off the wall, forcing Cole to drop down and roll out of the way as it crashed down. The bandit disappeared from the window, shutting it.

This was not how Cole was ending it.

He scanned the alleyway. Wall opposite the window held another ladder. The gap between wasn't too big.

He began to climb. He couldn't believe himself. He was officially diagnosed with Tabitha Delorous Syndrome on many levels.

He reached the window at the end, taking a deep breath and examining the gap between.

Ready, Johnson? No? Good.

He jumped, sending his body shattering through the glass, hitting the floor with a crash. He groaned, picking himself up to find an empty, concrete floor. He blinked a few times, his vision steadying. He spotted a grated stairway descending from a hole cut neatly in the stone. The building seemed to have been long abandoned for functional use.

He sheathed the Blade, creeping to the chairs, a shiver running down his spine as he heard the echoes of the floor below.

"—think that was a good idea?"

"I wasn't expecting *that* kid to follow me!"

If only he had the Medallion, he could go invisible and end this right now. He eased his Comm out of his pocket, slowly scrolling through his contacts.

"You have a new task to make up for this mess. The commission will not be compromised. And finish this one right!"

Commission? Could there be more kidnappings occuring…planned?

"But man—"

"I'm not taking excuses! We have ten at max!"

Cole's heart leapt, hitting send on his message. He heard the rustling and shuffling below. They were evacuating. If they got out, Dana was gone.

A pair of footsteps stormed off, and Cole took advantage of the noise to fly down the steps, ducking behind a table.

This level's windows were barred shut with planks and were dimly lit by yellow, tinted lanterns. A few fold-up tables were set here and there, mostly occupied with empty beer bottles and food wrappers, shoved aside for an occasional rusty projector. Wood, created cages stood along the wall. Most were empty, but a few held silhouettes of speechless victims cold and stunned in their new, little, confined space.

The blue-scarf man had a grip on Dana's arm and, with a jerk, tossed her in, where she instantly began to scream.

"Shut up, kid!"

Dana did not shut up. If anything, she got louder. The

man scowled, storming back toward her. Cole's heart seized in his chest. A figure jumped out in front of Dana, snarling right back at the man through the wooden bars.

The boy from the street fight. He was alive.

"I said stop—"

Cole slipped out from under the table, grabbing a bottle, and, in a fell swoop, crashed it against the back of the man's head. The man crumpled to the ground.

The feral-looking boy stared back at Cole, his cat-like eyes thinning in surprise. Dana's screaming ceased, joy lifting in her face before the boy rushed to slam a hand over her mouth and signaled her to be quiet.

They only had a matter of moments before the other guy came storming back in. Cole unsheathed the Illuminate, smashing a board clean off. The boy hesitated, watching Cole with suspicion in his glowing eyes before slinking out, Dana close behind.

The half-dozen begging eyes stared at him from around the room. Where had they all come from? The Market didn't legalize this. They had gone for a Marketeer child from right under the Market's nose.

The boy froze. Footsteps clambered up the downstairs steps. Cole grabbed Dana's hand and the boy by the shoulder, running to the dark corner between the far wall and an empty crate.

"Get the bait, and send Jerimonc to Imperial *now*. I shouldn't have to repeat myself! We can't let the situation get in the way!"

Hesitance. "Yes, sir."

Cole steadied himself, sword in hands, Dana cowering behind him. The boy tightened his fists, sliding to a crouching stance.

"What happened to Crute?!"

"Looks like he broke a bottle."

"That doesn't explain why he's knocked out!" The man groaned. "We don't have time for this—the boy's gotten out! The bait's escaped."

A shimmer sparked in the boy's eyes, a wicked smile growing on his lips as he watched his captors explode into panic.

"Where is he?" A loud *slap!*

The boy didn't even wait for them to look. He leapt from hiding, landing with perfect precision onto the table, tackling the man to the ground. Every punch was driven with power in his slim body, precise and accounted, hardly caught by the bandit's sloppy blows.

"Dana, get upstairs!" Cole shouted, running out. Dana obeyed, rushing for the stairs. Two bandits called after her, charging for the steps. Cole cried out, racing for him.

They removed their pistols.

Great. Another sword versus gun fight.

A shot fired. Cole dodged, rushing head on. The sword ignited. One man cried out in terror as Cole swiped for his hand, the pistol bursing. The other drew out a knife, dodging Cole's wide strike.

Dana screamed. Cole whirled around. "Dana, go—ah!"

Glass shattered. Pain exploded into his ankle. Cole was shoved face down into the floor. He slammed down, quickly rolling over and scrambling for his Blade. The bandit toppled on top of him, seizing his hair and holding him down to the ground. Cole fought and thrashed against him.

Just a little…farther.

Pain tore down the left side of his face. He couldn't bite down a cry, feeling the burning, cold blade pierce through his ear. He jerked to the side, trying to feel the rip. He grasped the hilt, swinging upward for his attacker, who toppled back, his knife tearing through Cole's ear till it was free and bathed in blood.

Cole's ears rang. He swiped, grazing the man's chest. The other was unconscious now, a happy-looking boy prowling nearby. Cole flipped the bloody knife from the sole bandit's hand with his Blade. The bandit's eyes widened with horror, beginning to turn to run. Cole caught his collar, slamming him up against the wooden cage, Illuminate to his neck.

"Don't kill me!" The man pleaded. "I—I'll give you whatever you wanna know! Don't let the savage kill me!"

"I want *this* to stop!"

"Chivalrous, eh?" the man joked between terrified breaths. Cole pushed the Blade closer.

"When is this commission happening?" a new voice thundered.

Cole glanced to his side, surprised to see the boy

glowering at the man with bared teeth.

"Fourteen days' time! 24.00!" the man cried.

"Where?" Cole said.

"You think I know?"

The boy snarled.

"Somewhere in the Dome probably!"

"What about the bandits heading to Imperial?" Cole said, remembering overhearing the conversation about not letting this situation get in the way. "What are they doing?"

The bandit froze. "They're—they're transporting an—an item…with—with intentions to dispose of a—a disruptor to the commission."

"Who?" the boy shouted.

The bandit's eyes met Cole's, his pupils narrowing in horror as he breathlessly choked out: "You."

Cole faltered. How could they dispose of him in Imperial?

"Kill him," the boy growled.

Cole's blood went cold. Doran's voice taunted him with the same command.

But I'm not a killer.

"Johnson!"

Relief flooded over Cole. "Echo!"

The Mater rushed down the steps, a large legion of armed Marketeers following after her. "We found a little girl upstairs and a group of bandits in the alleyway. They looked pretty beat up. I was worried."

"Dana." Cole gasped. "Is she safe?"

"She's outside," Echo said, scanning the room, her eyes settling on the boy before turning to her company. "Free the rest, take these into custody."

Cole staggered back from the bandit, the Marketeers rushing forward. He nearly toppled over to Echo.

"Ma'am?"

Echo and Cole turned to a Marketeer leaning over an unconscious bandit.

"What?"

"This one's dead."

Cole's eyes widened at the boy, who stared with no remorse, sitting promptly on the table.

"What is your name?" Echo said, her voice becoming

gentle.

"You wouldn't understand it."

Another language, perhaps? Though, Cole couldn't imagine a name being restricted by that barrier.

Echo raised a brow with a slow nod. "Perhaps we can help you. You'll be escorted to the Market."

"No!" the boy said. "I don't belong there."

"Where do you belong, then?" Echo said.

The boy opened his mouth. For a long moment, nothing came out. He shut it again. "Fine."

A Marketeer led the boy with no name out and a safe distance away.

Echo now spun with her full attention to Cole. She cringed, reaching for Cole's ear. He'd nearly forgotten about it in the rush, flinching in pain.

"That's a nasty wound," she said softly.

"There's only some ringing, but it's okay." Cole shrugged, sheathing his sword, his hands still vibrating with the adrenaline. He wiped the blood from his hands off onto his pants.

"That's not what I meant, child. He took a decent portion off."

Now Cole's nerves caught up with him, his heart running into his chest. He'd lost part of his actual ear?

And he totally missed training. "Doran's going to kill me."

"You don't have to worry about Doran," Echo said with a shallow chuckle. "This is a matter of Cecileo's level."

The very top.

Cole was speechless. What had he gotten himself into? A no doubt further kidnapping commission happening in ten days. He couldn't let it happen. And now, the bandits were transporting an item to Imperial, of all places, in an attempt to destroy *him* for messing with it? It didn't make—

Cole's heart skipped a beat. An item. An item related to him. *Stolen* from him.

The Medallion.

The Medallion had a history before Cole. A history connected to him. A legacy he was protecting. The Outowns.

"No." He couldn't breathe.

Echo frowned. "What? Are you all right? Do I need to

call a Medic?"

Cole turned on Echo. "Did any of the bandits you encountered get away?"

Echo frowned. "One managed to scale a wall," she admitted. "His arm was injured, and I sent a team after him. He couldn't get far—"

"No." Cole shook his head. "It's already too late. He's on his way to Imperial."

22

Kennedy, 15 Days Until

MERCY HADN'T COME to wake Ray up, and he knew that he'd slept in. He had lain there in the dark, waiting to hear her storming feet, trying to think of anything but his little sister. He was helpless. Thousands of miles away while she was in the hands of the very monsters who had created him. Ten minutes passed. Then twenty.

In fact, the entire day, Mercy was distant.

She gave him plates to take out and instructed him to do his regular duties, but nothing past that. At 8.00, she simply slunk away to her room with a click of the lock behind her.

Twenty-four hours of peace had been torture.

Ray was up early. He hadn't been able to sleep, anyway. Really. The lack of drama was killing him. He'd already spammed their group chat to oblivion about the creepy revelation about the Exerticus being literal magical zombies. How fun.

He grabbed his denim jacket from the pile, not bothering

to tie his boots as he opened his door.

"You're up early."

Ray jumped, swiveling around to Mercy, a basket of laundry in her hands.

"Disappointed?"

She deadpanned at him. "What do you want me to say? Annoying, talks too—"

"Okay, okay! Never mind!" he said, waving her words away dramatically.

She rolled her eyes, shifting the basket in her arms.

"Let me help you with that," Ray said.

Mercy hesitated, looking from the basket to Ray before handing it over to him. "Thanks?"

"What?" He laughed. "Didn't think I had chivalry in me?"

"I didn't know you knew what a word like that meant," she said with the crack of a smile, gracefully moving past him down the hall and down the staircase.

He followed her, careful not to fall and slip with the load in his arms. "You underestimate me, Remembrance."

"Do I, now?"

"There's plenty you don't know about my charming personality."

She raised a brow, pushing the door to the kitchen open, letting Ray in. "If it's any 'better' than what you already got, I think I'll pass."

Ray gasped, slamming the basket down onto the washing machine. "How dare you, ma'am?"

"I dare to do a lot of things, Mathews." She crossed her arms on her hips with the smallest teasing smile on her lips.

"Then will you dare to go with me to the research center?"

Mercy's smile dropped, her lips parting, breathless for a moment.

Ray knew that he'd screwed it up. *Stupid.*

"Smooth," she stammered, evening her speech with a deep breath.

"Look, Me—Remembrance," Ray said, flexing his hands, trying to shove together a semblance of an argument. "If we find out when this night takes *place*, it's as simple as that. We found our date, and we've basically found your dad."

To Ray's shock, Mercy nodded. "I know. That's why I'm going."

"Wait, wait, you're what?" Ray gaped.

Mercy shrugged, digging through the basket and dumping it into the machine. "It's just one time, right? It won't hurt."

He couldn't believe what he was hearing. He couldn't stop a smile. "Yes! I mean, you're totally right. It'll be real quick. In and out. We find out what we need to know, and get out."

Mercy nodded, quickly rushing from the machine. Ray shut the machine door, following after her. She jumped up onto the kitchen counter, opening the cupboard above the oven vent. His eyes widened, seeing her draw out the golden key hanging on a crimson ribbon.

She spotted his stunned gaze. "Don't get too excited, Mathews. I change its hiding spot every few days." She jumped down, pointing it at him like a blade. "I don't take risks."

He held his hands out in surrender. "I've noticed."

Mercy rolled her eyes, jumping down. "I just need to grab something, and then we'll be good to go *after* the shift, you hear me?"

"Loud and clear!" Ray rushed after her through the back door.

He tried to act nonchalant as Mercy wrestled the key into the keyhole. Mercy pushed the door open, the sweet aroma of the room filling Ray's senses as he stepped inside after her.

The large, leather book still sat on the desk, untouched.

Mercy opened the closet, boxes and tupperware shoved in every cranny. She muttered something under her breath, throwing a few aside and digging through. Ray's eyes darted to the book again.

Take it.

He shook away the thought. He couldn't deliberately betray Mercy's trust. Not when they were so close to getting an answer about something. He needed something easier.

He willed his mind to tug on the handle of the desk drawer. It didn't budge. Weird. It was locked.

Ray's eyes glanced back to the book. "The moon

cycles…They are important to your grandma?" He stepped slowly back from Mercy.

"She studies them," Mercy said, her upper half buried in the closet. "She thinks it has to do with our family legacy or something."

"Cool." Ray turned on his heel, holding his breath as he leaned forward to the desk. He twitched his fingers, willing the energy through them. The book shifted forward.

Bang!

Ray whirled around. Mercy was still in the closet.

"You good?"

"Hit my head. Aha! I see it!"

Ray swiveled around to the book, forcing it to fly into his hands. The cool, leather book was against his fingers. The pages stuck out unevenly and were yellowed at the edges.

He was running out of time. He gripped the book tightly, imagining his room to every little detail over and over and over and over—

"Uh, what are you doing?"

The book snapped from Ray's sight. He turned around on his heel, crossing his arms. "What? Me? Nothing. Just looking at the moon cycle stuff."

She frowned at him.

He held his breath, praying that she wouldn't notice the empty desk behind him.

She, instead, turned her attention to the shoebox in her hands. She took off the lid, removing an envelope from it. She slipped it into one of the many pockets of her cargo pants and tucked the box back.

"What was that?"

She closed the closet door. "None of your business, moon boy. Come on, let's get the shift over with."

Ray was more than happy to call the shift over, bounding out of the kitchen, his hands still wet from the dishes. He wiped them off on his jacket, rushing to Mercy scrubbing a dirty table top. "Come on, Remembrance!"

"I'm not—"

He tore the washcloth from her hand, quickly wiping down the table and tossing it into the bucket on the floor. "Now?"

She stared at him a moment before sighing. "Fine. We're ready. Now stop acting like it's Holiday or something."

"Oh, no, Remembrance, this wins by *far*."

Ray rushed to open the door, Mercy grabbing her coat and bag, seeming to take extra long on purpose. He tapped his foot impatiently.

"Probably the first person I've ever heard choose a research center over Holiday," she laughed, zipping up her coat.

The two left quickly down the steps.

Ray opened his Comm, quickly pulling up the nearest SpeedRail station. Not too far. A ten-minute walk. "Holiday was never fun for me, anyway."

She raised a brow at him. "Why's that, Mathews?"

Ray shrugged. "It was kinda just a normal day. My mom has to work, and my siblings try to make it fun, but it's always eh."

"Sounds rough," Mercy said with a surprising amount of sincerity, no matter how forced.

"It isn't really. Just never got the hype." He looked to her. "You know, I never thought *you* to be the type."

Mercy flustered. "What? Me?"

"Yeah, got a epic Holiday story for us?"

Her blush turned to a disapproving sigh. "No, not really. I enjoy it, though. The motel is closed…and I get to see people. Like Mechanic, the Nakusaks, and—and more."

Your dad, Ray was tempted to say, but he left it.

"We get a lot of snow here," Mercy continued tentatively, her eyes at her quickly moving feet. "When I was younger, we'd go to the small reservoir nearby just to play in it. There was a lake too that he tried teaching me to slide on." She snorted, a smile appearing for a split second. "But that was years ago. I can't afford to go that far anymore."

Ray's heart fell, just like the hope that seemed to spark in Mercy's face. He almost felt a pang of jealousy…and then, his thoughts turned. Who'd taken that from her? What changed to make Mercy so shut away?

They finally reached the SpeedRail station. It was hardly as large as the one in North Cordell and half as empty, but Mercy's entire demeanor went cold as soon as they stepped through the door. Ray gently nudged her forward, speaking for their tickets as she hurried to pay.

They chose a seat farthest from the door. Mercy squeezed herself in a corner, trying to hide herself behind Ray. Her height didn't help, but Ray pretended not to notice, or care, scrolling through his Comm.

The SpeedRail trip was relatively quick on Ray's standards, but as soon as they came to a hauling stop and walked out the door, Mercy gasped for air as if she hadn't breathed the entire time.

She shook herself off, swallowing hard.

"You good there, Remembrance?"

She gave a queasy smile. "Never been better. Now, can we hurry up and get this over with?"

He caught himself reaching for her. He snapped himself back. He couldn't comfort her. She'd probably punch him square in the face. He just had to settle for a quick grin. "Yes, of course, your highness."

The two raced up the steps out of the station, and Ray pushed his way out the glass door into the biting, cold streets of the outer Sycamore town. The sun was already tinting to yellow as the afternoon dragged on. The buildings were thinned out and mostly made of plaster and brick. There were no sidewalks, only a run-down road and a few sparse trees scattered through the fields that stuck up everywhere a building wasn't.

It was lonely, but it felt good to breathe.

Mercy stepped out beside him, her brows pinched. "Where do we go next?"

"It looks like they're off a branch of a dirt road," Ray said. He frowned, zooming into his Comm. Was that right? The red circle floated above it. It had to be.

Mercy leaned over his shoulder. "All right, then. I'll get there first."

"Hey, wait, what—?"

Mercy didn't wait. She broke out into a run, leaving Ray scrambling after her.

"I don't like races!" he shouted pathetically after her.

Why run when you can teleport? He snorted.

It wasn't hard to find the dirt road. There wasn't much else to find.

Ray spotted the large facility, which gleamed in the

setting sun. It was the only steel government-issued building seen in the town, and it sat proudly tucked away in the long, grass fields.

Mercy reached it first, giving him an unappreciated triumphant gesture, and Ray was still left halfway up the driveway, cursing her.

He reached her and said, panting, "Warning next time, Remembrance?"

She tossed her hair. "I *did* warn you," she said, turning on her heel to face the door at the top of the steps.

The entire building was the familiar, weather-beaten steel. The door was a dark-stained wood with a curious, golden knocker screwed into it.

Mercy and Ray exchanged glances.

"This was your idea. You do it."

Ray frowned at her. "What?"

"Don't argue with me," she said, hurrying to shove him forward.

He caught himself before colliding with the door. He staggered for a moment before taking a sharp breath and grabbing the knocker. The knocker opened, a camera pushing out.

Ray's heart leapt as it scanned over him.

"One moment!" a shrill voice broke out from inside. A thud followed.

Mercy cringed, her brow raising as she glanced at Ray. He could only step back and shrug.

The door flew open. A late-middle-aged woman stood in the door, wiping her face with a red towel, wearing a pair of thick-lensed goggles and a long, whte trench coat…that was tinted brown and probably in need of a wash.

She frowned through her goggles, pushing them up from her eyes and setting them into her thick, curly, red-tinted hair. "We weren't expecting a school trip this late, were we, Claire?"

"A what now?" another female voice cried out from behind her.

"We're not a school trip," Ray said.

"Tootega Nakasuk sent us," Mercy said quietly, stepping out from behind Ray. She kept her gaze down and firmly pulled her sleeves down to cover her exposed skin on her wrists.

"The last time that lady came around, she *stole* a tire!" Another woman pushed through from behind the other. She looked only slightly younger, the same goggles and jacket, yet this one was decorated in colorful pins. She had blond hair that was pulled in a tight ponytail perfectly, and her nose was smudged with soot.

Ray looked to Mercy, preparing to run.

"Tootega is a friend of ours," the red-haired one said with a long sigh. "The tire was part of a joke."

"An expensive joke," the other grumbled.

"If she sent you *here*, it must really be something."

Mercy and Ray exchanged glances.

Ray nodded. "It's important."

"Well, then come inside," the red-haired woman said, ushering them inside the tight entryway, closing the door behind them. "Call me 'Trinity,' and we'll get to business. This is Claire—"

"No Claire." The woman plopped her goggles back over her eyes. "It's 'Sader' to the children."

"It's not a field trip. They're from *Tootega*."

"Yeah? Your point is…?"

Trinity sighed, turning back to Ray and Mercy. "And who would you be?"

"I'm Ray…Johnson, and this is"—Mercy's eyes widened in panic, freezing up—"Marian…Giles."

Ray tried not to laugh, imagining the pompous, redheaded Defender next to Mercy.

Mercy just quickly nodded in approval. "Y—yes, that's me."

"Well, then, Mr. Johnson and Miss Giles," Sader said. "What can we do for you?"

"Uh…a night," Mercy started. "Where words had power and—and it was dark."

Ray quickly took over. "The night in Sycamore folk legend. Apparently, the night went entirely black, and using the power of words, the people were able to escape some sort of evil force to get to safety. We think this date could be important."

Trinity and Sader exchanged glances.

"The Soul Night?" Sader frowned.

Ray's heart leapt. "Yes! That!"

"The official date wouldn't really help you, considering the dates and moon cycles have shifted over the centuries," Trinity said, stroking her chin. "I'm sure, though, looking over the record and with some simple calculations, we can get you an official date as of this year."

"Really?" Mercy's face brightened.

"That's the simplest thing someone could ask about the Soul Night." Sader laughed. She turned to a metal cabinet hanging on the wall, opening the door, rows of goggles hanging on little hooks. She removed two and handed them to Ray and Mercy. "Wear these. The lights are specifically created to enhance the detail of our artifacts and collection. Without them…well, let's just say you might not be seeing great for a few hours."

That was enough motivation for Ray to quickly slip on the goggles that tinted the hall a hued yellow. Mercy did the same, and the two were led down the hall. They turned to a metal door with a red sign melted into the face of it, "WARNING" written boldly on it. Sader pushed through the door.

For a moment, Ray couldn't see anything. Had the goggles not worked? Was he blind now?

Then the room came into focus. Tables were set up everywhere. Neat piles were stacked up on each, either of old-looking possessions, an occasional tablet, or a paper held open by pins. A bot was rolling around, a little brush extended out from its side.

Sader glided over to a large hologram projection, swiping on a keyboard. "It shouldn't take too long," she grumbled.

"So, the Soul Night is real?" Mercy frowned.

Trinity shrugged. "It is known for sure that the sky did indeed go entirely black, and that there was a sort of attack and citizens made their way to safety, but the details are really only known by firsthand witnesses," she said. "But with the recent events, I think it's safe to say it's mostly tall tale."

Ray's heart sank. "Mostly?"

"We can't say for sure." Trinity sighed.

Trinity pulled up a hologram over the table. A curious symbol was portrayed in a photo. At first it only looked like a black blob till Ray saw the subtle spirals branching out from the side, bordering the entire shape as if it were turning. Ray's heart leapt. It was the *exact* symbol in the tapestry image Lincoln had sent him.

Trinity zoomed in on it. "This symbol is commonly connected to the Soul Night since many of the locals claimed it was in prophecy. From texts we've found they're not too far off."

"Where did you manage to find texts that old?" Ray gaped.

Actual texts about the Soul Night? Pre-Earthshaker? That information, freaking prophecies, had to be ancient. All Dow had been able to conjure was a few blurry screenshots of the '*Mors Vis*,' nothing like having a text.

"The Believers were intent on keeping old text, and apparently much of a forgotten history." Trinity sighed. "But their monasteries and followers are quite hidden away. These new, supernaturally growing woods have contained many unseen-before buildings, but not many who enter come out alive, or with much worth considering."

"Why don't you track down the people who *do* have it, then?" Mercy said, slamming her hand on the table. "They attacked Imperial, sent the regions into national crisis!"

Ray cringed, turning his face from Mercy.

"The government believes it needs more strength, not intellect, to solve the crisis," Trinity said sympathetically. "The Agent Aguirres would've agreed with you, though."

The Aguirres? Ray perked up. How much had these people gotten into?

"Lyell Aguirre was publicly confirmed to be a Believer after he died," Trinity said. "It explains why the couple were able to resurface as much history as they did."

"Got it!" Sader shouted, clicking on her keyboard, a machine beginning to print. She glanced over to them. "Not long from now. Quite fortunate, don't you think?"

Mercy and Ray tried to act surprised.

"Nice hilt, kid," Sader said casually.

Ray's heart almost fell out of his rib cage. "W—what?"

She tore a paper from the printer, striding over. "You have a sword in your backpack. Were you not aware?"

Ray tugged on his strap, feeling the hot stares of the room. "Uh…yeah. It was a…uh…gift."

"Real fancy replica of a legendary Blade or…?" Sader gave him a suspicious look as she handed Mercy the paper.

"*What?*" Ray said, with a fake laugh. "Legendary blade what now?"

"Now that Claire mentions it, it kinda does look like the Shadow Blade."

"A shadow blade? What is it with people and the word 'shadow?'" Mercy groaned. "I've said it before and I'll say it again: 'shadow' is cheesy."

Were the Shadow Holder member and the Shadow Soul related? Thriving in darkness? Isn't that what he was supposed to do?

He was the opposite of the Illuminate. The light, the good, his brother. He was anything but that. He was a murderer, a monster, and a liar.

His brain felt like it would pound right out of his skull.

"Now that you've given them enough information to make them regret their existence," Sader said, placing a hand on Mercy's and Ray's shoulders, "I think it's time for you to be going. It's getting late."

"Yes," Mercy said. "Thank you so much for all your help."

"Of course, little lady!" Trinity said.

They led them out of the room. Mercy and Ray returned the goggles, and Mercy held the paper close to her chest. Sader opened the door for them. Ray didn't hesitate to hurry out and down the steps into the cold, open air. The sun was setting farther now, the sky glowing pink now through the purple clouds and the open plains.

Mercy thanked them again and stepped out after him. "Mathews!" she cried, nearly laughing, running after him down the sidewalk. "The Night! It's in fourteen days! We did it! We're going to find my dad!"

Before Ray could even process what was happening, Mercy collided into him. She wrapped her arms around him and *hugged* him. He didn't hesitate to hug her back.

He wanted to. He wanted to hold her tightly. He wanted to feel elated and thrilled for her. He wanted her to be happy.

In that moment, he almost forgot the real reason he was there. He was here to trick her into getting information.

He stepped back. *You are lying to her. Straight to her face.* He forced a smile. "I know. I told you we would."

She laughed a giddy, uncontrolled laugh. It warmed Ray's chest.

"This is incredible!" she shouted, like it didn't matter for once who heard her. "Race me, Mathews?"

He groaned. "I hate running!"

"Too bad!"

He couldn't be angry as she ran into the field. He chased after her, not caring as the grasses stumbled him or how she managed to beat him with grace. Mercy was happy. He'd done something right.

For once, they had some control.

Mercy collapsed in the grass and Ray tripped, sprawling next to her.

"You win," he groaned, face down and laughing.

"You win for effort." She laughed back.

Ray sat back up, looking at the setting sky, the colors tinted yellow in the pink now as they smeared across the sky, meeting land. It was as if they weren't on planet Earth anymore, and he reveled in it.

Mercy sat up, her hair falling from its usually tight ponytail. She froze, scrambling to find her hair tie, only coming up with a snapped-in-half hairband.

"Don't worry about it. Your grandmother isn't here." Ray laughed. "You look good with your hair down."

Mercy blinked at him. "You—I—what?"

His face instantly went red. "I just—ugh—you look fine."

"Oh." She played with the broken tie. "Thank you."

He meant what he said. In the setting sun, her thick curls looked heavenly as they crowned her head, perfectly framing her face.

"I've never seen the sky like this," Mercy breathed. "I've never even been out this late."

"Then it's both of our firsts then, huh?"

Mercy pulled her knees to her chest, looking up at the illuminated sky. Her big, brown, beautiful eyes only glittered more in the sunset's glory.

Ray's heart swelled. "You've had so much stolen from you," he whispered.

Mercy paused, slowly looking to him. "But I've got a little

of it back."

A lump formed in his throat.

They just stared. He couldn't look away from them. Not when there was so much life locked inside those eyes that he'd never seen before. It was the hair, wasn't it?

He almost didn't catch her next words as she pulled the same envelope she'd taken from the office out of her jacket. She held it out to him. "I guess I should've given you your paycheck sooner."

Ray's heart skipped a beat. "My paycheck?"

"You've been working for me, haven't you?" Mercy said, seeming to grow uncomfortable with the moment of unexpected kindness. "It should be enough to cover a SpeedRail ticket back."

Ray paused. Enough money to get back. He could get out of this, back to the Council. Ditch whatever weirdness was here and let someone *else* come investigate Mercy potentially being a Member.

"It's okay. I don't need a SpeedRail ticket yet."

He still took the envelope. Who was he to pass up money?

Mercy gave the smallest breath of relief.

He grabbed his backpack, unzipping the front pocket and pulling out his purchase from the farmer's market.

"Look, I bought this on a whim at the farmer's market," he said, holding it out to her.

Mercy's eyes widened.

"But I think you should have it…just in case," he said.

Mercy took it hesitantly. She ran her fingers over the wood, her brows raising gently, her lips pursing. "It's very nice."

"Yeah. No pressure to wear it. It's just a thing I—"

Mercy shut him up, slipping it around her neck. "Of course I am, stupid."

She looked down at it admirably while Ray couldn't help but look at the nasty, blinking thumb rings and anklets. The things that trapped her.

She deserved freedom. He knew that they were keeping her captive.

Remember the mission. You're a monster. Complete the mission.

But Mercy needed help, no matter how independent and

self-reliant she was. She was strong. She was relentless. But she was trapped. And she needed someone to free her.

23

North Cordell, 15 Days Until

LINCOLN WAS ABOUT to break Dow's biggest rule, and he was trying not to be obvious about it. With this Soul Night Ray spoke about so fast approaching, he needed to get to Dr. Mathews for an update.

The problem? The doctor hadn't been to camp once.

Lawrence leaned over the table, half-blocking Lincoln's view from his scroll that was laid flat, Ray's message pasted to the side and the symbol from the tapestry on another.

"So we're going with that"—Lawrence pointed to the symbol, looking up, confused, at Lincoln—"stands for our mysterious Shadow Soul?"

Lincoln rubbed his arm, his brows pressed in thought. "Every piece of evidence points to it," he said. "Have you heard of the Soul Night before, Jack?"

Jack paused, halfway through chewing on a mouthful of noodles from his box. He hurriedly swallowed, coughing. "Not really. I mean, I've *heard* of it, but only from Kennedy

226

local Defenders who liked the legend. I never thought it'd become relevant."

"I can't believe you guys overlooked this Shadow Soul thing." Lawrence snorted. "It's turning out to be insanely important."

"And impending," Lincoln said. He bit his lip hard. Another reason he needed to get to Dr. Mathews.

"I'm calling the Exerticus are connected for good now," Lawrence said, zooming in on the image on the tapestry. "It can't be a coincidence that the symbol is right on the bloody mountains that we've already linked to them."

"They do seem to be organized and have a clear goal…that's not so clear." Jack sighed. "Nor do we know who this Shadow Soul *is* and what it's going to be doing in ten days."

"Cole is probably the closest possibility we'll get to answer." Lincoln sighed. "He's also close to these red-eyed guys like Ray, he might be able to find out who the Shadow Soul is and what they want."

"And quickly," Jack muttered under his breath.

Lawrence glanced at Lincoln, and Lincoln couldn't help but be empathetic to the frustrated, hard eyes staring at him. He knew exactly what Lawrence was feeling. *Helpless.*

"How's the progress with Matteo going?" Jack asked, seeming to also notice Lawrence's hardened expression.

Lawrence shrugged. "Taryn's list of 'Wingor tips' is pointless," he said. "And Miriam's method scared the crud not out of just him, but Miriam too."

"Then, why don't you teach him?" Jack said, as if it should've been obvious.

Lincoln cleared his throat. "But, no offense, you're a Ywondie and have, like, zero experience in anything Impure as of, like, a month ago."

"I don't think race or Impure gibberish has anything to do with what's holding Matteo back," Lawrence said.

So Lawrence *was* considering doing the training himself.

"The *Cors Vis?*" Lincoln frowned.

"He's insistent it still exists, so maybe it won't be an issue?"

"A lot of maybes."

"Look," Lawrence said, rubbing his temples in

frustration. "It's just a plan. We're not getting anywhere with Matteo, and his essence breaking is apparently insanely important because the longer we wait, the more this *Cors Vis* thing could become an issue."

"All right, all right. I got it." Lincoln plopped down into his spinning chair. "What can I do for you?"

"Can you make a device, like gloves——?"

"To keep you from scarring your hands when you touch fire?" Lincoln jumped in.

"What?" Lawrence frowned, shaking his head. "No, that's not what I—wait, did you?"

Lincoln shrugged. "Been an idea for a while." He'd had a lot of time sitting in the MedTent.

"While that would be cool, I'm thinking gloves that don't have direct contact…for training. That way Matteo doesn't actually have to get hit."

"Isn't that the point of fight training?"

Lawrence sighed for the hundredth time. "I don't think fighting is Matteo's greatest weakness. It's what it causes him to spiral into. If we could just give him a better understanding…" Lawrence's words trailed off.

Lincoln picked up the Cube, hitting the projection, pulling out a base file for a glove.

"Is that a model of my hand?" Lawrence frowned, leaning over Lincoln's shoulder.

"What would give you that idea?" Lincoln faked a laugh, swiping away the hand model.

Lawrence deadpanned at him, holding up his hand with its unique burn scar.

Lincoln cleared his throat. "Moving on. I think I can get that done for you. Just give me a day."

"Awesome," Lawrence said with a small smile. "Thank you…seriously."

Lincoln nodded. "It's not a problem."

It gave him something to do other than let his thoughts eat him alive. He glanced down at his Comm, quickly clearing his throat and jumping to his feet. "I—I should be going." He scrambled to roll up the Scroll and shove it into his bag, grabbing his green jacket off the bench beside him.

"In such a hurry?" Jack frowned.

"I'll be right back!" Lincoln laughed dryly. He spun

around, racing to the tent flap. He broke out into the cold air, strong with the aroma of the storm.

He took a deep breath and ran. His heart beat louder in his ears than usual, a small shiver crawling up his spine, like the smallest spark of energy. It swelled in his chest.

What is your name, child? I have saved her. You owe *me.*

He tried to ignore the echo, counting his breaths as he ran down murky roads.

Tell me your name.

Leave him alone! A new voice shattered the echoes.

It felt like someone had torn the fog from his lungs, gasping for a clean, deep breath.

The lights of the MedTent came into view over the hill.

Lincoln's foot slipped out from under him. With a curse, he came crashing down to the mud below him, tumbling down the road, helplessly clawing at the mud below him. He rolled to a stop.

He groaned, getting to his feet, shaking the mud from his arms. *Too* much energy there. But at least he was here now.

He broke out into the final stride toward the MedTent. He was so close to her.

He slipped into the main lobby. The lobbyist hardly batted an eye as Lincoln passed by, controlling his racing heart as he walked through the dimly lit night hallway. He'd never get used to the eerie silence of it.

"Dr. Mathews?"

He turned into Nikki's hall, her flap closed. The hall was empty.

She was most likely in the room with Nikki…but if he went in there, he was *really* disobeying the Defending Sergeant. But he needed to find the doctor and warn her about the Soul Night.

His heart seized in his chest as he ducked into the room, finding the room empty.

And then he froze.

Nikki was asleep as always, flat on the bed, her machines hooked to her and beating rhythmically. He couldn't believe his eyes, emotion swelling up his chest. He tried to push it down. He stepped slowly toward her.

Her face was relaxed, a scar cascading down the right side of her face, despite it. His eyes heated, but he blinked the tears away. He wouldn't feel. He closed his eyes.

Hey, Nik.

No response.

It's fine. I—I don't even know if you're really there, but I'm still waiting. I'm waiting and hoping you still have your same favorite color…that we didn't break you too much. I'm really sorry, Nik.

He opened his eyes, looking at her. *Is it selfish to say we need you? It is. You're just trying to survive, and I've been sitting here pouting like I even deserve to hear you speak again.*

He looked at her again. No response. It was worth a shot.

He gently brushed her hair from her face and got to his feet. "Please come back soon," he whispered.

He took a deep breath and, despite the crying of every cell of his body, turned to leave.

Beep!

Lincoln's heart leapt. No, not again. Please not again. "Nik!" he cried, rushing to her.

The vitals were rising up and down. He didn't understand it. Was she dying?

His eyes burned. What had he done?

"Nikki, please, no. Please!"

She was still.

He grabbed her hand, squeezing it. "Help!" he shouted. "Someone, she needs—"

The machine's alarms wailed. Lincoln's heart dropped into his stomach.

Her hand squeezed back.

Lincoln froze, unable to breathe. A tear slipped down his cheek.

"N—Nik?

Her hand went slack, his sweat going cold. "Lincoln?" her voice cracked.

"Nikki!" he shouted, not even thinking, just throwing his arms around her, holding back a sob. He held her, her beating heart against his.

"L—Lincoln?" came a small, fragile voice.

Lincoln's heart leapt, beating in his ears. He slowly sat up, fighting the tears. "It's me, Nik."

Her eyes cracked open, her right eye still swollen from the new cut. She stared at him for a long moment, and Lincoln couldn't breathe. She was alive.

Nikki trying to sit up was enough to snap him from his daze. "Nik! No, you're going to hurt yourself."

She shook her head, trying to fight. "Linc." She gasped. "She's coming. She's coming."

He grasped her shaking her hand. "Nik, it's all right. No one's coming. You're safe."

She squeezed his hand, shutting her eyes. "No, she's al—already here," she said, pained tears slipping down her pained face.

Lincoln paused. Was she talking about the person who did this to her? "Who?"

"Ka…ka…" Her voice trailed off. "Everything…so…heavy."

His heart swelled, a lump forming in his throat. "It's all right, Nik." He pushed back the bangs from her sweaty forehead. "Sleep. You can explain later. It's okay."

"Later," she repeated, the word seeming sweet on her lips, her panicked breathing slowing. She weakly brought Linoln's hand up against her burning face and closed her eyes. "S—stay."

"Nik." He paused, gathering his strength. His chest hurt, trying to keep the swelling in it away. He couldn't feel. He had to keep it down to protect her. He couldn't be weak.

But why was he so weak for her? "I—I can't stay. I'll come back. I promise."

"I c—can't go—go back." Nikki pressed her face into his hand, like she'd never let go. "N—not to her."

"You won't," Lincoln assured, wanting nothing more than to gather her back into his arms and never let her go. "I won't let them."

A small beep went off in his pocket.

He heard the nurses running, shouting for someone to call for Dr. Mathews, knowing that in moments he would be torn away from her. He had to hold his breath to keep tears from falling, wiping her own from her cheek with the thumb of his hand.

He slipped out of the room, rushing down the hall before the nurses turned the corner, shouting for support.

He didn't know how to feel. He felt heavy with guilt and elated with relief.

Your relief is selfish. Your mission isn't over. Your name will give

you your power.
But now that Nikki was awake, did he need the power? She was going to be okay—

Will she? Someone messed with her mind. It was all too planned.

What if they came back?

PART THREE

THE NAME

24

Liberty, 15 Days Until

"COLESON JOHNSON!"

Cole didn't hesitate, grabbing his satchel from off the bed. He could hear Doran storming through the dirt street. Cole knew that he should stay and face him, but he didn't have time. People were in danger. Their safety took priority over politics.

Cole ducked out the back flap of the tent, racing through the back way against the wall, seeing flashes of the crowd gathering around his tent. He slipped around the corner, out of the residential street, pulling over the hood of his jacket. He couldn't have much time if he wanted to beat the bandit.

He only had one advantage.

He turned the street into the crowds of tents, his eyes setting on the emerald tent.

Felicity Bentsworth.

He threw the flap open, instantly greeted with a knife to his throat. Cole staggered back, whipping his hood off.

"Giles!" he cried. "It's me!"

Giles faltered, frowning. "What the heck is going on?"

Cole pushed past the Defender to see Felicity curled up in her wheelchair, scrolling on her tele. She perked up, her eyes wide. "Cole, your ear—"

"I know, I don't have time to explain." He knelt beside her, trying to catch his shaky breath. "Felicity, I would never ask this of you unless it was vitally important."

Her brows furrowed, her eyes darting to Giles. "W—what is it? What's going on?"

"I have strong reasons to believe someone is on their way to hurt the Outowns…because of me."

Felicity's jaw fell. "What? Who? Why?"

"I don't have time to explain. I just need the fastest way to Imperial."

Felicity's face was blank before the smallest hint of a sly smile crept onto her lips. She plopped her legs down, speeding to Giles, turning impressively on her wheel to Cole. "I'll get you there."

"You will what now?" Giles said.

"Felicity, no offense, but—" Cole's eyes darted to her legs.

"What? You're saying because I'm bound to this thing, I won't be able to help you?" She glared at him.

"No! I'm just—fine! Let's just hurry!"

The two ran out of the tent, Giles recovering from his shock and dashing after them. "You can't just leave! I'm sworn to watch you!"

"I didn't say you couldn't come!" Felicity called.

Giles, the responsible Defender he was, ended his complaints there.

They reached the exit. Giles quickly entered his guest code, and they made their way out into the street.

"What's your big idea, Liz?" Cole asked, running alongside her. "Is there some sort of high-tech, private Bentsworth Express Rail?"

Felicity laughed.

"I don't like the sound of that," Giles said.

"We're heading in the same direction of the SpeedRail station," Cole said, frowning. What else was there besides an auto ride, which would take them *way* too long?

Giles's eyes widened. "Bentsworth, you better not be thinking what I think you are."

The trio turned onto the next block, the out-of-the-way station standing proudly. Cole gave up trying to understand when Felicity rolled up. Her confident demeanor faltered as she approached security, her face flooding red.

She glanced at Giles, who stepped up for her, not without sending her a disapproving look. He looked to the security in their glass booth. "Bentsworth Inc. access."

Felicity pressed her hand against the sensor pad. The security guard's eyes went wide, their expression frozen in shock.

"I'll take that as a we're clear. Thanks," Giles said, giving Felicity a shove into the station.

She shrieked. "Don't do that."

He dodged her easily. "Remember, no time, Bentsworth."

She glared at Giles and turned for an employee door. Cole stopped in his tracks.

"Come on, Johnson!"

"But I don't think we can—"

The door opened, the light above blinking green.

Cole sighed, jogging after them. "Bentsworth privilege, got it."

Cole burst into the hallway after Giles and Felicity. It seemed like your standard employee shipping ward. Dozens of people in blue polo shirts moved out of the way, confused faces as they tried to make sense of it among themselves.

"Official business! Department certified!" Giles shouted back as they ran through automatic, metal doors.

Giles caught the back of Felicity's chair before she went rolling down the sudden ramp.

Cole's breath caught in his throat.

Before them was the empty wasteland that he knew surrounded most of Liberty, but here was a huge runway, full of autos and flight Carriers sitting through the lot, crates being wheeled in by pounds.

"Felicity." Cole couldn't believe what he was about to say. "We're going to—"

"We're going to fly." Felicity smirked.

All it took was that one second to realize exactly why Felicity and Tabitha were friends.

"Carriers are nearly impossible to get clearance on," Cole said, his stomach churning, staring at the enormous, black machines and their giant wings. Post-Earthshaker flying machines had all been destroyed in hopes of hindering easy access to bombing. Carriers were only introduced in the past century as a luxury means of transport and exclusively for the shipping industry…which the Bentsworths dominated.

"Not when you're the heiress to them."

Right, the anxious girl trapped in a wheelchair was the heiress to the greatest cooperation in all ninety-five regions. And for once, she looked proud of it.

Giles let her slowly wheel down the ramp, slowly approaching a guard in a bright-orange vest.

Her recognition was almost automatic. "Miss Bentsworth?" The guard nearly dropped their Scroll.

Felicity nodded. "Good day. Which one of these flights is heading to Imperial?"

Cole braced himself.

"Carrier #391971 is taking off in ten minutes," the guard said, showing Felicity the Scroll.

Giles and Cole exchanged impressed looks.

"Thank you!" Felicity said cheerily, rolling at full speed toward the Carrier, leaving Giles and Cole to keep up. "In a Carrier, it should take us two times the speed of a Rail."

Perfect. And assuming that the bandit didn't have enough to afford a high-class, direct ride, they'd have plenty of time to warn the Outowns and formulate a plan to intercept them.

The news apparently traveled fast. This time, no questions were asked, the pilot himself escorting Felicity to the flight of steps before seeing the dilemma.

Giles solved the issue quickly, carrying an unpleased Felicity in his arms up the steps and Cole following after them with her folded chair. He caught sight of a running attendant in a red suit as she dashed for the steps.

"A Bentsworth is on this trip?" she asked, out of breath, leaning against the railing.

Cole nodded, unsure of what else to say. "You heard correctly."

That seemed to straighten the attendant, who followed Cole inside.

Despite the Carrier's massive size, the room was small. It made sense, though, considering that it *was* a craft meant for carrying cargo and didn't receive a passenger frequently. The floor was carpeted, and the window had light curtains. The walls had plenty of charging stations, a space for a film projector. White, leather couches were placed around the room, accompanied by small tables. Cole felt starkly out of place as he set down Felicity's wheelchair and awkwardly settled into the seat beside Felicity. He gripped his seat.

"You'll hardly feel anything," Felicity said, noticing his tenseness. "The weirdest part is when they drop the shield. It's all dark for a moment, and then back to normal."

"Oh. Doesn't sound terrible."

Her eyes fell, laughing softly. "That's what I keep telling myself too."

Cole hesitated before offering his hand. Felicity stared at it, surprised. She grasped it, squeezing it hard.

Felicity had been right.

The takeoff wasn't bad. It gave him an odd sensation seeing the world move higher and higher before launching into a riveting speed that he couldn't feel, but could only see. Felicity buried her face against his arm the entire time.

There was a shimmer crawling across the windows, and then it all went black. Cole felt Felicity tense.

The light flew back, the clouds and pen-blue sky racing past them out the windows.

Felicity slowly looked back up and bashfully removed her hands from his. She took her water, taking a long, shaky sip. "Wasn't too bad, right?"

Cole shook his head.

The two sat in silence, only with the sound of an occasional Giles snore. Cole reached to his chest, grasping at the empty space where the Medallion should've been.

Imperial, 14 Days Until

Any sleep Cole had was light, full of vague voices and figures he'd tried so hard to forget. Even pleasant ones were twisted with a simple word. The kind eyes and smile of his father, who now all Cole could see was the stark image of Ray standing before him in disapproval, turning him from the only home he ever had. Echoes of voices as the University students' gossip turned to harsh shouts and disapproval, accusing him of everything he'd done wrong, seeing right through his ruse.

The worst was the image of his mother...or, at least, he thought that it was his mother.

He'd been told that he'd never met her, as she died shortly after he was born, but his memories betrayed him with one vague, blurry image of a woman, her warm hands on his face and gentle eyes fragile with tears.

But now instead of a smile... it was terror.

"Cole!" Felicity shook him. "We're landing!"

Cole opened his eyes, feeling more tired and heavier than before. He sat up, his heart leaping as the sky outside the windows dipped down, the insane skyscrapers appearing through the clouds. Felicity grabbed his arm and Cole gripped the seat.

Giles just watched them, amused, getting to his feet seeming to simply mock them.

Cole could breathe again once the Carrier hit solid ground, the pilot speaking through the speaker: "Should I call an auto, Miss Bentsworth?"

Felicity wiped her shaking, sweaty hand off on her pants. "We should be good."

"You want us to *walk* to the Outowns?" Giles groaned. "An auto would be faster."

Felicity blushed. "I got us this far. No more autos."

Cole didn't argue. He currently owed Felicity everything. If all she wanted was to not ride in an auto, he wasn't going to complain.

He smoothed out his frumpled jerkin, this time volunteering to carry Felicity out, learning that she was unhappy no matter who had to carry her and was happy to get to the ground in her chair.

They left the facility quickly and out into the Imperial streets.

Cole felt a shiver come over him, seeing the streets that he'd one seen covered in the destruction of battle and felt the weight of the world come quickly crashing onto their shoulders. The streets of the infamous city were not as bustling as they used to be, as if the entire city were scarred from the past six months.

Cole ducked his head, praying that no one recognized them.

"We better hurry if we want to get there before dark," Giles muttered, looking up at the dying sky.

"I promise you, I'm only going this slow because not all of us can have wheels," Felicity said dryly.

"You act as though you're an expert already, Bentsworth."

"Seeing how I'll probably be in this for the rest of my life, I might as well begin to be." Felicity looked down at her unmoving legs. "I better get good biceps from this."

Cole laughed. "I'd love to see it."

"Watch Ray's surprise when I can suddenly beat him in an arm wrestle," Felicity said with a laugh back.

"I don't want to miss that."

Cole began to recognize the streets, and soon they were running down the sidewalks to beat the dark.

"How soon do you think the SpeedRail will get here?"

"An hour at the very most!" Felicity called back.

Cole clenched his jaw. Only an hour to formulate a way of attack? He'd work with it.

Finally, the enormous houses became familiar. He spotted the long, winding driveway leading up to the enormous home, which towered with its pillars and tall windows, trimmed with vines…

He didn't wait any longer. He broke out into a full sprint, racing up the path and up the steps, nearly crashing into the door, banging with all his might.

No answer.

His heart hammered. Had the bandits already gotten there? Was he too late?

The moment of horror was shattered when the door creaked open. "Hello, I'm Coleson Johnson. I need to speak with Lud—" Cole stopped frowning at the kid frowning back at him through the door.

"Who's Lud?"

"Who are you?" *Great job, Cole.*

"I'm not supposed to talk to strangers," the kid said, with

a smirk. "But I'm Eleazar. And technically, I'm not supposed to answer the door. But you were banging like a maniac, so I assumed it was—"

"Eleazar Outown!" A shriek came from inside. "Get away from the door right now!"

Eleazar was torn back, the door flying open, a Defender shoving his way to Cole's face, a woman standing behind him, clutching an exasperated Eleazer to her.

"Officer!" Cole heard Giles shout from behind him. "This is official Council affairs! That is the Outown's patronage, Coleson Johnson, and this is Felicity Bentsworth."

"DNA check us if you must," Cole pleaded. "But I have serious reasons to believe this family could be in grave danger."

The Officer paused for a moment, raising his Comm. "Call in security, and the Outowns. Some kid named 'Johnson' is here claiming danger."

He stepped back, ushering them in.

They lined up in the lobby of the manor. The Officer glared hard at them, especially at Giles as he scanned his pin on his jacket.

The woman who clutched Eleazar was very clearly his mother. Same eyes and dark hair. Eleazar's face showed light freckles and a far more fearless stare than his mother.

"I'll escort you back to the parlor safely, Mrs. Outown," the Officer said, ushering the woman toward him. He turned quickly back to the three of them. "Do not move until security arrives."

"I'll make sure of it," Giles said coolly.

The woman stayed close to the Officer as they left, but Eleazar's eyes were still glued on Cole as he disappeared.

Then it struck him. "That was Aaron Outown's son, wasn't it? *The* Eleazar Outown? The son of a Curatrix member?" His jaw fell.

Giles nodded. "Rare sight. I saw him once at my trial completion ceremony when they honored the Team." Giles sighed, lowering his voice. "And that was undeniably his mother, renown Agent Rallie Shi Outown…but I guess she isn't really an Agent or Defender anymore at all."

"Don't talk so loudly," Felicity whispered, her eyes falling.

"There's a reason."

Giles's expression quickly fell, nodding.

Cole frowned. "What reason?"

Felicity raised a brow. "You don't know?"

"She was there when Aaron was murdered," Giles said bluntly.

Cole blinked, guilt striking him wordless.

"She's the reason they got an attacker to interrogate. She killed one and the other unconscious," Felicity said, keeping her voice low.

But Aaron…the fear in her eyes flashed back in his mind. Felicity didn't need to say any more.

Rallie Shi had been too late to save her husband, the father of her son. He'd only heard of the horrible ways that the Curatrix team had been murdered. He couldn't imagine watching it.

Taryn had survived it. Nikki had lived through it. And Rallie…Cole's heart hurt for her.

"Surprised they're back in Imperial," Giles said. "I'd think she'd be too paranoid with the recent attacks."

"Whatever it is, it's not our business," Felicity said, giving Giles a look.

"Coleson!"

The cheery voice of Ann Outown rang through the echoey room. Cole jumped to his feet, meeting the older woman rushing toward him, trying to force a smile even though everything in him felt otherwise.

"Mrs. Outown," he said with a nod. He couldn't deny that she was Miriam's mother with the same round face, sharp features, and dark eyes…but it was still hard for him to remember that she was an immortal protector of an entire supernatural human sect. "Mrs. Outown, I have reason—"

"No harm will come to us on our watch," Miriam's father, Ludwig Outown, grumbled into the room, his hands in his coat pocket. He looked at Cole, his face emotionless as usual, planting himself at his wife's side.

"I don't doubt that, but I don't know if that's all there is to it, sir," Cole said. He had no time to fear this man's glare and power. "Bandits have stolen the Medallion. I thwarted them in a kidnapping scheme, and they meant to come injure my cause. Since you're my patrons…and your son the previous Illuminate, you were my first conclusion."

Another innocent group of people roped into his mess.

"Bandits would be fools to try to attack Imperial, much less our home." Ludwig Outown snorted.

Ann placed a gentle hand against Cole's shoulder. "Your concern is endearing. We'll heighten security. Ludwig, we should have Rallie and Eleazar moved from the city."

Ludwig snapped to a guarding Officer.

Ann looked back to Cole. "I do think your coming to Imperial was on the right track. You and the Medallion have a connection. You're the one who made the announcement during the battle that inspired people to act," Ann said. "Your face is remembered."

"But that doesn't key in to what they're planning unless they're here to hurt Imperial itself." Cole gave an exhausted sigh. He was tired of the confusion. He just wanted answers and the Medallion with Aaron's legacy safely back around his neck.

"Well, now that you're here, that does mess with their plans a bit," Ludwig said.

Cole thought on it a moment. That was their advantage right now. "I need to intercept them," he said, looking up.

"How do you plan on doing that?" Giles frowned.

"They're traveling by Rail, right? So let's station ourselves there. We can take on one person."

Everyone was quiet, looking around at each other before Ludwig said, "Sounds simple, yet plausibly effective. If they manage to make it past you, you have time to warn us to intercept."

"I'll go with him." Giles got to his feet.

"What about me?" Felicity said, her eyes looking around, pleading.

"You'll stay here, where it's safe." Ann gave her a warm smile.

Felicity didn't say anything.

"Felicity, we owe the fact we're even here all to you," Cole said, squeezing her hand. "We'll be back for you. Don't worry."

She forced a small smile. "Just go and save the world already."

Cole and Giles left without much further discussion.

More Defenders had already been unloaded in front of the manor. Giles took a squad auto, definitely speeding past the limit.

At night, Imperial City was incredible…even with its damage. Giant holograms were displayed against glass skyscrapers, and the sidewalks almost seemed busier than when the sun was out, shops alight and prepared for the night's business. The SpeedRails station was also unusually busy, crowds standing outside with bags and suitcases.

Cole began to doubt that his plan was actually going to be that effective. If they were going to find the bandit, it wouldn't be interception.

"We have to search," Cole said, jumping from the auto as soon as Giles rolled to a stop.

Cole burst into the bustling crowd. It was almost as if the world stiffened. He pushed through the door, and slowly, he could feels eyes moving. Comms went aglow in hands. Speakers were blaring run schedules.

He dashed to the giant, holographic display against the concrete wall.

#329 Rail from Isledowle, Arriving 17
#249 Rail from Algery, Arriving 10
#019 Rail from Liberty, Arriving 3

They had three minutes. He found Giles's face across the crowd, nodding in a stern understanding. Rail 019.

Cole ran through the station. People began to move away from him. He heard a woman gasp and clutch her bag as he passed. He slowed, realizing that all eyes were on him.

A man looked from his Comm to Cole. Cole tried not to think of it. Ann had said that he had a reputation in Imperial. That had to be all there was to it.

He jumped down the stairs, reaching the departing platform. He scanned the lined-up arriving Rails.

634.

192.

He found it. Last Rail to the right. 019.

The crowds were loading out. A few caught sight of him, pushing past.

He heard mentions of his name ripple. *Coleson Johnson.*

He broke into the lead, ducking under the plastic rope guarding the Rails, climbing to the other side. The crowd gasped and shouted as he pushed himself up onto the platform forming a circle as he pushed through.

"*Richard Mathews...*"

What? His father's true name now?

A Defender shouted at him, but Cole ignored them, leaping over the barrier and into the track. He could see 019 clearly now. He burst over the other side. The doors must have just opened, this crowd still thick at the exit and not spread throughout the platform.

He scanned around. No Giles. He was on his own.

He dashed for the crowd. It was now or never.

"*Terrorist's son...*"

The crowd peeled from him, Cole shoving his way into the Rail car. All the occupants froze, staring at him, jaws open. Where in the world was the bandit?

He looked out the window. And his stomach flipped.

There at the ticket station was the bandit in a bulky cargo jacket and his blue, silk scarf, glancing around anxiously as the handler counted out the pounds.

Cole unsheathed the Illuminate. The crowd screamed. He ran from the Rail car, pushing through the line. The bandit caught sight of him, tensing, whirling around to the handler, almost ripping the ticket from the startled man's hand.

He wasn't getting away this time.

The bandit was running to the open door of the boarding Rail directly opposite. The crowd's fear came to an advantage. He pushed himself faster. There were only feet between them.

The Iluminate ignited. The bandit leapt onto the boarding door, the Rail already moving.

Cole's sweat went cold. This couldn't be happening. He chased after the slowly accelerating train as it dove into the tunnel. The bandit only watched him snidely as he disappeared into the dark.

Cole couldn't stop now. He needed to chase him.

Board the next flight, or ride. He needed to catch them. His chest burned, clenching his jaw as he turned on his heel back for the ticket booth. The entire line ran back in shouts and screams. He slammed his hand down against the counter.

"Where is he going?" he shouted.

The man stared at him, his face pale as he staggered back. "You're—"

"We don't have time!"

"Glorgory!" the man shrieked, cowering behind his arms. *Glorgory.*

This wasn't about the Medallion at all. Cole felt weak, the Illuminate's flames dissolving. He leaned against the counter, trying to remember how to breathe.

Ray's family lived in Glorgory. *Cole's* family that he'd never met. And they were going to get hurt by the half-brother they never even knew they had.

"Please don't hurt me." The man's tiny voice thrust Cole back into reality.

He stood upright. "I—I'm not going to hurt you," he said, slowly turning. The crowd cowered around him.

"*Out of wedlock…Court Illegia destruction…*"

Cole blinked, the words all piercing themselves in his mind. Words from strangers. Words of things they couldn't possibly know.

He stepped back. What was happening?

Giles tore through the crowd. Cole looked at him, unable to find words. What was there to say?

"No need to crowd around. I'm handling the situation," Giles shouted to the crowd, rushing to grab Cole and drag him out of the mass of people.

"They're going to Glorgory," Cole managed to whisper. *After Ray's family.* That's the only thing they could possibly be going to Glorgory for. The region Cole was born in. The region Ray was raised in. His family.

Why did they have to be so cowardly? Why couldn't they just face him head on?

"We have a lot more to worry about right now," Giles said with a low whistle. "What they already *did* complicated everything."

Cole stopped. "What did they do?"

Giles snorted, turning to him. "Please don't tell me you haven't picked up on it."

"That everyone seems to know more about me…and hate me for some reason?" He could still feel the stares.

"About that." Giles laughed hoarsely. "Johnson, your

entire government files appeared to have been leaked to the net...publically. All the links, past records, relation to an Oquelite, Court Illegia, everything. I think you're about to win for being the quickest person to become the media's most hated subject of interest."

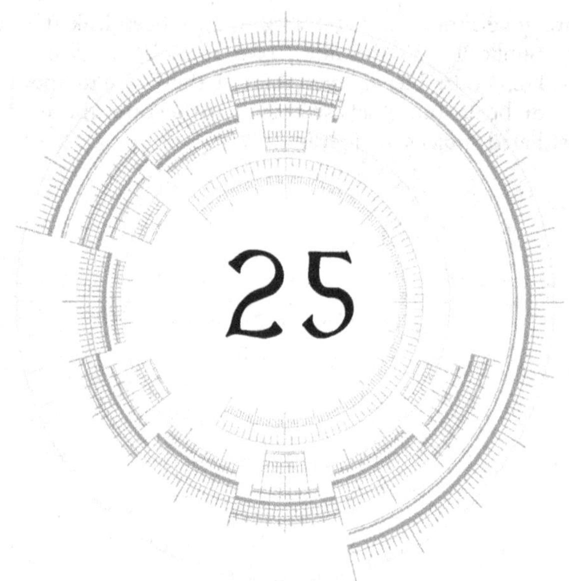

25

Kennedy, 14 Days Until

RAY NEARLY DROPPED his tray the moment he saw Cole's name plastered on the headline of an article.

The customer was absentmindedly scrolling through their Comm and frowned seeing Ray standing, mouth agape, behind her.

He closed his jaw, setting the tray down on the table. "Y—your order."

"Thanks," she said, turning her attention from her and back to her Comm.

Ray tried to read over her shoulder, his mind still reeling. Cole. What had Cole done?

"What are you doing?"

"Sorry." Ray cleared his throat. "Just…cool article."

"Creepy," the woman grumbled. "Yeah, some kid from the Imperial attack's file got leaked by some guy. M.E.D.I.A. picked it up, like, as soon as it dropped. Been trending for, like, an hour."

He hadn't even touched his Comm in the past few minutes. *Don't panic.*

"So, uh, the net is vibing with some guy's *private* records?" Ray said, not feeling up to mustering any sort of enthusiasm.

The woman laughed dryly, picking up her drink and taking a long sip. "You're cute. They're tearing him to pieces."

Ray faked a laugh back. They were *what*?!

He left the table in a hurry, nervously looking around the room. Nearly everyone was on their Comms.

This was not good.

He ran through the kitchen door.

"You're not done yet." Mercy sighed from the counter.

He ignored her, snatching his Comm from the shelf. His heart skipped a beat seeing the dreaded news notification, just as the woman had said.

Imperial "Savior" Coleson Johnson, File Leaked. Destruction in Court Illegia revealed.

Mercy groaned. "Please don't tell me you aren't into this too. That's the only thing anyone's mentioned since it hit."

"Someone leaked a *file* and you're just bored by it?"

"I don't find it interesting."

"That's not the point!" Ray waved his Comm in the air. "A file was leaked, and not even an hour later, it's been pitched to the biggest MEDIA corps? It's on an official Comm notice. This wasn't an accidental hack, this sounds like reputation sabotage."

Mercy shrugged.

Ray's thumb hovered over the notif.

"Don't bother. I've heard the gist of it," Mercy said with a whistle under her breath. She swiped away an order on the screen. "Golden-region populationists are freaking out because he's an out-of-wedlock birth. They're only freaking out about it because he's a public figure, not because it's oh-so-rare. Others are freaking out about how his dad's one of the literal terrorists who tried to take down Imperial—"

Ray's heart skipped a beat. *His* dad.

"—and that he blew up some building during the Court Illegia attack. A lot of people suspect he's a double agent or something."

Ray was speechless. People were suspecting that *Cole*

could be an Oquelite traitor? He was the one who had actually betrayed his friends. He was the one who had inherited his father's abilities. He was the one who had helped almost destroy Imperial. He was the one that had gone evil mode when Nikki was stabbed.

Cole didn't deserve this. *He* did.

He'd never scrubbed dishes with more outrage. Every passing moment, he itched for the shift and endless pile of dishes to be over. The only thing that calmed him was the thought of the thick book tucked under his dresser, heavy with answers. Once he was done, he would finally have a chance to get somewhere.

Mercy closed up shop early, leaving Ray to himself.

He had set his Comm on the counter behind him, turning every so often in hopes to see the screen light up with a message from Cole. He knew that it was a pointless hope. Ray wouldn't be the first person Cole thought of in a crisis.

He turned off the sink, wringing his wet hands and wiping them off on his shirt. He swiped his hand over the sensor, the lights shutting off. He stood in the lonely hall, the shadows of the trees scattered over the table through the windows.

He took a deep breath, clenching his fists, letting a surge of energy swell around his fingers. If he could just go and use his power as he pleased, he knew that he could accomplish more than just sitting here. He wanted so badly to give into the Voice. But it would suffocate his reason, or what little of it he had left. He'd sworn to himself he'd help Mercy get out, and he intended to keep it.

He ran up the steps quietly and slipped into his room, creeping so as to not creak against the old floorboards. He knelt to the ground, scooping up the old book from under the dresser.

A plethora of paper dumped out onto his lap. *Shoot.*

He desperately scrambled to collect them all into a pile. Maybe he could shove them between random pages and no one would notice.

It appeared to be a journal, the pages yellow and now obviously loose from their binding, the weathered cover scratched with time. He lowered the lights with a thought, holding his breath as he set it out in front of him. He carefully pushed back the cover.

The first page had an old photograph taped onto the bag and, in swirling handwriting, "*NAVAL BOUNTY (Post-EarthShaker 25)*."

"Naval Bounty?" What was it with this family and peculiar names?

Ray turned his attention to the photo of the seemingly normal young man, till Ray noticed a familiar mark crawling up the collar of his shirt and onto his cheek. Another one…just like Mercy. Over three hundred years ago.

He ran his fingers to the red pen scratched at the bottom: "*Waning Gibbous, Defective*".

He frowned. How did a part of the moon cycle make this man defective?

He took a photo with his Comm, turning to flip to the next page when the thickness caught him surprised. It wasn't one page. No, they were *two* pages glued together.

Ray held the book up. The two pages formed a pocket, and inside was tucked another piece of paper. Every single page of the journal was glued in a similar fashion.

That explained the mess he'd made.

Ray unfolded the yellowed page.

"*In the preservation of the Holder bloodline, the Bounty line keeps record and recollection with the effective partnering lines. Having survived the EarthShaker, Naval had a unique circumstance and precise study to ensure that there would never be a time without a Keyper.*

"*The conditions were simple:*

"*They be preserved through his line.*

"*There be no more and no less than one Keyper alive at all times.*

"*Naval was born…*"

Ray lost focus at the infodump of a life story. He sat, dumfounded, staring blankly at the page. He shouldn't have been surprised. They knew that there was a Keyper in Kennedy, and Ray was nearly sure that Mercy was a Member.

But now, he wasn't sure how to feel. This made things so much messier.

This family was terrifying. He flipped to the next page. Naval's daughter, whose birthdate conveniently was the same year as her father's death.

Ray didn't bother reading much, hurriedly flipping

through the others. Every single page had a man or woman with the same marks. The same story of their Keyper parent dying their birth year. And every single one was defective.

"First Quarter, defective."

"New Moon, defective."

"Third Quarter, defective."

"Waning Gibbous, defective."

None of the dates listed overlapped, each dying when their Keyper child was born.

Peculiar.

Ray sped through the pages. The broken spine flopped open to the second-to-last entry. The photo printed was clear and worn with touch, the tape holding it to the page pulled.

The woman's name read clearly as "Glory Faithful." She wore a cheerful smile, unlike the others before her. The mark on her face had a perfect, small curve that almost felt too coincidental with the "Waning Crescent" defective label. Her coiled hair was cut short and tied with a bright-red bandana.

Ray didn't need to turn the page to confirm who he knew Glory was. He still lost his breath seeing the image of a young, smiley, little girl facing the camera, the sleeve of her oversized shirt falling off her shoulder and thick hair too short to be contained. He opened the pocket on top, his sweat going cold finding it empty. Of *all* of the information to be missing.

He glanced nervously to the pile.

He flipped back to the image, feeling the hair on his neck rise as he moved his hand to reveal the name that he knew was coming. The name of the current Keyper.

"Mercy Remembrance."

Ray's eyes fell down the paper, his heart hammering against his chest.

"Full Moon, Effective."

Lucas had been right all along: Mercy was a Council Member.

North Cordell, 14 Days Until

"Bwenah dahs."

Matteo paused, frowning and looking over his shoulder.

"'*Buenos dìas?*'"

Lawrence had been trying to find a segway into telling Matteo about their new training all morning, but after the morning run to town when a group of unruly farm boys made it their mission to tease Matteo for his impulsive attempt to find Jenna and then the fight with guards, Matteo hadn't been in the mood for conversation with anyone.

And those boys almost got fireballs to their faces. Even with healing ribs, Lawrence could've beat them easily.

Lawrence cleared his throat. "That's what I said."

They'd been working on the Inn all morning with Jack. They'd been given a tour of the progress, including the second story, set aside exclusively for the Council, which included two halls, one for the girls and the other for the boys, and a conjoined kitchen and living space. It was small, but it was something that Lawrence hadn't been expecting.

The moment Jack showed him his room, he hadn't been sure how to process it. He hadn't had a room since he was seven.

It was unsurprising that they'd chosen Matteo as his roommate, seeing as he seemed uncomfortable around anyone else, especially now since all he ever heard about was his humiliating run-away. It was the first time Lawrence saw Matteo set down the brush.

Matteo shook his head. "Bwenah dahs," he said in a mocking impression. "Bweh-nohs dee-ahs."

Lawrence repeated after him. It worked.

Matteo simply sighed. "Sí," he said. "Your accent really ruins it."

"I've got time to get better, don't I?" Lawrence snorted.

Matteo's eyes widened in surprise. "You—you want to learn—"

He wasn't given a moment to respond as a chorus of "Cents" screamed into the air. Charles came barreling through the opening doors, sliding off of the Wolf's back, collapsing onto the floor. Both Matteo and Lawrence ran to him.

"Cents!" he shouted as Lawrence picked him up to his feet. "She's awake, Cents! Nikki's awake!"

Lawrence froze. "What?"

"Yeah!" Charles said, practically dancing. "I saw Lincoln.

Some Defenders were—were taking him to the big place and—and I heard them talking about her, Cents!"

"Lincoln?" Lawrence frowned deeper. What was Lincoln doing around Nikki? They were banned from that.

Those stupid Defenders were probably having a meeting about it right now. And, of course, not a soul had bothered to tell him about his family member not being dead.

He turned to Matteo. "I have to go," he said, patting Charles on the head on the way out. "Stay here, Charles! You hear me?! Do not wander off!"

Lawrence tore through the downhill path to the camp. Someone would scold him for coming alone, outside being dangerous with the loose Oquelite, but Lawrence couldn't have cared less.

He broke into the camp, running up the steps of the cabin. "Nikki's awake?"

The door slammed so hard, the weak walls of the cabin shook. Lincoln looked surprisingly relieved to see him. *They're debriefing the situation*, he sent through the telepathic link. *Help.*

It always sent a weird feeling in Lawrence, but not enough to over power his rage. *You saw Nikki?*

It was an accident, I swear!

"Williams, I thought you were supposed to be with Lopez." Taryn frowned.

Nikki's in trouble…or was. I'm sure of it. She seemed scared of a "she," Lincoln continued.

Keep talking, Lawrence said, keeping his face unaffected.

Lawrence stormed into the room. "My *cousin* is awake, and no one's said anything?"

"It's classified," Dow's hologram said.

I'm beginning to think Nikki being awake is classified for a reason. Either because of her information in her head…or because of her last time.

Lawrence could feel the pain in Lincoln's thoughts. "It's my family!" Lawrence turned on Lincoln. They needed to get vocal. "Is she okay?"

Lincoln rose to his feet, ignoring Jack's warning look. "She's speaking. She asked for help, but no one's given me updates, either."

"This information affects your emotions," Sergeant Dow

said, his voice pained. "It's affecting you right now as we speak. I know it's not easy, but we need to focus. We've hardly gotten anywhere with the Wingor."

"Don't look at me," Miriam grumbled, staring at the table.

Lawrence was *working* on that. More than anyone else here.

"Williams, this is final," Dow said. "Don't get yourself in the same boat as Lincoln."

Lawrence snorted.

"Perhaps we'll continue another time, Sergeant Hunter?" Dow said.

Taryn agreed, Dow's hologram shutting off. The group of Defenders rose, trickling out of the cabin accordingly. Lawrence made his way to Lawrene, non-compliance alive in his eyes. Lincoln bred to let himself do the same, but they both knew that they couldn't disobey the Department on such a minor issue.

Taryn sighed from the head of the table, letting her head rest in her hand a moment before looking up. "I have a mission for you."

Lawrence frowned. That came out of nowhere. "You do?"

"Yes," Taryn said, striding over to the two of them, quickly glancing to where the Defenders had left. "I need you to speak to Nikki. About this woman she mentioned."

Lawrence's heart leapt as he exchanged shocked glances with Lincoln. "What?" Lawrence said. "Dow just said we were basically forbidden."

"By the Department, maybe," she said, a glimmer in her eye. "But you're supposed to follow my orders on Council affairs, and I consider this to be one of them. And besides, Williams already has a pass into the HCS due to his ribs."

"You're serious?" Lawrence said. A small smidge of respect grew for Taryn that he didn't want to admit.

"Thank you," Lincoln breathed, looking like he was not believing what he was hearing.

"Report back to me with how she's doing. That's your only condition…and maybe try not to get caught."

Lawrence saluted. "We won't let you down."

Taryn smiled. "I believe that."

Lawrence stopped as soon as they slipped past the check-in and into the hall.

Lincoln looked over his shoulder as soon as the footsteps stopped. Not *now*. They were so close, and this time was actual permission. And now Lawrence was freezing up?

"Lawrence!" Lincoln snapped in a shushed voice.

Lawrence jerked his head back to Lincoln, his eyes darted around quickly. "I—I'll stand guard. Go without me, I'll meet you there."

Lincoln raised a brow. This was unusual for Lawrence. "She's your—"

"She probably wants to see you more than me, anyway," Lawrence said quickly. "Now, go! I'll be there in a moment."

Lincoln swallowed hard, just giving Lawrence a single jerk of a nod. Her voice had opened the NMA files disc, and it sat in his pocket. It belonged to her, but the Voice held him back.

You don't owe her that.

He approached the door, his body slowing down. He was really doing this.

He pulled the flap back. Nikki was asleep.

For a moment, anxiety crawled over him. Had she woken too early? Was she dying again? Had this mysterious woman killed her—?

The vitals breathed some sense into him as they fluctuated up and down with a healthy bounce. He let the flap fall closed, enveloping him in the dark.

He walked slowly to the bed, gently sitting on it. It had almost been two days.

Nikki rustled in her sleep.

Lincoln hesitated. "Nik?"

"Lincoln?" Two tired, blue eyes opened slowly. "Lincoln!" Her voice cracked, the exclamation sending her into a coughing fit. "You—you c—came."

Lincoln flinched, shushing her. "Yes, it's me. Lawrence is here too," he said, his breath caught in his throat as Nikki pushed herself up slowly against her pillow.

"It's okay," she whispered. "They said I'm—I'm getting stronger…My weird blood. Don't cry."

"I'm not—"

Her hand reached his damp cheek.

Lincoln laughed hoarsely, once again fighting the tears. "It's just that…" he choked. "You're alive."

Emotions are for the weak.

"I told you to trust me," she said, grabbing his hand with both of hers, inspecting it.

He grasped her hand in his, feeling the living warmth in them rather than the feverish burn. "You're alive, Nik."

He wasn't here to catch up. He had a mission. But he couldn't stop himself. He'd locked it away too long. She was *alive.*

He hugged her gently, even though everything ached to hold her as tight as she was grasping onto him, lying her head on his shoulder. "I—I missed you so much," she whispered.

"I missed you too, Nik." He finally sat back, not willing for Lawrence to choose that moment to walk in. He tried to calm himself.

"Don't cry," she said, her brows creasing with gentle concern.

He laughed, choking. "I—I'm not."

"You smiled," she said with a small, tired smile of her own.

"Hey, Nikki." Lawrence stepped into the room. He froze, looking as if the air had been knocked from him.

Nikki's eyes lit up. "Lawrence!" She tried to turn to him, but she stopped, her face contorting with pain and grasping her side.

Lawrence rushed to her. "Nik, be careful! You got stabbed."

She groaned, burying her face into her pillow. "I feel it."

Lincoln's heart skipped a beat. "How bad?"

"It's okay," she said, rolling onto her back, taking deep breaths. She looked back to the two of them. "I know you're here for answers."

"And for the girl we thought was dead for two weeks," Lawrence said, taking a seat.

That hit a little close to home.

"They told me you weren't allowed," Nikki said, disappointment falling on her face. "But I assume it must be extra important."

"You might not be in good condition for this," Lincoln

warned, glancing at Lawrence, who didn't look back.

"How did you know you'd be back?" Lawrence asked, his voice wavering.

Nikki hesitated, clenching her blanket. "I didn't. She—she just said was coming for me. I knew I'd have to leave…" Her face grew pained. "I *had* to come back."

"Who is *she?*" Lincoln asked, hoping to get to the point so as to not tire her.

Nikki's eyes drooped, but she forced them open again. "She showed me—me things. So—so many things. I felt it over and over and over…"

"But why? Was what 'she' told you important?" Lawrence asked.

Nikki's eyes shut. "I don't know. To her it was…and any—anything to her that's important…very important."

Well, they knew whom Nikki was talking about.

Lincoln didn't want to press her more. "Nik, you need sleep."

Her eyes shot open. "No," she said. "I—I need to show you."

"You might not have enough energy—"

I said—Nikki's eyes glimmered with a small, weak smile—*let me show you.*

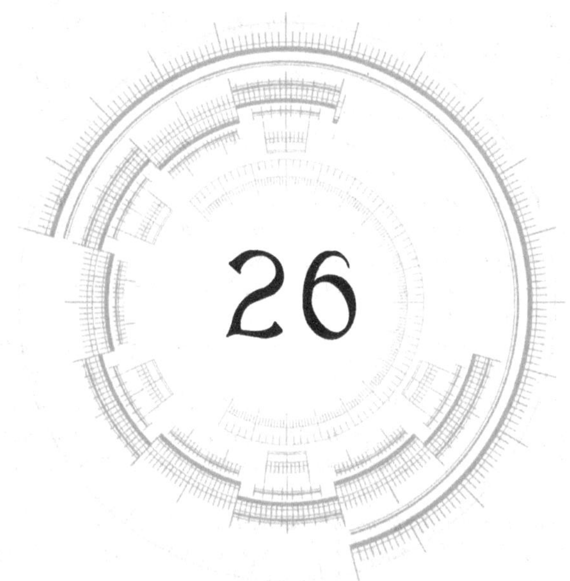

26

The Ewyon Coastal Alliance Palace—Before Recorded Time

WOLVES PROVIDED THE song that cut into her soul as clean as the cold night straight to her lungs. As unknown and unkind as those answers were.

She sat comfortably on the sill of the window, the knife in her hand as she casually twirled it against the stone. A beautiful Sublinight blade. What would it do to her?

"Adrienne, get away from there!"

Adrienne snatched up the knife with a heavy sigh, looking over her shoulder. "Why, dear Sergia? Are you afraid I'll fall?"

"You've had enough injuries to last you a good while now." Sergia snorted, twisting her long, dark hair up into a bun, a pin between her teeth.

"Just an injury?"

He stabbed the pin through her hair. "I don't believe your tall tale," she said, her face softening as she turned to Adrienne. "Don't you have attendance to keep today?"

Adrienne held up the knife, letting the sunlight glint off its clean surface. "That I do."

"Don't keep him waiting," Sergia said. "He might be the only thing keeping you in the court."

Adrienne's face darkened. "You speak of marriage."

Sergia's face fell, looking up with reluctance. "What else?"

Adrienne just laughed, jumping down from her seat at the window, slamming her knife down onto the table. "Humor yourself, dear."

"The Queen hasn't given up on you."

"My aunt hasn't spoken to me in months!" Adrienne grabbed the sheath from the armor.

Sergia sat down on the sofa, watching her with the deep concern that she always held in those dark eyes. "It's better to suspect the best."

"Or prepare for the worst." She sheathed the knife strapped to her thigh, letting her slip fall over it. "No need to lead me to the meeting."

Sergia sighed, getting to her feet, dusting herself. "I'll see you at supper?"

"Of course." Adrienne gave her a smile.

Sergia nodded in return, and the maid promptly swept herself from the room.

Adrienne dressed quickly, tying down her long, blond mane, letting it swing at her waist. Sergia, unbeknownst to Queen Carastene, let Adrienne roam the halls free of supervision.

And in her eighteen years, she'd never been caught.

She went quickly through the empty main hallway, where the one side stood high with the enormous windows, sending sunlight glittering down on the red carpet and glass sculptures that decorated the floors. This wing was hardly part of a guard round this early in the morning, making it ideal.

"You're late." Hadeon stepped out from the shadowy corner, his brilliant, violet eyes dazzling in the sunlit display, though she didn't find herself breathless at the sight of them.

"I'm never late."

"You're meeting Our Highest this morning, I hear."

"Sadly," Adrienne said. "But I believe it is best to seek answers straight out before pursuing…other options."

"Wise and beautiful."

She quickly dodged his lean with an amused scowl. "Did you discover the location of the Shadow Soul?"

He smiled, flashing a brilliant smile. "I know where it's moving as we speak."

"Perfect," Adrienne breathed. She dug the heavy, golden key out of her skirt pocket. "This enters the servant corridor. I will meet you in a fortnight to investigate this."

Hadeon snatched the key eagerly. "You will not regret this, my lady. Finding the Soul will be an incredible mark of nobility. Perhaps the Council will even acknowledge you."

"I don't care for the Council."

Hadeon only took the comment as amusing with a chuckle. "I better be leaving."

She nodded. "Quickly, before your heavy feet give you away."

He winked and dashed to the glass door. She spat, clearing her throat. At least Hadeon had done one thing right. Finding the Soul would be giving her an upper hand.

She spotted Caratene's pen office doors, approaching them to see the Queen painting an uncertain wait as Adrienne stepped inside. "Aunt."

Carastene didn't even bat an eye. "What happened to 'Majesty?'"

"Sorry." She bowed. "Queen Majesty."

"Enough, Adrienne."

"Ah, right," Adrienne said, smothering a smile, leaning on the chair beside her. "I want to know what happened that night."

Her aunt stiffened. "What about it? Your lack of essence to maintain so much as a simple glow?"

Adrienne's face burned. "Why am I not dead?"

"You fell."

"My neck snapped."

"You were unconscious," Carastene said, turning on her heel, her voice fierce, as if she were trying to convince fear into herself. "You were a fool running about to high balconies—"

"Aunt, I am not dead. And according to every eye witness, I should be!"

"Hysteria," the Queen huffed.

"You are hiding answers from me."

"You are a invalid child with no right to speak to me this way!"

Adrienne almost laughed at the blood rushing to her aunt's face. "You won't even tell me my father's name and leave my mother's to echoes of gossip and scorn."

Carastene's jaw clenched. "Silence."

"I demand to see my records."

"And I deny."

"So, you admit you're hiding something?"

Carastene was taken aback for a moment. "I admit you are too *immature and are only further proving my point.”*

Adrienne started back at the outburst. She'd never seen her aunt so out of control with her words. So quick to fear…to anger.

“You do know why I survived. Why I don't have abilities like the rest?”

“Get out,” Carastene growled.

“You know and your niece let me live like a horrible disgrace. Like I might as well be the Shadow Soul.” Adrienne stepped forward. “And we all know how weak you've been in handling that issue.”

She watched fear flicker in her aunt's eyes. “Leave, Adrienne.”

“I am of royal blood. I will not be tossed out and manipulated out of answers—”

Her jaw stopped moving, her lips closing without her consent. Her entire body wouldn't move, not under the heated gaze of the Queen.

“You have no rights,” Carastene sneered. “Guards!”

The doors burst open. Carastene walked slowly around her desk to face her frozen niece with a smile. Adrienne itched to scream and lash out.

The guards rested their hands on her, and her gaze dropped, life flowing back into her limbs.

Adrienne tore away. “I can show myself out.”

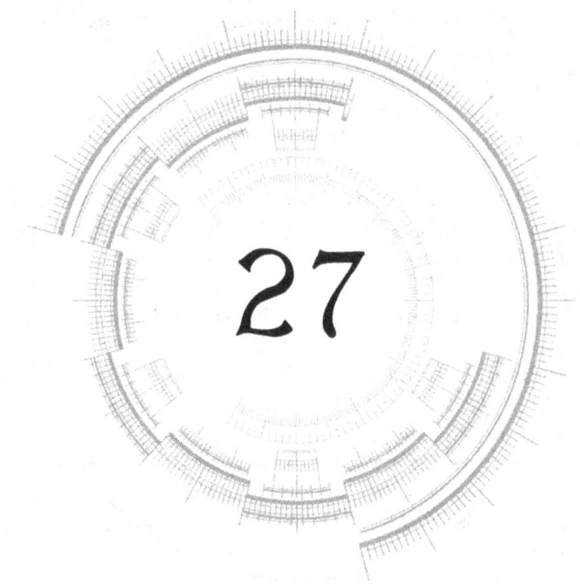

27

Glorgory, 13 Days Until

THE CARRIER RIDE would only be twenty minutes at most, but Cole felt that it was still twenty minutes too late.

Catching a flight hadn't been so easy since they had to go back for Felicity and convince the Outowns to not keep them here. Cole didn't know how long it had been, and that worried him. He couldn't stop pacing, running his hands through his disheveled hair. He didn't know what to do. Everything was falling apart.

Cole sank down into his seat, taking out his Comm, swiping away the news notification.

His eyes first settled on Ray's message. His stomach flipped.

RAY: *Hey are u ok???*

If only he knew where Cole was heading…

COLE: *I'm doing all right. Don't worry about it. Just try to make sure it doesn't affect you.*

Ray, surprisingly, messaged back quickly.

RAY: Don't worry. I've dealt with public scandal before ha
Cole sighed.
COLE: What about your mom? Your siblings?
Ray took a moment before saying, *Us Mathews are durable. And ur one of, u know?*
COLE: I know.
It felt like a lie to type out. Ray proceeded to like the message. As much as Cole longed to speak with his younger brother, he scrolled on.
*ECHO REUDER: 52 unread messages**
Cole's heart skipped a beat. He opened the chat. Most messages were just repeats of his name over and over, demanding his location and where he had run off to. And then there was a change of tone.
He could imagine why.
"It makes sense now," Echo had typed. *"Cole, when you mess with bandits, you mess with people like us Marketeers…but without the moral foundation. They know they're too weak to face you straight on, so they'll use whatever else to make you forfeit. Leaked files aren't uncommon with them. They're just not usually this big."*
Ten minutes
"We haven't known each other long, but long enough to know how you treat yourself. Do not let this crush you. That's exactly what they wanted."
Cole was still for a long moment. For a second, it felt like Echo's word carried even the smallest ounce of the weight. He shouldn't have been running from her.
He typed quickly before he could regret it. *"We're in Glorgory."* He added the address that Ray had given him months ago along with it.
The Marketeers wouldn't get there in time, but maybe if they overcame the bandit, they'd have someone to turn him over to.
A notification pinged.
"The File the Regions Have Been Talking About: Educate Yourself."
Cole froze. He could swipe it away and be rid of it, but the answers nagged at him. Even he hadn't read his private file. It was government information.
So many unanswered questions about himself that he'd never known. But there was only one he'd always really

wanted to know.

He clicked on it, scrolling past the commentary till he reached the end, and a green link for the reader to read the leaked file for themselves sat. It prided itself in being one of the few since the officials had been trying to take it down rapidly.

Cole entered the link, glancing up to check on Giles and Felicity. Giles was busy on a tablet, and Felicity was dozing. Cole turned back to his Comm.

He held his breath as the illegal file loaded before him. It was odd to see an image of himself he'd never seen. It was outdated, from last year during University…before he was expelled by an undercover Oquelite professor.

That was probably another mark against him.

He clicked quickly away to the place labeled, "GUARDIAN." Three names were listed.

Richard Mathews [Pseudonym: Richard Blythe] | Biological Father | File Subject Status: LIVING

Marie Blythe Mathews | Stepmother | File Subject Status: LIVING

Colette Johnson | Biological Mother | File Subject Status: DECEASED

Cole stared at his mother's name, pressing on it, but the link was blocked, her file still protected.

A small body of text was attached below: *According to those interviewed and resources found on the net, the search for Johnson lasted a few months before the case was declared finished. 26-year-old Johnson was officially declared dead when her body, along with a few others, were identified in a river bank not too far from her last sighting and location of a now known terrorist base.*

Cole didn't need to investigate further. He shut off his Comm.

It was final. Oquelite had killed his mother. And he knew the rest of the story. That Oquelite's fear of the Shadow Soul, an Oquelite hybrid, was so great that they'd go to any length to make sure that no possible half-Oquelite would survive.

Cole was the reason his mother had died. Not Ray's. Not his father's. His.

"Cole, you good?"

Felicity's voice caught him off guard, and he spun around

in his seat to face her. "You're awake." He coughed.

"Hard to sleep knowing what's on the line," she said with a hollow laugh.

The two sat in silence.

"So," Felicity said, raising her voice. "How are things with Tabitha *really*?"

Cole's face flamed. "Felicity, right now?"

"We have time."

Coles threw his head back and groaned. "Awful, so it's not worth discussing."

"Please, Cole, I know that's not true." Felicity shifted forward. "This isn't all about the building thing, is it?"

Cole locked eyes with Felicity before falling in shame. "I yelled at her," he said quietly.

Silence.

"Hold up, *you* yelled?"

"Yes! I get that's shocking, and I did it to *Tabitha* of all people!" Cole wanted to groan and melt right where he was. If the Mathewses being in danger wasn't enough, he didn't want to fight all the emotions that raged when Tabitha was brought up. He buried his face in his hands. "I was horrible."

"Did you leave on bad terms?" Felicity's face was pinched.

Cole tried not to let his face show the warm feelings he had about their last encounter. "She gave me a list of things to do."

"Have you done them?" Felicity said, her brows furrowing with force that practically said that if he hadn't, she'd make him do it herself.

"I've been trying," Cole said, thinking of the pathetic song attempts crumpled in the trash files of the notes application on his Comm. "I can't go back to her until I do."

Felicity's face brightened. "So you plan to go back to her?"

Cole frowned at her glee before shaking it away. "I do, and as someone she deserves."

Felicity's smirk dissolved, slowly placing her hand on Cole's. "You really care for her, don't you? You're in love with her."

"I—what? You—I didn't—" He knew that he didn't even have to answer, his bright-red face already saying everything that Felicity was here for.

To his surprise, her face remained lax, a gentle, studying look in her eyes, before she patted Cole's hand again. She turned without a word to her tele, leaving him alone in the deafening silence.

What was that supposed to mean?

He tried to sit back and relax his nerves, but his thoughts were wild. He tried to focus them on how to appeal to Doran and Cecileo once he got back, but they kept drifting back to the one girl he swore that he wouldn't think about. It almost physically hurt with how much he missed her. How much he wanted to run back to Court Illegia and take her up into her arms and apologize all over again.

He squeezed his eyes shut. He couldn't do that. He wasn't ready yet. He needed to keep working. Keep trying. No matter how long it took.

"We've landed!" Giles leapt from his seat, tugging his Defender jacket.

Good. Enough sitting around.

Cole shoved his Comm into his coat pocket.

They rushed from the Carrier. The early morning sky still had not fully risen. Cole wasn't taking any chances this time. He whipped out the Illuminate. "Giles, do you have the location?"

"On it!" Giles broke out into a run. "Bentsworth, if you can't keep up, stay back! This time is too close."

A begrudging Felicity nodded, rolling back on her wheels. "Meet you when you get back."

Cole and Giles wasted no time.

The SpeedRail station was small and the streets of Glorgory uncrowded, though Cole could still sense the horror and surprise of anyone around. From what he could see, Glorgory was as flat as the eye could see, besides its own growth of the supernatural woods far off in the distance. A local rebellion had devastated most of the region, making it a less desirable place to live in, even with the rebellion now thirteen years over.

Cole had been born during that rebellion. Sulfur wasn't his birth region. Glorgory was.

He shook off the thoughts, catching up with Giles. "How much further?"

"We cross into residential streets in a few feet. They're the neighborhood closest to the bordering wasteland." Giles handed Cole the Comm.

The small town was just a small dot in the vast plains, but Cole's entire world had been here at one point. Ray's entire family was here.

They burst down the border, ankles against the grass that flowed over the sidewalk. It wasn't much farther. It made sense now that Lincoln had wandered to it. There wasn't much else to wander to.

"There!" Giles shouted to a lonely neighborhood of spaced out houses. "The third!"

Cole spotted it: a smaller brick house with a basic, white trim beaten by the weather. A small, rickety, black, metal fence guarded it, overgrown with vines in an almost aesthetic manner. To Cole's relief, the gate wasn't locked. He ran up the path, his hair rising on his neck. Had he been here before?

He banged on the door. "Hello?" he shouted. "Is anyone home? You need to get out of there *now*!"

No answer.

"Open up!"

No response.

Cole stepped back, swinging the Illuminate and cutting the security door straight in half. He kicked the red door. It creaked open. He rushed inside. "Hello?"

His voice echoed back.

It smelled oddly familiar too…or was it just Ray?

Giles ran in after him. "The place is too clean to have three kids running around in it." He grunted, opening an empty dishwasher.

"They're not here," Cole breathed, unsure whether to be relieved or worried.

"And haven't been for a while, it seems," Giles said, opening the refrigerator.

"Hey! We're not here to raid them."

"All of this stuff is going bad, anyway." Giles shrugged, shutting it. "Proves my theory."

"At least they're out of harm's way," Cole said, leaning on the hilt of his sword. "But it also gives us an upper hand on the bandit."

"I see what you're thinking, Johnson." Giles smirked. "Ambush. Not a terrible idea."

Cole smiled back. "Take a room. Don't mess anything up. We attack the moment we're clear to trap them."

Giles nodded, surprisingly cooperative.

Giles went for the living room, behind the couch and near the front door. Cole went deeper in the house, slipping into a random room and keeping the door slightly open. With one glance, he could guess which sibling it belonged to. The only Mathews sister…and apparently his half-sister.

Jenna's room was the definition of an attempt. The walls were half-white and half-purple, and he couldn't tell which color was being painted over. A pile of clothes was shoved into a corner, and the bed was half-made. Her desk was closest to the door and cluttered with little, rainbow-colored rubber bands and disregarded tablets, photos taped around the wall.

One made his heart leap. His father.

Jenna had a photo of herself, he guessed, as a baby, who looked hardly two and his—their father.

Why did these faces seem to be haunting him?

He looked away, trying to shake it off. He tried to clear his mind, taking a deep breath, balancing the weight of the Blade in the hilt in his hands. He closed his eyes, listening through the quiet creaks of the house.

Your attempts are pointless.

A sharp scent flooded over him. Cole's eyes flew open. Smoke.

His heart skipped a beat.

He heard Giles cry out. Cole burst from the door. At the door, Giles tackled the bandit down. And to Cole's horror, the wall right behind him exploded in flaming. He was sent sprawling back, slamming against the floor. The bandit must have gone around the back first.

He scrambled to his feet, brandishing his Blade.

The bandit wrestled away from Giles with a deafening gunshot.

Cole's entire mind went blank. "Giles!"

The voice tried to taunt him again, but nothing breached his mind. He ran toward the bandit, who turned for the door. Giles jumped up, knocking the bandit back, picking the gun back up from the ground. The bandit backed away, glancing nervously over his shoulder to Cole.

"Giles! Get out! Let me deal with him!"

Giles opened his mouth to protest. The bandit tore a small, blinking disk from his pocket. Cole's heart leapt, swinging the blade for the bandit's hand that was thrown a second too early. Giles was already out the door as the front wall shook and splintered, engulfed in flames.

The bandit turned around to face Giles with a crude smile, slipping his blue mask up over his nose. "Nowhere to run this time?"

"I could be saying the exact same about you!"

The bandit brandished two long daggers from his sleeves, swiping at Cole. Cole threw back the blow, spinning out of the way of a chunk of the flaming ceiling.

The bandit ran at him with a cry, running and launching himself from the wall. Cole dove out of the way, ducking under the counters as the daggers screeched against it with a blood-curdling scratch. Cole kicked a stool up to his hand, jumping out from under the counter. He threw the stool. It crashed into the bandit, catching him off balance. In the moment of distraction, Cole swept the blade at the hanging light, letting it shatter down onto the bandit. He rushed at him, slamming him against the wall.

Pain spiked into the side of his leg. The bandit still clung to one knife.

Cole grit his teeth, threatening the Illuminate closer to the bandit's neck, kicking the knife from the bandit's grip. A thin, crimson line bled from the bandit's skin.

Cole almost pulled back in shock.

The bandit looked unphased, frozen in place with a snarl on his face.

"Any deeper and I'll kill you." Cole lied, ripping back the man's coat. Cole dug through his pockets, throwing out a few silver pounds and an info drive that made the man squirm. The smoke was threatening to suffocate him.

He still hadn't found what he came for.

The bandit coughed, as if to mock him.

Cole ripped the bandit's thin, worn shirt and, to both his horror and relief, saw the Medallion chained around his neck. He wretched it free.

A crack broke Cole's focus. He looked up.

A beam was split, flames quickly crawling along it.

The bandit took advantage, landing a fist to Cole's face, slamming him onto the floor and holding him down.

Cole struggled against him. "You'll be killed!" Cole cried out, his voice strained by the smoke.

"Act all humble, boy, but we all know what you really are," the bandit said, coughing.

Cole's eyes went back to the beam. At any moment, they were done for.

He kneed the bandit in the chest, thrusting them both through the glass window, shattering into the debris outside.

Cole pushed himself up, his arms trembling. He looked to the bandit, lying a few feet away. He only gave Cole a look of surprise before breaking out into another coughing fit.

Cole staggered back up to his feet, holding the Illuminate out in front of him. He looked up, the Mathews' house roof caving in, engulfed in flames. Walls that had held up memories long forgotten…destroyed.

"Cole!"

Cole spun around to see Echo racing for him. The Illuminate slipped from his hands.

Echo grabbed his shoulders. "You had me worried sick!" she said, shaking him. "And then I come here to this and—" She stopped. "Your leg. It's bleeding."

Cole only looked down at his hands, bleeding from being rubbed raw. "I—I found him," he choked hoarsely, turning to see the bandit still lying in the bushes behind him, Defenders were already arriving.

That was it, then. It was over—

Two forceful arms tore him from Echo.

His heart plummeted. "What?" he shouted, tearing at his scorched throat, pulling away from the Defender.

"He didn't do anything," Echo said, her expression darkening, her hand hovering over her hilt.

The bandit was pulled to his feet, the magnetic handcuffs clamped over his wrists. He sent Cole a pleased smile as he was dragged off.

"And, ma'am, who are you?" the Officer said, glaring at her. "I can take you in too for assisting the arson."

Arson?!

"I didn't set this building on fire!" Cole said. "It belonged to my family!"

"You're only making it worse for yourself, Johnson." The Defender removed the cuffs from his belt. "Don't resist or—"

The Defender dropped to the ground, convulsing with shocks. Echo held her electric blade in her hand. She grabbed Cole. "We leave *now*."

He didn't argue.

They leapt over the fence, dashing out into the streets.

"There!" he heard an Officer shout.

He looked over his shoulder as two leapt into an auto. Cole tugged his Medallion from his jacket and, with his shaking hands, slammed it against the engraved fit in the hilt. In a swift moment, he could feel the roll of invisibility and the momentary thrill of his feet disappearing below him. He grabbed onto Echo.

She didn't seem too fazed, clinging to his arm.

Cole didn't stop till he saw the SpeedRail station on the horizon. Guilt panged in him, realizing that he'd be leaving Giles and Felicity behind. He didn't have enough time to go back for them, or there wouldn't be any going back anywhere ever.

They burst through the front door, the security machine up in sparks. Cole guessed that that was thanks to Echo. She tightened her grip on him, taking the lead full forward toward the loading platform. She led him without hesitation toward the back end of the nearest Rail, where the luggage door was slowly closing and the lights were blinking with the Rail's start signal.

Cole held his breath, using every ounce of momentum and adrenaline to push himself off his feet and roll into the cart. He crashed against the freight car floor, submerged in darkness.

He lay on the floor, unable to breathe. Unable to process what had just happened.

But what about—?

He jerked upward. "Echo!" he shouted, his voice ragged. *No. Please no.* They'd find her and the Officers would no doubt arrest her on the stop.

He jumped to his feet, ignoring the pain in his thigh,

pushing through the luggage. "Echo! Please, Echo—"

"Coleson!"

Cole whirled around. Echo sat up on the floor, an emergency glow stick in her hand.

His body shuddered with relief, sinking to the ground. Why couldn't he stop shaking? He clenched his fists, trying to catch his breath.

Echo crawled over to him. "Breathe, Coleson. Your body's been through a lot. How's the leg?"

"Fine." He didn't even want to think of the wound.

Echo's glance said otherwise. Her lips pursed. "We'll be back in Liberty soon, and then straight to a medic. Doran can wait."

Right. Another problem to deal with.

The image of his unfamiliar mother seared in his mind, right next to the one of baby Jenna and his father, both up in flames with the Mathews house.

He thought that he was on the right track. He had a teacher. He was learning to use his sword.

"What am I doing wrong?" he said quietly, his voice cracking as he rested his head on his knees.

Echo pushed back his sweaty hair from his forehead, the gentle gesture feeling foreign to him. "You're too young to feel this way," she said gently. She held out her hand, the Medallion cupped inside. "Appreciate what victories you have made."

Cole starred at the Medallion—the small object that meant the world to a little boy to have something to call his own. A small object that gave him some sort of purpose…an identity, out of sight and out of trouble.

Cole folded Echo's fingers over it, meeting her wide eyes.

"Cole—"

He shook his head.

She clutched the Medallion in her fist, speechless. And Cole turned away.

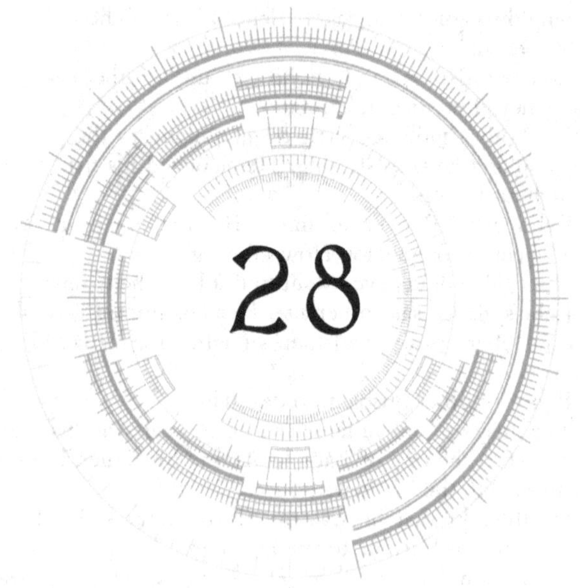

28

Kennedy, 12 Days Until

IT HAD BEEN two days, and still only one word repeated over and over in Ray's mind as Mercy Remembrance paced in front of him.

Keyper. Why did it stun him so much to know Mercy was the Keyper? A Council Member, like him. One of the four obscure ones: Guardian, Shadow Holder, Illuminate Holder, and then…Keyper.

What did the Keyper even do again?

He'd known that she had to be the one he was looking for the moment he laid eyes on her. So much mystery shrouded her, and those marks meant something beyond what he could comprehend.

What happened to her mother? Where were her papers? Surely not in the pile on his floor. He'd looked. Twice.

"Are you listening, Mathews?" Mercy said, slamming her hand against the table, jumping him from his drowse.

"Need more coffee," he grumbled.

She sighed, shaking her head. "This is important."

"I know it is, but just repeating the plan over and over isn't going to get anywhere," he said, lying on the table.

"Fine." She sighed, playing with a loose curl. She'd started wearing her hair down, and it brought so much life to her face. "But we do have one small, significant problem."

"And that is—?"

"I can't use the taxi." Mercy sighed, her eyes looking bashfully toward the window.

Ray frowned. "What?"

"They're region-run and my…family doesn't trust those kinds of functions."

"Mer—Remembrance, we literally just went on a SpeedRail the other day."

Mercy sank into the seat opposite him. "Ugh, I know, but we don't have another choice!" Her voice lowered. "I already pushed it with the SpeedRail."

Why step back when you can keep pushing till you knock it down?

Ray bit it back, the festering anger on Mercy's behalf being shoved away. "Lucas is a mechanic, right?"

Mercy perked up. "Yeah…"

"Maybe he has an auto he can loan us or something."

Mercy jumped to her feet. "That would work!" She halted. "Can you drive?"

Dang it.

"A little," he said, getting up after her. "My brother taught me a bit."

Cole had only let him and Lincoln routinely drive on the calm, short road to town. And the whole time, his older brother was having to grab the steering wheel to keep them alive. Ray didn't mention that part.

Especially since Mercy looked thrilled with the compromise of a plan as she rushed to grab her coat.

The timing was late as they rushed down the road, and how comfortable Mercy seemed with it surprised him. She hadn't bothered to wear the gloves that covered the small swirls on her hands, either, nor zip up her entire coat, leaving her neck, and the necklace, out in the open.

"You never mentioned having a brother," she said abruptly.

Ray blinked. "Yeah…I have three, and a sister. And an

older one." Still felt awkward to say. "He's busy, probably doing really important leader stuff."

Mercy raised a mischievous brow. "You jealous?"

"Me?" Ray laughed. "No. I'd be a disaster. Like, one time I got stuck—" Oh, wait. He couldn't mention that.

She frowned. "Stuck where?"

"On…the ceiling?"

Mercy laughed. "What?"

No questions asked. Phew. "My brother got me down, and here I am living for the world to admire." He combed his fingers through his hair dramatically.

She shook her head disapprovingly. "'Admire's' a strong word."

"Oh, come on!" Ray rushed in front of her, walking backward to face her. "We all know you get lost in my beautiful, golden eyes."

She shoved him back forward. "Lost in confusion on how you manage, that's for sure."

"Denial," he said, clicking his tongue.

"It's hard to swoon over your eyes when I have to look down to see them." She gave a dry laugh.

"Ouch."

"It's not awful being short," she said, flicking a tuft of his hair. "You can stay out of sight. No one's…staring at you."

She seemed to slouch only to make a point. In reality, Mercy wasn't much taller than him. Sure, she was taller than Felicity, Nikki, and Tabitha, but he hadn't realized that it wasn't something she was weary of.

"Nah, you're intimidating. It's a good thing. Scare people off with a punch to the face." He gave her a smirk, to which she only gave a quizzical look.

"Maybe I don't want to be intimidating all the time."

Ray didn't relate. He felt that his average height only added to the joke of how much he wasn't capable of. "Don't worry. Some other tall person will probably happily sweep you off your feet."

She laughed before her expression fell quickly. She cleared her throat. "Besides, I'm not supposed to indulge in things like that. Grandmere says we have to keep our bloodline pure. She has it figured out."

Ray's sweat went cold as Mercy hurried ahead of him.

This was lining up perfectly to the records he'd found. Each Keyper kept the line pure to make sure that there was another in the next generation. Mercy was just a teenage girl, but her identity wasn't her own. She was the Keyper, and that's all she was to her family.

And what made it worse was that Ray was getting the dreaded feeling that Mercy had no idea the half of it.

He needed to find those missing papers.

He ran after her.

They reached the mechanic shop, a small, steel, little shop that rented out half a building with a laundromat. There was a plated garage door; a hanging sign with a clever "MECHANIC" written out across it; and a little, wood door at the top of two concrete steps.

"Mechanic's manager should be out for the day, so only Mechanic should be left."

"Why call him…'Mechanic?'" And he thought the "last names" thing was odd.

She knocked with a shrug. "He's never told me his last name. Doesn't like being reminded of it."

"I mean, why not 'Lucas?' Why always call me 'Mathews?'"

"Names allow for emotional connections," Mercy said, her voice quiet. "Forbidden."

The door opened. No one was there. Ray almost went for his backpack before he spotted a small, can-shaped assistance bot, holding the door with its wrench hand.

"We're closed!" He heard Lucas call out, his heavy footsteps running for the door. He was wiping the grease from his face with his sleeve, reminding Ray of the eccentric blacksmith back in North Cordell, E.

Lucas stopped, frowning. "Wasn't expecting Queen Remembrance and her trusty knight of bad judgment."

Bad judgment? Who was he——?

"We need an auto," Mercy said, ignoring Lucas's statement.

"No extra laying around," Lucas said, nudging the bot out of the way, opening the door wide for them. "Last dude should not own a vehicle with the way he almost burned off my pride and joy."

Lucas gestured to his hair, kept up in a ponytail, and Ray

wasn't exactly sure if he wanted to hear the entire story.

The office of the mechanic shop smelled like rubber and gasoline, with a popcorn ceiling and yellow tint to the lighting.

"You don't have any?" Mercy pleaded.

"I mean, maybe I could have something useful to you if you want to look," Lucas said. He hung his gloves, swiping his hand over the door to the garage's sensor.

The door opened, a set of metal steps descending to the floor. Mercy and Ray exchanged glances before following Lucas inside.

There was a red auto propped up, but it was far from being useful: hood torn off, no windows, and a missing driver's seat. The walls were lined with storage shelves, full of tires and various car parts. Electric bikes were crowded by the right corner. Those caught Mercy's eye quickly.

"What about those?"

"How far you planning to go?"

"Twenty miles, maybe?"

Lucas chuckled. "You won't get very far with that plan, Remembrance."

Ray tuned them out, looking around the garage. Another section of the wall held busted engines as trophies. He smirked. Nice touch. There was so much here. Something had to be useful—

And then his eyes caught it. A hoverbike multiple generations old and the front tire patched countless times; a beaten, leathered seat; and duct-taped handlebars. It was nothing compared to the Defender cycles, but it was awesome. He walked over, his hands hovering over the bars.

"Hey! Earth to Raphael!" Lucas brought him down to reality, spinning around to face him and Mercy.

"You fixing this up?" Ray blurted out.

"Funny story about that one. The owner dropped it off for repairs, and then dropped off the face of the region. Not uncommon, but annoying." Lucas sighed.

Mercy eyed it suspiciously. "Don't tell me you want to ride that thing."

"Yes!" Ray turned back just to make sure he wasn't dreaming. The beaten-up thing was glorious. He and Noah would've drooled over it when they were younger back home. "Trust me, they're amazing!"

"Hasn't been ridden in months," Lucas said, walking over to it, dusting off the seat. He sent a kick to the charger, and it unplugged. "Might as well give it a go."

"What?" Mercy shrieked.

"Oh, come on, Remembrance!" Ray said, jumping onto the seat, feeling the handlebars. "If you don't come, I'll officially be better at something than you!"

"Better at dying."

He sighed. "Come on. Please?" He made a pathetic attempt at puppy eyes before she nearly thwacked him in the nose. "Fine," he said. "I'll go alone. But once again, you're letting your grandmother hold you back."

He shouldn't have said that.

Stupid, stupid Ray.

His heart leapt as Mercy plopped onto the seat behind him.

"Does a decent person have any protection riding this thing?" she said nervously.

"I'm your protection."

She kicked him.

"A helmet, usually, but we don't have any lying around." Lucas's eyes lit up, running up the steps and out of the garage. He burst back into the room in a second, holding a metal bowl.

"Just let me die." Mercy groaned.

Ray hit the start button, the engine roaring to life. Mercy cried out.

"Hold on, Remembrance!" Ray said with a grin.

She placed her arms loosely around his middle.

Lucas ran to the garage door, pulling up the holographic keypad, pounding in a few numbers. The garage door rose, the cold air of the night spilling inside.

"Just go around once, then come back," Lucas said, skidding out of the way.

"Got it!" Ray shouted, pushing on the handlebars, the sensors sending them forward.

Mercy cried out again, throwing her hands around him tightly, burying her face into his back.

The engine, despite the rickety exterior, ran smoothly, the bike speeding over the empty, dark street. The speed was thrilling, pressing forward. The sting of the air was cold, but he couldn't care less. In fact, it only wanted to make him laugh. All this open space around him. No one was trying to stop him. He felt so…free.

He turned the corner out of the town, racing down the dirt road through the never-ending flat grass fields. The sliver of the moon shined enough light down to see the wind brushing through the grass, casting the speeding shadows through the hovercycle's light.

Ray hadn't noticed the stars here before. They seemed so much brighter…so much closer. They didn't just decorate the night sky…They dominated it. That's all there was to the night. An open, never-ending sky full of stars.

The night was lonely. The darkness was beautiful.

He felt Mercy move her face to look out over his shoulder.

"As horrible as you thought it'd be, Remembrance?" He smirked.

"Keep driving." She scowled. She rested her head.

His smirk fell to a soft smile that he couldn't seem to erase.

Only one thing broke the mood: a terribly familiar, creeping feeling in his stomach, a subconscious shiver running down his spine.

It couldn't be, could it?

He slowed the hoverbike, feeling Mercy stiffen.

"What's going on?" she asked as they slowed to a stop. She let go of him quickly.

Ray clicked the standstill lever and jumped off the bike, narrowing his eyes over the dancing fields. He saw a small flash of a figure before it disappeared into the fold of air. His heart leapt.

"Stay low," he whispered. "I'll be right back."

She stared at him for a moment before giving a reluctant glare as she sank down to the ground. He walked out into the field, feeling his heart hammer against his chest.

The essence pounded equally hard against it. Where were they?

He glanced over his shoulder to where he knew that Mercy was ducked behind the hovercycle. He wasn't taking risks. He kicked the floor, pretending to fall, sending the dust flying in an enormous burst, falling straight into the void as he shut his eyes.

He felt like he was spiraling. With no clear destination, his body cried out for something to hold onto, but he pulled himself together firmly, reaching out.

A clear throb of cold beat against it. The feeling had a reddish tint.

You've killed a man, Mathews. What are you waiting for?
No! I didn't do it!

His eyes burst open, sending him sprawling to the ground with a thud. He scrambled to his feet, trying to catch his breath before the lifeless eyes caught him first. He looked around the field. The hovercycle was only a small speck now.

"Hello?" Ray called out, his limbs shaking. He took a steady step back.

Something rustled in the grass.

He whipped his head around to face it. His heart pounded. He balled his fists.

The guise dropped. A woman stood in the grass, her hand outstretched to her side. Her skin had a dark complexion, stark against the white over her hair. Her eyes opened.

Her eyes glowed red. A small smile followed, a blade dropping in red essence from her hand.

Ray cursed. An Exerticus.

He took a deep breath, beginning to charge the burn in his veins to channel his own…until a shrill scream sent his blood to ice.

"Mercy!" He spun around, seeing another Exerticus with Mercy in his grip, the blade nearing her throat. She struggled relentlessly against the muscled grip.

"I told you to stay low!"

"You said you'd be back soon!" She kicked her captor, who managed to hold her off the ground.

"Let her go!" Ray snarled pointlessly.

The Exerticus did just that. He grabbed Mercy, jerking her to the side, letting his energy shock her, and then flinging her to the ground.

The female Exerticus ran for Mercy.

"No!"

The other Exerticus charged toward Ray, dragging the sword in the ground before flinging it up. Ray dove into the crash, letting the anger burn in him. He could feel the Blade's hilt as it materialized in his hand. He leapt from the ground, launching himself into the air. He landed with it crashing against Red Eyes.

"You brought a—ah!"

Out of the corner of his eye, he saw the red-eyed gal's sword come crashing down onto Mercy.

His senses took over. Anger burned in his veins, trying to muster any sort of power to protect her.

He blipped away from his own attacker. He ran for her. And then his mind went quiet.

Tootega's voice whispered in his ear. *The power of words.*

And then the other voice chanting, *You're a killer. You're only my monster. You can't be there for your sister. You can't save Mercy.*

He raised his Blade and cried out. "Stop!"

He didn't know how it happened, only that it did. Almost as if torn from the earth, a dark power swelled, shooting out from under the swaying grasses, the shadowing of the Exeritucs's stunned face, and all came racing for his Blade. They bounced off and shot for the Exerticus, blowing them back, sending them sliding back through the field.

"Mercy!" Ray cried out. He needed to get to her.

Light radiated from where she should have been lying. Was she gone? Had they done something to her?

His heart seized as Mercy slowly stood up from the ground, clutching her bloody shoulder.

The glow wasn't from the Exerticus. It was coming from Mercy.

Her marks were glowing, her eyes having nothing but light, her hair having streams of glow growing throughout. With every heavy breath, she grew brighter.

Ray couldn't move.

Mercy looked at him, trembling, as his gaze dropped to her arms. "M—Mathews—"

The Exerticus charged back toward them. Ray screwed everything and jumped, appearing straight in front of him, battling with all his might. The man dove forward, cutting through Ray's shirt. He shouted, and in a moment, the man had twisted around his wrist, dancing the Blade out of Ray's grip and onto the ground.

And then a glowing flip-flop came and slammed into the attacker's face with such force, the attacker was blown off his feet.

Mercy shrieked. "It glows!"

Ray stepped back, turning around, his heart thundering. Had her touch just…superpowered a shoe? "*You're* glowing!"

And he'd just controlled shadows with a word. Tonight was full of surprises.

Mercy looked down and screamed.

"Stop screaming!"

"Mathews, I am freaking GLOWING!"

"Just—just stay calm!"

"How the heck am I supposed to do that?"

From a distance, the Exerticus stood, brushing himself off. The flip-flop had knocked him far.

Ray looked around, picking his sword off the ground and bracing himself. Where had the woman gone?

She'd just cut Mercy and left.

Ray prepared himself, watching as red energy grew in the man's hand. Ray took a deep breath, trying to think of a word.

It came flying for him. The flame exploded…

…into sand.

Ray blinked in surprise.

The sand man warlock raced through the field, charging for the Exerticus, sand spinning and rising high above him as he sent in glowing streams pummeling back against the red force exploding from the Exerticus's hands.

"Go!" Gorgon shouted. "Get out of here!"

He didn't hesitate to ask. Ray turned and ran for Mercy, whose hair was now all glowing. He reached out to grab her hand. It burned him at the touch, sending him back with a cry.

Mercy fell dark. "Mathews?"

He gripped his burned hand to his chest. "It's fine! Just *run*! Get to the hoverbike!"

The two of them tore through the field, fueled by the adrenaline and the surprising will to live. Ray nearly tripped over his own feet as they burst from the field, jumping onto the hovercycle. His hand seared in pain as he grabbed the throttle, kicking the hover-in-place lever off.

Mercy scrambled to get behind him, holding onto him with her life, screaming at him to go.

Ray wasn't sure what he should be more afraid of: crashing or being killed by Exerticus. Either way, it ended in death.

They entered the small Kennedy town, and Ray didn't bother to stop, even as a traffic bot ran after him. He sped to the motel, spinning to halt. Mercy tumbled off as soon as it was slow enough, dashing for the house. Ray turned off the hoverbike and ran after her.

He slammed the door behind him, locking every mechanism that lined the door, collapsing to the floor a few feet from Mercy. They both sat in the silence, gasping for breath.

"I should've listened," Mercy said through ragged breaths, her eyes crowding with tears.

"Yes. You should've let me handle it," he snapped back.

"Not you." She glared at him, stumbling to her feet. "I was glowing."

"Someone tried to kill us…again!" Shouldn't that be more important? In fact, he was surprised that she wasn't shouting at him for teleporting, but then again, she'd seemed too horrified by her own abilities to notice.

She's a Member, and it's incredible.

*I can manipulate shadows with words…*or, at least, he thought he could.

"My *grandmere* will kill me." Mercy said, as if that was worse. She grabbed a wad of napkins with her shaking hands, pressing them over her wound.

Dang it. How did Ray forget about that?

"I'm a Medic. Let me help—"

"No!" She scrambled out of the moonlight. Her breaths were ragged. "She'll already be furious. You don't need to touch me anymore."

"Why? You did nothing wrong. You couldn't control what happened." He stepped forward.

She flinched.

"The way you're terrified of her isn't normal," he said

gently, longing to reach out and help her.

Her face scrunched up, trying to keep tears at bay. She looked away. "Just go while you can," she choked, running for the stairs.

"I just want to help!" he shouted after her.

She slammed the door, letting it echo down the room.

Ray stood in the moonlit silence. He wanted to storm back out and finish Red Eyes once and for all, but he startled himself, shaking off the thought. No more killing.

Just…He glanced at his burned palm…Just healing.

He headed to the kitchen, flicking on the oven light. He climbed onto the counter, retrieving the HCS kit. The burn wasn't so bad. But the fact that it came from touching another human being's skin? It sent a shudder down his spine.

Just when he thought that he'd made a breakthrough. How was he supposed to get her to the Council now? He almost didn't want to. He'd burdened her enough.

He bound his hand, sinking to the kitchen floor. He was back to square one. A lonely, forgotten state. Tears threatened to overflow, but he fought them back. He opened his Comm, sending another worried message to Cole.

Oquelite. That's all you'll ever be.

He didn't want that.

He forced it away. It only fueled his rage. He was sick of the voice. He was sick of the silence. He was sick of being reminded.

Someone had finally seen him without the reputation that weighed on him. But now, he'd lost her too.

He clicked on another contact. One he hadn't touched in years. One that he doubted even still had a Comm.

He wasn't going to give up. He'd keep fighting for the Council no matter how much it might not want him. He'd keep fighting for Mercy. She deserved to be free.

He didn't want to be a Member. He didn't want to be an Oquelite. He wanted to be loved again.

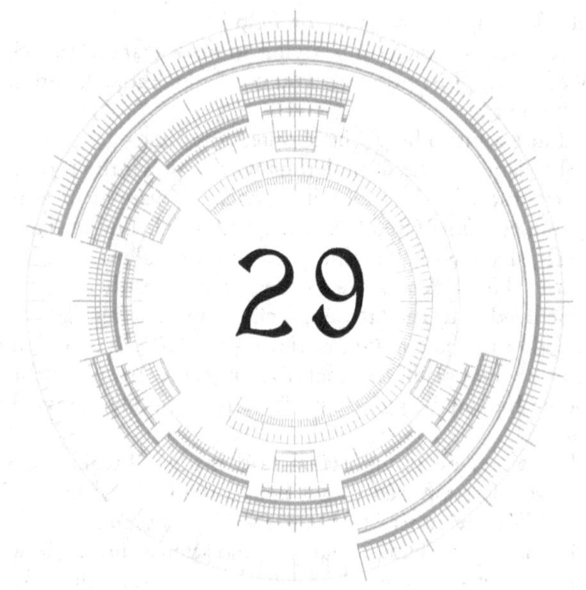

29

North Cordell, 12 Days Until

THE FLASHBACKS NIKKI had given them of the woman Adrienne replayed in Lincoln's mind as he walked down the path to the MedTent. Lawrence wasn't able to come this time, and he wasn't even sure if Taryn would permit him alone. His heart hammered against his chest.

The flashbacks were a bigger deal to worry about. How was he even supposed to process this ancient Ewyon woman lurking in Nikki's head? Why was she there?

They slipped through the side flaps.

"I had strict orders from Sergeant Rayder Dow *not* to permit another one of you kids in here," a nurse said, standing guard of the hallways.

Lincoln kept himself cool, pulling out the signed pass Taryn provided him.

"But Dow—"

"—isn't the Sergeant of the region," Lincoln finished for her. "This is important Department work."

The nurse glared at him, begrudgingly stepping out of the way and watching him go.

He saw that the lights were on in Nikki's room, spilling out from under the cracks of the flap. That was a first.

"Nik?" he said softly.

"Lincoln?" Her voice still sounded tired, but her excitement instead of lying lifeless was so refreshing that Lincoln almost didn't worry.

He stepped inside. Nikki was sitting up, holding her arms out straight in front of her.

It had only been four days. He frowned. "Nik, what are you doing? Shouldn't you be resting?"

"I was doing that for weeks."

"From what Noah was telling me, that's not the case." Regardless, he was happy to see her up at all. He set down his bag and quickly sat down at her bedside.

"I heard the doctor say I was healing faster than she'd seen before," Nikki said, as if that justified it.

Right. Nikki had the P9F, a healing file in her bloodstream.

She narrowed her eyes at her still injured wrist. Once upon a time, they'd been stressed only about *that*.

She looked at him with a tiny shrug. "You look worried."

He opened his mouth to deny it, maybe too quickly.

"I'm all right," Nikki insisted, dropping her arms. "I've been dreaming about walking again."

"Nik, I really don't think—"

"Can we try?" Her face pinched in determination, throwing off her covers.

"Nik, you're hooked up to a whole bunch of machines and hardly a week out of comatose." Lincoln shook his head. "Not safe."

Nikki looked at him, almost begrudgingly, as if searching for some ulterior motive. She sighed in reluctance with a small shrug. "It's too cold."

Lincoln moved to help her adjust the covers. The room was cold, and the fact that the hospital was quite literally a tent probably didn't help, but it didn't feel too noticeable. Lincoln frowned, pressing his hand against Nikki's forehead. It was warm.

"Nik, have you been having chills?"

She looked at him, confused.

He sighed. "Have you told Dr. Mathews about this?"

Nikki looked at him for a long moment. "It's just cold," she said quietly.

"You have a venom inside you from the Oquelite blade, and they can't treat it till you're stable enough." It was enough to make him feel nauseous just remembering it. "You're still infected, and you can't get any more sick."

NIkki didn't respond, her eyes glossed over, her breathing stopping.

"Nik?"

She squeezed her eyes shut. "I can't go back."

Guilt panged Lincoln's chest. "No, no, no. You're going to be fine," he said, forcing himself to believe his own words, afraid that the Voice would come and tell him otherwise.

She kept her eyes shut, her face pained and fighting something he couldn't see. She shivered. He unzipped his jacket, gently laying it over her.

"You're going to be okay, Nik," he assured.

She forced a small smile at the name before it fell again, her eyes drifting away. "Turn off the lights," she whispered.

"Why—?"

I feel her watching. Nikki's voice trailed into his head. Much more soothing than the Voice's.

Lincoln didn't argue, tapping the button on the monitor, the lamps submerging them into the darkness. She held his jacket close, burying her face.

Everything was supposed to be better once she was back. He had been so concerned about how it would affect him…but here *she* was. So broken and scared.

And yet, he couldn't reach out and help her. He knew that he'd break right there with her. And he couldn't risk that.

He put a gentle hand on her shoulder. She turned over to look at him. "Come closer."

"I don't want to hurt—"

She shook her head. "I don't want her to hurt *you*…" Her voice trailed off, lost. "…or anyone."

"No one is going to hurt me," he assured, but he moved off her chair, kneeling beside her cot.

She closed her eyes again. "You're afraid of her too," she whispered.

"The woman you've been seeing in your head? Adrienne?"

Nikki didn't respond.

Should we continue?

The Ewyon Coastal Alliance Palace—Before Recorded Time

Burning. It had a horrible smell. The heat that tore up your throat, every bone crying of escape and left drowning in your sweat.

Her thin shift was clinging on by the sweat and the fresh blood, and it was hardly enough to protect her from the cold and the eyes of the drunken creatures lurking beyond the stone wall.

She couldn't move. She couldn't breathe.

The dirt clinging to her wounds cradled her every ache.

Die. Die. Please die.

Her eyesight blurred.

Nausea overcame her. She tried to roll, her blood catching her with pain, before she vomited into the dirt. She reached to wipe her mouth. She narrowed her eyes as the dark substance dripped down her tied fists. Blood.

Let me die.

Air refused to breach her lips, trapping her in her burning skin, her mind spinning. Too vulnerable. Too weak. A cry escaped from her lips as she turned her back. A part of skin ripped from her flesh as the blood clung to the fabric.

Muffled voices caught her attention.

Voices.

She hated voices. He cowered so close to her eyes, his eyes, full of madness, into hers. The knives had voices as he tore it from her. Voices turned to screams. Screams echoed as she felt the blade sink through torn fabric, the cool prick against her skin—

And the numbness. The numbness as he drove the blade farther and farther across, and blood. She tasted war.

"Look, it's awake!"

It.

"Bruce, you're next with the little Shadow Soul?"

I'm not the Shadow Soul. The Shadow Soul killed my mother.

"For our legacy, brother!"

They laughed as if she'd just been thrust against the walls over and over and over… As if it would never end. As if everything in her body didn't burn to silence them.

She pushed her palms against the dirt, raising her quaking body from the ground. Nausea waved over her again. The silhouetted figure knelt before her.

"Good mornin'." He laughed.

The blade scratched against its scabbard. Left side. She felt him draw closer.

"You feeling awake?"

Who was he to ask her?

"Good. No trouble playing with that undying face—"

With a quick thrust, she sent her elbow into his body, forcing a cry of pain from her chest at the movement. She scrambled for the knife, but he rolled, threatening it to her neck. "Help!" he screamed. "Help me! Stop, or I'll kill you!"

She spat, a glob of blood splatting between his eyes. "You—you said it yourself," she choked. "I can't die."

Another fist to the princely boy's face. It felt…good.

"It's attacking Bruce!"

"He's fine! It can't do anything!"

"He's stronger."

I am strong.

He thrust the knife for her, catching her jaw, toppling off from him, sending her rolling into the brush, dirt and debris digging into her wet wounds.

She scrambled to her knees, her breath ragged. The boy tore after her. She tried to dodge, but the knife hit her chest. She screamed.

Don't show weakness.

This is a nightmare.

None of this is real.

She swung her other foot, catching his face. He reached to cradle his jaw, the knife falling. She didn't hesitate. She grabbed the knife with a cry and lunged.

It all happened too quickly. Her vision fogged. The males screamed. Her veins burned. It was unbearable, like it cut right through her skin, her pulse. Everything trembled.

She rose, shaking, to her feet, the pain numbing. Her hands were wet and sticky, her legs searing, but the burn numbed it all.

Oh, how she loved the burn.

"It killed Bruce!" A hysterical scream shattered her presence. "She murdered him!"

As you've murder me dozens of times, only to watch me live again.

Most of the pack ran in panicked screams, but a figure raced toward her. "Don't let it get away!"

Burn. She craved to watch them burn.

Violet flames burst from her fingertips, sending the grasses around her blazing red. And she ran.

Let them burn.

A tug sent her chest first into the dirt, her body's senses rudely awakening, her wounds sending her to a crippling cry of pain. She dug at the dirt with her nails, prying forward, but she slipped back.

They were pulling at her with their abilities.

Her heart dropped. She tried to pull herself to her feet. Burn.

Everything swirled through her, pain condensing in her chest. She collapsed, her body falling right through the ground. She opened her mouth to scream, but no sound came as the darkness enveloped her before she hit the cold, stone floor, the familiar moonlight cradling her as she curled up in pain, her vision spotting.

She'd teleported.

A shrill scream.

"Sergia." The name was gentle on her lips. The only gentle thing left.

She let her eyelids fall, the gentle, warm embrace cradling her against a beating heart. Life.

"Help!" A sob echoed down the hall. "She's dying!"

Oh, dear Sergia. I sadly don't believe I can.

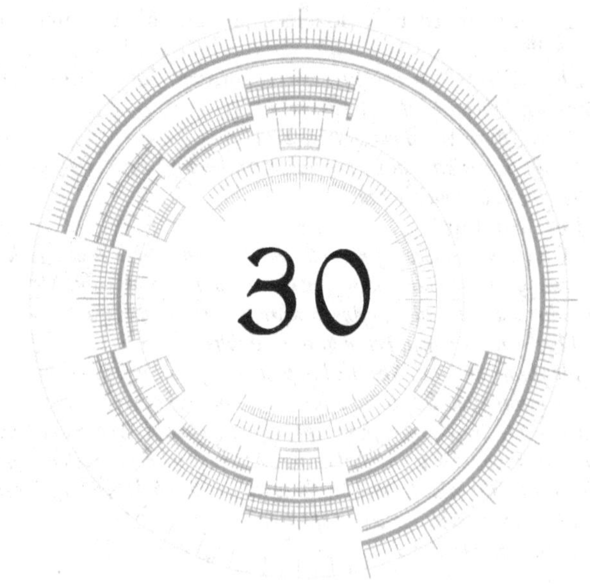

30

Liberty, 11 Days Until

THIS WAS THE moment he'd dreaded for days, sitting in his tent and trying to put together a semblance of a song for Tabitha and not pull a three-day-straight all-nighter. But now he was here, facing the room of Marketeers who probably wanted to kick him out for causing chaos.

"That was a lot. Let me get this straight," Cecileo said, running his fingers through his hair with a stylus in hand. "Our young Member guest stopped a bandit transport, now has information on a possibly commissioned kidnapping, and has multiple eye witnesses to an event to convict Victor, and that's a bad thing?"

"Exactly!" Doran said as soon as Cole tried to open his mouth. "He ran off against direct orders and is now charged as a criminal of Defender offense! It's taken us days to throw them off of his and your wife's trail."

Cole wanted to argue. There was so much more to this. Bandits had attacked a small town gathering in Kennedy, along with an Exerticus. They were linked.

He couldn't tell whose side Cecileo was on. He'd been the first to approach them outside the SpeedRail station, sending out search parties. He'd dropped everything just to pull Echo into a hug, holding her so tight that he might never let go.

He hadn't spoken to Cole at all.

Cecileo glanced at Echo, who sat beside him. "That's twenty-four kids free from enslavement."

"That's twenty-four over the world and our safety?" Doran said.

"The world doesn't end when a Council Member doesn't show up for training!" Cecileo jumped to his feet.

Cole almost stepped back in surprise. Doran's brow raised.

Had Cecileo just snapped at the swordmaster? *His* swordmaster?

"He's just defending the kid because of Echo's experience with bandits," a merchant in the room snorted.

"And does that make his argument any less valid?" Echo herself said. The first word she'd spoken the entire time.

The merchant shrank back.

Was Echo having something to do with the bandits the reason the Marketeers hated Echo so much?

"Personally, I don't see a single thing Johnson did as being wrong," Echo said, rising to her feet. "The only criticism you have of him is irresponsibility. But he was being responsible for the people, which our markets have been harboring from hurting others. No one was hurt more than his own reputation. And perhaps Doran's pride."

"Still far too impulsive," a merchant scrambled to rebuke.

"But it also shows a strong moral compass."

All heads turned to Doran, who slumped into a sigh with reluctance.

Cole had to keep his jaw from dropping. Doran? Of all people? His face burned.

"As much as I don't approve of many of his actions, Coleson has a strong sense, no matter ignorant, of morality. He saw saving that little girl as the top priority over anything else." Doran turned to face Cole directly behind him. "But the quality of a leader is to decide how much of a risk is worth taking."

"I'm sorry," he said, his voice raw.

"He came to learn," Echo said. "And the fact they got in and we got out as quickly as we did was thanks to his leadership."

His what? Please, not this again. He'd simply been acting on instinct. Get to Felicity. Get to Imperial. Get to Glorgory. And he'd still crashed and burned.

But he couldn't help but feel the smallest smidge of relief. They'd succeeded in capturing the bandit. Dana was home safe. That was all that made it worth it.

"He came to learn." Doran agreed. "And I can't teach him."

Doran didn't say another word. He turned and he left straight out the tent. The commotion was deafening. Cole's heart dropped.

And just like that...it was over. Just one step too far—

"I'll teach him, darn it!" Cecileo shouted, jumping to his feet. "Everyone, shut it! I'll teach the kid!"

The room froze.

Cole was speechless. Doran had just left, and now Cecileo was—

"You—you don't need to—"

"Oh, shut it," Cecileo said, waving his hands dismissively. "First lesson, Johnson. Get some self-confidence."

Cole shut his mouth.

"The rest of you are dismissed. Get out. Record this in your tablets for politics when the Market condemned stopping a kidnapping."

The crowd gradually tickled begrudgingly out of the tent.

Cole and Echo still both stood in shock staring at Cecileo as he casually poured himself another steaming cup of tea. Mid-sip, he paused, looking from Echo to Cole. "What?"

"I can't believe you." Echo shook her head.

Cecileo laughed.

"Why are you laughing?" Echo was failing to hide a growing smile. "This is serious."

"You're adorable when you're angry."

"Shut up, Cecil."

Cecileo took a long sip of his tea and turned to Cole. "I'm proud of you, kid."

"You are—" Cole tripped over his own words.

Something about the words made something inside feel tight and made him stand a little straighter. "Thank you, sir."

"I don't believe in training aimlessly. Let's get straight into your weaknesses."

Cole had plenty of those to work with.

"You've also never taught," Echo snorted.

Cecileo set his teacup down. "This was originally your grand idea."

"Yeah, well, I'm angry. Remember?"

Cecileo pretended to pout, and Echo just rolled her eyes. Cecileo turned back to Cole.

"So Coleson, first-name basis?"

"Sure?" Calling the leader of the Market—and now his teacher—"Cecileo" out loud would be weird.

"So, you know that odd boy you found?"

The one without a name and a relentless killer? How could Cole forget him? "Yes."

"He knows something about this commission. I want you to investigate to stop it."

Cole's heart leapt. "Aren't you supposed—?"

"Yes, you. And I'm going to help you smooth out the kinks, don't worry about it." Cecileo smiled. "What do you think?"

Cole didn't know *what* to think. "That—that's great."

"You know what, Echo?" Cecileo said, spinning on Echo with a sigh. "You were right."

"I'm always right, Cecil."

"Oh, right. Sorry, I forgot." Cecileo kissed her, and she pushed him away, laughing and gesturing to Cole standing there.

"Go shower. Sleep for a week," Cecileo said with a nod. "You look like you need it."

Finally. An order Cole could follow.

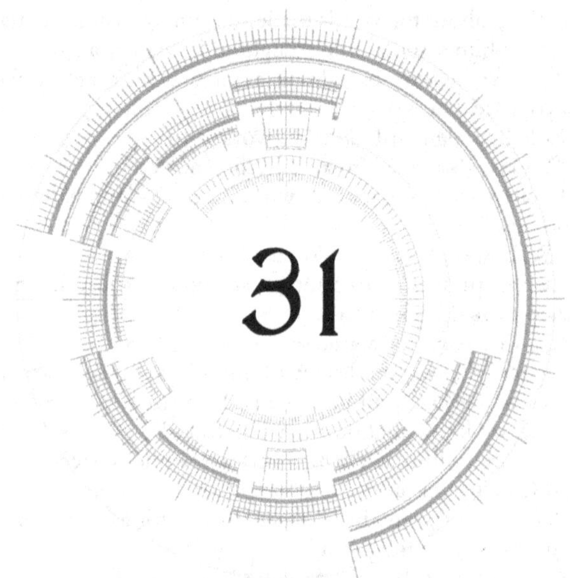

Kennedy, 10 Days Until

RAY HAD SEARCHED the pile over six times now and was still completely empty handed. The papers had to have been hidden, and Ray had the perfect idea of where. Except for the fact that he had no idea where the key was.

Ray was exhausted, but he settled for a cold shower and headed down the stairs, nearly having a mini heart attack at the three faces pressed on the glass, looking in.

Where was Mercy? Why wasn't the motel open?

He ran to the door, quickly undoing the locks and opening the doors to the visitors and, in a mad scramble, running to take down the chairs.

"Mornin', Mathews."

Ray froze. Lucas.

Ray turned on his heel, bracing himself for a lecture about the hovercycle. "*Hey.*" Ray laughed nervously. "About the hovercycle."

Lucas tightened his hair tie. "I did notice it was never

returned…and Remembrance isn't here."

"Asleep," Ray guessed.

Lucas stopped and frowned. "This late?"

Ray clenched the back of the chair he'd set down, trying to hold Lucas's gaze casually. "It was a…rough night."

Lucas glanced at the hovercycle, parked in the parking lot. He looked back to Ray. "Is it in any way related?"

"Mathews!"

A shrill shout caught him off guard from the kitchen door. His heart leapt. He thought that they were over the yelling.

"I thought you said she was asleep." Lucas's frown deepened.

Ray pretended not to hear him, dashing through the kitchen doors, where Mercy stood in a T-shirt and sweatpants, her frizzy hair scooped up in a bun, desperately trying to scrub dishes. She hadn't even bothered to turn on the lights. "We're late. We're so late! I prepared nothing! No, no, no…"

How had she gotten down here so fast without him seeing her? The open door to the forbidden hallway answered that.

"Calm down!" He rushed to pull the plate from her hand.

"I am calm!" A washcloth slipped from her hand as she spun around. He quickly sidestepped it.

Mercy's eyes were shimmering, squinting to keep them from overflowing, her shoulders pinched.

Ray froze. "Are you okay?""

Her face softened, her body wavering before she sank to the ground, burying her face in her hands, her shoulders quaking.

Ray hesitated. He wasn't qualified to comfort her. He was lying to her. He—

He shoved his doubts aside and sat beside her. "Do you want to talk about it?"

She glanced at him with her watering eyes. Her voice fell to a whisper. "I don't even know what to say."

"Believe me, I know how that feels."

She snorted, desperately trying to scrub the tears from her eyes. "Really?"

He clenched his fists shut. Right here, right now, he could

spark energy between his fingers and show her that she wasn't the only freak in the world. Instead, he kept them shut tight.

Panic seized Mercy again, her pupils narrowing. "She's going to be so mad," she whispered. "She's going to call off the search for Papa."

That darn grandmother. The fear she struck into Mercy sent a shiver down his spine.

"Why would she do that? She has no reason to."

"Because of my stupid marks!" Mercy began scratching at her arms.

"Hey! Don't!" He grabbed her arms, holding them tightly. He gave her a warning look. "It's not your fault, whatever this is."

"She's the only one who knows." Mercy sobbed, her head hanging helplessly. "She told me it's not supposed to happen. She's going to blame Papa."

"She's not the only one." His voice became gentle, his entire mind telling him otherwise. "And neither are you. There's a whole group like you."

Mercy tensed, with a scoff. "Stop with the folk tales."

"So you've heard of it?"

"Uki talks a lot," Mercy whispered, curling her knees to her chest.

"That there's a group of special, unique, individual abilities…just like this? Just like you? Those kinds of people are regarded as heroes, with a purpose to save the world. Why would your grandmother hate something with a legacy like that?"

"Because there are the Purizies," Mercy said, shaking her head. "They have abilities, and they use them in awful ways." Mercy shuddered. "Mathews, she's going to be so angry."

Ray gently let go of her arms, wrapping a hesitant arm around her shoulders. She didn't shove him away. He gave her a reassuring squeeze. "We all have choices. Perhaps people in that legendary group had choices to make too."

Mercy leaned her head against him, quiet.

"You can't restrict what you were made to do. I'm not sure what that is yet, but I do know it's your choice of what to use that for."

They sat in the silence for a long moment, where Mercy's

big breaths were the only sound.

"I—I'm so tired," she choked. "I don't know what else to do."

"Leave."

The suggestion even surprised him.

Mercy jerked up. "What?"

"Leave," Ray said again, more sure of himself this time. "Come to North Cordell with me."

Mercy stared at him, her lips trembling. "I can't."

"Another rule?" He thought that they were at the point where those were beginning to not matter.

"No." She held out her hands, the thumb rings glowing in unison with the anklet clamped around her ankle. "I literally cannot leave."

Ray's jaw fell in horror. "And you say she isn't—"

"Don't say it." Mercy squeezed her eyes shut, her body cringing away.

He set his eyes firmly on her, unclenching his fists, getting to his knees, now taller than her. "If I can do anything to help—"

"Why?" She wiped her nose. "You don't have to."

"Maybe because I'm a good person."

A hint of humor glinted in her eyes as she laughed hoarsely. "Fancy that."

"You got really lucky, I know." He smirked.

He got to his feet, offering Mercy his hand. To his surprise, she grabbed it. He pulled her to her feet.

"I'll cook," he said before she could open her mouth to panic. He headed for the light sensor.

"Mathews, I forgot to go to the grocer's this morning. We're short—"

He flicked on the light. "Trust me, Remembrance. If my family has taught me anything, absolutely anything can become soup."

A small smile crept onto Mercy's lips, making her entire face light up, even with her swollen eyes. "I swear, you're not even human."

Ray laughed hoarsely. *If only you knew.* "Look who's talking."

"As far as we know, I'm at least still human!" She dashed to the door, turning on her heel to call back to him. "Get on it, Mathews!"

Mercy proved herself to be far more handy with a knife than Ray was comfortable with, and for once she seemed to listen to his orders without more than a few snarky comments. The serving bot, B0bbl3, was on a roll this morning, literally, rolling in and out with the trays.

Or, at least, it had been.

"Has B0bbl3 come back yet?" Mercy frowned, looking up from her tablet and pile of receipts.

Ray frowned. "It's been awhile…"

The door kicked open, and their missing bot almost comically appeared…in Lucas's arms.

Mercy leapt out of her stool, rushing to him. "He broke again?"

Lucas carried the machine to the central counter, giving the bot a pat. "Good thing the hall's closed. Best time for his battery to go out…again."

"Can you fix him?" Mercy said, looking to Lucas with pleading eyes.

"I'm an auto mechanic."

"You did it last month. Please!"

"Fine." Lucas smirked, looking at Ray. "Only if Mathews makes us dinner too."

Ray wiped his hands off on the towel hanging from the oven handle, still sweaty from the heat of the stove. "Yeah, sure. I guess I'm everyone's mom now."

Mercy rolled her eyes, turning back to Lucas. "You know where the spare batteries are, right? Closet in the left-hand hall?"

"Got it." Lucas gave her a nod. "Mathews, help me out."

Helping Lucas out apparently meant carrying the bot half of Ray's size as Lucas walked empty handed across the motel. They entered the left-wing hall, most of the motel rooms empty and out of order. Lucas reached the door with a plaque stating "MAINTENANCE" embossed in it.

He opened the door, the light flicking on.

The closet was small, but the high walls were packed: cardboard boxes full of clothes and paper boxes with flower print tied up with cords and countless filled, plastic bags.

Ray's eyes crept up the tall walls. It honestly felt unnecessary. Was it built just for a Remembrance? Seemed to fit the height quota—

Ray's heart ceased. Dangling from the ceiling, right beside the light on a little hook, was the golden key.

"Found it!" Lucas said, picking a battery the size of his hand out from a grocery bag. He tucked it under his arm. "We're good."

Ray tore his eyes away from the key as he stumbled outside of the closet.

Lucas shut the door behind him. "You good, Mathews?"

"One cool closet."

Lucas raised a brow. "If you say so."

The last piece of the puzzle. The literal key to the room of answers he'd been searching for.

He followed Lucas out of the hall with every intent of coming back for that key.

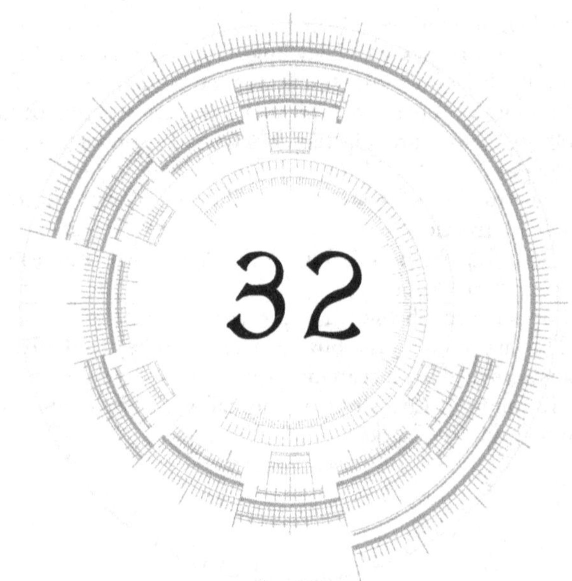

32

North Cordell, 10 Days Until

MATTEO SAT TUCKED away between the far-left cabins, staring out over the empty fields toward the dark storm brewing over the woods. Even a flash of the distant lightning made him jump. He only felt guilty knowing that Jenna was right under it.

He clenched his hands around his headphones, taking in a deep breath of the cold air, his senses sharp with the smell of the rain and the sensation dancing in his chest. It pulled him toward the woods.

He could hear the loud Defender's voice clearly in his head. *You're Impure. You can feel the presence of other Impure.*

He liked to try and imagine it otherwise. That explanation felt so…tight in a way he couldn't explain. He imagined that he was feeling more than just the presence, but a future. A certainty. Any certainty he could cling onto—

Something slammed into his back, a wet tongue immediately meeting his face and planting him to the ground.

Matteo laughed nervously at Fire Wolf staring down at him. "*Buen perro.*"

"Fire Wolf, off of him!"

At Lawrence's command, the giant wolf leapt off of Matteo. He sat up, brushing himself off, turning to scratch the giant dog behind the ears.

Lawrence came to a stop, catching his breath. "Are you all right? I feel like he's impossible to control…Supernatural wolf acting more like Charles every day."

"I'm all right," Matteo said.

And so was Fire Wolf. As heavy and startling as he was, the animal's eyes held an intelligence and silent compassion Matteo found soothing. The wolf had no need for noise, just a nudge of his nose for affection.

"Are you ready to begin our training?"

The question caught Matteo off guard, his heart skipping a beat. "We start today?"

"If you're not feeling up to—"

One glance at the forest, and Matteo was on his feet. He nodded.

Lawrence's eyes widened in surprise, though it was slowly replaced with a sly smile. "We're heading out to the fields. We better hurry to beat that storm."

Matteo glanced at Fire Wolf, who, without a second canine thought, ran to Lawrence's side. Matteo only met the dark-green eyes behind the glasses for a moment. They were intimidating, but one could see so much truth in them. Maybe it would help if Lawrence didn't loom over him.

He picked up his headphones, hanging them around his neck, and followed after the boy.

The knot in his chest loosened as they trekked through the worn trail in the grass. While one part knew that he should be terrified at the fact that they were going out unguarded, the other couldn't help but feel somewhat thrilled at the fact that he was training, as Lawrence said, with Lawrence instead of a Defender.

He hurried to keep up the pace with Lawrence, who removed a pair of fingerless gloves from his satchel. He held them out to Matteo. "We'll be using these."

Matteo frowned, taking them in his hands. He hesitantly

slipped one through his fingers. The material was surprisingly comfortable, not at all irritating against his skin. That was a first.

"It's made of your burned shirt from Liberty," Lawrence explained casually. "I thought you'd work better with a more familiar feel."

"It's perfect." Matteo couldn't think of a word to describe it. No one had ever done something like that for him before. "What's the metal disk for?"

Lawrence pulled out his own pair as they slowed their pace to an open patch of trampled grass. "They're repulsive of each other," he said.

Matteo raised a brow. What did that do for them? His heart stopped.

He blinked. "You can't hit."

"Right. Just a bounce. The focus should be more on mentality and confidence than actually landing a blow first." Lawrence shrugged, as if this wasn't the biggest deal that Matteo had ever laid eyes on.

It was genius.

He tempted himself to look into his eyes again. Relief. Lawrence looked relieved. His posture was more lax and his breathing longer. He shedded himself of his coat.

What was he relieved about? Matteo liking the gloves? Or for the same reason Matteo was?

But it couldn't be. Lawrence worked well under pressure. He'd seen it. He'd never seen Lawrence overwhelmed by the sounds, and the pain, and the oaths of the past.

Matteo tried to shake it away before it became more than just a chill.

Lawrence settled easily into a stance with a hard swallow. Easy to ignore, but Matteo hadn't. Lawrence was nervous, wasn't he?

"Just try a stance. Be comfortable. It helps your grace."

Matteo took a deep breath, taking in the silence of the wind. He began to shift into a stance, but it didn't feel right. He felt lopsided and disconnected. How was he supposed to feel?

Grace. Comfort. Feel.

He dropped to a knee.

"Are you—?"

Matteo untied his boots, tossing them aside. He stood back up, his bare feet against the soft dirt and grasses. He remembered Miriam's every move before him. He slid into it.

Lawrence shrugged. "Sure, whatever works." His brows furrowed, his gaze settling on Matteo. "Now, I want you to try and repulse yours off of me. That's all."

The shouts and screams as he hit the floor taunted the back of his mind. "Oh—okay." He narrowed his eyes, trying to focus. "Ready?"

"Whenever you are."

Matteo jumped out. Lawrence ducked and, with one quick movement, swung his hand out. Matteo's heart skipped a beat as he stumbled back. No contact made.

They both froze.

Matteo's breath caught up with him, energy sparking in the pit of his stomach. Slowly, he felt the tiniest smile creep on his lips. *Increíble.*

He leapt out at Lawrence again. Lawrence deflected. Quickly, Matteo could feet the swing of it. Lawrence used the same method of throwing himself out of harm's way with arms as a guard. There was a definite swing. Step, step, take back, lunge, turn.

Lawrence caught against his attack, knocking him back.

Recalculate the swing. Hit. Deflect. For the forward. Side to side. Deflect. Now, run.

He dove into the grass, waiting a moment to jump. Lawrence broke his pattern, swinging outward. He hit Matteo's field, and the two fell back.

Matteo tripped onto his back and into the grass. The landing was soft and the feeling exhilarating. He held up his hands against the stormy sky. There was rhythm to it. Rhythm in the silence.

He sat up, seeing Lawrence, wiping his brow of sweat. He stared blankly at Matteo for a long moment without blinking. "That—that was impressive."

"I didn't beat you," Matteo said, frowning.

"I'm sure you will in time…with what we've learned today." A surprised smile glowed on Lawrence's face. "You're proving them wrong, Teo."

Matteo's eyes fell. He shook his head. "It won't work like

that."

"You're right. Not now."

Not ever. Nothing works. Nothing they like, anyhow. Thunder crashed through the sky, and panic seized through Matteo, pain pinching him.

He looked up. The storm had grown.

Lawrence was looking up too. "Did you do that?"

Matteo rose to his feet. "No."

The winds picked up quickly, beating at the grass, pulling them at their roots. Lightning flashed through the mountains. Matteo stumbled back, the sky shaking with thunder.

Lawrence cursed breathlessly. "What is going on?"

Fire Wolf crouched low. Matteo met the wolf's eyes, the golden pupils staring with a fear Matteo felt shiver down his spine. He ran to his boots and quickly pulled them on. The wind picked up louder, and so did the noise.

Matteo reached for his headphones, tempted to block out the whistling.

"Matteo—"

The sky cracked. Matteo cried out, rain drops falling with the crash.

Fire Wolf growled. Something shot at him. Matteo's heart leapt as he jumped out of the way. Fire Wolf stumbled back in a pained whimper.

His heart beating into his ears, Matteo rolled over to face the blast. He nearly screamed, but the sound wouldn't come. He felt too frozen with fear.

First he met Lawrence's face, and then everything zoomed out to the ragged, pale Oquelite holding him hostage with the purple flames growing in his hands. Out behind them dozens...no, hundreds of small figures ran across the fields, some flashing in and out of sight but all coming with no slowing, streaming out of the woods, running in every which direction.

Another blast split, this time a visible stream of purple energy exploring through the trees and rain suddenly pouring harder, some Oquelite dropping.

"Finally," the Oquelite said, a curved smile on his face as he blew a loose, greasy hair from his face. "Some full-bloods."

"Matteo, run!" Lawrence cried out. The Oquelite scowled, slamming his fiery fist into Lawrence's side.

"No!"

Lawrence cried out in pain. "Go!" His expression twisted, darkening. "Now! I'll—ah!—catch up!"

Matteo couldn't disobey. He needed to warn the others.

Tearing himself from Lawrence, he raced through the field. His balance was off. Nothing felt settled around him. He could fall over at any minute. The wind worked against him. He leapt onto the worn path, pumping his legs with all his might. Harder than he ever had in Court Illegia.

He wouldn't hesitate this time. He wouldn't let his fear get the best of him.

If the Oquelite were here…His heart was racing.

The camp was fast approaching. He tried remembering the few words Lawrence had said only half an hour ago. He had to be comfortable.

But he wasn't. He was frozen with fear. He didn't have time. He burst into the camp, tripping and rolling into the dirt. He scrambled to his feet, shouting, "They're coming!"

The Defenders around the central fire jumped to their feet, stunned by his display.

"Matteo!"

Lincoln came racing down the steps from the boy's cabin. "Are you okay?"

Matteo pushed away from Lincoln's touch, his head feeling light, his mind tripping over himself for words. "Guys—people in cloaks." He whirled around, pointing to the massive woods in the rolling hills. He didn't need to say their name. They were already in sight.

"Oquelite." Lincoln gasped.

The Defenders began shouting, rushing off. A few simply pulled out a weapon and ran for the hills. "Evacuate the camp! Call a warning!"

"Why were you out there?" Miriam's scolding voice approached fast behind him.

Matteo didn't have enough room to fear her right now. Officer Outown and Jack Sallow rushed to them.

Lincoln turned to Matteo, his face holding the same question.

"Lawrence," Matteo managed to spit out. He didn't have

time to explain. "He's still out there."

Jack's eyes went wide. Miriam groaned.

"Stupid Williams boy always disobeying orders."

"We've dealt with Oquelite before," Lincoln said, starting for the cabin.

"Wait!" Matteo shouted after him. "The cape guy mentioned s—strong essence. He—he wanted strong essence."

Lincoln's face paled. "Nikki!" he cried out before Miriam grabbed a hold of him.

"Don't be irrational or you'll get her killed! We need you to get everyone you can to the Inn before the protective barrier drops. I'll get to Squirt and the Sergeant so she can alert the second camp, and Jack, you go to the barrier."

Matteo had only heard of the protective barrier around the new Inn. It wasn't tested. Would it be able to hold them off?

Jack nodded, running off. "Got it!"

Lincoln growled, but gave Miriam a hard nod before she ran off. Lincoln took a harsh turn on his heel and raced toward the cabin. Matteo froze, unsure what to do.

He knew that he needed to go to the Inn. The Inn was safe. But this could be his chance. The Oquelite were here. Right in front of him. He could see them running through the fields. He could hear the chaos and panic around him.

And yet, he didn't run. If the Oquelite were here, so was Jenna.

North Cordell, A Few Moments Earlier

Lincoln never saw the day where he'd meet the eyes of someone who'd forgotten how to use them. The pupils were so pale and the veins so ravenous, the creature didn't look human at all beneath the cape. They hadn't met eyes, technically. Lincoln was still tucked under the cot.

The Oquelite had stumbled in, and Matteo had cried something Lincoln hadn't heard.

He just hoped that the Wingor boy wasn't dead.

The Oquelite gasped for breath, his foot dragging, leaving a trail of blood with it. His tiny brows furrowed, his head snapping in Lincoln's direction. Lincoln stopped breathing, clenching his jaw.

A moment passed. The Oquelite looked away.

Lincoln followed the Oquelite's gaze, falling to the bow. "Oh no, you do—!"

In a flash, the Oquelite snatched them. Lincoln rolled out from the bed, grabbing the Cube from his satchel. He threw it, landing smack on the Oquelite's back, exploding into sparks. His heart dropped as the Oquelite simply frowned. "Aviduous…"

Lincoln jumped for the bow, pulling it with a harsh thrust against the Oquelite's frail body. Fury hardened in the Oquelite's face, twisting the bow, straining Lincoln's wrist with a painful twist.

This would be a great time for some abilities! he mentally shouted at the Voice.

Tell me your name, Aviduous. Then I will grant your wish.

Lincoln grit his teeth, throwing his weight back and slamming the Oquelite wall to wall.

"I've heard about you," the Oquelite rasped, a youthful giddiness in his crazy eyes. "How pleasant it'll be to brag with *your* essence in my veins!"

"Glad to see I have a reputation!"

The Oquelite Lincoln slammed into a cot, its wooden frame splintering under the pressure, ramming the bow right to Lincoln's face. Pain tore up his nose, blood red and flushing through his senses.

He gripped the bow tighter, trying to see through the painful tears. The burning swelled in him. He gave in to the sensation, letting it ignite his veins.

Now do my bidding.

With a cry, he tore the bow from the Oquelite's grip, surprising himself, and rammed it against *their* face. He landed his knee to their gut, rolling out from under, and delivered a kick to the Oquelite's chin. He tore his quiver off the chair and ran out the door, nearly colliding straight on with Matteo.

"Matteo! What are you doing?" Lincoln shouted, pushing past him, pulling out another arrow. "Get to the Inn!"

Matteo didn't listen, pushing back in front. "Jenna!"

Lincoln stopped in his tracks.

Matteo didn't need to say another word. His pleading

eyes said it all. Matteo was right.

Lincoln slowly turned toward the woods. If there was any time to get Jenna back, it was now.

He could hear the echoes of Ray's rage in his mind.

Don't let him distract you. The priority here is staying alive, remember? Think about that Ewyon girl.

Ray's voice drowned out the Voice's.

"Let's go!" he shouted back to Matteo, tossing him the taser arrow, which Matteo fumbled to catch.

"But—but how? Do you have a plan?" Matteo scrambled to keep up.

"Yep. Totally have a plan." Lincoln lied. So far that plan consisted of running right toward the people he should be running *away* from.

"Just try not to die, and look for any familiar Oquelite!" Lincoln shouted.

Matteo looked horrified at that command, but Lincoln didn't stop to elaborate, just broke off into the field.

Hey, Lawrence, where are you? He pushed mentally. The telepathic link didn't seem too great with distances. *We kinda need you right now.*

Are you getting to safety? Lawrence's internal voice was even out of breath.

Lincoln ducked a blat, rolling into the grass, glancing up at the oncoming, raging Oquelite. *Not exactly…safe.*

Lincoln! What the heck are you doing?

Matteo suggested it!

Suggested what?

We look for Jenna. We have the best shot at getting her back when everyone is in disarray.

Lawrence's mental voice was quiet a moment. *Don't get hurt. I'll try and find you.*

Well, at least they had someone's approval.

"There! A Member!"

That stupid name. "Member."

Lincoln pulled back the bow string, spinning around and releasing. An Oquelite froze on the path in horror, the arrow grazing their arm, drawing blood. The Oquelite cried out in pain but didn't burst into dust. Not even a small wither. Just grasping his wound in pain, looking up, desperate and confused. Lincoln's heart faltered, stepping back. This

Oquelite was young. They usually weren't put in upfront fights like this…

You have sympathy for the people who made your entire youth a misery? Kill him.

The Oquelite whipped up a free hand, gathering air in his grasp, and, with a thrust, knocked Lincoln off his feet. Lincoln rolled back to his feet.

The burn was back.

He drew another arrow, exploding on impact as it hit the mud in the path of the oncoming group of caped figures.

"No!" The wounded Oquelite threw himself onto Lincoln, wrestling him to the ground.

He tore out a blade and, with a cry, sent it straight for Lincoln's face. Lincoln writhed away, the blade landing an inch from his face. His newfound strength thrust the Oquelite forward, tearing out a taser arrow as he staggered to his feet, raising it to throw.

Another Oquelite dropped from the air. Lincoln landed a kick to the first Oquelite's face, drawing his bow on the hooded figure.

"No!"

The second Oquelite whirled around, their hood falling to their shoulders.

Lincoln froze. A girl. But not Jenna. An Oquelite *child.*

She hardly looked his age, tired and sweaty with the same pale eyes and scarred veins crawling down her cheeks. She scrambled back in fear, energy gathering in the palm of her hand as she sank back into a stance, trembling.

Young Oquelite never left the Labyrinth until they were battle fit or were of royal descent. Silas was the youngest Oquelite Lincoln knew.

No. The Oquelite weren't attacking.

Lincoln's gaze shifted to the forest, his heart stopping. They were *running.*

His foot pulled out from under him, slamming him into the mud. The male Oquelite ran for the younger girl, grabbing her arm, pulling her into a run.

Lincoln lay there, unmoving. The power faded in his chest. What were they running from?

He picked himself up. They weren't attacking the camp to attack the camp. They were getting essence to escape.

Supplies from the cabins.

But why?

You don't have time.

He shook himself. *Remember Jenna. Find Jenna.*

He stopped Matteo not too far off, running like his life depended on it, clutching the arrow with all his might. How were they supposed to find Jenna? All the Oquelite looked the same in their uniforms.

A figure dropped behind Matteo, turning with an insane delight, but Lincoln quickly whipped out an arrow, feeling numb as they fell.

Do not begin to feel empathy for your enemies.

Right. He couldn't have those feelings. Those feelings led to death.

Lincoln raced to Matteo. "Any sign of anything familiar?"

Matteo shook his head, out of breath. He looked scared out of his wits.

Lincoln didn't blame him. He could feel the tiniest twist of terror as he stared at the woods, the slowly turning storm clouds above as the Oquelite leaked out in a rage.

There was no order to it. It was chaos.

I think I see the Oquelite from the palace! Lawrence's voice broke so loud into Lincoln's mind, he cringed.

Matteo evidently heard it, his eyes going wide.

Where? Lincoln demanded.

Border of the woods? Big, overgrown trees. I can't see him super well. He's stopped.

"I know where that is!" Matteo shouted, turning left as Lincoln ran after him, stringing another arrow to taser a charging Oquelite out of their path.

If only he could take out the Super Cube to help decipher the location…His hands were too full for that. He was forced to rely on Matteo's memory.

They grew nearer to the woods, and Lincoln's heart leapt as he spotted Lawrence, sleeves rolled and his hands aflame…but no Oquelite.

"Lawrence!" Lincoln called out.

Leave him. Get rid of him. You're better off with the Ywondie dead.

Lawrence spun around, his eyes widening. "Watch out!

He's inv—"

A blast grazed Lincoln's shoulder as he spun around, pulling back another arrow. "Matteo, get down!"

Matteo didn't listen. He kept running. True Council Member fashion of him.

Lincoln saw the tall, ragged figure behind him: his cloak was gone, pieces of his armor missing, the fabric of his tunic burned around his shoulders. His eyes were pale, the veins deep and dark down his face.

Just like the Oquelite in the cabin…the sanity was gone.

"Where is the girl?" Lincoln shouted.

"He's beyond reason!" Lawrence shouted.

"The Lady of the Universe," the Oquelite sputtered, shooting another blast at Lincoln before disappearing.

"The half-Oquelite!"

"The Shadow Soul." The Oquelite seemed to glitch as he surrounded Lincoln, going faster and faster.

"I will spare you if you can just tell us where the Mathews girl is."

"Mathews. Mortalizer. The only way to escape her."

He moved faster, growing closer and closer. Lincoln held onto the bow tighter, trying to focus, but he couldn't.

"Tell us where she is!"

"She already found you!"

The man stopped, leaping; and Lincoln didn't have a moment to process before the man cried out, dropping back, his uniform engulfed in flames.

Lawrence stood behind, breathless. "He's beyond reason. It's not worth it!"

"We need to get to Matteo!" Lincoln didn't stall, breaking out back into a run, Lawrence right behind him.

It felt like with every step, the more Oquelite that appeared and the more Lincoln didn't have a moment to think when he pulled the string back on his bow. He was numb. And that almost made him feel terrified.

Matteo broke into the entrance of the woods, stumbling in the low-cut ditch as he scrambled into the woods, Lawrence and Matteo following. He slowed.

"We don't have time to stall," Lincoln said, his heart hammering in his chest. "We're three full-blooded Council Members in a forest of essence-hungry Oquelite."

"He came out of here, right?" Matteo said, ignoring Lincoln and turning to Lawrence.

"Yes. I'm sure of it," Lawrence said, his fists tightening on the flames in hand. "But I don't see her anywhere. Maybe we should just—"

Matteo ran farther, stopping at a twisted wall of trees, getting to his knees to crawl into the tunnel of roots.

A purple blast of flame shot out, sending Matteo scrambling back.

"Matteo!" Lawrence threw himself in front of him, bracing himself with his flaming hands.

Lincoln pulled out an arrow. "Show yourselves. You are surrounded. Any wrong moves—"

To Lincoln's surprise an Oquelite stumbled out in a hurry, her hands up in the air. Her face was streaked in blood and dirt, her pale eyes were darting around, and her hair was cropped close to her head, her body shaking.

Lawrence and Lincoln exchanged looks.

"Matteo?"

Lincoln's sweat went cold. Climbing out of the roots was a girl, her face dirty and her black curls frizzy and in disarray. She had a cape draped around her shoulders, tattered and ripped. Her face looked thinner, but her amber eyes were as bright as ever.

"Jenna," he breathed.

"Don't hurt them!" she shouted, throwing herself in front of the Oquelite.

The Oquelite grabbed her shoulder firmly.

"She didn't do anything wrong. You're looking for the wrong person." Jenna's eyes were crowded with tears. "Please."

With a shove, the Oquelite sent Jenna forward, collapsing into Matteo's arms. The Oquelite woman gave Lincoln a long look before running, jumping, and teleporting out of sight.

"They're going to kill her. All of them." Jenna sobbed, not fighting Matteo's arms that gently wrapped around her. He spoke to her in a different language.

"We have to get to the Inn before they drop the barrier," Lawrence said. "And get Jenna to a Medic."

"Don't hurt them," Jenna rasped.

"You feel up to running?" Lawrence asked.

Jenna nodded, straightening herself, clinging to Matteo's hand. And here was Lincoln, unable to feel anything. Was he glad? Disturbed? Worried?

His mind just felt like it was spinning. He just ran back out into the field, racing with all his might toward the Inn.

"I'll hold them back!" Lawrence shouted. "Go!"

Lincoln only glanced over his shoulder to see Matteo and Jenna running after him. The Inn wasn't too far. They just had to go faster.

Tell me your name, and that ability will be yours.

Lincoln pumped his legs faster. He just had to focus. If the barrier closed, they'd be stuck out in the brewing storm and the Oquelite.

"We're almost there!" he shouted back.

"What about Lawrence?" Matteo cried out.

Lincoln stopped, spinning around. Lawrence was far behind them, more Oquelite following behind.

"Go!" Lincoln shouted.

He grabbed his bow, shooting down two of the Oquelite. Jenna screamed. Lincoln felt his heart leap.

She's scared of you.

He shoved it away. He took a short breath and fired.

"You missed," Matteo said, his wide eyes turning to him, his brow arched.

Lincoln smiled. "Wait for it."

The arrow hit. The field burst into flame.

"Lawrence!" Matteo screamed.

Lincoln jumped out, holding Matteo and Jenna back. "Wait! He's fine!"

Matteo held his breath. For a moment, Lincoln only faced flames.

Good. You've gotten rid of one.

But he hadn't meant to. He never wanted to kill—

Lawrence burst out from the flames, sending out a sputter of curses.

Lincoln's heart leapt. "Faster! You don't have much time!"

"Oh, yeah. Because I'm just taking a walk through the park!" Lawrence rolled his eyes in visible disgust. "I'm being chased by psycho cape people, idiot!"

Lawrence burst past the fence, tripping over his own boots. He doubled over, clenching his side. Lincoln's heart dropped. Matteo tore free from Lincoln's grip, racing toward Lawrence.

"Matteo!" Lincoln ran after him, panic overtaking him, looking at Jenna standing, terrified.

"It's going to go off any second!" Lincoln shouted. "Go!"

The four of them ran toward the Inn, Lincoln counting the steps till they were over the barrier line, taking his time to keep the Oquelite back with his arrows as Matteo and Lawrence ran ahead.

Matteo, Jenna and Lawrence crossed the line.

An Oquelite dropped from the air, slamming against Lawrence, eyes crazed, cape burned and shriveled like the wound across his side. Lawrence didn't hesitate to send a fist to his face.

The Oquelite paused a moment before turning slowly, a bloody smile creeping onto his lips.

Lincoln tore faster up the hill, hardly breathing. The world felt slow. He wouldn't make it in time.

You do not need him.

A ball of energy formed in the palm of the Oquelite's hand and…

…he collapsed.

Matteo stood behind him, a taser arrow shaking in his hands.

Lincoln's jaw dropped, speechless, jumping over the barrier line and skidding into the mud as the forcefield dropped.

Lincoln sat on his knees, taking deep, trembling breaths. They'd just barely made it. His eyes drifted to the unconscious Oquelite lying face first in the mud a few feet away.

"G—good job, Teo," Lawrence stammered, struggling to stand upright, his eyes unblinking, staring down at the Oquelite as if they'd awake at any moment. "That was the same Oquelite who came after us in the fields."

"Wasn't real bright, was he?" Lincoln said, walking on his knees to the Oquelite's side.

The way he attacked was so untactical and desperate. His

uniform was ragged and suffered burns all throughout his body. He hadn't hesitated to run straight through the flames.

Unlucky for him, he wasn't burn resistant like Lawrence.

With a heave, he pushed the Oquelite over onto his back. Lincoln's heart stopped.

"What's wrong now?" Lawrence frowned.

Lincoln couldn't look away. "You know the Silas guy?"

"Yeah. That dumb-looking, monologuing prince?"

Lincoln forced himself to look away, his hands shaking as he met Lawrence's eyes, before he whispered the name. "We have his brother. Lord Matthias Idicous."

33

North Cordell, 10 Days Until

"WHERE IS THE Oquelite?"

The Sergeant burst into the room, slamming the door against the wall. She was drenched to the bone, her lip bloodied and her uniform spayed in mud, her braid loose and hair sticking to her face. It made her look all the more ferocious.

Her body went rigid as her eyes settled on Matthias Idicous, the Oquelite Crown Prince, tied to a chair between Lawrence and Lincoln, a whole dozen Defenders crammed in the room with them.

"You weren't joking," she breathed, walking slowly forward. She carefully lifted the unconscious Prince's chin. "Incredible. Even he was running."

But what had made them run? That was the question Lawrence couldn't seem to get an answer to. There was no order any longer. They were splintered. Heck, they had one of their leaders tied up in front of them.

"You two have done more than I could ask for," she said, turning to Lawrence and Lincoln.

Lincoln looked away.

"Go clean up. And don't leave the barrier," she said, turning her attention to the window. Even through the shimmer of the barrier, you could see the force of the rain falling in violent sheets, the grass and trees bending farther than Lawrence thought possible. "The Oquelite aren't the only thing to worry about."

"Is there a connection to the storm?" Lawrence asked.

Taryn didn't respond for a moment, her eyes firm on the storm. "I hope not."

She knew. And, of course, she wasn't going to tell them.

Lawrence and Lincoln left the room quickly, and Lawrence took everything in himself to keep his composure calm and not burst out the door.

They hurried past the crowds of drenched refugees into the kitchen.

Lincoln turned the knob on the door to the stairs. His eyes drifted to Lawrence, his face red. "Do you think she'll be okay?"

"Nikki?"

Lincoln nodded before quickly hiding his face as they rushed up the staircase. Was he...ashamed? Lawrence frowned. What for?

"I hope the rest of the recovery hurries so we can deal with...that venom problem," Lincoln said quietly.

The final point of her recovery. Removing the venom. The process sounded unpleasant, but Lawrence understood that it needed to be done, and if anyone could endure it with a smile, it was Nikki.

"Please—please call me when she's fine." Lincoln looked away from the steps and turned to leave the hall. "I—I'm sorry."

"Lincoln, what?" Lawrence shouted after him.

The door was already slammed shut.

Lawrence gave a frustrated sigh. Even Lincoln was running now?

He turned back to the kitchen, dimly lit by the raging storm outside and a lantern sitting on the partially installed counter. Fire Wolf sat on a stool, waiting patiently as Matteo gently finished applying the wrapping over the wolf's wound.

"You're back!"

Lawrence's heart leapt, spinning to face Jack, his arms full with a cardboard box. "Jack," he breathed.

"Funny, I was just going to bring this to your sister."

"My sister?" Lawrence's head went spinning. Isabel was safe in the camp over the mountain, and Lawrence hadn't been able to see her for weeks. It pained him to think that he'd almost forgotten.

He glared at the Defender. "What are you doing with my sister?"

"Whoa. Chill, Williams. I ordered her some supplies for the baby. She told me she didn't have anything yet," Jack said.

Lawrence's face heated. How had he not thought of that? Isabel was three months along now.

Jack scanned over Lawrence. "You're bleeding."

Lawrence frowned. He looked down to himself, lifting his trench coat. Ah, yes, his bloodied side.

"It's just a burn." He sighed, letting his drenched coat slip off his shoulders, and dropped it onto the coffee table in the living room. "It's hardly past my skin."

"Still not healthy. Anyone want tea? Our Doctor Mathews requested it to be *lemon*," Jack said, setting down the box and flicking the kettle on. He turned, his eyes still narrowed on Lawrence. "Take off your shirt. I'm patching you up. Lopez, can I have the Med kit?"

Lawrence panicked, stepping back. "No."

"No?" Jack frowned. "Williams, that wound can't stay exposed forever."

"I'll deal with it myself."

Jack raised a brow, glancing at Matteo and then back at Lawrence. "If you insist."

"I do." Lawrence stormed to the counter, taking the blue Med kit box and plopping into a stool. He grit his teeth to keep from flinching from the pain.

Jack opened his mouth to protest as the kettle went off. He took it off, still glaring at Lawrence as he filled the cups.

"You helped my sister, I hear," Lawrence said, desperate to change the subject.

Jack dipped in the tea bags. "I suppose so. It wasn't a difficult recovery. She has a very lively personality. Do you want some, Lopez?"

Matteo shrugged. Jack added a third.

"Did...*they* show up?

Jack frowned. "Who—?" His eyes went wide before his face faltered. "Oh. Your...legal family."

Matteo looked at Lawrence in surprise.

Lawrence's gaze dropped, staring intensely at the cup. "Are they going to take her back?" he asked quietly. He held his breath, bracing himself for an answer.

"Not now," Jack said. "They came in looking. A large group of employees from the farm, I assume. Demanding Isabel come back, saying she was legally bound due to her marriage and her...child."

Lawrence tried to keep his breathing even, squeezing his fist underneath the counter. Cain, Isabel's husband, didn't deserve any right as her husband and much less a father.

"I'd talked to Isbel before," Jack continued. "She told me the circumstances. Quite the character, she is, even when she was sick, she was always in the mood for conversation. She was tired and terrified most nights. And once they showed up, she came running to me. I lied a bit...told them I was like the Sergeant's right hand Officer and told them off."

"And Charles?" Lawrence dared to ask.

"They mentioned him too. Something about his mother." Jack's eyes fell.

So it wasn't over. They were still fighting.

Miz couldn't take back Charles. She may be his biological mother, but Lawrence had raised the little boy, his mother too drunk to notice him.

They hadn't escaped. Lawrence's eyes heated, but he squeezed his eyes shut.

It was quiet, all except for the rain pounding against the windows outside.

"I'm really sorry, Lawrence," Jack whispered.

Lawrence got to his feet, holding the Med kit close. "It's fine," he said, forcing his voice not to quake. "Thank you for protecting her."

Jack gave him a gentle smile. "Always."

Lawrence left without touching the tea. He moved quickly into the bathroom, locking the door behind him to deal with the wound. He wanted to remove his glasses, trapping himself in a blurry realm where he didn't have to face reality. He didn't want to face the past again. He didn't want to feed the wounds that stung so much stronger than the burn on his side.

The unfurnished bathroom only had a rag. He filled the tub with warm water, dipping the cloth in to soothe the dried blood from clinging to his shirt.

He finally managed to free himself, dealing with cleaning the bloody wound, when a soft knock came from the door. He frowned. "Yes?"

Silence.

"Are you okay?"

Lawrence blinked in surprise. "Matteo?"

"Are you okay?" he repeated.

"I'm fine," Lawrence stammered, turning back to his burn. He knew that Matteo was probably only here because of what Jack had said.

Matteo was quiet for a moment. "Is that true?"

Lawrence flinched. *Was it true?* How long did he have to keep lying? "I'm okay. It's almost patched up."

"That's not what I mean."

Lawrence swallowed hard, unraveling the bandaging. He pretended that he didn't hear him, taking his time to wrap the wound, waiting for Matteo to leave. On the third wrap, he heard a small thud outside the door.

Lawrence sighed. "I told you, I'm fine. And mostly thanks to you... You did incredible today."

Now it was Matteo's turn to be quiet.

"Thank you," he said finally. "You were right."

"Right?" Lawrence snorted. "About what?"

"I'm going to become a Member," Matteo said, not directly answering. Lawrence could hear him take a deep breath. "Thanks to you."

"To me?"

"Yes."

Lawrence sighed. "I didn't do much, Teo."

Matteo didn't respond.

He ripped the end of the bandage before pulling on a new shirt. He removed his glasses, rubbing the bridge of his nose. "Matteo, how do you say 'thank you?'"

"*Gracias?*"

"Grass-ias?"

Matteo sighed loudly. "You're terrible."

Lawrence smirked. "I'm trying."

"Grah-cias."

"Gra—"

"AH."

"Grah-cias."

"Very good."

Lawrence smiled, savoring the tiniest bit of praise Matteo had given. Matteo was growing, and Lawrence felt like he was struggling to keep up. How much longer until Matteo knew who he really was? He was no teacher. No role model.

"Williams!" Jack's voice tore down the hallway.

Lawrence heard Matteo shuffle to his feet with a bang to the door. Lawrence leapt to his feet, pushing on his glasses. He rushed to the door, unlocking it and swinging the door open. Matteo had already moved out of the way.

Jack stood in the frame at the entrance of the doorway.

Lawrence's heart skipped a beat. "What? Is something wrong?"

His breath caught as Dr. Blythe stepped in the silhouette beside Jack. "Nikki is settled and requesting your presence. Urgently. 'Lawrence,' is it?"

"Yes, that's me." Lawrence felt bad having to ignore Matteo, rushing to Dr. Mathews.

The doctor was quiet for a moment before nodding. "Thank you for bringing my daughter back."

"I hope she's all right."

The doctor tensed. "A bit shaken, but physically fine."

Lawrence felt a pit of guilt. "And Nikki?"

Dr. Mathews chuckled. "Fine. Quite spirited despite the hectic ride. She's insisted she's all right only about seven times. And made a request for lemon."

Jack handed Lawrence the steaming, plastic cup.

Lawrence let himself breathe again. Those flashbacks seemed to be torturing her, and he was terrified that it would worsen her condition. But if she was rambling about lemons…that was better?

Why lemons?

He pulled out his Comm, quickly messaging Lincoln. "Good."

Dr. Mathews narrowed her eyes, ushering him to follow her. "You're her cousin, aren't you?"

Lawrence tucked away his Comm as they entered the next hall. "I am."

"You two look very different," Dr. Mathews said, reaching Nikki's door. "Highly resemble your sister, I can say."

Dr. Mathews opened the door, stepping aside to let Lawrence through. His heart leapt, seeing Nikki sitting in a cot by the window, her machines still trapping her. She was alert, her eyes sparkling with excitement. "Lawrence."

He couldn't breathe. "Nikki," he breathed before clearing his throat and holding out the cup. "Tea?"

"I'll go deliver your other friend," Dr. Mathews said with a nod. She closed the door, leaving Nikki and Lawrence alone.

"You look terrified," Nikki said with a small frown as she took the cup.

"You really have no idea how crazy it is to see a dead girl alive, do you?" Lawrence laughed hoarsely, slowly taking a step closer to her.

Nikki shrugged. "It feels weird," she admitted softly. "That life just went on…and I wasn't there."

"You're back now." Lawrence tried to offer a smile.

She laughed softly, taking a small sip of the tea before her face scrunched up. "What is this stuff?"

"Lemon tea."

"Why tea? This is fake lemons." She stared with disdain at the cup.

Lawrence snorted. "Miriam put us on a coffee ban. Replaced them all with these tea bags overnight. Not a pleasant morning," he grumbled.

"So no lemons?" Nikki asked.

"No lemons."

She sighed, looking out the window. "I guess we'll just have to plant some," she said, digging out a satchel tucked between the bed and the wall, drawing out a wooden lemon, looking to be carved by her. With a small twist, it opened. "That's what Ray said the little, white things in my first lemon would do. It's fascinating, really."

"Yes…the magic of biology."

Nikki set down the tea cup, entirely uninterested. "So what has gotten you so busy?"

"Currently, we're dealing with a lovely situation," Lawrence said with a halfhearted chuckle. "A lot of things, actually. Ray's got a situation with a Member in Glorgory, and both he and Cole can't seem to get away from these Exerticus—I mean, red-eyed guys. Everything basically wraps up into two words: Shadow Soul."

Nikki froze. "S—Shadow Soul?"

Lawrence frowned. "Uh, yeah. Have you heard of it? Does it have to do with those memories in your head?"

Nikki didn't answer. She just threw off her covers and swung her legs off the bed.

"Nikki!" Lawrence jumped up. "What are you doing?"

"I need to go to Algery."

He rushed to stop Nikki from pushing herself fully up onto her feet, grabbing her shoulders. "You're not even fit to leave the Inn, much less another region."

Her brows furrowed. "You don't understand. We're running out of time. It makes sense now. It makes so much sense now."

"What time are you talking about?"

"Something is in Algery…something she wants." She tried to wriggle free from Lawrence's grip.

"Nikki! Calm down! If you want to get better, you can't exert yourself!"

She stopped fighting with a scowl. "Shadow Soul. That's why she needed me." Nikki's eyes were frantic around the room. "I'm an Aguirre."

"Nikki, none of this is making sense."

A thud came from behind him. Lawrence whirled around to see Lincoln with his bow fallen onto the floor.

"It makes absolute sense," he said, his voice strained. "The Aguirres were in Algery, and the Agents were involved with all sorts of Council-related projects. If there is anywhere someone wanting Shadow Soul-related information…it would be where the Aguirres were."

Lawrence glanced from Nikki to Lincoln. "And we haven't thought of this before because…?"

"It's burned to the ground," Lincoln said, his voice entirely monotone.

Right. How could he have forgotten that tiny detail?

"Nik, when is this person going to Algery?"

Lawrence's eyes widened, realizing what Lincoln was trying to confirm. The fact they'd been trying to tie together ever since the information had dropped.

"The night…with no moon," she stammered. "Ten days."

Lawrence and Lincoln exchanged glances.

"The Soul Night."

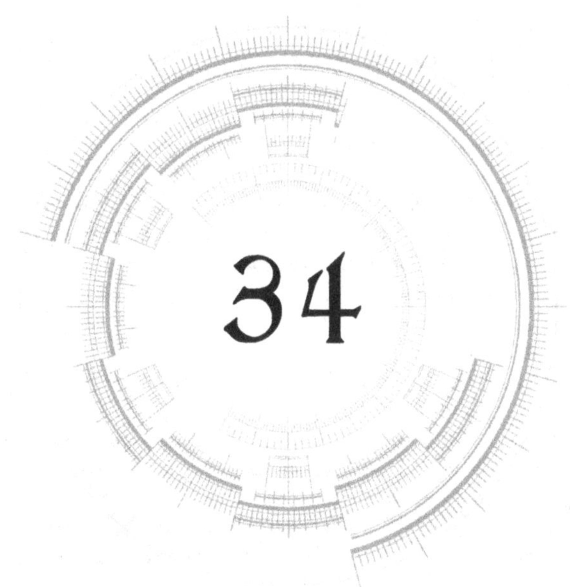

34

The Ewyon Coastal Alliance Palace—Before Recorded Time

THEY WEREN'T NIGHTMARES.

The world passed in slow motion as she hugged herself, her back pressed against the wall, feeling the glass doors, its curtain drawn.

Sergia's voice echoed in her mind: "Remember to breathe."

How could she breathe when it didn't matter whether she did or not? Her face was numb as she stared blankly forward.

If she breathed, she'd remember the last time she lived.

Die. Die. Die.

The door creaked open: a man, his posture firm and lightly muscled. She could bring him down. Not much of a fight. Just another pathetic male with the air of importance as he smoothed the silver tassels of his sleeves. "Our Highest will see you now."

She rose lifelessly from her seat, brushing past the guard through the open doors of the office. There Caratene stood, shorter than herself, and her arms lay daintily at her side, but her eyes were truly the killer.

"I think you'll be glad to know Abbadon's son is on prohibition."

"What?!" The burning shot through her eyes, anger shattering the stone of her face. "He kidnapped and murdered countless woman on a witch hunt for the Soul—"

"We do not want to cause rumors in our kingdom, especially in its rebuilding state."

"These aren't rumors." Adrienne slammed her fists against the table, startling Carastene. "There were other victims. Just ask them—"

"I am not to be the one to ruin our valuable ally's son's reputation for his immature ways of finding the Soul."

"It's all reputation with you, isn't it?" That's all the Soul search was. To appease the Council. That's all anything was. "I thought I was your niece. Family."

Carastene's face twisted. "I want to be related to no such thing as yourself."

Adrienne snorted, trying to control her breathing and the hot tears threatening her eyes. Her heart burned to hate her aunt, but her disapproval cut deeper than the healing wounds.

"So it only took being stabbed multiple times and every bare human decency stripped away for you to believe me?" Her voice cracked. "I can't die."

Anger swelled in her chest. The curls of energy began to flow around her fingers—the unfamiliar sensation that she savored. Carastene went pale and cried out, flattening herself against the wall behind her.

"W—when did you—?"

"This?" Adrienne whipped her blue, flaming hand toward Carastene. "It took killing to activate this."

Adrienne clenched her fist, the flame extinguishing.

"I'll have you arrested," Carastene stammered.

"For what?"

Carastene's eyes searched the room for an answer. Her eyes finally settled on the floor. "F—for being the Soul."

Adrienne snorted. "I'm no Soul. The Soul is prophesied as an Oquelite hybrid."

"Look in the mirror."

Adrienne reluctantly did as instructed, turning to the full-body mirror set on the wall. A frail frame stared back at her. A woman dressed in black, her body covered tightly, her braid flat on her shoulder. Her face was pale and thin.

"Look at your eyes, Adrienne."

They were violet, just as every full-blooded Ewyon born had.

She watched in the reflection as Carastene slowly stepped behind her, her face tight. She held up her hand, flexing her fingers.

Adrienne frowned, feeling a tickle through her face. She carefully pushed the blond locks from her face, revealing her opposite eye.

A steel-gray one stared back.

Adrienne scrambled back, muffling a scream.

"You—you lied to me." The words were cold, chilling her veins as the shock slowly turned to rage. "What am I? Who am I?"

Carastene stuck a hair in place casually. "You are Adrienne Emberson, daughter of my sister, Avalon."

Adrienne knew that. "Show me my record!"

Adrienne's hand whipped in the air. Carastene froze, fear flashing over her face. She opened the drawer to the desk, setting out a Scroll tentatively.

No arguing? No screaming?

She took the scroll hesitantly. She unraveled it, the swirling handwriting sending chills down her spine.

Kathryn Adrienne Emberson Idicous

Born on the fourth day of the autumn cycle by Avalon Emberson.

"Kathryn? My name is Kathryn."

"It's a name from the slave culture. I helped you by addressing you by your Ewyon given name."

She always had her name.

Child claimed to be fathered by east-sector farmhand, Orion Idicous, Oquelite.

Oquelite.

Everything came crashing down.

"Oquelite blood. I kept you from the humiliation."

Claim to be wed under Oquelite custom. Under Ewyon jurisdiction, the child is deemed out of wedlock and Avalon is condemned to masking. The child shall not assume the throne order.

This was information she'd known even far too young. The stories of how her mother's fling had ruined her, but with an Oquelite? And only because the Ewyon dismissed anything to do with the servant class as valid?

The scroll slipped from her trembling hands, clattering against the desk. "I—I am the daughter of the eldest Emberson Princess…a queen. I was born validly."

"Not of Ewyon law," Carastene snapped back.

She clenched her fists closed, her eyes squeezing shut. The burning longed to overcome her. It longed to form blades and fight for the world she was owed.

It had been taken from her and hidden from her. What was she?

"Am I?"

"What?"

"Am I the Soul, then?" Her eyes burst open, energy zapping through the air. "Am I the one we've hated so much all these years?"

"That's her there!"

The doors burst open behind her, two guards tearing into the room. "Your Majesty, are you all right?"

Carastene quickly snatched the scroll from the desk. "Take her to her tower."

Her mind begged to destroy the entire room, watch her aunt bleed and the hideous scroll burn.

A guard reached for her hand, but she jerked it back as his skin met hers.

No. Never again.

Her arms were jerked behind her back. She could take them if she wanted.

It was pointless. She was turned out the door.

Carastene called after her. "I tried to protect you, Adrienne!"

You lied to me.

"My name is 'Kathryn!'"

And the doors slammed shut.

The knife ran along her collar bone, the wicked, glowing, violet gaze trapping her. "The best part about you"—the laugh echoed against her skull—"is that I could do this forever."

Kathryn woke up in cold sweat.

The world came into focus around her. Moonlight lit the room, casting shadows on the wood floor. Cold air nipped at her skin. Her trembling fingers ran over the scar dragging across her chest.

"Adrienne!" Sergia flew in around the corner of the room from her place on the couch. She hadn't slept in her quarters since the incident. "Are you all right? I heard—"

"I'm fine."

Sergia's face softened. "It's just nightmares."

But they weren't.

Her silence made Sergia creep closer. "Adrienne, I'm worried about you. You're hardly eating. Hardly sleeping…"

"It's fine." Kathryn hung her head in her hands.

"No." Sergia sat down beside her. "It's not."

She placed a hand on Kathryn's. Without warning, Kathryn wrenched it away.

Sergia jumped.

Kathryn froze. "I—I'm sorry." Kathryn tried to relax, but the air felt stiff between them.

"It's not all right," Sergia said, her brows knitting. "You've proved that. Adri—"

Kathryn flinched. "Please. Please don't call me that," she whispered, hugging her legs to her chest.

"'Adrienne?'"

Kathryn nodded.

Sergia's lips parted, her eyes widening. "What happened in the Queen's office?" she said, her voice gentle now. "You've hardly spoken for days."

Her gentle voice soothed the tension, and her gentle, familiar hand methodically brushed through her hair, as if she was just a child again.

"My name is 'Kathryn Adrienne Emberson Idicous.'"

"So? There are many with longer names."

Kathryn squeezed her eyes shut. "No, Sergia. You don't understand."

"What don't I understand?"

Kathryn opened her eyes, slowly turning to face Sergia. "Kathryn. It's an Oquelite name."

Sergia's eyes went wide, unblinking. "No. You're not saying…"

Even the one closest to her would run too.

Kathryn nodded, letting the purple energy collect in rings around her fingers. "Oquelite…the Dark Force…the race which gets its power from the essence of others. The other half of the Shadow Soul."

Sergia looked to the power in Kathryn's grasp, cold realization flooding her face. "If you can do that, that means…"

"I killed someone," Kathryn said flatly. Saying it out loud was far less thundering than she'd expected. It was a fact.

Sergia stared at Kathryn for a long moment before her head fell. "I—I don't know what to say."

"Then don't."

Sergia pressed her lips together firmly but didn't leave Kathryn's side, letting them dwell in the silence, fiddling with a piece of Kathryn's long hair.

"Do you want me to call you 'Kathryn?'"

"It does not matter."

"Well, then, Kathryn." Sergia laughed quietly. "What do you plan to do next?"

What did she plan to do? She hadn't thought much of the question before. She couldn't just sit around and wait to die.

She couldn't die. Even if she wanted to.

"I need to learn more about the Oquelite hybrid," she said, shaking off the faint glow of her palms.

"They harbor the essence of others in their own." Sergia shivered. "That would mean killing someone."

"But what if it didn't? What if there was a way to only take what you needed? What if there was another way to harbor it?" She had an Ewyon's blood also flowing through her veins, didn't she? Essence was part of a person's being and could be controlled by an Oquelite.

An Ewyon could control basic functions of someone's person.

What if there was a way to use someone's being to control them?

Something as simple as a name.

Kathryn was the Shadow Soul after all.

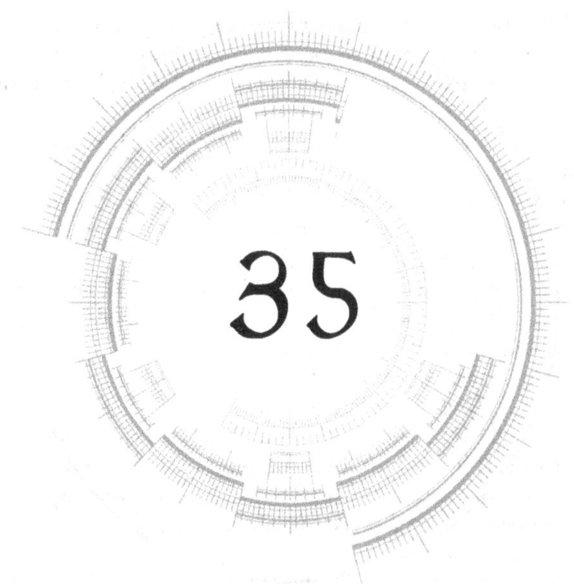

35

Liberty, 10 Days Until

THEY KNEW WHO the Shadow Soul was. Some lady named "Kathryn" in Nikki's head.

It meant nothing. They had no lead.

The woman was thousands of years old. She was immortal and unkillable, but they didn't have a single lead on her. And, apparently, she'd planned something on the anniversary of the Soul Night tall tale. How symbolic.

Cole tried to sleep, but it was pointless; so instead, he sat over the wrinkled piece of paper, stylus pen in hand, a messy stanza written out.

How did Tabitha manage this?

A love song was out of the question, even if that was the only kind of songwriting he was remotely familiar with thanks to his writing teacher with an obvious crush on the professor across the hall.

Cole didn't do very well in that class.

Right now he had the equivalent of a stupid poem.

I miss you, he scribbled out before quickly erasing it.

Everything seemed to be going on track now with the discovery of the Shadow Soul identity, besides the fact that he was a wanted man and he was utterly alone in it. But it would be worth it. He'd see Tabitha again. He'd say sorry again. Even if she wanted nothing to do with him.

Maybe he'd go home and visit his father for answers. He'd go find Ray soon. And he'd say sorry.

I will always be sorry. What rhymed with "sorry?"

He flipped the pen to erase the line when his Comm buzzed off across the carpet. Cole dropped the pen, scrambling to snatch the Comm.

A new message from Echo.

ECHO: Dinner tonight. You and Cecileo.

Just Cole and Cecileo, so soon?

His heart leapt. He'd been lying around, running on two energy drinks and the Shadow Soul's name running in his head as he stared at a piece of paper.

COLE: Okay.

He ran to change from his sweaty, day-old clothes. He rushed for the tent flaps before he caught his image in the mirror sitting on the dresser.

He hardly recognized the face looking back at him. His hair was longer than its usual close-cropped style. The Marketeer attire fit him better now than it had weeks ago, his bare arms less pale and more freckled from the sun. The Illuminate hung comfortably in its sheath around his waist. In fact, he looked more muscular too.

It made his heart skip a beat. How much had he changed?

He reached for his chest, clasping around the empty air where the Medallion should have been. He shook it away, walking out of the tent. The lights of the day were fading, the daytime merchant rolling carts. Cole stayed out of the way, feeling the smallest spark of importance as he walked the familiar path to the Pater's tent.

"Hearty." Did that rhyme?

He sidestepped quickly as an official stormed from the tent, nearly ramming into him.

Cole frowned, blinking. What was that about?

He picked up his pace and ran to the tent, nearly forgetting to wipe his feet. He burst inside.

The office was empty, but he could hear Echo shouting. "You are in no position to argue!"

"It's fine—ah! Hey!"

Cole's heart leapt, and for a horrible moment, he thought that they were fighting.

"You're bleeding all over your collar."

That wasn't much better.

"Are you okay?" Cole shouted, bracing himself. "Do you need me to get a Medic?"

They dropped silent. Cecileo cursed. Echo scolded him.

"No! Everything is fine! Cecileo, hold that to your nose and change!" Echo rushd out, wiping her hands on her coat. "This is why I deal with diplomats."

"Look, Echo, it was fine—"

"Change, Cecil!" Echo turned her attention back to Cole and his pale face. "Don't worry. It had absolutely nothing to do with you. Just a…frequently occurring *issue* these diplomats like to argue. Nothing strikes his temper more."

Cole caught the smallest, shameful blush on Echo's face, but she quickly erased it, clearing her throat. She snatched a satchel from Cecileo's desk and handed it to Cole. "Here's dinner. Cecileo wanted to be on the move for your lesson."

Lesson? Cole's heart leapt. This was their first training session.

"Thank you." He slung the bag over his shoulder.

Echo smiled. "Good."

Her eyes faltered. No matter how hard she tried to hide it, whatever had happened earlier shook her. Despite it all, she held the strength on her shoulders and the sincerity in her dark eyes, so warm and full of life…and something so much more sinister.

Cecileo rushed out into the room, still buttoning his jerkin. "Got a coat, kid?"

It had been so warm, Cole couldn't even remember where his was.

"I've got this." Echo rushed into the back.

Cecileo had a dried stream of blood from his nose, but besides that, he looked fine. He tore his fingers through his hair, tossing his circlet to the desk.

Echo raced in with two coats. She handed the smaller, more worn one to Cole.

"This was Cecileo's way back when he won the title of 'Pater.' Hardly out of his teen years."

Cole took the jacket gratefully.

Cecileo snorted. "'Won?' More like 'hardly survived,'" he grumbled. He pulled on his own coat, rubbing the blood away. "We good?"

"As long as you don't pick any more fights," Echo said with a heavy sigh.

"Good," Cecileo said, turning to Cole. "You can hurry ahead."

Cole nodded, slipping out into the dark street. He felt bad having walked in on whatever mess of a meeting had occurred.

Why had Echo seemed so guilty about it?

He walked slowly down the street. The white tents were aglow softly inside, the silhouettes of the Market medics along the outer walls, some leaving with bags and a bow to the Pater tent before scampering off and not batting him an eye.

"Safari…" That rhymed with "sorry." But it had nothing to do with the song.

He reached the end of the street, waiting against the wall. A breeze sent a chill through him, realizing why Echo had insisted on a jacket. He hadn't been out much on a Liberty night.

The soft, muffled voice and footsteps brought Cole's attention back to the Pater's tent. Echo stood in the doorway, tent flap held open, Cecileo standing on the mat in front of her.

They spoke to each other gently, genuine sorrow in the shadows of Echo's face. Cecileo said something, and Echo nodded.

Echo slumped into a hug, wrapping her arms around his neck. Cecileo hugged her tightly. He let go, but she pulled him back to kiss him before letting Cecileo go and slipping back into the tent.

Cecileo stood still for a moment before turning and dashing toward Cole. "We're taking a shortcut. Come on!"

Cecileo raced ahead, Cole hurrying to match his pace.

Cole quickly learned that Cecileo's shortcut was a turn through the space between the border buildings and expertly climbing to the roof without breaking a sweat.

He looked down on Cole, who'd managed to take a considerably longer time, pushing his back up against one wall and his feet on the other.

"You good, Council Kid?"

Cole moved a foot to another brick, stretching for the farthest hold. "Almost…there."

In an awkward struggle, he pulled himself up onto the roof, where Cecileo sat and gave an exaggerated yawn.

"All right, let's get a move on!" Cecileo didn't give Cole a moment to catch his breath, dashing across the rooftop, grabbing the fire escape ladder, and crawling higher.

Cole ran after him. The cold night air nipped at his face as he climbed. The sensation rose in his chest as they rose higher and higher, reaching for the highest rooftop after Cecileo.

Cole admired his youthful agility. Despite his hot-headed instinct as a diplomat, Cecileo worked with brilliance. Confidence. That's what Cecileo said that Cole lacked. A sense of confidence that refused to be shattered climbing higher and higher so that Cole could hardly catch his breath, not worrying about tripping and falling to his death.

Finally, he hoisted himself up to find Cecileo standing on the edge of the scraper. Cole stumbled into place beside him.

The view was astonishing, nothing like he'd ever seen before. Dark land stretched for miles till it breached the enormous, glowing Dome, its faded towers and buildings lit against the sky amidst the darkness of the wastelands around it.

"The Liberty Dome." Cecileo sighed. "Incredible work of engineering and human adaptation of the EarthShaker survivors, isn't it?"

"Only five like it." Cole agreed. The five golden regions were the hubs of survival among the two decades of winter after the war.

Cecileo snorted. "Riddled with a self-imposed righteousness and a prideful system to strangle a generation."

He plopped down fearlessly onto the edge. He took Echo's bag, pulling out a tinfoil package. He handed it to Cole.

Cole carefully sat on the edge, not as daring as Cecileo to hang his legs over. He unwrapped a sandwich and tried not to stare at the ground far below and more at the dazzling lights of the city Felicity inhabited.

"So," Cole said, daring to speak. "Where are we going?"

"Far side of the market," Cecileo said, retrieving a thermos, no doubt full of tea. "That's where we'll find your bandit survivor friend."

Cole's heart leapt. "Already?" He couldn't say that he was disappointed. In fact, it took everything in him to keep his face straight.

"We have to, unless you'd rather—"

"No. You're right! The sooner the better." With the Soul Night coming up, Cole needed to be prepared.

"Tarry?" That didn't rhyme at all…Was it a word?

"Good. And now that we actually have a living Illuminate." Cecileo chuckled, taking a long sip of his tea. "How long have you known now?"

"Si—seven months." The past month was an utter blur. Hard to believe that seven months ago, the height of his adventures were sitting in the back of history classes while receiving glares from a short, blond girl.

"How long have you had the Medallion?" Cecileo said.

"I found it…Well, it was given to me when I was seven." He paused. "Around the time the Curatrix team died."

"I was fifteen at the time. I remember the day well." Cecileo sighed. "Most of the Market didn't care. Another Defender dead was a good thing, though it really hit Echo hard."

"She likes Defenders?"

"If anyone despises Defenders more, it's Echo." Cecileo laughed harshly. "No, the Curatrix team was her hope that the system wasn't entirely broken."

Cole sat in the cold silence. He knew Defenders who'd die for him. Defenders he loved and called his friends…but he'd seen the fear they struck into anyone they passed. He'd seen them break up brawls on Sulfur street corners.

"Why Echo specifically?" His curiosity took the best of him.

Cecileo tensed. "She had a rough childhood," he said, his gaze falling to the streets below. "Let's just say, things were done to her and things seen by her that a child should never know."

Cole swallowed hard, trying hard not to let his mind ponder further.

They didn't speak for a moment, sitting and feeling the cold wind that picked up with the smell of rain.

"That's what she has against bandits too. They're the ones who sold her as a child to a few Officers for a pretty penny." Cecileo gave a harsh breath. "But that's what the Market's for. Saving people given up on by society and giving them something more than that. A home."

"What about you?" Cole dared to ask.

Cecileo simply shrugged. "Boring story. Parents moved from Avvio, killed in some riot by an Officer. I didn't speak Anglish, funny considering how I hardly remember a word of *Italiano* now. Jumped off a building when I was fourteen."

Cole's lips parted in horror, and Cecileo took a sip, as if it was just common knowledge. "Anyway, I didn't die, thanks to Miss Metal Hand and the Market's search for 'Sons' to become the next Pater. It all worked out."

"Echo saved your life?" Cole's eyes widened.

"It was hardly romantic." Cecileo laughed. "I told her I hated her for years for saving my life that day." Cecileo's gaze became lost in the thermos in his hands before looking back to Cole with a small smile. "How about you, kid? Any family?"

The change of subject made the food taste bitter. "My dad," he said, simply. Could he count his half-siblings that he didn't know existed for a decade?

"No mother?"

"Dead."

"What a coincidence," Cecileo said casually. He crumpled up his tinfoil, shoving it into the bag. "That's when Echo's influence comes in handy. I bet she'd send me to my room if she could."

Cole couldn't help but laugh. "You do manage to make her quite mad. Today?"

Cecileo snorted. "That disgusting excuse of a man grabbed her, Johnson. And she thinks I'm overreacting. Politics isn't an excuse to touch her." He shrugged with a proud smirk, with no regret of his brawl. "More than anything, it reminds me how much of a past has been stolen from us. The world would be better off if everyone had a mother, but all we can do is appreciate what we can have."

He never thought that he'd hear such intelligent words from Cecileo, getting to his feet to brush himself off. Cecileo had spoken so casually about events that Cole knew would eat him alive. He could barely handle what was going on, but how would he handle both his parents being murdered and never knowing the answers? Being forced into a system to become a ruler of a system of outlaws?

He wouldn't be able to let himself live with the knowledge of someone having been tortured so inhumanely. What if it was Tabitha? His blood burned. He knew that if he ever met her parents, it was done for.

But he also knew that revenge wasn't right.

Cecileo had let go of the past. Cole was holding onto every last thing until it crushed him.

He snapped out of his daze, scrambling after Cecileo, who hadn't bothered to wait for him.

They reached the far end of the Market, the border buildings mostly abandoned and stretching out into the wastelands. Cecileo signaled him to crouch down on the roof in the cover of the shadows.

The tents looked to be made of far cheaper material, and the life that seemed to thrive in Cole's street was dormant among them. Lanterns lit tent entrances, and primarily men walked in harsh, drunken conversation.

Cecileo pulled the hood of his jacket over his head. "You're leading. I'm just your follower. Got it?"

"Wait, what?" Cole frowned in a harsh whisper. "You want me to lead?"

"That's what you're here to learn, aren't you?"

Cole opened his mouth to argue. He wasn't fit to be a leader, but something tugged inside him, and he shut his mouth.

Cecileo flashed a triumphant smile. "And we can't have anyone reporting back to those complaining officials that they saw the Pater sneaking around the slum."

Great.

Cole scanned the area from above. "Do you know which tent he's in?"

"Nope." With that and without warning, Cecileo leapt from the low roof of the building to the ground, taking Cole with him.

Cole quickly collected himself before he drew too many eyes. He straightened his posture, and with a nod from Cecileo, he pressed forward into the street.

He moved between disgruntled drinkers, scanning the faces for anyone seeming reasonable enough to help. He stopped at a man standing outside a large, dirty carpet tent, tending to a table, flipping holocards.

"Hello." Cole cleared his throat.

"Aren't you a bit young to drink in this here region?" The man's voice cracked with a chuckle, and Cole couldn't figure out if he was joking or not.

"I'm not here for that."

"And your companion?"

"He prefers tea."

Cecileo raised his thermos proudly.

Cole leaned forward on the table, towering over the man casually. "I need directions."

"You lost?"

"No. I'm looking for someone. Reddish hair, marks on his face and chest, kind of hard to miss."

The man's face lit up. "You mean Box?"

"Box?" Cole frowned but quickly scolded himself for the doubt. "Yes. Him."

The man laughed. "Better not cross paths with Zion Hakuri if that's who you're looking for," he chuckled.

"Excuse me, who?"

The man ignored him. "Box has been staying in a little, white tent by the exit gate. Last owner died a few weeks ago. Perfect timing for the kid."

Cole and Cecileo exchanged glances. Cole turned back to the man. "Thank you. We'll be on our way."

With that, they hurried away.

"I thought the Market was a place of peace and prosperity. And who is this Hakuri guy? Another bandit?"

Cecileo sighed. "Zion Hakuri's not an issue, don't worry about it."

"But that guy—"

"Trust me, Johnson." Cecileo's voice was stern.

They made their way through the street, though it felt like they were nowhere near the Market. No one looked unhappy, but not many looked exactly sober, either. They managed to stay out of the bumbling person's way, finally breaking out into the abandoned dirt lot behind the line of tents.

The small tent was hard to miss, the sole glow in the dark lot.

"This is it," he breathed, rushing to the door, knocking on the wood support.

A sputtered curse came out from inside. "I said go away! I don't have any darn—" The boy's head popped out of the tent, freezing. "It's you."

Cole waved awkwardly. "Box?"

The boy's surprise quickly fell to an eyeroll. "Sure," he grumbled. "How did you find me?"

"I have my ways."

Box snorted. "Council Members."

"How did—?"

"'Have my ways,'" Box imitated. "Do you need something?"

"I have questions."

Box studied him for a moment. "I am in your debt," he said reluctantly. "Come on—no! He has to stay."

Cecileo gave Cole a reassuring nod before sitting outside. Cole took a breath and stepped inside.

It smelled strongly of cigar smoke that was long stained into the fabric walls, the tone more gray than white. The space was small and could fit the two of them. Box plopped down onto a mat and Cole sat tentatively opposite of him, a small, electric fire between them.

"Tell me what you know about the bandit commission," Cole said.

Box's eyes widened. "Look. I don't know everything, but I can tell you it has to do with…my kind." Box shifted uncomfortably.

Cole's brow furrowed. "And that is?"

"It isn't obvious to you, almighty Member?"

Cole had to admit that it wasn't. Box was beginning to remind him of Ray with his snark. It made the whole situation a bit less intimidating.

Box sighed. "I'm Lyntox." He bared his teeth, flashing sharp canines.

Cole froze. "Like the shifters? How? What are you doing here of all places? And in such a human form?"

From what Jack had told them over his lecture lessons, Lyntox were commonly most comfortable in an animalistic form, but Box had to have been human for weeks…maybe months. And all the way out here in Liberty?

Box's yellow eyes fell to the dirt floor. "It was a mission."

"You were sent on a mission? By who?"

"We're not savages, Member." Box scowled before his face faltered. "My pack received…a threat from a group of undeads with glowing, red eyes, under the command of some 'Lady of the Universe.'" He snorted.

The Lady of the Universe…That's what the Voice so persistently in their heads had named herself. She was in charge of the Exerticus?

"Anyway, they came thinking the Council Member was there. No idea how they found us, or even made it in there. Only happened once before. Found some weird, red-headed girl running through the woods months ago, that's when I first realized we were out of the Void."

Right. The supernatural world had been confined to the magical, growing woods. The reawakening was bringing it back from the Void…all of it.

"'They ravaged the camp, thinking we were hiding them—"

"Hold up…If they were looking for a Member in the Lyntox camp, this means a Member is Lyntox?"

"Don't you know all the Members?" Box groaned again. "The Guardian represents the Mythic. It was foretold to the Soroz that the next to live in the cycle would be a Lyntox. And considering they were searching for the Soroz, it's simple to come to the conclusion they were looking for the Guardian Member."

Cole opened his mouth to ask what this "Soroz" was, but Box beat him to it. "The Soroz is the eldest of the leader's clan, usually. It was said she'd be the mother of the next Guardian Member."

There was an awkward silence as Box cranked the lid of a can of beans open. Cole scrambled his mind for a potential

Soroz. So far, none of his friends' mothers were Lyntox. The marks, feline eyes, and sharp canines would make it obvious.

If this Soroz person was supposed to be a Member's mother…Cole's heart skipped a beat. "Where is the Soroz now?"

"Probably dead." Box shrugged, tossing a now empty can into the fire. Cole cringed as it sparked and popped. Box watched, unmoving, the flames, his cat-like eyes narrowing. "When the forest first began to awaken back into this realm, before I was born, she ventured out. Humans killed her. That's what I was told."

Cole blinked. That was a setback. Did he know that a Member with a dead mother? Plenty of them, including himself, but all had known positions already.

"Was the Member born already?"

"We don't know." He gave a heavy sigh. "We told the creatures they were on a wild, pointless chase, but they didn't seem to care. They headed here." His voice lowered. "A brother was sent after them."

Box squirmed, his eyes falling to the pit of the flames. "A month ago, the Rex declared him dead."

It suddenly hit Cole. Why Box had been such a mess and so defensive.

"You're not even supposed to be out here, are you?" He almost laughed, but it felt too serious. He had a brother too…even if he'd only known him for seven months. "You went after your brother, and seeing the fact you got captured by a bandit, it didn't go well."

Box flinched.

"If you're a Shifter, why didn't you just…shift and leave?"

Box toed the dirt floor. "I—I'm a runt."

Cole blinked, unsure of what to ask.

"A runt means I was born too small, and my 'natural' state isn't creature, it's human," Box spat. "I'm not even supposed to be here. I'm far from the woods, or any energy source at all. I can't—shouldn't leave." Box buried his face. "It's hopeless."

Cole's heart flipped, feeling the need to ditch his confident disposition and comfort him. Promise that they'd find his friend. But he stopped. As much as it hurt, there was too much at risk.

A potential Member was in danger. That took priority.

"What can you tell me about the commission?" Cole asked again, gently.

Box peered up. "The bandits are doing dirty work for the glowing-eyed idiots," he said with a scowl forming on his face. "Apparently they failed breaking into some Liberty manor, a place filled with historical artifacts or something. Now they're offering the bandits a hefty price to do it themselves. I bet it's something related to the Soroz."

So Cole had been right. The Excerticus and the bandits *were* connected.

Something in Liberty the Exerticus wanted? He knew that the Aguirre chip had been kept in Liberty. Had any historical Lyntox artifact made its way into a holding place?

"Do you have any idea where it'll be?"

"They did mention a location." Box's brows raised. "But I warn you, whatever warrior fended the Exerticus singlehandedly off might still be there. She sounds dangerous."

"Where?" Cole's heart leapt. How much worse could it really be?

"Bentsworth Manor. A place called 'Bentsworth Manor.'"

Cole almost started laughing. "We're in luck. I know that 'warrior' quite well."

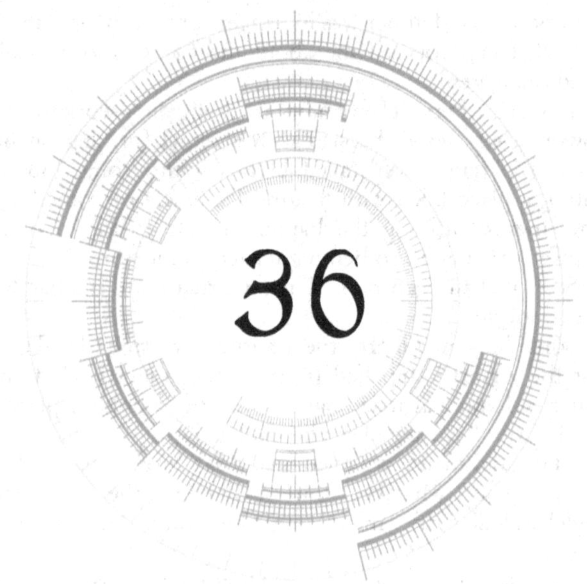

36

Kennedy, 8 Days Until

RAY HATED GETTING up early. It was the usual result of Lincoln hitting him in the face.

But today was different. His Comm blinked "4.03 AM," and he was fully dressed. Yesterday was a busy day, and Mercy acted as if the night wasn't on the brink of happening and they still had no plan. She just smiled and delivered meals, and everything felt like small talk with her.

If there was any time for this Shadow Soul to show their face, it would be the Soul Night.

At least she wasn't bawling on the floor, but he didn't really feel comfortable with her pushing her emotions down either.

His door creaked open as he hesitantly peered out into the dark hall. He let out a sigh of relief, seeing it empty. He crept to the edge of the balcony, finding the dining room empty and free of Remembrance. He shut the door soundlessly behind him, cloaked himself in invisibility just in case, and crept down the staircase.

The moon peered down through the windows. A waning crescent. The Keyper records had engrained the cycle in his mind.

The crescent moon was mysterious in its own right, just like the mark on the side of Mercy's neck…but it was even closer to the sky being entirely dark.

He was running out of time.

He ran across the room, breathing with relief to find the door unlocked.

Luckily, only one guest was staying here, but hearing something scamper across the dark hallways didn't make him feel entirely comfortable. He wanted to shush the stupid rat for possibly blowing it.

The guest checked in yesterday, a disheveled school teacher who was on her way to Sulfur and hadn't had a very good taxi ride. She was only here a night and already seemed uneasy.

Hopefully she was a deep sleeper.

Ray crept across the hallway, the boards creaking under his feet. He cringed until he reached the end of the hall, turning the knob of the closet slowly. The door opened with a loud creak. He slipped inside, shutting it softly behind him.

A squeak caught Ray off guard. He nearly cried out, clamping a hand over his mouth and slamming his hand over the light sensor. The light burst on.

A rat sat in the center of the closet, looking confused as to how the light came on and the noise it heard having no source. As soon as Ray dropped his invisibility, the rat nearly had a heart attack and scampered off for his life into the mass of boxes and bags of the storage closet.

"Sorry…rat guy," he said, feeling compelled to name it.

No, he had to focus.

He turned his attention up the ceiling, where the golden key still hung freely. He breathed a sigh of relief. Mercy hadn't moved it. Perfect.

He looked around the closet. All there was were cardboard boxes and bags. Nothing stable enough to support his weight to reach it. Taking a chair in here would cause too much noise.

Shoot.

He jumped, his outstretched hand hardly reaching the key. He hit the floor with a thud. He froze, holding breath.

Stupid idea, Mathews.

To his luck, no one stirred.

He got to his feet, cursing his height. When was this teenage growth spurt going to hit him like everyone said? It was making world-saving really difficult.

There had to be another way. He needed the key to unlock the desk drawer. If only he could just teleport his hand inside…

He cringed at the idea of it. Nope. Retrieving the key was the only way. But how?

An idea struck him. It was brash and stupid and didn't work the last time he tried it, but he wasn't exactly thinking of much else. With a quick jump, he landed his foot against the wall. His heart fell for a split second, panicking that he'd crash on the floor below. His feet stayed put against the wall.

He blinked in surprise, adjusting the strain of standing sideways. It felt awkward, gravity trying to pull him back down to the ground. He put a foot forward, gluing it to the wall.

He took a breath, maintaining his focus, taking small steps up the wall. The key glinted in the light. So close.

And this is where it usually went wrong.

He bit his lip, casually moving his foot up to the ceiling. Without warning, his foot stuck, swinging his entire body hanging upside down. He muffled a cry, letting his mind catch up as he hung from the ceiling.

He set both feet down, taking a deep breath.

Ray pushed himself up, stretching for the key. He held his breath, straining himself harder. The metal brushed against his fingers, pushing it farther off the hook. Almost…there…

The key fell from the hook and clattered toward the floor. Ray panicked, throwing his hand out, pulling at what little breeze the room contained, the key dropping into his hand.

Ray almost cheered. He'd gotten the key; now all he needed to do was get down.

He took a deep breath, closing his eyes. *All right, footsies, it's time to drop.*

Nothing happened.

Ray cracked an eye open, scowling at his feet still planted firmly on the ceiling. Maybe he could use his newly found word power?

"Drop!" he whispered.

Nothing happened.

He groaned. Did he imagine it? Or did it only work with the Blade?

He flailed his arms around helplessly.

He heard a familiar scamper, the creature tentatively crawling out from the boxes and sitting itself right under Ray, his beady eyes almost mocking him.

Ray scowled at it. "Don't make fun of me, rat guy. I could squish you if I wanted."

The creature cocked its head as if to remind Ray that he was the one dangling upside down from the ceiling.

"Do you happen to be a magical rat? Because, honestly, that'd be helpful."

He decided against it as it ignored him to sniff around the wooden floorboards.

Ray crossed his arms. "You didn't deserve a name, anyway."

A loud slam of the door caused the rat to dash away with a squeak. Ray froze.

"Is anyone there?" came a worried voice.

Why had he opened his mouth? He was so stupid.

"Hello?" The woman's voice quaked. Ray heard her footsteps creak closer.

He hadn't closed the door all the way, and no doubt that the light was spilling out into the hall. He was going to be discovered, and it'd be over. He had to think fast. He swung himself, knocking his head against the wall. He bit back a cry.

The woman didn't hold back a scream.

Yeah, he was done for.

He tried lifting his foot, but it wouldn't budge. How was he supposed to move?

Ray's eyes widened. He was an Oquelite, known for moving around with their most notorious ability.

Ray smirked. Why hadn't he thought of it before?

He didn't have much time to celebrate as his heart skipped at the sound of the woman quickly rushing for the door. *This better work.* He closed his eyes, trying to calm his nerves. Deep breaths.

The world around him began to envelope him, his nerves going numb as the woman's screams were cut off and—

—he clattered at Mercy's bedroom door.

He panicked, jumping to his feet as the door opened, Mercy half-awake. She frowned. "Who's screaming? Mathews, what are you—?"

Ray shoved the key into his pocket, their guest running, screaming from the hallway.

Mercy snapped awake, shoving Ray out of the way and bounding down the stairs. "Are you all right?" she asked.

The woman was trembling, and Mercy slid her a chair.

Ray decided that it would be best for him not to intervene, ducking behind the pillar of the railing.

"I—in the closet, there was someone." The woman began to dab her forehead with a napkin that Mercy had provided. "I—I went in and they were gone!" She shook her head miserably. "This region!"

Mercy blinked in surprise. "In the closet?"

Oh no…He could tell from her worried expression that she suspected the key.

"No one at all."

"I'm so sorry, ma'am. I'll investigate right away. You can make yourself comfortable in a room upstairs." Mercy turned to look up toward the railing. "Mathews!"

Ray popped up. "Remembrance?"

"We have something to look into."

Ray made sure not to make eye contact as he passed the shaking guest as they crossed on the stairs.

He rushed to Mercy's pace as she flew into the back hall, his heart beating against his chest.

"You don't think it was one of those red-eyed guys, do you?" she said, her voice breathy and panicked.

"Couldn't be," Ray said, his throat tight as Mercy swung the closet door open. His heart ceased.

Mercy looked up instantly with a horrified gasp. "No."

"What?" Ray asked stupidly, guilt piercing his gut.

She spun on him. Her eyes welled with tears. "They took it." She gasped. "The key to the room. They were after us in the field, they must want whatever Grandmere has hidden with that key."

Ray's heart swelled, taking everything in him not to flinch. "I'm sure it wasn't—"

"That's the only explanation!" she cried. "We need to find them."

It was me, Mercy. Please forgive me.

"How do you plan on doing that?"

Mercy stopped, stumped. She thought on it for a moment.

She looked up, a fearful boldness in her eyes. "We're going to find that sand man."

37

LAWRENCE OFFICIALLY HATED Council business.

He left Matteo at the door of the training basement after handing him his headphones and making him promise not to avoid the kitchen if he didn't come back. He enjoyed the time in the training basement, which was apparently created as a replica of Taryn's in her old Defending Base: hologram pads and simulations. It made things much easier, and Matteo was progressing, but here was Lawrence being called out to interrogate the captured Oquelite.

Lawrence followed Miriam out and down into the general Inn halls.

Isn't he just another one of your Council duties you didn't ask for?

But I don't mind that one. I don't mind spending time with a boy who's broken…like me.

"You found him. Good." Sergeant Taryn Hunter tore through the crowded hallway, packed with various officers and North Cordell officials all staring at the security feed displayed on their devices.

Taryn frowned at him. "You're a bit sweaty, Williams. When was the last time you brush—?"

"Don't baby them, Serg."

"This is being broadcast to the highest positions of government, Outown. I'm not babying them," Taryn said protectively.

Oh, great. More people who hated them.

"I would do it myself." Taryn huffed. "But apparently the regal pain Dean herself needs to witness the Council in action…and we're not each other's biggest fans." Which she followed up with a colorful string of words under her breath about the acting Commander.

"And you're the Aguirres' nephew. Dean has no idea about Nikki yet." Taryn gave a heavy sigh. "I'm hoping to keep that a secret as long as possible. You're representing what's left of the Curatrix team. And me. Essentially—don't screw this up."

He drowned out the voices, catching a glimpse of a familiar, green jacket.

Lawrence slipped into place beside Lincoln, who looked as frustrated as Lawrence felt.

"Worst timing yet."

"Tell me about it." Hopefully Matteo didn't try and follow.

Lincoln looked to Lawrence. "Did you hear?"

"Hear wha—?"

"The Commander is online!" Rayder Dow's voice echoed through the hall. "Quiet. Lincoln, you have the questions."

They didn't have another moment as the hall fell silent. Lawrence stiffened. The door opened.

The two boys stepped inside, the door locking shut behind them. The room was cold and smelled of drywall, the light source being the dim light of the window from the lightly storming day and lantern hanging in the corner.

Matthias Idicous knelt drenched, his loose, brown curls in his eyes, his upper uniform stripped to an undershirt, displaying how truly pale he was. His cuts and burns were mostly unattended too, and his breaths were ragged, no doubt from the shock collar to keep him from escaping.

Fire burned in Lawrence's chest as the Oquelite Prince turned his head up to assess them.

His gray eyes were pale, but his pupils had begun to show through, unlike his younger brother, Silas, the last time he saw him.

"Oh, lovely. They sent their Council *children* to do all their hard work for them." Matthias gave a ragged laugh. "As they always seem to do."

His eyes narrowed on Lincoln, whose face was tight and pained. Lawrence doubted if Lincoln had heard Matthais.

"Oh, how the roles have been switched, little Aviduous." Matthias smirked. "Yet you still aren't satisfied."

Lawrence jumped in before Lincoln could bite back. "We're not here for exchanging insults."

"I see that quite well…The Ywondie who burned my pathetic brother, I assume?" Matthias laughed hoarsely, wincing as a zap protruded from the collar. He shook it off, pushing himself as far as he could go with the chains holding him down.

Lawrence held himself firm. "If you lie, we can confirm with our source."

"Your source is a fourteen-year-old daughter of a mortalizer traitor with a memory wipe." Matthais laughed. "You think I'm scared?"

"You did wipe Jenna's memories?" Lincoln said, his voice as strained with shock as Lawrence felt. "You're lying. There is no way—"

Matthias continued to laugh. "The girl remembers how it *felt*, but any useful information? The Lady of the Universe is no fool."

Lincoln and Lawrence exchanged looks. That would explain why Jenna could only get emotional when asked questions. The thought was terrifying. An empty void of the mind…but feeling, knowing something was there.

"You're the big heroes now, coming to confront me, the bad guy." Matthias continued to drone on. "Is that what your little Sergeant told you? The First *Council* created the very Soul you run from." He laughed, his voice cracking to a choke. "And now children? How pathetic has fate become?"

Ignore him, Lawrence warned, as he could see Lincoln tense.

Lincoln nodded. But Lawrence didn't listen to his own command. So the Council was truly responsible for the existence of the Shadow Soul? They had that much power? They hardly knew the Council capabilities once united.

Matthias was nothing more than a desperate lunatic, and the sensible part knew that he shouldn't be taken seriously.

"Where is the rest of your troop heading?" Lincoln said, holding the tablet tightly, his breathing deep.

"Wouldn't know," Matthias spat.

"You're lying." Lincoln pressed forward.

"Why would I lie, Aviduous? We are on the run. We have nothing. I have nothing to lose…unlike you." A wicked smile crossed Matthias's face.

Lawrence's heart dropped.

Lincoln was already acting off the last time he saw him, and now Matthais was only digging at that. He knew something Lawrence didn't…and he could tell by the paleness in Lincoln's face.

"Really, I know this is broadcast. Does everyone know that the Aviduous was a thief and opened his mind to her—?"

"You're a murderer!" Lincoln quickly shouted. "Answer the question."

Lawrence frowned. *What is he talking about? Opening your mind to who?*

Lincoln didn't acknowledge Lawrence.

"I kill with dignity, which I know you have none of."

Lawrence frowned, watching Lincoln's eyes begin to twitch. Lost in his thoughts. His mind.

At first Lawrence just thought that it was him processing a sort of grief after he found Nikki. He was beginning to suspect it was something deeper. Why *now?*

Matthias's face flickered with fear. Lawrence saw it too.

For a quick moment, Lincoln's entire eye swelled as black as his iris.

Lawrence quickly ripped the tablet from Lincoln's hand, backhandedly slapping him with it.

Lincoln flinched, his eyes flying back to normal. He looked around, breathless for a moment, and Lawrence glared at him. The cameras were behind them and facing Matthias, so hopefully no one saw it.

Whatever that was.

Lincoln rubbed his eyes.

"He's telling the truth," Lawrence said to no one in particular. Matthias may be cruel, but he wasn't exactly in the position to gain anything.

"Why would he—?"

Another slap.

Shut up! You're making a scene. Lawrence eyed the cameras.

You're freaking hitting me!

Act like it was normal, then!

"Fine. Williams has a point." Lincoln glared at Lawrence to prove that he did not, indeed, agree with him.

His brother killed Nikki.

Lawrence was sick of this. *What's in your head?*

Lincoln blinked, a flash of his old self flashing back. He looked away.

Lawrence almost felt bad. Lincoln had multiple valid reasons to be upset. The Oquelite were his tormentors for years and took the one person Lawrence ever saw Lincoln be genuine with. But when did that start affecting his *eyes?*

They had a mission.

"Then why all the rampaging?"

"Escaping," Matthias said simply. "We're escaping."

"What?"

"How about you let Demon Eyes interview me again instead?" Matthias's eyes gleamed. "He's very convincing."

Look away from him if you know what's good for you, Lawrence commanded.

Lincoln begrudgingly obeyed.

"Are all the Oquelite fleeing?" He prepared himself for a lecture for going off script. Not like Lincoln was thriving, either.

"I suppose some, like my weakling of a brother, are following to Algery." Matthias spat like a bitter taste was in his mouth.

Lawrence and Lincoln exchanged surprised glances. *Algery?* Nikki had mentioned needing to get to Algery.

Lawrence couldn't breathe. "Following who?"

"The Lady of the Universe. She woke up the woods and brought hell with it," Matthias spat. "Those who follow her are traitors of our race. She controls their minds. Our efforts were pointless. Kill them if you please, and if they kill you, I'll be happy either way."

This Lady was…controlling Oquelite? Was that why Jenna said that it wasn't the Oquelites' fault? They were being…controlled?

It all lined up. When the magical woods began reawakening and growing rapidly across the planet, the Oquelite all gained the courage to rebel.

"Ray," Lincoln breathed. "Someone's controlling Ray?"

Lawrence turned back to Mathews. "Why Algery?"

"Something to do with some reversal to the First Council's decree."

Lincoln and Lawrence exchanged glances. The First Council's first decree was the one that created *the Shadow Soul.*

A reversal to the Shadow Soul.

"Session has ended," the speaker announced. "Head to the door."

Lawrence held a stare with the sneering Oquelite before turning to the door, having to shove Lincoln forward, or he might have taken Matthias, chains and all.

They were led through the door, slamming shut and locked firmly behind them. No one came to fetch them, all glued on their Scrolls and teles. Lawrence quickly caught sight of Jack standing outside the crowd beside Sergeant Taryn, signaling them over.

Lawrence led Lincoln through the crowd to Jack's side, looking over his shoulder to the screen in his hand. On the screen sat a woman, perhaps in her early sixties, sitting tall with her pristine, cropped, white hair, her white uniform adorned with gold tassels and medals, her red lips pinched for a moment.

"Impressive."

Lawrence took a double take. The acting Commander said…"impressive?"

"But as your Aviduous points out, the Curatrix link is blatantly in Algery. Unfortunately, the Aguirre site has been burned for the past decade."

Taryn snorted.

"We'll check our sources and send out a scout as soon as possible," Dow said.

"Very good," Cadissa Dean said. "You're doing fine work."

Dow was doing fine work?

Cadissa Dean signed off, and all at once, the hall was

thrown into conversation.

"She credited us to Dow," Lincoln pointed out flatly.

Jack sighed, clicking his device off. "Taryn's rep isn't as favorable as Dow's, so we may have slipped in a *little* misinformation in the report of who's handling Council affairs."

"Why?" Lawrence turned to Taryn.

"She's Curatrix," Dow answered before Taryn could open her mouth, slipping into the circle. "And Dean…disliked the Curatrix team."

"A bit of an understatement," Taryn grumbled.

"How so?" Lawrence said. He'd heard of Taryn's disdain for her, but how much could an Assistant Executive really do? The Commander had been James R. Kordin, Taryn's uncle, for years.

"She's the one who convicted the Aguirres for conceiving a full-blood, for one thing," Taryn said without missing a beat.

Lawrence blinked. Cadissa Dean was the one who tried to kill his cousin?

"Ewyons are illegal," Dow said matter-of-factly. "When Reyna conceived one, Dean went to court hoping to kill both the unborn child and Lyell, since he had more Ewyon blood. She won partially. The unborn child was terminated…or so we thought, considering our very own Nikki Aguirre is upstairs."

Well, screw thinking that the woman was tolerable.

"But she doesn't know about Nikki yet, and it's probably best that way," Jack said.

"You said she hates the Wents for strong Ewyon roots. I'm a Wents by blood too, by my mother." Lawrence clenched his fists. "Isabel. Will she go after Isabel?"

Taryn's eyes widened, looking at Dow. "We should keep a close eye on her," Taryn said, her brows pinching. "As well with Nikki…now that Dean's more invested in the operation. For now, our concerns lie in this Lady of the Universe heading to *Algery.*"

Wherever Nikki was imprisoned for the remainder of her childhood was still unknown, but considering that they inserted the dangerous, experimental P9F into her blood, Lawrence had to guess that it wasn't pleasant.

And now someone was after her home region, Algery.

Nikki had been right.

They spun around to see Dr. Mathews standing at the door of the hidden staircase. "Lincoln, you have an assignment."

Lincoln jumped. "M—me?"

"You and Williams, I suppose."

Ah, another mission he didn't ask for?

"I'm sure you've been informed of Miss Aguirre's Exil Libium injection."

Lawrence spun on Lincoln. "The what?"

"That's what I was trying to tell you," Lincoln said. "Nikki reached the level of stability to receive the file Exil Libium to expel the venom."

"I guess that's good news," Lawrence said, slowly turning back to the doctor.

Exil Libium was a dangerous file, created for killing, unlike the P9F healing file in Nikki's blood. But he guessed that it was best, considering that it'd be killing the venom.

"But considering how the transfer of Matthias and mass briefing of the Department troops, and relocation for the patients happens tonight,"—Jack groaned at the reminder—"I won't be able to watch her progress. Isabel knows what to do. So do Noah and Jenna…if you can get her to help."

More watching helpless children. Lawrence was good at that.

Jenna Mathews had refused to leave the upstairs. Her insistence that the Oquelite weren't as guilty was beginning to add up, but Lawrence still couldn't help but feel bad for her now knowing the state of her mind.

Why had the Shadow Soul…Lady of the Universe, whatever, needed to hurt the mind of such a young girl?

"Nikki should be out most of the time anyhow," Dr. Mathews said, crossing her arms. "Understood?"

"Yes, ma'am."

"Good, Sallow?"

"The trucks are ready, Doctor."

Dr. Mathews nodded to them. She and the two Sergeants followed Jack out the back door, leaving the Inn to the mercy of teenagers once again.

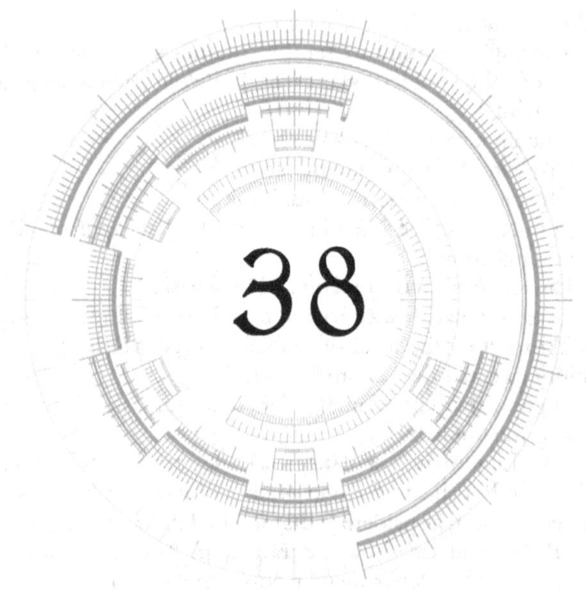

38

Liberty, 7 Days Until

"WHAT I DON'T understand is why the Lyntox would even have something in the Manor," Giles said. "Why would the big man, Bentsworth, find any interest in anything of their possession? How can you trust this boy…dog…person?"

"You should've seen him. There would be no advantages for him in stealing from the Manor," Cole said, wiping the sweat from his sword training with Cecileo.

The recap didn't go fairly well. Felicity was quiet, her eyes somewhere else as Giles went off on how ridiculous the source was.

Cole couldn't blame her. She'd been in disbelief when he told her that the Exerticus had been scared off by *her*. So much so, they hired bandits to do the dirty work out of fear of Felicity.

Felicity's leg was propped up for Echo's inspection, who seemed a bit miffed by Giles voice. "Perhaps you give

Johnson too little credit," she said.

"And why does your opinion of him matter?"

"Smart mouth for a *boy* soldier."

Felicity slapped her hand over her mouth to smother her smile. Giles's face went red at the mention of his age. He didn't seem to enjoy the fact that he was nineteen, Felicity's age, and only a mere year older than Cole.

"Not like the Market sends out young scavengers," Giles retorted. "The Department isn't perfect, but there's always a reason for when a teenager enters it."

"Perhaps you haven't considered the same for the Market."

Echo's and Giles's eyes met for a long moment before Giles's fell away. "Some of us are still trying to follow what the Curatrix team started."

"And the Curatrix team was notorious for listening to people with a voice, so give Coleson a chance." Echo settled back into her work without a second glance.

So Echo did approve of the Curatrix team.

Giles turned back to Cole without a word.

"I have a plan," Cole said.

"Well, I have one too, and no one seems to care about me," Giles grumbled.

Felicity groaned into her hands.

Cole ignored Giles, turning to Felicity. "So, do you have any idea where this Lyntox thing would be in the Manor?"

"There's only one place," Felicity said, sitting a little straighter. "My father has a bridge to his office, which holds this artifact gallery. If anything important is being held in that house, it's there. That's where I got the Aguirre chip and fought off the Exerticus last time."

That was perfect.

"Giles, inform the Defenders of a potential break-in, but don't make it too urgent. We just need them on stand by," Cole said. "Our biggest advantage is that they know we know when it takes place, but not where. Cecileo could lead a decoy mission elsewhere, since the Bandits will no doubt be watching the Market for our activity. They think they have me beat…Sucks for them."

"So you want to have a surprise attack?" Felicity said.

"Yes." Cole nodded. "I can assemble a smaller team to

attack once they breach the manor.”

“So more Defenders?”

“People more reliable than that. You, Felicity?”

Felicity’s eyes widened. “You want me?”

Cole smiled. “Of course I want you. You’re the one who got the chip and figured out the Curatrix code. Your quick thinking with the planes was insane, and the progress you’ve made with your spear is impressive.”

Felicity blushed, shaking her head. “I can’t Cole. I—I can’t even walk.”

“Not yet,” Echo corrected with the band of a tool against the brace. “I’ll have this up and running by at least tomorrow.”

Felicity’s jaw fell. “Really?”

Echo laughed. “Don’t underestimate me. Wearing this will tire you out quicker due to all the extra needed brain power, though. You’re far from free from a wheelchair, but it should be enough to let you do some field work.”

Felicity thought for a long moment before turning back to meet Cole’s eyes. She gave him a firm nod. “I’m in.”

“Awesome. I’ll call you later to discuss more.”

“Looking forward to it.”

“Giles, you up for it?”

Giles blinked in surprise, frowning. “Me?”

“All right, if you don’t—”

Giles panicked. “Wait! I’m in, gosh darn it, Johnson.”

Cole smirked. “Great.” He turned to Echo. “Could you?”

Echo gave a heavy sigh, getting to her feet and dusting her hands. “Marketeers and Defenders don’t mix well. And with Cecileo already recruited, someone will be needed to keep things stable back here.”

Cole sighed, disappointed. “So it’s a no?”

Echo gave a sad smile.

“I have two suggestions.” Felicity perked up. “My sister, Veronica. She’s only fourteen, but she knows the Manor and all its weird facts better than anyone. And my friend, Falcon Armstrong.”

Giles groaned. “Not the two nerds! That’s who you chose?”

“Veronica wouldn’t be in the front lines,” Felicity said, rolling her eyes at the Officer. “Maybe more tech. And

Falcon's much more than a 'nerd' than he appears to be. Being friends with Tabitha Delorous puts anyone in dangerous situations. You can thank Falcon for us escaping quite a few."

"Tabitha?" Cole said.

"Coleson's favorite thing to stress about?" Echo joked.

Cole shot her a frown, which she only returned with a non-remorseful smile.

"Yeah. Before we left for North Cordell," Felicity said, twisting a piece of her long, red hair in her fingers. "It was Falcon, Tabitha, and me for a while."

"Sounds like a disaster," Giles said.

"We were." Felicity shrugged. "Liberty's Dome isn't the most…accepting place when it comes to third borns, or anyone out of place"—she shot Cole a quick glance—"even though laws against it were dispelled years ago. Falcon's family isn't wealthy. His father works for the higher ups and by no means poor, but out of place. And I've always…been a little strange. It worked for the best, and now Falcon's stronger than ever. Tabitha had me." Felicity quieted. "But I don't think I was enough."

"You're her best friend," Cole said, confused. "I don't think that will ever change."

"Yeah, I guess." Felicity quickly cleared her throat, casting glances to the others standing in the room. "Is the meeting adjourned yet?"

Oh, right. "Yes, I guess. I have to go collect our final member…or a few more. I'll talk to you later." Cole ran for the tent flap.

"I won't be going anywhere till this leg thing is finished." Felicity shrugged. "I'll meet you later."

Cole nodded and raced out of the tent. He had a Shifter to collect.

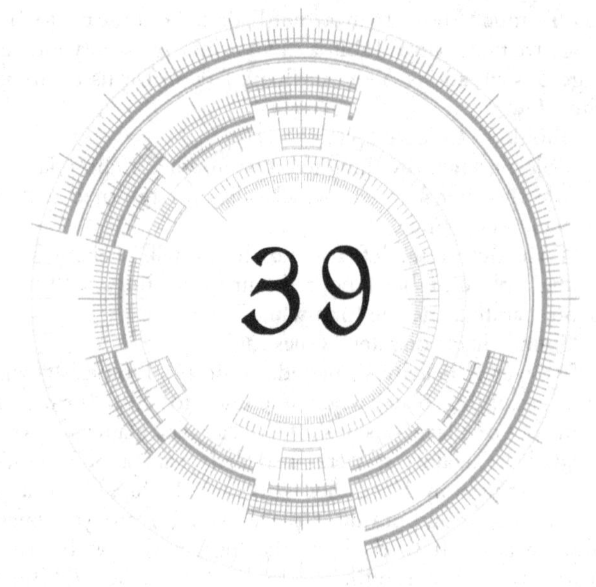

39

Kennedy, 7 Days Until

"YOU JUST WANT to ride that hovercycle and are using this serious situation as an excuse, aren't you?"

"I have a plan, Remembrance! Trust me."

Mercy scowled, walking beside him, her jacket zipped all the way to her chin and her eyes darting around nervously. Ray looked away, the pit of his stomach pinching with guilt. She was convinced that a red-eyed guy had broken in to steal the key. He'd never wanted so badly to admit the lie, but he couldn't. Not now. Not when they were so close.

They approached Lucas's mechanic shop, the sun setting on the horizon and the dark settling in. Ray looked up to the moon, nearly gone now. Three days. And then the sky would go black. And who knew what would happen then?

Ray raced up the steps, banging against the door till a surprised Lucas opened the door.

"You again?"

"Surprise. We need to borrow your hovercycle…and

some tape."

"Why not just buy it already?"

Mercy snorted from behind. "Too broke, but I bet he'd marry it if he could."

Ray glared at her. Mercy smirked.

"We only need it as a diversion." Ray explained. "We won't be too far…and I'll take it back this time."

"Saw a guy roll in with a tire and door missing on his auto while eating a burger today. How much worse can it get?"

Ray helped Lucas roll the beloved hovercycle out into the street. Lucas shut the garage door behind them with a wink, and as much as Ray was tempted to leap on, he walked beside Mercy down the street. It was foggy out. Perfect.

"You said we needed the lights on it?"

"Yeah. The brake lights are red." Ray smirked. "Just like those guys who attacked us."

Mercy frowned. "You don't think he's that stupid to fall for it."

No, Ray didn't. "Just trust me."

She sighed, pressing her lips together and her hand going to the necklace around her neck. "Fine."

They stopped once they were in a decent portion out in the street, the shops abandoned for the day. Ray kicked the stand down, starting the hovercycle. He took out the tape, holding down the brakes, the red lights glowing brightly. He tossed the tape roll into his bag with his sword.

"You're sure this'll work."

"Positive. As long as you're up for being bait." He winked at her before dashing into the shadows of the alley.

Mercy paced for a moment before glancing at him. He gave her a thumbs up, and she nodded with a small smile.

And she screamed. If there was one thing that girl was good at it, it was yelling.

"Help!" she cried. "They're back!"

He took a deep breath, letting his essence rush through his veins, letting it warm the chill that ran through him. Who knew he'd miss his abilities?

He muttered a quiet apology to Mercy, and with the guide of his hand, the hovercycle moved forward.

Mercy's scream now held genuine terror. "What the heck? Mathews!"

Ray panicked. No. Please don't let her run to him.

With the other hand, Ray willed the fog to crowd around her and, in a moment, teleported to the other side of the street. He pinched his gaze, following the glowing, red hovercycle light as it wavered slowly around Mercy.

"I'm not afraid of a stupid machine!"

A loud bang followed.

Ray blinked. Was she fighting the hovercycle?

He spun the hovercycle around her.

"Mortals curse you! What the heck is going on?" she shouted.

He let go of the hovercycle, turning for his most dangerous move. He took a deep breath, slowly closing his fist and feeling the air around Mercy. He closed the grip tighter and tighter around her till he could almost feel her writhing grip.

"Help!" she cried, her blood curdling. "Let me go!" She began pathetically kicking the poor hovercycle, letting loose a string of curses.

Ray felt horrified when a small smile crept onto his lips. She did seem more angry than scared.

One day he'd tell her...or not. She'd probably kill him.

"You should probably let her go before she gets suspicious."

Ray almost screamed as he spun around to meet the warlock, leaning against the alley wall casually behind him. Ray could clearly see the glowing specks in his eyes and the golden tips of his hair. He was the same warlock Miriam met, Gorgon.

Ray dropped Mercy and scrambled back, willing the fiery purple energy into his palms. "Don't move or I'll—"

"Oh, shush." The guy pushed past Ray and into the fog after Mercy. "Oquelite, always so dramatic."

"Hey! No!" Ray smothered his fiery hand into his shirt and raced after him. Would he hurt her?

He burst into the ring of fog.

Mercy looked shaken, still catching her breath as the sand man strode for her.

"You!" She fearlessly stormed forward. "You controlled that stupid hovercycle, didn't you? You trapped me!"

Gorgon cast a glance at Ray.

Ray's heart dropped. His secret was done for—

"I did, but you and your friend did intend to trap me."

He...covered for Ray?

Mercy scowled. "I didn't appreciate it."

"And I didn't appreciate you being out in the open to attract some Exerticus to cause trouble."

Ray's eyes widened. "We're attracting Exerticus?"

"Who are you?" Mercy said. "And why are these Ex—arti—cush doing here?"

That was the question the entire Council was asking: what did the Exerticus...and, more specifically, the Shadow Soul want?

"We need to get inside," Gorgon said, unfazed by Mercy's rage. His eyes darted to Ray. "The scent of *his* blood is particularly strong since they've already collected his."

Mercy frowned. "Him? But he's just—"

"Now."

Mercy's face quickly melted into submission, rushing to Ray, and the two followed the not-really-a-warlock man into an empty shop. The man shut the door behind them.

"That took you long enough."

Ray's blood went cold as the familiar voice trickled into his veins. There was no way. It couldn't be.

Ray slowly turned, his heart thumping against his chest. There in the shadows stood Silas Idicous.

"What are you doing here?" Ray said, trying not to panic in front of Mercy.

"*You're* the one who messaged me about the whereabouts of your sister," Silas scoffed.

Ray's face went red. He'd almost forgotten about that. It was a spur-of-the-moment, impulsive thought. He didn't think he'd actually—

"You're friends with that creepy guy?" Mercy squeaked.

"No way."

"Not even close."

Mercy looked back and forth, confused. Ray just glared at Silas. Any wrong move, he'd make sure that that Oquelite Prince would pay.

"I didn't really come for *you*, Mathews." Silas scoffed, stepping beside Gorgon. "I came to warn the warlock."

"A what?" Mercy's lips parted, moving closer to Ray.

Gorgon snorted. "An informal slur. As if I'm the most extraordinary thing in this region." He smirked to Ray, turning to Mercy. "It's a good thing I've been tracking the Exerticus down. Otherwise, both of you would have been dead the other day. White Hair here finally gave me answers about what they're here for. Taking blood."

Why would Silas tell Gorgon the Exerticus' plan?

"Blood? Taken?" Mercy blinked. "We were doing fine."

"You didn't even know what you're up against," Silas said. "If you even want a chance, you have to get out."

"Exactly. Get out and stop bringing those darn glowing-red-eyed monsters with you." Gorgon scoffed.

"Out?" Mercy's voice cracked.

"They were sent for very specific blood," Silas explained. "Twelve very important persons, to be exact."

Ray's eyes widened in horror. It all came crashing in. They were looking for *Council Members'* blood. That's why they didn't kill him during the Oquelite attack in North Cordell. They just cut him and left.

"I don't know the exact reasons, but they're very clearly looking to collect the blood of all twelve…for something," Silas said.

All twelve Council Members together had the power to create an entire curse. What could someone do with each of the members' blood? That could be detrimental. He had to warn the others.

Ray had been cut in North Cordell. And so had Cole. Who else?

"Why are you telling us this?" Ray snapped. "You're the one who started this whole mess."

Silas's face hardened. "I don't have to explain myself to *you.*"

"All I care about is that you get out of this region." Gorgon pointed an accusatory finger at Mercy.

Ray's heart leapt. The Exerticus wouldn't have found Mercy if it hadn't been for him. They had tracked him down. They already had his blood.

He'd put Mercy in danger. He'd led them right to her.

"M—me?" Mercy stumbled back speechless. "H—how do you know I'm one of these twelve?"

"It doesn't matter," Gorgon said.

"Remembrance, you could always come back to North Cordell with me," Ray blurted out. He'd explain everything, EVERYTHING, to her on their way back.

"I—I—" Mercy stumbled against the wall, her eyes squeezing shut. "I can't."

"We don't have time for this."

"My grand—"

"Screw her rules!" Ray shouted desperately, grabbing Mercy's shoulder. "You're in serious danger!"

Thanks to him. How had he not put it together sooner? Why had it taken that idiot Prince?

"It's not that simple!" She shoved him away.

"Oh, it really is," Silas said.

"And what do you know?" Tears fought to stay contained in her eyes.

"This isn't all about you!"

Mercy didn't even wait. She ran for the door, bursting out into the dark street.

"Mercy!" Ray didn't even care that he'd said her real name. He ran after her.

Gorgon grabbed his shoulder. Ray ripped himself from his grip.

Anger boiled in him, the voices taunting him, pulling at his mind. He couldn't think straight. He spun around, shoving Gorgon out of the way, flames exploding in his hands.

"What are you doing here?"

Silas stepped out into the light, unfazed. His skin was pale, and his hair was longer, dark roots beginning to show, but the most startling thing was his eyes. The color was almost all gone, and veins crept down his cheeks. "She broke a promise...I'm getting my revenge."

"Who is 'she?'"

"Names have power, hybrid. You should know."

He needed to warn the Council. They couldn't risk anyone else's blood getting into the Exerticus' hands.

Kill her. Kill her. The voices taunted.

He stumbled backward through the door. He broke out into a run. Kill her? Kill Mercy? Was he going mad?

Raphael Mathews—

No! Please! I don't want to hurt anyone!

He ran with all his might, ignoring his essence begging him to jump and embrace the instinct to teleport.

That's what you're good at, isn't it?

He wouldn't turn again. Not again.

He wouldn't kill again. He wouldn't add another set of lifeless eyes to his nightmares.

He could feel it swelling in his mind. It threatened to consume him. Imprison him in his own mind.

The motel lights glowed in the distance. Mercy was there. She was safe.

He gave in, teleporting, landing with a thud in the motel lobby. He heard Mercy's door slam.

Kill. Kill. Kill.

Go away!

His vision blurred.

He crumpled to his knees, gasping for air.

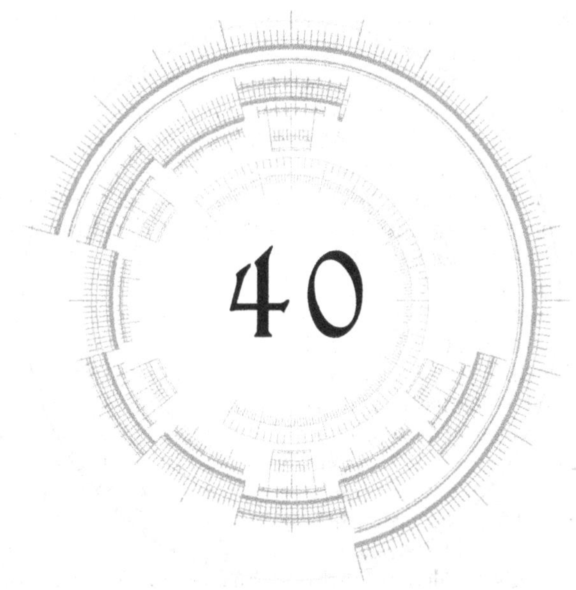

40

North Cordell, 7 Days Until

LINCOLN COULDN'T FOCUS on anything. He'd already cleaned the whole kitchen…twice, and made tea for everyone in their plastic cups and began designing goggles on a napkin.

Nikki was almost better. Nikki was almost okay.

Matteo sat in the corner of the kitchen on the floor beside Jenna, who rested her head on his shoulder as he showed her his tablet.

The adults wouldn't be back until the early morning, if not later due to the storm picking up again. The lights flickered as it thundered outside. Lincoln stirred his tea, looking back at the scribbles on his napkin.

The night was chaos, but he was all right.

He was all right till a hard thud and cry broke through the silence. He jumped to his feet, his heart skipping a beat. "Nikki."

He rushed for the door, tearing it open.

Nikki lay on the steps, her entire body shaking with a sob, tears streaming down her face.

"Nik!" He dropped to the ground, beginning to help her to her feet. She pushed away from him, turning to vomit. A sob tore through her as she staggered back, sinking. "Help," she choked. "It's so hot. I—it hurts."

Lincoln scooped Nikki's shaking body into his arms, rushing past Lawrence and into the kitchen. What was going on? She was supposed to be okay.

No. Please no.

"Lincoln, I—"

"Shh, Nik, it's okay. It's all right."

"Nikki!" Jenna cried out. Both her and Matteo leapt from their seats, Matteo frozen.

Jenna rushed to Lincoln. Nikki's face was coated in sweat, and he could feel her warmth radiating. "Is she—?"

"She's going to be fine," Lawrence said quickly, his face firm. "Matteo, go upstairs. Now."

The boy didn't hesitate.

Nikki struggled in Lincoln's arms, her breathing uneven, her eyes open and dazed before drooping.

"Someone call Dr. Mathews!"

"I'm doing that right now!" Jenna tore out her Comm.

Lawrence turned to Lincoln. "Lay her down. Now. She's burning up. I'll get rags."

Lincoln didn't argue. He rushed into the large lobby living room, laying Nikki out on the couch.

"Hot. So hot," she grumbled through her tears. "Lincoln? Lincoln…"

Lincoln unzipped her jacket. "I'm right here, Nik. It's okay. I'm right here."

"I—I can't breathe." She sobbed, and Lincoln slipped off her jacket, pushing back her sweaty bangs. He'd never seen her so scared. So helpless.

Lawrence dropped beside him with a bucket of cold water, splashing onto the floor. Lincoln took the rags, quick to dab at her face.

"It's going to be okay, Nik," he whispered. "I'm right here. It's going to be okay."

Look what happens when you deny me your name. I'm losing my patience.

"Her pulse is low." Lawrence's face was blank, moving his hand from her wrist. He shook his head. "I—I don't understand."

"Get the Defenders."

They cannot help you, fool. Tell me your name.

"In this storm?"

Lawrence was right. It wouldn't be logical.

He looked to Nikki, fighting to breathe, tossing and turning weakly. He clenched the rag. "I'm not going to let her die."

Tell me.

"Linc—" Lawrence's brows knit. Fear shivered cold through Lincoln's veins, like Lawrence's eyes could pierce right through him. Like he knew that Lincoln was falling for the voice in his head. That he was so weak.

"I'll stay with her. All night. I promised to make sure she was okay."

She's my best friend and I can't live without her.

Reject your feelings. You will only be weak—

Nikki grasped his arm, squeezing it.

Lawrence nodded. "I'm going to help Jenna. Message me. I'll be back to check in."

He left quickly, leaving the two alone in the large room. Lincoln dipped the rag back into the cold water, dabbing the sweat from her forehead as she struggled, muttering unintelligible words under her breath between attempts to breathe.

"It's okay, Nik," Lincoln said, trying to stop tears from burning his eyes. "You're okay. I promised you."

I promised you her safety, your power, all for a name—

Nikki seemed to settle at his voice. He clasped a hand over her feverish hand. He was here for her, not the Voice. He dipped the rag again.

"You know, Nik, before I met you, there was this thing that always bothered me," he whispered, his voice threatening to break. "I—I didn't remember anything. You—you know that. I wandered around when I was younger, stole some things, ran from a few angry farmers." He snorted, tears clouding his vision, ignoring the pain swelling in his throat. "Kinda a pathetic human being."

Her eyelids fluttered with a cough.

No, boy, embrace your anger. Don't be tempted by her. Tell me your name.

"I probably deserved Matthias to find me. They were probably pretty excited to find a stupid, thirteen-year-old Aviduous hanging around North Cordell." He wrung the rag. "I didn't understand why they kept me alive. I wanted them to kill me rather than chain me to a wall like some sort of prize."

His arms fell to his lap. He took deep breaths. The voice was shouting for him.

"Nik, they asked me over and over about an Ewyon. They asked me and only let me go on one condition: when I found the Ewyon, I'd tell them."

He couldn't look at her now. He didn't deserve to.

"I ran away. I fought them off for years. I told them the Ewyon was Felicity and then Silas took her."

He clenched his jaw. He would not cry. "Nik, they were looking for you, and if I'd known the truth, I would've turned you in. Seven months ago, I would've let them go."

His breath was ragged. "I am not good, Nik. But you—you still saved me. Remember you saved my life in Imperial? You broke me out from the Labyrinth. You didn't even know who I was."

It hurt, but the pain felt so good. It felt so good to hear the voice weaken.

He looked up at her still face. "Why would you save someone who would have let you die? Would you haved saved me if you'd known?"

He knew that he hadn't sent the Oqualite to kill her, but it felt like he had. His own fears had condemned her, and he still couldn't escape them. The moment the blade impaled her replayed over and over in his mind. He did that to her. He did that to her, the pathetic, demon-eyed monster.

You don't deserve a friend like her.

The tears fell.

"Lincoln?"

Lincoln's eyes flew open, meeting her dazed eyes. Her hand drifted to his face. "Don't cry." He clasped her hand, the tears falling freely now. He couldn't stop them anymore. "I—I'm so sorry."

"I forgive you." Her eyelids gently fell, her body suddenly

still.

"N—Nik?" He quickly checked her pulse. Still low, but she was asleep. He wiped his face of the tears, checking over his shoulder in fear that Lawence had walked in.

Lincoln curled up by her couch side on the floor, letting her words echo in his mind.

I forgive you.

For the first time in what felt like an eternity, those words rang louder than the Voice's ever could.

Lincoln woke to Nikki gasping for air. He shot up from his seat on the floor, grabbing the rag from the now lukewarm water.

"Nik? Are you—?"

"Cold," she muttered.

The cold nipped even at Lincoln's face. The heaters must have gone out in the storm.

Shoot.

He felt her forehead. Still warm, but no sweat. She shuddered.

"I'll get you blankets, Nik. Hang in there."

He rushed to the few boxes set up by the wall near the front door. He ripped one open, finding a few thin sheet covers likely meant for Inn beds. They'd just have to make do.

He rushed back to her, tucking the sheets over her. She took his shaking hands.

He quickly took out his Comm, sending the twentieth message to Taryn.

LINCOLN: Heater quit working.

He looked at Nikki and, with a quick breath, sat beside her, letting her have the warmth of his arm in her clutch and his jacket.

She fell back asleep on his chest, and Lincoln lay awake in the darkness, letting the heat of her feverish body warm him and the lull of her harsh, short breaths.

Everything that could go wrong was going wrong. His heart still echoed the panic of the hours before. But now Nikki was close to him. She was safe, no thanks to the Voice in his head.

He could protect her. She could protect him.

What are you doing? Get away from her. You cannot save her.

Leave me alone.

Oh, really now? Just because you've had one moment of air doesn't mean you don't have a mountain still suffocating you.

Leave me alone.

Not until you tell me your name. Remember the promise of your power.

Lincoln hesitated.

She's weaker, boy.

I—

You're tempted. You don't entirely trust. She was right about that. You know you're a defective Aviduous without me. Who are you to comfort her? You're conspiring with me, boy. The Lady of the Universe, after all.

Who are they to trust you?

Lincoln jolted awake, the world crashing down in a moment. The dim morning light shone through the windows, light rain hitting a windowpane, the stiff couch underneath him, the lack of a blanket…and a girl curled up beside him, his arm protectively around her, and the other in her possession.

His heart was racing, blinking a few times to make sure that he still wasn't dreaming.

Was the Voice right? Did he have no right to comfort her? No matter how right it felt…and how easy it had been to fall asleep in a long time?

He wiggled his arm from her grip, pressing his backhand against her forehead. The fever had dropped drastically, and her pulse seemed to have returned to normal. She also hadn't thrown up in the past few hours. A good sign.

He turned on his back, not willing to wake her.

It seemed that no matter what he did, the Voice knew how to kick him down. He hated it, yet the thought of entirely escaping it terrified him. The Voice was powerful. He needed that power.

But it ate at him. The guilt and pain and fear…the death. They weren't getting anywhere with the Soul Night, Matteo, Nikki…and who knows what else? Who knew when it could strike—?

"Lincoln?"

He jumped at the drowsy voice. Nikki's eyes opened with

a crack.

"Morning, Nik," Lincoln said, his face suddenly burning being so close, moving his arm back.

Nikki didn't seem the least bit embarrassed as she rubbed her eyes open.

"I feel bad," she said hoarsely.

"For what?"

"My body. Feels bad." She closed her eyes. "It's okay."

She'd reverted to her simple words. At least she was talking.

He pushed her sweaty hair from her face. "You scared everyone last night."

She frowned, her eyes cracking open. "What?"

"Do you not remember?"

Nikki closed her eyes again. "It's kinda blurry."

She was quiet for a moment. He didn't disturb her. She probably needed more sleep.

"Lincoln?"

"Uh huh?"

"The stab hurt."

Lincoln's heart skipped a beat. "The what?"

She felt for her side. "The—the stab."

"Your stab wound?"

She nodded drowsily. How many painkillers had Lawrence given her?

"I was stabbed," she muttered.

Yes, Nik. I see it over and over in my nightmares. "But you're healing."

She nodded. "Thank you."

"'Thank you?'" For what? He'd hardly done anything thank-worthy.

"You're the one who taught me what that means," she said, her eyes opening. "For saving me."

"I didn't save you."

She shook her head. "I know what 'save' means."

He almost laughed. "Good."

"Some people wouldn't be so lucky," she said, her voice quieting. "You won't be able to save everyone…or me all the time."

"I—I know."

She frowned at him, her eyes glaring at him with clear

disbelief.

Lincoln sighed. "I just…I just can't imagine if someone died…again."

His breath caught in his throat. Or if he died.

The world coming to an abrupt end—snuffed out of existence. It all ended the same. An irreversible nothingness. That was it.

"Remember when I asked if people go to places when they die?"

He remembered the conversation clearly. It was only hours after the whole Aguirre revelation. "Yeah."

"I think there is now. I know."

"Nik, you were probably hallucinating, as that Kathryn-Adrienne person was messing with your mind. It's unreasonable, unscientific."

"My Da believed it."

"Your—your father?"

Agent Lyell Aguirre, the infamously scientific Curatrix member, believed in an afterlife? Something outside of this world?

"You believed in the Void."

"But that…makes sense."

"You don't think it's connected?" She looked at him with curious eyes.

A tiny part of him believed her. She knew better than anyone the mysteries of death. "Though, it doesn't make killing good."

"Why not?" he said, somewhat curious in her lack of fear.

"We should all have the right to live…but don't you think we all have a time?"

"Life seems pretty unpredictable to me. Nothing's going to stop me from dying right—"

Nikki grabbed him suddenly with a burst of unexpected energy. "Me! Remember the Glass Tower? Jack said you weren't going to make it, but you did."

"Because of the P9F file."

"And it could have failed." Nikki bit back a pained cry as she rolled up. The pain resided quickly. "Why are you so terrified of the idea of something beyond this life?"

"I—I—" He looked away from here. "I don't want false

hope."

"But what if it's true hope?"

"You're an optimist, Nik. I'm a realist."

"You believe in me, Lincoln." Nikki was quiet a moment. "Even when everyone else thought I was dead and had every reason to think so, you believed me. You trusted me, even though it wasn't realistic at all."

Hot tears pricked at his eyes. Lincoln tensed, trying to hold it in.

"Don't try and tell me that your 'trust' was scientific," Nikki said. "Trust is anything but realistic."

"Nik." Lincoln quickly dabbed his eyes, looking over his shoulder. "I do trust you, more than anyone else in the world, I just can't seem to…I can't seem to—"

"Trust yourself?"

"Yeah. That." How could he? Everything he ever thought he knew was constantly being scattered. Why was it so hard?

"I believe in you."

Lincoln laughed, brushing away his tears. "Of course, you do."

Nikki shrugged, drawing her knees to her chest. "You are one of the strongest people I know, you just haven't even realized it yet."

"Glad you finally realized my undeniable muscle tone." Lincoln joked, his throat hoarse.

Nikki rolled her eyes.

They laughed, and it felt so good. So good to be able to breathe.

Lincoln took a deep breath and rolled back to face her. "Nik?"

Her eyes widened. "Yeah?"

"Is there any more the Shadow Soul showed you?"

The Ewyon Coastal Alliance Palace—Before Recorded Time

Kathryn knew the routine.

The knife was strapped to her thigh under the light, fabric skirt, which was rich and flowing, a slit masterfully cut to make it accessible. Her wrists hung with golden ornaments, her pointed ears heavy with looped earrings. Her golden hair was down and swept to her knees, ever so carefully tended for.

She stood outside the manor in the gardens as guests rushed by to be out of the whipping wind, not stopping to notice that it had no effect on the woman.

She flexed her hands, the thrill of the wind overcoming her, a smile breaching her painted-red lips. She made her way with confidence toward the open doors, the warmth of the manor's gala room pricking her skin.

"Name?" The guard looked up from his list.

"Kathryn.'"

The man frowned. "I don't believe—"

What is your name?

The guard's eyes flooded with horror. She furrowed her brows, satisfied when his entire body froze.

Tell me your name.

Marculus Eavon.

"Marculus Eavon." The words were sweet on her tongue. "Please permit me."

A smile broke out on the man's face. "Of course, my lady! Welcome! Enjoy your time!"

He scribbled a check mark stupidly on his scroll and stepped aside. She stepped into the hall, the music wrapping her within. She looked at the crowd, the laughing faces and spinning, colorful gowns.

The stench of perfume and humanity was strong.

She stepped forward, the world absorbed around her, and she moved smoothly among them. Not many caught her eye. A few older women with shocked looks at her loose hair and eager looks from a few boys, but that was as usual. The atmosphere of giddy thrill dominated.

She spun out of the way of the dancing guests as easily as a slight flicked off her. She moved toward the banquet table.

"Might you be in need of a partner?"

She spun to see a boy of raven-black hair and sparkling, orange eyes offering a hand. His scent was weak…and so was his build. A Ywondie for sure.

"Eymyst, son of Feir," he said with a wink.

She clenched her fists, feeling his emotions begin to swirl at her command. The first moments were the most thrilling. She saw his pupil narrow, his hand began to shake.

"I might not be looking for a partner," she said calmly.

He dropped his arm. "Ah. I see. I'm sorry. I feel a little—"

Nervous? *She smirked as he shrank away, back into the crowd.*

She picked up a golden goblet, the wine smelling strong as she brought it to her lips.

"Lord Merck has fallen ill too."

The conversation of the bustling women, not a threat by their builds and loud, gossiping mounts, perked at Kathryn's ears.

"I heard it wasn't an illness," the second said, her blond pin curls bouncing as she chased after her friend digging into a tray of pastries. "He was lifeless, besides a few moans. He could only lie there."

"I bet he ran into a faerie." The other girl joked.

"But last year, remember Lord Erie? He's still cold, living dead."

Kathryn set her goblet down, catching the girls' attention.

"Good evening," Pin Curls said.

Kathryn tipped her non-existent hat. "Lovely night."

She turned and left, drowning out the voices. So, her reputation was growing.

She stepped into a quick step, sending her quickly teleporting to the corner. She watched the room sway like a hazy fever.

She caught snippets of conversation. Very few useful for finding the described target.

"The Ewyon Queen has stopped all refugee flow after the Azar visit...The paralyzed noble boy? Of course I've heard of him...The Council spoke at the stone circle last moon...Can you hand me the goblet?"

Kathryn froze, the one thing she knew that she shouldn't do on an outing like this.

It couldn't be.

She let herself go invisible, pushing through the crowd.

"Thank you, darling."

It couldn't be.

She brushed past a group of suited men and stopped in her tracks. She'd found the target. He'd dyed his hair, but those eyes...They still burned.

Hadeon Abaddon stood, a girl on his arm and a goblet in hand.

Her mind threatened to betray her. This was the assignment?

She knew that it was a duke's son...but this particular one?

She almost laughed. She wouldn't feel a thing.

She let the invisibility fall, coming into view. Immediately, his violet eyes caught sight of her. He frowned, his laugh drowning out. "Do I know you?"

Right. She was no longer bony Adrienne of braids and forced smiles. She had circled herself with distortion, but she couldn't help the *burning anger. He couldn't remember the woman whose life he'd made a living hell.*

"No. I don't believe so."

The girl on his arm looked from Hadeon to Kathryn, a pout trembling on her lip.

Hadeon smiled with a laugh. "Ah, I see. I've met a few females in my life."

Have you? Does the one on your side know of the ones you've murdered?

"As one does."

"And you? Don't you have a partner tonight?" the girl spat.

"I don't believe in such a thing." No, not anymore.

Both Hadeon and the girl burst out laughing. "You're quite amusing…I don't believe I caught your name."

"I never dropped it. Names have power."

"She's quite smart." Hadeon winked.

Hadeon Abaddon, follow me.

No shock even fazed the stupid boy as he unhooked his arm from his partners. "Let me follow you."

"Hadeon!" the girl shrieked. "You promised me!"

Hadeon ignored her, offering Kathryn his arm. She rejected, not willing to even feel the fabric of his arm against her. They waltzed out into the dark outside corridor, Hadeon chattering the entire time.

"The elaborate parties never really suited me. I'm more of an in-the-open, one-on-one man."

Open in the woods. With knives and flames and burning touches. Dominating the nightmares and every waking memory.

The hall was lit by torches with a wave of her hand. A drunken Hadeon didn't take notice, his hazy eyes stuck on Kathryn.

Be numb. Be numb.

Stop looking at me.

His eyes drifted to the wall behind her. "How do you feel about me, darling?"

"It's something very sinister."

He laughed, stumbling closer. Kathryn summoned her knife, smoothly backing him to the wall.

"Are you sure we haven't met?" He frowned, though his smile still dwelled. "Those eyes…are familiar."

Carastene's essence was too strong for her steel eye's true color to show. She wanted to destroy it. She didn't want to be the woman he knew.

"*Like the Soul. I met the Soul once.*" He laughed hoarsely. *A hand tried to soothe her tense arm, but she willed her skin to burn. He pulled away. "She was beautiful. But everyone knows she's a witch…an accursed evil.*"

Control yourself, Kathryn.

"*And you know what princes do to witches?*" *Pride gleamed in his eyes.*

"*They burn them.*"

Control became an essence of the past and the knife became the words, tearing through Hadeon's side.

Don't scream.

He crumpled to the ground, his voice strangled, his eyes wide in a sober horror. "You…you are her."

"*I am she.*" *She knelt down, grabbing his hair to force him to face her. "And you will never burn me.*"

With a clench of his fist, the blue glow of his essence tore from his wound. Her command not to scream tormented him, and he wrenched in horror and pain on the floor. His face paled and teeth clenched through forsaken breaths.

"*You will burn.*" *He gasped. "All villains do.*"

She would not be the villain they all said the Soul was.

She didn't even care with an extra thrust and essence burning through her veins, his eyes rolling back, his limbs shaking. His body fell to the ground, unmoving. Not a breath escaped him.

Dead. And Kathryn felt nothing. Nothing at all.

She got to her feet, wiping the blood of the knife off onto her skirt. "The only person who will ever burn me is myself."

Watch the world crumble around you as you stand still to not be hit.

Panic.

Duke's son murdered in royal territory. Oh, how the court erupted within the following day.

Kathryn watched the halls pack, the panicked nobles scream and point fingers as Carastene sat stone faced on her throne. The amounts of accusations of the weakness of Carastene's efforts brought a thrill to Kathryn.

"*It must have been a refugee! You yourself know what goes down at those banquets held by the youth. Politics and strong drinks.*"

"*It was a clear assassination!*"

"*But the wound was hardly fatal.*"

"Then he bled out!"

"Our poor Hadeon!"

The sympathy they gave the Duke's district made Kathryn's veins burn. The ignorant fools knew not how many their darling boy had killed and covered as a foolish mishap. She was not the murderer.

If the standards were set that low, what was a group of boys torturing and killing women in the woods? Why was Carastene slaughtering refugees and hybrids even when she knew that the Soul already lived? What were the foolish nobles who still sent out their people to be swallowed by the Oquelite's growing force?

She knew exactly what they feared. It disgusted her. They feared the truth...the reality that their dreams were nothing but an illusion, just as the Ewyon race was the master of. They were slaves to it.

She was the murderer? She was the balancer. She wouldn't be the villain that the Council prophesied her to be.

She stormed down the hall, her boots clicking against the cold, stone floor.

"Adrienne!"

She didn't stop. She didn't respond to that name...that lie.

"Adrienne, if you don't stop right this instant, I swear, I will have you locked up once and for all."

Kathryn slowed, snorting. She looked over her shoulder to the shaken Queen trembling in the moonlit halls, her red dress hugging her frail frame, as she clenched her skirt in her hand.

Kathryn felt Carastene's tug on her mind, but she thrust it away. How satisfying it was to smell the fear ripple from her aunt.

"Lock me away now?" Kathryn said, turning to face her. "And why not years ago?"

"I'm not merciless."

"Oh, but you are cruel."

"I know it was you who killed the Abaddon boy."

"And if so, why haven't you reported this to your silly little court...? How about the Council?"

Carastene tensed, her jaw clenched. "I—I don't know how to prove it yet."

Kathryn smiled. "Well, then."

"Do you admit it?" Carastene took a shaky step forward.

"No. I don't."

"You're everything the Council said you would be." The Queen cowered as she spoke. "They said you'd be heartless...end the world as we know it."

Kathryn scoffed. "The Council is a bunch of pathetic, political tools. If I'm so dangerous, why haven't they taken care of me yet? They're the ones who created this curse."

Carastene paled. "That wouldn't be right."

"Then I'll just have to find another Council." Kathryn didn't wait for her aunt to respond. She stormed down the hall, Carastene screaming after her.

"You're insane! I shouldn't have to be part of this!" Fear echoed in her aunt's sob.

Kathryn slammed the glass door out into the courtyard, shaking angry sparks from her fingers. If the Council wouldn't willingly revoke their curse, she'd do it herself.

She raced up the steps to the tower, the cold night air beginning to pierce and the moon sinking behind the darkening clouds that swelled in her chest. She pushed past the guard, running higher and higher. She pulled the heavy, wood door open and froze.

Sergia stood across from her, her long, dark hair down from her tight bun, dressed in a beige dress that Kathryn had never seen before, a bag slung over her shoulder.

"Where are you going?"

Sergia's face hardened. "Away."

"For the night?" Kathryn breathed.

"Forever."

Kathryn went cold, the burning in her veins chilling. Thunder crashed through the sky. "What do you mean?"

Anger glowed in Sergia's eyes, clasping the strap of her bag. "You promised it wouldn't go this far."

"How far?"

"Stop acting oblivious," Sergia shouted with a pained cry. "Kathryn, you killed someone!"

Silence. The curtain began to swing in the grounding wind. Lightning flashed in the sky.

Kathryn couldn't breathe.

"And?"

Sergia's jaw dropped. "Do you have no remorse?"

Kathryn didn't know what to do. Say. Think. She'd never seen Sergia like this, tears streaming down her face.

"You promised me this wouldn't get out of hand." She sobbed. "Kathryn, you promised you weren't killing."

"I wasn't——"

"No!" Sergia screamed. "I have no more time for your excuses.

You've become far too much like Carastene."

Kathryn stumbled back. "I am nothing like my aunt."

Sergia laughed breathlessly. Her shoulder trembled as she tried to catch her breath. "Please. Just let me leave," she choked. "I—I can't."

Kathryn's lip quivered, speechless. This wasn't happening.

"Please, Kathryn." Sergia's eyes begged. "I can't watch you fall any further."

Kathryn slowly stepped away from the door. Sergia ran past. Kathryn stood, unmoving, listening to the echo of Sergia's racing steps down the stairwell, and finally…

…the door slammed shut.

The echo. Bang. Bang. Bang.

Sergia was gone. And it was all Kathryn's fault.

She sank to the ground, her hands tearing through her hair, and screamed.

No one heard her over the thunder. Lightning shattered the sky. Rain poured down as the wind threw the curtains up.

She fell, her hands against the ground, staring at the stone floor. She was a killer. She was falling right into line.

No. She refused.

She couldn't live. It was too dangerous. She'd fulfill what they said she'd be as long as she still breathed.

She'd find a way no matter how much she had to break. She'd find a Council that would.

She lay on the floor, letting the storm rage. Hours passed. Hours and hours.

Sergia's words echoed in her mind.

Hours. And hours.

Tears streamed down her face.

I can't watch you fall any further.

Morning came, but no sun came to greet it. The storm only raged harder.

She couldn't take it anymore. She eyed the open window, slowly getting to her feet.

She couldn't turn back. This could be the evidence Carastene was waiting for.

But what was Kathryn waiting for?

She ran, jumping over the sill and plummeting to the ground below her. She spun and, with a flash, landed on her feet in the stable, the stallion rearing in horror.

Submit.

The animal's weak mind calmed and moved to her outstretched palm. She climbed quickly to its back, tangling her hand into its mane, sending it a command.

Go.

She raced out from the courtyard and into the storm. The gates were open, and no one was out in the rain to watch as she tore out into the muddy road for the empty woods.

Sergia was right about one thing. Kathryn had made a promise. They meant little but words to her, but some hearts, unlike promises, were too painful to break.

PART ONE

THE PHOENIX

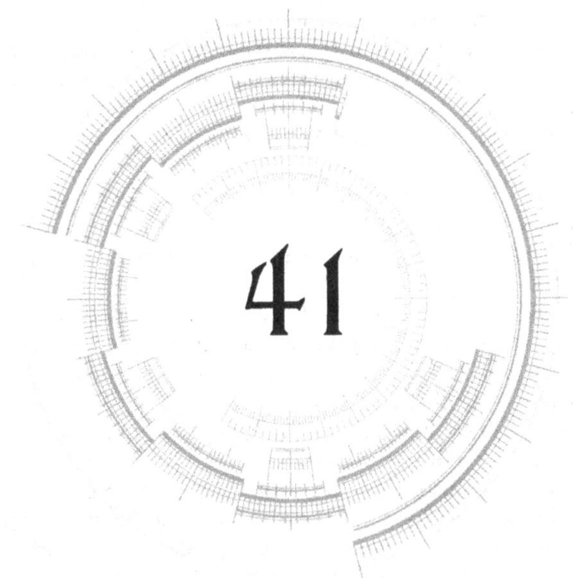

41

Liberty, 7 Days Until

WITHOUT CECILEO, NAVIGATING the rooftops was harder than Cole had anticipated. His sword was at his side with the cold night breeze through his loose shirt as he looked down at the shacks of the drunken, far side of the Market. It seemed like its inhabitants were only just now waking up from their sleep, laughing and jingling proud coin pouches.

Cole took a deep breath. He just had to get through, to Box, and out. One step forward toward stopping this "commission" and proving himself to the Council.

He descended quietly down the side of the building into the camp, quick to bow his head from any unwanted gazes, moving between the tents till he reached the desired sheet shack sitting alone in the back dirt lot.

"Box? Are you here?"

No light was on. Maybe he was actually sleeping.

Cole pulled back the flap, finding the fire smothered and

the tent dark. His heart flipped.

He dusted himself off, scanning the tents from behind. This Market section wasn't too big, and Box stood out as well as a small canine boy did in a society of humans.

How hard could it be? Apparently, pretty hard.

Cole trailed the streets until he swore that he'd seen the same guy on the street corner go through three rounds of cards.

Don't panic. Box wouldn't leave, would he? He had too much to lose.

Cole caught sight of the large tent he remembered from when he and Cecileo first traveled to this sector of the Market. This time a bored-looking woman guarded the door instead of the old man.

He groaned internally and walked quickly to the entrance. He cleared his throat. "Hello."

Her eyes shifted upward, annoyed. "Enter or get lost."

"I'm looking for someone," he said, ignoring her remark, despite his face heating. "Reddish hair. Sharp ears. Marks on his face. Hard to miss."

The woman looked at him for a long moment. "You been drinking, kid?"

Cole blinked. "What? No! Can you just answer the question?" He sighed. "Please?"

The woman snorted with a smile. "Saw a scrawny, little guy enter earlier. Don't think he's coming out considering his *company*." She threw her head back laughing.

Box's company?

She looked back to Cole with a wink, stepping aside. "Don't get eaten in there."

That…didn't sound good.

The pit in his stomach deepened. Cole just turned to the dark entrance to the tent. He held his breath and walked inside. He pushed through the dark entrance and through heavy flaps into a dimly lit, orange room, the smell of cigar smoke strong and the pounding of thrilling music and laughter drowning out anything else.

Folding tables and chairs were set up, and the bar seemed to have been rebuilt far too many times and on the verge of collapse. The place was crowded. Cole wanted to turn on his heel and walk right out, but he forced himself to stay put.

What would Tabitha do? No doubt she'd storm right into the building, demanding for Box and maybe a drink if she was really feeling the spite.

Most of the inhabitants didn't seem to notice him with more than a glance. He scanned the crowd. No small Lyntox boy in sight.

Cole was slammed forward from behind. He caught his balance quickly, whirling around, bracing himself to a middle-aged man, unshaken and not very sober.

"I'm sorry, sir—"

Before Cole could finish, the man clapped Cole on the shoulder. "Look what we have here!"

"Jin, we don't know him." A man sighed from the table beside him.

"Jin" waved him off. "Of course we do. Sit down, kid."

"I actually have to be—"

Cole was shoved down into a chair without warning and didn't dare get up when the man with a knife across from him smiled.

All right, then. He guessed he was staying. Maybe he could find more information on Box here, anyway.

"We new to the Market, kid?"

Play it cool.

Cole leaned back in his chair. "Fairly. Been here over a month."

"Explains it," a tattooed woman chortled. "Got a pretty puny imperfection."

Imperfection? Is that what they called each of their scars and missing limbs? He didn't think he had any—

"Yeah. How did you get your ear thing?" Jin leaned in.

Oh, right. His torn ear.

Cole resisted the urge to reach and feel it. "Stopped a…kidnapping. And they stole something off me."

"Huh." The group looked unpaused, almost bored. There was a high chance that they were thieves too. Cecileo, their leader, literally was one. It didn't seem to be uncommon.

"Not a result of a Defender run-in? A rebellion? Yen lost her foot to an ugly Tigia Sergeant."

The woman proudly slammed her foot up onto the table.

The group laughed, and Yen called for another round to

an annoyed-looking, passing waiter.

"Mater's imperfection is a fraud." The woman laughed all too casually.

Echo? Cole frowned. "I think her metal hand looks pretty real."

"It was cut off by Marketeers, not won by honor," Jin huffed.

A platter of jugs were set onto the table.

Cole's heart dropped. Echo's hand had been cut off by Marketeers? Cecileo never bothered to mention *that*.

Yen laughed. "You're pale, kid. Commonly known fact. She's a fraud. Don't let her deceive you."

"Why did the Market cut off her hand?" he said, trying not to shout.

"Crimes against the Market about two decades ago. She nearly exposed the entrance to the Elery Market running from an Officer."

Two decades ago…Echo was only seven. Cecileo told him about Echo's traumatic past connected to the Defenders, and being only a kid, he couldn't blame her for being rash.

And taking her hand as a punishment?

"That's hardly a crime," he managed to say.

"So pure, isn't he?" One snorted.

"Have a drink, kid."

They pushed a drink toward him, as if his mind wasn't already rushing enough. He picked it up just for show, but the smell was strong and bitter.

"She's a child killer. That's what she is," a man said, scratching his beard and slamming down his jug. "Preventing an heir. No doubt she wants to restart the bloody son tournament."

"Those seem like wild allegations," Cole said. Child killer? Echo had been nothing but motherly toward him since he arrived. And both she and Cecileo always spoke badly about the bloody contest that won Cecileo the role of "Pater." "From what I see, she's very against the son tournament after what misery it brought people.

"Did you happen to see a boy with marks, reddish hair, and sharp ears?" Cole said, trying to steer from the conversation before he lost all focus. "Goes by 'Box.'"

To his disappointment, the group looked around, confused. Cole decided that it was a lost cause and got to his feet.

"Like that kid with Hakuri?"

Cole's heart leapt, recognizing the name from the warning the man gave them on crossing paths with a certain "Zion Hakuri."

"Yes!" Cole jumped up.

The table blinked in surprise.

Cole cleared his throat. "Yes. Him. Do you know where I can find them?"

"You want to seek out Hakuri?" Yen raised a brow. "It's usually the other way around."

"He's always out back. The back alleys are too narrow for habitable streets," the bearded man said with a strong sip.

"Thank you!" Cole took off without so much as a nod. He was running low on time. He'd fight this Hakuri if it came to it.

He tried to replay Cecileo's instructions in his head as the back flap of the pub tent flew open. The night was cold, and the lot was empty. A shiver went down his spine as he heard the harsh vices nearby.

Cole unsheathed the Illuminate, took a breath, and advanced carefully forward. He leaned up against the alley wall, creeping closer to the lantern light spilling from across the corner. His heart leapt. They'd been right.

He crouched into a stance, peering out: a small group crowded with knives strapped to their belts, and the shadow of what appeared to be a man cast along the wall, a struggling figure in his grip. Cole tightened his hold on the hilt, taking an even breath.

"Again, I don't know where you got that information into your malformed, little skull!"

"It's common knowledge! No one even mentioned paying any pound—" Box's clear, barking voice was cut off with a shove.

"It's pay or leave—" The shadow suddenly turned and groaned. "Out of the shadows, idiot."

Cole leapt to his feet, brandishing his sword in front of him and fearlessly stepped into view to face—

—a teenager?

A boy who looked, at most, only a year older than himself with an angry scowl and a knife poised at Cole's head. His eyes were dark and his hair dyed at the roots with silver.

Box, who was wearing the dirt, looked back and forth, a frown deepening. "What the heck are you doing here?"

Zion, Cole guessed the boy to be, circled Cole slowly. "Who are you?"

"Someone looking for that fine friend of yours."

Zion stopped at Box, lifting him by the collar of his shirt, and shoved him forward, barreling in the dirt at Cole's feet. Box rolled gracefully back to his feet, sending Zion a glare.

Cole blinked in surprise.

Zion groaned. "Please, get him out of this darn Market!"

"He's the Modified who swore to protect the Northern Regions!" Box said, leaping to his feet. "He didn't mention his knife was special when I broke it."

"Wait, you're a warlock—I mean, Modified?" Cole's eyes widened. "Like, you have abilities?"

"I'm NOT." Zion threw his head back in frustration. "Stop saying that, stupid boy fox. And if you want me to go on your stupid mission to that manor, I told you. I take two hundred pounds per commission. No negotiation."

Cole stepped between the two before another brawl broke out. Zion's bystanders leapt for their weapons. Zion waved them off, glaring hard at Cole. "I know who he's talking about. Some Modified called 'Gorgon' from Hai."

"I only know of him," Zion said, his voice becoming quieter before sparking with anger. "But I am not that man."

Cole's brow furrowed. "So you know of him?"

"I already said yes, street rat, what more do you want?"

"So you know of his mission fighting Exerticus?"

Zion froze. His gaze fell with a curse. "I do."

"Do you know how to fight them?" Cole's heart was racing.

Zion turned the tip of his knife against his pointer finger before sheathing it. "Yes."

"I'm putting together a mission—"

Zion's head snapped up. "I take pay."

"I'm aware, and I can provide the two hundred."

For once, having the Outowns as patrons might come to

his favor.

"Four hundred," Zion said with a cool smirk. "Now that Exerticus are involved."

Cole flinched. That would be a lot to request, but this was a golden opportunity. "Fine," he said, tense. "You have a deal."

"Break the deal, and I get to take a limb," Zion said. There was no laughter in his voice as he simply crossed his arms. "My team is in."

Cole looked down to Box, offering a hand. "And you?"

Box got to his feet on his own. "Do I get paid too?"

"Uh—"

"I'm joking." Box sighed. "You're dense. Humans."

"Good," Cole said, ignoring the comment. He turned back to Zion and his unnerving, murderous glare in his young eyes. "I'll coordinate with you later. I am—"

"Coleson Johnson. I'm aware," Zion said, his brows deepening. "I've heard quite a lot about you."

"All good things, I hope."

"I hope so too." Zion chuckled. "For your sake."

42

North Cordell, 5 Day Until

"IT WAS AN allergic reaction," Lawrence said as he moved out of the way of Fire Wolf and beside Matteo in the dirt patch directly behind the Inn. "Apparently, my dear cousin is allergic to Exil Libium."

"Odd." Matteo's gaze shifted nervously to Miriam, who stood distracted by Charles showing off his dirt clot collection.

Lawrence dropped his stance with a sigh, doubting that Matteo had heard a word he'd said the entire session. "You good?"

Matteo turned, startled. He forced a smile and nodded. Something about him seemed to have shifted back to his uneasy self, whatever spark of confidence he'd had hidden away, and thanks to their unexplainable physical connection, Lawrence felt it.

Lawrence wanted to blame it on Miriam, but that wouldn't explain the new nightmares. They never lasted long since Matteo was up quickly and didn't fall back asleep for what seemed like hours. Lawrence thought that they'd passed, but last night proved otherwise. Not that Lawrence's sleep was any better.

"How do you feel, caterpillar? Good to go?" Miriam said, turning to them. "I have a feeling today will be the day we get something."

Whether you get something or not is entirely up to him.

Lawrence gave Matteo a nod of assurance, though he much rather would've turned and ran. Matteo returned the nod, a small glimmer of determination with it as he turned after Miriam into the Inn.

Lawrence took a deep breath and followed.

He felt guilty knowing that he had little faith in this working, even though Matteo's entire hope relied on the lie that he did. He felt heavy, everything weighing him down.

They reached the closet, and with a swipe of Miriam's hand, the floor dropped to the glowing, holographic staircase, the automated voice reading off their identification. Lawrence held his breath as he descended.

The platform was already raised, the Sergeants standing off to the side, studying it.

This was the moment they'd been waiting for since they heard that the Wingor member had arrived.

Lawrence reluctantly took his place beside Taryn, her foot tapping away.

"How do you think he'll do?" she asked quietly.

"No idea."

"You don't appear thrilled, Williams."

"I'm not."

Taryn sighed, her eyes darting to Miriam and Matteo. "I understand you feel this is rushed, but we don't have much of a choice."

Lawrence huffed.

"Williams."

"What?"

"Do you realize the importance of this at all?" Taryn's voice was harsher, her eyes boring into him.

Lawrence stared back. "I'm here for my family."

"Noble of you, but what about the actual result of the Council?"

Lawrence shrugged. "To save the world from some inevitable destruction or something."

She raised a brow. "That doesn't faze you?"

Guilt panged his side. His pride refused to let his indifference fall. "No."

"You're lying." The Sergeant's forehead erased between her brows with subtle frustration, her eyes glimmering with a hint of…pain? Sadness.

Lawrence looked away, trying to shake it off. He'd never intended to care for the Council or its mission. And especially its Sergeant. But he couldn't deny the growing pit in his stomach when he realized the very real possibility of failure. He couldn't show that.

"We're keeping the weird magnetic gloves, right, Serg?" Miriam called out from across the platform.

Taryn turned her attention to her Officer. "Yes, Outown. we don't want a replay of last time, but full simulator mode now. An essence break is vital, no matter its elements."

This is how she thought to break Matteo's essence and activate his wings? It was a weak idea.

"Why is fighting the way it's going to happen?" Lawrence asked. If he knew anything about Matteo, it was that he was far too gentle hearted for punching to be what brought his wings out. The happiest he saw him was sitting in a quiet room with Fire Wolf and mending one of Charles's socks.

"Since you refuse to tell us how *your* essence was broken, we have to resort to this." Taryn sighed. She raised a brow at him.

He looked away, tightening his fists. There was no way he would ever tell her what really happened the first time he held fire.

Miriam hoisted herself up onto the platform, fleshing her hands with the gloves. "All right, ready, caterpillar?"

Matteo followed up after her, settling into his usual place on the platform, casting a quick glance to Lawrence. "D— don't you need the *Cors Vis*—?"

"While I don't have half the power of a Member, I still broke my essence by myself. And the *Cors Vis* wasn't destroyed too long ago. We're riding on those chances. Good?" Miriam said, tying her short hair up.

Matteo didn't look "good," but he slid into his stance

anyway.

"Full simulation starts in five," Dow announced, looking up from his Scroll. "Lower your goggles."

Matteo and Miriam put on the goggles, and the light of the room fell, the holographic platform and its thin walls glowing.

The countdown hit zero, and Lawrence held his breath, preparing to shout for Dow to shut it off.

And then Matteo lunged.

Lawrence blinked in surprise.

Miriam was caught off guard, whirling to strike back, but Matteo skirted gracefully away from the strike.

Lawrence saw Taryn's mouth fall open.

He looked back, speechless for a moment. He couldn't help but smile.

Like a dance. That's how Matteo had described it, and how fitting of a description it was. While Miriam's method was fierce and direct, she was not used to Matteo's evasive, colorful turns and ducks that went to a rhythm only he understood.

Miriam hit the holographic wall…hard. She stumbled back, dazed.

The opportune moment to strike. Get it over with.

But Matteo stood, waiting patiently for Miriam to regain her senses.

"Strange," was all Lawrence heard Dow murmur.

Dow pushed the bar of intensity of the simulator up on his screen, the lights of the hologram shifting to warmer, red tones.

Miriam regained her balance, pushing quicker, managing to land a blow to Matteo's field. He recovered quickly, sensing Miriam and leaping up onto the stacked obstacles, descending onto Miriam, and knocking her back.

Another notch up. The room grew darker.

Matteo moved forward, ducking. Bad luck for him, Miriam came from below. He toppled to the floor.

Pain suddenly swelled through Lawrence's senses. *Not again.*

He held back a cry and gasped. The pain tingled at the back of his skull, his palms burning as if they held fire.

Was the connection getting *worse?*

Taryn cast him a quizzical look. He clenched his jaw and stared straight forward.

Matteo struggled slowly upward, and Miriam didn't give him the same mercy. He was knocked down again.

Pain shot through Lawrence again. He stumbled against the wall, trying to steady himself.

Holy mortals. What the heck—?

Matteo struggled up, his brows furrowed.

Miriam turned for another blow, but Matteo rolled out of the way, trying to scramble to his feet. He pushed himself up, his eyes darting everywhere.

Something was wrong.

He grabbed the goggles.

"What is he doing?" Dow said.

"You're overdoing it!" Lawrence shouted. He wasn't even sure if it was true. He just needed Matteo out of there. Now.

"But the simulation has no noise."

Did it matter?

Matteo successfully tore off the goggles. The simulation and holographic walls fell.

Matteo didn't wait for someone to confront him. He ran off into the dark, the door slamming open and his footsteps echoing up the stairs.

And then, silence.

"Williams."

Taryn's unusually stern voice froze him.

Lawrence spun on her. "This is your fault this keeps happening! Fighting doesn't work."

He knew that it wasn't true. It wasn't really the Defender's fault. Something else was going on. And he felt it. But he was too angry to admit it. He wanted to blame it on someone.

Before it gets blamed on you.

Miriam tore off her goggles, letting them slip from her fingers to the floor, staring blankly.

"He's just cowardly," Dow said. "He needs to learn to get over whatever is going on."

"It only matters he…we are Council Members to you."

"Do not speak to him that way." Taryn stepped forward. Lawrence scowled.

"Sergeant, the boy isn't a coward." Miriam looked up, her

eyes dazed and focused on Taryn. "You saw the way he fought. The way he let me get up…If anything, he might just be a little too compassionate, but Williams isn't all right, either. That boy is terrified of something."

The mere mention of his uncle, mother, his fear of Defenders…It was like a cry for help right before his eyes, but Lawrence didn't understand. What was it supposed to mean? What could he even do?

Taryn sighed, rubbing her temples. "It's never easy with these kids, is it?" She turned back to Lawrence. "I have no intention of becoming this dictator you've made me up to be, Williams. Do not make me."

Lawrence snorted and left.

He ran up to the second level. No Matteo in sight. Was he hiding again?

His anger dispelled as he slumped against a step in the dark, empty hall, slamming the door shut. He buried his face into his hands. What was he supposed to do? He didn't want Matteo to be forced into this battle against his will. He wanted Matteo to be all right. Stop torturing himself. Feel brave enough to live.

Someone had to get through to him.

Lawrence stopped himself. Who was he to want that? Matteo wasn't the only one keeping secrets, after all.

Lawrence couldn't sleep. He stared at the wall for what felt like hours, missing the closeness of his little brother, who'd fallen asleep in Nikki's room during a visit and insisted to be left there.

He tried to close his eyes and focus on the darkness instead of the voices, echoing and threatening to emerge from the grave he'd left them.

The darkness no longer provided safety.

The air was bitter and cold. The only sound was Matteo turning across the room.

Lawrence squeezed his eyes shut, forcing himself to take in long breaths. His mother cherished the long nights, often admiring the stars at his bedside. He was too young to appreciate it. Too young to ever imagine his mother's watery grave.

If she was still alive, he liked to think that she'd still do the same. She'd take Charles up into her arms as her own, help Isabel with the baby, and Lawrence? He didn't know what she'd do. He imagined that she wouldn't be horrified. She'd hug him and look at him with those blue eyes.

"No!"

Lawrence's eyes burst open, throwing off his cover and jumping up. Matteo tossed, shivering as he hugged himself, trying to fight with breathless and desperate words in his mother tongue. His body shook with tears.

"Matteo? Matteo!" Lawrence jumped from his mattress, not even bothering to grab his glasses. "Are you okay? Matteo!"

Matteo didn't respond, his arms pressing over his ears as he cried. Lawrence rushed to his side, quick to pull his hands from hurting his face. "Matteo, look at me! Breathe. It's okay. You're okay!"

Matteo didn't fight against Lawrence's hold of his arms, his eyes squeezing harder shut, shaking his head, sputtering words that Lawrence didn't understand through gasps for air.

"Matteo." Lawrence lowered his voice, trying not to let it quiver. What was going on? "It's okay. You were just dreaming."

"No," Matteo whispered, shaking his head furiously. His eyes burst open, glassy with tears as he tried to catch his breath. "N—not a dream."

He broke down again, slumping forward. Lawrence caught the boy, freezing in speechless surprise. He slowly wrapped his arms around Matteo's shuddering frame.

"It won't leave," Matteo choked. He grit his teeth. "It won't leave me alone."

Lawrence held him tighter to keep him from shaking. How could he help? He was no one. "I—I know how you feel."

"No, you don't," Matteo spat bitterly. "You have no idea what it's like. Shameful. Disappointment. Slow. Useless." He shivered. "I want it to stop."

Lawrence's throat tightened. *I know more than you ever will.* "I'm sorry."

Matteo didn't respond, his breaths still ragged. He pushed himself away, hugging himself.

Lawrence closed his eyes. It hurt. Everything hurt, like it

was ripped raw and the wound was bleeding…all over someone else.

Who was he? No one. No one at all.

"When I was thirteen—" What was he doing? Lawrence went on. "—I—I was dragged outside to a dirt lot behind the fields."

Matteo suddenly stilled.

Heat burned behind Lawrence's eyes. *Stop. Stop now.* "My sister's husband…I got in his way." The field hands already didn't like him. Thought that he was privileged, being the son of Miz's new husband. They were giddy to see Cain strike him first. "They hurt me…in all sorts of ways."

Echoes. So many echoes. Stings. Burns.

He'd shoved them away. Waking up to blood, alone in a field and the slow horror and sobs.

He moved to the end of the mattress and, with his shaking hands, slowly pulled his shirt off and over his head to reveal his scarred back.

He couldn't see him, but he could hear the halt in Matteo's breath. A small, gentle hand brushed gently against the crevice of a scar.

Tears burned at his eyes. Lawrence swallowed hard, struggling to breathe. "It stopped hurting once I learned to go numb."

Quiet.

Lawrence squeezed his eyes shut. "I do know how you feel," he choked. "I know what it feels like to be ashamed."

I could've done something.

"That—that isn't right," Matteo stammered. "You shouldn't be ashamed. You didn't do anything wrong."

Tears flowed down his face. Lawrence tried to hide his face. "I could've tried harder. I—I could've just left. But I just—" His voice broke, and he buried his face.

What was he doing? What was the point? He was broken and angry. He was always angry.

A hand gently rested on his knee. "Don't blame yourself."

Did it matter?

Matteo moved closer. "Is it hard to tell yourself it—it's not your fault?" he whispered.

Lawrence tried to swallow, but it hurt. It hurt more than

anything. It felt like he was drowning right next to his mother. "It hurts...so bad."

Silence.

"I know."

They sat in silence till Lawrence could breathe again. He took back his shirt, avoiding even Matteo's direction. He'd sworn that he'd never tell a soul so directly.

Nothing else seemed to make him listen.

"I tried to die when I was eleven."

Lawrence froze.

Matteo took a deep breath, playing with his sleeve. "*Mi papá*...was sick. He was always sick. He knew what it was like to be...broken. But he still worked. All the time." Matteo was quiet. "I was there when he died."

"Oh, I'm—"

"I was with his body for four hours in the back of the casino warehouse."

Lawrence was speechless. The questions in his mind went silent. It was best not to press.

Matteo's face hardened. "I tried to get him help." He dug his fingers into the mattress. "The door got jammed behind me."

"Matteo..."

"Voices get louder. Without him, no one understands them. They thought I was crazy." Matteo fell quiet, wiping away the tears. "I thought I was crazy." Rain began to pelt against the window. Matteo took a deep breath. "I wasn't thinking straight. He'd been dead for hours when they found us. I saw how much I hurt them. I kept seeing his eyes." His voice quieted. "I didn't want to hurt them again. I wanted to be able to save him. I wanted the voices in my head to go away. So that's why I thought...I thought if I was gone...it would fix everything."

The room was quiet.

"And now all I want is for her to look at me again."

His mother.

Matteo looked Lawrence in the eye. "I have scars too."

The two boys sat in silence.

"You're a lot stronger than people give you credit for," Lawrence finally managed to say.

Bottled it all up. Self-inflicted pain. Crying for help all

alone. Alone.

That was one thing Lawrence had been lucky enough to never be: alone. He'd had Charles and Isabel. They kept him alive.

But Matteo?

Lawrence looked back at him. "You're not alone anymore."

"I know." Matteo sniffled. "But now I have people to lose again."

"Who?"

"The Council…You."

"Oh."

"You act all tough to everyone all the time, but—but you always act so…gentle to me and Charles." Matteo struggled a moment. "You make me remember him."

Lawrence shrugged. "Maybe it's because our dad stopped trying. Charles deserved someone to take care of him. Besides, I'll never become a father." Lawrence tried not to squirm. "Yeah. Or courting. I don't want to."

He wasn't sure whether it was because of the horrors he'd seen it lead to or because he truly felt comfort in another path. He wasn't sure what the future held. He just needed to keep living right in the present.

"I'll tell Calynda to knock it off, then."

Lawrence laughed. "It's fine."

"I will," Matteo insisted. "And anyone who dares."

"Thanks, Teo."

"Any time."

More silence. A comfortable silence. Matteo rested his head against Lawrence's shoulder. "Thank you," he whispered.

Lawrence, for a moment, braced himself for a cold flash of terror—the flood of thoughts and memories he couldn't stop, but instead…his thoughts were empty.

The cold breeze pricking at his wet face did not compare to the warmth of the boy on his shoulder. A boy who looked up to him. A boy who'd defeated the horrors in his mind…at least for tonight. A boy Lawrence would protect like another little brother.

Miriam was right. Matteo was no coward. He was someone that Lawrence had sworn to help heal, but instead,

Matteo was helping him?

Lawrence closed his eyes and breathed. "Thank you."

"My father always always said sweet bread helped improve moods." Matteo opened his eyes with a small smirk. "Are you in the mood for a midnight snack?"

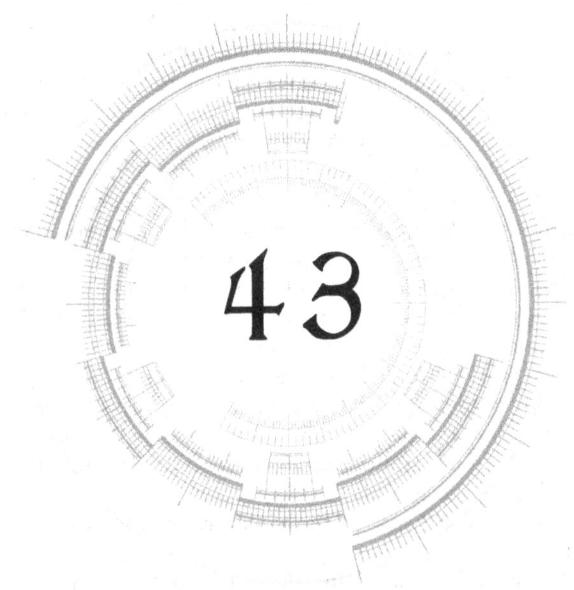

Kennedy, Mission Day

2 Days Until

RAY HAD HAD enough. They were two days away from the moon being submerged in utter darkness, and Mercy wouldn't so much as talk to him.

He stood outside her door. "We're running out of time!" he pleaded.

Nothing. He heard her walk across the room, her footsteps loud, almost mocking him.

"You want to find your father, don't you?" he said.

No response.

He scowled. He was sick of this. She knew that there was so much more at stake now, and she chose to be quiet.

"Fine," he snarled. "Be that way."

He stormed down the hallway. His friends were in danger. He was in danger. Mercy was in danger.

He slammed his door open.

And she didn't care? Who cared what her grandmother thought? There was no reason to stay in Kennedy anymore. Ray was trapped. He felt temptation building inside him, the numb, beautiful voice of the woman creeping into his thoughts. He shook her away.

He rushed to the desk, opened the drawer, and grabbed the key. If Mercy didn't want to talk, then he wasn't going to wait around. He wouldn't let guilt get to him. He wouldn't let himself be the reason more people got hurt again.

He turned quickly and, with a leap, fell through the floor, landing with a thud in the library room. His breath caught in his throat as he stepped back. He did it.

The window spilled with moonlight and, to his surprise, cast tiny shapes of stars all across the bookshelves. All around the room the silhouette of the moon cycle surrounded him, and the eerie silence made it triumphantly loud that he was intruding.

He clenched his jaw. He didn't have time to care about that.

He stormed toward the desk. He took a deep breath. What if he'd been wrong? What if this was all for nothing? And they were doomed? All because he'd gotten the wrong key?

The golden key slid into the hole. He held his breath and turned, bracing himself.

It clicked.

His heart leapt as he slowly drew it away and took hold of the handles. He pulled it back. He almost gasped with relief as a weathered page and a sealed projection disc lay neatly in the drawer.

He picked them both out. The disk had a note with "balance keeping evidence" and a date written on it.

Ray looked at the paper, which, to his relief, had the name "Mercy Remembrance" neatly printed at the top…and the same date written underneath. It must have been her birthday.

His eyes traveled down the paper.

Previous Keyper [Mother]: Glory Faithful
Genetics Match [Father]: Chance Remembrance

Ray's eyes widened. Her parents' names. An odd way to call them, but it didn't seem like these people really cared about much more than keeping the Keyper legacy going.

Born midday during heavy storm. My arrival was nearly delayed due to the storm and Chance Remembrance's stubborn refusal of the upholding of the balance keeping.

Ray glanced at the disc.

Exact lunar state at conception also unknown. Glory was difficult on communication.

Child is female, disruption of the pattern in which indicated a male.

Child has no face marking. She is the one of the Council, though the alignment of times doesn't correspond. We must wait for a further date to know how to contain.

Balance keeping was successful. The fire after was held at the lake.

Like a bonfire? A celebration of Mercy's birth? Ray frowned.

The record ended there.

He looked up from the paper, out the window. That was it? Mercy was born, and she was most definitely meant to be part of Council…since he guessed that that's what made her effective, but not much else.

His eyes drifted back to the disc.

All except one thing. Whatever this "balance keeping" was about.

He opened up the case, propping the disc upward in its case. It clicked. Ray glanced over his shoulder. He took a deep breath and clicked the small button on the side.

A projection burst from the disc onto the wall. The footage loaded the pixels. It looked to be the back of the motel. Chunks of snow lay in the dirt. The time indicated 2.36 AM, and it was dimly lit by a backlight.

A few minutes passed and nothing happened. And then the door creaked open.

Ray leaned forward.

A familiar woman stepped out, wearing a long coat, her coiled hair kept up in an efficient manner. She walked quickly with an authority in her step.

"Mama, I—" A voice from inside.

The woman stopped in her step, turning with an annoyed huff. "Glory, come before I have to move you myself."

The woman was undeniably Mercy's grandmother, Virtue.

A young woman with the familiar, swirling marks crept out the back door. She was wearing thin leggings and an undershirt stained with blood. Her face was stained with tears and her hair misshapen and uncared for. She seemed to hardly keep herself upright as she hugged herself in the cold.

Ray panicked for a moment before remembering the date. This was recorded on Mercy's birthday…Glory must have only given birth a few hours ago, at most. Had she not even been permitted to change?

"Don't slouch, child."

"Mama, why am I here?" Her voice quivered, yet it still held a fierce demand to it as she looked her towering mother in the eyes.

Virtue's face was cold. "There is a balance to restore, Glory."

"Not another lecture, is it?" Glory's face flashed with pain. "You got what you wanted," she said through a weak gasp. "I failed, you won."

"You simply were more resistant to the legacy." Glory moved farther to the back, examining her daughter from a few feet back.

"This isn't a legacy," Glory said, her eyes quivering as they followed her mother's every step. "This is absurdity."

"You do not believe the signs, do you?"

"I do, Mama, but you are not the one who needs to enforce them," Glory pleaded. "The universe keeps itself balanced."

"I will do what I will to keep the line pure," Virtue spat.

"Even if it means siding with the foretold force?"

"In order to protect our new Keyper? Yes." Virtue's face was cold as Glory's mouth hung speechless. "Any information I have gained from infiltrating that pathetic believer organization will be used for her good alone."

"They don't know every Member yet," Glory said, straightening with hope.

Virtue laughed. "No, they don't know about the Bentsworth yet."

Virtue knew that Felicity was a Member? How could that be?

There was silence between them.

"Turn around."

Glory's face fell. "Mama—"

"Listen to me."

Tears flooded Glory's eyes with the tiniest shake of her head. "Please, Mama, give some mercy."

"Turn around."

Glory slowly did as Virtue demanded, turning slowly to face the wall, tears streaming down her face.

Ray heard a familiar click. His blood went cold.

"Have mercy," Glory sobbed.

Virtue didn't say a word. A gunshot rang out.

Ray stumbled back, tearing his eyes away. Too late. Blood. The hologram shut off.

It wasn't a bonfire party. They'd burned Glory's body at the lake. The balance restored was to keep one Keyper at a time…by murdering the other.

Ray stared at his hands, unblinking.

Every Kerper in that book. They'd all been murdered.

Every. Single. One.

Mercy's grandmother wasn't just strict…She was a murderer.

She knew about Felicity when Felicity was only three years old. She had plans to use that information if something ever got in her way. What unforeseen force did she plan to tell?

Ray stared at the disc, suddenly feeling guilty for his previous anger toward Mercy. She deserved to know.

His Comm buzzed. He picked it up out of his pocket.

He'd missed a message from Cole to the group a few hours ago. Ray opened it.

COLE: Heading to Bentsworth Manor tonight to intercept Exerticus-commissioned attack. Will keep you updated.

Bentsworth Manor.

Exerticus.

Ray's heart dropped. No.

They were walking right into a trap. That's what the Soul Night was. All of it. It was all a big trap.

44

Liberty, Mission Day

2 Nights Until

"STAY STILL, JOHNSON, or you'll be missing another part of your ear."

"Yes, and keep your mouth still…and shut," Cecileo said, grunting as he sat back in his seat. "If I hear your plan one more time, I might go insane."

Cole snapped his mouth shut, even though he squirmed to remind Cecileo the emergency street name again. A lock of his blond hair fell in front of his face.

"The plan is fine…impressive, actually."

Cole was tempted to look down to the Bentsworth Manor blueprint in his hand. "Are you sure? Even plan B?"

"Positive," Cecileo said with a sigh. "Now the real question is, are you sure?"

Cole had poured hours over this, memorizing every detail of their paths through the Manor and any possible way it could go wrong. The beats were set to the very minute. It felt so fragile that, just like the Exhibit House, in one fell swoop it could be burned to the ground.

But one of Tabitha's conditions was to have confidence.

"I am sure." And he meant it. He wasn't going to fail this time.

"Done," Echo said, setting down her pair of scissors, stepping back to examine her work. "And now he doesn't look like such a mess going out on his big mission. Brush off your shoulders, Coleson."

"It's just a mission, Ech, not a gala."

She rolled her eyes. "Yeah, Cecileo. It's a mission, not a tea party."

Cecileo picked up his mug as if to prove his point. "What's wrong with a little tea? Want some, Council Kid?"

"Uh…no thanks."

"More for the addict here." Echo laughed, slapping Cecileo on the shoulder. She moved to the desk, taking up her circlet, placing it on top of her braids she'd tied up. She was fully decked out in assorted leather, boots, and metal bracelets she'd worn when he first met her. "I'll keep watch here as planned."

Cole nodded, still silently wishing that he could take one of the leaders with him. They'd gotten him out of the tight spots before. But that wouldn't happen again, he reminded himself.

Cecileo gave his wife a side hug, kissing her temple. "So when do we head out?"

"I thought you already knew the plan." Echo laughed.

"My group arrives at Bentsworth Manor at dusk," Cole said. "So I'll be leaving soon."

"I'll go with you," Echo said, stepping out from Cecileo's arm. "I assume you'll be collecting Felicity Bentsworth, and I want to make sure her leg braces are up and running."

"Sounds like a good idea."

Was it? The taunts of the Marketeers at the bar still rang fresh in the back of his mind. He knew that they couldn't be trusted…but something still nagged at him.

"Fantastic," Echo said with a smile, turning to Cecileo. "Be back tomorrow, don't do anything stupid."

"You know me, very responsible." Cecileo winked at

Cole.

Echo sighed. "This is serious business, Cecil."

"I know. I've done worse." He waved them off. "Hurry, you two, and—"

Echo caught Cecileo off guard, kissing him.

She pulled away with a smirk and Cecileo's face red. "Come on, Illuminate Boy. We better do as the almighty Pater demands."

She was out the tent flap before Cole could catch up.

"Wait!" Cecileo called out.

Cole halted.

Cecileo ran to him, one foot undoing one of his anklets. He tore it off and held one out to Cole. It was a metal wire with multiple metal, round beads with small, red crystals in each. "If you get stuck in a situation, this contains multiple shots of a fatal sedative. I'd prefer you use it on someone other than yourself."

Cole took it carefully into his hands, clipping it to his wrist. He looked up at Cecileo with a nod. "Thank you." *For everything.*

Cecileo smiled. "Any time, Council Kid. Better hurry before Echo starts getting worried."

Oh, right. Cole shouted another thanks and burst out the tent flap and into the dirt street after Echo, waiting patiently for him, communicating to her security team through the Comm in her metal arm.

His head tugged at his chest as he ran alongside her. He didn't want to believe the allegations against her. It didn't seem possible that she was manipulating Cecileo, he finally decided.

But it didn't mean that something wasn't off…The way the higher ups despised her, the way she stayed out of the public eye, and Doran always seeming unsure about Cecileo's protectiveness of her.

He just couldn't think of what.

Echo shut off her arm Comm. "You have a specific Manor location to meet?"

"Base of the Manor," Cole said coolly. "We'll be taken to the top by some person named 'Renee Kitts.'"

Another friend of Felicity's.

"Kitts?" Echo's brow raised.

"Sound familiar?" An employee of the Bentsworth and a Marketeer didn't seem to have much of a chance of crossing paths.

"I believe so," was all Echo added.

They approached the emerald tent, slowing. Cole followed Echo inside.

Felicity turned her head, hearing them come. She was standing, dressed similarly to Echo, her braces over her leather pants and a tightly fitted, bulletproof bodice and leather shoulderpads buckled across her chest. Her hair was braided back and around the titanium headband, her legs braces on full display. A new feature was a spear strapped to her back.

Despite her epic appearance, Felicity looked away bashfully, fidgeting with her fingerless gloves. "Does it look stupid?" she asked.

"What?" Cole gaped. "No, not at all! You look fantastic, Felicity!" He laughed. "I dare say you look more prepared than the rest of us. The braces look epic."

Felicity rolled her eyes. "Or a robot?"

Echo flexed her metal hand. "Robots are cool," she said. She circled Felicity. "How does movement feel?"

Felicity stepped forward, bracing herself. "Natural... painless."

"Good. It might take a bit to get used to, but I have no doubt you'll manage this mission." Echo gave a warm smile, squeezing Felicity's shoulder.

Felicity gave a small smile in return. "I trust Cole's got that taken care of."

"I hope that's the right call," Cole half-joked, ignoring the flip of his stomach.

"That's all we really ever have. Hope." Felicity straightened, stepping cautiously from Echo to Cole. "You ready?"

Cole took a deep breath. Hope. "Let's go."

"See you on the other side of success, Coleson!" Echo saluted.

Cole saluted back, offering his arm to Felicity. She took it, squeezing his arm.

"Just for now," she whispered, blushing. "If I pass out..."

"Don't worry about it, Liz. I'll make sure you don't," he

assured.

She exited, quickening her pace alongside him.

The streets were already getting dark. Time was ticking. Felicity's pace was becoming steadier as they went and her hold less clammy and clenched.

Good. They'd need Felicity in action, but he didn't want to push her. She was their secret weapon. For once, he would see her in action instead of the sidelines.

This was her chance.

They turned into the dark alley, and almost as soon as Cole stepped in, someone broke a glow stick light, illuminating Zion's face and his entire group behind him. "Slightly late, Illuminate."

Box snorted, crawling down the fire escape into the light. "Or you're just too early."

Zion rolled his eyes before they stopped halfway on Felicity. His mouth fell. "I—is that—?"

"Felicity Bentsworth," Felicity finished for him. She eased onto her own feet, taking a step forward.

The group was still for a moment before Zion shook himself to his usual, jaded senses, his steel eyes studying her. "Interesting."

Cole stepped forward, clearing his throat. "Zion, Box, and the rest are taking the rooftops to the Manor to lower suspicion, and we'll be meeting Felicity's friend, Falcon, there too. All clear?"

"Yes, Mr. Illuminate, sir."

Cole deadpanned at Box, who just shrugged.

"All right, let's go."

Zion was quick to lead them to the ladder to scale the wall, and Cole and Felicity passed through the crack in the fence and into the open street.

He turned to Felicity, who was tugging on a loose curl. "When did Giles say he'd be here?"

"Any moment now," she whispered.

After an agonizing four minutes, Giles finally pulled up in a long, black auto, shimmering away the window with a tilt of his sunglasses. "Get in, Council Idiots. Don't scare the nutrition-fact guy there in the back."

W—what did he just say?

Cole didn't have a moment to ask as Felicity quickly

pulled him into the cab.

"Falcon!"

The door shut behind them, Giles starting off without warning, sending Cole back into his seat with a thud. Felicity's excitement was replaced with a flash of sheer terror, gluing herself in the seat beside the reddish-haired boy, a few years than Cole. He was taller and had light freckles mixed with his array of scars. Cole couldn't help but notice the similar flash of fear in his green eyes.

"Raphael Mathews, right?" Falcon said as the fear fell from his shoulders.

He thought that he was Ray? A first.

"Cole Johnson," Felicity corrected behind a nervous laugh.

"Raphael…Ray's my brother, though," Cole said quickly to soothe the blush of Falcon's embarrassment.

"Wait, so you're the one on the news?" Falcon's brow arched. "Holy cow…"

"Falcon." Felicity gave her friend a warning look.

"Liz, it's a compliment." Falcon turned to Cole. "Trust me. Not too many things top Veronica's '53' obsession."

Cole blinked. Fifty-three? "Wait, like the number?"

"Yeah…and no," Felicity said. "'53' is a number part of a linked file to the Aguirres and some DNA harvesting organization. She's got a whole closet dedicated to figuring out what it means."

That was not what Cole was expecting to hear about the younger daughter of the infamous Gordon Bentsworth.

"Interesting person, that Veronica Bentsworth is." Falcon whistled. "Shame you won't get to meet her in person."

Felicity's eccentric, fourteen-year-old sister's role was solely on surveillance and communication through the earbuds that Echo had provided. Being a Bentsworth Manor resident, she knew it better than any patrolling Defender.

"Speaking of siblings," Felicity said, turning to Falcon. "Did Finch get suspicious?"

"She left for Uni in Sycamore, Liz," Falcon said, raising a brow.

Felicity's lips parted in surprise before clearing her throat. "Well…I've missed a lot."

Cole quickly moved his attention from the conversation that he felt like an intruder in to the window, the border wastelands spinning by as the Dome grew larger and larger, approaching them with an increasing speed. No stars were in the sky tonight.

Cole touched the cold windowsill. The auto began to slow, the light of the Dome growing brighter.

Giles pulled into the checkpoint, and a flash of a Defender ID and a Bentsworth permit got him quickly into the world's most perfect city within moments.

And instantly, Cole saw why Tabitha hated it.

The city at night was beautiful. Scrapers reached toward the sky, where stars that hadn't been there before glittered an equal distance apart from one another. There were elevator pavilions and bistros with cute, cut curtains and flashy, holographic advertisements.

Everything was just as was meant to be. Nothing was out of place. And that was all Tabitha was to this city: not meant to be.

A sense of dread flooded him as they moved quickly through the mostly empty streets, passing the smartly dressed citizens going about their nightly amusement. Women had close-cropped hair, and most wore short skirts or shorts, loose dresses, and painted faces. Men dressed brightly, loose fitting, and the variations of their hair were fantastically put together piece by piece.

"Welcome to the Liberty Dome," Felicity whispered, drawing Cole back.

The ride wasn't long after that and solely occupied by Cole trying to rerun the plan in his head, being interrupted by thoughts about how absurdly incredible the Dome was…and his own words replaying in his mind.

His own words shouting at her to go back to this place. He'd acted no better than the very people who made her home torture.

I'm sorry, Tabs. Please forgive me.

When they arrived at Bentsworth Manor, it didn't need an introduction. The manor was bigger than fifty Cordell shop units combined—twice the size of the University, the top with a glass dome, rising higher than Cole imagined was possible.

Guards lined the courtyard as Giles pulled to a stop in the circular driveway around an enormous, pouring fountain, its spouts weaving and pouring artistically as they splashed back into a basin below.

Felicity and Falcon did not even hesitate to get out of the auto, throwing the door nearly into a startled guard as they rushed out.

The Manor was even bigger once he was out in the open air standing before it. Cole saw it many times as a child on the news recordings his father would accidentally leave on after a late night. Rich man. Big house. Pretty city.

Now Cole stood at the foot of it. If only his younger self could see this now.

"Johnson, close your mouth before I throw a bullet in it. Hurry up," Giles said, slamming the car door shut behind him.

Right. Cole was the leader of this operation, no time for slacking.

He hurried after Felicity and Falcon up the enormous steps, into the Bentsworth Manor.

The room was bustling with security. Zion, Box, and the rest of Zion's crew were waiting under anxious Defenders, who definitely didn't seem too comfortable with the idea of Marketeers standing in the Bentsworth Manor.

Zion jumped into step beside Cole as he strode by. "Beat you."

"What an accomplishment."

"Johnson, you'll need this," Giles said as they turned the corner. He handed Cole a key card. "Security access key."

"Thank you." So far, all part of the plan. "Ear Comms on?"

Everyone rushed to tap the ear buds. Cole took a deep breath as they approached a golden elevator door at the end of the hall. Most tech in the manor had been shut off, which was why Cole assumed that he hadn't experienced the infamous moving floors yet, but the elevators had been left on for a purpose of being the only way to access the office.

He swiped the card for the elevator door. The door shimmered away, and everyone rushed in.

"And we're live!" A youthful voice filled the ear Comm. "This is so cool."

Cole tried to suppress a smile. "Veronica, right?"

"Yessir," the voice said.

Good. He was already informed that Gordon Bentsworth's office was situated at the top level. With the speed they were going, they'd be there in a matter of moments.

Cole looked to Felicity, crushed in the corner beside him, fidgeting with the zipper near her neck, her eyes nervously darting around the quiet elevator.

Cole quickly squeezed her hand with a nod. She sent him a small smile.

The elevator came to a stop. The doors opened, the hallways dimly lit. Cole led the group out. "Veronica, what does the lower level look like?"

"They're mostly cleared," she said. "Give it a minute."

Not that he suspected that the bandits would even enter via the lower level. They would break in some other way, but their path would inevitably lead here. The appearance of no one else being present would be their most valuable asset.

Cole took a deep breath as he stepped into the glass hallways, looking down at the impossibly far drop of twists and turns of halls and floors, hanging colorful vines and soaring trees. The glass hall was lit by blue lights below them.

"Lower level cleared."

He tried not to think of it and moved along quickly to the other side, signaling the other to follow. They reached the opposite hall with a, thankfully, solid door below.

If they'd taken a different elevator that a select few had access to, it would have led them beyond the solid door that stood as a precaution, but right now, they were only looking for a trap. Cole looked up to find the walls just as they were described. Tall pillars and enormous tapestries.

The lights dimmed.

Zion and his crew had no problem silently crawling up the long cords that hung on the tall walls and shifting behind a hanging tapestry. Giles took a moment longer, whereas Box disappeared as quickly as he had come.

Cecileo's excessive tower limping came in handy, allowing Cole to hoist himself up fairly easily, Felicity struggling up below him. He finally looped the rope around his foot, holding it steady with his opposite heel. He reached out for

Felicity. She hesitated before reaching out her hand. He grabbed her wrist and hoisted her up. With a squeak, she grabbed onto him for dear life, pushing her face into his side to catch her breath. She carefully peered out, taking a deep breath, and moved a ready hand to her spear.

And now, they waited. Veronica was prompted to give them any update when seen, and so far, nothing.

Felicity's breathing was harsh. Cole longed to comfort her, but was restricted to the silence and holding her tightly as the wait stretched on.

Time passed. Not a sound.

Cole's heart beat against his chest. This was it. There was no going back.

I'm sorry, Tabs. I'm not going to mess up again.

He wasn't. He knew what he was doing, and he would not turn back.

"Intruder's breaching top dome window." Veronica's voice broke through, breathless. "Prepare for a full-on break-in."

He had been right. This was it.

He slowly unsheathed the Illuminate from his back, shifting his arm from Felicity to the cord as she held onto him firmly.

Quiet. The hall was still.

A minute. Two min—

Footstep. They were here.

"Drop!"

All in a moment, Cole and Felicity slid to the ground, rolling out into the hall.

Three figures jumped into the hall, not even hesitating with surprise before they charged.

A gunshot rang out. Cole dodged and a ping came from Zion's metal armguard. Zion was hardly fazed, whipping out his own weapon.

"Go around back!" Cole shouted to Felicity, swinging the Illuminate, the blade engulfing into flames.

Felicity nodded, gripping her spear and breaking out into a run.

A holographic shield burst from the bandit's wristband. Cole dove into a full charge, the Illuminate shattering on impact. The bandit staggered back, pulling out a knife as he turned and, with a quick glance, realized his mistake. Cole swiftly pinned them to the floor, slicing his bag open.

Empty. The bag was empty.

If the mission was to enter and take…it wouldn't be empty. They'd need more than just weapons…unless—

That's all they were anticipating.

"They're not what we're here for!" Cole shouted, jumping to his feet. "Veronica! Find the rest of them!"

"The—the rest?"

A pause. The bandit tried to get back up, but Cole slammed his foot down on his chest.

"The roof garden." Veronica gasped. "They're coming in through the garden! B—but that makes no sense…"

The garden at the top of the building? How were they supposed to get there?

Cole whirled around to Felicity, guarding the doors with Box. "Felicity!" he cried out. "We have to get to the roof garden!"

Felicity's eyes widened before her brows hardened to a firm expression, flipping her spear back into its holder and breaking out into a run. Cole ran after her, the clamor of the others shortly echoing after.

What in the world were they doing in the garden? Had the other three simply been a diversion? Why? What had they missed?

"The only way to the roof garden is through a non-tech stairwell," Veronica informed, her breath panicked, the sound of clicking and banging ringing through. "Liz should be leading you to it now. The system's going a little whack."

"Is it bad?"

"It seems like they've tapped into a server. I can probably override it."

Cole let out a sigh of relief. "We have it handled on this end. You go."

Felicity burst from the hall, running with no hesitation along the hall suspended in the air, without a wall in sight. Cole almost jerked to a stop. And he thought the glass bridge was odd. He didn't stop, not wanting Zion to crash into him and send them both to their dooms.

How did the Bentsworths prevent that sort of thing? Their house wasn't even adult-proof.

He chased after Felicity, up to a golden, winding stairwell. Felicity caught the rail and tore her way up the stairs. Cole reached them moments after.

"They're tearing up the garden!" Veronica shouted.

A loud crash above confirmed it. Felicity reached the entrance first. A masculine cry followed. Cole burst in after her.

Felicity's spear was drawn, her body poised in a stance. Bandits had shattered pots and a crushed statue worth more than Cole's childhood apartment on the floor. They stood with proud faces, armed…and Victor triumphantly with his own sword.

Disgraced Marketeers…Bandits hired by a supernatural enemy. Just what Cole needed to face off right now.

If they wanted the Council's attention, they'd gotten it. He was tired of the tricks.

But a sword? It felt like an odd choice till he caught a glimmer of the familiar, red glow.

His blood went cold.

"Cole! We're getting an emergency call!"

"We're a bit busy!" Falcon shouted.

A gunshot echoed. One of Zion's men appeared behind the bandits, slamming an electric shield down.

"Cole! You have to listen! It's from the Marketeer Pater!"

Cole's heart leapt. Cecileo?

He dodged a swipe of a knife, shoving the hilt into the attacker's gut with a hard thud.

"Glowy, red eyes…" Veronica's voice cut out. "Exerticus."

"So they have a name?" Cole shoved his attacker off of him, his eyes meeting Victor, standing with a sly smile.

Veronica screamed. "It's fine!" She gasped. "They've broken the upstairs camera!"

"It's all right, Veronica!" he shouted. "It's not your fault." Cole glared at Victor and charged.

Felicity screamed. "Cole!"

Cole ducked. A shot rang out. His shoulder skimmed it. He grit his teeth, spinning off balance. He caught himself. Victor ran. The Exerticus sword was heavy in the bandit leader's grip as he beat back on Zion.

With a cry, a bandit ran to give Victor the upper hand, but

Cole took only a moment to dismantle the weapon and shove the man aside.

"Pathetic fun, isn't it, boy?" Victor laughed, standing around, bracing the Exerticus blade. "You might be disappointed to learn you're not what we're here for. Seeing that you brought Boy Fox here, you've probably put it together."

"You're here for the Soroz's Member."

Victor shrugged. "Something like that."

"Good." Because they didn't have it.

He swung the Illuminate, causing Victor to fall back. Cole sliced the strap of Victor's satchel, catching the bag in his hand.

A gun clicked.

Cole's heart stopped, slowly looking up the barrel starring him in the eyes.

A wicked grin on Victor's face. A flash.

A spear struck down. Victor cried out in pain. Cole stumbled back, scrambled away, clenching Victor's satchel, catching his breath.

Felicity stood, her fists clenched, face red and stern like Cole had never seen. Her yellow eyes had a glow to them…and her pupils thinned.

"Don't you dare," she snarled.

Victor was only frozen for a moment. He grabbed the blade and charged straight for Felicity.

Cole's heart leapt, jumping to his feet.

"Cole!" Veronica's static erupted into his ear.

A bandit leapt for him. Cole flicked the Illuminate, the flames igniting. The bandit ducked. A gunshot went off. Cole turned, setting the pistol and the bandit's glove aflame.

Felicity had reclaimed her spear, rushing for the giant, twisting tree in the center of the gardens. It must have been beautiful with all the lanterns that decorated it…when they weren't smashed below.

Cole grabbed Victor's bag and ran for Felicity. "Veronica!" he shouted. "Send Defenders in if you can! We have them contained!"

Zion was mercilessly storming through, now guarding the door with Falcon. Blood streamed down the side of his face from his Victor encounter, but beside that, the fire was well alive in his eyes. Falcon looked less well at the violent display, the pistol shaking in his hands.

Cole ran for the tree.

Another shot. Again, his arm throbbed in pain. He cried out, whirling the flaming blade toward a screaming bandit.

Felicity balanced on the edge of a branch as Victor crawled after her.

Pain stabbed up Cole's arm as he ran, feeling the blood beginning to soak his shirt. "Veronica!"

"I'm calling Def—" Static.

He saw Felicity jump down from the tree and bare her spear as Victor followed after her. Cole leapt over the smashed fountain, shoving a bandit over into the gushing water. The bandit grabbed hold of the collar of Cole's jerkin and dragged him in.

Cole wrestled for air, losing grip of the Illuminate as he kept the bandit's hands from his neck. "Ver—ica!"

"I got the server back!"

Cole threw his weight onto the bandit, slamming him against the stone basin of the fountain. The bandit's eyes rolled back. Cole caught sight of Felicity beating Victor back with the help of—Cole frowned—Box.

Cole scrambled out of the fountain, fishing out the Illuminate.

"Stupid Boy Fox. You have no idea what lies you're fighting for. You could be in on the profit."

Box snorted, leaping forward, but Victor slashed him. Box fell back with a painful grimace. He clenched his chest.

Cole ran for him.

"Cole! Echo said the Exerticus—" Veronica cut out.

His ear piece must be damaged.

Felicity's eyes widened at Box. Victor took the moment of distraction. Cole's voice refused to cry out in time. Felicity spun back, throwing out her spear like a staff as the blade hit the wood. With a shove, Felicity was thrust to the ground.

Cole was so close. He tried to ignore the pain in his arm as he raised the Illuminate.

Victor had no mercy. The Exerticus blade fell, cutting clean into Felicity's thigh. She didn't scream.

A siren went off. The room dropped red.

Victor lifted the Blade triumphantly, slicked in Felicity's

blood.

"Hands up!" The door burst open.

Defenders flooded into the room, heavily armed, their light targets blinking as they met the bandits. Everyone froze, looking around, confused. All except Victor, who looked all too smug with his bloody blade towering above Felicity. Defenders ran for the bandits, not even bothering with Cole…He, apparently, was the least of their problems.

He sheathed the Illuminate and ran to Felicity.

Giles got there first, landing a punch to Victor's face, tackling the bandit to the ground. "What the heck did you do to her?" he shouted.

Victor was laughing victoriously, even as the Defenders tore his bloody sword from him. "You'll all be dead, and I'll be a rich man!" he boasted as the cuffs locked around his wrists. "They'll come for their prize, and I'll get the quarter-million pounds promised. Just wait and see."

The Defenders seemed uninterested. Giles looked like he was about to kill him before turning to Felicity.

Why did Victor think he won? He got nothing the Exerticus found of value.

Felicity wobbled to her feet, shooing Giles away. "They need you," she grimaced. "I'm fine."

Giles pressed his lips together with a small nod.

Whatever energy had consumed her earlier drained as she released a staggered breath, collapsing into Cole for support.

He wrapped his arm around her shoulders tightly, guiding her away from the commotion to the Defenders calling for them. He could hardly make out their voices.

Did we do it? Felicity's voice echoed in his mind as an Officer guided her away.

He met her eyes. He shivered, almost forgetting the odd Council telepathy. He couldn't muster a response. He was forced to sit, a Medic dabbing at the wound.

His ear Comm began to crackle again. Cole cringed.

"Are you all right?" the Officer asked.

Cole nodded, his eyes drifting to Victor still triumphantly monologuing to the recording Defenders.

"'Echo,' I think her name is," Veronica said.

"Yeah," Cole breathed, ignoring the startled Defender.

"Is she all right?"

"She got a transfer from your…brother?" Cole's heart leapt. "Yeah, your brother Ray had a message. About the Exerticus."

Cole frowned.

"They're after blood," Veronica stammered. "They didn't come for anything. They're looking for each Council Member's BLOOD."

They what? They'd shot Cole a few times but hadn't—

Cole froze. The Exerticus already had his blood. The rooftop in Court Illegia. They'd just cut him with their blade and left.

The Lyntox Council Member. The Soroz's child. The Exerticus Blade. Felicity.

His blood went cold. Cole jumped up.

He didn't wait. He ran, pushing through the crowd of Defenders. "The sword! We need the sword!"

He burst out into the open toward Victor, the blade lying in the grass. He couldn't let them get the blade…the blood. Not when they were so close.

"Kid, what do you think you're doing?"

He didn't stop. He was so close. It was right there. He dropped to his knees, reaching for the hilt—

But the blade disappeared.

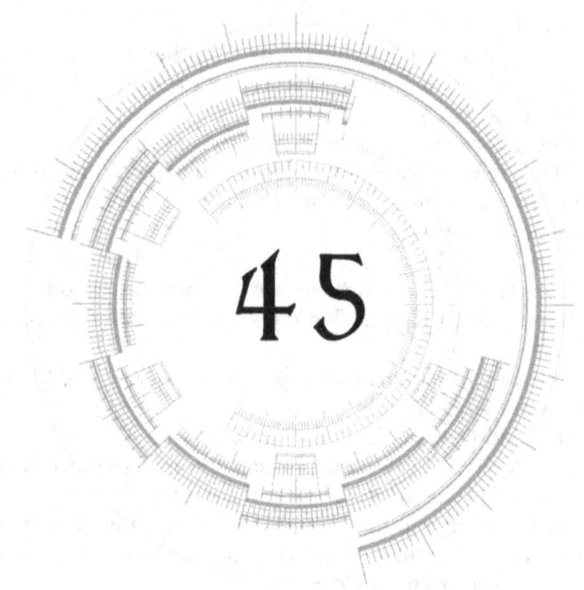

45

Liberty, A Few Hours Later

"THIS DOESN'T MAKE any sense!" Box said, staring wide eyed at Felicity, his hands in his hair.

Felicity was huddled under a blanket, sitting quietly beside Giles, who had a protective arm around her.

"They were after the Soroz! Why would they be asking about the Soroz if they were looking to take a Council Member's blood?"

Felicity shifted in her blanket, raising her chin slightly. "Maybe…it's because I'm the Soroz's daughter." She looked as horrified as Box did.

"You?" He choked. "There's no way. The Guardian Member born from Hannah Bentsworth? There is no way that woman is a Lyntox. There is no way *you* are Ly—"

"Just be quiet," Giles snapped.

So Cole wasn't the only one who noticed the tears building in Felicity's eyes.

"I—I'll talk to my parents," she said, her voice trembling

428

in a whisper. "They've lied before."

Everyone stood quiet, Box glancing from Cole to Giles. Cole didn't know what to say. This meant that Felicity was a Lyntox, a shape shifter…It meant that Hannah Bentsworth wasn't human and had done an incredible job at hiding it.

He hated to see how it crushed her as she brushed away the falling tears. "But we did it," she choked, forcing a smile. "We stopped the bandits."

But the Exerticus still got what they wanted.

"You were amazing," Cole said gently. "You're the reason the plan worked."

Felicity shook her head. "Don't discredit yourself. Your plan was brilliant."

If so, why had it failed so miserably? Why did it hurt so much to see her cry? It hurt more than anything, feeling like it was his fault as Felicity buried her face into the blanket as Giles tried to console her. She was so strong. And he'd failed to protect another one of his friends.

Cole forced a smile and slipped out of the room. He left Bentsworth Manor, no one batting an eye. They had more important things to worry about.

He traveled back, alone, to the Market. He watched the rain as he traveled rooftop to rooftop. He arrived, sliding down a fire escape, slipping, unnoticed, behind the market tents. He could hear the voices and the rush of the Market despite the rain. The crowds were excited. News traveled quickly. Zion had returned. The mission had been a success.

The bandits were now in Defender custody.

Cole pushed out from the shadows, running through the muddied streets. He heard his name. He didn't look back. Just step after step after step.

Pointless. Failure. Pathetic. Nothing.

Failure. Failure. Failure.

He had failed. Again.

Tears burned in his eyes. He gripped his bag even tighter. Why was he even trying? Did it even matter anymore?

He'd failed. He'd failed Felicity. And he'd done everything right.

He couldn't fail.

His feet gave out in the muddy street, crumpling down on the curb. He tried to catch his breath. Begging the burning of his lungs away. The voices still taunted him.

Victor's bag was heavy in his hands. He stared at it through his glassy eyes. Everything he thought he was after.

A Council Member. A leader.

With a cry, he thrust the bag out into the street.

He tore his hands through his hair. He was no leader. He'd tried, and now the Exerticus had almost won. They'd taken Felicity's blood. He couldn't stop it.

A gentle hand rested on his shoulder.

He jumped, looking up to see Echo, her brows knitted as she rubbed her hand over his shoulder. "Coleson."

He looked away. The woman who'd given him the very information he'd failed.

"It wasn't your fault."

"I could've stopped it."

"You didn't know."

"I should have." And he hadn't. And now everyone was going to—

"Coleson Johnson, look at me right now."

He made the mistake of not listening, so Echo cupped his face into her hands, forcing him to look at her.

"It wasn't your fault," she repeated. "Okay?"

Just say "okay." Just say "okay" so she'll leave. Don't let her see you're weak.

"Then why does it hurt like this?" he whispered, new tears burning the knot in his chest, aching.

Echo was quiet for a moment before her brows pinched. "Because you care," Echo said softly. She gently brushed her hand against his cheek. The small, tiny, affectionate gesture made him want to break down even more. "Because you care so much for your friend Felicity. You care about that Defender Giles. You care about that girl back in Court Illegia. You care about your Council. The reason you came here is because you cared, Coleson."

"But I keep failing them." He clenched his jaw, fresh tears falling. He tried to turn away.

"No…Cole, keep looking at me." Echo's big, dark, loving eyes were set on him. "You can't let a failure set you back. If you do that, you will never win. You cannot let your fear consume you."

You cannot let your fear consume you.

He stared at her, unsure of what to say.

She was right. He was terrified.

"Echo?"

"Yes?"

"Why do they hate you?" he choked. He couldn't understand it. Who could hate her when she put up with him? His fears…his failures. "Why does the stupid Market hate you? Why do you still care about me…all of them?"

Tears burned.

Echo's lips parted, quiet for a moment. "Sometimes," she said, "we love people who might not love us in return."

Cole swallowed hard. "They call you a child killer."

Echo's eyes flashed, and for a quick moment, her gaze fell. "I know." A pause. "I was never well regarded. My hand was removed as punishment as a child, and it was the cause of ridicule. The Market is one consumed by fear. It chose its leader by the Son Tournament that caused so much loss and chaos in the Market. They thought once Cecileo became Pater, the bloodshed would end and we'd have a real heir. No more fighting." She looked away. "They say we failed to provide that for them."

Cole's heart dropped. "That's—"

"—not my fault." Her voice was coarse, tears glistening in her eyes. "I know. It's taken me years to accept I'm not the reason my small, unborn child died. It's taken me so much longer than I'm willing to admit. Those rumors, the words, they are a constant reminder."

That's why Echo didn't go out in public often. One of the reasons Cecileo was so protective of her.

Cole was speechless. Before he knew what he was doing, he was hugging her. Echo jumped before throwing her arms around him and hugging him tightly back. Her arms were strong, warm, and comforting.

"I never knew my mother," Cole whispered. "Thank you for being there for her."

Echo was still a moment. He heard her voice crack. "Any time."

The two sat in the rain for a long moment, and despite being drenched and exhausted, Cole felt safe.

His Comm went off. Perfect timing.

He sat up and breathed, missing the warmth of Echo's

strong arms as he pulled away. A message from Cecileo.

CECILEO: EMERGENCY. Report now.

Cole and Echo exchanged glances. Cole wiped his face. "I—I have to go."

Echo grabbed his arm. "Wait! Before you go," she said, looking him sternly in the eyes.

He frowned as she reached into her coat pocket. His throat clenched as the Medallion unraveled from its chain in front of him.

She clipped it around his neck. "I believe that belongs to you," she said, sitting back with a proud smile.

Cole looked down, speechless, at the golden medallion hanging around his neck.

"You better hurry." She laughed, a tear escaping.

"Thank you," Cole breathed.

He got to his feet, turning to run for the Pater's tent.

He stopped, his heart leaping in his chest. He took a deep breath, spun around, and hugged Echo one last time.

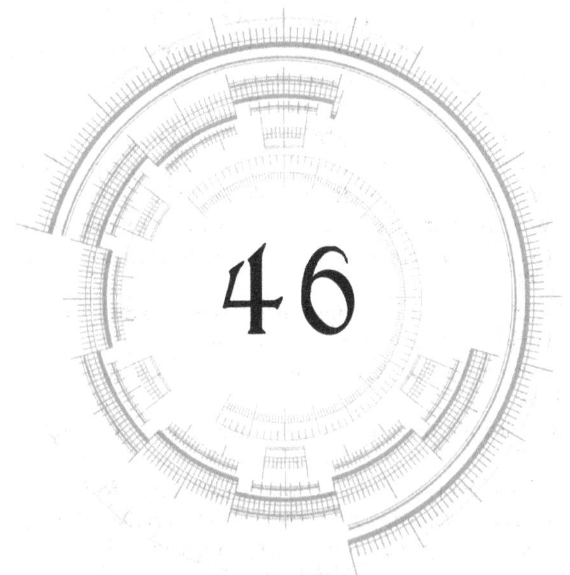

46

Kennedy, 1 Day Until

RAY NEEDED TO tell Mercy. He could only hope that the information got to Cole fast enough. But now how was he supposed to tell Mercy that her grandmother killed her mother and probably had no problem murdering Mercy once her use was up?

Mercy wouldn't believe him. He knew it as he ran from the library with the horrifying video disc in his pocket and out into the kitchen. But it was worth a shot. This was so much more than the Council now.

"Mercy Remembrance!" The voice echoed throughout the dining hall.

Virtue.

Ray's heart hammered in his ears. What was she doing here? She couldn't know…could she?

He burst out of the kitchen door, freezing under Virtue's glower.

"Grandmere?" Mercy stood at the bottom of the stairway.

Her form was hunched in submissive fear, her eyes nervously darting to Ray. Everything in him screamed to teleport and take her away.

"What is that boy doing here?"

"She killed your mother!" Ray blurted out.

Virtue spun on Ray with a horrified gasp. "What a horrendous accusation from a child." She spun to Mercy, marching toward her. "This what you've invited into our home? And you allowed the key I entrusted to you to be stolen?"

Mercy froze and her lips parted, but no words escaped as Virtue clamped down on Mercy's wrist.

Mercy jerked back, her eyes welling. "Grand—"

Slap.

Ray leapt forward. "Leave her alone! You have no right—"

"I have every right!" Virtue thrust Mercy forward, who was limp in her grip, eyes wide as she cradled her cheek. "You have no right to speak, demon spawn. I know exactly what you are and what you've done."

Ray's sweat went cold against the burning of his face.

"You," Virtue snapped, grabbing Mercy's face. "You disobeyed me. After all I've done for you? You pathetic, ungrateful child."

Virtue pulled Mercy to the door. Ray didn't even think, grabbing Mercy's arm with a quick jerk, pulling her from Virtue's unsuspecting gasp. Mercy stumbled behind Ray.

"You!" Virtue screamed.

"Do not hurt her." Ray braced himself, trying to keep the heat of the flames spinning in his chest down.

Virtue took a heavy step toward him. "You turned my own granddaughter against me." Virtue clenched her fists. "Mercy, get in the auto. And you, boy. I'm calling the Defending Officers on you."

"Grandemere," Mercy cried. "He—he didn't do anything! It was my fault. Everything was my idea."

"Remembrance—"

"Shut up, Mathews." Mercy stared at him hard, tears welling in her eyes as she stepped out.

Virtue grabbed her with a quick twist of her arm. Mercy bit back a cry. Virtue hauled her to the door.

"Please, listen to me!" Ray ran for her.

Virtue slammed the door shut, swiping the keycard over the lock with a successful click. She met Ray's eyes with a murderous glimmer and snapped the card in her hand.

All hope drained from Mercy's face.

"Mercy!" Ray shouted after her, banging on the window, not even caring that he'd said her name. Virtue shoved her into the back of the auto. "Mercy! No!"

Panic flooded him. Teleport. He needed to teleport. He tried to contain his swelling emotions. He needed to think clearly. He needed to save the Keyper. Defenders were probably on their way to arrest him. They wouldn't care whether or not he'd done anything wrong.

Only that he was an Oquelite. A killer.

The auto was driving off.

Ray took a deep breath. Screw teleporting. "I'll pay for it later, Remembrance."

He charged, flinging himself full speed into the window. It shattered, sending him tumbling onto the porch.

The auto was already nearly out of sight, going far faster than legal. He wouldn't be able to catch it. He wouldn't be able to teleport onto a moving object. He couldn't even visualize where it was going. It had to be the lake house that Mercy and Virtue had mentioned.

The Soul Night.

He only had one option.

He ran down the steps, tripping over himself. He had no time. He needed to get to her.

The Soul Night had been his idea and he had gotten her into this mess. The lake could be hours away. He tripped over the sidewalk, scrambling to his feet.

Raphael Mathews.

He felt his eyes begin to warm with the glow.

"No!" he shouted aloud, ignoring the stares. "Please, not now!"

Not now. Never again. I have to save her.

You will save her, but only with my help.

Your help has gotten too many people hurt!

It didn't matter what he said. The angry, shadowy voice swallowed him.

Submit.

NO. Ray stumbled back against a wall, tearing his hands through his hair. *I will NOT let you make me hurt anyone again!*

Oh, foolish boy. Thinking you ever had a choice.

Ray's breath was smothered, his vision clouded. His body went numb. He could see the blurry figures around him. He could feel himself moving. He could feel the pain fighting his consciousness, the shadows searing through his mind, strangling his control—

NO. YOU CAN'T CONTROL ME.

He felt the thoughts leaking in. Anger burning through him, rage threatening to overcome him. Why should he care? They'd cast him out. They'd tried to hide the Blade that was rightfully his.

He had every right to burn them to ashes. He had the power.

She would not let him grow weak.

No. That's not true! They cast me out because of you. *Being an Oquelite doesn't—*

His own father had cast him out, hadn't he? An Oquelite too, at that. He chose a powerless brother over him. A powerless brother that they said Ray would kill.

And he could. He could get this over with.

He felt the whirling sensation, the image of Liberty forming in his mind against his will. He could kill his brother.

He could finally be free. He could finally have his father who ruined his life.

Cole didn't do anything wrong!

Ray fought the image, trying to distort it. Cole was his brother, and no matter how much he'd been lied to, he loved Cole. Cole had been there when he'd embraced the truth. Cole had kept him in line. Cole wasn't afraid.

The whole world turned its back on him. Everyone except for his friends, who'd done everything for him. People who loved him. People who expected him.

People who fought to keep him alive. And he would fight to keep them alive. And not a *stupid* voice in his head was going to make him feel different.

The image cracked. Ray felt his body fling to the ground. *Foolish boy.*

He was not going to be the monster they told him he was.

He was going to be the hero Mercy believed he was.

Pain shot through his skull. He cried out...all on his own.

Feeling overcame him, and for a moment, he thought he was back. And then, it burned. It felt as though his very bones were embers, his blood boiling in the heat. Pain shot through him. Weight pulled him, pressing against his chest, refusing to let him breathe.

You don't have a choice.

He ignored it, pushing against the weight with all his might. *You are not a monster. You are not a monster. You are not a...*

Pain shot through him again. He stumbled, releasing a pained gasp. He could feel a warm trickle down his face from his nose to his lips. The sweet taste of blood.

He fought against the pain, pushing harder till he felt his palms steady against the asphalt. He felt energy crackling through his hands.

If they really cared for you, why would they leave you alone?

A ragged breath escaped him, a moment of cool air before the Voice returned her control over his throat.

Ray squeezed his eyes shut, willing all his energy to his hands, feeling a flicker of energy growing and heating. Faster and faster.

Why do you lie to yourself?

Ray's eyes burst open. "The only liar here is *you*."

He let the power go, and with a blast, he was thrown back, sent crashing into the road and rolling back. His ears rang, screams muffled behind them. His body was sore, sweat drenched his face, and the crisp smell of blood and scrapes overwhelmed his senses.

He slowly opened his eyes.

The world was crystal clear around him. He sat up. Civilians cowered away, many rushing to their Comms, or rushing into a shop. He searched the crowd, struggling to his feet.

You don't have time to think. Mercy is in danger.

Mercy. Right. He needed to save Mercy. He owed her that. He broke out into a run, his path now fairly easy as people jumped with fear out of his way. He caught their words and curses.

"Demon child."

"Hellspawn."

"Killer."

I am not a monster. I am going to save Mercy.

He tore around the corner, catching sight of the flickering sign above the mechanic shop. Ray ran across the road, nearly tripping over himself as he crashed against the door, banging with the full force of his fists.

"Lucas! Lucas! I need your help! *Lucas!*"

The door flung open, Ray toppling inside. Lucas caught him swiftly by the arm and shut the door quickly behind them. "Wow! Dude, what's going on?"

Too much.

"Mercy." Ray rasped, trying to catch his breath as he paced. "I need to get to Mercy."

"Remembrance?" Lucas's eyes shot wide. "What happened to her?"

"She was taken."

"What?! Did you call the Defenders?"

"No. No. It's not that simple!" Ray shouted, banging his fist against the counter in frustration. Why couldn't anything be *simple*? Ray's gaze settled on the tele beside his hand. "I need that hovercycle."

"Done," Lucas said, a frown creasing across his brow. "Do you need to make a call?"

"I already called my brother…and some weird guy named 'Cecileo' picked up and—" Ray shook his head, trying to control his breathing. "I just need to go."

Lucas gave a reassuring nod. "I'll get the hovercycle prepped."

"Thanks."

Ray didn't need another word. He hung up, and ran out the door past Lucas to see the hovercycle sitting in the garage, its red light lit.

"Two requests," Lucas said, slamming a helmet onto Ray's head from behind and walking forward to the hovercycle. "Wear that at all times. Don't give me that look. Safety over aesthetic."

Ray begrudgingly buckled the helmet under his chin and walked over to the hovercycle. He hesitantly placed his hands over the cool, leather handles.

"And I want you to give my ID number to my sister."

Ray's head whipped back to Lucas. "Hold up, your

what?"

Lucas stared at him. "My sister."

"Who—who is your sister?" Ray didn't need another quest to go on. Time was already running thin. Every moment, Mercy was getting farther and farther away.

Lucas frowned and then threw his head back, groaning. "She didn't even mention me, did she?"

"But how? No one has a bro—"

Felicity had a sister. Nikki's family was all dead.

Ray stopped mid-sentence, cursing. "You're a Delorous."

"Took you long enough," Lucas grumbled.

A Delorous, here? The Delorouses were a wealthy family with close ties to the Bentsworths, and from the way Tabitha spoke of her brother, he was fairly well known.

"What are you doing here in a mechanic shop in Kennedy? I thought you were a M.E.D.I.A. star." Ray's mind was reeling.

Tabitha's brother. Mercy in trouble. Could the world just be straight foward for one gosh darn second?

"You're thinking of Clarence." Lucas snorted, finishing scribbling on a sticky note. "Look, we don't have much time. Just give her my ID and tell her to contact me."

Right. Tabitha had *two* siblings, which made her being a third so disgraceful.

"I don't think she's going to like that idea."

Lucas glared at him, handing Ray the sticky note. "Make her."

Okay, so the glare was a family thing.

Ray jumped onto the hovercycle, thumb hovering over the gas. He nodded to Lucas. "I will. Thank you."

Lucas nodded back, tucking his oil-stained cloth into his belt. "Go get Remembrance back."

Ray clutched the lever and, within a moment, was thrust full speed into the night. He was getting his friend back, and no evil grandma or supernatural Voice could stop him.

North Cordell, 1 Day Until

Nikki stood in front of Lincoln on her own two feet, not shaking or quivering, though slightly disappointed.

"Just because you couldn't react as quickly to the

simulation *doesn't* mean there's something wrong with you," Dr. Mathews said, instructing Nikki to take a deep breath in as she checked her back. "You're still recovering, and you haven't been in a fight in a while." She patted Nikki on the shoulder with a small smile. "You're fine. You should be proud. Your recovery is nearly miraculous."

Lincoln knew that the smile Nikki returned wasn't genuine, and disappointment still settled behind her eyes as she looked back to Lincoln as if he would be too. In all honesty, it was relieving. She didn't need to be jumping right into the thick of battle so soon after the venom extraction proved to be successful.

"You still must take small doses every evening," Dr. Mathews instructed for the one dozenth time, scribbling something down on her Scroll. "Since Exil Libium proved ineffective, we'll need extra long-term doses."

Nikki cringed at the words "Exil Libium," and he couldn't blame her. That night was nightmarish, and he'd wished that he could push it from his mind. Every time he thought that she might be okay, the replay of her gasping in pain wouldn't leave him.

Another super-powered plant, similar to the phenonomena flux already in her system, and yet it had given her an extreme allergic reaction.

Why do you care so much? Leave. We have better things to handle right now, boy.

"So, do you think Taryn will approve?" Nikki asked, her voice cutting cleanly through the woman in his mind.

Lincoln watched Dr. Mathews, who glanced at him and then back at Nikki. "I'll give her the report, and I'm sure the Sergeant will get back to you. Now, get some rest. Don't want you collapsing and ruining any chances of approval."

Dr. Mathews tucked her Scroll under her arm and walked toward the door, but not without a nod to Lincoln. "I see your feelings on your face. It's all right."

Right. No need to panic.

Dr. Mathews left the room, leaving just Nikki and Lincoln to the vast basement. Nikki sighed and took a seat beside him.

"It has to be in there somewhere," Lincoln said, trying to muster some sort of positivity. "Even if it takes extra training, we'll get it back. I promise."

Nikki smiled, only for a moment, before it faltered. "What if I've forgotten other things too?"

Lincoln stood up after her, gently grabbing her hand that tried to nervously pick at the healing scar on her face. "I'll teach you." He shrugged.

"You're confident of that?"

"I'm the Joined World's best teacher." He shrugged.

"You're illiterate."

"Hey!"

Nikki imitated his shrug. "It's true."

Lincoln froze, realization hitting him like a wall. "You're teasing me."

She only smirked back.

Now, he couldn't help but laugh. "Fine, you teach me to read, and I teach you whatever you might be lacking. Sound like a deal?"

Her eyes lit up. "Yes! Let's start right now!"

"Whoa, whoa!" Lincoln caught her by the shoulders as she turned to run off toward the training pad. "You're still recovering."

Nikki's face fell, but she shrugged it off. "You're right." She sighed. "I—I'll try to rest."

"Good."

"Tell me if Taryn calls," Nikki said, turning to go up the stairs and out of the basement.

Lincoln nodded, hoping that she wouldn't. "I will."

The confirmation seemed enough to lift Nikki's spirits, and she walked away and out the steps. Lincoln turned to the empty basement with a heavy sigh.

The Sergeant would be reasonable and deny a mission to Algery. She had to be.

He shut off the lights and followed Nikki out.

Lincoln's Comm went off, and it may as well have been a personal attack with it lying on his face.

He jumped up, his vision blurry, toppling off the mattress and onto the hard floor, making a triumphant echo through the otherwise empty room. The Comm still buzzed away on the floor till he slammed his hand on top of it.

He sat up, rubbing his face awake, taking a moment to

look around the empty room with his racing heart.

He picked up the Comm and tapped the screen to life, the device reading the message aloud. His heart sank.

TARYN - 6.42

REQUEST FOR MISSION WAS APPROVED. MEET ME IN OFFICE.

Office…as in kitchen, but the Sergeant's pride was too high to fully embrace the fact that her actual one had been burnt to the ground. But the fact that would usually humor Lincoln fell flat and cold.

The mission to Algery was approved. *Nikki's* mission.

He didn't even bother to change, just grabbed his jacket from its designated place in the middle of the floor and ran out his door and into the hall, slamming through the door out of the boy's hall.

Jack Sallow jumped up from the couch with a shout, pulling out the knife from under his pillow. "Ah! What's going on? Everyone ca—oh. Hey, Lincoln."

"I got a message from the Sergeant," Lincoln said, hurrying for the stairs. "It's urgent."

Jack tossed the knife to the coffee table and settled back down onto the couch. "I'm making Miriam take the supervisor duty tonight."

Lincoln raced down the steps and went right through the door into the main kitchen, where he was greeted by Taryn sitting at the kitchen counter, a Scroll below her and a hologram in front of her. And Nikki was sitting, with two layers of jackets and a turtleneck, on a stool beside her, her hand on the Stone fixed around her neck. Her eyes lit up upon seeing him. "You were fast."

"You were faster."

"She's been here since 4.00," Taryn said with a sigh.

"Nik, you promised to rest."

"I *did*, and then I couldn't anymore." She shrugged.

Lincoln looked to Taryn, hoping that she'd side with him, but Taryn tilted her head and eyed him to sit down. He did as he was instructed.

"I know you think this is a bad idea," Taryn said.

"It is," he said quickly. "What if she gets hurt? Again?"

"Those are valid concerns."

Nikki frowned at this.

"But," Taryn continued, "that is why she is not going alone. With Matthias Idicous's information about this…new threat heading to Algery, and the only connection we have is the Aguirre residence there."

The Soul Night was in less than forty-eight hours. It could be dangerous.

Yes, she's fragile. You'll need me to protect her.

"But why are we throwing *her* into danger? She just began recovering."

"I think you forgot who I am," Nikki said quietly, tracing circles on the counter. She looked up at him, her face hardened. "My name is 'Nikki Aguirre.' I have to be the only one to get us access to the secrets connected to them."

Lincoln suddenly felt stupid. The words had come so strong. Nothing like the childish, curious remarks he was used to. She wasn't a child. She was his age and had been through things neither knew, but it showed in the blue of her eyes.

He couldn't meet them.

Taryn sighed. "And there is our dilemma. Time isn't on our side, Lincoln. This is where those strange scenes in Nikki's mind and the Oquelite keep leading us to: Algery."

"I know," he said, staring at his feet.

"Did I miss anything important?"

All three heads turned to Lawrence, who, unlike Lincoln, looked like he took the time to get dressed, and wore his coat, Matteo on the side.

"Hello, Lopez," Taryn said, nodding to Matteo. "I should've known you would've been bringing a tagalong or another."

"Fire Wolf and Charles were busy."

"Well, good to know." Taryn's eyes settled regretfully on Matteo. "As much as I would like to say Lopez will be included, due the last test, I don't think we can risk him leaving. He'll stay and continue with Miriam."

Even Lincoln's eyes widened.

"He can't exclusively train with Lawrence, and if Williams accepts, he can't just stop." Taryn clasped her hands together. "There are stakes. I'm sorry, Matteo."

Matteo didn't say a word but simply nodded.

If Lincoln hadn't just been shot down about the Nikki

issue, he'd be tempted to argue for Matteo, just out of spite.

"I think the evidence you're going off of is still weak," Lawrence said, taking a seat, and Matteo only followed when Lawrence beckoned him. "That 'if we can get him to break his wings sooner, maybe we can still get some *Cors Vis* energy' sounds more hopeful than realistic."

Lincoln agreed. It was a pathetic theory. Even Matteo's "maybe the *Cors Vis* is still out there" theory seemed more plausible.

"We don't have much of a choice, Williams." Taryn sighed. "We can discuss your frustrations later. Right now, we have another matter to attend to."

"Going to Algery," Lawrence said. "I know. Nikki likes to talk about it."

"It will be quick. Two days at the least," Taryn said. "That way it doesn't mess with Nikki's progress, and we can get back here as soon as possible. You scout the Aguirre remains for anything that could be attracting this powerful entity. And come back, even if it's empty handed."

When Taryn said it like that, it didn't sound *that* bad. Lincoln looked to Nikki, who was practically bouncing in her seat.

"Officer Jackson Sallow will be there for your protection; though, it wouldn't hurt to bring that bow of yours, and Williams—"

"Light something on fire. I know." He rolled his eyes.

Taryn gave him a deadpan expression. "Yes. I plan on you leaving as soon as Dr. Mathews officially says so. Are you in?"

As soon as possible? The Soul Night was fast approaching. Was that safe?

"Yes," Nikki said, not surprising anyone.

Lincoln straightened. "I'm going too."

That earned him a small smile and nod from Nikki. He couldn't help a small smile in return.

Lawrence took a moment longer. He looked at Nikki, locking her gaze before turning to Taryn with a slight nod. "I'll go, just to make sure it doesn't end up like last time."

Taryn stood up, pushing her stool back and shutting off the hologram. "Well, then, I insist you pack."

47

Kennedy, 1 Day Until

THE ONLY THING Ray could hear was the whistle of the wind, and he was grateful for it as it drowned out the taunts that were triggered on repeat in his head.

The Kennedy winter was ruthless, feeling as though it was cutting the surface of his skin, but he'd felt worse. He pushed the hovercycle faster. He would've been more thrilled with the fact that he was riding as fast as he wanted on a hovercycle for the first time in his life, if Mercy's terrified face wasn't ingrained in his mind.

If Mercy was afraid, he should be horrified.

It was his fault that she was in this mess. He would not leave her to suffer.

The trees began to grow thicker, and the air began to smell of earth and distant rain. He craned his neck for some sort of water through the trees. So far, nothing, just the dark shadows of the trees. He slowed as the road grew darker and darker.

Aponi's story still taunted his mind. Any moment now, he suspected a guy with red, glowing eyes to burst out of the trees with a wail and chase after him at full speed.

His heart hammered against his chest, and he sped up.

There. A glint.

He slowed, straining his eyes through the trees. A lake with a reflection of a moon proudly shown on it. The bump of wood jumped the hovercycle.

A bridge.

He was getting close. He pulled off to the side of the road, shutting off the cycle and jumping off. He dragged it over into the brush and set the helmet onto the seat.

Ray took a deep breath, and with a swift motion of his hand, his body vanished from sight. Instead of the small pang of exhaustion he usually felt, a burning sparked in his chest.

He didn't have time to ponder it, just hoped that it wasn't deadly and moved on down through the trees. It was only a quick jog down to the sandbar, the ground damp under his feet. The lake was still and longer than it was wide, reaching farther than he could see.

He caught sight of a yellow flicker. He teleported closer, landing beside a log cabin. His breath caught in his throat. The lake house.

It had to be. There wasn't another one on this freaky bank.

A small flicker glowed from inside the window. Someone was inside. Ray unsheathed the Shadow Blade. He wasn't going down without a fair fight this time.

He crept around the building, facing the front. Creaky steps and a no doubt locked door stared him in the face. He draped himself in invisibility.

"Open," he commanded, the shadows of night swirling around the Blade, exploding the door open.

He ran into the cabin. It was dark.

A muffled scream followed. He froze.

There in the center of the room was a dining table, and atop it was a candle, nearly at the end of its run. Standing opposite was a girl, her fists bared and her jaw clenched, sweat across her forehead as she searched the room.

Ray dropped the invisibility. "Mercy—ah!"

Pain tore through him, his body seizing, his vision flashing white with a swift crack of electricity. He crumpled to the floor, the Shadow Blade slipping from his grip.

A deep laugh followed. "What did I tell you?" Virtue's voice echoed from above.

Ray groaned, looking up at Mercy cowering away, her eyes going back and forth between her grandmother and Ray.

"Mer—" A kick to his side.

"He's one of them," Virtue said, stepping over Ray, her taser gun still poised at him. "He came for you."

"No! That's not true!" Ray shouted.

Virtue pulled the trigger. He cried out again.

"You—you didn't tell me you could—could teleport," Mercy rasped. "You lied to me."

He could see tears beginning to crowd in her eyes, her shoulders beginning to fall.

"I didn't lie, I just—I just…" *…never told you. Just like your grandmother never told you who killed your mother. You're no better.*

Another shock.

"If given a moment of release, he'll be able to escape," Virtue said. "We'll kill him. I'll protect the legacy, Mercy."

"No!" Ray shouted through the pain. "Mercy, you need to get out!"

Strong arms pulled him to his feet, a dirty gag forced into his mouth and tied too tight. A collar was clamped against his neck. He thrashed against his captor. A shock burned him against the collar.

"He was coming because that's what he's supposed to do." Virtue huffed. "You were just a check on a box, and *I* saved you."

Tears burned in Ray's eyes as he saw Mercy creep closer to her grandmother, a look of disgust flooding her face toward him.

"Look him up in the cellar." Virtue instructed the man. "I'll deal with him in due time."

Another shock.

Ray thrashed, trying to shout for Mercy as he was dragged off, the shocks repeating over and over. Nothing hurt more than the pain in her eyes as she looked away. He was shoved down stone steps and into a damp, moldy-smelling room lit by a dim, fluorescent light.

Ray turned and ran. Just one jump and—*shock*.

He crumpled to the floor in pain. He was thrust from his feet against the wall, the jingling of chains echoing in his skull. No. No—*shock*.

A cold cuff locked around his hand. Ray fought for his opposite hand, throwing a punch, but it was quickly caught and slammed against the wall behind him.

Shock.

The second cuff was clamped against his wrist. His captor let him go, letting him fall forward, the chains whiplashing him to a stop.

He hung breathless as he watched the captor walk to the steps.

Shock.

The lights were shut off. The basement fell to darkness. He'd fallen into a trap.

Shock.

He squeezed his eyes shut, feeling the damp air pressing around him, the light dropping off in the distance, the skittering of an unknown creature. And worst of all, the creaking of the footsteps above him.

Shock.

Ray slumped forward. He was defeated. He was trapped. Even when he tried to do the right thing, he screwed up. It was pointless.

Shock.

You are a monster…To Mercy, you are a monster.

Ray couldn't take it anymore and cried out as loud as he could to drown the voices out.

"He lied to you." Her grandmother wrung the towel under the only lit light above the sink. "And you fell for it. After all I've taught you?"

Mercy looked away as her grandmere turned her head. She spotted l'oncles sitting on the sofas in the corner of the room, the hologram playing a flashy program. There were only four this time. All as faceless as the rest and refused to speak to her when she asked them why she was here.

The only woman caught Mercy's eye. She upturned her nose and waltzed to her grandmere's side. She handed her grandmere a key. "The boy has been situated. Shock sequence every thirty seconds, as per request."

Every thirty seconds? Mercy's eyes widened.

Her grandmother nodded the woman off and set the key onto the table. "Don't give me that look, child. If he gets a moment of relief, he'll use his *abilities* to escape," her grandmere said, leaning across the table to stroke her face. "And we wouldn't want that."

Mercy flinched. They didn't want that, did they? Why didn't she want Mathews to escape?

Because he'll kill you. He wants to take your power.

That's what the smile on her grandmere's lips told her as she straightened and dusted her suit off. But if that was Mathews's intention, wouldn't he have done that a long time ago?

She watched her grandmere pop off the cork of a wine bottle, pouring it into a glass, her back turned.

Mathews always told her that doing the right thing was better than doing what you were told. Could it have been the same with him? Or was he just as her grandmere said? A liar?

Her grandmere took a long sip of the wine before passing Mercy with a pat on the head. "*Bonne nuit, mon héritage.*"

She left, going up the creaky staircase, leaving Mercy alone at the table in the kitchen and the low murmur of the l'oncles' voices.

She watched them in the low, blue glow of the hologram as they promptly ignored her. Mercy set her eyes on the largest-looking, half-asleep in his recliner. The one who'd dragged Mathews away.

I hope Mathews gave him a fight.

She shook her head. No. Why would she hope that? Mathews deserved whatever happened to him…being shocked every thirty seconds. She swallowed hard, digging her fingernails into the polish of the table.

She glanced at the corner quickly before raising to her feet. She stretched, giving out an exaggerated yawn. "Well, good night, fools! Tomorrow, another day and time for sulking in the dark!"

They ignored her. Good.

She took the key from the tabletop and grabbed the

lantern from the hook by the door. She crept toward the lower stairs. She sat down on the first step and slowly made her way down with one soft thump at a time. She was getting answers. She didn't trust her grandmere, and she certainly didn't trust Mathews.

Her feet hit the cold stone of the first floor, completely dark now. She slowly got to her feet, waving her hand over the lantern's sensor.

She caught sight of the basement's wooden door and ran for it before her mind could try to reason with her. She set the lantern down and, with all her might, heaved the door up, letting it fall open with a shuddery slam.

She cringed. Hopefully, no one heard that. She grabbed the lantern and stared down the dark descent. Was she really doing this?

Yes. We are. I'm taking things into my own hands. I won't be deceived again.

She moved quickly down the steps, almost gagging on the putrid smell of the humid air. The basement came into sight. A dirt floor, stone walls, and discarded cardboard boxes. Mercy held her breath as she stepped off the last step.

"Mercy?"

Mercy nearly tripped over herself, swiveling around to see Ray chained up on the far wall. He had cuts on his face and arms, his jacket and sword missing, sweat dampening his face and shirt, his hair stuck to his face. He seemed breathless, his voice ragged and his eyes wide.

The stillness was ruined as the collar let out a shock, Ray tensing, biting back a cry.

Mercy flinched, trying to straighten herself and harden her expression. Her grandmother said that he was danger-ous. He *was* dangerous.

It was harder to convince herself when he lay by the support of chains, bleeding and in pain.

"So, you're a demon?" she said, raising her voice.

Ray's face hardened with determination. "I'm an Oquelite."

Shock.

She diverted her eyes for a split second. "That doesn't change the fact you have supernatural abilities and didn't tell me! How can I trust you?"

"You have supernatural abilities too," Ray spat back with a glare.

"I didn't know I had those!"

"You would've freaked out if I told you!"

Shock. Ray stumbled back.

She wanted to spit out that she wouldn't have and that he was, once again, underestimating her; but she froze, watching as he took in deep, pained breaths, and she couldn't argue with him.

How would she have reacted? Would she really have just accepted it?

"If you hate me so much, why are you here?" he croaked.

"Because—because—" She stumbled over her words. Why was she here? "I want answers for myself."

Ray cracked a smile. "Hey, look at that! You're doing something for you."

Shock. The smile was torn from him.

"Why did you come for me?" she asked.

Ray squeezed his eyes shut, taking a deep breath, turning toward the ceiling. "That group I told you about?"

Mercy stepped forward tentatively. "Yeah?"

"It's real." He gasped, turning back to her, his amber eyes wide open. "I'm part of it."

Shock.

Mercy's eyes widened. "If it's real, why haven't I heard of them before?"

"You have." Ray begged. "Mercy, the people your grandmother is trying to keep you away from. The six kids on the news who prevented Imperial's destruction. They're one in the same. She *knows* what I am. Please you have to belie—ah!" *Shock.*

Mercy turned away. She couldn't process this.

"In my pocket." Ray gasped. "It's proof. It's proof about what really happened to your mother."

Mercy froze. He—he had a disc?

Her heart raced. She shouldn't look. She should walk back up the stairs and forget it. But she couldn't. She needed to know.

She turned toward him, swallowing hard as she tried not to look at his pained face. She felt his pocket, removing a metal projector disc.

"Remembrance, it's really intense—"

"Be quiet," she said, her voice cracking. She activated the projector, the video popping up on the wall. For a moment, all she heard was her grandmother's voice and saw how she looked the same even sixteen years ago.

Then, there was her mother.

Mercy couldn't breathe. She couldn't process it. She was seeing her mother right before her eyes trembling in the cold.

"Turn around."

Her grandmother's grave words echoed in her mind. Her mother sobbed.

"Have mercy."

And then the gunshot went off. Mercy dropped the disc, muffling a scream. The disc cracked as it hit the floor, the image flicking off. Tears burned her eyes.

She sank to the floor, trying to catch her breath. She may as well have never breathed again.

"My name," Mercy choked. "My name was her last word."

And her grandmother was wrong. Grandmere was *a murderer*.

Everything was wrong. The legacy was wrong.

The Keyper was part of a group. A legendary group. *Shock.*

Mercy turned to Ray, tears crowding in her eyes. She dropped the lantern and ran to him, clicking the latch on the collar, letting it fall to the floor at their feet. Ray's eyes widened in shock, staring at her, seeming unable to speak. The skin on his neck was raw, and she cringed.

She pulled the key from her pocket, quickly undoing his chains.

"What are you doing?" he hissed, immediately rubbing his neck before cringing in the pain.

"I need you to get me out," Mercy said.

Ray stared blankly at her.

She groaned. "Mathews, it's not the time to doze off."

Ray blinked a few times. "Sorry, I just—"

"No time," Mercy said, holding out her wrists. "Take them off."

"You want me to—"

"Yes!" How stupid was he? "Take them off. You already *lied* to me, and you're lucky I'm unlocking you."

"Okay, okay! I'll do it!" Ray gently gripped her bonds. "Sorry if this hurts."

It wouldn't be anything compared to the pain that had caused the nasty, red burn on his neck.

She watched, holding her breath, as small, literal sparks came from his hands. A small zap went up her arms, and the bonds fell free.

She stared at them in utter disbelief. It had been years since she saw them empty of the bonds.

"Now my ankle," she instructed, trying to suppress her excitement. Her head was light, her stomach rocking. She was really doing this.

Ray knelt down, and with another shock, the anklet fell off to the floor.

She was free.

He stood up, his eyelids heavy.

"Mathews, you good?"

Ray slapped himself. "Yeah! I'm good. Just get drained from using...or trying to use abilities."

Had he really been trying to use them the past few hours?

"So teleporting is not an option?" Mercy said, her voice weary.

Ray shook his head.

And there went her entire plan.

"There's a hovercycle by the lake," Ray said. "We can make a run for it and get to it."

"And *I* take you as far as town, and we split separate ways and never speak to each other again," Mercy finished for him, but by the frown on his face, she could tell that that's not how he had intended to finish it.

"But what about the Council?"

"Even if I do join, I'll still ignore your pretty, little face."

Ray closed his mouth and nodded. "Sounds fair."

"Good."

Mercy turned for the steps, picking up the lantern and shutting it off. She motioned for Ray to follow. The two slowly ascended the steps, Mercy's heart hammering in her chest.

Her head hit the door. She slowly heaved it open and

crawled out from the stairwell. And there sitting waiting for her was Grandmere, her drink in one hand and a pistol in the other.

An Undisclosed Speed Rail Station, An Hour Later

A thrilling new record. A distress call from Ray only a few hours ago, and now Tabitha sat at the edge of a bench in the SpeedRail station, her foot tapping.

She almost laughed to herself, but that would have been morbid. Her friends were in danger. Their reason for reunion wasn't joyous.

That's what happens when you leave Tabitha Delorous back in Court Illegia.

They now knew two vital things: the Exerticus were after Council blood, and Ray had found a Council Member.

Cole had given no details, which was disappointing. Tabitha hoped that they'd at least get there in time to meet them…and, you know, save their life.

She shut off her tele, trying not to stress. They *would* save them. There was no other option.

The SpeedRail came speeding through the station and slowed to a stop. Tabitha jumped up from her seat, shoving her tele into her bag. The doors of the Rail opened, and almost instantly, the crowds flooded out. Tabitha rushed head first into the crowd, scanning the crowd for a familiar face. Her height didn't help, having to settle for weaving between passengers and looking up.

Were they wearing a disguise? Had they taken a different Rail? Did they go on ahead without her?

Something rammed into her legs. Tabitha swiveled around.

"Tabitha!"

Felicity.

Tabitha spun around, freezing.

But…not Felicity. Both excitement and confusion. Did she hug her or did she—?

Hug her. Never hold back a hug. She hugged Felicity, and her friend hugged her back, pulling back with a brilliant smile on her face.

Now, Tabitha stared. "Liz…you're in a wheelchair."

Felicity glanced down as if she'd just noticed that she was confined to the chair that comfortably held her legs and had holographic wheels on the side. Felicity looked back up with a small shrug. "It's minor compared to everything else that's happened," she said quietly. "Believe me."

"I mean, if anything, you now have an epic ride."

Felicity laughed. "I guess so."

What else had Felicity discovered? Why was she so calm? It was nice to see, but different. A good different. Tabitha was so happy to see her friend being, well, happy.

"Tabitha?" a voice asked from behind her.

Tabitha rolled her eyes to Felicity. "I wonder who that could be."

Felicity shook her head and sighed.

Tabitha turned around, stopping mid-step to face the one person she'd been waiting to see. She couldn't breathe. He looked…different. Taller, shoulders broader.

He stared in equal disbelief at her. After all this time. After every late night of hoping that maybe, just maybe, it wasn't broken.

And she couldn't even open her mouth to greet him.

Finally, his eyes diverted to the ground, holding a piece of crinkled, folded paper in his hand.

Before she could even speak, he held the paper out and blurted out, "I'm sorry."

Tabitha tentatively took the paper, and a bracelet slipped out. Her eyes widened. "Did you get me—?"

"No, it's, uh—for killing people."

Cole and Tabitha stared at each other blankly.

Tabitha broked out a smirk. "You know me very well, Johnson."

"It contains several shots of deadly poison, and I trust you'll use it wisely," Cole said, slowly straightening to his stoic self.

Tabitha hopped on one foot, clipping it around her ankle. "I murder wisely, Cole."

Silence.

"I promise," she said with a small smile. It made her sick to even think of using it as she looked into his solemn eyes. She quickly looked away and began to open the paper before Cole clamped his hand down over it.

"Wait!" Tabitha looked up to his red face. "Probably should read that in a place where you won't die from secondhand embarrassment."

"Oh, it can't be that bad."

"No, Tabs." *Tabs*. He called her "Tabs" again. "It's that bad."

She shoved it into her pocket. "Fine," she said. "But only because we have your brother's behind to save right now."

Cole breathed a sigh of relief. "Good. You ready, Felicity?"

"As I'll ever be," Felicity said, rolling ahead.

Tabitha's heart panged with worry. "Will she be able to protect herself?" It might be safer to leave her there.

Cole snorted. "Oh, I wouldn't worry about her protection."

"I feel like there's a lot you're not telling me," Tabitha said.

"I'll catch you up on the way!" Felicity called out.

Tabitha turned to Cole, and he caught her eye. Her face flooded with heat, kindly reminding her of their last in-person conversation.

It wasn't the time to discuss it further. Right now, they needed to get to Ray.

They broke out into a jog after Felicity, and Tabitha's mind was still churning. In a matter of hours, she'd be thrust back into battle and possible death, but right now, she was happy. She was happy that her friend was happy, and that she could struggle to keep up with Cole again.

48

North Cordell, 1 Day Until

"MATTEO?"

Lawrence checked their room for what felt like the tenth time, and it was as empty as the last nine. He shut the door behind him, hurrying out the hall.

"Still no sign of him?" Jenna asked, her face pinched with concern. She sat at the upper level's kitchen counter, a mug in hand and her hair tied up, her old cape still folded in her lap. Charles sat beside her with Adam, watching Lawrence with wide eyes.

"I have no idea where he could've run off to!" Lawrence said, walking to the siblings. Matteo had been missing for the past few hours, almost right after the meeting. Taryn assured him that Matteo was fine, and she had already issued a Defender to scout for him if he went too far, but it didn't help relieve his worry. The Soul Night was tomorrow, and he hadn't seen Matteo since last night.

"This doesn't seem like him at all," Lawrence said,

checking his Comm. No response.

"I'm sure he'll show up. You have to leave. You can't hold up everyone," Noah said with a reassuring nod. "We'll make sure of it."

"Yes!" Charles said. "And then we'll drink tea together, and watch a film together, and all sortsa stuff!"

Lawrence cracked a smile. "I'm sure you will." He turned back to Jenna. "Keep them from all going crazy."

Jenna forced a smile. "Stay safe."

"I will." Lawrence started for the stairs, calling goodbye to Charles, who was still rambling about Matteo and for Fire Wolf.

Jenna opened her mouth again, hesitating. "Lawrence?"

Lawrence stopped. "Yes?"

Jenna's eyes shifted downward. "I—if you see Ray," she said, forcing her voice louder as she raised her eyes. "Can you let him know I know it's not his fault?"

Lawrence swallowed hard with a nod. "I—I will."

Jenna gave a small smile. "Thank you."

"You're welcome."

"Now, go!" Noah shouted from behind the counter, only to be seen by a waving fist. "Don't want to be late to your big Algery debut!"

Lawrence rolled his eyes and rushed down the steps. The downstairs was bustling, as most of the Defenders had returned from their rounds, and Lawrence had to push through the crowd to the front door.

The fact that the "Council Members" were going to investigate Aguirre property was quite a popular topic as he tread through; though, no one seemed particularly concerned about the Council Member they were blocking from getting out the door.

"Hey, Williams! Come on!"

Jack was waiting at the Defender truck outside. The Mathewses had promised that they'd make sure that Matteo was all right…which probably wasn't ideal, but it was something.

He took a deep breath and left the front door.

Fire Wolf claimed shotgun beside Jack, which meant that Nikki, Lincoln, and Lawrence were crammed into the back, with Nikki's small frame squished in the middle, which she didn't seem to mind. She was basically a pillow with the amount of layers that had been packed on her.

She sat, fairly content with watching Jack drive with the utmost curiosity, and Lincoln looked too busy nervously fidgeting with the Cube for conversation. Lawrence couldn't exactly blame him.

Jack informed them that Algery wasn't an inherently long drive from North Cordell and shared North Cordell borders with Court Illegia, though the Aguirre property was closer than the Lopez's in the Skyline. Lawrence couldn't help but notice Nikki perk up at every mention of her childhood home.

Lawrence didn't want to remind her that it had burned down. Everyone knew the story. The assassins had broken into the two Curatrix members' home. No one escaped the burning house, not even the ones sent to kill them. Everyone died, including Reyna and Lyell's two infant children.

All except for Nikki, who still somehow escaped.

The trip was long and quiet. No one bothered to say anything other than to get something, and by the time Jack sounded a horn, Lawrence jumped.

He must have dozed off. The night had fallen, and they were now parked along the side of a building with a "Defending Department" sign plastered in the front.

"All right, up and out, magical children. Let's go!" Jack said, leaving the auto and Fire Wolf bounding after him.

Lawrence stumbled out of the door, taking his bag with him. The air had a bitter cold like North Cordell, though smelled more of soot and garbage.

He helped Nikki out of the truck, who took the help begrudgingly. Her eyes were wide and seemed incapable of blinking as she looked around the grungy Algery street.

Lincoln followed them out, far more cautious.

"Don't be getting your first impressions here," Jack said, laughing at their stunned faces as he strolled up to the automatic doors of the Defender building. "The Aguirre residence is a bit farther up in the woods, and we'll be looking at it soon. But we need in-region clearance."

"That's relieving," Lincoln muttered.

"I think it's nice," Nikki said, following them in.

Nikki nearly tripped over the door. Lawrence and

Lincoln jumped to her aide, Lawrence quickly supporting her side.

"I'm fine," she said breathlessly with a shrug. "Just… getting used to it."

Lawrence eyed her. "Let me help you."

"I don't—"

"Come on, Nik. Be reasonable."

Nikki sighed, letting Lincoln take her satchel and Lawrence support her. She felt so tiny against him, it was unnerving. Maybe Lincoln had been onto something about letting her come…

But as the Sergeant liked to say: they didn't really have another option.

They spotted Jack leaning against the counter as a receptionist clicked away on his hologram.

"There they are!" Jack said, perking up.

The receptionist frowned, tilting his head at the curious trio that made their way to meet Jack. "Is—is she all right?" he asked, raising a brow to Nikki.

"Yes." Nikki answered for herself. "Just tired…He's my cousin."

As if that made it less odd looking.

"Are they really?" The receptionist sat back, looking bewildered between the two of them.

"Genetic differences—now, the clearance?" Jack said, stepping in front of them. "Did you receive Sergeant Hunter's message?"

"I did, and I should have badges by tomorrow." The receptionist sighed. "The Aguirre property is a *highly* restricted area, and I expect you and your kids and, uh, your dog to treat it as such, Sallow."

"Why would you doubt me?"

The receptionist snorted. "Look, your screwup isn't super secret."

Right, the unknown incident that made Jack demoted to more of a janitor than an Officer. Jack's face flamed at the mention of it, and he just squeaked a nervous laugh. "It's been years."

He handed Jack two keycards after an ordeal of listing their IDs and gave the Members a glare as Jack led them through the back door and out into the steel hallway that smelled of chemicals and was lit with fluorescent lights. The base was mostly quiet that night as Jack led them up a flight of echoing, metal steps to another hall lined in closed doors.

He took one keycard for himself and handed one to Nikki. "Do you think you'll be all right alone?" he asked.

Nikki nodded. "I'll be fine."

"I'll trust you," Jack said, swiping the keycard on the boy's door. "Call if you need any help."

Nikki nodded, easing out of Lawrence's support and swiping the key over her own door handle. She looked at them and laughed. "You should see yourselves, all wide eyed and pale. I'm fine. Good night."

Lawrence nodded. "'Night."

Are you awake?

Lawrence's eyes shot open to Nikki's voice in his head. Far more comforting than the creepy woman's.

Well, I am now.

Lincoln rolled on the bunk above him. *Are you okay, Nik?*

I told you. I'm fine. I just remembered something else from the Kathryn story.

Perfect timing for tomorrow, Lincoln's voice said, Lawrence hearing him give a shallow laugh. *We're going to get all the Shadow Soul info we can get.*

And we're calling her "Kathryn" now? Lawrence thought.

She seemed pretty insistent, so why not?

A curious name for the Voice, daughter of Orion Idicous, who nearly destroyed Imperial and was a proven murderer. *All right. Fine point.*

What was it this time? Lincoln asked.

Nikki paused. *It's less unsettling than the last one…depending on how you look at it.*

I've already seen this woman pull the life force out of multiple men with little to no emotion. Seriously. Nothing could be more unsettling than that. Lincolns shuddered.

Need someone to hold your hand as you have nightmares, Lincoln?

Haha, very funny.

Are you boys done yet? Nikki butted in.

Yes, Lawrence said quickly.

Good. Because it starts like this…

Border Woods of the Ewyon Coastal Alliance—Before Recorded Time

Just a little…farther.

Kathryn nearly tumbled out of the tree, bag and all. She caught the branch by her legs, swinging upside down.

A cow stood in the field, staring at her with its unfocused eyes. Stupid animal.

She hoisted herself back up, zapping the apple from its branch. It landed in the bag with a thud, and she leapt to the ground, slinging the bag over her shoulder.

Her skirt was tied up to her knees and her bare feet were free, moving quickly across the forest, her long hair swinging up against the inside of her knees.

She walked inside the tiny house, the fire slowly burning in the fireplace, warm against the cold fall outside. She set the bag down onto the table, splashing the lukewarm water from the basin on the table onto her dirt-streaked face.

She blew the droplets from her hands, watching them freely dancing in the air. With an exhale, they fell against the table.

She focused on the bowl, dipping her hand inside. The droplets swirled around her arm, crystallizing at her command. It formed along her arm, sharpening around her fingers.

Sergia told her that she didn't need weapons. You didn't need weapons when that was exactly what you were. Racing through the woods, riding winds, and fighting tree limbs had proved that.

She clenched her fist, the ice blade dissolving back into the bowl. It worked best when emotion didn't consume her. Anger, joy, nothing. That way nothing irrational would happen ever again.

If she killed, it was now with purpose.

The cottage door swung open. "Kathryn, can you—ah!—help?"

Kathryn spun to Sergia's aide, grabbing a sack and basket from Sergia's overflowing arms. She sent Kathryn a thankful smile and unloaded the rest off onto the table.

"I trust everything went well while I was gone," Sergia said, wiping the sweat from her brow, tucking loose hairs back from her ponytail.

Never had Kathryn seen Sergia…healthier.

The past year in the thick of the woods had done wonders to the light of her eyes. Her complexion was darker and healthier, with more fullness to her, that she looked so much stronger and more alive than an overworked palace servant.

Kathryn still stood taller than Sergia, her shoulders broader and more muscle on her bones, but Sergia's voice always carried more life and authority as she beckoned Kathryn to help unpack.

"Everything went well," Kathryn said finally, taking up a sack of flour discarded by the door with ease.

"That's good to hear," Sergia said with a smile.

Kathryn couldn't help a small one in return.

Sergia's gentle face slowly fell. "Though, the town had other news."

Kathryn's heart stopped. "What happened?"

"Nothing…yet." Sergia plucked an apple from Kathryn's batch. She forced another smile. "I'll tell you later."

Kathryn didn't press her. She hadn't dared in the past year. Sergia had let her come stumbling in from the storm she'd created, Sergia's eyes still red from the tears.

Kathryn would never hurt her like that again. Sergia was the closest thing she would ever have, and she couldn't break that. Being submissive was the only hint she could think of to make Sergia forgive her again.

She was miles from the palace, and she had no desire to see its stone face again. Let the unclean Lady be lost to time.

Time. Oh, she had all the time in the world.

Dinner was a cheery event. It was small, considering their lack of income with an unstable, tiny farm, but it was every bit as filling and every bit more enjoyable. Sergia spoke excitedly over the upcoming renovation plans and how they almost had enough to to pay off the land. Carastene didn't give Sergia her last check because of her sudden quitting, but Sergia always managed, and the sight of her talking happily by the candle light made Kathryn sure that everything up until this moment was worth it.

They cleaned the small kitchen, as they did every night. Sergia went to prepare for sleep earlier than Kathryn, who promised to check on the animals. In her dressing gown and leather pants, she teleported quickly out into the cold, clutching Sergia's shawl, her blood quickly adjusting to the harsh pasture.

She walked into the barn, and with a flick of her finger, the lantern hanging by the door lit. As usual, the barn was unfazed by their magical companion, as they had been long ago.

Whatever Aviduous essence she had managed to take was strong in her veins. Perhaps that was why the adjustment came quickly. She heaved the doors shut, letting the gust of wind blow out the lantern as she rushed back to the cottage.

She entered quickly, her movements silent as she moved to drape the shawl over the chair in the kitchen. She moved to the sheet that separated the bedroom from the kitchen. Across the room, Sergia was still in her cot as Kathryn slipped quietly into her own.

"Can you turn on the light?"

Kathryn's heart leapt, and without warning, Sergia's bedside candle lit.

Sergia sat up. "You wanted to know what was being said in the town?"

Kathryn nodded, taking Sergia's pat as a signal to take a seat beside her.

"In my bag. There's a scroll."

Kathryn eyed Sergia's bag, hanging on the knob of the night stand, and with a flick, as Sergia said, a scroll slipped out and flew to Kathryn's hand.

She could feel Sergia's anxiety pounding on her, and she toyed with a long strand of Kathryn's hair.

Kathryn uncurled the yellowed paper.

Two Thousand Credits to those who pledge loyalty to Queen Carastene of the Emberson House and the dynasty against the dark force.

Join front lines by decree.

"She's paying for soldiers?" This was a new Carastene ploy.

"Against the dark force," Sergia pointed out. "On the way to the royal town, I passed a refugee camp. Ewyon refugees. Not foreigners to this place. Just a few days ago, their town was ransacked to the ground. They escaped."

Kathryn's eyes widened, the pieces slowly coming together.

"Town was full of panic. The dark force is coming, and at this rate, a little less than a week—"

"For Castarene," Kathryn finished.

"To the throne." Sergia's eyes met Kathryn's. "The dark force…The Oquelite, if they make it—"

"That's the end for the coastal alliance," Kathryn said solemnly.

Thousands seeking refuge would arrive at Ewyon towns to flames and sudden death. Thousands of refugees of mixed blood, accused of the very curse she fulfilled, would meet a much grimmer fate.

"Kathryn." Sergia's eyes held fast onto her.

"You want me to do something about it," Kathryn whispered. "Don't you?"

Sergia nodded, and Kathryn wished that she'd gone insane. "You think I, the Shadow Soul they hate so much, should save them?"

Sergia's gaze fell to Kathryn's hand, clenched in a tight fist. As usual, she kept back from touching her, but Kathryn could see the pain it took to hold back.

"They're not asking for your help," Sergia said quietly. "Carastene would probably prefer it if you stayed far from this whole mess. But…but are politics and hurt feelings worth the loss?"

Due to Carastene's negligence, the entire coastal settlements could fall. The dark force had wiped out the original kingdoms. A group of Oquelite who had once been deemed nothing more than serf material.

The people who killed her mother. The people who fathered her.

The glowing burning in her palms threatened to overcome the chill in her veins. Did the people under Carastene's rule deserve to fall at their queen's hand?

Their unrightful queen. One who'd taken a Lady's throne.

Kathryn wanted to be no such ruler. She didn't want that kind of power. She wanted the curse broken. It didn't matter what she did. She would live through it whether she wanted to or not.

And then she'd live to find revenge.

She turned to catch Sergia's desperate eyes. "When do we begin?"

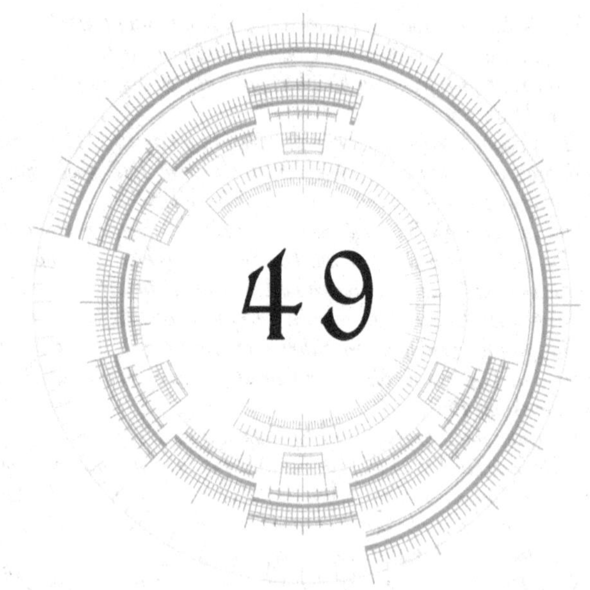

49

Kennedy, 2 Hours Until

RAY COULD AT least feel Mercy's warmth as she lay with her back against his. He'd woken up groggy, his head in pain and a blindfold tied tightly around his eyes. All in all, he assumed that their flimsy escape plan had failed.

Go figure.

"Mercy?"

Still no response. Hopefully, it *was* Mercy. Hopefully, they were alive.

Of course they're alive, genius, they're warm and you can hear them breathing.

A shuffle of footsteps echoed through the room. Ray went stiff.

A pair of hands pulled him to his feet and shoved him forward. He nearly toppled over, spinning around and catching his balance.

And then something bit at his arm, feeling as though it burned his very skin, stinging and aching his bone. He grit his teeth and gripped his arm, struggling to control a pained gasp.

"You escape your collar, we treat you even more like a dog." Virtue's voice.

Ray turned in the direction of her voice. "You're insane."

Another lash. This time he couldn't help a cry. Didn't they see that he was too weak to teleport away? He wanted to crumple to the ground and hoped that exhaustion would take him.

Boy, I could save you.

Get out of my head.

He was grabbed by the shoulder and forced forward. He heard a small groan belonging to Mercy. At least she was alive.

A door swung open, and Ray was shoved out into the cold air, tripping over a step and landing hard into the dirt. Pain scraped down his face. He felt it grow warm and wet. What if he lay there—?

He was jerked up by the collar of his shirt and forced forward, a cold metal forced against his shirt. He had no desire to find out what it was, so he walked.

The trek was quiet. Not another noise from Mercy, and it terrified him. Almost as if they could sense it, he was lashed in the ankle, causing him to trip again.

He struggled to his feet before he was grabbed. He was suddenly jerked to a stop.

"A fitting punishment for a traitor to the legacy…and the one who refuses to follow it." No doubt Virtue.

What punishment?

Ray nearly tripped over something, but he may as well have fallen as he was shoved down, hitting something wood.

A body was shoved beside him. No doubt Mercy. Were they being buried alive? Fear seized him as something slammed above them, the steady rhythm of a hammer following.

"If this Keyper won't carry on the line, no Keyper will!" he heard Virtue shout.

Had the woman lost it?

He could hear Mercy's fearful breath as the hammering continued. Ray wriggled his tied hands up to pull down his blindfold.

He was right. With Mercy crammed beside him, they were in a box.

He couldn't move. He couldn't think. They were going to be buried underground. No one would find them. And they'd die.

The coffin was hoisted up. This was it.

All in a moment, he was spinning and crashing, and neither of them knew who'd screamed. Then it slowed.

Nothing followed. An odd sound flooded the coffin. Mercy peeled back her blindfold. "What—what's happening?"

The sound…A fluid, rhythmic rush and crash. Not dirt at all.

Ray's eyes widened. "No."

"Mathews?" Mercy's voice quaked.

Ray looked at her, his mind scrambling. "We're underwater."

Algery

"I can't believe Taryn only requested clearance for you three!" Jack said as they trekked up the dirt path in the woods.

Apparently, Jack also forgot that the roads to the Aguirre property had all been blocked and dismantled; so no civilian, or forgetful Defender, could access it, meaning that they had to walk the rest of the way to the checkpoint.

"Honestly, how rude!" Jack said, sighing. He looked behind him. "How's little miss Aguirre?"

Due to Nikki's condition and limited energy, she'd begrudgingly settled to let Lawrence and Lincoln carry her on their backs until they reached the checkpoint; that way she wouldn't be too exhausted to do their actual job.

She rested her chin on Lincoln's shoulder. "I'm fine."

Besides her pride, Lincoln had to give her credit. She woke up with a surprising amount of strength, which he wasn't sure was genuine or just from her determination to see her childhood home again. Either way, she had been incredibly animated that morning.

"How much longer?" Lawrence asked from behind Lincoln. Fire Wolf barked, as if to agree.

Afternoon wasn't going to last forever. Tonight was the night, and Lincoln didn't want to risk it.

"Only a few minutes," Jack said, holding his Comm up as he walked. "Or, at least, this is what it says."

"It *feels* familiar," Nikki whispered. "Something about it."

The woods were peaceful and less densely wooded than the ones in the North Cordell. The woods were light in the chilly afternoon air, and there was a soft breeze through the green trees. Nikki's hair brushed against his cheek as she lifted her head.

He caught sight of two blinking lights and a gate, suited persons pacing in the distance.

Nikki began to wriggle in his grip. "Put me down! Put me down! I can walk from here."

There was no denying her as she slipped back down to her feet. She quickly grabbed his hand, and for the first time in over a month, she ran. It wasn't as quick as she had been and in no way straight or coordinated, but she was running for the checkpoint and pulling him with her.

He tripped over himself, trying not to topple over onto her. They ran past Jack and pulled up first to the checkpoint.

"This is a restricted area!" the Defender in a helmet shouted.

Nikki was quick to pull her clearance card from her pocket, squeezing Lincoln's hand. "We've been given permission. Sergeant Hunter."

Lincoln pulled his out too.

The Defender's helmet scanned the card and, with a huff, said, "You are clear. What about them?"

Lawrence and Jack burst through the checkpoint.

"Good day," Jack said with a wave as he caught his breath.

"Clearance card, Officer?"

Jack frowned, straightening himself. "I was just the escort."

Lawrence pulled his card from his shirt pocket and was checked out. The Officer tilted his head at them, glancing at his partner.

With a sigh, the Officer turned back. "You kids are cleared…for some reason. Your officer and that dog must wait."

Fire Wolf pouted, and Lawrence consoled him with a pat to the head. Nikki cast Lincoln a thrilled smile as the gate opened. She, Lincoln, and Lawrence walked through.

"The remains of the residence are up the path and over the hill," the Officer instructed. "Only do as your Sergeant instructed, or you will be punished accordingly."

Sounded threatening enough.

"You ready for this?" Lawrence said.

"I don't know," Lincoln said. His head reeled. They were really doing this.

"Yes!" Nikki said, pulling Lincoln along as they slowly rose higher and higher up the hill.

His breath caught in his throat. He slowed. It was nothing like he had thought.

An entire plot of ash, cleaned and trimmed appropriately and marked with glowing holograms. The Aguirre house was gone. But the very fact that it once stood there hit him like a door.

Lawrence and Nikki were frozen in place on both sides of him. "Very familiar," Nikki whispered. She slowly let go of Lincoln's hand, slowly stepping forward and down the path.

Lawrence and Lincoln exchanged looks and followed her.

Nikki's face was unreadable as her eyes searched, cautiously stepping off the path and onto the flat ground toward the burnt remains.

Lincoln stepped to go after her, but Lawrence held out his arm to block him and shook his head.

Leave her.

Lincoln took a deep breath. Lawrence was right.

Nikki knelt down in front of the ruins, carefully reaching out to the untouched ash. She picked up a small piece of charred wood, examining it in her fingers for a moment. And then she crushed it.

She let the ash seep through her fist and crumpled down to two knees, falling forward with her hands to the ground, completely still.

Lawrence dropped his arm, and with a forward gesture, he and Lincoln walked toward her.

Nikki rose to her feet. "It's okay," she stammered. She

turned back to them, rubbing her face with her sooty hand. "It's okay." She turned to scan the rubble again, frowning. "I feel like I remember."

Nikki turned, walking quickly around the house, closing her eyes.

She was going to trip herself. "Nik!"

Nikki ignored Lincoln. She walked along the edge of the house. "There were steps here…" She moved along farther. "A…garden? It died a lot, right under the bedroom window." Her feet hit the dirt road. "The driveway. Up a hill. Two vans and a truck."

Her eyes opened, welling with tears.

Her eyes froze, and Lincoln's gaze settled on the sight. Three grave markers, the holograms cared for and strong with their projections.

Agent Reyna Wents Aguirre
Agent Lyell Aguirre
Emil Aguirre & Jeana Aguirre

"And now it's all gone," she choked.

Lawrence stepped forward, gently slipping his hand into hers.

Lincoln stood back, unsure of what to say. He bowed his head. More people who were killed…More grief and pain.

And it was all so incredibly unfair. No matter what Nikki said about a life after death didn't stop the fact that it was unfair. The Curatrix team shouldn't have been killed. Nikki shouldn't have had to live without her parents and her siblings.

After a moment of silence, Nikki finally let go of Lawrence and turned back to Lincoln and the Aguirre property. She wiped her eyes. "Let's continue what we came for," she said, walking quickly toward the ruins.

Lincoln looked to Lawrence. "Is she okay?"

"I can't imagine it's *easy*," Lawrence said, trekking after her. "People died here."

Her people.

"There's nothing here but ash and memory," Lincoln said, running after Lawrence.

Lawrence shrugged. "And maybe that's all we need. I trust her, don't you?"

Do you trust her?

He watched Nikki sift among the vast space of rubble, her brows knit with determination. She squatted down, brushing ash away.

"I found it!" she called.

Lincoln frowned, glancing at Lawrence, who shrugged. The two broke out into a run.

In the wreck of the floor was a metal door: one that was dented and scratched, looking as if it had already been attempted to be broken into before and failed.

Nikki pressed her palm against the door. For a moment, nothing happened, and Lincoln was ready to pull out an arrow and blow it. But then it began to glow, and a soft *ding!* followed.

A familiar, automated voice spoke, and the door slowly opened: "Nikki M. Aguirre detected."

Weird. The automated voice here was the same as the basement in the Inn…

A set of stairs unfolded into view, lights bursting underneath each step. Reyna and Lyell must have had something to do with Taryn's basement too.

Or maybe they just had a thing for underground tech.

Nikki eagerly began the descent, and Lincoln and Lawrence followed after her. Every step Nikki took ahead of them, a light burst on with an echo and whir of machinery and a smell of wet earth. Lincoln's eyes grew wide as, bit by bit, an enormous basement revealed itself. A half-circle desk sat with dull monitors and an uncharged hover chair. A few file cabinets set along the walls, but nothing compared to the amount of cardboard boxes. Halls led out of the main room and into darkness.

Lincoln's breath caught itself, turning to take it all in. This had been hiding right under the Defenders noses for a decade?

"This is incredible," he gasped. He turned to Nikki, who sank into the hoverchair with her legs crossed, her eyes lost in the room. "Did you know about this?"

"It was part of the memories," she said, her voice low. "I remembered a door."

"Did all the Curatrix members have weird basements?" Lawrence said with a jagged laugh.

Lincoln shook his head. "This is different from Taryn's.

Hers is more of a simulator, seeming to have been made for training. This? This seems more personal."

"And where do *those* lead?" Lawrence said, pointing to one of the open halls.

Nikki frowned. "I don't know."

They all stood in the silence until Nikki rose from the seat. "We should begin our search. Anything that *she* might be after."

Lincoln and Lawrence didn't argue.

First box was a lot of busted discs, cords, and wires. Plenty of outdated tech scraps all stored away in a box. Lincoln began to worry when the second one was just that.

He stripped the tape away from the third box and opened it. Inside were...binders? He gently picked one up and flipped it open.

Oh, great. Words. He hated those things.

"'Last test was incomplete. The runes have only a slight re...'"

Lincoln whirled around to Nikki, who had knelt beside him, her eyes glued to the paper.

"Runes?" Lincoln asked. "What runes could they possibly be deciphering?"

Nikki didn't answer him, entirely engrossed in the words. She flipped the page, muttering under her breath.

Nikki took the binder from him and set it into her bag and peered farther. She picked up a small, flimsy, plastic-like paper. On it was a...photo.

The photo depicted only what Lincoln could know as Reyna, but different than how he always saw her in the M.E.D.I.A., slightly older, her hair shorter and mussed, glaring at whoever the photo taker was.

Lincoln looked from the photo to Nikki, who seemed to be unable to blink, her eyes only getting wider. Her fingertips gently traced the outline of her mother.

"She kinda looks like you," Lincoln said. Same face shape and darker skin shade, and something else he couldn't place. Almost as if they *felt* similar.

Nikki huffed, folding the photo and tucking it away into one of her many jacket pockets. She wiped her face and got to her feet. "The rest of the box looks like photos."

And she didn't want to look at more than one? This was

a basement full of memories. If he had such an opportunity, he was sure that he'd savor it. To know who his family had been and have everything that they'd kept.

But she'd just gotten up and walked away with that tiny frown. The same look Reyna had. Determination. Even when everything he could imagine she wanted to see was set before her, she was still choosing the darn mission.

Life is unfair.

He got to his feet, leaving Nikki to continue to search alone, and went to Lawrence, sitting amongst a few unloaded boxes, which, so far, seemed to consist of uniform and armored gear.

"Find anything?" Lawrence asked as he examined a shoulder pad.

"Notes. Something about deciphering runes." Lincoln got to his knees to help Lawrence sort. "You?"

"Nothing so far." Lawrence sighed, tossing the shoulder pad aside. "You'd think they'd leave something in these uniforms…but I'm beginning to think it's not exactly storage."

Lincoln frowned. "What do you mean?"

"These aren't full uniforms."

Lincoln scanned the piles. Lawrence was right. They were only the Agent body armor and bulletproof shirts. A rare material only higher Defenders possessed. One chest plate was bigger than the other too. Different sizes…

"Do you think they were collecting it?"

"They have to have been." Lawrence shrugged. "And for more than one person, at that."

Lawrence rummaged through the box, pulling out a shirt. Something fell through, hitting the floor with a ping. Lawrence frowned, scooping it up.

"What is this?" Lawrence said, holding up the chain, a small, silver cross dangling on the end.

Lincoln shrugged. "I'm not sure."

"Seems odd to have left something like this in here," Lawrence said, examining it as it glinted in the fluorescent light. His trance broke as Nikki slammed a file drawer, and he slipped it into his pocket.

"Paperwork," Nikki said when she noticed their stares.

Lincoln moved to her, looking over her shoulder. Photos

were paperclipped to the edges, fine print on little lines with numbers and more words.

"Defender files?"

"But it doesn't say 'Defending Department,'" she noted, pointing to the logo at the head of the page.

"What does it say?"

"'NMA File,'" Nikki muttered.

Lincoln's eyes widened. "Wait, NMA? When we unlocked the Curatrix machine, it mentioned something about those files being unlocked."

"But what *are* they?" Nikki said, flipping through the pages of the file. "I've never heard anyone mention it before."

"I heard it had to do with a back up plan...if Reyna didn't make it," Lincoln said, his face burning, hoping that neither questioned how he learned the information.

"If she didn't make..." Nikki's voice trailed off.

She put the file back and eyed the hologram monitor, and then looked to Lincoln. "Do you think you can download—?"

"Oh, yeah. Easily."

It took Lincoln a matter of minutes to hook the machine back up to power, and he found it in considerably good condition. With the flip of a switch, a holographic keyboard popped up over the desk. He pressed down on a key, and the whole monitor flashed red.

Nikki quickly pushed through, and with her touch, the monitor reverted back to blue, and the automated voice read, "Unlocked."

A blinking bar appeared on the screen, and Nikki began typing the familiar "NMA."

Bang!

Lincoln's attention whipped to the far end of the basement. The light of the outdoors had disappeared from the stairwell...The door had closed.

Lincoln glanced at Lawrence, who was slowly creeping for the door, in step with Lincoln.

"Hello?" Lincoln said. "Jack?"

Silence.

Maybe it was just the wind. One strong wind it would have been, then.

A creak came from the steps. A person definitely.

The lights flickered.

Nik, hurry.

I am. I'm transferring the file to a disc.

Lincoln eased his bow from his shoulder, reaching back to the quiver for an arrow. He held his breath. "Ja—"

A whir of a red cloak and a wicked blade spun from the shadows, dashing right for Lincoln. *Not* Jack.

Lawrence smashed a glass case, tearing out the decorated sword. Lincoln whipped out the arrow, letting it loose as it caught the skin of the neck, sending tiny volts to convulse the body.

"Nikki!" Lawrence shouted. "Hurry!"

He swung the blade at the Exerticus, but before it could meet it, another blade interceded.

Lincoln's heart skipped a beat. *Another one.*

This one was a woman, white hair tucked behind her ear and braided back and her skin a shade darker than Nikki's. She slammed Lawrence back against the wall, and Lawrence pushed back with his blade.

The other quickly recovered, swinging at Lincoln. Lincoln ducked, rolling backward onto the floor, whipping out another arrow, hitting his shoulder with a thump.

The Excerticus only grunted, swiping at Lincoln. Lincoln rolled away. The Exerticus slammed the blade into the ground, blocking his escape, landing a knee to Lincoln's chest.

Lincoln struggled against it. "NIK!"

He didn't hear a response, only the scrape of the blade torn from the floor and held above him. The burning spiked in his chest, and he tore an arrow from his pack and jammed it into the Exerticus's hand, digging it deep as the Exerticus cried out. Lincoln twisted it till the Blade fell, nearly missing his face.

Relief washed over him. Too long. The other hand came down as a fist to his face, blinding him with pain as the Exerticus wrenched the arrow from his hand.

There were only seconds before he picked up the blade. *You're trapped.*

No, not entirely.

I'm going to regret this.

Lincoln smashed his head into the attacker's face, sending another taser to the neck. The Exerticus reared back. Lincoln's head spiked with pain, but there was too little time to address it. He scrambled to his feet, kicking the sword as far away from the Exerticus as possible, and raced for Nikki, still bent over the desk, the whir of the machine printing the disc.

Pain tore through his side. He cried out, not daring to check what had happened. Nikki grabbed the disc from the implanter, and he swiftly grabbed her arm and burst into the dark tunnel.

A crash followed, and Lawrence's voice joined the commotion. "They're only held off for a matter of freaking seconds!" he shouted.

"I thought you were supposed to be some magic fire boy!"

"Ha! I thought you were smart! I can't conjure fire. I can only *control* it!" Lawrence snorted.

Another crash followed.

Lawrence shouted a curse. "They're coming!"

Another glowing, red blast shot through the tunnel. Nikki pushed herself and Lincoln out of the way, taking the lead down the tunnel.

Three new branches appeared in the darkness, and Lincoln pulled faster, trying to will the powerful burn back, but it refused to come. Nikki tightened her grip on him.

FASTER.

They tore through the middle hallway. "Lawrence!" Lincoln cried, not hearing his voice in a moment.

"I'll hold them back! Go—ah!"

A blast shook the hall, sending Nikki and Lincoln flying across the floor. A thunderous crash followed.

Lincoln's eyes adjusted to see the ceiling above the entrance cave in, crumbling closer and closer...

He scrambled to his feet, pulling Nikki up with him. "We have to run!"

Nikki nearly slipped but pushed herself after him, the collapsing tunnels chasing at their heels, the hall thick with dust.

Run. Run. Run.

You have no other option. Turn to me.

Nikki slipped, crying out.

A spark lit inside. He pulled her back to her feet, supporting her, and ran.

He spotted a turn, a tiny divot in the hall, the size of a small, carved-out room. It would either cave in with the rest and kill them both or be their chance at surviving.

Nikki gasped for air, and he turned. They didn't have another choice. He jumped, tucking and rolling, holding onto Nikki as the rubble crashed, blocking their only exit.

He lay still for a moment, hugging Nikki tightly as they both tried to catch their breath.

Lincoln slowly sat up, his eyes adjusting to the dark: an Aviduous skill that came in handy. The tiny room was entirely enclosed by the stone. They were trapped.

Nikki sat up, coughing on the dust. Exhaustion leaked into her eyes as she held his gaze. "You're bleeding," she whispered.

The pain came all at once as Lincoln's eyes dropped to his side, flashing blood, his shirt burned around the blast wound.

He removed his jacket with his shaking hands and pressed it against his wound with a harsh breath.

"Are you okay?" she asked, crawling forward.

"It's fine." Lincoln lied. "How about you?"

"I'm tired," she admitted, hanging her head. "I hurt a little."

"You need rest."

She nodded. "Help will come," she said as Lincoln tried to single handedly lead her to the wall. "We won't die."

"Nik…we—we'll be stuck here for the Soul Night."

"We don't even know if that's dangerous," she said.

It might be detrimental. Tell me your name.

"But it might be. We don't know what the Exercitcus are planning…They'll be powerful…They'll get to our blood just like Ray said—"

"You're worried about dying," she said, her breath uneasy as she watched him through her dazed eyes. "You can solve a lot of things, but you can't solve death, Linc."

She nodded off against his shoulder and Lincoln stiffened, his throat tight, trying to keep fearful tears at bay and the pain from overcoming him.

You can't solve death.

Then what was he supposed to do? Just die?

Tell me your name. Accept me. I am the Lady of the Universe and I can provide you power.

He stopped. When death came, it would come. He couldn't stop it. And it scared him.

Tell me your name.

He was scared, and he felt so pathetic about it.

Tell me your name. And you will not die.

But it was the truth. He was terrified, and he couldn't stop it. He didn't have any other option.

TELL ME YOUR NAME.

He took a deep, shuddery breath. "No."

What?

"If I die," he stammered, "so be it."

And if she dies?

Lincoln couldn't breathe. He couldn't think. He could feel the Voice entering his mind. His thoughts weren't his own. She was *in* his mind, and he could do nothing. He was too tired to fight.

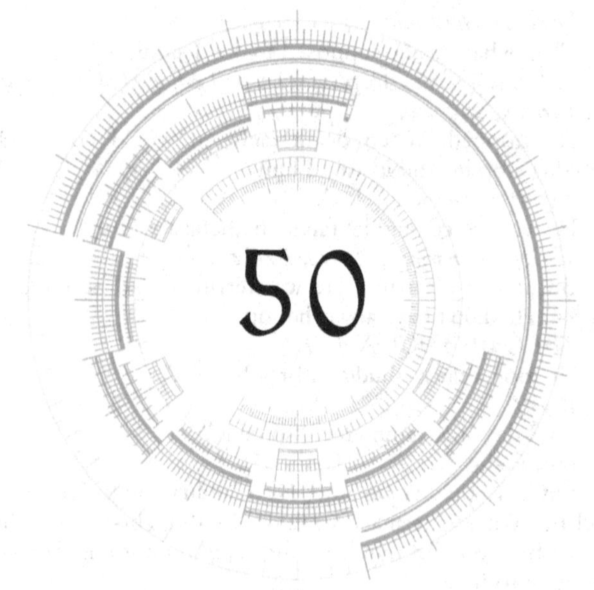

50

The Ewyon Coastal Alliance Palace—Before Recorded Time

BREATHE.

The darkness was her only companion. No emotion. No feeling. Suspended in the air. The strong smell of rain. The cold air pricking at her face.

Every day, the feeling swelling inside her grew stronger. It threatened to swallow her whole, her body trembling with essence.

Power. So much power. And it was all coming here. For Carastene. The foolish Queen. All this blood would be on her hands.

Kathryn would hold nothing.

The wind whipped harder, not by her command. The feeling crept through her, her burning veins rising.

Her eyes opened. She dropped to the forest floor, turning to Sergia, cloaked beside her. She nodded. "They're here."

Sergia pressed her lips into a tight line and nodded back. She stepped forward, hesitating before brushing a loose hair from Kathryn's coat.

The coat was one of Sergia's proudest projects: a thick fabric that could withstand the surplus of Kathryn's abilities. It was a dark navy with silver embroidery, a maroon cape draped from the shoulders that Sergia insisted was necessary, but Kathryn didn't argue otherwise.

For long nights leading up to this day, Sergia had been occupied by the candlelight, and since Kathryn couldn't comfort her herself, she was glad something helped keep Sergia's mind calm.

Sergia tried to hide her fear, but being one who could sense the overpowering emotions, it wasn't hard to see through her brave face.

"I'll protect you," Kathryn assured quietly.

Sergia nodded. No doubt in her feelings. She trusted Kathryn entirely.

Kathryn swallowed hard.

The sensation raged. The dark force was here. They didn't have much time.

"Are you ready?" Sergia asked, straightening. The air fell still around them.

Kathryn nodded. It didn't matter how ready she felt or not; they would come and destroy without permission.

She placed a tentative hand on Sergia's cloaked shoulder, seeing the relief relax Sergia's face at the rare touch.

A deep breath.

Sergia closed her eyes. Kathryn followed, placing her opposite hand on Sergia's other shoulder.

One breath, one blast of energy. The burning coursed through her.

The world blew past her, dropping only for a moment as her body came full circle, her feet hitting the ground.

The flames started there.

Sergia's eyes flew open with a startled gasp.

One of the biggest concerns was Carastene suspecting Kathryn's arrival, but from the looks of standing out in the open of the town burning around them…no one had a moment to care.

The world slowed.

Village aflame, peasant and noble alike running in the midst of the night, mouths open in the terror of a scream.

And then Kathryn saw it. The top of a roof. Caped, black tunic, masked, and stoic.

The world flew back into motion. An Oquelite.

"Kathryn! We can't stall!" Sergia shouted over the commotion. "Come on!"

Kathryn blinked away, breaking out into a run after Sergia.

A wheeled cart broke loose from the steed, the horse rearing up in the air. Kathryn weaved out of the way.

A scream tore out. Kathryn's head jerked to the sound, her heart skipping a beat at the sight of the familiar, blue essence in the corner of her eye as it was pulled from its victim.

So they really could take essence too. Excitement raced through her.

They turned onto a new, stone road, the palace now hovering over them. A carriage raced from the foolishly open gates. A caped figure flew down on top of it.

One leap, and Kathryn dropped onto the moving carriage beside them.

The Oquelite paused in surprise. He drew a sword. Kathryn effortlessly dodged. She had no such chivalry. With a blast of power, they were sent down into the trampling crowd.

She teleported back to running at Sergia's side. If the Oquelite were this weak, Kathryn might as well take them all out herself.

They tore up the bridge, the sounds growing finer: the scrapes of her boots against the stone, the distant echoes of screams, the crackling of wood under fire, and the startling sounds of blasts that she once thought could only come from her hand. She ran through the gates, not batting an eye at the two court women who foolishly ran out into the open courtyard.

There was no mercy in sight. Bodies were strewn across the ground, and the towering fountain she'd once watched from her tower crushed to flooded rubble, misting with the dirt and blood.

Almost as if they'd sensed her, heads of the nearby, cloaked warriors turned from their Oquelite fights.

Kathryn shifted into a stance. "Run, Sergia!"

Sergia didn't hesitate, tearing toward the brandished doors.

Kathryn exhaled and strode after her. A cloaked figure flew in front of her. She willed a block of the destroyed fountain stone to fly crashing into them, throwing them out her way.

The others began to turn their attention. She kept up her stride, mustering the bloodied water as they charged for her, solidifying the icy blades around her arms.

And all senses went numb. And, oh, how sweet it was.

One slash, body crumpling, the familiar, wonderful sensation blazing with power through her veins. A blade met hers, quickly throwing it off and sending a guard to meet him, others falling to the ground.

Fire flew for her. It only took a snap to send it flying the other way.

One after another, they fell. Not once did she slow.

She strode, untouched, through the doors and into the main hall of the palace, the air thick with the smell of smoke.

Sergia stood waiting. The halls were eerily empty. Kathryn let her bloody blades melt into a puddle below.

The draw was stronger. Their leader was here.

"They must be heading for Carastene," Kathryn said, rushing past Sergia.

The tactic was smart. Take out the Queen, burn the village, and consume the powerful Ewyon essence…or what was left of it, and flee. But Kathryn had no intentions of letting such a thing happen.

Sergia unseathed her knife and chased after Kathryn. Kathryn was surprised by how calm Sergia's demeanor was as they raced up the steps, ignoring the bodies here and there. They ran up into the next hall.

The smoke slowly settled away, a harsh, unliving cold setting in as Kathryn sent a blast to the Oquelite guarding the door of the royal quarters, ignoring Sergia's flinch as the fell to the floor.

With a gust of air, Kathryn sent the doors flying open. She braced herself for an attack.

Darkness. She raised a brow. Nothing.

The overpowering essence pounded at her temples, but the entire hallway was dark. Kathryn stepped hesitantly into the hall. She slowly waved her fingers, the torch lights lighting.

Her heart seized in her chest. Across the dark hallway were blood and bodies—the strong, undeniable scent of death.

Do not let it overcome you.

"Adrienne?" A weak voice broke through the silence.

Kathryn spun around. In the doorway of the first room in the hall, a frail figure of a teenaged boy cowered. Blood was smeared across the Crown Prince's pale face, his violet eyes wide and trembling. She could smell the fear rolling off him, almost stronger than the death.

She turned her gaze and kept walking. She stepped over the still figures.

It was too quiet. Too still. Her hair stood at the end of her neck.

The door slammed shut. Sergia screamed.

Kathryn's hands flooded with flame. Oquelite dropped from the shadowed ceiling.

"Run!" Kathryn screamed, throwing a blaze at the cloaked predator.

Kathryn and Sergia raced through the hall. The once tall and magnificent windows were shattered, drafts of the cold night air infecting *the moonlit halls.*

"Kathryn!" Sergia's shrill cry pulled Kathryn to a stop.

Kathryn flew around. They were so close—

No.

Sergia was pinned against the wall, and a shaken Oquelite, their cape still smoking, held up a shard of glass in their gloved hand.

Kathryn's whole world went slow. "Stop!"

It was too late. The shard pushed right through Sergia's fabric.

Kathryn watched in horror as blood soaked her friend's stomach. Anger settled in.

No. No. No.

Everything burned. She felt everything.

The shard tore itself from Sergia's body, smashing into the Oquelite's face as Kathryn demanded it to splinter and sink deeper and deeper. Every pained cry fueled her.

Another Oquelite leapt for Kathryn.

She thrust Sergia's attacker at him, sending the window shards flying to them both. They collapsed to the floor.

She scrambled to Sergia, who lay gasping through her bloody lips.

"There!" The enemy's voices echoed.

Kathryn scooped Sergia up into her arms and ran.

"Kathryn," Sergia choked, her head nodding off against her chest. "Leave me."

No. She could heal her. Kathryn could do almost everything. Almost.

"That one! The blonde! She's the Shadow—"

Kathryn cried with anger, stomping her foot, the floor splitting. She ran, the split following at her heels. She could feel the warmth of Sergia's blood seep into her coat. The scent was overpowering. Sergia's essence was weak, but Kathryn's senses were hungry.

No. Not Sergia. She refused to take Sergia's.

She tore through the heavy curtains to the marble-floored halls. The cracks stopped. The throne room was fast approaching.

Guards lay still at every door. Kathryn could feel the power burning at her skin, begging to be released.

Burn. It. All.

The throne room's heavy doors were ajar. Kathryn dropped to her knees, laying Sergia against the wall. A small groan escaped from her lips. Kathryn swept Sergia's hair from sweat pooling on her face.

"Please stay with me," she said, trying to keep tears from choking her. "I'll be right back. I'll come back for you."

Sergia grasped Kathryn's arm. Kathryn grit her teeth, resisting the urge to pry free.

"Promise me," Sergia begged, her breathing heavy. "Promise me, Kathryn."

Kathryn blinked back the tears burning in her eyes. Promises meant little to her.

"I swear on my life." Her never-ending life.

Sergia let go, and Kathryn tore away before she lost control of her emotions. The storm was growing inside her. She stormed instead into the throne room. She took a deep breath, let herself fall away to the invisibility, and slipped inside, letting violent sparks dance around her fingers. She faced the room.

She always knew that names had power. But never before had she been able to feel it hit her so hard.

"Lord Orion Idicous."

Orion. Idicous.

Orion. Orion. Orion. Orion. Orion.

An Oquelite soldier dropped to the center of the room, facing an unmasked Oquelite who stood on the throne's podium.

Kathryn caught her breath. The man stood tall, his shoulder red, his eyes...a steel gray, so familiar that the spell keeping her mismatched eye hidden faltered. Blond curls coated his head, winding around a circlet on his head. He held a sword, the blade shimmering with a violet energy every child only heard stories about.

The Shadow Blade. Its tip met the neck of her aunt, who sat plastered against the throne, shaking in her nightgown.

"We have a complication," the solider announced.

The General's face hardened.

His name spun in Kathryn's head. Orion. Orion. Orion.

"An entity has breached the palace. We can't sense its essence rate."

"A creature," Orion murmured.

Carastene paled.

"No, sir," the soldier said. "A woman."

Without warning, Orion swung the blade before her aunt could even cry out, and before Kathryn's eyes, she watched Carastene topple from her throne, lifeless, to the ground.

The powerful, blue essence seeped from Carastene's fatal wound, dancing around Orion's fingertips. "Where is this woman?"

Kathryn thrust out her hand, Carastene's essence from Orion's hand flying to her grip. Her invisibility dropped, the essence colliding with her chest, sending her body aglow.

The Ewyon essence overcame her, a smirk growing on her lips. "I am she."

One wave of her hand and she sent the soldier sliding across the room.

A slight waft of surprise fell from Orion. "Have we met?"

"No," Kathryn said, her words bitter on her tongue. "But you knew my mother quite well."

Orion's brow raised. Not a word left him. Had he put it together?

Perhaps that was all it took. His daughter was right here in front of him.

Embrace her. Teach her. Rule with her.

He charged her.

Kathryn sighed, evading his attack, her arms going alive with flames. He swung the blade for her.

The world slowed. She bent back, sliding underneath, setting his cape ablaze. He dropped the flaming cape from his shoulders. She summoned the wind from the open window, throwing herself to the wall. She ran. Orion leapt up to join her. He threw a flame.

Kathryn dodged, jumping to the opposite wall. She ran, jumping with the wind, catching hold of the long, wood bars along the castle wall. A mistake as she watched Orion's red hand burst with a red blaze, aiming it for the wood bar. Kathryn quickly set it out with a gust and ran.

Orion jumped after her, pulling down tiles from the ceiling, the stone sharpening at her will. A tactic that she thought she'd created.

He threw stone blades. Kathryn flipped back, falling to the floor below, landing on her feet.

A shrill scream followed. Kathryn's heart stopped.

There on her knees amidst the stone blade, cuts adorning her face and fresh wounds across her body, was Sergia.

Orion dropped from the ceiling to his feet, his face emotionless. He towered above Sergia.

"Please," Kathryn whispered as she stepped forward. She tried to muster something…anything. The emotion crashed inside her.

Her only rule: not to feel. She was breaking it.

She stared Orion dead in the eyes. "Do. Not. Harm. Her."

"K—Kathryn."

"Just look at me, Sergia. Look at me," Kathryn said, trying to keep her breathing straight. "It's going to be all right."

Sergia trembled as her eyes raised to Kathryn's, tears mixing with the blood on her face as Orion stalked behind her.

Orion unsheathed his sword, his eyes boring into Kathryn.

Orion Idicous. Listen to me.

Nothing. His mind was completely numb.

He raised the sword. Kathryn threw out a blast. In one swing, he deflected the blow, the blade sliding right though Sergia's chest.

Kathryn watched helplessly as Sergia's eyes widened. Orion kicked her, Sergia's body slumping forward against the floor, her essence rushing to Orion's fingers.

Kathryn couldn't think. There was nothing left to think for. She sank to her knees and screamed. The windows burst, sending glass flying.

Her veins burned with power. She felt the glow overcome her eyes. She flew to her feet, Orion rushing to meet her, his blade meeting her shoulder. She hardly felt it.

A monster. A cruel, insane monster. That's all her father was.

Look at the monster you have created, Father.

Ice blades formed through her fingers as she clawed at him. He battled her back. She tore his hand, pulling at the blood, causing him to cry out. His grip hardened on the sword he swung. Disappearing.

And it stopped…slamming her right to the floor, sending the bloodstained blade through her side. Pain ripped through her, but a strained cry escaped her lips from the pain in her heart.

One agonizing moment later and Orion frowned, shoving the blade deeper.

Tears streaming, a bloody laugh bubbled in Kathryn's chest. "I wish that worked. Trust me."

With a blast, she sent him flying off her and staggered to her feet, a groan forcing its way as she pressed her hand against the fatal wound in her side.

A blast slammed into her, sending her flying to the wall. She formed her bladed fingers. He charged after her.

He thrust the hilt into the open wound, forcing warm blood into her mouth. He tossed her to the ground. She skid helplessly, trying to scramble to her feet with her sticky hand.

He tore out a dagger and thrust it to her chest. She cried out, her body writhing. Please. Please stop.

"H—how…?"

He raised to strike again. She redirected his hand, pulling the dagger from his grip, and it hit the stone floor beside her. In anger, he cried out, slashing a flaming hand into her arm, letting her scream. "Who are you?"

A sob wretched her as the burning raged and he took her by the collar, tearing out the blade. He dragged her writhing body across the floor.

His vision blurred before her eyes. The pain was all she could know. No sweet reward. No death. Oh, sweet death.

He hoisted her up, thrusting her up against the windowsill. His gaze was bewildered, his scent horrified her as he choked her.

She couldn't breathe. She couldn't scream. She couldn't die.

Orion growled and, with a thrust, pushed her to the windowsill, the glass shattering behind her. Kathryn gazed over the blurry village drowning in flames.

All. Her. Fault.

The Girl Who Should've Died. The Shadow Soul.

She was nothing. Nothing but desperate.

"The Lady of the Universe," she said with a ragged laugh. "That's who I am."

Orion's icy eyes stared into her dark, immortal soul and thrust her out the open window, falling just so that maybe, just maybe, nature would take its toll, give her mercy, and let her die.

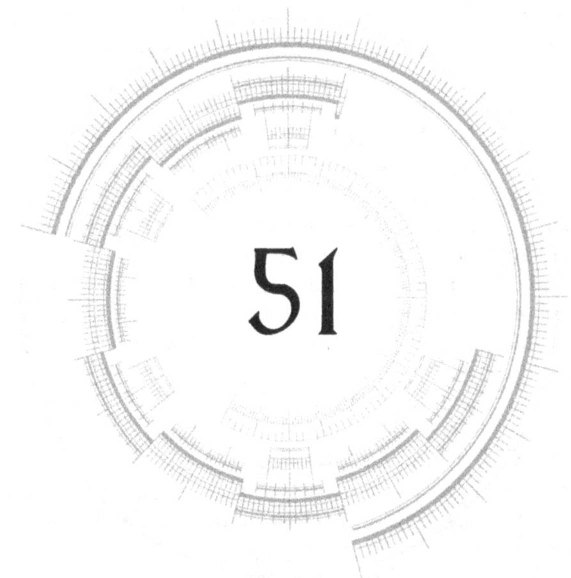

51

Algery, 2 Hours Until

LAWRENCE LIFTED HIS face from the dirt, his entire
body aching. He rolled onto his back, staring up at the forest
ceiling as it spun above him. He quickly felt for his glasses.
No cracks. Good.

He sat up. Where was he?

There was no remnant of the Aguirre property anywhere. By the fact that he was covered in dirt and bloody
scratches, he must have been blown out. Memories came
back to him in a fog. He remembered running. A sharp back,
the burning of his hands.

Fire Wolf licked his face, appearing above him.

Lawrence patted the wolf's face. "I owe you, boy."

He sat up, the aches rolling fresh through him. He grimaced and took a breath through his gritted teeth as he got to
his feet and examined the woods around him.

The sun was falling quickly. The night was coming.

That's when it came to him that he hadn't come alone.

No.

"Nikki? Lincoln?" he shouted, swiveling around. "Nikki!"

Nothing.

"No, no, no," Lawrence whispered. They couldn't have. But they were. He'd seen them run into the tunnel. They were trapped.

He pulled out his tele from his pocket, the cross on a chain falling out and onto the ground. The Comm was cracked. No amount of pounding on it burst it back to life.

He let it drop to the ground and, with a cry, kicked it. "Why does *everything* have to go wrong? Why can't anything go right for *once?*"

HELP! he screamed mentally. Not like a darn person would hear him.

Fire Wolf whimpered, backing away.

He crumpled to his knees, something poking his knee. He lifted his leg to find the cross on the ground. He lifted it, examining its scratched and worn edge in the sunlight.

Fire Wolf's nose brushed up against the chain, beginning to sniff Lawrence's palm.

"What are you doing?" Lawrence frowned.

The wolf's head perked up, and he bound off into the woods. Lawrence stood and watched him go, raising a brow. Fire Wolf stopped and turned, wagging his tail in patient waiting.

Lawrence looked back down at the necklace and then back up at Fire Wolf. He didn't have any other lead. He chased after the wolf, who excitedly leapt back into a run.

Lawrence ran with all his might, his sore body threatening to slow him down. This was his only chance at being able to contact people.

He needed to get to Taryn. He needed to get help. *Please let Nik and Lincoln survive.*

They began to descend down a hill, and a strange adobe building sat in a small clearing. A window was lit as the night began to fall.

"Help!" he yelled. "Please, someone! We need help!"

He heard a door swing open.

Of course, he tripped and toppled downhill till he could roll back to his feet and run to meet them, out of breath, and his scabs already ripped anew.

The women, around three or four, rushed to him, eyes wide in shock. They were mostly young and wore an assortment of simple, long, beige-to-brown-colored dresses and a veil to go along.

But one thing stuck out in particular: the necklace around their necks, with a cross attached.

One in particular, who couldn't have been much older than nineteen, pushed through the group. "Oh, goodness, you really are in need of help."

"Thanks," Lawrence managed with a tight breath. "I—I need help. I need to call Defenders. My friends…They're trapped. Potentially dead. I don't…"

"Whoa, whoa," the girl said, gently grabbing his arm. "Calm down. It's all right. We have a cell station inside. Please, come inside."

Go inside some strange building full of strange women all because of an odd necklace he had found in the Aguirre house? Yet he didn't feel panicked. Maybe it was because it couldn't get much worse or because something about them was overpoweringly safe.

She shooed the others back to work, and he followed her through the wooden door and into the adobe, into a courtyard.

"Were you attacked?" she asked, scanning over him.

"Yeah," he admitted bluntly.

"You really must get to the Defenders, then," she said with a nod.

She opened a door to an office. A middle-aged man wearing a similar garment to the women sat at his desk. He raised his eyes to Lawrence, looking not at all surprised by his appearance.

"This boy needs to use the tele, Father. It's *urgent*."

The man gestured to the small tele that sat in a small booth in the corner. Lawrence nodded in thanks, running to the device and quickly dialing Taryn's ID. It rang, and he tried to ignore the girl's stare, tapping his foot anxiously.

Unable to reach.

He didn't have time for this. He tried a new ID. Almost instantly, it picked up.

"Lawrence?" Miriam's panicked voice filled the tele.

"Miriam! You need to get Taryn! Something went wrong! We need backup…We need Matteo. Anyone!"

"Taryn's not here." Miriam hesitated. "She went after Matteo."

"What?" Lawrence's heart beat faster in his chest. "He never came back?"

So all that progress and exposing himself with Matteo had been for what? For him to run away?

Taryn was gone. *Matteo is gone.*

"Miriam, contact Cole. Now. He might be our only chance."

To his surprise, Miriam didn't argue. "I'm on it right now."

"Thank you." He tried to keep his voice from breaking.

The tele hung up, and Lawrence couldn't move, just staring at the blank screen.

It took him a moment to remember that people were still there, watching him. He hung the tele up and turned to them. "Thank you," he managed to stammer. "I—I need to be going. My friends…"

"They're in danger," the man said with a nod, getting to his feet. "But, young man, do you really think you'll be suitable to help them when you look, and no doubt *feel*, like this?"

He had a point. His bones ached, and the burns on his hands stung, his stomach hurting from being so tense.

"Come," the girl said. "Let me help you, and then I promise, I'll let you on your way."

Lawrence stared at her.

"I don't bite." She laughed. "I promise."

With a second glance at the older man, who offered him a nod, he followed her out.

The girl was, for the most part, quiet but by no means shy. She led him to a small Med Center, where she sat him down and instructed him to remove his coat and shirt.

He did so tentatively, trying not to cringe in the pain, and was probably more embarrassed about it than her. She was quick and direct about tending to the wounds, not making a single comment about the scars that littered his back.

"I don't believe I ever caught your name," she said.

"'Lawrence,'" he said. "'Lawrence Williams.' Seventeen.

North Cordell."

"North Cordell…That's far from here," she said with a small frown. "There aren't many who know of this place, and especially not of those who live in other regions."

Was she going to kick him out?

"My…dog found you," he said, digging out the silver necklace. "Using this."

The girl's eyes widened. "Where did you find that?"

"Do you recognize it?"

"Not personally, but I know of it. It belongs, well, belonged, to Lyell Aguirre. I'm sure of it," she said, peering closer. "The Aguirre property isn't too far away from here. Did you steal it?"

"I—I was allowed to *go* there. It was an accident. I just—"

"No. It's all right," she said, pressing an alcohol-dipped cloth against a cut on his shoulder. He winced. "If you found it, it must have been for a reason."

"It belonged to Lyell?" Lawrence said, wondering why it mattered.

"Yes." She nodded. "Our organization gave it to him once he moved here. Reyna had one too, though I'm not sure where it ended up."

"What is your organization, exactly?"

The girl stopped and frowned. "You mean to tell me you don't have missions in North Cordell?"

Lawrence shook his head, since he had no idea what she was even saying.

"Or Believers?"

"I've only ever heard about you," Lawrence said. A broad term for the various groups of people who believed in a higher power. Something that was more or less mocked by the farmhands. "Do you all look like that?"

The girl laughed. "No, goodness. Only some who've dedicated our life to it." She turned to the cupboard and brought him a clean shirt. "But those who *do* believe wear variations of those. A bit of a secret, but seeing as how you've stumbled across us and have far bigger things to worry about than burning down an organization, I believe you are safe."

Lawrence buttoned up the shirt and took back the coat.

"But I need to get back to the Aguirreses'," Lawrence said, turning to her. "As soon as possible. I don't have *any* time to waste."

The girl perked up. "I can take you," she said. "I know the woods better than any guide."

"Perfect. Thank you."

She nodded, grabbing her bag off a nearby stool, before she ran for the opposite exit, surprisingly nimble on her feet. Lawrence chased after her.

They sped through the woods, passing unfamiliar trees and slopes. The girl didn't once slow down. She wasn't lying when she said that she knew what she was doing.

Finally, she began to slow down, signaling Lawrence to be quiet. He slowed with Fire Wolf beside him, whose ears perked up curiously. The girl peered around the thick brush down the slope. Lawrence peered over, his heart lurching.

Along the forest floor, there was a line of fallen-in earth…and now four Exerticus. Three were focusing their energy along the ground, and another, the woman, stood scanning the trees.

The girl ducked her head, her eyes wide. "What are those?" she asked, her voice low in a whisper.

"They're called 'Exerticus,'" Lawrence said. "Not much time to explain."

"It looks like they might be making more progress on finding your friends," she said with a sigh. She took the bag off her shoulder and handed it to him. "I think you'll need a MedKit. No doubt they'll be a bit banged up in there."

Lawrence took it graciously.

"I should be going," she said. "I'll send over any Defenders if I can get a hold of them."

"Thank you," he said with a nod.

She nodded back. "If you ever need me, I'm just known as 'Sister Lillian.'"

Funny name, but he nodded again. "Thank you again for the help. You have no idea."

She flashed him a smile. "I am glad I was given the opportunity."

She peered back at the Exerticus and, with a final squeeze to his arm, skittered off into the brush.

Lawrence watched the Exerticus, his breath threatening

to reveal him. If he jumped out and attacked now, he would probably die, and they would have no way of finding Lincoln and Nikki. But if they waited too late, the Exerticus would get to them first, and that was it. It was almost certain death either way.

Or he could run away. He had *that* choice. He could run like Matteo had and be free of all this. He had no obligation to stay.

The Council, with a destiny beyond what anyone should have and a bond with people he'd grown to care about…or himself.

For what felt like the first time since forever, he had a choice to make.

Kennedy

"His tracker hasn't moved," Tabitha shouted from the back. "Keep going down this road!"

They tried reaching Ray's Comm multiple times, but it wasn't exactly going well. Especially not when a message from Miriam popped up on his Comm, warning them that Lawrence needed help in Algery just a second ago.

The Soul Night was finally here. Hopefully, Ray's rescue wouldn't take long.

Cole pressed harder. Getting from Kennedy to Algery in as quickly as needed would be near impossible.

Not without Ray. If he could even teleport so many at once.

They tore into a thicket of the woods. It didn't seem as supernaturally infested as North Cordell, but no doubt the anxious look of the twisted trees had still come from the same awakening. Another plague of woods sprouting from the Void, with no doubt long-forgotten Mythic creatures not far behind.

"There!" Felicity cried.

Cole caught sight of a small lake house, supported by wood beams in the sand. It sat alone, not a hover in sight.

Cole took a harsh turn, the truck bouncing down the road rapidly toward the house. Felicity slammed her hand over the final disk connected to her knee, tapping on the power to her braces, and held onto her spear for dear life.

The truck came to a halt, Tabitha's head appearing briefly as it jerked forward.

Cole jumped from the truck, whipping out the Illuminate.

Tabitha followed on foot, her fists clenched and a convenient pistol on her belt, which she'd been instructed not to touch unless the situation was really that dire.

It was oddly quiet, only the sound of rolling waves and the soft rustle of the trees. Cole side-stepped up the porch stairs, bracing himself for the door. With a swift kick, the door burst open, and Cole swung the Blade in front of him.

Empty. The house was completely empty. A table sat dead center, covered in a sheet. The room smelled of dust and was cold.

"How?" Felicity breathed.

Cole turned to Tabitha. "Tabs, hand me the tracker."

Tabitha handed over the tele, and Cole stared at the blinking dot. They were in that location.

Panic. You've failed again.

He zoomed into the dot, closer and closer. His eyes widened. "He's not in the house," Cole said, his heart hammering, looking up. "He's about twenty-five yards left."

Felicity frowned. "But that's—"

"In the lake," Tabitha finished, her eyes going wide. She cursed under her breath.

Cole's sweat went cold. That could be right.

Please don't let it be right.

He sheathed his sword and tore out the door, sprinting through the sandy banks, following the little, red dot on the screen. It had to be a mistake. It had to be.

The dot led him to a short dock. He ran, staring at the dot, praying that when he looked up, someone might be there.

He nearly tripped, falling back, the tele clattering against the dock. Out in front of him was the dark lake and its slow, rolling waves.

He gave out a shuddery breath, reaching back for the tele. The dot marked a foot out and who knew how deep.

"Cole?" Tabitha ran up beside him.

Cole turned to her, seeing the concern deep in her brown eyes.

"Where is he?"

Cole looked toward the lake. "There." He pointed to right off the dock, his throat tightening. "Right there."

They stood frozen for a moment, the crash of the water only growing louder in his ears. The taunts of failure came for him.

You've failed. Again.

No. He wouldn't fail again. If it was tears or the wind that burned his eyes, he wasn't sure. If there was one person he refused to fail, it was his brother.

He unbuckled his belt and sheath, shoving the sword to Tabitha, who stared at him, stunned, as he quickly undid his boots.

"Cole, please don't be doing what I think you're about to try to do."

"You told me to take a risk, Tabs." He tossed his coat aside, stepping to the edge of the dock and staring into the cold, dark waters. If there was any chance he could save Ray, he was going to take it.

"Don't die," was all Tabitha breathed.

Cole nodded to her, taking a small step back and then diving into the water.

"We're going to die." Mercy gasped, her body trembling as her eyes trailed along the coffin. Her eyes finally met Ray's. "We're going to die!"

"No, Mercy. Please don't think like that."

Ray's own mind was in panic mode. It was taking everything in him not to utterly shut down. He wanted to kick and thrash and break the wood coffin. But then he'd drown. They'd die.

Ray's eyes widened. His heartbeat slowed. There was no escape.

"I shouldn't have disobeyed," Mercy whispered, burying her face into her hands.

See, foolish boy, the fate you have put upon yourself. To them, you are nothing more than a liar.

Ray wished that he could squirm away from Mercy, not have to face her. Not have to be constantly reminded that he, in fact, was a liar. He lied to Mercy, and he thought that it would keep her safe.

And so had his mother. And his father. They'd thought that lies would keep *him* safe.

Suddenly, all anger just...vanished. His grudge against them felt so small now.

It didn't matter. He didn't want to be angry at his mother. He just wanted to see her again. Because even though the entire world saw him as some sort of Oquelite demon spawn, it stood no different with her.

"I'm sorry," Ray whispered.

Mercy stilled. "What for?" she whispered back.

"Everything. For lying to you, getting you in this mess. You were right...I was only trying to find you to fulfill a duty."

Mercy turned her eyes away, closing them.

"But, Mercy, it isn't like that anymore. I know you have no reason to believe me, but you're still a friend to me. It's selfish, I know. But you told me the same thing when you didn't know what I was. I don't care if your grandmother's stupid rules say otherwise." *And it felt nice...to be seen.* He squeezed his eyes shut. "I don't care what happens as long as you're okay. I'm really, really sorry."

She didn't respond, and he didn't blame her. He was probably the last person she wanted to be crammed in a box of death with. He tried to will the energy to pull for the Void, for anything to escape. But his mind was too cluttered. It was too pointless. Even if he managed to find the energy, there was no way he could—

A sudden warmth caught him off guard. His first thought was fire, but he was harshly reminded of where they were as he slowly opened his eyes.

The marks along Mercy's skin were glowing lightly, seeping into her hair.

"Mercy?" Ray's heart quickened. "Mercy, your marks!"

Mercy's eyes flickered open with a frown. She looked down and nearly screamed. She looked at Ray. "They're glowing."

"Mercy..."

"I'm going to get us out of here." With a quick twist of her wrists, she snapped away the rope, quickly undoing Ray's, careful not to touch his skin. "I really hope you can swim."

"Mercy, it's dangerous. We're probably too far down

now."

Mercy threw the rope aside. "You may be a liar, but I've never known you as a quitter. You have too much of an ego for that."

Ray stared at her, dumbfounded.

Her hair was fully aglow now, her marks shining brighter and brighter. She braced her feet against the roof of the coffin. She turned to face Ray. "If we don't make it, I want you to know something. We *are* friends, Raphael."

She said his name.

She said my name.

His mind was too busy going crazy that he forgot to shout when Mercy's glowing feet slammed right through the wood top of the coffin. The sheer force shattered the top, water flooding in, instantly suffocating him.

It took him a dazed moment to hold his breath, spot Mercy's glowing body, and swim with all his might. She grew farther and farther away.

Curse her enhanced abilities.

He swam harder. His lungs screamed for air. How far down were they? Too far?

He tried to force energy through himself. Water squeezed him, fighting to force its way to his oxygen-starved lips. His limbs burned.

Higher. Higher.

His heart threatened to grow light. His lungs burned. His wounds stung and ate at him.

Air. Air. I need air.

No, you don't. Keep going.

Higher. Harder and faster, he pushed. His vision began to grow blurred. His thoughts collided. His limbs wouldn't push hard enough.

Light was approaching. What kind of light?

Light was always good. He wasn't very light. He was Shadow.

But the light seemed comforting. What if he just stopped…?

Something jerked him. Something pulled him toward the light. This was it?

And then he hit air, pairs of arms dragging him up onto the surface. He gasped for air. Real darn air. His vision was still blurred, his mind reeling. He wasn't dead.

He sat up, his entire body shivering.

His vision cleared to Cole kneeling in front of him, drenched and shivering, his eyes full of concern.

Ray couldn't help himself and threw himself onto his older brother and hugged him, tears burning down his freezing skin.

Cole hugged him back tightly. "Hey, it's okay."

"I know." Ray shuddered, burying his face. It was okay now. It was all okay. He could breathe.

Cole gently pulled away, holding Ray's shoulders, staring with his own glassy eyes. "It's good to see you again."

Ray laughed through his tears. "You have no idea."

Cole helped Ray to his feet.

Tabitha stood on the dock, holding Cole's sword. Felicity was helping Mercy dry off with her jacket.

"This is the Keyper," Ray said, swallowing hard with a nod to Mercy, who gave him a tight smile back.

"And I take it you're his brother he doesn't shut up about," Mercy chattered with a glint of humor in her eyes.

"Aw, you talk about me?"

Ray rolled his eyes.

"Holy cow, you two really are brothers," Tabitha said, suddenly breaking her silence with a laugh. "You're both total *idiots*." She shoved his sword back to him. "But you're both alive, and that's kind of the important part."

Ray cracked a smile. "Really."

"Hate to break the mood," Felicity said. "But we have the whole our-other-three-friends-are-in-danger situation to deal with, and we were riding on Ray being able to teleport…which he doesn't seem to be in ideal shape for."

"Wait, *they're* also in trouble?"

"You guys are kinda making it a theme tonight." Tabitha shrugged.

"Right," Ray breathed. "The Soul Night."

It turned out to be a bigger disappointment than he thought. A trap by Virtue Faithful…not some second coming of the Shadow Soul or ultra powerful word power. It was a tall tale.

"The Soul Night is a trap," he said. "It's just a whole plan to get the Council's blood."

Cole re-buckled his belt to his waist, whipping out the Illuminate, which burst into warm flames.

Mercy jumped. "So you—you're all a little weird." She laughed nervously.

"Whatever you think is weird, glow girl." Ray shrugged, warming by the sword.

"Mercy, you said your name was?" Tabitha asked, turning to Mercy.

Mercy hesitated, but nodded.

"I'm Tabitha," Tabitha said, offering her hand. Mercy tentatively shook it.

"So you're now part of this thing we call a 'Council?'"

Ray froze. He should've explained the whole mess of a situation he and Mercy were in. He cringed watching Mercy's eyes blink a few times. He braced himself.

"I suppose I am."

"What?" Ray blurted out.

Ray's mouth hung open. *You, Mercy Remembrance, confuse me.*

"Well, then. Do we, like, knight her or something?" Tabitha said, turning to Cole and Ray before frowning. "Ray, where is your sword?"

"It's—" His heart sank. It was taken when he was chained up in the basement. He had no idea where it had been taken. But he had one stupid idea on how to get it back.

He scanned the faces of his confused friends, and he raised his hand. He'd had a moment of clarity when he fought off the Voice, like his veins had been cleared. If he could just focus.

Think of the Blade. Think of its smooth edge, the cool, stone grip. A slow burning rose in him as he flexed his fingers. The dark, reflective edge of the Blade. The glow of violet—

Something crashed against his hand, but instead of catching it, he jumped back with a cry. The sword clattered against the dock.

"It worked!" he shouted, grabbing the Shadow Blade. "It worked! And I don't even feel drained! It worked!"

"Wait…did you say you don't feel drained?" Cole asked, a brow raised.

"I'm also confused, probably more than you are, but also

confused." Mercy butted in.

"Usually, when I use my abilities, it takes my energy," Ray said, pacing. The cold had been replaced by the heat of power and excitement. "But I was able to deny the Voice…the Lady of The Universe creep…when I was coming here! What if she was blocking my abilities' fullest extent? Preventing a full breaking?"

"All Oquelite, no matter how powerful, get tired after too much exertion," Felicity said, not seeming to understand.

"Yes, but now she can't *control* how much I exert."

"Wait," Mercy said. "He was being controlled?"

"Long story. Multiple long stories, actually." Tabitha shrugged. "I'll get you caught up after this mess. I'm the most trustworthy source."

Cole raised a brow. "Oh, really?"

"Cole just likes to live in denial…of quite a few things, actually."

Ray couldn't ignore his brother's blush.

"Do you think you can teleport?" Felicity said, stepping forward. "All…five of us?"

"It sounds dangerous," Cole said, extinguishing the Blade's flame, sheathing it. "We have no idea what situation we could be dropping into and no idea if you'll be able to teleport *five* cross country and come out okay."

Ray cracked his knuckles. "Bring it on."

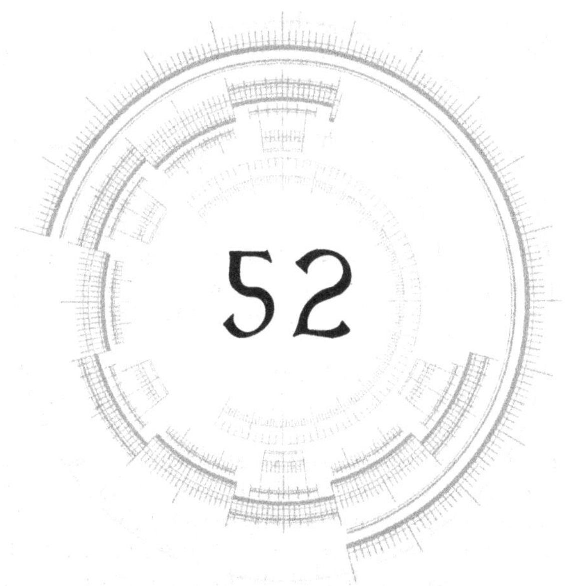

52

Algery, 0 Days Until Night

LINCOLN WAS RUDELY awoken by dirt. He blinked, frowning at the shaking, dirt ceiling above.

Wait. He looked around at their earthy prison. *No.*

He turned and shook Nikki awake beside him. "Nik, wake up! Nik!"

Nikki's eyes fluttered, her face pinching with discomfort. "Lincoln?"

"Are you feeling okay?"

She nodded, even though her eyes were rolling back. She caught herself. "I'm fine," she said, her voice scratchy and thin.

Lincoln stared hard at her. Guilt threatened to punch him square in the face at how weak she was. How strong she was trying to be by sitting up and, with shaking hands, checking her bag. She should've been back at the Inn, resting comfortably after a successful mission.

The ground shook above them again.

Nikki froze. "What was that?"

Their eyes met, Lincoln pulling an arrow from his pack. "I—I don't know."

Thump.

Now something was hitting above them. Lincoln's eyes widened. Dirt began to rain down on them.

Before he could even fully process what was happening, he threw himself over Nikki, pressing the both of them against the wall as the dirt collapsed, sending dust and dirt flying, showering them in a thick coat.

Lincoln slowly peeled away from Nikki, his eyes drifting upward to their saviors.

Just empty trees and a dark night sky…Then a pair of glowing eyes had to step into the beautiful sight of freedom. Darn it.

The Exerticus dropped into the pit, whipping their blade. Lincoln scrambled to his feet, grabbing his bow and pulling back an arrow, aiming it at the Exerticus's face.

Neither of them moved. Lincoln's instincts cried for him to shoot, but his mind fought for control of reason.

Another Exerticus dropped into the pit, and then he realized that they weren't going to be civil, anyway. He released the arrow, spinning on the second attacker, meeting their blade against the bow, thrusting away from Nikki, and ducking back as the second blade came for him, flipping into a swift kick to the Exeritcus's face.

He swung around to meet the second with his fist. They caught it, twisting his arm and slamming him against the ground. Lincoln struggled to pick himself up, a blade quickly unsheathed above him.

And then the Exerticus collapsed.

Lincoln frowned, looking up at Lawrence with a pistol in hand with a look of little remorse on his face. "Get Nik out!" Lincoln shouted, turning to the Exerticus, suffering a bloody, crooked nose.

They ran for their blade. Lincoln kicked it away, throwing his fist. It was quickly blocked, and he was beaten back.

The Exerticus suddenly stopped, sparks shaking him until he stumbled back, and Lincoln spotted Nikki at the top of the ditch, his bow in hand. He breathed a sigh of relief.

Don't underestimate her. He scrambled his way out of the

ditch.

Lawrence had the gun pointed at an Exerticus standing a few feet away, and Lincoln spotted the woman sitting in the trees, observing.

He took the bow from Nikki and aimed for the female Exerticus. A flicker of a smile appeared on her lips.

"She looks familiar," Nikki breathed.

"Like Kathryn familiar or…?"

"No. Not her."

Good. He wasn't willing to see the Voice in the flesh. If she had this much power over his mind, he couldn't imagine how it'd go down in person. He hoped that that's all she was now. Just a Voice.

Lawrence suddenly cried out, sent skidding in the dirt. Lincoln whirled around as two Exerticus crawled from the ditch, a blast of energy smoking from their fingertips.

Lincoln cursed. This was not good. "We can't let them get Lawrence's blood!"

Nikki's back was pressed against his as they turned. Lawrence scrambled for his pistol, shooting aimlessly, but the Exerticus were more on guard now, blocking the bullets with quick slashes of their blades.

Fire Wolf charged for them, but the blade clashed against him and he fell back in pain.

"No!" Lawrence cried out, turning to glare at the attacker.

"Lincoln?"

"What, Nik?" He met her eyes as she clenched the Stone around her neck.

His eyes widened, realizing what she was about to do. "Nikki, don't you *dare*—"

"We don't have any other options."

"You need it to stabilize your essence! You're not healed yet!"

She couldn't die again.

He pulled her out of the way of a blast, shooting an arrow and catching an Exerticus, who swiftly caught the arrow.

They were learning. Fast.

His heart thundered in his chest as they slowly backed away. The woman dropped from the tree, whipping out her blade. Lincoln caught his reflection on the clean blade.

Lawrence stumbled to his feet, throwing the empty pistol to the ground and clenching his fists.

"Hey! Zombie losers, how about you pick on—uh, someone considerably shorter than you?!"

"Tabitha!"

Lincoln's heart stopped. Five people who had definitely *not* been there before stood by the ditch. Ray, Cole, Felicity, Tabitha, and…another girl?

Lincoln couldn't believe his eyes. *No freaking way.* He almost laughed.

Cole didn't even take a moment of hesitance to charge forward, unsheathing the Illuminate blade. The presence of plenty of new Council Members gave the Exerticus quite a bit more to focus on.

Nine…well, eight considering Nikki's condition, versus four. Not terrible odds. They just had to keep them from getting any new blood.

Lincoln sneaked out of the way of a hacking blade. Okay, maybe the odds still weren't great.

He scrambled away from the Exerticus, pulling out another arrow. He spotted a bloody spot on its back. It must have been from where Lawrence had shot him.

But it was healed.

If they kept fighting like this, they would get nowhere. It was a battle of who got exhausted first, which was most likely to be the Council.

The Exerticus were quick on their feet but were un-amused by Ray's thrilling excitement of jumping around teleporting. He appeared beside Lincoln. "Need help?"

"Wait, Ray—"

The two dropped to an Exerticus and Ray clashed against their blade, shouting a command, and to Lincoln's shock, shadows peeled off the trees and began to swirl around the Shadow Blade.

Lincoln took the moment of distraction and took out another taser arrow. They were stunned, struggling as they crumpled to their knees and shot another arrow for safety measures.

"We need a plan!" Lincoln shouted as he and Ray ran for Oquelite-succumbing Cole and Lawrence. "We're going to be overtaken. And we can't risk them getting blood."

"Whose hasn't been taken?" Ray shouted.

"Tabitha's and Lawrence's," Cole shouted back.

Lincoln snorted. "They have to have a weakness. There isn't a creature whose essence encapsulates everything."

"Well, why don't you just ask them?"

Ray joined Cole quickly. The Exerticus batted them away with a glide, spinning out of the way, sending a blast of energy to Lincoln. Lincoln skidded to the ground.

What had they not used? What were they missing? Brute force wasn't working. Ray's abilities were definitely frustrating them, but not defeating them.

If only he could use his own abilities—

He shook it away. He didn't need *her* help.

He hurried to his feet, landing an arrow in the Exerticus's ankle. It grunted, spinning around and sending another blast. It caught Lincoln's already injured side. He cried out.

Water? No doubt not destructive enough. Besides, they had no Aguarious. Sky, air? No. It wouldn't be possible. What else was there?

He sent an explosive to the feet of an advanced Exerticus, blowing them back.

And then it struck him. Their only source they hadn't used. The only source the enemy had gotten out of the way with the wolf: *Fire*.

Lawrence's mind was consumed with one thing: he *really* hated these things. How pathetic did you have to be to go after a wolf?

He took hold of his puny knife and dared them to come after him. Besides, he was one of the main targets of this raid. He didn't feel really special.

"Lawrence!"

Lawrence kicked back his attacker and only looked for a split moment looked to Lincoln, running up the hill toward him. "Fire!"

"Fire?" Lawrence shouted back.

"That's the only plan of attack we *haven't* used!"

Huh. Not a terrible idea.

"I can't just make fire, though! And I thought we trying to make sure they *didn't* get my blood!"

The Exerticus came running back. Lawrence ducked, turning out of the way, his knife slashing their side, which seemed to hardly affect them as they turned for a punch. Lawrence dodged, kicked their ankle, and spun out of their shadow.

Lincoln shot an arrow, the ground exploding, sending both Lawrence and the Exerticus back. "We don't have any other options! They'll get to you either way!"

Lawrence scowled, shaking off the dirt. "Where do you plan to get fire from? You have any fire arrows?"

"Not with me."

Lawrence scrambled to his feet. Fire…fire. He scanned the mess of the woods and locked eyes on Cole. Perfect.

Without a word to Lincoln, he wiped the dagger against his pants and ran. "Cole!" Lawrence shouted. "Illuminate the Illuminate!"

Well, that sounded dumb. No time to consider it.

Cole frowned only for a moment before he whipped the Blade and it burst into flames. Lawrence ran up beside him, and it felt as though only for a moment, the world slowed as the flames caught his fingers and he rolled away to his feet, the little flame sitting happily in his palm.

Cole jerked the flaming Blade toward the nearest opponent, and to Lawrence's excitement, the Exerticus *backed away*.

Lawrence heated the flame in his palm, watching as it grew larger and larger.

No way Lincoln's idea just worked. It *worked*.

He didn't have a moment to celebrate before an Exerticus came barrelling for him. Lawrence focused, jumped, and tossed a flame. The Exerticus shouted an inhuman cry and stumbled back as part of its arm began to dissolve. The new girl's eyes grew wide in horror as she stepped back. The Exerticus scowled, running for him. Lawrence grew the flames, whipping out another, the Exeritcus crumbling back. The focus began to turn to him.

Cole's fire sword proved to be almost equally effective. The Exerticus began going for the trees, trying to attack from below.

Lawrence dove out of the way, careful to keep his flame lit, rolling to his back, sending a fistful to engulf the

Exerticus's red scarf.

One turned for a retreat, his arm practically melting due to the blow. Lawrence turned with a blast to the nearest Exerticus, thrown off course by Lincoln's blast.

The flames grew stronger as the thrill grew inside him. He thrust forward with the flames, and every step back felt like a victory till they tore away, reaching for the trees to go farther and farther.

Lawrence turned, and suddenly a blade slammed into his chest, sending him back and toppling into a roll down the slope, slamming against the ground. He tried to catch his breath, pushing himself up, his eyes widening in horror. The slope was now roaring with flames, spreading around through the brush and grasses. *No.*

He slammed back to the ground, his face smashing against the dirt. He rolled over, scrambling away from the female Exerticus, her Blade in hand as she stalked forward.

Lawrence jumped to his feet, stumbling backward. He glanced behind him to the flames, willing a flame to his fingers, then turned on her, throwing with full force.

More easily than the others, with nearly lightning speed, she dodged each throw, running toward him with the blade, her face solemn, her actions quick and decisive. It left Lawrence in a mad scramble for an idea.

He collected more flames, blasting them for her, and ran. She deflected it back to him and rolled out of the way. Why wouldn't she just leave?

A flame licked her cheek and she flinched as the area swelled. She sent a full blast for him again as he blew back on his feet.

Could he shape the flames? Through his panic, they wouldn't listen. With every anxious breath and dodge from death, it grew harder to control, burning warmer and warmer.

The female Exerticus leapt forward, the blade slicing through his shirt. His blood went cold. *No.*

Lawrence stumbled back, his hands falling to catch himself against the ground, the flames extinguishing.

He watched helplessly as all within a moment, the blade slid through the crook of his arm. He cried out as she pushed farther, smashing his face against the ground with a strong hand. He watched helplessly as blood seeped from the wound as she withdrew the blade, blood spilling faster as she lathered the blade.

"Let him go!"

The shout was familiar. Too familiar. Seeming out of nowhere, a glowing figure dropped from the air to the ground. Flames adorned them….like wings.

The Exerticus stood, kicking Lawrence in the gut as the Exerticus brandished her bloody blade.

Matteo's face hardened, nothing like the fearful boy Lawrence knew so well.

How was he here? How had his essence broken? All on his own?

The Exerticus ran for him, and the enormous, fiery wings wrapped around him. Lawrence summoned the flames and, with a blast, caught the Exertius woman off guard. She stumbled back, her arm sizzling. Lawrence sucked in a painful breath as he ran for the blade, kicking it to Matteo, who peeked out of his cocoon.

The woman grabbed it, now directly near Matteo's flames. With one step she stumbled back, looking toward her blade, turning back for Lawrence, and ran.

"No!" Matteo cried.

The wind picked up, throwing her off balance, the flames raging.

Well done, Teo.

Lawrence directed the flames toward the Exerticus and blasted her side. She fell back, and in a moment, the bloody sword disappeared from her hand.

Injured and in pain, she sent Lawrence another blast and ran for the trees.

Lawrence tried to push himself and chase after her, but his arm gave up on him and he crumpled to the ground. He lay there, trying to catch his breath. His arm was wet with blood, his throat dry from the flames.

She'd gotten away with his blood. It was over.

It was okay. At least Matteo and Tabitha were still spared.

A raindrop hit his face. And then another. Rain began to come down harder.

Matteo fell to his knees beside him. "Lawrence? Lawrence! Are you—?"

"I'm fine," Lawrence croaked, sitting up with Matteo's help. He looked at the boy's face, his big, brown eyes full of worry, his green T-shirt singed with sparks…and the lack of the long-sleeved shirt underneath. "They told me you ran away."

Matteo looked away. "I did," he said, quietly.

"Why?"

Matteo looked off toward the flames sizzling out from the new downpour. "Because I didn't think I could do it. Without you. I didn't want to."

"So you ran away?"

Matteo buried his face. "I didn't know what else to do." He was quiet for a moment. "But then I heard your voice in my head. You said you needed help."

The mental cry for help from the woods. Lawrence's eyes widened. Matteo had heard that?

"And then something just clicked," Matteo said, looking up and resting his chin on his knees. "All of the sudden, I couldn't just run. I needed to help you…because of how much you helped me."

"And that's when your essence broke," Lawrence breathed.

Matteo gave a breathy laugh. "I guess so. I didn't really fly. I had no idea what I was doing. It's like they have a mind of their own." He shook his head. "I don't think I could do it again."

"Flames have a way of doing that." Lawrence looked hard at Matteo, who frowned back at him. Tears burned in his eyes. "You finally realized what you're capable of. All without that stupid *Cors Vis*."

"Unless *you're* the *Cors Vis*," Matteo said.

Lawrence was about to laugh till he realized that Matteo's face was dead serious. "Wait, what? That's insane."

"You were there when the *Cors Vis* was destroyed. You *felt* my pain, and I've felt yours. There's a connection there."

But it made sense. The answer to why Lawrence felt random spasms of pain that felt oddly linked to Matteo. He was there when the *Cors Vis* was destroyed.

Balance always restored itself.

Lawrence laughed at the absurdity of it. "So, you need me, a screwed-up teenager with fireproof hands, to teach you how to use gigantic fire wings?"

Matteo gave a small shrug. "You—you've helped me this far."

"I'm glad you're confident."

"You could learn a bit of that." Matteo snorted, muttering under his breath.

Lawrence rolled his eyes. He got to his feet and held out his hand to Matteo. "Well then, Council Member Lopez, why don't we start?"

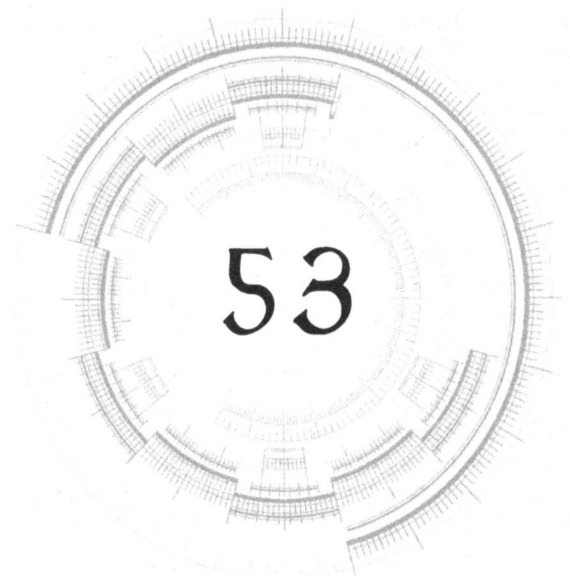

53

Algery

TABITHA SHOT ONE last photo of the damage before turning to Cole, heaving along her impossible bag with him.

"So, we got everything?" he said with a hopeful glint in his tired eyes. He had a cut on his cheek and a few along his arms, with plenty of burns and bruises. The rain was washing away most of the remnants of battle and, to Tabitha's disappointment, the collapsed tunnels too.

"I wonder where they lead to," she said, looking off toward the thick of the woods.

Cole stopped beside her, dropping her bag with a clatter. "You ever think you want to find out?"

Tabitha smirked. "Only if you think it's a good idea."

He rolled his eyes.

"Maybe one day." She sighed. "But right now, I'm content with surviving."

"The world seems to be trying to make that difficult."

It was, wasn't it? How much damage had they seen only

in the past month? Nikki's dying…but then not. North Cordell ravaged with a fever. A building burned at their own doing. And now damage to Aguirre property.

But they were alive. She was alive. Cole was alive.

"So, how'd your list go?" she said, turning to him with a sly smile.

He smirked back, raising a brow. "Drill me, Sergeant."

"Song?"

"Done…badly."

"Oh, really?" Tabitha said, pulling it out from her pocket, watching his face go pale. "I didn't think it was *that* awful."

"Tabitha, don't you—"

Tabitha cleared her throat. "'I'm so sorry,'" she read. "'The star here is starry.'"

Cole groaned into his hands.

She spared him further humiliation of reading it aloud, but she couldn't help but feel warm reading the words over again.

> *I'm really bad at writing songs.*
> *But this is what you want.*
> *And for you, I'd complete the task.*
> *All you have to do is ask.*
> *I'm just trying to find my way.*
> *No, it's hardly very long.*
> *I hope you accept this song.*

She looked up to him. "I love it."

"Don't lie." He laughed.

"I'm not," she said with a small smile as she gently folded the paper. "I—it means a lot."

Cole's face softened.

"Act of confidence?" she said before she could stare at him too long. She remembered quickly his words before jumping into the stupid lake and shook her head before he could continue. "Never mind. Passed that one and also scared the living daylights out of me."

She looked to her ankle, where the deadly anklet fit snugly, waiting to kill an unsuspecting victim. "A really epic souvenir. I'll give you extra credit for that one."

Cole smiled. "I thought you might. Both nice looking and deadly. A perfect resemblance of yourself."

"Ha, nice try at a flirt there, Johnson, but you have a long way to go." Tabitha laughed. She wasn't going to tell him that she took it as a compliment.

He blushed but laughed with her anyway. "I didn't say I was—"

"You're very pretty too, don't worry, Johnson."

He rolled his eyes. "Ah, yes, thank you very much for that."

She racked her brain through the list. There was only one left.

She turned to meet his eyes. "Something impulsive?"

Cole froze, his brows pinched in thought. The wind beat against Tabitha as the rain poured down as she waited for what felt like an eternity.

Cole stepped forward, gently placing a hand against her wet face. "I have an impulsive idea…if you'll let me."

Tabitha's heart beat in her chest. Any snarky reply was caught in her throat. "Then do it."

Even though she knew what was coming, her heart still leapt as he leaned down and placed gentle lips onto hers. She drew her arms around his neck and kissed him back, never wanting the moment to end. Like she'd waited her entire life for this. Waiting her whole life for someone not to give up on her.

They slowly pulled away.

Tabitha couldn't breathe, her entire face red.

He stared at her with wide, bewildered eyes and she at him, his face so close that she could feel the warmth of his breath.

And then she burst out laughing, hugging him and laughing.

"What's so funny?" He laughed breathlessly.

"You're an idiot…and I love you. It's funny."

He hugged her back. "I like you too, stump."

There in the rain and wind, she felt perfectly warm, inside and out. For once, she was utterly certain that she would never be alone.

North Cordell

Cole was exhausted and sleep hadn't been an option with

nine people crammed into a transport auto back to camp. Not like he could sleep if he could. In fact, his entire mind and heart were going a million miles a minute, even if it had been two hours. He couldn't even look at Tabitha, or Ray would break out laughing and comment on how red they were.

Put simply, everyone guessed within two minutes.

"So we now have nine Members with Mercy as the Keyper, the Shadow Soul and the Lady of the Universe are the same person named 'Kathryn,' Tabitha has a brother with a man bun, and Tabitha and Cole are *finally* a thing." Ray listed everything off.

Tabitha elbowed him. "Is that important?"

"I'm surprised it took this long," Lawrence grumbled.

"See?! If Lawrence agrees, you *know* I'm right," Ray said, leaning over Tabitha's shoulder, wiggling an eyebrow at Cole.

Tabitha elbowed him in the stomach, leaving Ray gasping and Mercy smothering a laugh in her hand.

"How do we know this Kathryn person is really 'here,' though?" Cole said, hoping to change the subject. "All we have proof of is she can control Exerticus and people who tell her their name, and talk to people through their minds."

"She kicked me in the face!" Lincoln said.

"How do we know it wasn't an Exerticus?" Lawrence shrugged. "Not sure some all powerful 'Shadow Soul' would want to honor you with a kick to the face."

"No matter if she's here physically or not, she has the Exerticus." Felicity shivered. "And she's after each Member's blood, which we can, by no means, let happen. Matteo and Tabitha are the only ones whose blood hasn't been taken."

"The fact it was put into Nikki's mind has to have importance," Cole said, pursing his lips in thought. "In fact, every interaction must have."

"Like when we were traveling to Imperial," Felicity said, her eyes wide. "And the Voice…Kathryn led me to the woods. I met Box."

Tabitha frowned. "Who?"

Cole met Felicity's eyes. She hadn't spoken on the Lyntox topic since it came up.

"A Lyntox," Felicity said, quickly noticing Mercy's and Matteo's confusion. "They are shapeshifting creatures, or

Mythics, that go from a mammal to human form."

"Huh. Of course they do." Her brows knit together in a deeper frown.

"And why is that important?" Ray pressed.

Felicity stared at her palm, running her thumb in circles. "Because we have reason to believe I might be one."

The whole car went silent, exchanging glances.

"The Exerticus told Box they were after a woman who was thought to be the mother of a Council Member…and the Council Member they went after…was me." Felicity's eyes rose, looking at the stunned faces of everyone but Cole, who must've known, his eyes firmly on Felicity.

"Your mother is a Lyntox?" Tabitha said with a frown. "I don't see how that's—" She stopped herself with a small frown. "She did tend to wear that scarf. You don't think *that's* how she could hide it all these years. That seems ridiculous!"

Felicity shrugged, sitting up and clasping her hands together. "I have no idea, but Taryn said I'm the one to figure this out, and that's exactly what I intend to do."

"We'll help you out, of course," Tabitha said, scribbling something onto her paper. "Because we're a Council… without a good name."

"A name?" Mercy said. "You guys have a group of potentially all-powerful teenagers and you just call yourselves 'The Council?'" She laughed.

"Giles calls us 'idiots,'" Tabitha said.

"'Idiot Council' does have a ring to it."

"I like your thinking, Remembrance." Tabitha smiled, nodding to Mercy.

"Hold up, if we're naming the Council, it's *not* going to be 'Idiot Council,'" Lawrence said.

"Fine." Tabitha scribbled it off the list. "Suggestions?"

"I have an idea!" Ray said, cracking his knuckles. "How about 'Taco Council?'"

"Vetoed."

Ray shrugged. They were just missing out on a genius option.

"How about 'Phoenix?'" Lawrence said.

"Cool…but why?"

"Fire's kind of what saved us…not to mention Matteo's wings. We have a habit of always coming back despite odds."

Lawrence glanced at Nikki. "I just hope it stays that way."

"I mean, it does *sound* cool. The Phoenix Council," Ray said, jazzing his hands. "I'd put that one into strong consideration."

The auto jerked to a stop. The driver looked back through the glass window separating them. "Here's your stop!" he yelled through the glass.

Cole hadn't realized that they were so close. One glance out the window, and it was just as he said. There, only a short walk down the hill, was camp.

The door of the auto opened and Cole stepped out, the others trailing after him. He took a deep breath, a shiver running down his spine as the familiar North Cordell air nipped at his face.

"Nervous?" Tabitha stepped beside him.

"Is it that obvious?" He laughed softly.

"Well, quit being nervous, we have things to do!" Nikki pushed between the two, breaking out into a run down the path.

Lincoln shoved between them after her. "Nik, no running!"

"The sooner she gets that NMA file disc into the Curatrix machine, the better." Tabitha laughed, turning back to Cole. "I'll race you."

"What if we just walk—?"

"You have no choice!" Ray grabbed Cole's and Mercy's arms and pulled Cole with an impressive strength down the path, Tabitha laughing after them.

Cole wasn't mentally prepared for this at all. What would he do when he had to face Taryn? What would she say about the news articles plastered all over the net? About him joining the Market? He'd drop down and beg her to forgive him.

A small crowd had formed at the edge of the camp, and Cole braced himself as he approached. Ray slowed.

A woman pushed through the curious Defenders, and Cole's heart stopped in his chest. The woman had long, dark hair braided back with a few stray, gray hairs; perfectly trimmed bangs across her forehead; and a white coat tied around her waist, her brilliant, amber eyes so familiar.

But they weren't on her. "Raphael!" the woman cried.

Screams of "Ray!" followed soon after, three children tearing past the Defenders after their brother.

Dr. Mathews collided with her son, hugging him tight. Tears began to stream down her face as she kissed his hair. She pulled back, clasping Ray's face, rubbing his cheek with her thumb.

"Hi, Mom," Ray choked. "I—I'm—"

She shushed him. "No, baby, it's okay. It's okay," she said, hugging him again.

This time Ray wrapped his arms around her and held his mother tightly for a long moment before he wiggled out of her grip. He wasn't even given a moment of freedom before his siblings tackled him into their own embrace.

Jenna hugged him till he couldn't breathe, not letting go, tears trickling down her face. "I'm so glad you're okay," she said.

"I'm fine, Jen. I'm okay."

She let go of him, looking up at her older brother with a trembling smile. "And you aren't crazy. They all said you'd be crazy, but you're just stupid, old Ray."

Ray cracked a smile. "Just stupid, old Ray."

Jenna laughed and began to cry, though her smile never left, another one of her brothers comforting her.

Ray wiped his eyes and slowly turned. "Mom, this is Mercy," he said, gesturing to Mercy, who stood nervously off to the distance.

"Hello, child." Dr. Mathews gave Mercy a kind smile.

Mercy gave a shy wave.

Ray tightened his grip on his mother's hand as he turned toward Cole.

Cole's heart leapt to his throat.

Dr. Mathew's eyes widened, her lips parting with a breath. "Cole?" she said, her eyes glinting with tears.

Cole couldn't breathe. He thought he had one blurry memory of his mother.

Dr. Mathews stepped toward Cole, cradling Cole's cheek in her hand. "You've grown up so much," she whispered.

But the woman in that memory stood right in front of him, her warmth bringing him back fourteen years. She reminded him of Echo with the strength in her eyes and the gentleness in her touch.

"H—hi," he stammered.

Dr. Mathews laughed. "I'm sorry," she said, drawing her hand away. "It's just—it's just been so long. You're a man now."

"Nah, Mom." Ray smirked. "You should see how boyish his face gets when Tabitha's around."

Dr. Mathews raised a brow. "Who's—?"

Lawrence saved Ray from being strangled as he burst through the crowd around the corner. "Guys! We need you *now*!"

Cole, Ray, and Mercy all exchanged glances. "What happened?"

"Nikki got the NMA disc into the machine," Lawrence said, catching his breath. "Come on!"

Cole looked back to his stepmother.

"We'll catch up later," Dr. Mathews said, shooing him off. "Go!"

Cole ran after Ray, tearing into Taryn's cabin. The Curatrix machine was set out on the main table, its holographic screen covering the entire tabletop.

"What's going on?" Cole said, pushing through the others crowded on the map.

The red and purple marks were still there...but three new, yellow ones were indicated on the map.

"They're alive." Nikki looked up, out of breath. "We can get to them before the Exerticus do."

"Who?"

"The last three Council Members."

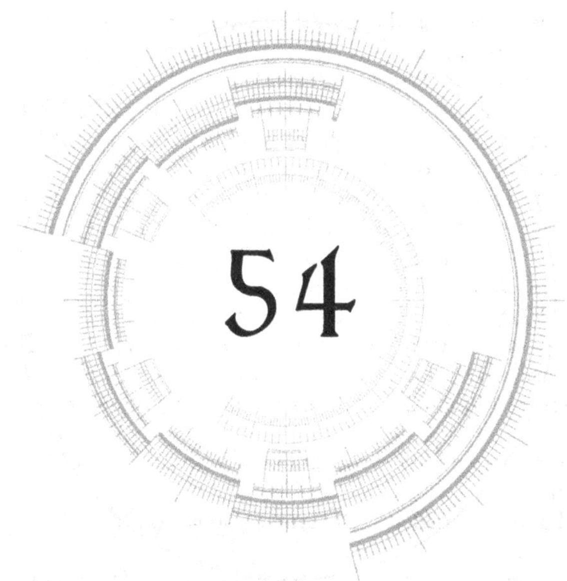

54

Defending Department Artic Prison, Capitol North

SHE STRODE DOWN the freezing hall, every step echoing, her cape dragging behind her, bars of flickering light slowly lighting the hall—a dark and cold existence below the earth…neither of which bothered her.

She had business to take care of.

Now that she had secured the Creature, she only had one matter of business to deal with to keep *them* loyal to the cause.

And rage she'd held for over a millenia to release.

Doors lined the walls with small slits for windows and bars for handles.

"Hey! Hands up! You're not supposed to be down here!" Two guards jumped forward, their curious sticks aimed for her.

She threw her arms out, both guards slamming against the walls, collapsing, unconscious, to the ground. She dusted off her hands and stepped over them.

She stopped at the end of the long hall, wiping the frost from the plaque.

Orion Idicous, Prisoner #019384

She grabbed the handle, feeling the energy trickle from her fingers, hearing the pops and clicks of the machinery. She swung the door open with a slam.

The man, chained on the floor, jerked his head up. A collar was strapped around his neck with an occasional zap. His eyes twitched, his long hair falling across his face.

The almighty Idicous Lord.

"Who are you?" he said, his voice strained.

She spat with a harsh laugh. She snapped, Orion flying forward, slamming onto the ground before her. She knelt down, grabbing his face to meet hers. "You don't recognize me?"

Orion trembled as he fumbled with lips. "No," he said firmly.

Kathryn scowled. "Of course you wouldn't."

Father.

She raised her hand, the ice in her hands forming into a blade, glinting in the dim light. Orion cried out, trying to pull against his chain,

Kathryn slashed the blade across his face. The blade melted in her hand. She dropped her father to the ground, watching him writhe in pain as the essence flew into her fingertips.

Power swelled inside her, burning and churning, growing and living. But she didn't feel warm. Her body felt like ice.

Finally, Orion stopped moving, his eyes staring up at the ceiling. She snorted, whipped her cape, and strode out of the cell, flexing her hands.

I kill with purpose. I kill without remorse. And I will break this curse, no matter what I have to do.

With her next step, she was back outside in the barren, icy terrain above. She looked down at her hands, scowling at the smear of blood. She wiped it off.

"I am sorry for the failure," the voice beside her said.

Right on time, as expected. Kathryn spun around.

Sergia dropped to a knee, a hand on her blade hilt as it was buried in the snow. Her arm was bandaged, and the burn on her face was scarring nicely.

Her new appearance was still something to get used to. The glowing, red eyes and the frost-white hair. "I was only able to acquire the Ywondie boy's blood."

"Sergia, you do not bow to me."

Sergia's newly red eyes peered upward in hesitance before pushing herself to her feet.

"That makes seven successes of your mission," Kathryn said with a nod and a hand on her friend's shoulder. "It might only be a little over two quarters till you are freed. No doubt the final few will be simple."

Sergia shook her head. "You haven't faced them all together. They're far stronger than you may be suspecting."

"The stronger, the better."

She looked back toward the door. Kathryn let out a harsh breath. So, that left five Members' blood to acquire. The Wingor and the Humanic, both tucked away safely in the hold of the other Members, and the Aguarious, Oquelite, and Sublinight Members locations still unknown.

Wherever it was, she intended to find it.

"And did they get away with that…disc?" Kathryn asked.

Sergia's glowing eyes fell. "Yes. I apologize for the failure—"

"Very good." Kathryn placed a hand on Sergia's shoulder.

Sergia's eyes widened in surprise. "But we failed to get the location of the last three."

For the first time in 200,000 years, Kathryn was tempted to smile. "The Council is about to lead us right to them."

The Unanswered Questions

BOOK FOUR

COMING NEXT WINTER

GLOSSARY

THE JOINED WORLD

95 REGIONS OF EARTH, ALL JOINED UNDER ONE GOVERNMENT AFTER THE EARTHSHAKER

THE EARTHSHAKER – APOCALYPTIC WAR 340 YEARS AGO, WHICH SENT HUMANITY INTO REBUILDING EARTH

THE DEFENDING DEPARTMENT – THE "DEPARTMENT" OF LAW ENFORCEMENT TO KEEP EACH REGION IN ORDER

    COMMANDER – IN CHARGE OF ENTIRE DEPARTMENT

        NOTE: EXECUTIVE CADISSA DEAN IS ACTING COMMANDER AFTER THE DEATH OF JAMES R. KORDIN

    EXECUTIVE – ASSISTANT TO THE COMMANDER

    GENERALS – IN CHARGE OF MULTIPLE REGIONS

    AGENTS – SPECIAL TASK FORCE UNDER GENERALS

    SERGEANTS – IN CHARGE OF A REGION

    OFFICERS – UNDER SERGEANT'S COMMANDS

THE CURATRIX TEAM – WELL KNOWN TEAM OF DEFENDERS, MURDERED OVER A DECADE AGO. MADE IMPORTANT CONTRIBUTIONS TO THE DEPARTMENT

    MEMBERS: AGENT REYNA WENTS AGUIRRE, AGENT LYELL AGUIRRE, SERGEANT JESSICA HUNTER, OFFICER AARON OUTOWN

COMMON TECH

SCROLL – UNRAVELING DEVICE THAT CONNECTS TO NET AND CAN PROJECT HOLOGRAM

TELE – GLASS DEVICE THAT FUNCTIONS AS A SMALL SCROLL AND COMM

COMM – GOVERNMENT ISSUED COMMUNICATION DEVICE

BUDS – EAR BUDS THAT READ TEXT TO ITS USER

IMPORTANT PLACES

DEFENDING DEPARTMENT HEADQUARTERS – LOCATED IN THE GLASS TOWER IN IMPERIAL, HEAD OF OPERATIONS

THE MARKET – HIDDEN SYSTEM IN THE REGIONS, AND HOME TO IT'S OWN SOCIETY, AND CULTURE. VERY OPPOSED TO DEFENDERS.

THE LABYRINTH – OQUELITE UNDERGROUND LIARS. LOCATED IN MULTIPLE REGIONS.

THE (EVER GROWING) WOODS – THE WOODS COMING FROM THE VOID AND BRINGING THINGS BACK FROM THE PAST. RAPIDLY GROWING THROUGHOUT THE WORLD.

THE INN 2.0 – THE ALL IMPORTANT HOME BASE OF OPERATIONS. (INN 1.0 BURNED DOWN...)

THE IMPURE

OVERALL NAME FOR THE SUPERNATURAL BEINGS AND HAPPENINGS OF EARTH

ILLIAH/ESSENCE — THE "SECOND BLOODSTREAM" CONTAINING THE SUPERNATURAL ASPECTS OF HUMANITY

THE IMPURE RACES— THE SEVEN "TYPES" OF ESSENCE, WHICH ADAPTED TO A CERTAIN WORLDLY ELEMENT

    EWYON — ILLUSION, APPEARANCE

    AVIDUOUS— EARTH, STRENGTH, CREATURES

    OQUELITE — ESSENCE ITSELF?? (UNKNOWN)

    YWONDIE — FIRE

    AGUARIOUS — OCEANS, WATER

    SUBLINIGHT — EMOTION, FEELING

    WINGOR — SKY, WEATHER

    HUMANIC — TECHNICALLY "PURE" AS THEY HOLD NO SUPERNATURAL ASPECTS IN THEIR ESSENCE, EVEN IF FULL-BLOOD

MYTHICS— SUPERNATURAL CREATURES, CREATED BY IMPURE

SHIFTERS — MYTHIC CREATURES THAT CAN SHIFT BETWEEN A HUMAN FORM AND ANIMAL

    LYNTOX— SHIFTS TO MAMMALS

    REPITOX — SHIFTS TO REPTILES

The Council

LEGENDARY GROUP OF 12 MEMBERS CHOSEN BY 'FATE'.

Members

(EACH MEMBERS REPRESENTS A RACE/IMPORTANT ASPECT OF THE WORLD)

Ewyon (ILLUSION, EXTERNAL) X
Sublinight (EMOTIONS, INTERNAL)
Aviduous (EARTH, NATURE) X
Oquelite (THE SUPERNATURAL?)
Ywondie (FIRE.) X
Aguarious (WATER, THE OCEANS)
Wingor (SKY, WEATHER) X
Humanic (THE PURE) X

ILLUMINATE HOLDER — HOLDER OF THE ILLUMINATE BLADE; REPRESENTATION OF LIGHT X

Shadow Holder — HOLDER OF THE SHADOW BLADE; REPRESENTATION OF DARK X

KEYPER — HEREDITARY ROLE, CAN FORM/BARE KEY??

Guardian — REPRESENTATIVE OF THE MYTHIC

X = FOUND

ACKNOWLEDGEMENTS

Another year, another acknowledgements section.

So much has changed in the 364 days since *Of The Curatrix Code* dropped in 2021. Little LDF in 2020 wouldn't even believe it if she saw us now.

I admit it all hasn't been good, but the fact we're here, living and breathing is something I want to thank my Lord for every single day. If anything, this year has taught me I am nothing without Him.

* First and foremost to my mother: I love you with my entire heart, and am so beyond blessed to be your daughter, even if I'm a mess sometimes. Like I always say, "you're my favorite mom."
Don't worry, we'll get a cover with a bird on it soon. XD
* To Millie Florence, for giving me a reason to smile again. God really knew I needed someone like you. I can't wait to give you a big hug again soon, and rant about Minecraft bois.
* To Ariana Tosado, my honorary big sister, and my absolutely fantastic last minute editor. I owe a lot of who I am today to your influence. Thanks for fangirling over Kathryn with me >:)
* To Ellie. We might live across the country from each other now, but I will never stop sending you all the TUQ rough drafts. Thank you for agreeing to read this book when I was on the verge of tears and you had no idea. You're a lifesaver, and the OG Cole stan.
* To my author friends who've stuck with me through thick and thin. I can't remember you all, but a few honorary mentions: Lorelei R. Jensen (best coffee shop date EVER), Brigitte Cromey (Author Mom ™), Susan Markloff (Author Godmother ™), and Naomi Kenyon (for being here so long <3)
* To my IRL friends (*cough cough* my children).

- To my beta readers, who I originally wrote a few sentences for each but then realized that I made this acknowledgements section too long *again*. I love you all dearly: Laurel (she gets a shoutout for being the best Kathryn actress), Leigh Cresent, MT Zimny, Lydia, Julie Mozart, Kate, Samantha Crago and Lexy.
- To my Kickstarter supporters because without them this book wouldn't even exist: Leigh, Lorelei R. Jensen, Madison, Allison, Tuesday, Susan, Amanda, Lydia, Mitchell, Susanne, Susan, Andrew, and THE Brandon Sanderson (??!!).
- To the people who put this book together: my fabulous editors Micheala Bush and Ariana Tosado, my amazing illustrator, Anna, and cover designer, Beck (who both whipped out yet another killer cover), and my incredible formatter Benita! <3
- To Black Rock Coffee (b/c I literally go there 3 times a week and the employees now know my name…), and my coworkers at Chick Fil A (b/c they asked to be mentioned).
- To my little sister, Grace.
- The manager of Scottsdale B&N for being the coolest.
- And last but CERTAINLY not least, my loyal readers. You're the real ones. I wouldn't trade y'all for the world. Have a lemon. <3

The Council Kids call me so back to writing I go---

Lauren D. Fulter is an young American fiction author, after publishing her first book at the age of sixteen. After learning the word 'author' at age five, she's been captivated by the art of storytelling, and the little people roaming her mind. Though she longs for the cold, she lives in the desert with her large family, spending her days drawing, dabbling in fictional dimensions, and attempting to make something edible.